Stay Awake

Megan Goldin, author of novels including *The Escape Room* and *The Night Swim*, worked as a correspondent for Reuters and other media outlets where she covered war, peace, international terrorism and financial meltdowns in the Middle East and Asia. She is now based in Melbourne, Australia where she raises three sons and is a foster mum to Labrador puppies learning to be guide dogs.

STAY AWAKE

MEGAN GOLDIN

CANELOCRIME

First published in the United States in 2022 by St.Martin's Press, an imprint of
St.Martin's Publishing Group

This edition published in the United Kingdom in 2022 by

Canelo
Unit 9, 5th Floor
Cargo Works, 1–2 Hatfields
London, SE1 9PG
United Kingdom

A CIP catalogue record for this book is available from the British Library.

Print ISBN 978 1 80436 006 4
Ebook ISBN 978 1 80436 005 7

Cover design by Lisa Horton

Cover images © Shutterstock, Trevillion

Look for more great books at www.canelo.co

Printed and bound in Great Britain by Clays Ltd, Elcograf S.p.A.

1

To "TLEA." With love...

Chapter One

Starbursts blink from streetlights like they're sharing a secret as I wake to find myself slumped in the back of a cab, without any recollection of how I got here, or where I'm going.

I stare hypnotically out the window as city lights streak by against a blanket of darkness, lulled by the pensive hum of the car radio.

"Not much longer," the driver murmurs, braking suddenly at a red traffic light.

Our eyes lock in the rearview mirror until the traffic light changes and the city slides away in a swirl of neon.

"This tune is for all the insomniacs out there, looking for sleep like it's a star-crossed lover." The DJ's laconic voice disappears under the strum of an acoustic guitar.

We cross the Brooklyn Bridge listening to Paul Simon sing about the moon's desolate eyes. I look up, above the jagged skyline of the city's silhouette. There's no moon in the murky sky tonight. A siren wails ominously in the distance as we cruise through a maze of sleepy streets.

"We've arrived." The driver's voice breaks through the jumble of my drowsy thoughts.

I pay with a crumpled fifty-dollar bill clutched in my fist and cross the one-way street to the apartment I share with Amy. It's on the second floor of an old brownstone that's been transformed into a modern apartment block with a sundeck on the roof.

I

When I'm at the street door, I realize I don't have my keys or purse. I rest my forehead wearily against the rough brick wall next to the entrance and reluctantly press the intercom buzzer to wake Amy.

"Come on, Amy. Please be home."

Leaves fall from half-naked trees like autumnal rain. I do a double take. The leaves are not just an anomaly. They're an impossibility. Who ever heard of fall leaves in midsummer?

Watching the leaves float ethereally onto the sidewalk deepens the disquiet I've felt since waking in the cab. The last thing I remember before opening my eyes was working at my sun-drenched desk by the office window until I was startled by the sudden ring of my desk phone.

"This is Liv," I said into the receiver as I looked out at a magnificent summer sky.

Everything after that is a blank, until now.

My breath hovers in the frigid air like a restless ghost. Summer, I realize with a shiver, has disappeared like a wrinkle in time.

I press the intercom buzzer again, and again. Each time, I keep my finger on the button for a little longer until eventually the kitchen lights turn on, illuminating the stoop. I hear a clatter of footsteps on the stairs.

"Amy, I am so sorry…" I begin as the building door swings open.

It's not Amy standing on the threshold. It's two strangers. The woman is tall with straight hair. Salon gold. She wears pajamas with a blue bunny print. Her pedicured feet are bare. Next to her is a tall, athletic man with tousled blond hair and matching stubble. He wears gray sweatpants and a white top that he lifts to scratch his taut belly.

"What the hell are you thinking, ringing our doorbell in the middle of the night?" It's the woman who chews me out.

"I didn't know that Amy had friends staying tonight," I stammer, taken aback by the bite of her tone.

This is not the first time I've returned home to find strangers staying at my apartment. Amy is a brilliant doctor who graduated at the top of her class. I love her to death, but she can be scatterbrained about updating me on what she considers mundane things, such as friends from back home camping out on our living room floor for a couple of weeks.

"I'm Liv," I introduce myself. "I'm so sorry I woke you. I forgot my house keys. Again." I roll my eyes self-deprecatingly.

The woman's humorless gaze remains fixed on me.

"That's why I rang the doorbell...." My voice fades out.

Neither of them moves out of the way. Their blank expressions unnerve me.

"Well, I guess I'd better go upstairs and get some sleep. It's been a long day." I step forward, eager to get into the warmth of my apartment and, hopefully soon, the comfort of my bed. As I move across the threshold, the woman slams the door shut to try to keep me out.

"Ouch." I wince when the door hits my foot.

Despite the pain, I don't move my foot out of the way.

"You need to go," she tells me.

"That's my apartment." I point to the top of the landing.

"That's where we live," says the man. "You've made a mistake."

I almost believe him until I catch a glimpse of the distinctive tiled hallway floor and the dark timber staircase banister with its curved edge. They're unique period features preserved to maintain the building's heritage character.

"I've lived upstairs with Amy for years."

Recognition flashes across his face at my mention of Amy. I exhale in relief. We're no longer talking at cross-purposes.

"Amy Decker?" he asks.

"Yes!"

"That's the doctor whose junk mail we get," he tells his girlfriend, as if I'm not here.

3

I want to tell him that Amy still lives here. As do I. I bite my tongue, aware they have the upper hand. After all, I'm the one standing out in the cold.

Soft warm light beckons from the partly open apartment door upstairs. I ache with a crushing longing to go up there and resume my life. The only way to do that is to convince them to let me in.

"I'm so sorry for the mix-up," I grovel. "It's been one of those nights! I've lost my purse and my phone." I shiver in the cold. "Can I at least use your phone to call my boyfriend, Marco, to come and get me? It's freezing out here."

The woman gives me a death stare. I could die of hypothermia on the doorstep for all she cares. Her boyfriend is more sympathetic.

I look up at him, my eyes wide and pleading. He hesitates and then pushes open the street door to let me in. His girlfriend stares daggers at him for caving in. Her feet stomp angrily all the way up to the landing.

Chapter Two

All my certainty disappears like a popped bubble when I'm inside. I've made an embarrassing blunder. It isn't my apartment. Sure, the layout is the same. But the decor is entirely different.

The apartment looks like the cover of an Ikea catalogue, its interior designed to an inch of its life in a mélange of whites and natural accents. Even the kitchen cabinets are new.

My seasoned teak dinner table, my tattered Persian rug, and my colorful artisan bookshelf filled with my eclectic collection of books and magazines have all been replaced with minimalist designer chic.

I'm about to make my apologies and leave when I catch a glimpse of brightly painted flower boxes in the apartment window across the way. I've stared at that view for years. This is definitely my apartment.

My head spins with questions. Who are these people? Where's my stuff? Most importantly, though I can hardly bear to dwell on it, why have I forgotten that I don't live here anymore?

"Where's Shawna?" I ask, sticking to practicalities.

"Who?"

"My cat!"

"There was a one-eyed ginger cat that kept sneaking in last winter. We took it to the shelter."

"You had my cat killed?" I'm horrified they'd be so callous.

"We didn't have her killed. We gave her to the animal shelter."

"What do you think they do to half-blind cats?"

"Look," the woman cuts in impatiently, handing me a phone. "We need to get back to sleep. We both have work meetings first thing in the morning. Call your boyfriend, and then go down and wait for him on the street."

I wander through an open doorway, barely hearing her as I enter my bedroom.

"Hey, you can't go in there!" she yells, coming after me.

The ultramodern platform bed with rumpled bamboo-cotton sheets is not mine. Neither is the metal floor lamp, or the abstract zebra print on the wall. I pick up a photo frame from next to the bed. Everyone in the picture is a stranger.

"Don't touch that!" She snatches the frame from me.

I'm vaguely aware that her face is too close to mine. Her skin is mottled red, draining all her natural beauty. Her yelling is drowned out by a crackling sound inside my head. It gets faster and faster until it sounds like a Geiger counter hitting a radiation contamination site.

"Grant, call the cops," she orders.

The noise in my head stops abruptly. The last thing I want right now is a confrontation with the police. I'm acutely aware the police won't take my side. Even in my confusion, I know it looks bad for me. I can hardly explain myself to the police when I don't have the faintest idea what's happening.

"Wait!" I say, louder than necessary. "I'll leave."

I hold the staircase handrail tightly so that my legs don't buckle under me as I walk down to the street entrance.

"Don't come back. If I ever see you here again, then we *will* call the cops," the woman calls from the landing. I open the building door and step out into the cold.

Lowering myself to the top stair of the stoop, I lean weakly against the brick wall under the intercom as I try to think of somewhere to go. I've been cast out of my home into the cold in the middle of the night. I remind myself that it's not my home anymore. The couple upstairs have clearly been living there for some time.

My head throbs with confusion. I pat down my pockets on the off-chance that I have my phone tucked away somewhere. In the front pocket of my jeans I find a wad of cash. There's an object wrapped in a T-shirt in the pocket of my long cardigan.

I prop the T-shirt on my lap and carefully unwrap it. Inside is a stainless steel knife streaked with blood so fresh I can smell it. I flinch instinctively, repulsed by the thought that this was in my pocket. The knife tumbles onto a step, hitting the concrete with a metallic clatter.

I'm reluctant to touch the blade. After a moment of hesitation, I pick it up with the T-shirt and toss both the knife and the shirt into a trash can set against a brick wall. As I close the lid, I hear car doors slam farther up the street. It's a cab dropping off passengers. I stand in the middle of the street and wave down the cab as it drives toward me, its headlights shining on the wet street ahead.

"Where to?" the driver asks once I'm inside.

I give him Marco's address even though I don't know how Marco will react when I turn up at his place in the middle of the night. Our relationship has clear boundaries. One of them is that we don't drop in on each other without calling first. We don't even have keys to each other's apartments. I reassure myself that Marco wouldn't want me wandering in the dark with nowhere to go.

City lights pulsate in the distance as the cab weaves through thinly trafficked streets to mournful notes of Billy Joel singing good night to his angel on the radio. As we pass a streetlight, I notice writing on the backs of my hands. I look like a human graffiti board.

A few messages are legible. Most are so washed out that they're virtually indecipherable in the streetlights strobing intermittently across me.

Above my knuckles are letters written in black ballpoint pen. I put both fists together. The letters spell out the words STAY AWAKE. Above my right wrist I've written the name and address of a place called Nocturnal.

I lean forward and tell the driver to take me there instead.

Chapter Three

There's nothing familiar about Nocturnal when I press my face to the stippled glass door of the bar entrance. Smudges of color move behind the thick art deco glass like an impressionist painting coming to life.

The roar of the bar spills into the street when the doors open. The blur of colors I saw through the mottled glass turn into people in long overcoats, arranging scarves around their necks. Their inebriated eyes scan for passing cabs as they talk loudly among themselves in voices not yet modulated for the quiet of the street.

Once they pass, I grab the door before it shuts and enter a cavernous room filled with moody lighting and a deafening hum of laughter and clinking glasses.

"We're closing soon," an attendant tells me as if she knows me.

She disconnects a velvet red cord. It flops behind me as I walk inside. To my right is a closed-off section with empty restaurant tables. A cleaner in a white uniform silently mops the floor as if he is slow-dancing in his sleep.

I go down two steps into the busy bar area, where I get tangled in a party of eight rising from their table. They scrape their chairs against the floor as they get to their feet and drunkenly stumble toward the entrance. They take the bulk of the noise with them.

A few hard-core drinkers remain, swilling their drinks as they perch on stools. None of them talk to each other. They

9

keep their eyes firmly on their liquor glasses as if that's their only source of solace. Behind the bar is a 1930s-era triple-paneled mirror.

It feels as if I'm looking at a distorted version of myself in a carnival mirror. My hair is very long and much darker than my natural honey-brown shade. It's the color of coffee: Americano. I plait it to get it out of the way, surprised at how practiced I am at a skill I don't remember learning.

A bartender with a dark goatee and white shirtsleeves rolled to his elbows to reveal a tattoo pours a drink for a man slouched on a barstool. The bartender looks directly at me, flashing a broad smile filled with warm recognition.

"Liv!"

I'm so surprised this stranger knows my name that I instinctively glance behind me to see if some other woman with the same name happens to be in the vicinity.

"I knew you'd come back before we closed." It's as if he's picking up the thread of a previous conversation.

"What can I get you, Liv? It's on the house."

"Thanks, but all I want is water," I tell him as I squirm onto a vacant barstool. "I'm not drinking tonight."

"That's not what you told me a few hours ago," he chuckles, handing me a glass of ice water.

"I was here earlier?"

The bartender's eyes dance in delight at my brain freeze. "Sure. At around ten. You had a few drinks and then you left."

"Alone?"

"You were with a dude, Liv," he says, watching me carefully. "You don't remember?"

My chest tightens with unease. The bartender clearly knows more about me than I do right now.

I must have been here with Marco. Maybe we were drinking. That would explain the out-of-body sensation I've felt since I woke in the cab.

"Everything's fuzzy right now," I explain. "What did he look like, the guy I was with?"

"I only saw the back of your heads as you left. The place was jam-packed. You know what it's like when we have a live band playing."

I smile knowingly, even though I don't remember anything. Not the bartender. Not this bar. Not the man I left with last night. I change the subject and ask whether I left my purse or my cell phone when I was here earlier. They both appear to be missing.

"Not that I've seen, but I'll ask the staff once we close and let you know when you come in tomorrow." He pours liquor into a cocktail shaker.

I'm so focused on trying to reconstruct last night from the tiny scraps of information he's given me that I jump when he puts a cocktail glass in front of me and asks me what I think.

"It's a new take on a gin and tonic. I use ginger ale instead of tonic. Try it."

I shudder as the liquor hits my throat.

"You don't like it?"

"It's pretty good, actually. It's just that I'm not in the mood for alcohol tonight."

I stifle an exhausted yawn. The brass clock on the wall says it's close to four in the morning. "I should go. It's way past my bedtime," I joke.

"You're never in bed at this time," he assures me.

"Then where am I?"

"Here. Drinking. Talking to me. Taste-testing my new cocktails. Anywhere but in bed."

"Why?"

"You hate sleeping. Especially at night."

The manager announces the bar is closing in five minutes. As if in unison, all the stragglers sitting along the bar swallow what's left of their drinks and trail out of the main doors to the street. I hang around talking to the bartender as the staff pile chairs on tables.

"How do you know so much about me?"

"You tell me all your secrets," he teases.

"What secrets?"

In answer, he gestures toward the ballpoint letters above my knuckles that spell out the words STAY AWAKE. I snatch my hands away in embarrassment.

"I sometimes write reminders to myself," I explain, self-consciously. "It's a bad habit. From when I was a kid."

"You do it so you don't forget stuff. Like this." He points to writing on my hand that says: DON'T SLEEP! Below it, partly hidden by my sleeve, it says: WAKE UP.

"What do I have against sleep?"

"You're afraid of what you do in your sleep." He flips a white cloth off his shoulder and wipes a beer glass dry as his words sink in. "At least, that's what you told me the other night."

"What could I possibly do in my sleep?" I ask.

Then I remember the bloodied knife.

Chapter Four

Darcy Halliday pushed through the crowd pressed against police barricades outside the entrance of an apartment building. A television crew was setting up a camera and sound equipment near a patrol car with its siren lights whirring. A reporter in pancake makeup paced nearby, rehearsing her lines.

Nobody paid much attention to Halliday as she moved toward the police tape. She wore navy running shorts and a pink Lycra tank top. Flushed and sweaty from her morning run, she looked like any other curious jogger stopping to find out what was going on.

"Move along. There's nothing to see here," ordered a cop manning a police barricade outside the building. Halliday pushed through a gap in the crowd and ducked under the police tape.

"Miss, I need you to step back," the cop barked. He was about to block her way when he noticed the detective shield she held out.

She stepped around him and took the steps to the lobby. She'd been on her morning run to the precinct when a message popped up on the precinct group chat about a homicide on East Fifty-Third. The captain had asked if any of his detectives were in the vicinity.

"I'm a block away," she'd messaged back, even though she was more like three blocks away.

Still, that put her closer than anyone else. She sprinted past gridlocked traffic with the certainty she'd be the first investigator at the scene.

In the two months since Halliday moved to homicide on a six-month temporary transfer, she hadn't once worked her own case. She didn't even have a regular partner. She was the extra pair of hands assigned to help other detectives with their investigations. She knew the drill. It was all about paying dues. Two months into the job, she was done proving herself. As far as she was concerned, she'd already paid every due she ever owed. With interest.

Halliday had served in the military for six years with distinction, during which time she'd done multiple tours in Iraq and Afghanistan. She joined the NYPD after her discharge. Her first two years were spent as a patrol cop, with occasional stints in vice, dressing as a hooker to act as bait. Halliday did a stint in forensics after she aced the detective's exam and then five months in Major Case while she waited for an opening in homicide. It came in the form of a temporary position to replace a detective who'd gone on long-term sick leave.

Halliday had more than earned her badge. Yet her time in homicide felt like her first year as a beat cop, where she was treated as a wet-behind-the-ears rookie despite her military service and combat experience. So when she saw that she was in the vicinity of a homicide, she jumped at the chance to get in early on the case.

"What floor?" she asked the doorman, flashing her badge.

"Sixth."

Halliday jogged up the stairs to avoid waiting for the elevators. On the sixth-floor landing, she unzipped her runner's pouch and took out an NYPD zipped top and blue nylon warm-up pants that she kept for such emergencies.

She put them on and brushed her shoulder-length chestnut hair with her fingers before swinging the stairwell door open, coming out into a corridor where a cop was questioning a red-haired woman near an apartment sealed off with crime scene tape.

The woman spoke in broken English with a strong Eastern European accent. Halliday assumed she was the person who'd alerted 911 after finding the body.

"The cleaner's name is Olga Kuznetsov," the patrol officer told Halliday when she took him aside for a quick update. He mispronounced the name. "She says she arrived to clean just after seven. Found a dead man in the bed. Apparently, she cleans the apartment a couple of times a week. The owner stays some nights. The rest of the time he puts the apartment up on Airbnb or some other website."

Halliday turned to the cleaner. "Is the dead man the owner?"

"I never seen owner before. He always at work when I clean. Doorman give me key. I give key back after I finish," Olga explained in halting English.

Next to her was a cleaning trolley. Olga told them that she worked for a company that provided maid service for short-term apartment rentals.

"Olga, did you take anything out of the apartment? Towels, bedding, garbage, anything at all?" Halliday asked.

"I throw out one bag from kitchen." She pointed at a garbage chute near the elevator.

The police officer who'd been questioning her groaned softly. He knew what that meant. He'd have to take Olga down to the garbage room to identify the trash bag she tossed down the chute.

Halliday took crime scene gloves out of her runner's pack and put them on, along with shoe covers. Another cop stood guard outside the apartment's front door, which was crisscrossed with crime scene tape.

"Any other detectives arrive yet?" Halliday asked, taking a clipboard and signing in.

"You're the first," he answered.

Halliday held out her phone to film her movements as she ducked under the crime scene tape and entered the apartment.

It stunk of ammonia. The faux marble tiles by the entrance were damp from fresh mopping. Streaks of cleaning fluid were drying on the mirrored living room walls.

"Looks like Olga cleaned the place before she found the body," she called out to the cop by the doorway.

"She cleaned the living room and kitchen before she went into the bedroom. That's where she found the stiff. In bed with a hole in his chest. Push open the bedroom door and you'll see him."

The apartment was the size of a hotel room and just as impersonal. It had a compact kitchen and living area. There was a gray leather L-shaped sofa and a round coffee table with a freshly vacuumed shag rug underneath. On the wall was a large-screen television. The kitchen counter had two metal barstools for meals. The apartment was too small for a dinner table.

Halliday filmed the living room and kitchen area before opening the stainless steel fridge. Inside were shelves of deli containers of salads and cut-up fruit from Whole Foods, an assortment of yogurts and a half-drunk bottle of orange juice.

Next to the sink were two tall drinking glasses that had been cleaned and left to dry. More evidence washed away. "Damn. We really can't get a break," Halliday muttered.

She popped a piece of mint gum into her mouth and cracked it as she pushed open the bedroom door, holding out her phone to record her entry into the room where the murder had taken place. Halliday felt a rush of cold air from a rotating ceiling fan as she stepped inside.

She didn't turn off the fan. Nor did she turn on the bedroom light. Nothing could be tampered with until the forensic team officially photographed everything exactly the way it was found.

The bedroom was semidark. The lights were off and the window shades were pulled down. Halliday could see enough to determine the victim was male, likely in his thirties.

The wildly rotating ceiling fan tousled his hair as it spun, making it look as if he was still alive. Halliday squatted down to get a closer look at him. The indents in his square-jawed cheeks suggested he had dimples when he smiled. He looked like a man who smiled a lot. His jaw was square. His nose was aquiline. His lips were decidedly blue.

He was naked except for black boxer shorts. His clothes were in a pile on the carpet. An ugly gash under his rib cage suggested the murder weapon was a sharp object of some sort, probably a knife. Halliday hadn't seen a knife lying around during her cursory inspection of the scene. She wondered if the killer had taken it.

She guessed the victim died instantly. It explained the lack of any notable blood splatter at the scene. It did not explain the serene set of his mouth. Nobody looked that relaxed while being stabbed to death.

She saw nothing lying around to help identify the victim. There was no wallet on the bedside table. No cell phone. The bedside drawers were all empty.

"How did you get here so quickly? Traffic's backed up for miles this morning."

Halliday spun around to see Dr. Franklin, the medical examiner, entering the bedroom.

"I was on my morning run to work when the call came in," Halliday said. She knew Franklin from her time in forensics.

"You're still running?" he asked.

"Six miles a day. Five times a week. What about you?"

"Gave it up after my knee surgery."

Dr. Franklin's narrow face was pursed in concentration as he checked the room temperature from three different locations. He was close to retirement and had given up any pretense of adhering to dress code conventions. These days he tended to wear polo shirts and chinos rather than suits and ties. It gave the impression he'd abandoned a golf game to come to the murder scene.

"I assume the ceiling fan was on when the victim was found?" he asked. "It might affect my calculations on the time of death."

"I believe so. We'll double-check with the cleaner," said Halliday, poking her head into the en suite bathroom while Franklin examined the victim.

Splashed water on the floor suggested someone washed up in the preceding hours. A long strand of dark hair was balanced on the sink. The forensics team would collect it when they processed the scene.

"Any idea of how long ago he died?" Halliday opened the bathroom cupboard.

"The ceiling fan would have kept things cooler in here and slowed down decomposition. So I'd guess he's been dead for between six and nine hours. I'll do a more exact calculation later. Cause of death appears to be from a stab wound to the heart. That's why there's not much blood. His heart would have stopped midbeat."

"Does anything about the vic strike you as strange?" Halliday asked cryptically.

"Other than the gaping hole in his chest?" he asked flippantly, before realizing Halliday was serious. "What's troubling you, Detective?"

"Looks to me like he slept through his own murder."

"You think he was drugged?"

"I'd say it's a distinct possibility. There's no bruises or scratches on his body. No sign of a struggle. The victim was at least six foot tall. He was in good physical shape. A man that strong would have fought like a demon."

Halliday squatted next to the victim and examined his hands and nails with the flashlight of her phone. There were no obvious defense wounds.

"I don't see abrasions or trauma to his nails or fists. I'm betting he never put up a fight." She stood up and took a step back, bumping into what felt like a brick wall.

Chapter Five

It wasn't a brick wall. It was Detective Jack Lavelle. He was surveying the crime scene with the jaded gaze of a homicide cop who'd seen too many murders to count over his fifteen years on the job. He wore jeans and a brown leather bomber jacket. He, too, had been heading to the precinct to start his shift when the call came through.

Halliday gritted her teeth as she prepared to fight her corner. There was no way she was going to get bumped off this case just because the hotshot detective decided to mosey on over and steal her case.

"Detective Lavelle," she said sweetly. "I guess you stopped by to see if I need a hand. I don't."

"I can see that, Detective," he said, making no effort to move.

"Good. I presume you're heading back to the precinct."

"I can't."

"Why not?"

"The captain wants me to work with you on this case," Lavelle responded. "As partners," he added, when he saw Halliday's eyes flash angrily.

"I thought you don't work with partners."

"I don't," he said, squatting on his haunches to take a closer look at the victim. "But I don't always get what I want. Catch me up here. Any ID for the victim?"

"Nothing so far," Halliday said after a frustrated pause. "No wallet that I could find. No cell phone. The body was found by the cleaner. We believe the victim rented the apartment on Airbnb or something similar," she said. "The cleaner doesn't usually clean on days when the apartment is rented out. Apparently, the owner forgot to cancel the cleaning service this morning."

"Anything else?" he asked.

Halliday moved to the other side of the bed and shone the flashlight on the pillow next to the dead man. "My guess is that he wasn't here alone," she said, fixing the beam on an indent in the pillow. "Someone was lying in bed next to him. Most likely a woman."

"Why a woman?"

Using the flashlight beam, she traced a single long hair on the pillow. The forensics team would bag it when they arrived.

A half-empty bottle of wine was on the table next to the bed. "There are no glasses. I'm guessing they drank straight from the bottle."

"We'll get the lab to do a rush job on the bottle. I'll tell them to check for fingerprints and DNA. Maybe there's saliva on the rim."

"We'll need toxicology as well," Halliday added.

"Why toxicology?"

"I think the victim was sedated. That would explain the absence of defense wounds. We'll need to get the apartment owner's name and find out who booked it," Halliday said. "We'll also need to rustle up some extra hands to see if the murder weapon was discarded in a Dumpster nearby, and collect and run through security footage. I'm sure this building has plenty of surveillance cameras."

"I took down the owner's name and details from the doorman on my way up here," Lavelle said. "The owner's on a flight to Hong Kong. Business trip. I've arranged for a team of uniforms to help with the grunt work."

A sudden racket outside the apartment announced the arrival of the forensics team. Halliday and Lavelle waited in the living room while the crime scene photographer filmed the bedroom. The rest of the crime scene team arranged their equipment in the hallway by the elevators.

"Detective Halliday," someone called from the doorway.

Halliday headed over to the threshold where a patrol cop who'd gone down to the trash room with the cleaner swung a white garbage bag in his gloved hand.

"How do we know this is the trash the cleaner threw out?" Halliday asked, unknotting the handles of the garbage bag and peering inside.

"Olga's one hundred percent certain. She'll put it in her statement. She says there wasn't much trash in the bag. This was the only bag that fitted her description."

Halliday rifled through the trash inside the bag with her gloved hands. There was an apple core and an empty yogurt container, the same brand as the ones in the fridge. At the bottom were yellow Post-it notes crumpled into balls of paper. One note, written in black marker, said: STAY AWAKE. The others had messages that were no less weird. DON'T OPEN THE DOOR. DON'T ANSWER THE PHONE.

"Detective Halliday, you'd better come over here," Lavelle called. "You're going to want to see this."

She handed the trash bag to a crime scene technician to collect as evidence and joined Lavelle in the bedroom. While she'd been going through the trash, the crime scene photographer had ripped off the bedsheet to continue photographing the victim. With the top sheet gone, the soles of the victim's feet were visible. They were cut up and drenched in blood.

"There are multiple slashes to his feet," Lavelle said.

"Strange. Why go to the trouble of shredding the victim's feet when there's only one stab wound in his torso?" Halliday squatted down at the end of the bed to take a close look at the gashes. "It's as if the killer couldn't decide whether to be frenzied or restrained."

"Maybe the killer had a foot fetish," said Lavelle. "Why else cut his feet to ribbons?"

"For the blood." Halliday rose. Her eyes scanned the bedroom. "The killer needed his blood."

"Why would the killer need his blood?" the crime scene photographer asked. He bent down and twisted his camera lens to take a close-up of the victim's feet.

Halliday ran her flashlight around the bed looking for the answer. The beam hit a tiny drop of blood on the plush gray carpet. And then another, and another. The trail led to the window shades. Halliday pulled at a toggle and lifted the shades to expose an expansive floor-to-ceiling window.

Written across a glass pane in blood was a message: !PU EKAW. A camera flash lit up the room as the crime scene photographer took a photo.

"It looks like gibberish," he said.

"It's sign writing. It was written backward so it can be read properly from the outside," said Halliday.

"What does it say?" the photographer asked, taking a burst of photos.

"It says: WAKE UP!"

Chapter Six

Wednesday 8:35 A.M.

Pigeons warble by my feet as I doze on a park bench. My body sways like a pendulum, moving left to right as I drift to sleep, snap awake, and then do it all over again. All the while, I'm riddled with a nagging feeling that something is wrong.

The urgent siren of a fire truck startles me. I open my eyes only to be blinded by the sun. Shielding my face with my arm, I blink rapidly as my eyes adjust to the explosion of light. My disorientation disappears like a burst bubble when a shape emerges from the blinding light and morphs into an arch.

I'm at Washington Square Park. The arch reassures me. I often come here in the summer to drink coffee in the sunshine before heading to the madhouse that's my office a block away.

On my lap is a paper bag with the remnants of an orange poppy seed muffin and an empty coffee cup with dried milk froth on the lid. It's my standard take-out breakfast. All that's missing is my phone, which I usually leave at my desk before heading out here so I can chill before being bombarded by work calls for the rest of the day.

Now that my eyes have adjusted to the light, I notice there's not a scrap of blue in the gunmetal sky. As I look around, I absorb other incongruencies.

People crisscross the pathways of the park in buttoned-up coats and scarves, or sweaters in bleak colors that match their somber faces. There's no lush summery foliage on the trees. Quite the opposite. The dogwoods and elms are a mass of brittle branches in the final throes of fall. Piles of dead leaves scatter across the pathway, blown by a wind infused with the unmistakable chill of approaching winter.

I'm baffled as to how it could almost be winter when my last memory before waking on this bench was sitting at my sun-streaked desk by the office window, typing on my laptop on a perfectly beautiful summer day.

My desk phone had rung abruptly. "This is Liv," I said into the receiver.

Next thing, I woke up here, on this bench.

I blink to clear away the cobwebs of sleep that must be to blame for my confusion. My hands feel numb from cold. I open and close them into fists to get the blood circulation back. As I do, I notice they're covered with writing.

I used to write on my hands as a kid until Mom married husband number two. Unlike me, Randal's daughter from his first marriage, Stacy, always came home from school pristine. Stacy never jotted messages or scrawled pictures on the back of her hands. Her ponytail was never askew.

"Why can't you be like Stacy?" Mom would say, sending me to the bathroom to wash my hands clean. "Try not to write on your hands again, Liv. It's unladylike," she'd tell me in the Southern accent she'd affected so she'd fit in with Randal's snooty country club set.

It was a far cry from her previous life as a single mom waiting tables at a Jersey restaurant that claimed to serve the best steaks on the Eastern Seaboard. That was where Mom and Randal met. He came to the steak house for a meal during a business trip. Mom served his table. Three weeks later they were married. I was the flower girl. I was the flower girl at all her weddings.

Despite Mom's efforts to cure my tendency to doodle on my hands, I've apparently returned to the habit. I stare at the swirls of blue-and-black ballpoint writing decorating my skin. The writing goes all the way under the sleeves of my sweater. There are letters written under each knuckle that form the words: s-T-A-Y A-W-A-K-E.

Near my wrist it says: DON'T SLEEP! I FORGET EVERYTHING WHEN I FALL ASLEEP.

I've underlined it twice for emphasis. I fell asleep right here on this park bench. I can't help but wonder what I've forgotten.

A rustle in the bushes sends pigeons squawking into the air in a tumult of flapping wings and falling feathers. Amid the fracas, I feel someone is watching me with a frightening intensity. Whoever's there has vanished by the time the birds have flown away. I'm in danger. I feel it in my bones.

I get up and rush out of the park, stopping only when I'm on the sidewalk outside the entrance of my office building. I pause to watch people rotate like spinning tops through the revolving glass lobby door. I don't join them. I'm reluctant to go up to the office feeling so dazed.

Down the street is the café where I often buy lunch. I decide to get a coffee to calm my nerves. When I reach the corner, I find the café is closed down. Its windows are boarded up.

Next door is my hair salon. I drift inside, drawn by an inexplicable desire to see a familiar face.

"Can I help you?" asks a woman with blue-tipped hair, folding salon towels behind the counter.

"Is Stevie here?"

"Stevie moved to Miami after the wedding."

"Stevie got married?" I ask, surprised. I consider Stevie a friend as well as my hairdresser. "Stevie never mentioned anything about getting married the last time she cut my hair."

"That must have been some time ago," she says.

"Why?"

"Because it looks like it's been a while since you had a haircut."

My eyes drift toward a long-haired woman standing behind the hairdresser. For a split second, I'm shocked at this woman's sudden appearance, seemingly out of nowhere. Then it hits me that this woman is me. I barely recognize myself. I've lost weight. My hair is very long and shades darker than my natural color. I run my fingers through it uncertainly.

The hairdresser misinterprets the gesture. "I have an opening now if you want a cut."

I like the idea. Maybe if I go back to looking like me, it will pop the surreal bubble that has enveloped me since I woke in the park.

She leads me to a chair by a salon sink where she pulls back my head and turns on the water with a hiss. Geometric patterns from an overhanging chandelier flit across the ceiling, mesmerizing me while she rubs shampoo into my wet scalp with long nails. I close my eyes and try to relax to the gentle splash of water.

"We're done," she announces, turning off the faucet.

She rubs my hair dry with a black towel and wraps another around my head like a turban before escorting me to the closest chair.

"You have gorgeous hair," she enthuses, running her fingers through my wet strands. She asks how I want my hair cut.

I describe my usual style. For years, I've worn it in a short chic cut that brings out the green in my hazel eyes and accentuates my wide cheekbones.

The first clump of hair drops to the floor with a snip of her scissors. More hair follows, until the white floor tiles by my feet are covered and the hair dryer roars in my ears.

I panic at the cash register when I realize I don't have my credit card on me. Fortunately, I find a roll of money in my pocket so I pay with cash.

As I open the glass door to leave the salon, I almost collide with a man in a charcoal suit striding along the sidewalk like he's in a rush. My heart skips a beat. He looks like Marco. He has a chiseled face and jet-black hair, and he walks with the same cocky self-assurance.

"Sorry," he says, stepping around me.

He's not Marco. For a moment I can't breathe as sadness crushes me.

Chapter Seven

Two Years Earlier

"Liv. Liv. Wake up."

I wake, blinking blindly until the fuzzy blur leaning over me morphs into Marco. His chocolate eyes look down at my sleepy face as he gently shakes my shoulders. I stare up at him; too paralyzed to say a word. My eyes are open. The rest of me is fast asleep.

"Liv. It's time to get up," Marco tells me. I nod and drift off for a second before forcing myself to wake.

"What's the time?" I mutter sleepily.

"It's just after eleven."

"You have to be kidding!" I pull myself up and lean groggily against a pillow behind me. "Marco, you were supposed to wake me an hour ago."

"I tried. Believe me. I've never seen anyone so exhausted before in my life."

Marco opens the window shades with a long tug of a cord. I cover my face with my arm as sunshine streams into the bedroom.

"Marco, close the shades. The sun is killing me." I throw the covers over my head to block the blinding light.

In response, Marco disappears into the kitchen. He returns with a steaming mug of extra-strong coffee. I drink it and sink back onto the pillow, immune to the caffeine surging through my body as I drift off again.

There's no pick-me-up on this planet that could possibly wake me. Not after the party that Marco threw for me last night. I haven't stayed up this late since college. Nor have I drunk this much champagne since I drowned my sorrows at my mother's third wedding when I was seventeen. It must have been a portent of what was to come. She was killed a couple of years later when the bastard she married drove into a semitrailer while he was blind drunk.

Maybe that's why I hate drinking champagne, although I didn't tell Marco that last night when he produced a bottle of Bollinger. We were celebrating my promotion to senior staff writer at the magazine. I'll be writing features and other assignments, but mostly I'll be writing about food. My editor says that food is the new pop culture.

My promotion was a long time coming. I've been working at *Cultura Magazine* for six years. I joined the magazine right after I left teaching after a year of hell at my first school. I was lucky to get a temporary job at *Cultura* editing copy. Over the past six years, the temp job became permanent. Now, I've finally been promoted. I savor my new title. It might not sound like much, but I've worked my ass off to get it. I drift off, vaguely aware of a violent crash of water as Marco showers in the en suite.

"You still haven't gotten up!" His amused comment jolts me awake.

I open my eyes to see Marco walking across the bedroom with a white bath towel slung around his waist. He puts on blue chinos and a fitted casual shirt with gray hexagons, which he buttons up before disappearing into the bathroom again. When he comes out, his jet-black hair is neatly brushed. His cologne smells like ocean spray.

"Looks like you're getting ready for a hot date!" I joke.

"I'm off the dating scene. I have a girlfriend."

"Really? Do I know her?"

He leans in to kiss me. I try to unbalance him so that he'll fall on top of me, my fingers working at his top button. "God,

I wish we could, but I'm going to need to take a rain check." He gently removes my hands from his shirt.

Marco and I have been dating for almost three months. He's different from my other boyfriends. Maybe it's because he's European in nationality and sensibility. He has a way of making me feel cared for that I haven't experienced before. I can't remember when I've been this in love. The downside is that I'm not sure if Marco feels the same way. I think he does, but I sure as heck am not going to ask him. I've learned from experience that asking too many questions is the perfect way to ruin a relationship.

Marco's a very compartmentalized person. We see each other two to three nights a week when he's not traveling for work, which he does a lot. Marco left a job in finance to set up a technology start-up. It's something to do with advertising software. He's on the road a fair bit, raising capital and doing deals.

"Where are you going?" I prop myself up against a large pillow.

"I'm meeting an investor for lunch. Remember? You said last night that you'd join us. That's why I woke you. Otherwise I'd have let you sleep longer."

"I totally forgot!" I groan.

That's not technically true. I have a vague memory of a drunken promise to join him. It was quickly followed by regret. Being an appendage at a working lunch while Marco charms an investor is hardly my idea of a fun-filled Sunday with my boyfriend. Marco's so driven, but I wish he'd give his wheeling and dealing a break on weekends.

"I'm a mess. There isn't enough time for me to get ready." I run my hand through my disheveled hair.

"There's plenty of time for you to get ready." He puts on his watch.

I make a comical face in the mirror on the wall, amused at how my hair sticks out in a dozen different directions. I look like an ingenue with hair this short. It makes my eyes bigger and my face pointier and uncertain. I look much younger than a woman who's just hit the big thirty.

"Marco. Will you hate me if I skip the lunch?"

Disappointment shifts across his face so quickly that I wonder if I imagined it. "You don't have to come, Liv. It's up to you. Dean's bringing Emily, but I never told him that you were definitely joining us." He shrugs, leaving the rest unsaid.

I like that Marco doesn't push me. I've always had a tendency to date overbearing boyfriends who expect me to be at their beck and call. Marco's not like that at all. He's easygoing. It makes me want to please him.

"On second thought, I'll go. It'll be fun," I say, with forced enthusiasm.

"Great! You'll love Emily." I suspect he knew all along that I'd agree. Am I that predictable?

"What does Emily do?" I ask a few minutes later after I've showered. I take out linen pants and a navy off-the-shoulder top from Marco's closet. I keep a few outfits at his apartment. Sometimes I go straight to work when I stay overnight because he lives a few blocks from my office near Washington Square Park.

"She's a designer. Handbags and accessories. She's very talented. Dean tells me it's a tough industry to break into."

I hear that a lot. The market is flooded with designers trying to get discovered. It's the Project Runway effect. Some of the designers are amazing and yet they struggle to survive in a saturated market. These days, it's not how good you are as a designer but who you know, or how many Instagram followers you have. Celebrity is what sells. I tell Marco some version of this as I get dressed.

"If you like Emily's collection, then maybe you could get *Cultura* to do a write-up."

He says it nonchalantly, but I sense his expectation. My eyes flick to his face in the mirror while I apply lipstick. He sits on the edge of his bed putting on his socks, his face inscrutable.

"It's not my beat, although I can always ask the style team if they're interested," I offer.

I'm starting to suspect the real reason that Marco wants me at this lunch is so I'll meet Emily and get roped into arranging free publicity at my magazine for her label. I immediately feel bad about my uncharitable thoughts. Marco is not manipulative. If he wanted me to help his investor's wife with free publicity, then he'd have come right out and asked. On the other hand, he doesn't usually take meetings on a Sunday.

I'm uncharacteristically quiet as we leave the apartment.

Marco senses my disquiet. He puts his arm around me when we're out on the street. "How about we go on a bike ride after lunch?"

Marco has a set of road bikes. I've always presumed he keeps the smaller road bike for his girlfriend of the moment to join him on weekend bike rides.

Until I met Marco, I hadn't been on a bike since I was a kid. My dad taught me to ride during a visit to see his family in England when I was five. It's my last vivid memory of him before he walked out on Mom the following year.

Marco's an avid cyclist. After our second date, I borrowed a friend's bike and went riding by myself until I felt confident enough to join him on his weekend treks. I'm starting to get the bug, too. In fact, we're talking about doing a cycling trip in France in October.

"I'd love to, but I arranged to go to a kickboxing class with Amy this afternoon. She's already signed us up."

"I thought you hated kickboxing."

"It's growing on me. The instructor says I have potential."

"What does he mean by 'potential'?"

"He says I have great technique, but I'm too timid with my punches. Why don't you come over tonight instead?" I suggest to Marco. "I'll cook. Name any cuisine and I'll make you a feast."

Marco looks tempted. He knows I'm a great cook. My love affair with cooking began after Mom was killed in the crash.

Cooking became my therapy. I studied *cordon bleu* cooking part-time as a hobby. I even thought about working in the industry until I decided I preferred writing about food to working in the restaurant business. I like nothing better than to spoil my friends with a restaurant-quality meal at home. Surprisingly, instead of jumping at my invitation, Marco suggests we go out to eat.

"How about I ask Amy and Brett to join us?"

Marco's frown is immediate.

"Come on, Marco! A double date. It will be fun."

"With Brett?" he mocks. "Dr. God Complex? All he talks about is his patient list and how he's single-handedly saving humanity. He has zero interest in discussing anything that isn't about him. As for Amy, every time we meet up, we argue over politics. It totally kills the vibe."

"There won't be arguments," I say, not particularly convincingly, because their political discussions can get heated. "I'll ask Amy to tone it down." We both know that's unlikely to happen.

"Liv, you're going to have to get used to the idea that Amy and I don't get along. I know she's your best friend and you want us to like each other, but the two of us are like oil and water. We don't mix."

Chapter Eight

Natalie with her singsong "good morning" greeting isn't at the reception desk as I come out of the elevator and head into the office. Instead, a receptionist with blond-tipped bangs is taking a call on her headset.

"*Cultura Magazine.* How can I connect your call?"

The receptionist looks up as I pass her desk. I flash a confused smile. She doesn't smile back. Instead she asks briskly who I'm here to see.

"I'm not here to see anyone. I work here. Where's Natalie?" My tone comes out more rudely than intended. An accusation more than a question. Natalie's been *Cultura's* receptionist for so long that it feels wrong for anyone else to be behind the reception desk.

She looks at me blankly. "Who?"

"Natalie." My voice drops off as I realize she must be a temp. Maybe Natalie is on sick leave. "Never mind."

I walk past the reception desk toward the main office, where I beeline to my cubicle, pausing at the expansive window by my desk to take in the familiar view of the street.

As I turn to sit on my black swivel chair, a leggy young woman with long red hair tosses a jacket over the back of the seat. She's dressed like a runway model in a tartan miniskirt with thigh-high boots and a black cropped sweater. She drops her purse on the desk and leans forward to plug in a laptop.

My gaze shifts from her to a photo montage pinned to a corkboard on the cubicle wall. The strangers' faces in the photos

34

blur into a kaleidoscope of colors as my head spins. I put my hand on the back of the chair to stop myself from losing my balance.

"Who are you?" I think she asks me. Maybe it's me who asked her.

"I'm Liv. Liv Reese."

Her mouth widens into a beaming smile of recognition. "Liv! I'm Josie." She talks as if I should know her. She opens her arms and gives me a hug. "I am thrilled to meet you. Finally."

"It's wonderful to meet you, too," I respond out of politeness rather than recognition. I try to place her but I can't. There's nobody called Josie at the magazine.

"It's so great to see you back at *Cultura*," she gushes.

I want to tell her that I never left, that I've been here all along, when I look around and realize the office looks different. It's had a radical makeover.

The carpet used to be dark blue. Now it's a textured concrete gray decorated with splotches of lime and electric blue that look faintly like hopscotch markings.

Desks are arranged in little island hubs across the open-plan floor space. Scattered under pillars are sitting areas of backless round sofas also in lime and electric blue. Jeans-clad people slouch about on the sofas like teenagers in their bedrooms, typing rapidly on their laptops as they sip from mugs of coffee.

The office is too fluorescent. Too pulsating. Too hard on the eyes. It's alien, and yet familiar. *Cultura* is written on the office wall in giant three-dimensional reflective silver letters in the same archetypal font used on the cover of the magazine. I'm definitely in the right place.

Farther along is a wall covered with glass-framed *Cultura Magazine* covers going back years. I've worked on every issue of the magazine since I started working here. I know all of the covers like the back of my hand, but I don't recognize any of the most recent ones.

Everything is out of sync. I need to figure out why. I glance at the writing on my wrist. DON'T SLEEP! I FORGET EVERYTHING

35

WHEN I FALL ASLEEP. I fell asleep on the park bench. What did I forget?

Josie's chatter washes over me as I try to remember. She talks about the magazine's new direction as she shepherds me around the office. My unease turns into near panic as I realize I don't recognize anyone. Everyone at the office is a stranger. I feel as if I'm in a parallel universe.

My eyes dart toward the entrance. I want to make an excuse and get out of here, but Josie is already introducing me to the team. Everyone is superfriendly, getting up from their desks to greet me with a succession of warm hugs. They treat me like I'm the prodigal daughter returning to the fold.

"You look wonderful, Liv."

They all give me different versions of the same compliments in saccharine voices that are too chipper to be authentic. They're being too nice. That bothers me more than the hopscotch carpet.

A woman rushes toward me and embraces me as if I'm a long-lost sister. I hug her back, thinking that I don't know who the hell she is.

"Liv, I wish we'd known that you were coming today. We'd have arranged a lunch to welcome you. It can't be easy...."

"What can't be easy?" I ask.

"Coming back here after all this time..."

I stare at her uncomprehendingly. Her cheeks flush. She looks away, squirming with discomfort.

She changes the subject.

"I'd love to hear about your life in London."

I'm lost for words. I don't know what she's talking about. I've never lived in London. Without pausing for breath, she inundates me with questions. What part of London did I live in? Did I do a lot of traveling around the UK?

I want to tell her that she's mixing me up with someone else. The only time I've spent in Europe was a six-week backpacking trip with friends after college. I certainly have never lived there.

"You must be very jet-lagged," she says. "It always takes me a day or two to adjust when I fly back from Europe."

Jet lag? Maybe that's why I feel so numb.

Josie sweeps me away toward the office pantry area. It's been remodeled into an open-plan lifestyle area with an assortment of white-and-lime tables and chairs. A giant white shelf of bright green ferns in white pots serves as a natural divider with the rest of the office. She prepares us coffees on a shiny new coffee machine as she jabbers on about *Cultura*.

She talks as if I'm aware of all the changes at the magazine. I'm not. If anything, I'm shocked by what she tells me.

It turns out that it's not just the office decor that has changed. The magazine was taken over by a European magazine publisher. There's been a radical change of strategy. Now there's an emphasis on a younger, millennial audience. The online and social channels get as much attention as the magazine. There's talk of turning the hard-copy magazine into a quarterly.

"I barely recognize anyone here. The staff is completely different."

"It's the restructure. They let a lot of people go," Josie explains.

I'm shocked to hear that Frank, my editor, and Sonya, the style editor, were retrenched along with Natalie and many others. Poor Natalie. She's a single mom. She really needed the money, and she loved working here.

"We're going for edgy. That's why they hired Niko to be the executive editor and why the editorial team has changed. It's a younger team to reflect the demographic of our new readership. Ted, as you know," she pauses meaningfully, "transferred here a few months ago to run the commercial side of the business. Neither of them is here today."

"Where are they?" I ask, largely because it seems expected that I show interest.

"Nico is at a cover shoot in L.A. Ted is home sick. It's bad timing. They would have loved to have been here to welcome you."

Josie prattles on at a mile a minute while I try to make sense of all these changes at the magazine. Everything is off-kilter. I need to get back in control. To do that, I need a laptop so I can check my emails and refresh my memory. It's not possible that I've blanked out for what seems like years.

"Actually," I pipe up. "Ted asked me to come in... to work on a project." I become more confident as I lie. "He was supposed to organize a loaner laptop for me, and somewhere to work. I hope he didn't forget."

"Ted gets more forgetful the closer he gets to his wedding day." She bites her lip and flushes as if she's said something out-of-line. I have no idea what she's talking about, or why I'd care.

"It's so great that you two are still..." she starts to say, and stops when she notices my frozen expression. "I'll find you a spare laptop."

Josie escorts me to a small glass-walled meeting room over-looking the lunch area. She tells me she'll be back in a minute with the computer.

While I wait, I stare at the morning news on a large TV screen. The footage cuts to police officers standing behind crime scene tape at the entrance of an apartment building. A graphic at the bottom of the screen says: MURDERER WRITES MESSAGE IN VICTIM'S BLOOD.

The camera crash zooms from street level to an apartment window. Painted on the window in red letters are the words

WAKE UP!

I've seen that message before. I push up my sleeve. The same words are scribbled just below my wrist bone.

Chapter Nine

The laptop Josie brings me is a clunky old beast with a sticky space bar. While she sets it up for me, I stand by the meeting room's internal window and scan the office looking for my missing handbag. I assumed I'd left it on my desk, along with my phone, when I went out to get breakfast and take a breather at the park.

I now know that my handbag's not here since I clearly haven't been in the office for some time. My desk isn't even mine anymore. It belongs to Josie.

"Is there something wrong?" Josie asks as she rises from the floor after bending to plug in the laptop charger.

"I think I've lost my purse," I tell her, without revealing that I'm more concerned that I might have lost my mind. How could I have forgotten that I don't work here anymore?

"Let's check with the police lost property," she suggests. "Maybe someone turned it in."

Before I can protest, she looks up a phone number for the local police precinct on the loaner laptop and dials it on the desk phone.

"I'll take it from here," I tell her, as the line rings. "I don't want to hold you up from your work."

She hands me the receiver and heads for her desk. I feel uncomfortable about involving the police. I have a deep distrust of cops, dating back to when I was briefly put in child protection after Mom was arrested for a DUI during her acrimonious divorce from Randal.

While I navigate the computerized phone system, pressing the various number options to get to the police lost and found department, I read the spidery ballpoint messages on my hands. STAY AWAKE, it says under my knuckles.

"I'd like to report a lost or stolen handbag," I tell a curt duty officer when my call is answered.

"Which is it?" she demands.

"What do you mean?"

She sighs impatiently. "Was it lost or stolen?"

"I'm not sure. I fell asleep on a bench at Washington Square Park. When I woke, it was gone."

"You fell asleep? And your handbag was gone?" she says with disbelief. "Okaaaay…." She drags out the word. I feel like an idiot.

"Can you describe your handbag and tell me anything about the brand and color?"

Since I don't remember which purse I had with me today, I describe the three handbags that I use interchangeably. I sense her impatience.

"You just described three different purses," she snaps in exasperation. "Are you missing one or three?"

"One."

"So which one are you missing?" She barely conceals her impatience.

"I don't know. I can't remember which I took today," I stutter.

"Let me get this straight," she says. "You fell asleep on a park bench. When you woke, your handbag was gone. You don't know if someone stole it while you slept or if you lost it. And you don't remember what color it was, or the brand." She pauses for breath. "Listen, lady, I have a suggestion for you."

"What is it?"

"Why don't you call us back when you remember," she says in an angry staccato.

The phone disconnects with a click. I'm so annoyed by the woman's rudeness that I take a pen from a container on the table and I write on my hand: DON'T TALK TO THE COPS **EVER**!!

It's a childish gesture, but it makes me feel better. That police officer treated me as if I was nuts. I'm not. I'm certain there's a perfectly reasonable explanation for my confusion. Perhaps I'm feeling the aftereffects of a sedative that's left me in a zombie state. Or maybe I really am jet-lagged. That might explain why everything feels as if it's happening to someone else.

I put my head in my hands and try to focus on what to do next. If I've lost my purse then someone may have my credit cards. I need to cancel them.

I pick up the phone again and call my bank. After I've worked my way through the self-serve system, twice, my call is answered by "Brad" from customer service.

I tell Brad that my wallet is missing and that I'd like to block all my credit cards and access to my bank account. We go through a verification process of my name, social security number, and all the rest.

Brad puts me on hold while he checks my details. The tinny hold music rubs my nerves so raw that I breathe an audible sigh of relief when his officious voice returns on the line.

"Ma'am, there must be a mistake. You don't have an account with this bank." His tone is patronizing.

"You are Chase Bank?"

"Yes."

"Then I definitely have an account with you. I've been banking with you since high school."

"Ma'am, our records show that your account was closed more than two years ago."

"Who closed the account?"

"You did."

"That's not possible."

"There's no mistake, ma'am. Perhaps you've forgotten? I suggest you go to a branch with your ID. Someone will help you further."

41

"But I don't have my ID. It's in my handbag. The one that's missing. That's the reason for my call; to cancel my credit cards."

"You definitely don't have any cards or bank accounts with us anymore so there's nothing to cancel," he says.

I hang up the phone feeling physically sick as I consider the possibility that my bank accounts have disappeared, which means I have no money. In a panic, I take out the wad of cash I found in my pocket at the hairdresser. I count the money, note by note, making a pile on my lap. There's over a thousand dollars in crisp notes.

My eyes well with tears. Everything has felt inside-out since I woke on the bench at Washington Square Park. My bank account at Chase has been closed, apparently for years. My desk at work has been taken over by bubbly Josie with her tartan skirt and legs that seem to go on forever. The office has changed almost beyond recognition. Almost everyone here is a stranger to me. They all think that I've been living in London, which is patently ridiculous. Who forgets relocating to a foreign city?

I look again at the message written on my hand. DON'T SLEEP! I FORGET EVERYTHING WHEN I FALL ASLEEP.

The sentence reverberates in my head. What else have I forgotten? I sense it's something important. No matter how much I try, I can't think of what it might be. The only thing I know for sure is that time has skipped ahead without me noticing.

"What's today's date?" I type into the search bar on Google.

"November 2," says the search result.

That surprises me. My last memory is from July 31. I distinctly remember seeing the day marked on the calendar pinned to my cubicle wall when I reached across my desk to answer the phone.

Three months have passed.

No, not three months, I correct myself. I focus on the date on the computer screen.

Two years have passed, and I remember none of it. It feels as if I've been catapulted into the future.

Chapter Ten

Two Years Earlier

Lunch is a disaster. Marco's investor, Dean Walker, is a cradle-snatching misogamist who makes it clear he expects me to use my contacts at *Cultura* to get free publicity for his young wife's fledgling design business.

It puts me in an awkward bind. Apparently, Marco's other funding options have fallen through. Marco tried to sound blasé about the whole thing, but he obviously has a lot riding on this pending deal with Dean.

Emily's in her midtwenties, a handful of years younger than me. She has coltish legs and long hair that's more strawberry than blond. Her bust, if real, would be a wonder of the modern world.

Dean's in his midsixties with dyed hair plugs and a face so Botoxed that he looks like a lecherous gargoyle. An ex-investment banker who runs a private equity fund, he met Emily at a green energy conference in Vegas. "The rest," he says, waving his hand dramatically in the air, "is history."

When we've settled at our window table, Dean and Marco jump straight into a discussion about their prospective business venture. I ask Emily about herself.

"I'm a dancer but my real love is fashion. I especially adore accessories," Emily enthuses. "They can make or break an outfit. That's why I designed my own handbag collection."

She confesses that she has no design background and no experience in the fashion industry. "Dean says all I need is good publicity and my designs will be snapped up. Plus, I have my Instagram account."

Her label is called Embr. "It's the first two letters of my first and last name. The name was Dean's idea."

Emily takes out her phone and scrolls through to show me her handbags and accessories designs on her Instagram feed.

It's obvious she's here to pitch to me and I give the appropriate encouraging responses.

Emily asks me about *Cultura*. "It must be amazing to work at such a prestigious magazine."

"Oh, it is," I respond. "I'm very lucky."

I try to move the conversation in another direction. Every time I do, she brings the discussion back to the magazine. Eventually, she gets to the point.

"So how does *Cultura* choose the fashion items it features in its hot new trends column," she asks.

Getting a spot in the *Cultura* design column is very sought-after since it is closely followed by fashion aficionados and department store buyers.

"To tell you the truth, I don't deal with the style side of the magazine. I generally write features and do interviews."

"Really? On what?"

Dean has apparently been listening to our conversation while talking to Marco and he intervenes to ask me bluntly whether I can arrange for Emily to be featured in the magazine.

"I was just telling Emily that it's the style editor who decides. Of course, I'm always happy to put in a good word for talented designers," I say, as diplomatically as possible.

His eyes get narrow and mean. He's about to say something when the waiter arrives with our meals artfully arranged on oversized white plates. The waiter moves around the table putting our orders in front of us, while telling us the names of the dishes and the key ingredients. When he reaches Emily, she asks whether the homemade aioli in her Caesar salad is vegan.

The waiter seems lost for words. Judging by the unease in his pale eyes, I can tell that he's wondering whether he should point out that a Caesar salad is a decidedly non-vegan menu choice regardless of whether the aioli has eggs in it or not. Eventually, he says in a masterfully polite tone that he'll check with the chef. He heads to the kitchen and returns a minute later.

"I'm afraid the aioli is not vegan. The chef tells me that since there are eggs, anchovies, and Parmesan cheese in the salad, he uses a traditional aioli. However, he can remake the salad for you with vegan mayonnaise if you prefer. Or if you prefer a vegan meal then you could choose one of the vegan items listed on the menu. They're all marked 'Vegan.'"

I admire the lack of irony in his voice.

"How long will it take to make her salad from scratch?" Dean snaps.

"About ten minutes," the waiter says.

"So we're all supposed to wait?" says Dean, staring him down.

The waiter holds his stare for a fraction of a second before his face goes blank and a servile expression magically appears. I sense it's far from sincere. Who could blame him? Dean's rudeness makes me blush.

"It doesn't matter. I'll keep the salad," says Emily, staring at the ground as if she wished it would swallow her up.

"No, you won't, honey," Dean tells her. "Choose something else. The chef will expedite your order. Right?" he challenges the server.

"We'll do our best."

She chooses a Greek salad instead.

"The Greek salad contains feta cheese, which is a dairy item," the waiter says haltingly. "Is that an issue?"

"Get her what she wants," Dean snaps. "Hurry up. We've been kept waiting long enough."

When he's gone, Emily takes out a designer shopping bag with her logo and presents it to me as a gift. Inside is a bright-yellow handbag with a tassel and a matching purse.

I'm about to refuse it as nicely as possible when Marco gives the slightest shake of his head. He's worried I might offend them.

The plea in Marco's eyes wins out. I thank Emily and gush over how much I love her bags, even though they're flashy and not at all to my taste.

Emily's salad arrives. The chef has cleverly put the cheese in its own container on the side. The rest of the meal goes in a blur of desserts and coffees. Dean uses every opportunity to get a gibe in at the waiter, who ever since the Caesar salad showdown can apparently do nothing right as far as Dean is concerned.

I look at Marco and silently beg him to say something. He gives an imperceptible shake of his head as if to indicate that he's powerless. I suppose he is if he wants Dean's money.

When the waiter brings the bill, Dean insists on paying. "Marco, you got it last time." They argue the point. Dean wins by snatching the bill and waving it in the air along with his credit card.

The three of us chat as the server processes the credit card and brings it to Dean to sign. I'm vaguely aware of Dean taking out his wallet and leaving cash before we rise from the table.

It's only as we're walking out of the café that I hear Dean whisper to Emily that the waiter will regret his rudeness and terrible service when he sees his tip.

When we're on the street, I turn and glance through the window of the café just as the server picks up Dean's measly ten-dollar tip, all in single bills. It was left under the salt shaker on our table. The waiter should have been tipped at least four times that amount based on my rough estimate of our bill.

The waiter looks up and sees me watching. I'm absolutely mortified. Dean and Emily get into a cab, while Marco kisses me goodbye and heads back to his apartment. I've already told him I'll go straight home from the café since there's a subway station at the end of the block.

When Marco's out of sight, I go back into the restaurant. Our table is already being set for the next customer and the waiter is taking orders at another table. I approach him during a brief lull.

"I'm sorry my, er, friends were rude," I tell him. Scrambling in my purse, I hand over forty dollars, which is by my reckoning the balance of the tip he was shortchanged on.

"You don't need to do that."

"You should have been tipped properly to begin with... Kevin." I read his name off his name badge. "I served tables when I was in college. I know this is your income."

"Thank you," he says, putting the cash into his pocket. As I turn to leave, he says: "By the way, I'm a big fan of your columns in *Cultura Magazine*."

"Thanks."

In truth, it creeps me out that he'd been listening so intently to our conversation while he served us that he knows who I am and the magazine I write for.

Chapter Eleven

Detective Darcy Halliday flicked through photos of the crime scene she'd taken on her phone as Jack Lavelle steered the navy Ford through heavy traffic on their way to the city morgue. Those photos were all they'd have until they received the official crime scene images sometime in the afternoon.

The crime scene photographer had still been snapping away at the scene when they'd left, accompanying the victim's body, which had been zipped into a black body bag and taken on a stretcher down to a morgue van on the street. Halliday and Lavelle had studiously ignored the reporters calling out questions from behind a police barricade as they exited the building.

"Our biggest problem right now is that we have no ID for the victim," Lavelle told Halliday as he drove. "Homicide investigations are exponentially harder when the identity of the victim is unknown."

The owner of the apartment wasn't due to land in Hong Kong until late afternoon New York time. Lavelle hoped the owner would be able to tell them who had rented the apartment for the night. That individual was most likely the victim, or possibly the killer.

In every other respect, the investigation was looking good, even though it was early days. The forensics team had found fingerprints all over the bedroom and the bathroom.

In fact, the embarrassment of riches of trace evidence found at the scene was something of a headache in disguise. They'd be lucky if they received the fingerprint results by the weekend. Hundreds of prints would have to be cross-referenced and collated before being run through the system. The lab had to exclude the victim's prints and the prints of everyone who'd been at the scene, including Olga, the cleaner. She'd be asked to provide her fingerprints and samples of her hair when she came to the precinct later to sign her statement.

At the morgue, Halliday and Lavelle waited at the entrance of the autopsy room while the pathologist finished a Y-incision on a morbidly obese middle-aged man who lay with his lifeless head hyperextended on the slab and a sheet pulled down to his waist.

The chief pathologist was a sixty-year-old doctor with a semicircle of white hair on an otherwise hairless pate. He had the somewhat apt name of Dr. Cutter, although he generally went by his first name, Richard.

"Can I help you, Detectives?" Dr. Cutter asked, looking up from the metal autopsy table once he'd completed the incision.

"Any chance you can expedite the autopsy of the stiff that's just checked into cabin twenty-four?" asked Lavelle. "So far we're stumped on the ID. We haven't found anything at the scene that so much as tells us his first name."

"There's a backlog of bodies waiting for autopsy, and I have two staff members out sick," said Dr. Cutter. "But we can definitely get dental impressions done today, even if the autopsy has to wait a few days."

"Whatever you can do, Doc," Lavelle said. "There was no murder weapon at the scene so we're keen to find out what sort of implement was used to stab the vic. By the way, this is my partner, Detective Darcy Halliday."

The pathologist picked up a round electric blade for cutting through the rib cage. "Detective Halliday, I don't know what you did to draw the short straw and get Jack as your partner. But either way, you have my deepest commiserations." He turned on the electrical cutter and began working the round blade into the body on the slab.

"And that," whispered Lavelle ironically to Halliday as they turned to leave, "is why no male detective ever likes to stand too close to Dr. Richard Cutter when he's doing an autopsy."

After their fleeting visit to the morgue, Lavelle did a quick detour to the forensics lab. He double-parked while Halliday ran out to drop off several pieces of evidence they wanted fast-tracked. Among them was an evidence bag with the wine bottle Halliday had found next to the bed. She hoped it would turn out to be the holy grail of evidence. There was as good a chance as any that the bottle contained the killer's fingerprints, and perhaps even saliva so they could extract the killer's DNA.

"We'll head back to the precinct," Lavelle said when Halliday returned to the car. "The first batch of security camera footage should be there soon. I'm expecting we'll get hundreds of hours of CCTV footage to trawl through."

Halliday glanced sideways at Lavelle. She wondered whether he'd try to put her in charge of reviewing all the security camera footage. That was the sort of desk jockey work she'd been assigned since she'd been transferred over to homicide. As if reading her thoughts, Lavelle told her he'd rustled up two detectives and a few uniformed cops to go through the video footage.

"We both need to be out in the field. Not chained to a desk," he said.

A small team of rookie cops had been assigned to search for the murder weapon in trash cans and drains in the vicinity of the building where the murder had taken place. Another team had fanned out across the neighborhood, knocking on doors to collect security camera footage and checking whether anyone had witnessed anything suspicious overnight. They were in the process of collecting surveillance footage from city CCTV cameras, as well as private security cameras in shops and buildings in the vicinity of the murder scene.

The only lead Halliday and Lavelle had to work with, at least until the security camera footage arrived, was the writing on the bedroom window. Halliday zoomed in and out of the photo she'd taken of the words WAKE UP! written in the victim's blood.

"Ever seen writing in blood at a crime scene?" she asked Lavelle.

"A few times," he conceded. "Usually when the killer was drugged out of his mind, or going through a psychotic episode. In those cases, they write lots of crazy stuff, sometimes in blood or feces. Usually whatever they write is rambling garbage."

"That's not the case here," Halliday said, staring at the two succinct words on her photo of the crime scene window. "The killer was making a point. The question is what point, and why go to the trouble of writing WAKE UP! in blood on the window?"

Even though Halliday had been assigned to Lavelle's precinct for a couple of months already, the two hours they'd worked together on the homicide was the longest she'd ever spent in his company.

They knew each other in passing. She'd nodded to him a few times when she'd seen him lifting weights at the fitness center near the precinct where she also worked out. They'd shared elevators and rubbed shoulders making coffee in the kitchenette by the Detective Bureau. They'd attended plenty of team meetings at the precinct. Their casual interactions had never gone beyond the most basic niceties, and they'd never worked together on a case.

Halliday had been in the unit long enough to get the impression that Lavelle rarely socialized with the rest of the team. Despite that, the other detectives treated Lavelle with the same deference they gave to the captain.

"What did the neighbors tell you when you interviewed them earlier?" Lavelle asked, making a left turn near the precinct.

"The teenage son of the neighbor who lives at the end of the hall said he was binge-watching a TV series in bed when he thought he heard a door slam. He thinks it happened at around two in the morning."

"How can he be so sure of the time?" Lavelle asked.

"It was near the end of his episode. He set his alarm and went to sleep as soon as it finished. It's possible the noise he heard was the killer leaving the apartment."

"Did you talk to anyone else?"

"The woman who lives diagonally opposite the apartment didn't hear or see anything last night. However, she did see a couple coming out of the elevator yesterday morning around ten, when she was waiting to take it down to get to work. She said the man looked like Ryan Reynolds. That's why she remembered him. The woman accompanying him had dark hair. Very long."

"Did the couple go into the apartment where the murder took place?"

"She didn't see where they went because she stepped into the elevator and the doors shut behind her. She did say that she'd never seen them before. That might not mean much. Two apartments on that floor are regularly rented on short-stay websites. There are always new faces around. My hunch is that the couple did go in there."

"What makes you think that?"

"The long dark hairs I found on the pillow and in the bathroom fit the neighbor's description of a woman with extremely long hair."

"So you think our killer was a woman."

"It's certainly possible. It explains why she drugged him. So he wouldn't put up a fight."

While they waited at a traffic light, Lavelle called the security company responsible for the CCTV cameras in the apartment building to find out when copies of the footage would be ready for collection. The supervisor said it might take a few more hours.

"I have a bad feeling about this," murmured Lavelle, hanging up before stepping on the gas when the light turned green.

"We really need that footage," said Halliday. "The CCTV video must have visuals of the killer."

"I agree. Unless, of course, the killer had wings and flew out of the sixth-floor window, in which case we really are screwed," remarked Lavelle.

"What did the doorman tell you when you spoke with him?" Halliday asked.

"He didn't see anyone or anything suspicious. Having said that, he only started his shift at six A.M., an hour before the cleaner found the body. He said we should talk to the overnight doorman. I called a couple of times, but his phone is off. I'm guessing he's asleep."

Lavelle glanced at Halliday as he pulled the car into the parking lot next to the precinct. She was relatively young for a detective. He figured her for late twenties. He hadn't had any personal dealings with her since she'd moved to the unit on a temporary transfer. He'd heard she'd received the highest marks in the detective's exam in seven years and that she'd done a standout job at Major Case. He happened to have seen her at the firing range the previous week and had been impressed at how she handled a weapon. She was an incredible shot. He'd heard she'd been a sharpshooter in the military. He also knew she was very fit because he often saw her running to work.

"You're a serious runner," he said.

"I run for fun, mostly. Although right now I am in training for an ultramarathon next spring in Arizona."

"What distance?"

"Fifty miles. Through the desert. We run at night."

"With the coyotes and the rattlesnakes?"

"Something like that," she laughed.

"Why would you put yourself through that hell?"

"For the challenge. And to raise money."

"Any particular cause?" he asked.

"An old friend from the military, Lieutenant Antonio Lopez. Lost a leg in a roadside blast near Mosul. It was on Tony's bucket list to run this ultramarathon. I'm doing it on his behalf. The money I raise will go to his baby daughter and to help other wounded veterans adjust to civilian life."

"That's very generous of him, and you. But he's also a wounded veteran. He doesn't need the help?" Lavelle asked.

"Well, that's a sad story," Halliday said, not saying anything for a long moment as she looked out the car window, blinking furiously. "It just so happens," she said finally, a crack in her voice, "that Tony took his own life earlier this year."

Chapter Twelve

Now that I know it's two years in the future, I quickly scroll news headlines on my loaner laptop, looking for something to jog my memory. A headline from this morning catches my attention.

"Killer Wrote Message with Victim's Blood on Bedroom Window."

When I click on the headline, an article opens up.

"Police believe a murderer wrote the message—WAKE UP!—on the window of an apartment after killing an unknown man," the article says. "The body of the man was found in bed this morning in a mid-town apartment. NYPD detectives are investigating."

Below the article is a photo of police wearing navy CSI jackets going up the stairs into the lobby of an apartment building. The article provides no information about the dead man. No name. No details of his identity.

There's a suggestion the man might have been killed during a robbery. The article quotes a resident of the apartment building where the man was murdered as saying there had been several incidents of petty theft and a home burglary in the complex in the past month alone.

Near the bottom of the article is the building's location. I give up on reading the news and open my personal email account in the hope that my emails will lift the fog that's surrounded me since I woke on the park bench.

The system rejects my password. A security notification tells me that "unusual activity was noticed in your account." It says a code has been texted to my cell phone to restore my account. The problem is that I don't have my phone.

When I try to access my social media accounts, the same thing happens. After three passwords guesses are rejected, I get locked out of my social accounts as well as my email. I've been electronically cut off from my life.

The meeting room phone rings suddenly, startling me with its insistent peal.

"Hello?"

"Liv, this is Dee from reception. I have a call for you. Please hold while I transfer it through."

There's a single beep followed by a man's voice. "Liv?"

Something about the muffled voice makes the hairs prickle on the back of my neck.

"Yes?" My throat is tight. I can barely raise my voice above a whisper.

"Where did you put it?"

"Put what?"

"The knife," he hisses. "What did you do with the damn knife, Liv? You took the goddamn knife when I was in the bathroom, and you walked off with it."

"I don't know what you're talking about. This must be a wrong number." I resist the urge to hang up the phone. I feel compelled to know more.

"Don't tell me you fell asleep and forgot everything again?" he says.

He frightens me with the accuracy of his comment. "How do you know I woke up with no memory?"

"Because you lose your goddamn memory every time you fall asleep. Listen, here's what I want you to do…"

The door opens with a rattle. I put my hand over the receiver as Josie pops her head through the doorway.

"The spring issue planning meeting is about to start," she says. "We'd love for you to join. As the guest of honor. Everyone's waiting for you."

"Okay. Um, sure. That would be great. I'll be there as soon as I'm done with this call," I tell her.

"Sure," Josie says, still hovering.

I hold the phone against my chest until Josie's left the room.

"Who are you?" I whisper into the phone once she's closed the door behind her.

There's nobody on the line. All I hear is an engaged signal.

I put down the receiver with a click. A sickening dread creeps through me. Something terrible is going on and I don't have the faintest idea what it is.

Chapter Thirteen

Two Years Earlier

We spend the better part of an hour passing around mood boards and swatches of colors as we discuss plans for the December issue of *Cultura*. December is almost six months away, but the Christmas issue is always a blowout, which means months of extra planning, pages of extra content, and pullouts with glossy advertising.

After canvassing our opinions on the design colors and cover proposals, Frank, our editor, assigns us the articles he wants us to write in addition to our usual beats. For me, that's food. For obvious reasons, food is always a big deal in the December issue. The other highlight is *Cultura*'s signature year-end articles.

"I always like our end-of-year features to have a fresh perspective," Frank reminds everyone. Naomi, who likes to think of herself as our resident arts writer, is visibly furious when Frank assigns me to write on the arts scene.

Naomi's never liked me anyway, not since I complained about George, a photographer she was dating, who put his hand on my thigh and propositioned me while we drove to cover a music festival. He was subsequently fired after it turned out that was his go-to move with young reporters. Naomi's pretty much hated my guts since.

When the meeting ends, Frank leaps out of his seat and rushes to his office so he doesn't have to hear everyone's complaints about their assignments. I go after him.

"Frank, you have writers here who are far more knowledge-able than me about the art world." Like Naomi, I think, who studied fine arts and considers anyone writing about the arts at *Cultura* to be not just stepping on her toes, but squashing them to smithereens.

"That's exactly why I want you to do it, Liv," he says. We walk past the wall of framed historic *Cultura Magazine* covers and enter his office.

"The last time I wrote a review on the Milo Zee exhibition, he sued me and the magazine. Do you really want to take the risk again?"

"It was all for publicity. He dropped the lawsuit," he says, dismissively. "Your article cut right through all his bullshit. It skewered him. The rest of the media took off their gloves after your piece came out."

Frank doesn't mention that the media frenzy led to Zee being accused of beating his girlfriend and ultimately being "canceled."

"It was just a review. I didn't intend to destroy his career."

"You have nothing to feel bad about, Liv. You were doing your job: giving a brutally honest review of his art show. I loved it, and so did our readers. It's why you were promoted."

He pulls last year's November issue from a shelf behind his desk and reads my review in a toneless voice.

> No wilting wallflower, Milo Zee describes himself as the ultimate bad boy artist and founder of his own school of millennial nihilism art. Zee has near-guru status among his more than one million Instagram followers who hail him as a #Zeenius.
>
> Zee's exhibition *Sum of Us* features enormous canvases created with paint made from his own bodily fluids. Zee says he slashed his wrist to produce the blood for the largest canvas, titled *Deathwish2*. He claims he almost died in the making of that curiously bland painting.
>
> The New York exhibit contains new works produced by Zee since his sellout shows in

London. Among them are an actual #Zeenius bowel movement displayed inside a transparent cube of resin hanging from the gallery ceiling, and a wineglass filled with Zee's own spit framed on a wall.

Zee's publicist describes his work as "an illuminating insight on the human condition. It reminds us that we are not the sum of our parts, but the parts of our sum."

I'm no expert on postmodern abstract art, but I have to admit that I found scraping mold from the grout between my bathroom tiles using an old toothbrush to be more illuminating than Zee's artwork, and a considerably more apt statement on the human condition.

Frank tosses the magazine onto his desk. "That's what I want in your year-end piece. That tone. That sarcasm."

"Frank, I wasn't being sarcastic. I was being sincere," I say, straight-faced.

"You cut him to shreds in a way that Naomi could never do. She's far too effusive to the artists she's trying to cultivate. Okay, get out of here, Liv. I have a budget meeting to prepare for."

Before returning to my desk, I stop at the office of our style editor, Sonya, and ask for her thoughts on Emily's handbag collection. I've given her the handbag samples that Emily gave me as well as a link to Emily's Instagram feed so she can see her other designs.

"At best, they looked like cheap and nasty knockoffs. At worst, well, let me suggest she finds a new hobby. I can't see how she can build a career as a serious designer if all she's doing is knocking off iconic designs."

She hands me back the handbag and purse that Emily gave me with the tips of her fingers as if they're contaminated.

I'm almost relieved at her candor. I can honestly tell Marco that I did my best to get Emily's collection written up in the magazine. Hopefully, if Dean has hard feelings, they won't be directed toward Marco. Remembering Dean's behavior at the restaurant, I have no doubt he's more than capable of petty acts of revenge.

When I return to my desk after a late lunch, I find a Post-it note on my keyboard. KEVIN ASKED YOU TO CALL, it reads. It includes his cell phone number.

Kevin is the waiter at the restaurant that I went to with Marco, Dean, and Emily. It's the third time he's called.

I returned his first message thinking I'd left something behind at the café. Of course I hadn't. He said he'd called to thank me for being so gracious by coming back to sort out the tip. Even though he was superpolite, the call creeped me out. As did his next call a few days later, which I didn't return.

I crumple up the note and toss it in the trash. Kevin's messages are starting to scare me.

Chapter Fourteen

Detective Darcy Halliday's hair was damp from the quick shower she'd taken in the women's locker room as soon as they'd returned to the precinct. She'd changed into a navy suit with a teal shirt which she kept in her locker. Her detective badge was clipped to her waistband, her service weapon was strapped in a holster on her left hip. Handcuffs hung off the back of her pants.

She stood back and observed the photo she'd printed and taped to the office window near her desk of the WAKE UP! message at the crime scene.

Lavelle wandered over from his desk to take a look.

"What are you thinking?" he asked.

"Was the message intended for the victim?" Halliday asked. "Regret for killing him? Or was it written for someone else? And why write the message on the window and then lower the shades? Why not keep the shades up? Or write the message on the bedroom wall near the body?"

"Because the message wasn't intended for the victim," Lavelle said, cottoning on to her train of thought.

"Exactly. That's why the killer wrote it in reverse; to make sure it was read properly from outside the building. The killer was making a statement to the outside world, not to the victim."

The glass door behind them slammed loudly. They both turned around to see Detectives Rosco and Tran from Central Robbery walking toward them between a row of desks.

"Looks like the cavalry's arrived," said Lavelle, holding out his hand to greet the two detectives.

He'd cleared two tables near Halliday's desk by the window, where both loan detectives would sit for the duration they'd be helping out. They'd be on transfer for a couple of weeks. It might be shorter or longer depending on how quickly they got a break in the case.

Halliday's cell phone rang just as Lavelle brought the detectives over to her for an introduction. She quickly shook their hands before answering.

"Halliday," she said, moving to the window where she'd taped the photo.

On the line was Owen Jeffries, an old friend from the military who had been recruited to the CIA when he finished his last tour.

"So you got my voicemail," she said.

"Sure did. What's up?"

While Halliday briefed Jeffries on the murder, she texted him the photo of the ghoulish writing on the window. "Any thoughts?" she asked.

"It shows premeditation," he said, once he received the photo.

"Why do you say that?"

"It's not natural to sign-write the message so it could be read correctly from the outside. It involves reversing not just the words but the shape of the letters. In my opinion, achieving this type of complex writing without any mistake, especially during a high stress situation such as after committing a murder, would require a cool head and planning."

"What sort of planning?" Halliday asked.

"It could be as simple as writing the message in reverse on a piece of paper before the murder. Or even on the back of a hand. That way it could be copied letter by letter to avoid mistakes. There are no mistakes, or reversing errors in the photo you sent me. That suggests it was preplanned."

The captain motioned for everyone on the investigation team to assemble in his office. Halliday covered the phone receiver and asked Lavelle to start without her. His expression suggested it wasn't a smart move for her to be late to her own briefing.

She pulled a notepad across the desk and wrote: *Talking to an old friend from my unit who's in the CIA. Give me a couple of minutes.* He nodded and headed into the office with Rosco and Tran.

Halliday asked Jeffries if he could run the message through the CIA's handwriting analysis database to compare the writing sample from the window to the millions of samples in the CIA and law enforcement databases.

"I can also do one better. I can run it through a new algo we've developed that gives a pretty good profile of the probable characteristics of the writer."

"What sorts of characteristics?"

"It can tell us with a high degree of probability whether the message was written by a male or female. The rough height of the writer. Left- or right-handed. Native English speaker. A read on the writer's age since writing styles taught at schools have changed over time. That sort of thing," he said. "Normally you'd have to request permission, but since we're old friends, I can cut through the red tape and run it through for you today."

"I was hoping you'd say that," she said.

"Make sure the lab cuts off the glass pane and scans it," Jeffries instructed. "It's more accurate than relying on photos or a tracing outline of the message."

–

The squeaking wheels of the portable whiteboard Halliday pulled into Captain Ken Clarke's office brought the conversation she'd interrupted to an immediate halt.

The captain was propped on the edge of his desk as he listened to Jack Lavelle give an overview of the case. Lavelle was leaning against a filing cabinet with his arms crossed as he spoke. Rosco and Tran sat on a sofa in front of a large internal window that looked out at rows of detectives' cluttered desks. Detective Tran half rose to give Halliday his seat, but she motioned for him to stay put.

"The ME believes the victim was killed by a single stab wound," said Lavelle. "Death was immediate, or close to it. No hesitation wounds. The crime scene was neat and organized. No signs of a struggle. Forensic evidence at the scene suggests that a woman might have been involved."

"Why a woman?" the captain interrupted.

Lavelle looked at Halliday, the incline of his head inviting her to answer the question.

"We found a long strand of black hair, believed to be from a woman, on a pillow next to the victim," Halliday explained. "A neighbor saw a woman with long dark hair exit the elevator with a man yesterday morning. We believe that man may have been the victim."

Halliday handed around packets of printouts of several photos from the crime scene that she'd taken on her phone. Among them was a photo of the victim's bloodied feet and of the writing daubed in blood on the bedroom window.

"WAKE UP!" The captain read it out loud. "Is it a political statement?"

"We don't know yet," said Halliday.

"I think it was a hit," said Rosco. "How often do we ever find a stabbing victim with only one wound? I'll tell you how often. Never. There are always several. Sometimes dozens, or more. I don't think the slashes to the feet count."

"They don't. They were almost certainly done postmortem," Halliday noted. "As far as we know pending the autopsy results, the victim was killed by a single knife wound to the heart. The victim died almost instantly. Blood spatter was minimal. You're right. It's rare, almost unheard of, for there to be a single stab wound in a homicide. There's usually defense wounds, overkill wounds, and sometimes hesitation wounds."

"Exactly," said Rosco. "Not too many people can kill a man with one slash of a knife. Not unless they have skills. Ex–special forces. Once we get an ID on the vic, we should look into whether he has any connections to organized crime. We should hone in on the Russians. The Russian mafia recruits former Russian special forces soldiers. Those guys sure like using knives."

"Knives and poison," said the captain. "Both seem to have played a role in this case." He tapped his finger on a photo of the wine bottle that Lavelle said might have been spiked with a sedative. "Do we know what kind of knife was used?"

"The perp took the murder weapon," Lavelle said.

"Well, there you go!" Rosco added. "A perp so attached to his blade that he can't bring himself to leave it behind. It adds fuel to the theory that it was a killer for hire."

"It wasn't a mob hit." Halliday's tone was so emphatic that everyone went silent.

"How do you know?" the captain asked.

"If it was a mob hit, the killer would have used a gun. Two bullets in the head is faster and more accurate than a knife."

Halliday swapped to a detached tone now that she had their attention. She knew from experience never to show that she was emotionally invested in a theory. It was the sign of a cop with tunnel vision, and a cop with tunnel vision was a lousy investigator. She wasn't blinkered. She just happened to have more information than they did.

"Even contract killers have preferences," said Lavelle.

"Contract killers do their job and leave. They don't get sidetracked with art projects," said Halliday. To emphasize her point, she slapped a photo of the WAKE UP! message under a magnet on the whiteboard.

Lavelle liked the way Halliday stood her ground. He hated when detectives, especially new ones, buckled at the first sign of an opposing opinion and embraced groupthink.

"The writing on the window could have been deliberate. A bum steer," Rosco remarked. "I've seen contract killers fixing crime scenes before to give the impression it's the work of a serial killer. A slogan in blood on a wall. A mutilated body that looks like it was cut up by a sicko to send everyone on a wild goose chase."

"I don't chase geese." Halliday was firm.

"So what's your theory?" Lavelle asked.

He agreed with Halliday that it wasn't a contract killing. There was nothing specific that jumped out at him when he was at the scene. His judgment was based on pure instinct honed by almost two decades working homicides.

"I won't speculate. It's too soon to have a theory. We don't even know the victim's identity," she pointed out. Halliday wouldn't be drawn on theories when there were no witnesses and the forensics information was still being worked on.

She knew about confirmation bias and how airing a theory led some detectives to inadvertently look for evidence that supported their hunch, while ignoring evidence that undermined it.

"Let's focus on the nuts and bolts of this investigation. Fingerprints, CCTV footage, and identifying the victim," said the captain. "Follow the evidence."

He rose to his feet to indicate the briefing was over. "Keep me updated. I don't want to find out anything on the evening news that I should have found out first here in this office. Detective Lavelle, stay back."

The captain waited until the last person left his office and shut the door.

"Jack, what's your impression of Halliday?" The captain sat back down behind his desk as he asked the question.

"She has good instincts and a real eye for detail. You don't see that combination too often," Lavelle said.

"Yup, she has a good reputation," agreed the captain. As he spoke, he sorted through a pile of files on his desk.

"You don't sound convinced?" Lavelle asked, noticing a file with Halliday's name on it.

"Between you and me, I'm being pushed to consider changing Halliday's status from temporary replacement for Al to his permanent replacement." Noticing Lavelle's raised eyebrow, the captain added, "Al's putting in his papers. We'll have a permanent opening next month." "I want your input on Halliday. I don't want to be arm-twisted into taking her just to meet a gender quota."

"Is there a reason why you have reservations about her?" Lavelle asked.

"Her military records are sealed."

"So?"

"I don't like sealed records. They make me nervous."

"I bet her records are sealed because she served in an intel unit," Lavelle said.

"How do you know that she worked in military intelligence?" The captain sat forward, his interest piqued.

"She was on the phone earlier to a buddy from her old unit. He's now in the CIA. I don't think you have anything to worry about when it comes to her military record. Her record's sealed because it's classified."

"Maybe." The captain shrugged. "Still, I need to know who's joining my team. Since the military won't tell me, I need you to find out. I won't risk hiring a detective who turns out to be a liability just to help boost the department's percentage of female detectives on the job."

"You're asking me to spy on her? It's not my style. You know that."

"Not spy, Jack. I want you to observe Halliday in the field and tell me whether you'd put your life in her hands. That'll be good enough for me."

Chapter Fifteen

Lunch is a crustless cheese sandwich with soggy alfalfa taken from an oversized platter ordered in for the design meeting. I have little appetite. I feel antsy, like I'm craving caffeine. I push a flavored coffee capsule into the coffee machine.

While the machine hisses and splutters noisily, I tune in to a whispered conversation going on somewhere behind me.

"I'm not surprised she seems so... lost and confused, with everything she's been through."

The conversation stops midsentence when they realize it's me standing with my back to them. They quickly launch into a contrived discussion about weekend plans. Apparently, I'm supposed to believe that's what they were discussing all along.

I take my coffee mug to the office window and drink, looking down at the street while trying to figure out what I should do. I tried to call Amy after the design meeting. Her phone wasn't on, which usually means she's at work. Marco's phone is also turned off. I suppose I should leave the office and go down to the police precinct in person to ask for their help, but I don't trust the police and I'm afraid of what I might find out.

A noise explodes behind me and I whirl around. Someone has unmuted the office TV to listen to the noon news break without realizing the volume was on the highest setting.

As the newsreader talks, footage appears on the TV screen from outside an apartment building where the anchor says a murder took place. I recognize the building from the article I read earlier.

Crimson writing on an apartment window appears on the TV screen. The camera settles on the words WAKE UP! I stifle a sudden desire to check my wrist, where the same message is written in blue ballpoint letters.

"Police will be trying to determine what the message means and why the killer wrote it as they investigate the brutal murder of an as yet unidentified male," the newsreader says.

Fresh footage flashes on the TV screen. This time it shows a close-up of two detectives quickly going down the stairs of the building to the street. One is an attractive woman with chestnut shoulder-length hair wearing a navy police jacket. The second detective has tightly cropped dark brown hair, stubble, and deep-set ink-blue eyes. They both ignore reporters shoving microphones in their direction and shouting out questions about the murder as they walk away.

The footage cuts to video of a stretcher with a black body bag being pushed into a van.

"Police aren't divulging the name of the victim or saying whether they have any suspects at this point," the newsreader says.

She calls the murderer "The Sleepless Killer." Almost immediately a graphic appears at the bottom of the TV screen saying the same thing. The news program crosses to a reporter at the scene standing in front of the police tape.

"Not surprisingly, the building's residents are afraid they might be next," the reporter says. "The good news is they might not need to worry for much longer. A police source told me that evidence has been found at the scene that could help identify the killer within hours."

The newsreader moves on to another story. I turn away and accidentally bump into a young woman holding a mug of coffee. It spills all over my clothes.

"I am soooo sorry," she says, looking mortified. "That was totally my fault. I was watching the TV instead of looking where I was going."

"It's not just your fault. I wasn't looking where I was going either," I reassure her, dabbing my wet clothes with a napkin to get rid of the stains. My clothes are ruined.

"Coffee stains are the worst," calls out Claudine, the magazine stylist, who has just finished eating her lunch. "Come with me, Liv. We'll find something in the closet for you to wear."

The closet is where the magazine keeps all the clothes and accessories we use for photo shoots. Most of the garments have been given to the magazine as freebies from brands hoping to get a plug in one of our issues.

I follow Claudine into a large rectangular room with huge windows. In the middle is an enormous table covered with bolts of fabric and color swatches. It's surrounded by long chrome racks of clothes pressed against the walls. The mood boards of color palettes presented at the meeting earlier are propped up against a window.

Claudine slides hangers along the rack noisily as she pulls out a few pants and tops and tells me to choose an outfit. I opt for a pair of dark skinny jeans and a loose navy cashmere sweater.

The changing room is little more than a booth with a black curtain for privacy. Inside are a stool and a full-length mirror. I pull off my coffee-stained clothes and drop them on the floor.

I'm about to put on the clothes that Claudine brought me when I catch sight of the reflection of my near-naked body in the mirror. My forearms are covered with scribbles in ballpoint pen that reach up to my elbows. There's so much writing that it looks as if I have tattoo sleeves. Some of the messages are washed out and illegible. Others are incomprehensible rants that strike me as paranoid and delusional. DON'T TRUST ANYONE and DON'T ANSWER THE PHONE are some of the more comprehensible ones.

Claudine reaches into the changing room to hang another garment on a wall hook for me to try on. "This will look great with that outfit. How are you going in there?"

"Good," I say absently, staring at myself.

My gaze moves down my bra and rib cage to the top of my abdomen. It stops abruptly at what I presume is a lipstick smudge on the mirror. I lean forward to wipe the red mark off the mirror. The stain remains. That's when I realize the red mark isn't on the mirror, it's on my skin, just below my rib cage.

I look down curiously to examine it with my fingers. It's not a mark. It's an ugly clump of puckered red scar tissue that I've never seen before.

Chapter Sixteen

When Detective Darcy Halliday came out of the meeting with the captain, she found a padded envelope lying on her desk. Inside was a black hard drive that had been couriered over by the surveillance company responsible for the CCTV cameras in the apartment building where the murder had taken place.

Halliday plugged the hard drive into her computer. There were dozens of files. Each file contained footage from a different security camera. The building was wired up with surveillance cameras on each floor, as well as in all the elevators and at all the entrances and exits.

Halliday clicked on the footage from the camera on the floor of the murder scene. The camera angle that appeared on her computer screen showed the corridor leading to the elevator doors. The video was in color, but the hues were washed out. Halliday wasn't looking for Hollywood production quality. All she wanted was a clear photo of the suspect's face.

The medical examiner had said the victim was likely murdered six to nine hours before he'd examined the body. That gave Halliday a rough band of time to focus on.

Halliday rewound the footage until she found the time code of the video taken before midnight. The corridor lights were off. Nothing was visible in the darkness. Halliday fast-forwarded through the dark footage. Eventually, a few minutes after two A.M., Halliday noticed a change in the dim light in the vicinity of the apartment doorway. The teenage neighbor had told her he'd heard a door banging shut at around that time.

A hint of movement was noticeable as the front door opened and then closed. Halliday re-played the video on slo-mo, pausing to freeze the frame every few seconds. Someone had surreptitiously left the apartment and gone into the stairwell in the middle of the night.

"You think that's the killer?" asked Lavelle, looking over Halliday's shoulder at a freeze-framed shot of a silhouette on her computer screen.

"It's very likely," Halliday said, trying to enhance the silhouette. "I can't get it clearer than this," she said in frustration. "We need to go through footage of all the exits. There has to be a clearer visual of this person leaving the building. Right now, all we can see is a shadowy blob."

"Rosco and Tran will follow up," Lavelle said. "We need to get going soon. Forensics called. They're ready to walk us through the crime scene."

Halliday was about to unplug the hard drive to give to Rosco when she remembered something important. "Give me a second. I want to see if we have a visual of that couple coming out of the elevator yesterday morning."

She quickly found the footage she was looking for, at 10:08 A.M. the previous morning.

Halliday recognized the older woman with short hair walking toward the elevator. That was the neighbor she'd talked with earlier. When she reached the elevator, the neighbor pressed a button and waited. Twenty seconds later, the elevator doors opened and a man and a woman stepped out.

Halliday paused the video. She was certain the man was the victim. He was roughly the same height and build as the stiff she'd found in bed at the crime scene that morning. The man in the video also had tawny hair, just like the victim, and he had the same distinctive dimples permanently indented into his cheeks.

The man's hand rested on the long-haired woman's lower back as they came out of the elevator, but it wasn't a romantic gesture. It looked as if he was propping her up. She wore jeans and a long cable-knit sweater. All Halliday could see was a curtain of hair obscuring her face.

The man unlocked the front door of the apartment, and they both went inside. Perhaps for the last time. Within twenty-four hours, the man was brutally murdered in that same apartment, and the woman had disappeared.

As she looked at the blurry security camera footage of the long-haired woman, Halliday couldn't help but think that they'd found their prime suspect. She rewound the video back to the moment the couple came out of the elevator. She pressed Play to watch it again.

"Look up," Halliday pleaded, but the woman continued to stare down at her feet.

"She's not looking up," said Lavelle, disgusted by their bad luck. "It's almost as if she's deliberately hiding her identity from the CCTV cameras."

Halliday took a screenshot of the best photo they had of the woman. Her face was largely obscured, but there was a chance that someone who knew her might recognize her anyway. Halliday printed off a hundred copies of the photo to give to the cops going door-to-door in the vicinity of the crime scene. From the photo, it looked as if the suspect was a slender Caucasian woman of average height with waist-long coffee-colored hair.

"We might get lucky. Maybe someone will recognize her," Halliday told Lavelle, as she scooped up the pages from the printer and followed him downstairs to the car.

Chapter Seventeen

Two Years Earlier

I'm taking the subway home from work when my phone vibrates in my handbag. It's Amy. She texts that she's going on a mini vacation over the three-day gap before her next shift at the hospital.

> Early birthday present. Plus I need to work on my tan!

A string of sunshine and beach emojis follow the message.

You deserve it, hon, I write back.

She does deserve it. Amy's in the final stretch of her internship. I've never seen anyone work so hard. Last week she worked six night shifts in a row. Other times she's up at five in the morning for an early morning shift that often drags on well into the evening. Her dedication to her patients is incredible.

Amy and I were introduced at a party by a mutual friend who knew we were both looking for a roommate. We immediately clicked. We come from different worlds, with different life experiences. Yet after sharing our apartment for almost five years, our bond is much deeper than just that of roommates, or even close friends. Amy's the sister I never had.

She's the only person I've ever told about my nomadic childhood, moving to different towns and schools every time Mom got a new man in her life, during which time she'd all but ignore me while she devoted herself to the relationship. Not to mention her meltdowns when her marriages broke up, and the way she'd guilt-trip me for being the cause of all her heartache. "Men don't want women with baggage," she'd tell me. Amy knows it all.

I know all her secrets, too, like how she began her affair with Brett months before he split with his wife, and her lifelong dream of going to Africa to work as a doctor with a humanitarian organization. There's very little we don't tell each other.

When I get home, I unlock the front door tentatively and push it open with a creak. "It's just you and me, kid," I tell Shawna as she rubs herself against my legs in greeting.

I pour her food into a bowl while I text-message Marco to suggest he come over and stay the night. He doesn't text back. I dial his cell phone. The call goes straight to voicemail.

When I examine the contents of the fridge, I decide it's a good thing Marco didn't respond. We're out of everything, other than eggs and cheese. I should go to the supermarket to pick up groceries, but I'm too beat. Instead I head to the bathroom, where I fill the tub with hot water and a splash of lavender oil.

I wish I'd joined Amy on her mini vacation. I'm also feeling burnt out. Work has been stressful. There has been more sniping than usual among the staff writers. Naomi's still furious that I've been assigned the arts roundup. Her only communication with me all week has been to take subtle potshots during editorial meetings. It's been exhausting.

I slide into the hot water and put a wet terry towel over my face. The water is so warm that I drift to sleep. When I wake, the bath water is getting cold and there's an intermittent thumping noise nearby. At first I think that someone is hitting a nail with a hammer somewhere in the building. After listening to more thumps, I realize the noise is coming from inside my apartment.

Amy's away so it can't be her. I think for a hopeful moment that Marco received my text and came here to take me up on my invitation. But Marco doesn't have keys to the apartment so it can't be him. The only possibility left is that there's an intruder in the apartment.

Cold fear slides through me like liquid mercury as I climb out of the bath, careful not to make any splashing noises. I throw my satin robe onto my wet body without toweling off and press my ear against the bathroom door. The thumping noise resumes.

Someone is definitely in the apartment. I haven't brought my phone into the bathroom so I can't call for help. Instead, I push down the bathroom door handle soundlessly and count to three before swinging it open and charging to the front door. My robe flaps behind me as I run. The lock opens quickly despite my slippery hands. I step out onto the landing dripping wet and feeling like a total idiot.

The building door opens downstairs. I tentatively move forward to the banister to see who's come in. It's a neighbor who lives on the fourth floor. She doesn't notice me as she strides up the stairs two at a time, her eyes peeled on her phone as she talks on FaceTime. When she reaches my landing, she glances up and makes eye contact before continuing to her floor.

Seeing the neighbor makes me feel more stupid than ever. Of course, there isn't an intruder. The banging must be from the new tenants assembling their flatpack furniture like they did the other night until late.

I return to my apartment and close the door behind me. Once inside, I call Marco.

"Is everything okay, Liv?" he asks.

The murmur of voices in the background and the clatter of cutlery scraping against plates tells me that he must be at a restaurant.

"Did you get my text about staying tonight?" I head down the corridor toward Amy's bedroom, where the banging noise came from. I feel more courageous knowing there's someone on the phone line who can call the cops if something goes wrong.

"I just saw your message. I wish I could come over, but I'm out of town."

78

"Where are you?"

A floorboard creaks behind me. I freeze.

"A tech conference. Chicago. I fly back on Friday night."

"I didn't know that you're away this week," I say, feeling incredibly alone and vulnerable as I realize there's no way Marco can come to my aid. I take another step forward.

"I thought I mentioned it," he says a little too sharply. Marco hates it when I pry. "You sound upset about something," he says, cottoning on to the fear in my voice. "Are you sure everything's okay, Liv?"

"I'm just disappointed that you can't come over. Amy's away and the apartment feels very… empty," I say, too embarrassed to tell him that I'm spooked being alone in my own home.

"I'll make it up to you." His voice is husky with promise.

"I'll hold you to it," I say haltingly before hanging up.

The banging resumes. It's definitely coming from Amy's room. I walk toward her bedroom door, holding the phone as if it's a weapon. When I reach her room, I gently kick the door fully open and turn on the bedroom light.

Amy forgot to latch the window. The wind must have blown it open and it's hitting the wall.

I close the window and turn around to examine the room. There's a walk-in closet and a desk in a nook by the window. When Amy was a medical student, the desk was always covered with books. Nowadays, it's empty other than a silver laptop.

On her bed is a small suitcase that she appears to have abandoned half-packed. I presume she opted for a bigger suitcase and more clothes. Amy always overpacks. It's not unknown for her to take two suitcases for a weekend trip. As I turn to leave the bedroom, I almost trip over Shawna's tail, which is sticking out from under Amy's bed.

"So that's where you are!" Shawna opens her one good eye and stares at me in disdain before returning to sleep.

I head to the kitchen to prepare something to eat, acutely aware that it will be slim pickings given the state of my fridge.

Besides the eggs and cheese, I find a jar of asparagus in the cupboard. I cook a cheese and asparagus omelet, which I eat while watching TV in the living room.

My eyes get heavy and I fall asleep on the sofa in the middle of the show. I wake to the sound of banging. It's Amy's window again. I can't begin to fathom how it could have opened when I closed it firmly earlier. Once again I go in to turn on the lights and close the window. This time, I double-check to make sure it won't accidentally open again.

The alarm clock next to Amy's bed tells me it's getting close to midnight. I stumble to the bathroom and brush my teeth before opening my bedroom door.

I turn on the light and stand stunned at the entrance of my room. It was neat when I left for work this morning. It's not like that now. My bedroom's a mess. The bed is rumpled. The closet doors and some of my dresser drawers are partly open. It looks as if someone was rummaging through my stuff.

One of the photo frames lies on the floor amid a pile of smashed glass. It's a photo of Marco and me on a weekend trip to Maine. I pick up the frame and the broken glass and put it on the table next to my bed. My chest tightens with fear when I see my bedroom window. Someone has drawn a heart pierced by an arrow in the dust on the glass pane.

I call 911 even though it goes against the grain for me to turn to the police. I have a deep-seated distrust of the authorities ever since the night a cop pulled me out of Mom's arms when I was taken by child protection as a kid. That memory has never left me. It doesn't help that when I was in college, I was roughly handcuffed and arrested when I happened to be in the vicinity of a student protest. The cops let me go after reviewing footage that showed I wasn't involved, but the experience only deepened my distrust.

Two uniformed police officers arrive twenty minutes later. By then, I've changed into sweats and curled up on the armchair in the living room, taking deep breaths as I try to stay calm. The officers listen politely as I give them a blow-by-blow of what happened.

"So you didn't go into your bedroom at all when you came home?" a heavyset cop with a thin mustache asks while his much younger dark-haired partner checks the window latches in the kitchen and living room for signs of a break-in.

"The last time I was in my bedroom was this morning before I left for work. It was neat. My bed was made. It didn't look anything like this." I gesture toward the mess.

I follow the younger cop to Amy's room when he checks the window. "Looks like the window catch needs to be fixed. That's why it's swinging open when the wind is up," he says, as he plays around with the latch.

He tells me that nobody could have scaled the external wall of our building to get in through that window. "Not unless it was a cat burglar. Do you know whether your roommate is missing any valuables?"

"It's hard for me to say." I rest my eyes on Amy's silver laptop. "Amy's computer is still here."

"That would have gone in a second if the place had been robbed. So would that." He points at a gold necklace and some other jewelry in a crystal bowl on Amy's bedside table.

He twists the catch to make sure the window closes properly this time and tells me to get the super to fix it in the morning.

"I suggest you go to sleep and talk to your roommate tomorrow. Maybe she drew the heart on the window as a joke," the burly cop with the mustache tells me when we return to the living room.

"I really think someone was here," I say dubiously.

"There's no sign of a break-in. We checked thoroughly."

"Just because there's no sign of a break-in doesn't mean it didn't happen. Can't you at least take fingerprints?"

"Ma'am, there's no sign a crime took place here. Nothing's been stolen. We don't take fingerprints when there's no indication a crime was committed." He talks to me like I'm a child.

"So you're saying I trashed my own bedroom and I don't remember?"

"There's probably a perfectly good explanation for everything that happened. Cats can be vindictive when they're left alone. They're smarter than people think."

"My cat is smart, but even she can't open and close drawers and closet doors. Nor can she draw hearts on windows."

"Maybe your roommate did that before she went on vacation," the burly cop suggests, trying to shut me down. "Maybe she borrowed some of your clothes and she was in such a rush to pack that she left a mess behind."

"Amy wouldn't do that. She knows that I'm a neat freak. Someone else was here."

He sighs impatiently. "Look, we've checked your apartment. There's nobody here except for you." He opens the front door and gestures with his head for his partner to follow.

"Someone must have come into the apartment and messed up my bedroom. Even if that person didn't steal something, it's still a crime. Breaking and entering. Isn't it?" I'm annoyed that they're literally doing nothing to get to the bottom of this.

"It would be a crime. If it had happened," he says, turning around enough for me to see a judgmental glint in his eyes. "But there's no evidence there was a break-in. Nothing's missing. There's no forced entry. Is there someone you think might have broken into your apartment just to mess with you? Someone with a grudge? An ex-boyfriend? A neighbor?"

"Nobody I know would do something like this!"

"What about someone you don't know?" the junior cop chimes in, earning an irate glance from his partner.

"What do you mean?"

"Have you been harassed recently, ma'am? Anonymous messages? Calls? Threats of any type?"

"You're asking whether I've been stalked?"

"Yes, I am."

Kevin, the waiter from Café del Mar, left three more messages for me at work. I wouldn't define his calls as stalking.

He's never done anything more than leave me innocuous messages. But I find it weird that a waiter, with whom I had a fleeting conversation, would track me down at my office and call me repeatedly.

I'm about to mention his name, when I change my mind. Some people are really bad at reading social cues. Kevin might be one of them, and that's why he keeps calling me at work. Plus, it might antagonize him if the police confront him about his calls to me. The fact is that bitter experience over many years has taught me not to trust cops. Things always go haywire when the police get involved.

"Nobody's stalking me," I say, with more conviction than I feel.

Chapter Eighteen

Claudine holds her hands together in delight and tells me to spin around when I come out of the changing room dressed in the outfit she's styled for me.

She inclines her head at an angle, as if not quite sure about how I look, and then scrambles in a closet and removes an asymmetrical silver-blue cardigan so long that it reaches the top of my thighs. It suits my outfit of skinny jeans and a cashmere black scoop neck top.

"It's still missing something," says Claudine.

She disappears into a storeroom and returns with a necklace made of different shades of blue-and-clear quartz stones. Standing behind me, she clips on the hook of the necklace.

"One last thing and then you can go," she promises.

She pulls out a handful of cosmetics samples from a box and sorts through them until she finds shades that suit my coloring. "This will finish off your look."

As I apply the makeup, I see my reflection in the small mirror morph back into... me.

I almost fool myself into thinking that everything is back to normal until I remember the jagged scar on my body. No matter how hard I try, I can't remember what caused it. There's a gaping hole in my memory from the moment I answered the phone on my desk on what was definitely a blue-sky summer's day until the moment I woke on the park bench this morning to the biting chill of an approaching winter. I tell myself my

84

memory loss is temporary, the aftereffects of a late night, or really bad jet lag. Clarity will return very soon.

The main office is deserted when I emerge in my new clothes and fresh makeup. I feel bereft as I watch everyone talking animatedly in glass-walled meeting rooms scattered around the office, probably planning the next issues of the magazine.

I don't belong here anymore. That thought pierces me with a visceral sense of irretrievable loss. I loved working at *Cultura*. Being here, doing this job was among the happiest times of my life. I don't know how I became an interloper in my own life. I could ask Josie or someone else to fill me in, but I'm embarrassed to reveal how confused I am.

I dial Amy again. She's a doctor. She'll tell me what to do. I can almost hear her faintly amused voice telling me to sleep it off, the way she has countless times when I was wooly-headed from a hangover, or a bad flu.

Unfortunately, Amy's phone is still turned off. I consider asking the hospital to page her, but I know that Amy hates getting personal calls at work. In the end I call Marco. Sheer relief runs through me when my call is answered.

"Marco!"

"Who is this?" a man snaps.

"Marco?" My voice lilts uncertainly.

"There's no Marco here."

"But... this is Marco's phone?"

"Listen, lady, for the millionth time, this is a wrong number. How many times do I have to tell you the same thing!"

A dejected click tells me he's hung up on me. I dial the number again. This time I double-check to make sure it's correct.

"Lady," says the same gruff voice as before. "I told you already. You've dialed the wrong number."

"It's definitely Marco's number." Hysteria rises inside of me.

"No, it's not. Just like I told you the last time you called. And the time before that. And the time before that. You get my drift."

I don't get it. I'm certain this is Marco's cell phone number. "Is Marco ghosting me?" I ask. "Tell him that Liv called. I'm his girlfriend. I need to speak to him. It's urgent."

"Trust me, lady. This is the wrong number. You need to stop calling," he shouts over a grinding truck engine before hanging up.

The conversation drains me. I put my head in my hands. Everything has changed beyond recognition. The office. Me. The scar, I think, as I absentmindedly rub it through my borrowed designer clothes.

On the office television set, a news report flashes again on the screen, with that shot of the words WAKE UP! written on an apartment building window.

I have the same message written on my skin. It must be more than a coincidence. I'm consumed by a powerful urge to go there. Maybe being there will bring back my memory and dissolve the confusion that has hung over me like a blinding fog ever since I woke on the park bench.

The article I'd read earlier mentioned the location of the building where the murder took place. I check the article again. It's near the corner of Fifty-Third and Lexington.

As I leave the office, the receptionist asks whether I spoke with the man whose call she transferred earlier. I shudder when I remember the frightening voice on the phone, his tone accusing and cajoling at the same time.

"I spoke with him."

"He called again. He said the first call was cut off. I trans-ferred him to you but you didn't pick up."

"I was in a meeting."

"Oh. He said he'll swing by later. In fact, he asked me to tell you to stay in the office until he gets here. He says it's important."

"I have an appointment and I'm already late," I lie, rushing out of the office even faster.

Nine subway stops and five minutes' walk later, I'm standing outside the apartment building that I recognize from the news bulletin.

A police car and a forensics van are parked on the curb near police barricades. Uniformed cops stand on the sidewalk at the entrance. A few residents wait to be allowed inside, visibly annoyed at having to line up to get into their own building.

Onlookers loiter behind the barricade. I don't join them. I feel intimidated by the heavy police presence. Instead I go into a high-end shoe shop directly across the street. I pretend to look at the boots in the window display, while surreptitiously watching the police outside the building.

"Can I help?" I almost jump as a shop assistant comes from behind me.

"Sure," I say, pointing to a knee-high boot in the shop window display. "Do you have it in a size seven?"

She disappears into a back storeroom and returns carrying an oversized shoe box.

"What's going on out there?" I ask.

"Someone was murdered in the building across the street." She whispers discreetly even though there're no other customers in the store.

She lifts up the shoebox lid and removes the boots, extolling the virtues of the Italian-made leather soles and inner lining.

She stops in the middle of her explanation as a police officer comes inside. "Why don't you try on the boots and see for yourself how comfortable they are," she suggests, before rushing over to the police officer and leading him to a corner near the cash register.

I listen intently to their hushed conversation as I put on the boots. He tells her the police are collecting security camera footage from the stores along the street.

"We think the killer might have been filmed leaving the scene of the murder," he says. "We're talking to all the stores along this block to get surveillance footage from early this morning."

The saleswoman noticeably lowers her voice. "We have cameras facing the street. You'll need to speak with my manager to get copies. Do you have any idea who might have done it?" she asks. "The murder, I mean."

"A woman with long dark hair down to her waist was seen with the victim. Have you seen anyone answering that description in the vicinity over the past few days?" he asks.

"Not that I recall," she says.

Self-consciously, I touch my short hair as creeping panic runs through me. My hair was long when I woke up in the park this morning, just as the cop described. The words WAKE UP! are written on my wrist. It's more than a coincidence. I have a terrible feeling that I'm connected to this crime.

I pace around the store in the boots, making what I hope is a convincing show of pretending to deliberate whether to buy them. By the time the police officer leaves the store, I've taken off the boots and slipped into my own shoes.

"Aren't those boots just to die for?" the saleswoman says.

"They're lovely, but I have very wide feet and they just don't feel right. I'll come again to try on another style when I have more time," I say, before hastily rushing out.

I barge straight into a throng of people craning their necks on the sidewalk as they look up at the apartment building across the street.

"Someone was killed there today. Murdered." A man in jeans and a khaki windbreaker points up at the sixth-floor window. "The killer wrote a message on the window. Can you see it?"

I look up, squinting. I can't see the writing from this distance.

"I heard on the news that the message is written in the victim's own blood. That's why I came down here. I wanted to see it for myself," says someone in the crowd as he holds out an iPhone and tries to zoom in on the window in question.

"What do you think it means?" a woman asks nobody in particular.

"The murderer is sending us a message," a man responds.

"It's a warning," says someone else, his voice rising hysterically. "We must wake up and repent for our sins before it's too late."

Chapter Nineteen

The crime scene was transformed by the time Darcy Halliday and Jack Lavelle signed their names on the log sheet and ducked under the yellow crime scene tape strung across the entrance of the apartment.

Kneeling on the floor in the living room, a forensic technician carefully removed fingerprints from the arm of a leather sofa. Another technician was painstakingly brushing black dust across the stainless steel fridge door to look for prints.

In the bedroom, numbered cards were scattered across the room to indicate where trace evidence had been found. The mattress was stripped bare. The sheets had been bagged as evidence. Bloodstains were evident on the mattress.

In the corner, Detective James Bowen was drawing a plan of the bedroom with precise measurements. Bowen was a bear of a man with a furrowed brow and a full beard that was a mix of brown and gray.

"Tell me you found something to help us ID the victim? A dry cleaning ticket? A cell phone? Better yet, his missing wallet?" Halliday asked.

She'd worked closely with Bowen when she'd done a stint in the forensics unit after she'd received her detective's badge. When it came to working a crime scene, nobody was more thorough.

"We've been through everything in the apartment with a fine-tooth comb. There's no ID, no wallets or credit cards or anything else that will enable a quick identification of the victim, or the woman who was with him."

"You're sure it was a woman?" Lavelle asked.

In answer, Bowen slid open the bedroom closet door to show a selection of women's clothes neatly hung on cedar hangers. Halliday pushed the hangers across the rack to take a better look. The clothes were largely fashion items from mass market brands. She noticed they all had the faintest whiff of mildew.

The odor was so subtle that most people wouldn't have noticed it, but Halliday smelled it immediately. She'd lived in a basement apartment in her last year of college and her nose had been sensitive to the smell of mildewed clothes ever since.

She handed Bowen the flyer she'd printed, showing the security camera image of the mystery woman with long hair exiting the elevator along with a man the previous morning. The date and time code were stamped on the image.

"The man, who we believe is the victim, entered this apartment with this woman yesterday morning," said Lavelle.

Bowen lifted up his glasses to take a closer look. "Long dark hair. It sure looks like she's our gal. Shame we can't see her face."

"She's awfully shy in front of the cameras," agreed Halliday.

Bowen rummaged in a metal case filled with evidence bags and retrieved several small sealed bags. Each contained a human hair. "Based on the unusual length of the hairs, I'd say it's likely these hairs put the woman in your photo in the bedroom with the victim around the time he died."

"How do you know the woman was here at around the time of the murder?" Halliday asked.

"One of the long hairs was found on the victim's body. With blood on it," he said. "I suspect she was leaning over him when the hair fell. I'd say the woman in the photo is your prime suspect. Unfortunately, there's no root sheath on any of the hairs we collected. We won't be able to run them for DNA without intact roots."

"That's a real pity," said Halliday, deflated.

Detective Bowen walked them through the bedroom pointing to different evidence cards and explaining what had been found in each location.

"There was a partial print on a lipstick applicator we found wedged behind a leg of the bed. We're testing the lipstick for DNA," he said.

"You think the lipstick belongs to our suspect?" Lavelle asked.

"Who knows. It might have been here for months," said Bowen.

In the bathroom, Bowen pointed out where they'd found fingerprints on the sink, faucets, light switch, and cupboard doors. They'd bagged the long black hair that Halliday had seen near the sink, and found a matching hair on the floor.

"We found some interesting items in the bedroom that we'll get the lab to do a rush job on," Bowen said.

"Like what?" Halliday asked.

"We found foreign matter on the pillow where the victim's head was." He showed them a small evidence bag containing tiny granules of a black substance.

"Any idea what it is?" Halliday held the evidence bag up to the light to get a better look.

"My guess is that it's flecks of paint. Black," Bowen responded.

He held up another handful of evidence bags with a single strand of hair in each. "I don't think these hairs are from the victim or the long-haired woman," Bowen said. "They're shorter in length and the color is different. It's a few shades lighter."

"You think there might have been a third person in the apartment?" Halliday asked.

"Could be," he said. "It's also possible the hairs are from someone who stayed here in the past. The owner or another short-stay guest. We need to get the owner's prints and hair samples for matching purposes."

"Can't," said Lavelle. "The owner's in Hong Kong until next week."

"That'll slow things down."

After they'd gone through the apartment, Halliday and Lavelle went down to show the doorman the photo of the long-haired woman.

"I don't think I've seen her before," the doorman said, after taking a close look. "But I wouldn't bet my house on it. There are people coming and going all the time. There are at least eight apartments in the building that are rented out on short-term rental sites. The night doorman regularly gives guests the keys to their rentals when they check in late. He might remember them."

"Yeah, I've been trying to get hold of him," said Lavelle. "His phone is off."

"He's probably still sleeping," said the doorman. "He starts work at six. Come again tonight. He'll be here," he said, before rushing to the door to help a woman arriving with an armful of shopping bags.

After talking to the doorman, Halliday and Lavelle split up. He went to talk to the officer supervising the door knocking and murder weapon search, while Halliday went down to the basement to check out the building's rear exits.

There were two service exits from the basement. Both came out into a narrow lane behind the apartment building. The first exit was where the garbage Dumpsters were located. There was also a rear exit at the bottom of the fire escape stairs. Black-fingerprint residue coated the metal door handles and light switches at both exits where the forensics team had taken prints.

Halliday pushed open the fire exit doors and stepped into an alley behind the building. Ten yards away was a street. On that street, directly facing the end of the lane was a liquor store. Halliday crossed the side street and went inside.

An elderly man with a drooping gray mustache hunched on a stool behind the counter manually checking an order book with a blue ballpoint pen. He looked up when Halliday approached, holding out her badge.

"How can I help you, Detective?"

"Do you have security cameras pointing out to the street?"

"We sure do. Had a robbery a few years back. They threw a brick into the store window, grabbed whatever they could, and drove off. We put up cameras after that."

He motioned toward a bank of small screens behind the counter. They showed footage from different angles in and outside the store. One of the camera angles showed a clear shot of the end of the alley across the street. That was the killer's likely exit route.

"Can I get a copy of the footage from that camera?" Halliday asked.

"My son knows how to do that. I barely know how to turn on a computer. He's out right now. Leave me your number and I'll get him to get right onto it as soon as he gets back."

Halliday left her business card and then walked back to the main entrance of the building, where she waited for Lavelle. Across the street, people were milling around on the sidewalk, craning their necks to look up at the apartment where the murder took place.

"What's going on over there?" Halliday asked a cop outside the building.

"The TV news ran pictures of the message on the apartment window. People are coming to take a look like it's a tourist attraction."

"Some tourist attraction!"

Halliday crossed the street and joined the group looking up at the window. Seeing it from this angle cemented Halliday's view the message was intended for the outside world. That's why the killer had written it on the apartment window instead of on a wall near the body, or on the body itself.

A glazier was due to arrive shortly to cut out the entire pane of glass for analysis at the lab as Owen Jeffries had requested.

It would be replaced with new glass. Within a day, the police barriers would be gone, along with the gawkers. Halliday knew from experience that in all likelihood the murder would be quickly forgotten in the shuffle of fresh news headlines.

While Halliday waited for Lavelle to return, she showed the onlookers the flyer of the female suspect leaving the elevator with the victim. Most shrugged blankly when she asked if they recognized anyone in the photo.

"Ma'am, have you seen this woman before?" Halliday handed a flyer to a fashionably dressed woman with a short asymmetrical hairstyle who'd joined the crowd after coming out of a high-end shoe store.

The woman took the flyer and studied it. Halliday noticed black-and-blue writing on the back of her hands. It struck her as strange that an otherwise smartly dressed woman would write on her hands like a schoolgirl.

Before Halliday could read any of the writing on the woman's hands, the woman moved them away self-consciously and handed back the flyer.

"I haven't seen her before," she said. "I'm sorry that I can't help you." She turned abruptly and disappeared into a throng of pedestrians.

Chapter Twenty

My gaze moves from the apartment window down to a female detective standing in front of me on the busy sidewalk. She's the detective I saw earlier on the TV news.

She holds out a flyer and asks whether I recognize the long-haired woman in the photograph. I freeze when I see the photo. Even though the woman's face is downcast, her long waist-length hair is distinctive. My hair was that long before I had it cut short this morning. The woman's clothes look a lot like the ones I threw away after I was splashed with coffee at the *Cultura* office.

Running through my mind is the horrible thought that I'm the woman the police are looking for. I hand the flyer back to the detective, mumbling something about how I don't know who it is, before I walk away as calmly as possible.

Once I've put some distance between us, I push up my sleeve and stare at the writing on my wrist. Just because the words WAKE UP! are written both at the murder scene and on my skin doesn't mean I have anything to do with what happened. Does it?

Then I remember the man who'd called the office earlier. He asked if I'd taken a knife. Fear rushes through me at the terrifying thought that there's yet another link connecting me to this crime.

"Liv?"

I flinch at the sound of my name.

"Liv?"

I walk faster, pretending not to hear. I'm afraid it's the detective coming after me. Ahead of me is a green traffic light. I stride ahead, willing myself to make it across the street before it changes to red.

It's too late. The light flashes amber and then red before I reach the curb. I'm cornered. I move deep into the knot of people waiting to cross the street, desperate to disappear into the crowd.

"Liv. Liv Reese."

Just as I'm about to bolt across the street against the lights, a hand squeezes my shoulder.

Reluctantly, I turn around. I'm both shocked and relieved to see it's Dean, Marco's investor. He wears jeans and a white shirt. His craggy face seems genuinely happy to see me.

Before I can say a word, he leans in and kisses me on both cheeks before stepping back to admire me, still holding my hands. "It's been a long time. How have you been?"

"Great. Really good."

"That's terrific. I heard you moved abroad? London, right? I guess you wanted a clean break."

His words ring ominously in my head. A clean break from what?

Before I can ask him, the traffic light turns green. We cross together, pushed by the tide of pedestrians behind us.

"How about we grab some lunch?" he suggests. "You're a foodie, right? Boy, do I know a place that will knock your socks off!"

Without waiting for my answer, Dean raises his arm to hail a cab. As the cab changes lanes to pull up by the curb, my heart drops when I glimpse a ballpoint pen message scribbled on the side of my hand.

DON'T TRUST ANYONE, it says.

Chapter Twenty-One

Two Years Earlier

I'm on the train heading home when Frank, my editor, texts me with a request to attend an art show preview.

> Now?

I text back with one hand, clutching the overhead rail with my other hand to steady myself when the train brakes suddenly to stop at the next station.

> I have plans tonight.

> Are you in or out? It's a huge deal. It's Q!!

> What's Q???

I immediately regret it the second I press Send. Note to self, never show ignorance about the arts scene when you're working at a culture magazine. Frank texts me an eye-roll emoji. A moment later my phone rings.

"Liv," Frank says, without any preliminaries. "Q is a guerrilla artist. He's one of the hottest new names in performance art."

The background noise gets louder as the train speeds up. "Q doesn't just test boundaries, Q takes them to a new constellation. Like Banksy, nobody knows Q's real name. Q could be the art gallery guard, or a waiter carrying a tray of champagne at the opening. Or Q could be someone in the audience. Nobody ever knows."

"Sounds intriguing," I respond, even though I'm not intrigued at all.

"You have no idea how lucky we are to get this invitation, and it was addressed to you. Will you go?"

Amy's arranged a dinner for her birthday at her favorite restaurant and I can't be late. "The thing is that I actually have another…"

"To be clear, Liv." Frank's voice is clipped. "If I have to ask someone else to do it then I won't ask you the next time an opportunity this good lands on my desk. I need to know that my reporters will drop anything for a good story."

"Text me the details and I'll be there."

In truth, I'm kicking myself. I would never say this at the office, but I've never been to a performance art event that didn't make me want to barf. Maybe I'm cynical, or maybe I've seen too much in my life, but I find these sorts of things fatuous and self-indulgent.

Also, I can't bear the thought of letting Amy down tonight by not turning up for her birthday celebration. I certainly can't stand up Marco. He's coming as my plus-one. It wouldn't be fair to him if I came late, especially since Amy is one of his least favorite people in the world. As Marco says, my boyfriend and my best friend don't actually need to like each other.

I text Marco on the way to the gallery to tell him that I have to cancel the predinner drinks we'd arranged.

> I have to stop off at an art show for the magazine. I'll meet you at the restaurant.

Fine, he responds. I can tell he's pissed.

The gallery is in a renovated red-brick warehouse by the Manhattan Bridge. A bronze plaque by the entrance says it used to store cotton at the turn of the twentieth century. The address that Frank sent takes me to an entrance at the rear of the building.

I go around the block into a narrow back alley alongside a wire fence until I find a doorway between two lots of Dumpsters that smell of rotting garbage. The door is turquoise. It has a sign on it that says: Q: ADVANCE VIEWING. ENTRY BY INVITATION ONLY.

I'm surprised such a well-known artist would have his preview in such an awful location. Maybe that's the point; Q is a guerrilla artist. Perhaps walking past Dumpsters to get into the exhibition is part of the "guerrilla experience."

I swallow my apprehension as I push open the turquoise door. There's no public relations person armed with glossy brochures to meet me at the entrance. I presume that's because I'm late. A hum of chatter and clinking glasses deep inside the gallery tells me the art show is in full swing.

Walking across a polished concrete floor, I reach a door with a sign that says: ENTER HERE. The door leads me into a dark room. Tiny fairy lights on the floor delineate a path in the dark. I can just make out a wall of lockers and another sign saying: CONDITION OF ENTRY: ALL BAGS, PHONES AND OTHER POSSESSIONS ARE TO BE LEFT IN A SECURE LOCKER.

It's inconvenient since there's no way to take notes or record interviews without using my phone, but I play by the rules. I lock my purse in a locker and put the key, which is on a multicolored elastic band, over my wrist like a bracelet. I'll take notes in my head and write them all down when I get out of here.

The ambient sounds of people talking and a string quartet moving into Vivaldi's *Four Seasons* gets louder as I move past the lockers toward a partly open door. Through the gap, I glimpse a bold red canvas on a wall.

Someone taps a wineglass with a knife to get everyone's attention. It's followed by an announcement by an MC asking everyone to gather for speeches.

I rush through the open door into the gallery, keen not to miss the speeches. When I'm inside, I halt midstep. The red canvas is not real. It's a projection on a white wall. All the other walls are empty. There's no artwork on the walls at all. No paintings. No people. No waiters wandering around with trays of glasses filled with red and white wine. No MC.

The door behind me slams shut. The ambient sounds of the gallery show continue on the other side of a wall. I feel trapped and disoriented, like I've taken a wrong turn in a maze. I'm trying to figure out how to reach the art show when the lights go off.

I stand still, blind and helpless in the dark. I focus all my senses on the hum of the art show behind the wall, until suddenly that sound disappears as well. It's replaced by a hollow silence. The only sounds are my own heartbeat and quickening breath.

A frisson of terror runs through me as I recognize how vulnerable I am, alone in a warehouse. A spotlight turns on. Its beam moves along the floor playfully as if urging me to join it. I follow the beam into another room, equally dark and silent.

Another spotlight turns on and settles on an exhibit surrounded by red velvet ropes. A woman sits on a wooden chair. Frayed sailing rope is wrapped around her torso. I can't see her face. There's a burlap sack over her head. Her ankles are tied to the legs of the chair. Her arms are tied behind her back.

A museum sign says: WOMAN ON CHAIR.

That's when I realize the woman is the display.

She groans and contorts her body as if trying to break the bonds that tie her to the chair. Her dress is ripped open, revealing a lace bra and smooth pale flesh.

Performance art has never been to my taste, but I'm here to write about it, so I walk closer to get a better look. A whispered chant gets louder the closer I get to the red velvet barrier, until it becomes deafening: "*Kill. Kill. Kill.*"

The woman emits an animal groan as the chanting roars louder. It sounds as if she's gagged under the burlap sack. The sounds she makes are barely human. On a table next to her is a glass box. Inside are a knife and a pair of scissors. Next to it is a hammer. A sign on the table says: DO NOT TOUCH.

"*Kill. Kill. Kill*," the chanting continues.

As the chanting reaches a fever pitch, I reach the velvet ropes cordoning off the "exhibit." I'm close enough to the woman to see a tattoo of tiny, brightly colored butterflies on her shoulder.

Black-and-white footage appears on the stark white walls of the room. The footage is badly scratched like an old-fashioned movie film reel.

On one wall is footage of a woman undressing until she is naked. She slides into a bath and fully immerses herself under water. All that can be seen are bubbles of various sizes at the top of the water until they, too, disappear and there is nothing.

On another screen is a young woman leaving an apartment building. It's filmed from the perspective of a voyeur watching the woman from the bushes.

On the third and largest screen, a woman walks across an empty parking lot to her car late at night. The heels of her shoes click with each step that she takes. Heavy breathing in the background gets louder and louder, mocking the woman's lack of awareness that she's being watched. She presses her electronic key to open her car. It beeps twice.

High-pitched violin notes rise deafeningly as the camera gets closer and closer, zooming in on her eyes widening as she realizes she's in danger. As the violin hits the highest note, the footage on all the screens disappears in a tide of spilt red.

The spotlight turns off and the room is cast into pitch darkness again. My heart beats rapidly, mimicking the terror of the woman in the video. I'm filled with a desperate urge to get out of here. Just as I'm about to turn and run, a light appears in a far corner of the room. Someone is sitting on a stool, backlit. I see only their silhouette.

"We're honored to have you here today, Liv. You can play with the display in any way you like," says the disembodied voice of a man who I assume is the famous Q.

"What about the signs saying not to touch the display?" I ask.

"It's like life." He shrugs. "Some people obey the rules. Others break them. We all have free will. You could have broken the glass box and freed the woman. That would have been a reasonable choice. Or you could have left her there, as you did. Another reasonable choice."

"Does she want to be free?"

"You're asking the wrong question. You should ask whether you wanted to free her. Whether you felt constrained by the rules, or whether ignoring her plight was your natural inclination. Did you want to break the glass box?"

"Yes."

"So why didn't you?"

"Because the sign said not to touch the display."

"I see." Silence follows. "There are no right or wrong answers. You can do whatever you like. To her. To me. To yourself," he says.

"What I'd like to do is interview you," I say, trying to get in control of the conversation.

"Why?"

"To get a broader understanding of your work."

"My work speaks for itself."

The spotlight returns. "Leave your business card in the locker where you stored your belongings," Q instructs. "I'll contact you."

The spotlight guides me back to the locker room. I leave my business card in the locker as instructed before I collect my things and rush out of the building. The turquoise door slams shut behind me with an iron clang that echoes long after it's closed.

I lean against an alley wall near a Dumpster, taking a series of deep breaths to calm myself and stop my legs from trembling. It feels as if this exhibition was designed for the sole purpose of terrifying me.

Chapter Twenty-Two

Detective Jack Lavelle was dubious about eating a vegetarian burger until he saw Darcy Halliday unwrap hers and take a bite.

"I'll have the same but with extra hot sauce," he told the waitress. "And hold the tomatoes."

"You won't regret it," Halliday said in between bites. She wiped a trickle of sauce dripping down her chin with a napkin and scooped up a handful of sweet potato fries.

Halliday had asked Lavelle to stop at the hole-in-the-wall vegan eatery on the way to the precinct so they could grab lunch. She hadn't eaten anything since the previous night, other than a couple of crackers from a box she kept in her desk drawer. There hadn't been time for breakfast in the crucial first hours of the homicide investigation.

"Not bad, right?" Halliday said, after he'd taken the first mouthful. His expression answered her question more succinctly than words.

They ate quickly, talking shop in between mouthfuls of food.

One of the most pressing issues was getting hold of the owner of the apartment. Lavelle was tracking the progress of his flight across the Pacific Ocean and would call him as soon as the plane landed in Hong Kong.

In Lavelle's car was an envelope with over a dozen evidence bags, each containing a USB drive with video footage from the security cameras of stores and apartment buildings. The police officers canvassing on their behalf were still in the process of collecting more footage. Lavelle expected there would be thousands of hours to go through by the time they were done.

After viewing the footage and following up on any information so far collected by the patrol cops canvassing the area, they'd go back to the crime scene in the late afternoon to question residents who'd been at work when they'd knocked on their doors in the morning. The night doorman would be on duty by then as well. They had plenty of questions for him, considering that the murder had taken place under his watch.

At a temporary lull in the conversation, Lavelle asked, "What made you want to work homicide?"

"I'm embarrassed to tell you. It sounds hokey."

"Try me." Lavelle stopped eating while he waited for her answer.

"When I was a kid, I guess around thirteen, I did a summer camp on law enforcement. One of the cops who mentored us was a homicide detective. He told us that homicide cops served a much more important purpose in society than just putting killers behind bars. 'Homicide detectives,' he said, 'are what keep us civilized. We are the last line of defense against the barbarians,'" she quoted, pausing to take a sip of her drink. "I guess it stuck with me."

"I'll bet you didn't expect the boring side of the job."

"Like what?"

"Like the paperwork."

It was a frequent gripe. They were required to record every aspect of their investigation in a log book. Nothing was too minor to be documented.

"To tell you the truth, there are days when I'm buried under so much paperwork that I wonder why I left the military."

"How long did you serve for?"

"Almost six years."

"What made you enlist?" Lavelle asked.

"It paid for my college education. I was in ROTC. Plus, I thought it would be a good way to get new experiences. You know. Make friends. Visit exotic places. The joke was on me. There is nothing exotic about three months on a military base in Helmand province."

"Why did you leave?"

She sighed. "Let's just say I did several tours of duty, the last couple in Afghanistan. I made friends. Some of them died. Others made it through, and then died. Like that friend I told you about who had his leg blown off and then decided there was nothing worth sticking around for. Not even his baby girl."

"Sounds like you went through a tough time."

Her jaw tightened. "At the end of my last tour, I decided not to push my luck, so I put in my papers. It turned out to be harder to adjust than I'd anticipated. It's not something a person can understand until they've done it."

"So you became a cop?" he asked.

"Not straightaway. There were job offers. Due to the nature of my service," she said cryptically.

"CIA?" he asked.

"I can't go into details. I turned them down. I wanted to be stateside and I wanted to be a civilian. No more taking orders," she said.

"If you didn't want to take orders, then how did you end up in this job?"

"Civilian life turned out to be harder than I thought. Starting from scratch. Building a network out of nothing. Getting recruiters to recognize that I wasn't a traditional candidate but that I had plenty of other skills. Coming to terms with the idea that most of the jobs I applied for were about money, nothing more. No sense of service, or community. No greater good. To cut a long story short, a friend suggested I join the NYPD. I did and I've never looked back. I guess I like being in uniform."

"Detectives don't wear uniforms!"

"Sure we do. This is as much a uniform as any other." She tugged at the lapel of her navy jacket. "Believe me, I wouldn't wear a suit if I didn't have to. I bet you wouldn't either." She smiled. "Enough about me. What brought you into this line of work, Detective?"

"Third-generation homicide detective," Lavelle said. "My dad used to say working homicide is like malaria. Once it gets in your blood, you can't get rid of it."

"My dad sold insurance. I'm grateful that didn't get into my blood!" Halliday scrunched up her wrapper and threw it in the trash. Her phone rang as they rose from the table.

"Detective Halliday," she said.

"Darcy, this is Grace from the lab. I have preliminary results from the wine bottle you dropped off earlier as a rush job."

Halliday followed Lavelle toward his car. "Go ahead."

"We have a fourteen-point match to a print in the IAFIS database."

The IAFIS was the FBI's national fingerprint database. A fourteen-point match was good enough to be presented as evidence in court.

"The fingerprint on the wine bottle matched the prints of a perp in the database?" Halliday asked, with barely contained excitement.

"The prints on the wine bottle don't match a perp," said Grace.

"Then who do they match?"

"They match the prints of a crime victim."

The FBI database contained every print ever put into the system. Many of them were those of criminals, or suspected criminals. But there were other prints, too, belonging to upstanding citizens. Among them were prints of victims whose fingerprints and DNA were taken as part of an investigation. It was always necessary to take prints of everyone who'd been at the crime scene, from first responders to cops and even the victims, so their prints could be ruled out from the evidence. The prints were almost always kept on file.

Halliday took out a notepad and a pen as she climbed into Lavelle's car. "What's the name?"

"Her name is Liv Reese. That's R–E–E–S–E," Grace spelled out. "I have a social security number and her last known address on file from two years ago."

Halliday wrote down the details. Liv Reese's last known address was in Brooklyn. "Grace, do you have any information about the crime in which this woman, Liv Reese, was a victim? I assume her prints were taken to eliminate them from the forensics at the crime scene?"

"There's no additional information in the system," the lab technician said. "Jerry Krause handled the case. Talk to him. He'll know more."

Halliday updated Lavelle after she'd hung up. "Do you know Jerry Krause?"

"Oh yeah. Jerry and I go way back." Lavelle's lackluster tone suggested he was no fan of the other detective. "I'll call him when we get to the precinct."

When they arrived, Lavelle gave Rosco and Tran the USB drives with CCTV footage to add to their growing pile of security camera footage to review.

"We haven't found any more visuals of the woman with long hair. It's like she disappeared into thin air," said Rosco.

"Nobody disappears into thin air," said Lavelle. "Take a closer look at people coming and going. Look for people wearing baseball hats, beanies, or hoodies. Even high-collared jackets. Anything that covers their hair. We estimate her height at around five foot six, so pay special attention to people of a similar stature."

Halliday opened her laptop to find out more about Liv Reese, but before she could run a search, Lavelle signaled to her to join him in an interview room. He wanted her with him when he called Jerry Krause in case Halliday had any questions for the detective.

The interview room was bland and windowless. It was used to talk to potential witnesses and informants. The table in the room was round rather than rectangular, to encourage collaboration.

In the middle of the table was a telephone. Lavelle pulled it over to the edge so they could both be near the speaker while they spoke with Krause.

There was no love lost between the two detectives. Lavelle had partnered with Krause when he first became a detective. Their partnership had been mercifully brief, and they hadn't had much to do with each other since. Over the years they'd drifted to different units at different precincts.

"Don't expect too much," Lavelle warned Halliday. "When I worked with Krause, he had lousy instincts and he always looked for shortcuts. I doubt he'd pass if he did the detective exam today."

He punched in Krause's number.

"Krause." The detective's crusty voice was tinged with a mixture of irritation and apathy.

"This is Jack Lavelle. I have my partner with me here, Darcy Halliday."

"I feel like I've won the sweepstakes. Two homicide detectives for the price of one! What's up?"

"Does the name Liv Reese ring any bells for you?" Lavelle asked.

Krause paused. Halliday could sense him trying to figure out the lay of the land before he answered. "What about her?" he asked cautiously.

"Her name came up in connection with a case you were investigating. We wanted to get the lowdown from you."

"I'm strapped for time here, folks. The case is an old unsolved. I can't recall all the specifics. Call my old precinct and they'll get you the file. It'll all be in there. Now if you'll both excuse me, I really need to..."

"Detective, we're not quite done yet. I have a few questions," Halliday interrupted. "The records say Liv Reese was a crime victim. They don't give details but..."

"She was never a crime victim," Krause thundered. Halliday had hit a nerve.

"What do you mean?" she asked.

"Liv Reese was a suspect. A murder suspect."

"Was she charged?"

"The DA never charged her," Krause acknowledged.

"Why not?" Lavelle asked.

"He claimed there wasn't enough evidence for a conviction." There was palpable derision in Krause's voice.

"Maybe that's because she didn't do it?" Halliday suggested.

"Detective Halliday, I'll give you a word of advice from an old-timer who has clearly done this job for a heck of a lot longer than you; absence of evidence is not vindication," Krause said, pausing to let it sink in. "I'll tell you something else, Detective. If Liv Reese didn't do it, then I feel damn sorry for her."

"Why?"

"Because that would mean she's the only witness to one of the most cold-blooded murders that I've ever investigated."

Chapter Twenty-Three

Dean presses his hand on the small of my back as he guides me toward the cab that's pulled up on the curb ahead of us.

"You're going to love it. The food's terrific," he says.

The closer we get to the car, the more my body resists. DON'T TRUST ANYONE, says the message on my hand. I don't trust Dean, but I very much want to talk to him. His is the only familiar face that I've encountered since I woke up in the park this morning. I'm bursting with questions, but I don't like the idea of being bundled off in a cab with him.

"On second thought, I'm kind of in a hurry. Can we go somewhere nearby?" I ask. "There's a place over there that looks good." I point in desperation toward a retro-looking deli farther along the street.

"Sure. If that's what you want."

Dean waves off the cab and walks with me to the deli. It turns out to be an old-school deli that does lunches and coffees on cheap Formica tables. The place is noisy and very crowded. A waitress shows us to a table in the middle of a crush of lunchtime diners. She hands us each a laminated menu and runs through the specials so quickly I barely catch them before she's moved away to take an order at another table.

I bury my face in the menu, but I have no appetite. A restless nervous energy has been racing through my body since the detective showed me the flyer with the photo of a long-haired woman linked to last night's murder. I'm starting to believe that woman may be me.

"What can I get you?" The waitress's wrinkled hands and stooped shoulders suggest she's spent most of her sixty-plus years leaning over tables asking diners that question.

"I'll have lemonade," I tell her.

Dean orders a Reuben on toasted rye. "Bring me sauerkraut and pickles on the side. Oh, and I'll take a bottle of Coke and a separate glass of ice. Ice chips if you have them. Ice blocks are okay, too, so long as they're not too big." The waitress takes his order with a blank expression.

"You're very specific about your food," I say once she's gone.

"I'm a very detail-oriented person. That's why I've been such a successful entrepreneur. It's the tiny details that make all the difference," he says, flashing bleached teeth that contrast sharply with his fake tan and dyed hair. Despite his obvious efforts to hold back the tide of time, Dean's aged since that lunch with Marco and Emily. For one thing, he's packing a lot more pounds.

I remember how he stiffed our waiter on his tip when we ate at Café del Mar that day. What was the waiter's name? Kevin. He's the one who started calling me at work. For days in a row, I'd come into the office to find a fresh Post-it note slapped on my computer screen. KEVIN CALLED. AGAIN.

It feels as if it happened yesterday. I shake the thought away. I know now that it happened more than two years ago. Two years that I inexplicably can't remember. That's why I'm here. This lunch is my chance to get Dean to tell me everything he knows.

I try to build a rapport by asking about Emily's handbag design business. He immediately shuts that conversation down.

"We broke up last year. Turns out the marriage game isn't for me," he says. "Tell me about you. How are you managing?"

"Fine. Fine," I say, dwelling on his use of the word "managing." It strikes me as an odd phrase, filled with a meaning that I don't grasp. "What about you?"

"I've been keeping myself busy with a new venture," says Dean, veering into a monologue about an organic vegan oatmeal latte company that he's invested in. "We've given baskets of the product to celebrities. They love how it fits in with their eco values. Hey, are you still writing about food at that magazine, *Cultura*? I heard you were working for them in London."

"Actually, I'm not there anymore," I say, remembering the alien feeling of not belonging when I visited the office earlier.

He visibly deflates and his eyes wander restlessly around the deli as if he's looking for an escape route. That's when I realize why he was so keen to have lunch with me. He brought me here to butter me up so I'd do a write-up on his oatmeal latte venture.

Dean glances at his gold Rolex and taps his fingers on the table impatiently as he looks longingly toward the waitress, almost beseeching her to hurry up and bring his food. When the silence gets too heavy, and he realizes he has no choice but to kill time with me until the food arrives, he asks what brought me to this neighborhood.

"Shoe shopping. I need boots for winter." I'm surprised at how easily I lie. "I went into a store that was having a sale on Italian boots. While I was there, the shop assistant told me someone was murdered in the building across the street."

"So that's why there were police everywhere!" he says. "The world is going back to the bad old days. You probably weren't even born in the eighties, Liv. Trust me, in those days a person couldn't walk down the block without getting mugged. Not to mention murdered. There were murders all the time. You can't imagine how crazy..."

He stops midsentence as if he's spoken out of turn. Then he breaks off a bit of breadstick from the complimentary bread basket on the table and pops it into his mouth, chewing it deliberately slowly as he stares at me with an intensity that fills me with trepidation.

The waitress puts a tall glass of freshly squeezed lemonade in front of me and places a Coke bottle and a glass of crushed ice in front of Dean.

"Your order will be ready shortly," she tells him.

He straightens his cutlery until the silverware is arranged with military precision. He moves the Coke can so that it's exactly above the tip of the knife. He puts the glass next to the Coke can, but not so close that it's touching. The salt shaker goes to the left. The pepper shaker to the right. The hot sauce goes just behind the salt. He puts the ketchup right behind the pepper. He does all of this with laser-sharp focus.

When he's done, he looks up as if he's just remembered I'm here. His eyes land on my hands as I sip my lemonade. I can tell he's noticed the messages scribbled all over them.

I lower the glass and put my hands in my lap so the writing is out of sight, but Dean's seen enough of it that I feel I need to acknowledge it.

"Bad habit. My mom used to make me scrub it off with soap and water when I did it as a kid."

"So why do you still do it?"

I instinctively shrug and then immediately regret it. This is the opportunity I've been looking for to segue into asking him to tell me what he knows about my life over the past two years. It's blindingly clear from his comments that he knows more than I do. I pluck up my courage. "I have issues remembering things…"

"Memory problems! Tell me about it," he cuts in. "I'm not sure if they're a blessing or a curse. There are some things I'd rather forget. Like my ex," he says, laughing at his own joke. "I mean, what was I thinking, marrying Emily? She sure wasn't the sharpest tool in the shed. All my kids said so, but I was in love. Lust. Whatever."

The waitress leans across and puts his sandwich and a bowl of pickles on the table. "How about you, Liv?" he asks, as he unfolds a napkin and puts it on his lap. "Tell me about your life since we last saw each other."

His question hits me like a sucker punch. I have no answer to give him because I don't know myself what my life has been like for the past two years.

For a moment I can't breathe or move at all. When I can, I scramble up and mutter something about needing the restroom. In the ladies', I lean over the sink to hold myself up as my body trembles violently. I'm having a panic attack. I splash my face and take in a series of deep breaths until I've calmed down. Then I lift up my top and stare at the scar below my rib cage in the restroom mirror. It's a horrible feeling, knowing that my body has been disfigured and I don't remember what happened.

Dean's eating when I come out of the restroom. I stand out of his line of vision and watch him add mustard and mayo to his sandwich. Two spoons of each. Three shakes of salt. Two of pepper. His obsessiveness chills me.

I steel myself before returning to the table, uncertain how much to confide in Dean.

As I move toward the table, a phone rings. I freeze midstep. The old-fashioned ringtone cuts through all the noise. It feels as if everyone in the restaurant has frozen, and time is standing still. The only sound in the deli is the insistent ring of the phone. Each successive shrill ring makes me more tense until I'm as taut as a high wire.

I feel I'll snap if the phone doesn't stop ringing.

Numbly, I walk to our table. "I'm sorry," I tell Dean, as he bites into his sandwich. He stares back at me, his beady eyes blinking rapidly. "I really need to go."

Before he can do anything, I run out of the deli and down a nearby set of stairs into the subway.

Chapter Twenty-Four

Two Years Earlier

A saxophonist plays a solo that sounds like a jazzed-up version of *Boléro* as I walk into Café Lisbon. Winding my way around tables in the crowded fusion restaurant, I catch sight of Amy and Marco. They're sitting next to each other at a long table that Amy reserved for the evening.

They're the only people at the crowded table not looking at the band. For once they're talking in a civilized manner. I'm relieved they're getting along.

On the way here, I worried that without me to act as a buffer, they'd get into another argument and it would ruin the evening. It saddens me that my best friend and my boyfriend can't stand each other. Those two have gone from barely tolerating each other when I first started dating Marco, to pretty much detesting each other. Things are at a point where Marco rarely visits my place at all if there's any chance that Amy will be there.

It started shortly after I began dating Marco. He and Amy got into an argument over politics. It became more than a little heated. She's progressive. Marco says he's a moderate. Amy insists he's actually a conservative in disguise.

It's true they have radically different views of the world. Marco's a lawyer turned entrepreneur who worships at the shrine of capitalism. Amy's an idealistic doctor who considers money to be a dirty word. Although, as Marco has cynically pointed out more than once, that might be because her family had so much of it.

I listen to the rising notes of the sax as I watch Amy put her hand on Marco's arm and hold it there as she makes a point. The gesture is typical of Amy. She's warm and incredibly tactile. She's always hugging, rubbing arms, or massaging shoulders. It's part of her charm, along with the way she bats her eyes like a femme fatale in a cartoon to get anything she wants.

And I do mean anything. Amy gets freebies wherever she goes. At restaurants, it's free meals. Bartenders always give her free drinks at bars. When she travels she gets flight upgrades. One time on a girls' trip to Aruba, she complained to the hotel manager that her assigned room stank of stale cigarettes. She was offered a free upgrade to a beach villa along with a complimentary massage at the hotel spa.

It doesn't hurt that she's drop-dead gorgeous. She has delicate features and long flaxen hair that she inherited from her Swedish grandma. But it's not just her looks that make her stand out. Amy has bucketloads of charisma. She's one of those rare people who instantly lights up a room just by walking into it.

Neither Amy nor Marco has seen me yet. Their seats are pressed back against a wall, which forces them to sit unnaturally close to each other.

I feel a twinge of unease when Amy flicks her hair—one of her go-to flirty gestures that I've seen a thousand times before when she sets her sights on someone. Amy falls in love so frequently that I honestly lose track of all her boyfriends, and she falls out of love even faster. Except with Brett, the surgeon she's been dating since last year. It's the first time I've seen her so in love that it's the guy who has the upper hand in the relationship. Luckily for Amy, Brett is besotted with her, too.

Unlike Amy, I'm always the heartbroken one who cries on her shoulder, while she consoles me with hilarious, and largely made-up, stories about being dumped by various boyfriends over the years. I know they're made up because Amy instigates all her breakups. It's one of many secrets she's shared with me over the years.

It's thanks to Amy that I met Marco in the first place. She was asked on a blind date; a friend of a friend's brother. She only agreed to the date if they could each bring a friend and make it a blind double date. Marco turned out to be that friend.

It was at a Japanese restaurant. We bonded over our terrible chopstick skills. Marco and Amy argued over whether sushi should be eaten with chopsticks or fingers. Amy insisted the correct way was using fingers. She lived in Japan for a semester when she was a sophomore and claimed to have survived on a diet of sushi and sake.

By the time the evening was over, I was head over heels. Marco, apparently, not so much. It took him three weeks to call me. He said it was because he was snowed under with work, although I later gathered, by joining a few dots, there had been another girl in the interim.

"There she is," Amy screeches when she sees me approaching the table. "Marco and I were wondering what happened to you."

Amy stands up and wraps her slender arms around me in a clingy hug. Compared to Amy in her sleeveless figure-hugging rose silk dress, I feel positively grimy. Since I had to come straight from Q's creepy preview, I didn't have time to go home and change into the sexy midnight-blue dress I was going to wear tonight. I put on makeup in the cab over here and opened up the collar of my wine-colored satin shirt to display a striking black pearl pendant that belonged to my mom.

Amy takes her seat at the head of the table. I sit where she was sitting next to Marco, surrounded by a cloud of jasmine that Amy left behind like a scent marker.

"You look stunning, Liv," Marco says, kissing me.

He puts his arm possessively around the back of my chair and caresses the nape of my neck as we talk. I explain that I didn't have time to go home and change.

"Liv, honestly, it doesn't matter. You look amazing in anything. Or in nothing," he whispers, laughing softly at the faint blush that runs across my cheeks. I lean my head against his muscular chest for a moment, reveling in the security of being with Marco after the unsettling experience at Q's art preview.

"What were you and Amy talking about when I arrived?" I ask eventually.

"You. It's the only topic Amy and I agree on."

"Really? What about me?" I say, amused, because he's right; I'm all they have in common.

"We talked about how you're never on time. You'd be late to your own wedding."

"It's funeral," I correct playfully, smiling at his inside joke. "I'd be late to my own funeral." Marco mixes up his idioms on purpose to amuse me, rather than because English is his second language. He speaks it as flawlessly as his Italian.

"Well, either way, you really are never on time, Liv!"

"You two can criticize my lack of punctuality all you want just as long as Amy wasn't discussing plans for my birthday. I have an awful feeling that she's planning a surprise party. I've told her so many times that I hate surprises, especially surprise parties. Everyone always tries to act so…"

"Surprised," Marco finishes my sentence.

"Exactly."

"Well, we were talking about you, but I promise that surprise parties didn't come up. I was telling Amy how lucky I am that I broke my ironclad rule against blind dates the night we met," he says. "If I hadn't gone that night then I'd never have met you." He kisses the back of my hand and squeezes it tightly.

A waiter comes by the table and fills my wineglass with Rioja.

The other dinner guests are mostly Amy's work friends from the hospital. The hospital crowd inevitably talk shop whenever they're together, which can get boring for the rest of us who have no interest in hospital politics.

The empty seat to Amy's right, opposite mine, is for Brett. He's always running late whenever he's working, or on call.

Brett is a cardiothoracic surgeon, older than Amy by over a decade. He turns forty next year, but he looks years younger. He's a fitness fanatic with a wiry frame and a great physique. He broke up with his wife shortly after meeting Amy. Apparently, it had been in the cards for a while.

Amy has dated Brett for almost eight months. It's her personal best. Sometimes I think the secret to their successful relationship is that they barely see each other. Their schedules at the hospital always seem to clash. And when Brett's off from work, he has family responsibilities. He has two kids from his broken marriage. Amy confided in me once that she both admires and resents Brett's dedication to his children because it cuts into the time they spend together, although she admits that he's an amazing dad.

The waiter brings me a menu and I order a grilled salmon dish with chili and lime. As I hand back the menu, my eyes flick to the bar where a man sitting on a barstool watches our table over a glass of bourbon.

Our eyes lock. His smile is so engaging that I unwittingly smile back for a fraction of a second. I look away to see that Brett's finally arrived. He strides toward our table holding an extravagant floral bouquet of pastel flowers wrapped in brown paper. He hands it to Amy, along with a Tiffany jewelry box. A smile spreads across Amy's face when she lifts the lid.

Brett mouths "thank you" to me as Amy puts on her new earrings. They're white gold with a stunning diamond and aquamarine setting that matches the color of her eyes. She's over the moon, as I knew she would be.

"I can't take all the credit," Brett laughs, after Amy kisses him. "Liv chose the earrings. She has wonderful taste. The second she saw them she knew they'd be perfect for you."

Brett doesn't tell Amy that the earrings came with a price tag that almost made me swoon. I was about to ask the saleswoman to show me something cheaper, assuming that Brett would balk at the cost. But he didn't blink an eye as he produced his platinum credit card.

He'd told me that he wanted to spoil Amy with something very special. For his birthday, Amy bought him a thousand-dollar pair of shoes for his custom-made shoe collection. He happily paid ten times that amount for her earrings.

We had coffee after we left the jewelry store, and all we talked about was Amy. Brett asked me to convince her to drop the idea of going to Africa to work for a medical aid group. He said it was a waste of her remarkable talent. He thinks Amy should specialize in pediatrics first and then they could both go together to Africa to do humanitarian work for a year.

"I've always intended to give back. Amy and I would make an incredible team," he told me.

It sounded like Brett had their lives all planned out. He even confided that he'd pull strings to get Amy into the pediatrics program at the hospital once she finishes her internship. When there was nothing more to say about Amy, he started talking about his kids and all the prep schools where they were being registered years in advance. He didn't once express the slightest interest in me. Marco was right. Brett is self-obsessed.

He orders a medium-rare steak without looking at the menu. It arrives after most people have finished their meals. When he's almost done eating, he gets a text message on his phone. He whispers something to Amy and kisses her before rising from the table and sprinting out.

"Brett's been called to the hospital," Amy tells me. "A three-car pileup at the turnpike. He says it sounds ugly. It's going to be a long night."

Amy does not appear upset at her boyfriend's fleeting appearance at her birthday dinner. I suppose she knew the drill when she became involved with a surgeon. Brett's soon-to-be ex-wife obviously did not. From what Amy's told me, one of the prime reasons behind their breakup was his ex's resentment at the way that Brett always prioritized his patients before his family. It's not something that troubles Amy. She's equally dedicated to her career. In that respect, they're a perfect match.

"Are you a doctor, too?" one of Amy's doctor friends asks.

"Hardly," I laugh. "I'm a staff writer at *Cultura Magazine*."

"Really? What do you write about?"

"All things food. The making of it. The eating of it. Celebrity chefs. I sometimes write about the arts scene as well when our art reviewer isn't available. In fact, I came here from an advance viewing of a performance art show."

"I've always wondered about performance art. What is it exactly?" he asks.

"Have you heard of Marina Abramović?"

"Is she a Russian scientist?"

"She's a performance artist. She's very famous. She did a performance at the Museum of Modern Art a few years ago where she sat at a table all day and stared at members of the public brave enough to sit opposite her. There was a documentary made about it."

"Are you telling me that sitting on a chair and staring at people for hours upon end is considered to be art?"

"It is for some people. Performance art is a type of conceptual art in which the public interacts with the artist's vision."

Through the corner of my eye, I notice the man sitting at the bar turning around again and unabashedly listening to our conversation.

"It sounds like pretentious, self-indulgent crap," the doctor says.

"It's all a matter of perspective," I say, trying to be diplomatic. "The show I went to earlier contained violent themes. It seemed very personal, and vaguely threatening. I'm not sure I'll do a write-up, at least not before I interview the artist to find out more about his motivation and inspirations."

A waitress arrives with a birthday cake for Amy. Through the bright flames of the birthday candles, I notice the man at the bar has disappeared.

When we leave the restaurant an hour later, I'm slightly tipsy. Marco ruefully declines my invitation to stay over. He tells me he's flying to Houston early in the morning and still has to pack.

"It's a last-minute trip. I managed to get a meeting with an investor who I've been trying to connect with for months," he tells me. That explains why he didn't mention it before. "I'll make it up to you, hon. We'll do something extra special on the weekend."

He kisses me before getting into a cab. As he closes the door, I realize that Marco will be going in the same direction as Amy. She's heading to Brett's place so she can be there when he gets back from work.

"Marco." I tap on the cab window. "Can you drop Amy at Brett's apartment?"

"Sure," he says. It's obvious that Marco's not crazy about the idea, but he knows it makes sense since they really are going in the same direction.

I hustle Amy over from where she's standing by the curb trying to book an Uber. We hug and she gets into the backseat.

Marco's cab drives off. I watch it disappear around the corner before I turn and walk away, encouraged by the thought that maybe the two people closest to me in the world have finally reached a point where they can be civil.

In truth, I wish Amy had come home with me rather than head over to Brett's place. I'm still rattled by that incident at the apartment the other night and I'd rather not sleep there alone.

Even though it's midweek, the streets are busy as people leave restaurants and stroll home in the refreshing night air, or head somewhere for a nightcap or dessert.

I get so lost in my thoughts that I don't notice the streets have emptied until I'm walking alongside a park on a dark stretch of street. I walk faster. After what happened at the apartment the other night, I want to get out of this lonely area as quickly as possible.

As I walk, I hear myself breathing. Heavily.

Too heavily.

My stomach drops like I'm plunging down a roller coaster. That's not my breathing I'm hearing. It's coming from someone walking behind me.

Chapter Twenty-Five

Wednesday 2:20 P.M.

"We have a problem."

Detective Tran signaled to Detective Halliday to come over to the desk where he was trawling through CCTV footage.

"What's wrong with your screen?" Halliday asked as she leaned over Tran's desk and looked at his computer screen. It was filled with static.

"There's nothing wrong with my screen," said Tran. "The static you're seeing is the footage from the security cameras at the rear basement exits of the building."

"You're telling me those cameras didn't film anything last night?"

"That's exactly what I'm telling you. They were both offline."

"Do we know if someone tampered with them?"

"The security company supervisor won't know until his technicians have physically checked the cameras this afternoon. I just got off the phone with him," said Tran. "He thinks it's more likely it was a technical fault rather than sabotage."

On the whiteboard, Halliday had taped a screenshot of the CCTV footage taken just after 2 A.M. in the hallway outside the apartment where the murder had taken place. The murky shadow of a person could be seen leaving the apartment and going into the stairwell. The investigative team were all working on the assumption that the figure was the killer. An innocent person would have taken the elevator rather than try to leave surreptitiously.

Tran had gone through the CCTV footage from all the other entry and exit points in the building trying to track the mystery person's escape route, but the figure hadn't appeared in any of the footage from the other cameras at the relevant time period.

He'd had high hopes of getting a visual of the killer in the CCTV footage of the basement exits. Instead, all he got was static.

"What's going on?" asked Lavelle, who had just finished taking a phone call at his cluttered desk.

"We've hit a brick wall," Halliday said. "It appears the security cameras filming the basement exits weren't functioning properly last night. Tran believes the killer used one of those exits to leave the building. He's already checked CCTV footage from the other exits."

Tran turned his laptop so that Lavelle could see the static on the screen.

"Unless the killer never left the building," Lavelle theorized.

"We won't know for sure because we're missing key footage that could tell us definitively if the killer left the building or not," Tran said.

"I think we might have a backup option," said Halliday. "The liquor store facing the end of the lane behind the apartment building is all wired up with security cameras. They would have captured anyone who came out of the lane."

Halliday called the liquor store again. This time the manager answered the phone. He told her he'd received the message she'd left with his elderly dad and they could come over anytime to download whatever footage they needed.

She would have left straightaway to collect the footage, but Lavelle had disappeared into the captain's office.

While Halliday waited for Lavelle, she ran a series of checks on the name Liv Reese, the woman whose prints were on the wine bottle found next to the bed at the murder scene.

First she tried the DMV's driver's license database. Four people by the name of Liv Reese had a New York driver's license, but they didn't fit their profile: a newly qualified sixteen-year-old driver and three women ranging from their sixties upward. There were no outstanding warrants in the name Liv Reese. She had no criminal record either.

Halliday searched for "Liv Reese" on Facebook and Instagram. She hoped to find photos on a social media feed that would resemble the long-haired woman who was seen getting out of the elevator with the male victim less than twenty-four hours before he was murdered.

The search results were extensive, and Halliday didn't have time to go through it systematically. She made a note to do it later.

She did a quick general internet search instead, not expecting much. She certainly didn't expect to find an Interpol alert near the top of the search results. Halliday read the Interpol yellow notice, which was an international missing person report posted the previous day, for a woman by the name of Liv Reese who had last been seen in London a month earlier.

The missing person alert was accompanied by an ID photo of the woman taken from a London public transport travel card that bore her name. The woman in the overexposed photo had dark brown hair of indeterminate length. Her eyes were wide and surprised, as if the photo had been taken before she was ready.

It wasn't possible for Halliday to determine categorically whether the woman in the photo was the same woman they had seen in the footage. But there were enough similarities between the two women to make Halliday think it could be the same person.

Halliday dialed Interpol to get more information and was directed to a desk officer at Scotland Yard, who in turn gave Halliday the number of the detective sergeant who'd filed the missing person report. London was five hours ahead, and it was well into the evening when she called. From the loud background music blaring over the phone line, she could tell she'd caught him at a bad time.

"Hold on. I'll move somewhere quiet so I can hear you," he shouted over the thumping beat of music.

Halliday could hear the British detective's footsteps and the hum of passing cars as he moved away from the raucous noise.

"I'm outside now. We should be able to hear each other properly," he said. "Sorry about that. I was having a pint with the lads when you called. Who did you say you are?"

"My name is Darcy Halliday. I'm a New York City Police detective and I'm calling about a yellow notice alert you gave to Interpol for a woman by the name of Liv Reese."

"Have you located her?" he asked.

"Not exactly," said Halliday. "Her name came up in connection with another case. When I ran a search, I found the Interpol missing person report. I need to determine whether it's the same Liv Reese. Can you tell me when your person went missing and why a yellow notice was issued?"

"We believe she went missing about three weeks ago. We only found out a couple of days ago when her social worker filed a missing person report. Apparently, she'd missed several hospital appointments and wasn't responding to repeated calls. When we went to Liv Reese's flat, it was apparent she'd packed in a hurry and left. Her credit card records indicated that she'd bought a train ticket to Paris. After that, I'm afraid we lost all trace of her."

"How old is she?"

"Thirty-one, I believe," he said. "She's a dual US–British citizen. I have a pending request with your Department of Homeland Security to find out if she entered the United States."

"Why is there so much concern about this woman skipping town?" Halliday asked. "People pack up and move all the time. Without Scotland Yard or Interpol launching international manhunts, I might add."

"This case is different."

"How?"

"Liv Reese has a serious medical condition."

"What's her condition?" Halliday asked.

"She suffers from memory blackouts."

"So she's an amnesiac who doesn't know who she is?"

"Oh, she knows who she is," he hedged. "It's complicated. She gets intermittent blackouts during which time she can't retain memories."

"You think she's currently suffering from a memory blackout?"

"Yes, we do. The blackout appears to have begun a few weeks ago. We believe she's still in the throes of it. She took almost four thousand pounds out of her UK bank account before she disappeared. She told the bank teller that she was going to Paris on holiday. She hasn't withdrawn any more money since then, nor has she used her credit card. That suggests she's either suffering a blackout, or..." His voice dropped off meaningfully.

"Or what?"

"Or she's dead."

"Tell me about the blackouts." Halliday opted against mentioning that she believed Liv Reese was alive and well, and that she had been seen one day earlier in the company of a man who was subsequently murdered hours later. "How exactly do these memory blackouts manifest themselves?"

"According to her doctors, every time she goes to sleep, she wakes up with no memory of anything that has happened in her life, going back to when she was still living in New York two years ago."

"That seems very specific. Why two years?"

"What do you mean?" he asked.

"Why not five years, or ten? Why does she forget everything going back two years?"

"It's two years and three months, actually," he clarified. "You don't know anything about the case, do you, Detective Halliday?"

"Not a lot. That's why I contacted you."

"Liv Reese was almost murdered two years ago. I gather that's why she moved to London. For her own safety. Her assailant was never caught. By all accounts, she was doing well, establishing a life for herself in Britain, until a few weeks ago, when she apparently woke in her London flat suffering a memory blackout. She didn't remember a single thing that had transpired going back more than two years to the day when she was almost killed."

"So she's living in the past," said Halliday.

"Something like that. Only worse," he said, "because every time she goes to sleep, she forgets everything all over again. The poor woman is absolutely helpless. In fact, she's a sitting duck, really. That's why we enlisted Interpol to help us find her."

"What do you mean, she's a sitting duck?"

"Well, if the person who tried to kill her two years ago finds her before we do, we're terribly worried that she'd have no idea this individual was a threat to her."

Chapter Twenty-Six

The rattle of a jackhammer drilling at a construction site gets louder as I climb the subway station stairs to street level. I emerge into daylight only to get body-slammed by a woman rushing past in a whirl of shopping bags.

"Hey, lady! Watch where you're going," the woman calls out.

Farther ahead, a tourist in a puffer jacket drags an oversized suitcase out of a budget hotel directly into my path. I step out of the way to let him pass. His wife and daughters, dressed in matching puffer jackets, walk behind him wheeling their own suitcases.

The family walks slowly, like their bodies are weighed down by fatigue, until I realize it's me who's exhausted. All I want to do is sleep. I walk into the narrow lobby of the hotel and ask a receptionist how much it costs to get a room.

While I wait for her to check the rates and vacancies on her computer screen, I look down at the knuckles of my hands resting on the counter. STAY AWAKE, they read.

The message immediately revives me. I can't get a room. I can't go to sleep. By the time the reception clerk looks up from her screen, I'm heading out through the smoked-glass lobby door.

"Stay awake," I repeat to myself until a constant hum in my head takes on the rhythm of those words. "Stay awake. Stay awake."

There's a Starbucks on the corner. I order two double expressos to go. The coffee is so strong I wince as I drink every drop of it. I swig the second expresso like it's a shot.

It doesn't take long until the caffeine kicks in, surging through me. After that everything moves in hyperspeed. Traffic rushes past and my mind races ahead at a thousand miles a minute. All I can think about is being with Marco. I ache to lie against his chest with his arms wrapped protectively around me and his scent on my lips. The thought overwhelms me, like I'm an addict needing a fix. I raise my hand abruptly to hail a cab. It pulls over and I scramble inside.

The scenery zips by through the windows of the cab. I talk so fast that the cab driver asks me to repeat myself. Twice. I hop out a block before my destination because the traffic is jammed. I can walk faster than the traffic can move.

At Marco's building, the doorman is signing for a delivery when I walk in. "Hi Bill," I say without stopping. I walk straight into an open elevator just before the doors close.

There's only me in the elevator, along with a woman in her seventies with champagne hair. She's holding a Whole Foods bag to her chest like it's a shield.

Nervously, I tidy my hair as the elevator rises. The woman in the elevator slowly edges away to the farthest corner as if hoping I won't notice. I do notice, but I don't care.

The woman looks at me strangely when she gets out at her floor. I realize that I've been muttering "Stay awake" under my breath the whole time.

I want to explain, but the doors have already shut and the elevator is pummeling up again at full speed. When the elevator stops on Marco's floor, I step out and walk toward his apartment at the end of the corridor. I freeze when I see his front door.

Someone is coming out. It's not Marco. It's a woman with shiny hair. She wraps a red scarf around her neck and buttons her navy overcoat as she walks toward me. Her cheeks are flushed and her mouth is swollen as if she's just been kissed.

There's something about her that reminds me of me. I stumble toward the apartment. The woman brushes past me without stopping. I feel an icy breeze as if I've passed a ghost.

I press my eye to the peephole of Marco's front door and stare at the concave reflection of my pupil.

"Marco. It's me, Liv. Can we talk?" I bang on the door with my fist and ring the doorbell at the same time.

A clatter of metal startles me. I turn around to see a cleaner pushing a metal bucket with a mop near the elevators. The cleaner stares at me as if she's telling me something. Her mouth opens and shuts. I don't hear any words. All I hear is buzzing.

"You've got to leave."

I'm not sure who says it. Either way I'm in the elevator again. The doorman yells out as I pass him. "Lady, every few days you turn up here. I've told you plenty of times not to come back. Next time I see you, I'll call the cops."

His threats are drowned out by the traffic as I come out onto the street and wait for a bus to pull up. Soon, I'm on the bus looking down as pedestrians stride along the sidewalk while we're stuck in traffic. My mind churns so many confused thoughts that I feel like I'm spinning on an out-of-control amusement park ride. I lean my head against the window and close my eyes for a moment of respite. I'm lulled by the hydraulic bus doors opening and closing as we move through snarling traffic.

I get off the bus and walk along the river to Bellevue Hospital. In the distance are the rectangular towers of the United Nations headquarters. I'm walking so fast it feels as if I am flying.

There's a long line at the ER reception desk so I head over to general reception and ask if they can page Dr. Amy Decker.

"I'm sorry, ma'am," the woman says after checking her computer. "There's no doctor by that name working here. Are you sure you're at the right hospital?"

"Yes. Amy definitely works here."

The woman shrinks away at my vehemence. "It's my first week here. Maybe I'm not looking in the right place," she explains. She taps the shoulder of a colleague sitting next to her to enlist her help. Her colleague has dark hair that curves against her neck and suspicious eyes.

"Why are you asking for Dr. Decker?" she asks.

"Amy's a friend. A close friend."

I rub my temples to soothe the painful throb in my head as the woman looks at me strangely. She picks up a phone and makes a call, swiveling around on her chair so that I can't hear her hushed conversation.

"Dr. Graham is coming to see you," she tells me once she's hung up.

"Brett?" My eyes widen in surprise. I want to talk to Amy, not Brett.

Brett turns up a couple of minutes later dressed in blue surgical scrubs that match his eyes. He beelines across the waiting area toward me. When he reaches me, he gently takes both my hands and helps me sit on an upholstered chair near the reception desk.

"Are you okay, Liv?" he asks, squatting down, as the receptionist watches curiously from her desk.

"Yes. No. Sort of." Tears well in my eyes, making everything look blurry. I self-consciously wipe them away with my fingers, but they keep coming back. "Brett. I don't understand what's going on. Everything's very confusing."

"I know it is," he says gently.

Brett's so close to me that I can smell a mixture of aftershave and antiseptic.

"I'm in the middle of ward rounds. I still have two more patients to see, but I promise that as soon as I'm done I'll be back to explain everything. Wait here for me, Liv. It's important. It's not safe for you out there. Do you understand?"

"Yes, of course."

"Good. I'll be back very soon and then we'll talk."

He takes a few magazines off a table and hands them to me to read. Then he has a quiet word with the woman behind the reception desk. She nods her head vigorously. I get the impression that Brett's asked her to keep an eye on me.

Live electricity crackles in my head like a warning signal as he walks away. It gets louder and louder until I can't bear it anymore. I feel restless and suddenly terrified of what Brett's going to tell me.

I notice the secretary is distracted by a call. I slip out of my seat and head toward the exit, bursting out of the glass lobby door into a buffeting draft. It feels as if the wind is blowing me along against my will. Eventually, I stop and lean against a rail overlooking the East River, gasping for air and wondering why I can't stop crying.

Chapter Twenty-Seven

Two Years Earlier

I was an idiot not to ask Marco to give me a ride home when he left the restaurant last night. I should never have walked home by myself. It was false bravado from drinking too much wine at Amy's party.

Now I'm hemmed in between the iron railings of a park on my left and a deserted trade school shut for the night on the other side.

The labored breathing and footsteps behind me make me acutely aware that I'm on a dark and isolated stretch of street. Nobody is around other than me and the stranger following me.

I deliberate whether it's tactically best to run and risk my pursuer catching up and overpowering me, or whether it's smarter to pretend I'm unaware I'm being followed while walking through this lonely stretch as quickly as possible. I decide it's safest to maintain the pretense since I'm unlikely to outrun him.

The headlights of an approaching car cut through the darkness enough for me to see a residential side street coming up after the trade school. I dash across the street as the car passes and then run full speed toward the side street, almost bumping into a couple getting out of a car near the corner.

"Sorry," I say, as I slalom past them.

The end of the street hits a well-lit intersection that connects to the street where I live. My lungs burn as I approach my street. Breathlessly, I slow to a fast walk as I tell myself I'm being paranoid and that I was just imagining being followed.

It was the product of alcohol and fear stoked by that awful avant-garde performance art show. That art show has probably spooked me for life.

Flashing through my head like a warning is the image of the bound and gagged woman writhing on the chair behind the red velvet exhibit ropes, and the black-and-white footage beamed on the gallery walls around her of a woman being watched by an unseen predator. I tell myself that it was only art. Bad art.

The thick foliage of the trees diffuses the streetlights, casting the street into a dark gloom. When I'm halfway down my street I hear footsteps again. They echo my own. I don't turn around to check who's behind me. Instead I assume it's my pursuer.

My building is very close. As I approach the stoop, I pretend to walk straight ahead. At the last second I bolt up the stairs and open the door with a well-practiced single turn of my key. I clamber inside and shut the door behind me. Once it's closed, I lean against it and gasp for breath until my racing heart slows.

Shawna meows insistently when I let myself into the apartment. I lock the front door behind me and hover near the kitchen window to look down at the street. I make sure to stand far enough away from the window so that nobody will see me watching. There's nobody there. Just rows of parked cars on either side. I feel like an idiot.

Thunder rumbles and Shawna rubs herself nervously against my legs at the sound of an impending summer storm. My terror from the other night returns even though there's no more banging windows and my bedroom looks exactly as it did when I left home this morning. I wish Amy had come back with me instead of going to Brett's apartment.

I'm still rattled by what happened the other night in the apartment, even though there's no logical reason for it to bother me. Amy admitted to borrowing a sarong from my closet and looking for a couple of other clothes she wanted to take with her on her vacation. That's why my drawers and closet doors were partly open.

She agrees with the police that Shawna might have accidentally knocked over my photo frame. I still don't have an explanation for how a heart was drawn in the dust on my bedroom window. Amy thinks it might have been there for a while and I just noticed it. She said one of her hometown friends who was camping out in our living room a few weeks ago used to do things like that when they were teenagers. There's probably a logical explanation for everything, but the fear I felt that night hasn't quite left me, especially now that I'm once again alone in the nighttime stillness of the apartment.

I open the fridge to take out milk for Shawna as a treat. The milk carton is empty, which means there's also no milk for my morning coffee. I close my bedroom door when I go to sleep, and push a chair up against the door handle, more to calm my nerves than because I think it will stop an intruder from bursting in while I sleep. I hear the storm overnight in my dreams. Pouring rain angrily hits the concrete outside.

When I wake in the morning, the alarm clock next to my bed is turned off. I've woken an hour later than usual. Exhausted, I go to the kitchen and robotically make myself coffee.

It's only when I'm taking an unopened carton of milk from the fridge door to pour into my coffee mug that I remember there was no milk in the fridge last night. I assume Amy came back early this morning and brought milk.

But when I go to the bathroom to clean my teeth, I notice that Amy's bedroom door is wide open, as it was when I came home last night, and her room is filled with daylight. I tentatively stick my head through her doorway. Amy's bed hasn't been slept in. Her window shades are up. I'm certain that she didn't come back last night.

How on earth did the carton of milk get into the fridge if Amy didn't bring it? There's obviously a rational explanation.

I must have been so distracted from being followed home last night that I didn't notice there was already milk in the fridge door.

I turn on my phone and check my updates as I stir my coffee. I drink it standing against the kitchen counter, basking in sunlight shining through the window above the sink. A message notification from an anonymous number comes up on my phone screen.

> Enjoy your coffee. I know how much you like it milky.

The message terrifies me so much that I instinctively toss the contents of the mug into the sink and peer surreptitiously out the window. Is someone watching me? How else would the sender know that I was drinking coffee? Or my preference for extra milk.

Even more terrifying is the realization that I was right the first time; there was no milk in the fridge last night. The implications of that make my blood run cold. Someone must have come into the apartment while I slept and put a carton of milk in the fridge, which means someone is watching me and has a key to my apartment. It's the final straw.

I grab my purse and head to the local police precinct, where I show the text message to the duty officer. Since this is the second incident, the officer calls a detective downstairs to talk to me.

The detective comes down five minutes later. He's a heavyset man in a creased suit, balding, with squinty eyes and an expression that exudes boredom. He tells me his name is Detective Krause.

"How much did you drink last night?" Detective Krause asks a few minutes later when we're in a cramped interview room and I'm sitting on the other side of a small desk facing his hulking frame. He scribbles my answers in a notebook.

"Two glasses of wine. Actually, three." I remember that I finished the meal with a Madeira port.

"After drinking three glasses of wine, you walked home thinking that someone followed you. You didn't see this person and you didn't report it. In addition, you are certain there was no milk in the kitchen fridge before you went to sleep, but you found a full carton this morning when you woke. Is that what happened?"

"Yes, that's right. That text message I received this morning telling me to enjoy my coffee suggests that whoever sent the text left the milk for me."

"But you said there was no sign of a break-in. So how did this intruder put the milk carton in your fridge?"

"Maybe he picked the lock while I was sleeping."

The detective stares at me, openmouthed, like I'm crazy.

"You're telling me that someone came into your apartment, put a carton of milk in your fridge, and then left without stealing a single thing?"

"What I'm saying," I say tersely, "is that the incident last night, in addition to what happened the other night, suggests a pattern. The officers who came to my apartment last time told me to look out for a pattern."

"I don't see any pattern," Detective Krause says, dropping his pen abruptly onto the table. "The police report from the other night says there were no signs of a break-in and there's no history of harassment. There was also nothing stolen. The officer who signed the report indicated the mess in your bedroom might have been caused by a domestic pet."

"My cat didn't do it. And, incidentally, my cat doesn't generally put milk cartons in the fridge or send me text messages either. It wasn't my cat," I sigh with frustration. "There must be something you can do, Detective!" I'm getting upset now. "Please, surely you can find out who sent me that text? I bet it's the same person who broke into my apartment the other night."

"You want me," he points to himself, "to get a federal warrant to access private phone records and use them to arrest whoever sent you this text message on suspicion that this individual broke into your apartment to put a carton of milk in your fridge? Miss Reese, no judge would sign off on a warrant based on the information you've given me."

"This message is implicitly threatening." I hold up my cell phone so he can see the text I was sent. "The person who sent it implies that he knows what I'm doing as well as my likes and dislikes. I *was* followed last night, Detective Krause. I'm certain of it. What more do you need in order to investigate?"

"A heck of a lot more."

"Such as?"

"Keep a journal. If you're being followed, write it down. When. What time. What happened. Keep any messages you get. Most importantly, never communicate with a stalker."

"How can I communicate with a stalker if I honestly don't know who's stalking me?" I'm horrified at the thought that someone in my orbit might be harassing me. "Nobody I know would do something like this."

"I've had cases where someone nursing a grudge acts months or even years later," he says.

George's bearded face flashes in my head. The veteran *Cultura* photographer lost his job when I complained about him deliberately putting his hand up my thigh on a work trip. When the HR manager called me into her office to tell me he'd been fired, she made it clear that I should let her know if he caused any trouble for me. I immediately knew that I'd made an enemy by reporting him. But that was ages ago. Surely George has moved on since then. Hasn't he?

"It could be someone from your past, or it could be, as I said earlier, simply a mistake. Maybe things have been stressful for you at work. Maybe you drank too much last night. There might be a perfectly innocent explanation."

"Detective," I insist, "I did not imagine it. I just don't know who'd do this to me."

"Okay." He holds up his hands defensively. "Don't assume it's someone you know."

"What do you mean?"

"Oftentimes, a stalker is completely unknown to the victim. Maybe the victim did something nice, like hold open an elevator door. The stalker creates a fantasy world about that person and becomes obsessed."

My stomach gets queasy as I consider the possibility that it was the waiter, Kevin, who followed me home last night and put the milk in the fridge. I tell myself that's ridiculous. I have not a scrap of evidence that Kevin has done anything other than try to call me at my office a handful of times, which is creepy but not illegal.

"What happens if I only have a hunch as to who might be doing this? No evidence, just a hunch. What do you do in that scenario, Detective?"

"Probably nothing." He shifts his big frame in his chair. "Without evidence, we'd watch and wait until the individual crossed a line."

"Detective, are you actually telling me you can't do anything to help me until this person hurts me?" I ask.

His silence is pretty much my answer.

Chapter Twenty-Eight

Detective Halliday immediately dialed Homeland Security after ending the call with the Scotland Yard detective.

"I need to know whether a woman by the name of Liv Reese entered the United States over the past month," Halliday told the clerk.

She tapped her pen on her desk impatiently while the clerk performed a data search. Through the internal window of the captain's office, she saw Jack Lavelle stand up. His meeting with the captain was wrapping up. She'd heard on the precinct rumor mill that they'd been partners for years, and that it was Jack whom everyone had expected to rise through the ranks.

"Are you there, Detective?"

"Yes." Halliday shifted her attention back to the call.

"Liv Catherine Reese arrived at JFK on a flight from Paris." The clerk gave the flight number and a date three weeks earlier. "According to our records, she arrived on a US passport. She holds joint US–British citizenship via her father. Do you need any other information?"

"What address did she write on her arrival card?" Halliday asked.

"It's an address in Brooklyn." The clerk hesitated. "Her handwriting is hard to read. I'll email it to you."

The scanned copy of the arrival card was already in Halliday's inbox when she ended the call. She opened it up and magnified the image so she could decipher the cramped handwriting.

"Bingo," she said under her breath.

The address Liv Reese had written in block letters on her airport immigration card was the same address as the one listed for her in the fingerprint database.

It proved that the Liv Reese who was the subject of an Interpol missing person search was the Liv Reese whose fingerprints were at the crime scene, and who in turn was the same woman whose prints were put into the system more than two years earlier when she was almost murdered. They were one and the same person.

"We have a Brooklyn address for the woman whose prints were found at the murder scene," Halliday told Lavelle as he came out of the captain's office.

"Let's head over there. You drive." Lavelle tossed her his car keys and Halliday snatched them in the air. "I'll meet you out front in two minutes."

–

Liv Reese's address was on the second floor of an old brownstone in Brooklyn, which had been remodeled into a modern four-floor building with a rooftop.

Fall leaves in the gutter swirled from the wind on the narrow tree-lined street as Halliday and Lavelle walked to the apartment. They took the stairs in unison up to the top of the stoop.

Lavelle pressed the intercom buzzer. There was no answer. He did it again. This time they both heard an angry thud of footsteps rushing down the stairs. The door swung open only enough for them to glimpse a woman with dark blond hair, who looked nothing like the Interpol photo of Liv Reese.

"You need to leave or I'll call the police," said the woman through the gap.

"We *are* the police." Halliday held up her detective's badge. "My name is Detective Darcy Halliday. This is Detective Jack Lavelle. We're looking for this woman. Have you seen her?"

She pushed the Interpol photo of Liv Reese through the crack in the door.

"You'd better come in," the woman said, opening the door. She introduced herself as Angela as she led them up the stairs.

"I don't have much time to talk. I'm between Zoom meetings," Angela said, swinging open her apartment door to let them in.

On the dinner table were a laptop and a pile of files. Hanging over a chair was a tailored jacket, which Angela obviously wore to look professional from the waist up for her Zoom meetings. Below the waist, she wore gray yoga pants and fluffy slippers.

"I have fifteen minutes until my next meeting. Let's get straight to the point," Angela said. "The woman in the photo you showed me downstairs rang our doorbell early this morning. She looked a bit different, but I'm certain it was the same person. I'm very good with faces."

"Run us through what happened last night," Halliday said.

"Our doorbell rings in the middle of the night. It rings and rings. Wakes us up. I had an early conference call with Shanghai. Let me tell you, I did not appreciate being woken at three in the morning."

"I can imagine," Halliday sympathized.

"I went downstairs to answer the door. Grant followed me. He knew I'd be furious. There's a woman standing on the stoop. She acts as if she lives in our apartment. She actually asks us if we're out-of-town guests staying the night! She seems to think her roommate invited us. Total nut job."

"What's her roommate's name?" Halliday asked.

"I don't remember. Wait! We sometimes get mail for her."

She jumped up from the sofa and removed a couple of unopened envelopes from a basket on a white oak bookshelf. "Dr. Amy Decker," she said, passing them the envelope.

"Go on," said Halliday.

"It was very weird. When we told the woman to leave, she got all teary and told us that she'd lost her purse and phone and she had nowhere to go. Grant felt bad. He's a pushover. He let her come up to use the phone. Next thing, she's in our apartment accusing me of killing her cat and acting as if she owns the place. I was furious. She even went into our bedroom. We threatened to call the cops and she left."

"Has this happened before?"

"Grant and I just came back from vacation a couple of days ago. Our neighbor mentioned hearing our doorbell ringing in the middle of the night while we were away. He said it happened more than once. Maybe it was the same woman. Maybe last night wasn't the first time she came here. I couldn't say for sure."

"Any idea where she went, or what direction she took after she left your apartment?" Halliday asked.

"Grant went to sleep. I waited by the kitchen sink, which faces the street, to make sure she left. She was hanging around our stoop. Then she sat down on the stairs. I said to myself that if she was still there in five minutes I was definitely calling the cops."

"Did you?" Halliday asked.

"No. She waved down a cab coming down our street."

"Did you notice the name of the cab company or get a plate number?"

"It was too dark out for me to see the plates," said Angela with a shrug. "I'm pretty sure the cab picked her up at about three in the morning, if that helps.

"She's not dangerous, is she?" Angela asked, suddenly wary.

"You never can tell," said Lavelle. "Call us if she comes back or if you think of anything else." He handed her a card with his contact details.

Halliday called Tran as they walked back to the car. She asked him to call every cab company in the city and find out if they'd had a car at the Williamsburg address at around three that morning.

In the old days, that sort of job would wear holes in the soles of a cop's shoes. It would mean going into the depots of every cab company in the city and looking through their log books. These days, cab companies worked with a GPS system. It would be a relatively quick and painless task for them to review their GPS data to see whether any vehicles had been there that morning.

"I need the cab driver's name and phone number. I especially want to know where he dropped her off. The cab GPS should have that information even if the driver doesn't remember," Halliday told Tran. "We're heading over to the liquor store now to look at the CCTV footage. I'm still waiting to get hold of Detective Krause's file. Did his old precinct call?"

"No," said Tran. "Do you want me to go over there and get the files?"

"We'll take care of it. Can you run a name for us, in the meantime?" she asked.

"Sure. What's the name?"

"Dr. Amy Decker." Halliday read the name off the unopened letter. "Apparently she and Liv Reese shared an apartment a few years back."

Chapter Twenty-Nine

The beep of a delivery truck reversing to offload goods cuts through the hiss of white noise in my head. Someone is talking to me. I turn around.

"I already told you, it's not open," calls out a stocky man with a bushy gray mustache wearing a white apron covered in flour dust. He stands outside the pizza place across the street, smoking a cigarette. I get the impression I've been standing here for a while, staring into space.

"Lady," he says, dropping cigarette ash onto the sidewalk. "The bar doesn't open for hours."

I look up. Above my head is a sign that reads NOCTURNAL. The bar looks seedy, as most bars do in the cold, hard light of day. Pressing my face to the stippled art deco glass doors, I look inside. The lights are off. From what little I can see there's nobody here.

"It opens at five. The place next door sells liquor if you can't wait until then," the man calls out. He gestures toward a bodega next to his pizza shop before stubbing out his cigarette with the bottom of his shoe and going back inside.

My mouth is dry and I feel woozy like I've just been roused from a deep sleep. I've felt this way since I woke on the E train, my head pounding like the beat of a war drum. I have no recollection of getting onto the subway and no idea where I was going. It feels as if time has skipped ahead without me noticing.

The last thing I remember before waking on the train was the sudden ring of my desk phone in the office. It was so loud and insistent that it startled me. "This is Liv," I said into the receiver.

Everything after that is a blank until I opened my eyes, my body swaying with the movements of the train as it shot through a subway tunnel.

My hands were covered with ballpoint writing. Amid the scribble was an underlined message with the name and address of a place called Nocturnal. Something about the name struck a chord. It drew me here like a magnet.

I cross the street to the bodega. My body's working on autopilot and my mind is a blank as I enter the store. A man with a wide friendly face beams at me from behind the counter; his smile is filled with warm recognition. I smile back stiffly. I've never seen this shopkeeper before in my life.

I stop at a wall of refrigerators to check out the assortment of drinks arranged neatly on shelves. Stifling an exhausted yawn, I remove a can of iced coffee espresso from the fridge. It contains enough caffeine to keep an elephant awake for the next twelve hours.

"How much do I owe?" I ask the man at the counter as I put the coffee can down with a thump.

He stares at me tight-lipped, his jaw protruding slightly. Hurt shines in his thickly lashed brown eyes. I get the impression that I've offended him in some way. Perhaps by not saying hello.

"I'll put it on your tab," he says.

I'm about to tell him I don't have a tab when he continues. "Every day it's the same, Liv. You never sleep. You're up all night. You walk around like a zombie during the day. Two, three caffeine drinks a day. It's good for business. My business. Not good for you," he says, shaking his head sadly.

He puts my purchase into a plastic bag and hands it to me by the handles. "You should take better care of yourself. You've lost more weight. Soon there won't be anything left of you."

I'm stunned into silence at the familiar way this stranger talks to me, like we know each other. I look down at myself. He's right. I've never been so thin, nor felt so fragile.

"Go home and rest," he tells me. "You look as if you haven't slept for days."

Standing on the sidewalk outside the bodega, I wonder if he's right. I'm utterly exhausted. I look up at the sky. It's overcast and steely gray. Even that confuses me. It's supposed to be the middle of summer. Yet it looks and feels like a blustery fall day. The buildings whirl around me with dizzying speed. I close my eyes and wait for everything to stop spinning.

"Are you all right, Liv?"

A man holding a box of groceries stands in front of me, his wide, pleasant face creased with concern. He looks like a younger version of the shopkeeper. He has the same strong, slightly protruding jaw and he speaks with the same Middle Eastern accent.

"Are you having another migraine attack? Do you want me to get you some water so you can take your medicine?"

"I'm fine," I insist, even though it's far from the truth.

"I'm delivering this order to a customer on your street. Come with me. I'll see you home."

I follow behind him like he's a pied piper. I'm too dazed and exhausted to explain that I don't actually live anywhere near here. Two streets later, he stops by a flight of stairs leading to the entrance of a light brick apartment building. He rests the box of groceries on a ledge.

"We're here," he announces.

I look around, blinking in confusion. He's brought me to someone else's street, and he's waiting outside someone else's apartment building for me to go inside.

I take a tentative step up the stairs. I figure I'll take a cab out of here once he's gone. It seems less awkward than explaining that he's mixed me up with someone else.

"That's not your building!" he tells me, as I take another step up the stairs. "You live across the street, Liv." He points to a dark brick building on the other side of the street. I stare at it, bewildered.

"You don't remember. Do you?"

"Remember what?"

"Your address."

"Of course, I know my address. I live in Brooklyn," I say.

"That's where you used to live." His voice oozes compassion. "You've moved, Liv. You live in the building across the street now."

His certainty leaves me baffled. "I know where I live and it's not here."

"Come with me. The doorman will explain."

He picks up the box of groceries and crosses the street, herding me along with him, until we're standing by a counter tiled with old-fashioned brown ceramic tiles.

"Good afternoon, Miss Reese," says the doorman, standing up from behind the counter to greet me. "I have your key here for you."

He hands me a key ring. My name and an apartment number are written on the tag in my own handwriting. The doorman gestures for me to enter a waiting elevator. It feels as if I'm being sucked into a vacuum as I step into the dimly lit elevator. I turn and stare helplessly at the doorman. I don't know which floor number to press.

He leans in and presses the button for the basement, unfazed by my confusion. It's almost as if he expects me not to know where to go. The doors slide shut and the elevator heaves down with a sudden jolt, taking me with it.

When the doors slide open with a rattle, I step out into a long poorly lit corridor. The ceiling is low and the walls are yellowing with age. A rancid smell of cooking fumes hangs in the air mixed with a faint tinge of mildew. I walk down the long corridor looking for the apartment that corresponds with the number on the key ring.

I find the apartment at the end of the hall. There's an envelope on the doorstep. It's an electricity bill and it's addressed to me.

Chapter Thirty

Two Years Earlier

My red boxing gloves are tied together and slung over my shoulders like a necklace as Amy and I walk home after kick-boxing class. I have never been so exhausted in all my life. Amy might have a great bedside manner when she's seeing patients at the hospital, but when she puts on her boxing gloves she gives a heck of a wallop.

I was so beat after class that I slumped on a bench in the locker room with a wet towel over my head and told Amy I wasn't physically capable of moving. She jokingly offered to order an Uber for the five-minute ride home. In the end, it was Amy's lighthearted mockery that gave me the push I needed to get up and walk back with her in the stifling morning heat.

When we reach the landing, we both see a special delivery outside our front door. Amy picks up an enormous bundle of bloodred roses wrapped in frothy paper. A gold box of expensive chocolate truffles is tied to the flowers with an enormous matching gold bow. It's the sort of grand romantic gesture that's typical of Brett. He loves spoiling Amy.

"Brett said he was arranging a surprise for me because he had to leave the restaurant early the other night. This must have cost him a fortune." Amy cradles the bouquet in her arms as we go inside.

Amy's cell phone rings. From the muffled conversation that ensues, I gather it's a call from the hospital. When Amy finishes the call, she asks me to put the roses in a vase for her.

"They've called me into work. I have to get changed quickly. My Uber will be here in ten minutes."

While Amy takes a quick shower, I go over to the dinner table where she's left the flower arrangement. The gold ribbon tied around the roses is tightly knotted. Shawna jumps onto the table and meows furiously as I ease the knot open with my nails.

Something sharp pricks my finger. I screech "Ouch" so loudly that the cat jumps down in panic and glares at me with her pale green eyes as if to say: "I told you so." A trickle of blood runs down my hand.

"Are you all right?" Amy rushes out of her bedroom, freshly showered and dressed for work. She grabs her purse and keys.

"I must have cut it on something." I clutch my finger tightly. It's throbbing like mad.

"There's a bottle of disinfectant in the bathroom medicine cabinet. Put some on. I'll take a look when I get back." The front door closes behind her as she leaves.

I wrap a Kleenex around my finger and then open the bouquet and spill the roses into a pile. There's a small envelope among the stems. I tear open the envelope and read the gift card inside. The flowers weren't sent anonymously. I'm surprised to discover the name on the envelope is not Amy's name. It's mine.

Tearing open the envelope, I pull out a generic florist's card with a brief message.

"To L." It's followed by a heart.

I'm moved by Marco's sweet gesture. I take the gold lid off the chocolate box. Inside are a dozen truffles, each individually decorated with swirls of contrasting colored chocolate drizzle. I call Marco to thank him for the thoughtful gift, but there's no answer, so I text him instead.

> Roses AND chocolates! You're spoiling me!!

I pop a truffle into my mouth and savor the heady taste of chocolate and liqueur as I lie on the sofa and relax with a

154

magazine. As I flick through the glossy pages, my eyes get heavy and I drift off, the magazine falling onto my lap.

I'm woken by a beep from my cell phone lying on a sofa cushion next to me. My eyes are so blurred I struggle to read the hazy message on the screen. It's from Marco.

> I can't take the credit for your flowers. You must have a secret admirer!

A stab of fear pierces me as I remember my discussion with the police about stalking. I try to get up, but I'm overcome by a paralyzing exhaustion. The front door opens. Through the drowsiness that envelops me, I wonder what brought Amy back so quickly. I try to ask her but my tongue is too thick to form words.

A shadow appears on the living room wall. It's too tall to be Amy. It's someone else. I try to lift my head to see who it is, but my muscles don't cooperate. Sleep overwhelms me. The shadow disappears into a black mist.

I'm stretched out on the sofa when I wake again. The apartment is cast in a twilight glow that suggests I've slept the day away. Keys rattle in the front door.

"Liv?"

I peek through my lashes. Amy looks down at me with concern.

"Is everything all right?"

"I was sleeping so deeply. Such strange dreams…" I mumble.

I gather enough strength to move into a sitting position on the sofa cushion. I cradle my throbbing head in my hands as I listen to Amy's chatter.

"I don't know who called me into work," she says. "Not only did they *not* need me, they were actually overstaffed. Since I was already in the city, I went shopping. Like I need an excuse to buy more clothes I don't need. Right!"

Amy puts her shopping bags on the floor next to the sofa and takes out an assortment of packages wrapped in reams of tissue paper. She tears open the paper and holds the various garments she bought against her slim figure while I gush approvingly.

The cobwebs of sleep disappear as I look away from Amy and her impromptu fashion show to the roses beautifully arranged in a glass vase on the coffee table.

"Thanks for putting the roses in water. I dozed off before I had a chance to do it."

"Liv, I didn't put the flowers in the vase," Amy says. "I was in a rush to get to work. You arranged the flowers. Don't you remember?"

Chapter Thirty-One

Detective Jack Lavelle checked the list of flights arriving at Hong Kong International Airport while Halliday drove them to the liquor store to collect copies of the store's CCTV footage.

The apartment owner's flight was due to land at any moment. "If we can find out the victim's identity then we can blow this case wide open by working backward," Lavelle said, refreshing the arrivals screen on his phone for the dozenth time.

"What do you mean by 'working backward'?" Halliday asked.

"We get an ID on the victim. After that, we figure out who his enemies were."

"What if he didn't have enemies?"

"Everyone has enemies. Ninety percent of homicides are about figuring out who the victim pissed off enough to kill."

"What if the victim didn't piss someone off at all? Maybe this murder had nothing to do with settling scores. What if the killer was trying to make a statement?"

"You're saying this because of the writing on the bedroom window?"

"Yes," said Halliday. "The murderer spent considerable time writing a message on the window with the victim's blood. Think about what it took to write that sign. The killer would have gone backward and forward from the window to the body to get more blood. It was a statement. This murder wasn't about the victim. It wasn't about revenge, or acting out a fantasy. This murder was about getting attention."

"Is it possible you're overthinking it?"

"In what way?" Halliday asked.

Lavelle shrugged. "Most homicides I've dealt with over the past two decades had one thing in common."

"Let me guess. Greed? Jealousy?"

"Not even close," Lavelle said.

"Then what?"

"Getting even."

"Getting even?"

"Yes. You can't imagine what some people will do to settle a score."

His voice trailed off as the word "Landed" appeared on his screen. He immediately dialed the owner's number.

Halliday listened to Lavelle's side of the conversation as she drove. The owner of the apartment was obviously shocked at first to hear that a murder had been committed in his apartment. His shock was quickly followed by concern. He wanted to know how much damage had been caused.

Lavelle told him the police department had arranged for the windowpane to be replaced since it was needed as evidence.

"Otherwise there's no damage and not much blood. You could get a cleaning service to steam-clean the mattress and carpet," he said. "Or you might want to replace them both given what happened in there. Either way, you'll probably need someone to clean up the place. For one thing, the fingerprint powder leaves a residue on all the surfaces it's brushed on," Lavelle told him.

"He sounded more worried about the state of his apartment than that a man was murdered in his bed," Halliday remarked when the call was over, flicking a sideways glance at Lavelle as she drove. "Did he tell you what you wanted to know?"

"The apartment was booked via a short-stay bookings website. The name of the guy who booked it is James E. Carter Jr. He put down his home address as 1600 Pennsylvania Avenue."

"That's the address of the White House," said Halliday.

"Yes, it is. The owner didn't notice he'd been given a fake address and the name of our thirty-ninth president. His main concern was that the payment went through. It did. He charges three hundred dollars a night plus tax. His guest paid for a week up front."

"How did the guest pay?"

"Visa," said Lavelle.

"We should be able to get a name for him from the credit card company. Hopefully, the card wasn't stolen along with the fake address and Jimmy Carter's name," Halliday said.

An international call with a UK country code flashed on her phone screen. Halliday answered it on the hands-free system.

"Is this Detective Halliday?" asked a woman with a clipped British accent.

"Yes, it is."

"Detective Halliday, this is Marcia Nichols. I'm calling from London. I heard via Scotland Yard that you might have found Liv Reese?"

"We haven't found her yet," Halliday clarified. "We saw the Interpol missing person alert and I contacted Scotland Yard for more information. What is your involvement in this?"

"I'm Liv's social worker," Marcia said. "I was the one who asked the police to file a missing person report when we couldn't locate her. We've been awfully worried about her. I'm not sure if you're aware, but Liv has a condition that makes her quite vulnerable."

"What can you tell me about her condition?" Halliday asked.

"Well, it's rather complicated. Maybe I should start at the beginning."

"Go ahead," said Halliday, signaling to take a left turn.

"Liv moved to London about two years ago after she was almost killed. Attempted murder, I believe. The killer got away."

"Do you know the specifics of what happened?" Halliday asked.

"I'm afraid I don't," said the social worker. "Neither did Liv."

"What do you mean?"

"Liv was in a coma after the incident. She never remembered what happened. She moved to London afterward to start afresh. As far as I know, her life here was relatively normal. In fact, from what we can tell, she had no memory problems other than being unable to remember the incident in which she was almost killed. That's perfectly normal given that she'd been unconscious for days afterward. In fact, it was probably a blessing in disguise."

"The Scotland Yard detective told me that she's suffering from a memory blackout," Halliday said, pulling to a stop at a red traffic light. "When did that start?"

"As best we can tell, it began five weeks ago."

"Can you tell me what happened?"

"Liv woke up one morning in her flat in Clapham. According to her neighbor, she was very confused. She didn't know where she was, or how she'd gotten there. Liv panicked and ran downstairs. When she attempted to cross the street, she was almost hit by a double-decker. She must have thought she was in New York because she apparently looked the wrong way when she tried to cross. Fortunately, someone pushed her out of the way just in time. She fell onto the pavement. An ambulance was called and she was brought to the hospital where I work. Saint Vincent's."

"Was she badly hurt?" Halliday asked.

"She had a few bruises. No head injuries or concussion. Usually she'd have been discharged straightaway but due to her obvious confusion, she was reviewed by a psychiatrist."

"What did the psychiatrist find?"

"That she had no idea how she happened to be in London. No idea whatsoever. She had no memory of moving to the UK, or of her life in London. In fact, she had no memory of anything going back two years. He diagnosed her as suffering from some sort of repetitive memory blackout."

"What do you mean by repetitive?" Halliday asked, pressing on the gas as the traffic light turned green.

"Liv was kept overnight at the hospital for observation. Her doctor discovered that every time Liv fell asleep, her memory reset back to two years earlier."

"How did they know that?" Halliday asked.

"Because each time she woke up in her hospital bed, she didn't have the faintest idea that she was in London. She consistently told her medical team that her last memory before waking up in hospital was working at her desk in her office in New York. She remembered answering her phone, but she couldn't remember anything that happened after that until she woke up in a London hospital. And what's more, whatever new memories she'd formed when she was awake disappeared once she went to sleep, and the whole process started all over again."

"Why would somebody suddenly lose their memory like that, out of the blue?" Halliday asked.

"Dr. Stanhope, her psychiatrist, says her condition may have been induced by insomnia. Apparently, Liv hadn't been sleeping properly for weeks before her sudden memory loss," the social worker said. "In fact, when I took her back to her flat after she was discharged, I found piles of medications. All sorts of pills to help her stay awake. NoDoz. Alert. She drinks a dozen cups of coffee a day. Dr. Stanhope thinks it's all connected. The insomnia and her blackouts."

"She must be high as a kite on caffeine if she's drinking so much of it," said Halliday, turning onto a street near the liquor store.

"It's a stimulant. It makes her very nervous and erratic."

"Enough to be violent?"

"Oh, Liv's not violent," said the social worker. "She's lovely. She's had a very hard time of it. She has nobody to look out for her, which is very difficult for someone who wakes up each morning without any memory. Usually when these things happen there's a family to support the patient. In Liv's case, it's just her."

"She doesn't have any family at all?" Halliday asked, backing into a parking spot.

"Her parents are both dead. There's an aunt who lives in Southampton. She's the one who told me that Liv moved to the UK after the attempt on her life. Her aunt also confirmed that Liv didn't appear to have any memory troubles when she first moved to London. She knows that Liv had a man in her life for a while, but she never met him and she doesn't know who he was. They're not particularly close, Liv and her aunt. Apparently, Liv grew up estranged from her father's family. Her parents' divorce was acrimonious."

"What is your role then? Are you a liaison between Liv and the hospital?"

"In a manner of speaking," Marcia said. "I taught Liv strategies so she could manage her day-to-day life somewhat normally, despite the memory loss."

"How does someone who can't retain memories live a normal life?" Halliday asked. "I understand that she may have gone to France, and there's a possibility that she's back in the US now? How would she travel like that without being able to remember anything?"

"Well, it's really about writing everything down. Keeping dynamic documents that become a surrogate for her missing memory."

"What does that involve exactly?"

"Simple things. I taught Liv to stick Post-it notes with reminders on her front door. I encouraged her to write the key things she needs to remember each day on her hands so that it's visible when she wakes up. Due to the insomnia, Liv sometimes nods off in the middle of the day in all sorts of places; trains, park benches. Each time she wakes with no memory, so the notes on her hands are often the first things she sees. They tell her what's going on," she said. "The most important tool is her journal."

Halliday turned off the engine.

"When I settled Liv back home at her flat in Clapham after she was discharged from the hospital, we put up a message in big letters on the wall opposite her bed telling her to read her journal. The message was supposed to be the first thing that she saw when she woke up. I wanted her to start her day reading her journal so she'd know about her condition and she wouldn't get anxious when she realized she didn't know where she was or how she'd gotten there. Her journal fills in all the missing pieces of her memory so she can function somewhat normally."

"What sorts of things does she write in her journal?"

"Everything. The journal is her surrogate memory," the social worker said. "She writes what happens each day so that when she wakes, she can read her journal posts and resume her life where she left off. The journal contains a detailed explanation about her condition. It has her address and her doctors' contact details, as well as other basic information that we all take for granted. Bank accounts. Her landlord's contact details. All sorts of mundane things that are crucial for a person to live a normal life."

"So it's fair to say the journal is her lifeline?" Halliday asked.

"Very much so," said the social worker. "I dread to think what would happen if Liv lost it."

Chapter Thirty-Two

The bill from the electricity company lying by the front door might have my name on it, but there's no way I actually live here, I think as I unlock the door with a loud rattle of the keys and step into a grim apartment.

The yellowing drapes covering the windows cast a mustard gloom. The apartment is furnished with a badly worn brown vinyl sofa and a cluttered coffee table. Rays of dust particles hang in the air.

This place couldn't be more different from my cute two-bedroom in Brooklyn. The view from my bedroom window is of my neighbor's brightly decorated flower box which overflows with vibrant blooms in spring and summer. It's most certainly not the ugly sight of Dumpsters in an alley that I can see through the grille windows set high up on the walls of this basement apartment with its claustrophobically low ceilings.

Dust chokes my lungs, already burning from the noxious smell of wet paint that fills the place. The delivery guy who escorted me here said I have problems with my memory and that I don't always remember this apartment is my home. He's wrong. Never in a million years would I live in such a dump.

I reach blindly for the front door handle to let myself out and come face-to-face with a black-and-white photograph stuck on the back of the front door.

What's Marco's photo doing here?

There are other photographs stuck on the door. There's a photo of Amy in a swimsuit, her sunglasses pushed to the top of her head. That photo was taken on the girls' trip to Cancun when Amy charmed the manager into upgrading us to a luxury seaside villa. There's a group photo taken at the staff Christmas party at *Cultura* when I first started working at the magazine. I've circled the face of the staff photographer, George, standing in the crowd. There's also a photo taken by the waiter of everyone raising a glass to celebrate Amy's birthday at Café Lisbon.

A sudden mechanical noise startles me. I swing around to see what's caused it. It's the motor of a clunky refrigerator. I head across the small living area to a narrow galley kitchen that's about three decades out of date.

A window lets in meager light from the rear alley. Underneath it, an overflowing bag of trash is slumped in the corner, swarmed by tiny flies. Some of the trash has spilled to the floor. Among it are blister packs of pills with names such as NoDoz and Alert. In the bag are piles of empty cans of caffeine drinks.

Colorful magnets in the shape of letters are arranged on the dented white fridge door. They're the type preschool kids use to practice spelling.

The magnets are arranged into colorful words and phrases. STAY AWAKE, it says across the freezer door. I look at the back of my hands. Under each of my knuckles is a letter spelling the same thing: S-T-A-Y A-W-A-K-E. Under one of the magnets is a doctor's appointment card with my name on it, along with an appointment date and time. I slip the card into my pocket.

Seeing another link between me and this hovel makes me light-headed. I open the fridge. Every shelf is stacked with caffeine drinks and individual bottles of store-bought coffee. Extra strong.

The sink is filled with a pile of black ash. It's the burnt remnants of paper. Among the ash are yellow bits of charred Post-it notes. There's also a badly burned book. The word "Journal" is embossed on the scorched remnants of a blue cover. The burned pages turn to ash when I touch them. Whatever was written in this book has been destroyed.

I rush away from the kitchen to the living room. It's filled with a headache-inducing odor of wet paint. I pull open the dusty curtains to get some light in here. The longest wall has been partly painted black with a roller brush. On the floor is an empty can of black paint. Alongside it are a roller brush and a paint tray stained black. It looks as if someone left in a hurry, perhaps to get more paint to finish the wall.

The white, as yet unpainted, part of the wall is graffitied with an array of random sentences. Most are written in pen. A couple are in marker. One appears to be written by a finger dipped in black coffee.

Memories lie.

Don't trust anyone.

He's coming for me.

The writing strikes a chord. I pick up a dusty pen lying on the floor and neatly copy the messages onto my arm. When I'm done, I move through a doorway into what must be a bedroom, although it looks more like a prison cell, perhaps because all the walls are covered with fresh coats of black paint.

A single barred window is set high up on the wall. A ray of light captures dust hanging in the air as if defying gravity. The only furniture in the bedroom is a bare camping mattress on the floor with a crumpled pillow and a half-open sleeping bag on top of it.

Across the room is a closet. I open the door to see what's inside. Empty wire hangers sit at odd angles on the metal rod, giving the impression that someone packed in a hurry. A couple of garments and a few socks are scattered on the floor.

Whoever painted the bedroom walls black also painted over several newspaper clippings stuck to the wall. A newspaper article in the far corner of the wall appears to have sections that weren't painted over, probably because the paint roller couldn't get into the corner. I peel the newspaper clipping off the wall and read the bits of text that aren't covered in paint.

"Police are hoping to question a comatose woman who they believe witnessed... Doctors are bringing the woman out of the medically-induced coma... Police hope she will be well enough to undergo questioning later this week.... Mystery continues to swirl around the brutal..." The rest of the article is painted over and indecipherable.

An old-fashioned telephone rings so loudly that I drop the clipping to the ground. The phone is ringing somewhere in the apartment. It makes my blood run cold.

Chapter Thirty-Three

Detective Darcy Halliday watched a live feed of CCTV footage on a screen behind the counter in the liquor store as the owner gave change to a customer buying a bottle of malt.

On the screen, she could see Detective Jack Lavelle walking out of a narrow lane behind the apartment building where the murder had taken place. He walked about eight yards down the lane to an intersecting street and stood in full view of the liquor store's security cameras, where he reached into his jacket pocket and answered his phone. It was Halliday on the line.

"It's a perfect angle," she said. "If the killer came out that way, then it's almost certain we'll get a visual. I have the USB stick with the CCTV footage from overnight. Let's watch it in the car."

Sitting in the Ford a few minutes later, Halliday plugged the memory stick into her iPad. They were silent as they watched the recorded footage.

Given that the CCTV cameras at the building's rear doors weren't working, the liquor store's footage might be their only chance of seeing the killer.

The time code–stamped footage was drained of color due to the low quality of the camera lenses and the poor light. They didn't need bells and whistles. All they needed was for the suspect to come out of the lane and look up so they could get a clear view of a face.

Halliday fast-forwarded the footage until she reached the section with a time stamp after two in the morning.

At seven minutes past two, they saw a movement in the lane.

"Here it is," Halliday said.

In the CCTV footage, someone was walking down the lane toward the liquor store. They both leaned forward in anticipation.

It was only when the suspect approached the curb that the detectives were able to see the suspect's face thanks to a nearby streetlight. Halliday froze the video.

"It's a woman," said Lavelle.

They stared at the hazy image. The woman's long hair was tied in a plait that was starting to unravel.

"Not just any woman. That's Liv Reese," Halliday said.

"I'm not so sure," said Lavelle dubiously. "The image is too murky. We can't see her face properly."

"Trust me. It's her," said Halliday, comparing the Interpol photo of Liv Reese to the woman in the CCTV footage. "I'll ask the social worker in London if she can give us an ID based on the footage. Otherwise we'll need to use facial recognition software."

Halliday messaged a screenshot of the woman's face to the social worker. **Marcia, do you recognize her?** she texted.

Halliday's phone rang seconds later. "You've found Liv!" Marcia called out. "I'm delighted. How is she?"

"We haven't found her," said Halliday. "She appears on some CCTV footage so we know she's here in New York City. We just don't know where. But we will find her."

Halliday tried to keep her tone light. She wasn't ready to tell the social worker that Liv Reese appeared to have fled the scene of a murder early that morning. That put her at the top of their list of suspects.

Not only did they have Liv Reese's prints at the scene, they now had visuals putting her in the apartment building at the time of the murder. That was more than enough to bring her in for questioning.

"Marcia, I know it's late there but I have a couple more questions," said Halliday, thinking ahead. They would need more to build a case against Liv Reese.

"Of course, anything I can do to help."

"You mentioned that you've encouraged Liv to write notes and messages as reminders. Has Liv ever written the words WAKE UP on her hands, or anywhere else?"

The social worker sighed. "I tried to get Liv to write practical messages on her hands, such as her address and emergency contact numbers. But when I last saw her several weeks ago, she'd written messages that came across as delusional. So in answer to your question, yes, I've seen handwriting on Liv's hands saying things like DON'T SLEEP, STAY AWAKE, and WAKE UP."

"Do you know why she chooses to write those particular messages?" Halliday asked.

"Liv tries her very best not to fall asleep. Perhaps deep down she knows that she'll forget everything once she sleeps. Dr. Stanhope, her psychiatrist, says her self-induced insomnia actually exacerbates her condition. She falls asleep all the time out of sheer exhaustion."

"It sounds like a terrible way to live," said Halliday.

"Lack of sleep does horrible things to a person's mind," said the social worker. "It can make some people psychotic."

Chapter Thirty-Four

The telephone rings and my nerves shatter. It traps me in an indecisive limbo. I'm desperate to leave this apartment, but the ring of the phone erodes my willpower. I'm powerless to resist its pull.

I find the phone plugged into a socket on the floor next to the sofa. It would be so easy to pull the plug from the wall and break the hypnotic hold the phone has over me, but I resist the urge. Instead I hover my hand over the receiver as it continues to ring.

DON'T ANSWER THE PHONE, says a Post-it note stuck to the phone.

It rings again. This time I snatch up the receiver and press it hard against my ear.

"Hello?"

Silence.

"Hello? Who's there?"

More silence, followed by a *click*. The line has been cut. It must have been a wrong number. I put the phone back on the console.

It rings again. I answer it immediately.

"Liv. I've been looking for you everywhere."

The man's voice is so muffled that I have to strain to hear properly.

"I knew you'd eventually return home, Liv."

"What do you want?" I ask, my voice tight with fear.

"I need to know where you left the knife." His muffled voice is drowned out by the roar of traffic.

"What knife?" I ask blankly. I have no idea what he's talking about.

"Don't tell me that you fell asleep again! Did you, Liv? Did you fall asleep?" he rasps.

I don't respond.

"Where did you wake up this time? Tell me, Liv."

"I woke up on the subway," I concede.

"You don't remember what happened last night, do you?"

"No."

"I thought so. You forget everything every time you fall asleep."

"How do you know all of this about me? Who are you?" I clutch the phone receiver tightly.

He ignores my question. "You try to stay awake all the time. You even write it on your hands as a reminder. It's taking a toll on you, Liv. The insomnia. It's taking a toll on your sanity."

I look at the back of my hands and read the letters across the knuckles. STAY AWAKE.

"How do you know about the writing on my hands?"

"Honey, I know more about you than you know about yourself," he rasps again. There's something about his muffled voice that's vaguely familiar, but I can't place it.

A car horn blasts. I hear it in stereo, over the phone line and through the apartment windows. The long aggressive blast goes on for seconds. A truck driver leans out of his window and shouts: "What the hell is wrong with you!"

A series of expletives follows. Once again, I hear it all unfold in stereo. It tells me what I intuitively know. The man on the phone is outside this building.

There's a pause as he talks to somebody. My heart skips a beat when I realize he must be talking to a doorman. I hear a door slam shut over the phone line, and then the tap of footsteps quickly going down stairs. He's in the building. He must be on his way down to this apartment.

I glance at the white unpainted section of living room wall. Pulsating on the wall is a scribble: HE'S COMING FOR ME.

It's too late to leave through the front door. I look around for another exit. The living room and bedroom windows are high off the ground. They're all barred. The only way out is through the kitchen window. It's lower and appears to have a hinged grille that can be opened in case of a fire.

"You've done something terrible, Liv."

I almost jump at the voice coming through the phone again. I struggle to hear as I run my hands over the kitchen window bars looking for a latch to open the grille.

"What have I done?" I force myself to hide my fear. I can't let him realize I know he's here.

"You haven't seen the news?" he asks.

"What's on the news?"

"The murder. Your fingerprints are all over the apartment. The police will eventually piece things together and determine that it was you."

"I didn't kill anyone," I say, climbing onto a stool to reach the latch, which is at the top of the window grille.

"How could you possibly know what you've done? You don't remember."

"I know I'm not a murderer. It's not in me to kill someone." I prod and pull at the window bar latch. It's unyielding. I break into a sweat as I wrestle to get it open.

"Everyone is capable of murder," he says. His footsteps thud as he walks down the stairs. "Given the right provocation."

"Not me."

"All the evidence points to you, Liv. Even the words WAKE UP! written on the window link back to you. The same slogan is written on your wrist."

A door bangs down the hallway. It's the stairwell door slamming behind him. He's on my floor. His footsteps echo as he walks down the corridor.

"The evidence ties you directly to the murder," he rasps.

"I didn't kill anyone," I insist.

"I know that. And you know that. But the evidence suggests otherwise. The police might think differently."

"What do you want from me?" My voice is barely above a whisper.

"I want to help you, Liv. All I need to know is where you put the knife. Is it in the apartment with you, Liv?"

I finally release the stubborn catch on the window bars. The security grille swings open.

"They'll find you, Liv. When they do, they'll put you away for the rest of your life. It's only a matter of time. I'm the only person who can help you clear your name."

"What do you mean it's only a matter of time?"

The window's stuck. I grit my teeth and use all my strength to lift it up.

"Every time you fall asleep, you forget everything. You'll forget this conversation, too, within hours. By the time the police track you down, you won't be able to say a single word in your own defense."

The footsteps pause in the corridor. There's a rattle of keys. He's outside the apartment. Using every ounce of strength, I push the window up enough to create a gap. It's too narrow for me to squeeze through. I try again, forcing up the window with my shoulder until there's enough space for me to crawl through.

A key enters the front door lock. The lock clicks.

He's here.

I wriggle through the narrow opening. My legs are still dangling in the kitchen when the apartment door swings wide open. I pull my legs through the gap and run out of the alley and into the street.

Chapter Thirty-Five

Two Years Earlier

Amy's hand hovers over the box of truffles as she decides which chocolate to take. She settles on a milk chocolate truffle with white chocolate drizzle.

"Don't eat it!" I call out as she's about to put the chocolate ball in her mouth.

"What?"

"Don't eat the chocolate."

"Why not?"

"It's spiked."

Amy looks dumbfounded. "What makes you think it's spiked?"

"I ate one earlier. I couldn't keep my eyes open afterward. It felt as if I'd been drugged."

"Liv, none of the chocolates have been eaten yet. Take a look."

Amy hands the gold foil box to me to inspect. "See! All the truffles are in the box. Nobody's eaten any of them."

Amy's right. The box is full. None of the chocolates are missing.

"I guess I must have dreamed it," I say, mortified.

"Liv, what has gotten into you lately?"

Amy sits next to me on the sofa and inspects the finger I hurt earlier when I opened the bouquet of roses.

"What do you mean?" I ask as she opens her first aid kit.

"You're paranoid about everything," she says, taking a sterile needle from the kit to remove what she says is a thorn in my finger.

"Like what?" I wince as she teases the thorn loose with the tip of the needle.

"Well, let's start off with the fact that you called the police because you thought someone had ransacked your bedroom when all I did was borrow a few clothes for my vacation," she says. "And then you wanted them to do a full-blown criminal investigation into how a carton of milk got into our fridge. Now this drama about the chocolates being spiked. Liv, I'm worried about you. Your paranoia is off the charts."

The way Amy puts it, I have to admit that my behavior does sound deranged. "It must be stress," I say, defensively. "Work has been intense lately."

I grit my teeth as Amy pokes the needle deeper into my skin and then takes out a set of tweezers from the first aid kit.

"You should take a few days off work, Liv. Go somewhere relaxing."

"I wish it was that easy."

"It is that easy. Tell that boss of yours, Frank, that you're taking a couple of personal days. You work long enough hours that he should cut you some slack."

"I need all my leave for my vacation with Marco in October."

"Vacation? Where are you going?" Amy hovers the tweezers over my fingers before pulling out the thorn.

"France. We're thinking about doing a cycling trip in the Loire Valley."

Amy doesn't respond as she cleans my finger again with antiseptic lotion and puts on a bandage.

"Your finger should be fine now," she says in a thin voice when she's done.

She gets up abruptly and takes her assortment of shopping bags to her bedroom. I rise from the sofa and follow the delicious aroma of food cooking in the kitchen. Looking through the oven glass, I see a delicious casserole bubbling in a ceramic dish on the oven rack.

"It smells amazing," I tell Amy, when she comes into the kitchen. "Where did you get the recipe?"

"Recipe? What are you talking about?"

"The casserole in the oven! And here I thought you couldn't boil an egg."

"Liv, you know I don't cook."

"Then who made the casserole?"

"You, of course," she says, looking at me weirdly again. "You're the only one of us who cooks."

I'm speechless. I'd know if I cooked dinner. Wouldn't I? Everything feels so out of place. That's when I realize that I haven't seen the cat since I woke up.

"Where's Shawna?"

"Probably prowling around the neighborhood," says Amy.

"She's usually back by this time."

I tap a can of cat food with a spoon by the kitchen window. The noise always brings her home. We both hear a faint sound in the hall closet. Amy opens the closet door and Shawna runs out, skittish and visibly distressed.

"How on earth did you get locked in the closet you silly thing?" Amy asks the cat as she picks her up.

Hanging in the closet is my dry cleaning. A receipt stapled to the front of the clear plastic garment bag indicates it was collected today. Payment was in cash.

"Did you pick up my dry cleaning? I'll transfer the money I owe to your account."

Amy doesn't hear me. She's deep in concentration, typing a text on her phone.

"What did you just say?" She looks up after she's sent the message.

"I thanked you for picking up my dry cleaning."

"What dry cleaning?" Amy looks at me strangely. "I didn't pick anything up today."

Her denial makes me wobble. I put my hand against the door frame to support myself. If I didn't collect the dry cleaning, and Amy didn't collect it, then who did? First, milk appearing in the fridge, and then a casserole in the oven. Now my dry cleaning miraculously turning up in the hall closet. Someone *was* here while I was sleeping. It's the only explanation. The question is who, and why.

"Are you all right, Liv? No offense, but you're acting really strange."

"I'm feeling a bit dizzy," I say, to explain my weird behavior.

Amy will think I've gone nuts if I tell her that I believe someone came into the apartment while I was asleep to heat up a casserole and bring in my dry cleaning. It's ridiculous. Even I think I'm crazy. Yet I can't think of any other explanation.

When I go into my bedroom, I find another bunch of flowers in a vase next to my bed. This bouquet is a combination of white and pale pink gardenias. They fill my bedroom with an intoxicating floral aroma.

My cell phone beeps with a message on my Snapchat app. I open it to see a photograph of the gardenias next to my bed along with a message.

> This is how a boyfriend is supposed to treat the woman he is dating, Liv.

Who is this? I write back.

By the time I press Send, the original message has disappeared, as if it never existed. I kick myself for not taking a screenshot of it.

I call the police. This time two detectives arrive half an hour later. The first is the surly detective I talked with a few days ago when I made the report about the milk carton. His partner, Detective Larry Regan, is around my age. He has rich chocolate-colored hair and matching velvet eyes.

"I remember you," says Krause, the surly detective. "Did someone leave you eggs this time? Or maybe a loaf of bread?" He laughs at his own joke. It makes me instantly regret calling the police, and reminds me why I've never trusted cops.

"A bouquet of flowers was left next to my bed. I didn't put it there and neither did my roommate." I tell them about all the other strange things that happened today.

"And you think what? That a stranger brought your dry cleaning to your apartment and cooked dinner for you?" Detective Krause scoffs. "I wouldn't mind a stalker like that. Do you think he irons shirts and starches collars, too? He'd be worth his weight in gold."

His shoulders shake with stifled laugher at his own joke. The younger detective doesn't laugh. If anything, he looks visibly discomforted by his partner's rudeness as he dutifully writes down the details that I've provided in his notebook. He tells me to come to the police station to sign the statement the next morning.

Amy shows the detectives out and stays on the stoop to make a call. I distinctly hear her say: "This has gotten out of hand."

A floorboard creaks when I step onto the landing to hear better. Amy must have heard it, too, because she leaves the building and continues her phone conversation down the street, where she stands with her back to me on the corner, talking intensely on the phone.

Repulsed by the thought that a stalker left me gifts while I slept, I grab the bouquets of flowers, the casserole dish, and the box of chocolate truffles and I throw the whole lot in a trash can by the street as the detectives drive away in their gray Ford. I go upstairs with a horrible feeling that my life is spinning out of my control.

Chapter Thirty-Six

Darcy Halliday could see that Jack Lavelle was getting increasingly frustrated as he paced the sidewalk alongside his parked car, where she sat in the front passenger seat.

So far everyone he'd spoken with at the credit card company had demanded a warrant in order to divulge the name of the credit card holder who'd booked the apartment where the murder had taken place. Lavelle could arrange a warrant, but it would take a while. In the meantime, his entire investigation was being held up by pedants, obsessed with dotting the i's and crossing the t's for the sake of it.

While Lavelle waited on hold for the fourth time, he bent down and spoke to Halliday through the open passenger window. "Call in a BOLO on the Reese woman while I deal with these idiots," he said. His jaw was tense. A BOLO was a "be on the lookout" alert that would be distributed across the NYPD.

"I think we should wait," said Halliday. "If it leaks to the media or Liv Reese gets wind of it, then she might run."

"It wasn't a request, Detective," he snapped.

"What happens if she didn't do it?" Halliday pushed. "A BOLO puts her in the sights of every trigger-happy cop in New York. And if the media gets hold of it, she'll be on the front page of every tabloid. Imagine waking with no memory and seeing your face on the front page of all the newspapers. It will freak her out," she said. "Who knows what she'll do?"

"It would make my job a hell of a lot easier if you would do as you're asked." Lavelle enunciated each word.

A senior manager came on the line and he stepped away from the car to explain the situation. Halliday dictated the BOLO over the phone to Detective Tran.

"Be on the lookout for a woman by the name of Liv Reese," Halliday said. "She is wanted in connection with a murder. She is described as approximately five foot six, around one hundred twenty to one hundred thirty pounds. She has long dark hair reaching almost to her waist. The suspect has a severe memory impairment that makes her erratic and disoriented. It is not known if she is armed. Officers should approach with caution."

To accompany the BOLO, Halliday messaged Tran a still photo of the security camera footage of Liv Reese in the alley behind the apartment building in the early hours of the morning, her long plait unraveling. She asked him to also include the photo from the Interpol missing person report.

"I shouldn't have lashed out at you. I was out of line," Lavelle apologized when he'd finished his call and climbed back into the driver's seat. "I bet those idiots had the information on the computer screens in front of them. They just wanted written requests to cover their collective asses. Stupid pencil pushers. The body was found nine hours ago and we still don't know the victim's name."

"The BOLO will be broadcast as soon as the captain signs off on it. The night shift will get hard copies at their briefing," Halliday replied, making no effort to hide her annoyance. She was used to taking orders in the military. That didn't mean she had to agree with them.

"Good," he said, turning on the car engine.

"I hope we don't regret it, Jack."

"We won't. If the Reese woman did it then we'll have our suspect. If she didn't, then she'll be safer with us than she is wandering the streets in a state of confusion. Especially if whoever tried to kill her two years ago finds out that she's returned."

"I don't know how safe she'll be with every cop in New York thinking she's a dangerous killer."

"Much as I hate to say that Krause was right, the odds are that she is a dangerous killer."

"Based on what?" asked Halliday, mostly to be contrary. It was true that Liv Reese was emerging as their prime suspect.

"Based on the laws of probability," Lavelle said. "The fact is that until we have an ID on the victim, this whole case rests on supposition. In fact, screw it. I'm going to call in the big guns. I'm cutting through this bullshit red tape. We're this close to knowing the victim's identity. I am not going to allow some credit card company to give us the runaround."

Halliday knew they couldn't begin to make a case against Liv Reese if they didn't have a pretty good idea of her motive to commit murder. Her potential motive and the victim's identity were indelibly connected. Knowing one of those unknowns would help them figure out the other. At the moment, they knew neither.

Lavelle called an old friend who worked financial crimes for the FBI on speakerphone as he drove through heavy traffic. He asked his buddy to use his contacts to get an ID on the credit card holder.

Minutes later, Lavelle's friend called back and relayed the credit card holder's details over the speakerphone.

"His name is Edward Cole. He's an executive at a magazine. Age thirty-nine."

"What magazine does he work at?" Jack asked, stopping at a red light.

"*Cultura*. Heard of it?"

"No," said Jack.

"I have," Halliday chimed in. "It's a high-end glossy magazine that claims to be the last word on music, arts, theater, style. Basically, anything cultural. Hence the name."

"That must be why Jack and I haven't heard of it. Our idea of culture is watching the Knicks. Isn't it, Jack?"

"Something like that," said Lavelle. "Hey, thanks, buddy. I definitely owe you one."

"Let's find out more about Edward Cole," Halliday said, dialing Tran.

"It's me again," she said when the detective answered. "Can you run a name through the DMV. We want a driver's license for a thirty-nine-year-old male by the name of Edward Cole. That's C-O-L-E. We need the name and contact details for him and his next of kin."

"Stay on the line and I'll take a look now," said Tran.

A moment later, he said, "Edward Cole received a driver's license... four months ago."

"That's weird. Who gets a driver's license at the grand old age of thirty-nine?" Halliday pondered out loud.

"Gimme a minute and I'll find out," said Tran, pausing as he ran another search. "Cole is not a US citizen. He's only been in the country for five months."

"Let me guess where he's from," Halliday said. "Britain."

"How did you know?"

"Shot in the dark," said Halliday, glancing at Lavelle.

"There's no next of kin listed in the database," said Tran. "There is an address for him. It's a few blocks from the murder scene."

"Why would Cole rent a second apartment near the apartment where he lives?" Halliday asked Lavelle after the call.

"Maybe his relationship broke up. He needed somewhere to stay for a few nights," Lavelle suggested.

"Sounds as if you're speaking from experience," Halliday said.

"Oh, yeah. Bitter experience."

Lavelle had done the same thing when his relationship with his girlfriend broke up a few months earlier. He'd rented an Airbnb for a few days and then extended it for a few days longer. Two weeks later, the penny finally dropped. He and Ingrid weren't getting back together.

"That doesn't explain why Cole booked the apartment using a fake name and a fake address," Halliday pointed out.

"Maybe he didn't want someone to find out he was staying there. Like a wife, or a girlfriend."

"You think he was having an affair with Liv Reese?"

"That would certainly explain all that sneaking around," Lavelle said. He did a quick U-turn and drove in the direction of Edward Cole's apartment.

Chapter Thirty-Seven

Outside a subway entrance, a man with a scraggly beard and a knitted orange beanie strums a guitar as he sings a 1970s pop song about a Californian hotel where you can check out but never leave. His twangy voice competes with the deafening clatter of construction across the street.

I throw money onto the torn red lining of his guitar case. I'm across town now, having jumped into a passing cab after I ran from the basement apartment. My heart is still racing after my terrifying escape.

I won't report it to the police. They'll treat me with derision, just like that awful Detective Krause did when he mocked me for making a complaint about the break-ins at Amy's and my apartment. As if to emphasize the point, just above my wrist is a handwritten message that says DON'T TALK TO THE COPS EVER!!

It's wise advice. The last thing I need right now is to explain a situation to the police that I don't understand myself. How does one explain the inexplicable? One moment I was answering the phone at my desk in the office, the next I woke on a train howling through the subway. Those two moments are like bookends. Everything in between is missing.

It's not just my memory that's gone. My phone and wallet are also missing. I don't recognize the clothes that I'm wearing, or the pretty beaded necklace around my neck. Or the writing on the back of my hands, so much writing saying so many strange things. It terrifies me to read it all. Mom would hate that I still scribble on my hands. She always said it was so unladylike.

A huge yellow sales sign in the window of an electronics store catches my attention. I go inside and beeline to a row of display computers arranged on a long white counter.

I choose a laptop in the middle of the row and immediately open a web browser to run a search. I want to see if there are reports about a murder last night. The man who called me at that apartment said it was in the news.

It turns out there was a murder. I click on the first article I see, which is accompanied by a photograph of an apartment window. The words WAKE UP! are written in red on the window.

There's not much information in the article. It says that an as-yet unidentified man was found dead in a midtown apartment and police are investigating. The article says the killer is believed to have used the victim's blood to write that message on the window. It's a chilling thought.

Lower down is another photograph. The caption says it was taken from a security camera near the murder scene. It's a grainy photo of a woman with long dark hair exiting an elevator with a man. The woman's face isn't visible because she's looking down at the floor. The face of the man accompanying her is obscured by a black square, obviously intended to block out his features. I assume he's the murder victim.

Through the corner of my eye, I notice a salesman heading toward me. I click the mouse to close the browser and it disappears just as he reaches me.

"Can I help you?" he asks.

"I'm looking for a lightweight laptop that's reliable and very fast," I tell him because I can hardly admit that I only came into the store for the free computer access.

He takes my query as an invitation to go into an excruciatingly long sales pitch that involves demonstrating all sorts of features on the laptop. I wish he'd leave. There are so many more important things that I want to find out about, such as this murder, and how the world went from midsummer to late fall without me noticing.

I mutter my thanks to the salesman and quickly leave the store. I'm more confused than ever from the scraps of information I've gleaned from my web search. All I have are more questions.

I stop to look at a pile of newspapers at a newsstand farther up the street. The date on the masthead says it's November, not July. The year is two years into the future. That makes no sense. But then neither do the headlines. They describe a chaotic, pestilent world I barely recognize.

The date on the masthead prompts me to take out the medical appointment card that I found on the fridge at the basement apartment. My appointment was today, almost three hours ago. I'll go anyway. Maybe the doctor will know what's happened to me.

As I make my way to the subway, I notice a public phone by an escalator. I pull loose coins out of my pocket and shove a couple of them into the coin slot.

Marco's phone rings and rings and then goes to voicemail. He's obviously rejected my call. He must be in a meeting. I hang up without leaving a message.

I dial Amy's number next. Her phone rings repeatedly until an automated message says the number is invalid. In a panic, I call her mom, whose number is the same as Amy's with a one-digit difference. Amy once told me with some embarrassment that her entire family has cell phones with consecutive numbers under a family plan.

Amy's mom answers on the second ring. "Hello?"

"Is this Margaret Decker?"

"Yes, this is Margaret," Amy's mom sings down the line.

"This is Liv Reese." I wait for an indication of recognition. There is none. Just a deafening silence that makes me squirm. "I'm Amy's roommate."

"I know who you are. What do you want?" Her voice is icy.

"I'm trying to get ahold of Amy. Her phone isn't working."

"Are you serious?" Her voice lashes me into silence.

"I really need to talk to Amy." I pause, confused by her belligerence. "It's kind of an emergency."

"You have some nerve."

Her tone stings like a slap across the face. "I'm sorry if I've called at a bad time, Mrs. Decker. It's just that I need to speak to Amy urgently."

"You, of all people, should know why you can't get ahold of Amy," she says.

My throat is paralyzed. I don't know what to say so I say nothing as she goes into a furious rant. Her voice comes and goes in between angry crackles of electricity inside my head.

"How could you! You are sick. Sick!! Calling me like this. Don't you have any decency, any…" She hangs up.

I shudder at the silence on the dead phone line. I walk numbly against a tide of pedestrians streaming toward the subway entrance. I'm surrounded by people jostling me, but I've never felt more alone in my life.

Chapter Thirty-Eight

The front door of the apartment opened as far as the latch chain would allow. Halliday flashed her detective's badge toward a woman peering through the gap.

"What is it that you want?" the woman asked, making no attempt to unlatch the door.

"It would be easier if we came inside to talk," Halliday responded, noncommittally.

The woman released the latch chain and swung the door open to let them in. She wore jeans and a cream cashmere sweater. Her honey-colored hair was arranged in a loose chignon. She told them her name was Elisabeth.

Halliday and Lavelle glanced at each other to silently decide who'd do the talking. Halliday nodded slightly. She'd do it.

"We're actually here about Edward Cole. What is your relationship to him?" Halliday asked when they were all seated.

"Nobody calls him Edward. We all call him Ted," said Elisabeth. "Ted is my fiancé. Why are you asking about Ted?"

"Edward Cole—Ted," Halliday corrected herself, "rented a short-stay apartment for a week. We found the body of a man in that apartment early this morning. We believe that man might be Ted."

"You're wrong." Elisabeth was emphatic. "Ted was here last night. You've made a mistake."

"Very possibly," said Halliday. "But we need to know for sure. I'd like to show you a photo, if you don't mind."

"Go ahead," said Elisabeth, steeling herself as Halliday turned on her iPad and found a crime scene photo that clearly showed the victim's face.

Halliday turned the screen around. Elisabeth inhaled sharply. Her complexion turned to ash. She put her hand over her mouth as sobs racked her body.

Ten minutes later, Elisabeth sat with a blanket over her shoulders, her body trembling as she cupped a mug of sweetened coffee that Lavelle had made for her. Despite her grief, she insisted on answering their questions.

"I met Ted at a dinner party. There was an instant chemistry. Within a couple of months, Ted and I had moved in together and he'd proposed to me."

"Sounds like a whirlwind romance," said Halliday.

"We didn't want to waste time dating when we both knew we wanted to be with each other for the rest of our lives. We were going to start a family straight after the wedding. Ted would have been an amazing dad." Elisabeth put her fist against her mouth to gain control of her emotions.

"Do you know why Ted rented the apartment nearby?"

Elisabeth nodded. "He was helping a friend who was in trouble."

"Which friend?" Halliday asked.

"It was more than a friend," Elisabeth admitted. "It was his ex."

"So he rented the apartment to help his ex-girlfriend?"

Elisabeth nodded. "Ted came here last night and told me everything. He said he didn't want to keep secrets from me."

"Do you know his ex's name?"

"Her name's Liv. Liv Reese."

Halliday and Lavelle kept their expressions blank. The dots were connecting.

"Are you aware that he rented the apartment using a fake name?"

"Yes," she said. "He didn't want anyone to know that she was hiding there."

"Did Ted give a reason for the secrecy?"

"He was worried she might be in danger."

"What danger?"

"She was almost murdered a few years ago. Ted was worried the killer was after her again. He wanted to protect her. Ted felt responsible for her."

"Did he ever tell you why he broke off their relationship?"

"Ted said their relationship had been rocky for a long time," Elisabeth said. "She suffered from severe insomnia. She wouldn't sleep for days. She was constantly popping pills to stay awake. Her condition was getting worse, not better, and she refused to get help. But what bothered Ted most was that she wouldn't let go."

"Let go of what?"

"Of her past," said Elisabeth. "Ted told me once that she was haunted by her inability to remember what happened the day she was almost murdered. It consumed her. It dominated her life, to the exclusion of everything else. All she ever talked about was finding out who did it and getting justice."

"Is that the reason why Ted moved to New York?"

"He took the job because it was a promotion, but mostly because he couldn't take it anymore," Elisabeth said. "He said he couldn't build a future with a woman who was trapped in the past. Deep down he must have known she wouldn't come with him to New York. She suffered night terrors that the killer would find her again. The thought of returning back here, to the place where it happened, terrified her. To cut a long story short, their relationship died a natural death once he moved here. And now Ted is dead. Because of her. It had to be because of her." Elisabeth broke down.

"Have you ever met Liv Reese?" Halliday asked, once Elisabeth was able to talk again.

"I met her for the first time two weeks ago when she turned up at our engagement party at my parents' house in Scarsdale,"

Elisabeth said, wiping her eyes. "She was dressed inappropriately for the occasion, in a white scrunched dress and bare feet. She'd walked across the waterlogged lawn. Her feet were splattered with mud and loose grass. Her hair was very long," she said. "Ted was shocked when he saw her. He took her aside to talk privately in the garden."

"Do you know what they discussed?"

"He asked her to leave."

"How did she take it?"

"She claimed to have no idea who he was. She told him she'd come to the party because she'd found the invitation that morning stuck to the front door of the place where she was staying with a Post-it note telling her she had to come. Her behavior was so bizarre that we honestly thought she was drunk, or on drugs. My mom called for a town car to take her home. Ted contacted the driver afterward to get her address. He wanted to see her."

"Do you know why?"

"He told me last night that he wanted to make sure she was okay. When he arrived at her apartment, she had no idea who he was. Ted realized she was suffering from amnesia."

"Did Ted mention whether Liv had suffered from memory problems when they were dating in London?"

"That's why Ted was so worried about her. She'd never had memory problems when she lived in London. Other than not remembering the stabbing incident, which Ted said was probably due to her being in a coma afterward."

"Do you have any idea how she found out about the engagement party?" Halliday asked.

"I sent her an invitation," Elisabeth said, color returning to her cheeks as she flushed with shame. "She brought the invitation with her that day."

"I don't get it," said Lavelle, who'd been standing by the window and letting Halliday ask most of the questions. "Why invite your fiancé's ex to your engagement party?"

"I didn't expect her to actually turn up. She was living in London," Elisabeth said defensively.

She paused for a moment as if unsure how much to divulge, then took a deep breath and explained in a rush of words, "Liv would call Ted constantly from London. Several times a week. I hoped the invitation would drive home the fact that Ted wasn't hers anymore."

"What did she say in these phone calls?" Halliday asked. "Did she ever threaten Ted?"

"Sometimes she'd call and tell Ted that she couldn't sleep and that she missed him. Other times, she'd cry and ask him to give her another chance. It tore him up. She'd been through a terrible ordeal. She was emotionally fragile. Ted felt guilty," Elisabeth said. "That's why we were so relieved when the calls stopped. We assumed she'd finally come to terms with the breakup."

"Then why did you send her the invitation to your engagement party?" Lavelle asked.

"Actually, I'd already mailed her the invitation a week before the calls stopped," Elisabeth said, her cheeks flushing again. "I sent it because I wanted her to know that our marriage was real. I wanted her to realize it was time for her to let go of Ted. When she suddenly stopped calling, I thought it had worked. That the invitation had given her closure. I was as surprised as Ted when she turned up at the party."

Halliday jotted down a quick timeline in her notebook. Liv's calls to Ted had stopped abruptly five weeks ago, around the time she'd received the invitation to his engagement party. That coincided with the time of Liv's first known memory blackout, according to the social worker. Halliday wondered if Liv Reese stopped calling Ted because she had a memory blackout. Perhaps she simply didn't remember him anymore.

It was possible that the invitation had been the catalyst that sparked Liv Reese's amnesia. Maybe the shock of learning that she'd lost Ted for good caused her psyche to block out everything that had transpired in the last two years, all the trauma and all the heartbreak. Without her recent memories, it was as if her life was back to how it had been before she'd met Ted and before she'd been stabbed. It was the ultimate form of denial.

"Was she violent when she came to the engagement party? Did she make any threats?" Lavelle asked.

"No," said Elisabeth. "Her presence alone was ruining our party. I should never have sent her the invitation. Ted was furious when he found out."

Her shoulders shook again with sobs. Halliday and Lavelle exchanged glances. It was entirely possible that Ted Cole might still be alive if his fiancée hadn't sent the invitation to his ex.

"Ted felt obliged to help her." Elisabeth kept talking through her tears. "He told me last night that he'd found a doctor who was a world expert at treating memory problems. Normally there's a long wait to see him, but Ted pulled strings to get her seen quickly."

"Do you know the doctor's name?" Halliday asked.

"Ted didn't say. Do you think Ted's ex is responsible? Did Liv Reese kill Ted?" Elisabeth looked up at them, waiting for their answer.

"Our investigation has just begun," Halliday responded. "Did Ted do or say anything when he came here last night that you think might help us figure out what happened?"

"Not really," Elisabeth said, after a moment's thought. "Except for maybe one thing." She stood up and went to her bedroom, returning a moment later with a piece of paper. It contained a photocopy of a sketch made from small dots that formed the shape of a lily. At the top was a phone number.

"What is that?" Halliday asked.

"A drawing of some sort," said Elisabeth. "Ted received a call while he was here. It was Lou, a menswear designer we both know. I gathered that Ted had asked him about this design and he was calling Ted back with information."

"Did you hear their conversation?"

"Only the start. Ted took the phone into our bedroom where he continued the call. It struck me as strange because he'd come here to tell me the truth about his ex and then he gets a call and he's being secretive again. He left in a rush straight after the call. He must have accidentally dropped the paper with the sketch. I found it this morning on the carpet next to the bed."

Halliday and Lavelle left the apartment carrying an evidence bag with the sketch, as well as evidence bags containing Ted Cole's toothbrush, hairbrush, and wristwatch. The lab would, hopefully, match the DNA and any fingerprints on his personal belongings to the body they'd found in the apartment.

Halliday drove through heavy afternoon traffic toward the forensics lab to hand in the evidence bags as Lavelle updated the captain on the phone. Even as she listened to his side of the conversation, she couldn't stop thinking of Elisabeth, Ted Cole's heartbroken fiancée.

"Worst part of the job, telling people they've lost a loved one," remarked Halliday when Lavelle was off the phone. "Worse even than the mountain of paperwork they bury us in."

"Tell me about it," said Lavelle. "I've done more of these than I care to count."

She double-parked and waited at the wheel, while Lavelle took the evidence bags up to forensics. Halliday called the phone number that had been scrawled on the sketch, which she'd photographed on her phone before Lavelle had taken it up to the lab. Her call went straight to voicemail. She hung up without leaving a message.

Since Lavelle was taking longer than he'd anticipated, Halliday turned on the radio to distract herself with music. She'd been in plenty of tense situations. She'd driven in military convoys along roads mined with bombs disguised as rocks. She'd been shot at more times than she remembered. Since she'd joined the NYPD, she'd been involved in drug busts and undercover operations. Halliday could deal with danger. It was grief that tore her apart.

The click of the driver's door opening interrupted her thoughts. Lavelle explained as he put on his safety belt that the lab technician had taken prints off Cole's toothbrush while he'd waited. She'd then done a quick comparison with prints taken from the victim at the crime scene.

"It's not an official ID, but it's just as good for our purposes. Ted Cole is definitely the victim," he said. "Oh, and there's another update. They found traces of sedatives in the wine bottle, just as you'd suspected. The wine was spiked. That's why Cole didn't fight back when he was stabbed. He was fast asleep."

"At least that's a small mercy for him," she said quietly.

As Halliday turned on the engine, Lavelle's phone rang. He took it on speaker. It was a detective at the Ninetieth Precinct in Brooklyn, Detective Krause's old precinct. His name was Larry Regan.

"We have the files you wanted," Regan said.

"Any chance you could have them scanned and sent over?" Lavelle asked.

"They're huge files," said Regan. "There's way too much to scan. I could send you the originals, but it might only get to you in the morning. Or you could send someone to collect them."

"We'll drive over and take a look in person," said Lavelle.

He and Halliday were eager to find out exactly what had happened to Liv Reese two years earlier. Krause had made it pretty clear he thought she was the perpetrator, not the victim. He'd been scant with details and deliberately cagey. Knowing Krause the way he did, Lavelle guessed that he resented other cops looking into his old case.

"What's the connection between the two cases?" Regan asked.

"We don't know," said Lavelle. "All we know is that Liv Reese's fingerprints have turned up at the scene of another homicide."

"Who was the victim?" Regan asked.

"Her ex-boyfriend," said Lavelle.

Regan was silent as he absorbed that information. "In that case it sounds as if we'll have plenty to discuss when you get here."

Chapter Thirty-Nine

Amy's lying on her back in a bikini on the rooftop of our building when I come up and arrange my beach towel alongside hers. Her oversized sunglasses reflect the pristine blue sky and a snippet of street art graffiti on the rustic brick wall behind us.

I hike up my mint-green sundress with spaghetti straps to avoid tan lines before relaxing on my towel. It's a rare treat for us to be here alone. Usually the rooftop is crowded on weekends. Judging by the pile of crushed beer cans and empty tequila bottles in the trash, I'm guessing everyone else is sleeping off hangovers.

I sit with my back against the brick wall and read my novel. Two chapters into my book, I glance up when the rooftop door creaks open. Someone watches us from the shadows of the stairwell before turning away. Footsteps clatter down the metal stairs and the door slams shut.

It's probably nothing, just another resident checking to see if the deck area is available. Still, it creeps me out. I've been getting that feeling a lot lately. Too many weird things have been happening. Each time, my anxiety builds to a boiling point. I'm constantly looking over my shoulder.

Amy thinks I'm being paranoid, but it's not just me. Shawna's skittish, which is totally out-of-character. She was a pretty chill cat, until recently.

This morning, I received a Snapchat message as I pushed my shopping cart along the canned food aisle at our local super-market.

Mint really is your color, the message said, referencing the color of my sundress.

Looking up from the phone, I scrutinized the shoppers in the aisle around me. They were too busy taking products off the shelves or pushing their carts to show the slightest interest in me. Within seconds, the message disappeared and I was left wondering if I'd imagined it.

This time I took a screenshot of the text before it disappeared. It's exactly the sort of evidence of harassment the cops told me to bring them so they can investigate further, although I still haven't decided whether to show it to the police.

What's that expression: "Once bitten, twice shy"? I haven't contacted the cops since I fell asleep on the sofa and woke to find signs that someone had been in the apartment. My face burns as I remember Detective Krause joking about whether my stalker will leave a loaf of bread in the fridge next time instead of milk. I'm not inclined to risk being mocked again by showing the cops a screenshot of another ambiguous message. They'll only explain it away, like the last time.

Thinking about the text message I received at the supermarket makes me look nervously around the empty rooftop. I feel like I'm being watched again, which is silly because it's just me here, and Amy. She looks dead to the world as she lies tanning in her coral bikini with her sunglasses covering her eyes.

I assume Amy's asleep until she reaches for her phone, which is ringing on silent mode. She rejects the call without even looking at it.

"Who is it?"

"Brett," she mutters. It's the first sound out of her in an hour.

"You don't want to speak to him?"

"I'm not talking to Brett right now."

I've shared an apartment with Amy for years. Usually I'm blasé about the ups and downs of her roller-coaster relationships. But Brett has lasted longer than any of Amy's other boyfriends. He wines and dines her. He showers her with exorbitant gifts, and takes her on luxury weekend breaks. He indulges her every whim and Amy laps it up. For the first time, I've wondered whether she might settle down.

"Why aren't you talking to Brett?" I ask, unable to hide my surprise.

"It's a long story. Let's just say that our relationship is getting close to its 'use by date.' It's been heading in this direction for a while. I haven't told Brett that it's over, so don't say anything." She changes the subject. "How's everything with you and Marco?"

"Pretty good," I say, still shocked Amy's thinking of dumping Brett. "I'm crazy about Marco. You know that! The thing is…" My voice drops off.

"What?"

"I'm not sure that he's as into me. Sometimes I think that he slots me into his life when it's convenient for him. Other times, I feel frozen out. And…"

"And? What?" Amy turns to her side, reclining on her elbow. She pushes her sunglasses onto the top of her head and stares at me, waiting for me to elaborate.

"He wanted me to get free publicity for his investor's wife, who's a handbag designer. The style team refused to do a write-up, and I don't blame them. Emily is not a great designer. She's not even a good designer. Marco was upset when I told him. He really wanted to keep Dean, his investor, happy. At first I felt guilty about it, but now I'm sort of annoyed."

"Why?"

"I'm annoyed that Marco expected me to help him in the first place. It makes me feel… used," I tell her. "I'm seeing him this afternoon. Do you think I should say something?"

Amy slides her sunglasses off her head back onto her face, hiding the expression in her eyes. "Liv, I wasn't going to say anything, but here goes. You're wasting your time on Marco. That relationship will never go anywhere. Break up with him. Go meet someone new."

"Aren't you a little biased because you two don't like each other?"

"I'm only biased against him because I think he's wrong for you. You need someone stable and reliable after your messed-up gypsy childhood. All your mother's marriages, going from having money to being dirt poor every time she had a breakup, being taken by child services when she went on drinking binges. Not to mention all the other crap that you've told me about. All that takes a toll."

"What toll?"

"Well," says Amy, choosing her words carefully. "For one thing, I don't think you're good at telling the good apples from the bad ones."

"You think Marco is bad?"

"He's an asshole. Don't get me wrong. That's okay. As long as a girl knows what she's getting into. You don't," she says pointedly. "Look, everything with Marco is a means to an end. He's a wheeler and dealer. That's literally his profession; a salesman." She pauses, seeing my hurt expression. "Liv, you deserve someone who loves you for who you are, not for what you can do for him."

"Does such a person even exist, Amy? Because if he does, then I sure haven't come across this paragon of virtue yet."

"You will," she says. "But not if you keep wasting your time on the Marcos of this world."

"I know you only want what's best for me, Amy. But I'm in love with Marco, flaws and all. He's awesome in so many ways. I'm not going to break up with him in the hope that I'll meet someone better."

"Then there's nothing more to say," she says, before turning around and lying on her stomach. She unclips her bikini top to prevent tan lines and falls asleep.

After a while longer, I'm getting thirsty from lying in the sun. I collect my things and go down to the apartment to get ready for my cycling trip with Marco. I don't wake Amy. She'll come down when she's ready. I'm halfway down the stairs when I realize I left my straw sun hat on the roof.

I go all the way back up the metal stairs and push open the rooftop door. I'm immediately hit by a sweltering blast of heat. Amy's standing by a rooftop wall, looking at the view of the East River, her back to me as she talks on the phone. She doesn't notice me retrieving my hat from under the ledge where I was lying earlier.

"You have to tell her."

Amy pauses midsentence as she realizes she's not alone. She turns around and sees me standing on the roof, holding my hat awkwardly to my stomach.

"I forgot my sun hat," I say meekly.

My cell phone rings with a blocked number as I open the front door of our apartment.

"Who is this?" I ask.

"Your partner in crime."

"Tell me who you are or I'm going to end this call. Now." I'm rude for a reason. I assume the voice on the phone is the stalker that the police don't believe exists.

"I'm Q. You were at the special advance showing of my exhibition. You asked me to contact you for an interview," he says, amused by my hostile tone.

It's the artist whose disturbing exhibition I went to last week. He's caught me unprepared. I grapple around for a pen and a notebook in a kitchen drawer. I was expecting a sit-down interview at a prearranged time. Instead he's called me unexpectedly and caught me off balance. I wonder if it was deliberate.

"Did you enjoy the performance?" he asks.

"It was certainly unique," I respond, thinking back to the bizarre exhibit in the warehouse. "Does it have a title?" I'm standing by the kitchen sink looking into the street as I talk.

"Mirror Four," he says. "That's the title of the show."

The name throws me. I don't recall seeing a mirror at the exhibition. All I saw was a gagged woman with a burlap sack over her head, bound to a chair. I remember that her clothes were almost shredded. It was more a macabre horror show than anything to do with mirrors.

"What's the significance of the name?"

"The exhibition is what I call a four-dimensional mirror," he says quietly. "It signifies a metaphorical mirror that shows my audience for what they really are."

"Which is?"

"Good. Evil. Banal. Maybe all three."

"Usually in performance art, the artist is part of the experience. What's your role in the exhibit?"

"I'm a voyeur," he answers. "I arrange the experience and then I step back and watch. What happens next is in the hands of the audience. They can do whatever they like. Free the woman with the scissors. Cut her with the knife. Or walk away as you did, Liv."

"I didn't walk away. I observed and then I left," I say defensively.

"There's no such thing as being an observer. Doing nothing is doing something. Being passive has consequences."

I roll my eyes, grateful we're only talking on the phone and he can't see me. As far as I'm concerned, Q's experimental sensory experience is nothing more than heavy-handed social commentary. It's fatuous, and it leaves me cold. Of course, I'm too polite to tell him that. Instead I ask him to tell me about his inspiration for the work.

"The Bible."

"In what way?"

"What's the greatest gift God gave humankind?"

I run through my lax religious education. "The Ten Commandments?"

Through the kitchen window, I see a white minivan stopping outside. Its engine idles noisily as the driver gets out and disappears into the entrance of the building across the street.

"Free will, Liv," he chastises. "Genesis Two. God told Adam not to eat the apple. Adam had a choice. He could obey God's order not to eat the apple, or he could exercise free will and eat it anyway. He chose the second option."

I check the time. I really need to get ready or I'll be late to meet Marco for our cycling trip this afternoon.

"How does the story of Adam relate to your exhibit?" I ask somewhat impatiently as I walk to my bedroom and take out a T-shirt and Lycra shorts.

"You had choices, Liv. You had free will. You could have rescued the woman in my exhibit. Instead you walked away. Why?"

"There were signs on the exhibit that said 'Do Not Touch.' I didn't want to interfere or break any rules."

"So you left? Because of a stupid rule?" he asks.

"Yes."

"Bystanders can be just as culpable as perpetrators."

"Perhaps in real life," I say. "In this case, it was an art exhibition. It wasn't real."

"The ropes. The duct tape. The gag. All were real." He sounds offended. "The woman. She was a real woman bound to a real chair. With real blood in her veins. The hammer was real. So was the rope. You could have smashed the glass box with the hammer and taken out the scissors to cut her bonds and free her. Instead you abandoned her there and left."

He's right. I should have cut the woman free. His accusation chills me. I want to tell him that his exhibition frightened me with its realism.

"I thought that was part of the performance. I didn't know I had a role to play."

"Everyone has roles to play. Sometimes we don't know it until it's too late. You were given a choice, Liv. Every choice has a consequence."

I walk to my bedroom and glance out the window. The minivan driver comes out of the building across the street carrying a large box. He slides open the van door and puts the box on a rear seat before slamming the door shut and going around to the driver's seat.

The van's engine pops and whines as it drives off. It sounds as if the same noise is coming over the phone line. As if Q is on my street. I look out the window, expecting to see a man on the street below. There's nobody's around except for a young couple walking a French bulldog on a leash.

When the call with Q is over, a text message comes up on my screen. It's from Marco.

> Something's come up. I can't go cycling today. I'll be in touch.

It's the sort of brusque message someone might send a business acquaintance, not a girlfriend.

I remember what Amy told me about Marco being a bad apple, and I wonder if she's right.

Chapter Forty

Wednesday 4:36 P.M.

"Your appointment was for this morning," says the doctor's receptionist when I give her my name. Before I can apologize for being late, she adds: "Nevertheless, Dr. Brenner left instructions to squeeze you in no matter when you turned up. He'll see you as soon as he's finished with his current patient."

She tells me to take a seat in the clinic waiting area, where several aqua chairs are pushed in a tight row by a frosted-glass wall. I take a corner seat opposite a wall clock. The slow movement of time lulls me into a semitrance. It's broken when the receptionist's phone rings with a loud and sudden peal.

"You can go in," she tells me.

Dr. Brenner's eyes are magnified by the lenses of his silver-framed glasses. He asks me how I'm feeling. I shift uneasily on the upholstered chair next to his desk and answer that I'm fine. That's a lie, but it doesn't matter, because I look fine on the outside. And that's what counts.

Isn't it?

"Ted couldn't make it today?" he asks. "I'd really hoped he'd join you so we could discuss your treatment plan." He stares at me without blinking as he patiently waits for me to answer.

"Something came up at work. He sends his apologies," I lie.

I'm too embarrassed to admit I don't know anyone named Ted. I only came here because I found the appointment card at that awful basement apartment. I figured that if I went to the appointment with this neurologist then he'd be able to tell me why everything has felt like a fractured dream since I woke on the subway.

Dr. Brenner is talking again. I stare at his mouth, trying to focus.

"Do you have your journal or any of the notes you showed me last time?" he asks.

"I didn't bring anything with me," I fib, once again not knowing what he's talking about.

He's about to say something else, but obviously thinks better of it because he clears his throat awkwardly and picks up a pen from the ink blotter on his desk.

"Let's begin. I'd like you to remember the following three things," he says. "Red flower, blue car, and a tennis ball. Can you remember that?"

"Of course," I respond. My eyes focus on the glint of the doctor's wedding ring as I memorize those words.

Dr. Brenner has my patient file open on his computer. I shift in my chair to get a better look, but I'm still too far away to see anything other than a blur of words on the screen.

"I have the results of the MRI," he says.

He twists his laptop in my direction so that I can see the image of my brain filling the screen. "There's no indication of any organic brain damage. Certainly nothing that comes up in the scan. That's good news. Great news, in fact," he emphasizes.

Dr. Brenner leads me to an examination table. I sit with my legs hanging over the edge as he examines me, running through a battery of tests to check my motor skills and reflexes as well as my muscular strength. When he's done, he shines a penlight into one eye at a time and asks me to follow the light.

"What's today's date?" he asks, turning off the silver penlight with a click.

I tell him the date. I remember it from the newspaper I saw earlier at the newsstand. He asks me to name the five most recent presidents. I do better and go all the way back to Nixon.

"Can you tell me what were those four things I asked you to remember early on?" he asks when I'm back on the chair next to his desk.

"There were three things. Red flower, blue car, and a tennis ball."

"Very good." He turns his swivel chair to face his desk and types something, then turns back to me. "Are you still taking caffeine tablets and anti-narcolepsy drugs to stop yourself from falling asleep?"

I squirm under his steady gaze as I remember the piles of NoDoz tablets I saw in the trash at the basement apartment where I've apparently been living.

"Not anymore."

"Excellent. I'm pleased you followed my advice." He nods encouragingly.

I press my hands to my side so he won't notice the messages on my skin telling me not to sleep. Although I suspect he already saw them.

"Do you remember the reason why you came to see me?"

"Yes," I answer confidently, even though I don't have the slightest idea. He is silent as he waits for me to elaborate. The faint tug of a headache gives me an idea. "I came to see you because of my migraines." My voice rises hopefully.

"Just your migraines?"

"Sure." I try to inject conviction into my voice. It comes out as a falsetto.

Both of us know I'm lying.

"What about memory issues?" he prompts.

"My memory is fine, as you just saw. I answered all your questions perfectly," I respond.

His eyes widen through the lenses of his glasses. He clicks his pen and leans forward in his black swivel chair.

"Liv, you came to see me not because of migraines but because of problems with your memory."

"What kind of problems?" I'm terrified to hear the answer.

I remember the phone call at the basement apartment earlier. The caller said I forget things when I fall asleep. Is it possible that he was telling the truth? And if he was right about that, then maybe he was right about all the other things he said.

"You appear to be in what I'd call a repetitive dissociative fugue. It's a rare form of amnesia," the doctor tells me. The word "amnesia" hangs in the air. It fits in with all the strange occurrences that have happened today.

"How long have I had it for?"

"I'm not sure. This is only your second appointment with me. We're still trying to get to the bottom of it."

"How could I possibly have amnesia? I remember so much about my life going back to my childhood."

"What things do you remember?"

"Well, for instance, I was cast in the role of Ophelia in a high school play. That was more than a decade ago, and I can still recite the lines, almost word for word."

"I don't doubt it," he says. "Our brains are highly complex. It's a different mechanism in your brain that appears to be blocked. You might remember dialogue from *Hamlet*, but unless you keep a written record of this conversation, you won't remember what we've discussed when you next wake up. You won't remember me. You won't remember being here. You won't remember anything that happened to you today. None of it."

"What happened to cause this?"

"I don't know exactly. Ted was going to make some inquiries in London to figure it out. What I do know is that it appears to be connected to your sleep patterns. Whenever you fall asleep, you wake up without any memory of events in your recent past."

I look out into the bright sunlight coming through his office window and lose myself in my thoughts. I've lost such a big chunk of my memory. It makes me feel bereft, like I've lost a limb, or an eye.

"Liv? Liv?" Dr. Brenner must have been talking to me. I didn't hear any of it. "Do you have any questions?"

"Is that why I drink so much caffeine and take NoDoz tablets?" I ask, thinking of the energy drinks filling the fridge at that horrible apartment. "Am I forcing myself to stay awake so I won't forget?"

"I believe so," he says. "Deep down you must know that you're going to forget everything when you sleep, so you try to fight it for as long as possible. Narcolepsy drugs, caffeine pills. Triple-strength coffee. You take whatever will keep you awake. It's a sort of self-induced insomnia. Sometimes you stay up for a full twenty-four hours. Or longer," he says. "I suspect it's affecting the levels of serotonin in your brain. The lower levels of serotonin, which controls moods, might be one of the causes of the fugues you're experiencing."

"It sounds like a vicious cycle. The longer I stay awake, the more it takes a toll on my memory."

"It is a vicious cycle. You need to break it if you're to get better."

He writes something on what looks like a prescription pad and hands it to me. I'm expecting it to be a script for drugs. Instead, he's written the name of another doctor.

"A psychiatrist?" I look up in surprise.

"Dr. Rosen specializes in memory problems. Due to the circumstances of your condition and the fact that we can't find any indication of damage to your brain in the scans, I believe this problem is most likely psychological. Dr. Rosen and I often work together with complex cases such as yours."

He holds up a palm as if he knows I'm going to push back. "We need to work out what triggered your memory disorder. Fugues with no organic cause are usually the result of trauma, extreme psychological trauma. Dr. Rosen can help you identify and work through that trauma."

"Trauma? What trauma?" I ask blankly.

He pauses as if contemplating how best to answer. "It's best you discuss that with Dr. Rosen."

I can barely hear him over an electrical crackle, rising in my head until it gets so explosive I want to put my hands over my ears and scream. When it stops, I realize I'm crying.

Dr. Brenner tries to comfort me. He tells me that his secretary will call Ted to come and get me. He says that he doesn't want me to be alone.

"But I don't know Ted," I say so softly that only I can hear.

His reassuring voice washes over me until I find myself on an aqua chair listening to a baby screaming in a pediatrician's examination room down the hall. Dr. Brenner's secretary squats next to me, holding out a box of Kleenex.

"I've left a message for Ted," she says. "I'm sure he'll call back very soon. Meanwhile, Dr. Brenner has asked Dr. Rosen to come down and talk to you when he's done with his next patient."

The minute hand of the waiting room clock looks as if it's frozen in time. I can't take waiting anymore. I get up from my seat and lean across the receptionist's desk to ask her what's going on.

"I've just left another message for Ted. His voicemail says if he doesn't answer then he's probably in a meeting. I'm sure he'll call back soon."

"Maybe you don't have the correct contact details for him? Can I check?" I'm curious to find out more about this mysterious Ted who is apparently listed as my next of kin.

"Is this his phone number?" she asks, rotating her computer screen so I can read it.

I don't recognize the phone number. The address, on the other hand, is a whole different story.

Chapter Forty-One

Detective Jack Lavelle navigated afternoon traffic to Brooklyn as he and Detective Halliday went over the shards of information they'd picked up so far on the case.

According to his fiancée, Elisabeth, Ted Cole had rented an apartment for his ex-girlfriend as a safe house because he was worried she might be in danger. It was in that apartment that he had been found stabbed to death early that morning.

"It seems straightforward," Lavelle said. "Liv Reese snapped. She stabbed her ex, Ted Cole, and fled."

"I think it's too early for us to focus on her to the exclusion of all other suspects," argued Halliday. "Ted believed that Liv Reese was in danger. That's why he moved her to a safe house. Maybe the person he was trying to protect her from confronted them both and murdered Ted."

"If that's the case then why wasn't she murdered as well?" Lavelle asked.

"I don't know," said Halliday after a moment's thought. "I still think we need to find out why Ted thought Liv was in danger."

"Maybe he made it up," said Lavelle.

"Why would he do that?"

"Maybe Ted told his fiancée that his ex was in danger to hide the fact that he'd rented an apartment to conduct an affair with her behind Elisabeth's back."

"If Ted and Liv were having an affair, then why would Ted tell Elisabeth anything at all?" said Halliday. "Why not cover his tracks by telling her that he was late at work, or on a business trip? No." She shook her head. "Ted told Elisabeth the truth. He had no reason to lie. He was genuinely worried about Liv's welfare. We need to find out why."

"We don't have limitless resources," Lavelle said. "Right now we have a likely suspect, and that suspect is Liv Reese. She found out that her ex was getting married. It upset her enough to pack up her life in London and travel back to New York. We know that for sure. Anger and betrayal. Liv Reese had one heck of a motive for murder."

"Not everyone with a motive kills," Halliday pointed out.

"True, but she had more than motive," said Lavelle.

Motive was the final piece in the trifecta. Liv Reese had opportunity, they both agreed on that. Security camera footage showed her leaving the scene of the crime. She also had means. Ted Cole was stabbed while he was sleeping, possibly after drinking wine laced with sedatives. Liv's fingerprints were on the bottle.

"You saw the long dark hairs on the pillow next to Cole. Liv Reese was most likely in bed with him on the night of the murder," Lavelle said, sounding exasperated by Halliday's refusal to be swayed. "And we know she was having mental health issues in London. She'd seen a psychiatrist. Even her social worker agreed that her insomnia might make her psychotic."

"I'll admit that it doesn't look good for Liv Reese," Halliday conceded. "Call me contrary, but I'm still keeping an open mind."

The facts all lined up to support Lavelle's theory. Liv Reese looked as guilty as sin. Still, Halliday felt in her gut they were missing something.

She looked through the windshield as they drove, trying to figure out what it was that bothered her enough to seriously consider the remote possibility that someone else had done it.

"You're very quiet," Lavelle commented after a while.

"That's because we're missing something."

"What makes you think that?" Lavelle asked, flashing her a sideways glance.

"I don't think any of this is as straightforward as it appears. It's true all the evidence points to Liv Reese. She's rightly our prime suspect," Halliday admitted.

"Yes, she is. So why aren't you convinced?"

"I worry it may be an optical illusion," Halliday said. "We have only some of the pieces of the puzzle. It's made us think the emerging pattern is something other than what it actually is."

Halliday knew a thing or two about puzzles. When she'd left the military and was dealing with the emotional withdrawal of being alone after spending years with a tight-knit group of military buddies, she'd taken up doing complex jigsaw puzzles to keep her mind preoccupied.

The veterans' counselor had recommended it as a strategy to eliminate stress and give her a sense of achievement. It helped lift her out of the depressive hole that so many veterans fell into during their transition into civilian life, especially those like her who'd spent so much of their service in combat zones.

Halliday took out her phone and Googled a phone number for Saint Vincent's Hospital in London.

It was well after 11:00 P.M. London time when the switchboard operator answered. Halliday asked for a phone number for Dr. Stanhope, Liv Reese's psychiatrist.

"I'm a police detective in New York," she explained. "I need to speak to Dr. Stanhope urgently. It's about one of his patients. She may be in serious trouble."

The operator gave her a cell phone number for the doctor. Halliday dialed it immediately, hoping that he kept his phone on after hours. He did.

"Stanhope." His voice was husky from being woken.

"I'm sorry for disturbing you so late in your night, Doctor. I'm a detective in New York and I'm investigating a case involving a patient of yours, Liv Reese," Halliday said.

His bedsheets rustled over the phone line as he climbed out of bed.

"Liv Reese has turned up here in New York. I'm one of the detectives looking for her."

"The hospital social worker told me earlier that you might get in touch," he said. "I hope you understand that I'm quite limited in what I can tell you. There are certain things about my patient that I am not at liberty to discuss. Patient confidentiality. You understand."

"I believe she may be in danger. I hope that gives you some leeway to talk to me about her. Incidentally, I know she has some sort of amnesia and I'd be interested in your take on it."

"It's a very rare condition. It's a type of dissociative fugue. Except instead of one fugue episode, Liv is experiencing a series of repetitive fugue episodes. They begin every time Liv wakes and end every time she falls asleep."

"Help me out here, Doctor. I'm not great with medical jargon," Halliday said. "What do you mean by dissociative fugue?"

"It's a type of amnesia that has a psychological cause. It's often sparked by trauma and it presents with quite unusual characteristics."

"Such as?"

"A person tries to resume his or her old life after suffering a trauma. They don't realize that time has passed. We've had cases of people with dissociative fugue who have taken on new names, started new lives. There are even cases of people who have begun speaking in different accents, or languages." He paused to let his words sink in. "You must have heard of the crime writer Agatha Christie?"

"Of course," said Halliday.

"In 1926, after she discovered her husband was having an affair, Christie disappeared. The police dredged the local lake, believing she might have drowned. Thousands of volunteers searched for her in the countryside. Meanwhile, a woman claiming to be a grieving mother from Cape Town checked in at a health spa under a name very similar to the name of the mistress of Agatha Christie's unfaithful husband. Eventually, one of the guests recognized her as the famous crime writer and alerted the authorities. Christie regained her memory, but she never remembered anything that happened to her during her time at the health spa."

"You believe the same thing happened to Liv Reese?"

"It's very possible. If anything, her situation is significantly more dire."

"In what way?"

"Her fugue incidents are repetitive. They happen every time she wakes up," he says. "That puts her in a constant state of confusion and makes her extremely vulnerable. It's very rare. In fact, I don't recall ever seeing another case with that presentation."

"Do you know what might have prompted her to leave England and return to New York?"

"I'm afraid I haven't seen Liv for a while. My wife and I have just returned from a visit to Australia for the birth of our first grandchild. Liv was supposed to see a colleague while I was away. It appears she didn't attend her appointments. We only found out she'd disappeared when I returned to work a few days ago. I asked the social worker to contact the missing person department at Scotland Yard when she couldn't get hold of Liv," he said. "From what you're telling me, she's in New York again. Her old stomping ground."

"That's correct," said Halliday.

"That's very interesting. Very interesting indeed."

"Why is that?"

"I suspect Liv's subconsciously trying to find out the source of the trauma that caused these fugue states," he said. "Killing her monster, as it were, may be her way to assert control. To break the cycle and get her memory back."

Chapter Forty-Two

Two Years Earlier

I stare at myself in the window as the train roars through a subway tunnel with a deafening howl. I wonder if the silk scarf tied jauntily around my neck is over the top, especially on such a sweltering summer day. Marco gave me the scarf as a gift. I thought it would be nice to wear it when I see him later tonight.

We've arranged to meet for dinner at Stefanie. There's a two-month wait to get into the restaurant, but Marco pulled strings to get us a table. I'm impressed. I'm a food writer and even I couldn't get a table at Stefanie on short notice. Marco hinted he's taking me there because he wants to discuss something important. I'm filled with a nervous anticipation.

I sway in tandem with the passengers in the train car. It's like we're a single seething organism, moving to the familiar rhythmic ritual of the morning commute.

When the train reaches my stop, I push my way out of the car and through the mass of passengers waiting on the platform. My phone rings as I climb the stairs to street level. I answer it as I walk into my office.

"Liv? Where are you?" Amy sounds sleepy.

"I'm almost at work," I respond, pressing the elevator button. "Why? Is something wrong?"

"No," she yawns. "I just woke and heard creaking floorboards. You didn't answer when I called out your name so I figured I'd call and see what's going on." She yawns again.

"It wasn't me. I've just arrived at work."

"It must be the new people in the apartment upstairs. They make such a racket when they leave in the morning. Listen, Liv, since I have you on the line, I think Shawna needs to see the vet."

"Why?"

"She's limping. She won't put pressure on her right front paw. I think she might have been injured. Maybe she was in a fight or something. She seems spooked…" The rest of her sentence is swallowed up by the noise of the elevator doors opening.

"Amy? I can't hear you."

Her voice has been replaced by crackling silence as the call drops out. I take the elevator up to the office. Once I get out, I dial Amy's cell phone again.

Her phone's engaged so I leave her a message. "Amy, your call dropped out. Bad reception. I'm in the office now. Call me on my cell or my desk phone when you're free."

I push open the glass office doors and walk past the reception desk, turning my head to smile at the dimple-cheeked receptionist. "Good morning, Natalie."

She mouths a greeting before answering a call.

It's late morning when Marco's number flashes on my screen. It's unusual for him to call me at work and I'm afraid he's calling to cancel our dinner. He canceled our bike ride, and now this. My body tenses as I wonder whether he's planning on breaking up with me tonight. Maybe that's why he's taking me to such a smart restaurant: it guarantees him a cordial breakup without any histrionics. I could always tell when Mom's relationships were about to explode. Canceled dates. A sudden coldness. I can't believe it's happening to me, too. The more I think about it, the more convinced I am that he's going to break up with me tonight.

Marco's call eventually goes to voicemail. I quickly turn off my cell phone so he can't get through. It's childish and counterproductive. All it does is make me anxious to find out why Marco was calling me in the first place. I'm about to ring him back when Frank calls me into his office.

"Where's the draft of your story on the Q preview show?"

"It was horrible. Gratuitous violence and pop philosophy. It was the performance art equivalent of a snuff film. I don't think *Cultura* should deign that sort of thing a write-up."

"That's my job to decide, and it's your job to write," he tells me. "I want your copy on my desk tomorrow. Once I get it, then we can talk it through." Before I can respond, we're both called into a meeting on the January issue of the magazine.

When the meeting finally breaks up, I return to my desk and start working on my write-up of the Q exhibition. I do preliminary stuff first, transcribing my notes and going over Q's quotes from the phone interview before I get started on writing the actual article.

Outside, it's a perfect summer day. The sky is a canvas of unblemished blue. I bask in the sunshine streaking across my desk, typing rapidly on my laptop. I'm startled by my desk phone ringing abruptly.

"This is Liv," I say into the receiver.

"Liv?" It's Amy. There's a strange inflection in her tone that sends a shiver down my spine. "Liv, can you come home?" I can tell she's been crying.

"Now?"

"Yes."

"Is it Shawna?"

"Yeah." Her voice wobbles. It sounds as if she's swallowing back tears. "Please come quickly. There's been a... I'm... sorry. Just come. Please. As soon as you can...." The phone line clicks. She's hung up.

I grab my purse and rush out of the office, muttering something about an emergency to Natalie as I race past the reception desk. I try to call Amy again on my way home in the back of a cab. She's not answering the phone. I stare out the window, sick with worry, as the cab navigates through midday traffic. When the driver finally drops me off on my street, I don't bother to wait for my change. Instead, I stride to the building and race up the stairs to my apartment.

"Amy?" I call out once I'm inside. "Amy?"

There's no response. Her bedroom door is slightly open.

"Amy, is everything all right?"

I push open her door and step into her dimly lit bedroom.

Amy and Marco are in her bed. Naked, with the sheet down to their waists, their heads propped up against the headboard.

"What's going on? The two of you…"

I'm so shocked at their betrayal that I don't immediately notice the terrible details. Their eyes are unblinking and there are holes in their chests. Blood trails down to their navels, pooling on the sheets like crimson inkblots.

"They've been sleeping together behind your back for weeks."

I'm about to turn toward the chilling voice behind me when powerful arms restrain me, pulling me into a macabre bear hug. His arms are like steel clamps around my body. I open my mouth to scream, but only a terrified whisper comes out.

"What have you done?" I ask.

"Not me. What have *you* done, Liv?" His breath hits the nape of my neck as he whispers in my ear. "The police will conclude that you were so devastated to find your best friend and your boyfriend in bed that, in the heat of the moment, you went to the kitchen and took out a chef's knife. A nice touch, I might add, given that you're a food writer. You took the knife and came in here, killing them and then yourself," he says. "A double murder and suicide. Tragic but neat, at least from my perspective."

Before I can speak, he takes my hand and forces me to grip the smooth metal handle of a kitchen knife. I look down and see his shoes, which are the color of blood with a unique dotted pattern by the toes.

As I try to squirm out of his arms, he lifts up my hand and forces me to thrust the blade deep into my torso. The pain is excruciating. I crumple onto my knees and collapse on my side. He turns and walks out of the room as I lie on the carpet and stare at Amy's pink kimono rocking on the hook behind her door.

I slide toward Amy's desk and desperately tug the cord of her landline phone until it tumbles onto the carpet next to me. I grab the receiver and dial clumsily. My hands are slippery with blood as I try to apply pressure on my own wound. I'm vaguely aware of the front door closing.

"Nine-one-one," a woman says. "What is your emergency?"

"I've been stabbed," I gasp into the receiver.

I whisper my address to her, panting heavily as I choke on my own blood.

"What's your name?" the dispatcher asks.

"Liv," I murmur. I can feel myself drifting into unconsciousness.

"Liv, there's an ambulance nearby. It's going to be there real soon. I'll stay with you on the line until it arrives. Okay?"

"I'm so tired," I slur.

"I know you are, honey. But you can't go to sleep. Try to stay awake.... Liv, honey," she says. "I need you to stay awake. Okay?"

I don't have enough strength to answer her. I lie with my head on the carpet and stare at Amy's kimono. It turns from pink to black and I pass out.

The dispatcher's strained voice calls out: "Liv, are you awake?"

I snap my eyes open, focusing on the kimono like it's a beacon. "Yeah," I rasp. My voices fades away as darkness engulfs me again.

"Wake up, Liv." Her voice is loud and urgent. "I need you to wake up. Can you do that for me? The ambulance is almost there. Stay with me."

"I'm trying," I gasp.

"You need to stay awake, Liv," she orders. "The ambulance is downstairs. The paramedics are on their way up. Stay awake. You have to do that. Liv? You have to stay awake."

Chapter Forty-Three

The white bricks of the Ninetieth in Williamsburg had dulled over time, giving the Brooklyn precinct with the second-highest murder rate in the borough the grim air of a military-style bunker.

Detectives Lavelle and Halliday were met by their counterpart, Larry Regan, at the top of the stairs. Regan wore a thin black tie with a white business shirt, his sleeves rolled up to his elbows. He was a gangly young detective with chocolate-brown eyes and a crop of dark hair. In his arms was a huge document box with the files they'd come to collect.

"I'm going to need you to sign for it," he said, handing over a clipboard.

Lavelle leaned the clipboard onto the stair railing and signed the forms before taking the box. The hefty weight was unexpected.

"There's a lot of paperwork in there. It'll take a lot of time for you to go through it all," said Regan. "I worked on the case early on. I can give you a quick overview if you have a few minutes."

"Sure. We can make time," said Lavelle.

Regan fed coins into a vending machine and bought them each a can of soda. Drinks in hand, he led them to a "soft room" at the end of the corridor.

"We won't be disturbed here," he said, turning on the overhead fluorescent lights.

It was called a soft room because it was used for the families of victims and traumatized witnesses. Hard rooms were the hard-core interrogation rooms for suspects, often painted in sickly colors, with minimal furniture and no windows other than a one-way mirror.

The soft room had a table and chairs, a couple of sofas and a bookshelf with scuffed toys and magazines. At the far end was a square window that looked out onto the precinct parking lot, where squad cars and unmarked police vehicles were parked in untidy rows.

Regan unpacked three bulging files from the document box. Each file had several strategically placed elastic bands around it to stop documents from falling out.

"That's a lot of material," said Lavelle.

"The investigation was extensive." Regan tapped the document box. "This case happened almost two and a half years ago. It officially remains 'unsolved.' Right now, it might as well be a cold case."

"Why?"

"It's been open season around here lately. We're getting homicides every day. There's no time to deal with unsolveds right now. Plus, it was Krause's case. When he moved to Queens, it was given to another senior detective. He's on leave right now, which is why you're talking to me."

"You were Krause's partner?" Lavelle asked.

"Briefly. We didn't see eye to eye."

"I bet you didn't," Lavelle said. "Why the interest in this case?"

"Because I think we screwed it up," said Regan, not mincing words.

"Why?"

He let Lavelle and Halliday flick through the pages of the files while he recounted the basic facts of the case and the investigation.

"It was a double murder," he said. "Liv Reese's boyfriend, Marco Reggio, and her best friend, Amy Decker, were killed.

Liv Reese was the only survivor. She suffered a near-fatal knife wound. Amy Decker was a doctor finishing her internship at Bellevue. Originally from Wisconsin. She was killed a couple of weeks after her twenty-seventh birthday. Reggio was an ex-finance guy turned entrepreneur. Age thirty-four. They were having an affair behind Liv Reese's back. In fact they were in bed together when they were killed."

"Do you think Liv Reese killed them?" Halliday asked, looking up from the file.

"The way Krause saw it, Liv Reese caught them in bed together. Killed them both and then stabbed herself. Murder-suicide. She covered it up by calling nine-one-one and pretending she'd been attacked."

"Why would she call nine-one-one if it was a murder-suicide? She didn't need to worry about covering it up if she was dead," Halliday pointed out.

"Exactly," said Regan. "There are other inconsistencies, as you'll see in the files. It didn't help that her recollections of the murders were almost nonexistent."

"She didn't remember anything at all?"

"She barely had a pulse when the paramedics reached her. She was in a coma for almost two weeks. When she came out of it, she remembered almost nothing about the murder. She did have flashbacks months later, but her recollections weren't consistent with the evidence."

"How so?"

"For example, she had a flashback about shoes covered in blood, except there was no blood trail on the carpet."

Halliday shuffled through the crime scene photos. She paused to look at a ghoulish photo of Amy Decker and Marco Reggio. They were sitting in bed, naked, with a bloodied sheet at their waists. Both had been stabbed in their torsos, much the way that Ted Cole had been stabbed.

She handed the photo to Lavelle. He nodded. It was uncanny. A single stab wound. Same location. Similar MO to the Ted Cole killing.

"It sounds as if you didn't agree with Krause that Reese did it?" Lavelle asked.

"Krause believed it was an open-shut case; jealous girlfriend stabs cheating boyfriend and his lover who happened to be her best friend. Jealousy and betrayal, prime motives for murder."

"It is a convincing scenario," said Lavelle.

"I agree. Amy Decker's family thought so, too. But the anomalies bothered me. I carried out my own inquiries after hours. The more I learned, the less sure I was that Liv Reese had done it."

"Why?" Halliday asked.

"I consulted with a top forensic expert on knife wounds. He told me there was no way the stab wound in Liv Reese's torso was self-inflicted. She's left-handed. The wound would have been made by someone who was right-handed due to the angle the blade penetrated the body."

"Forensic experts can be wrong," said Halliday.

"There were other leads that we never followed up on. Potential suspects."

"Like who?"

"An artist whose exhibition Liv Reese reviewed. Have you ever heard of Zee?"

Halliday nodded. Lavelle shook his head.

"Zee's an avant-garde artist who was accused of beating up his pregnant girlfriend," Regan said. "He was outed on social media, and his career was basically over. He reinvented himself as a guerrilla performance artist known as Q. At least, that's what a recent exposé in *The New York Times* suggests."

"What does Zee have to do with Liv Reese?" she asked.

"She wrote a scathing review of Zee's last exhibition before he went underground. Her review was the beginning of the end of his career," Regan said. "Shortly before the Decker-Reggio murders, Liv was invited to a preview exhibition by Q. She found it violent and disturbing. She didn't want to write about it, but her editor insisted. She was working on the article on the afternoon of the murders."

"So you're saying that if Zee and Q were one and the same person, then it's possible he was trying to get back at her for ruining his career."

"Yes," said Regan. "I went through her notebook after the murders. The Q exhibition was creepy as hell. It was almost as if he brought her there to scare her."

"Why do you say that?"

"Because the exhibition that she described in her reporter's notebook contained themes of violence, misogyny, and bondage that were completely different to the actual exhibition that ran months later."

"Were there other suspects?"

"A photographer, George Yanis."

"What's his story?"

"He was fired after Liv Reese filed a sexual harassment complaint against him at the magazine where she worked. She wasn't the first, but he blamed her. He told people he'd get even with her. Krause flatly refused to look into him as a possible suspect. Then there were the stalking complaints she made in the weeks before the murders."

"Stalking? She was stalked?" Lavelle asked, snapping to attention.

"The police reports are in the files." Regan flicked through the folders until he found several reports, which he handed to Halliday and Lavelle.

"You're telling us that Krause didn't look into the stalking when he was investigating the Decker-Reggio murders?" Halliday asked, surprised.

"He thought it was bogus. He thought she'd made up the stalking incidents because she'd intended to kill Amy and Marco and wanted to create an alternate suspect. He said it showed premeditation. He believed Liv knew Amy and Marco were sleeping together. According to some of the neighbors, they were hardly discreet."

"What did you think?" Lavelle asked.

"I went with Krause to her apartment after one of her stalking complaints. This was a few days before the double murder. She was terrified. It wasn't acting. Krause thought it was a big joke. When we left, he told me she was a nut job. Maybe he was right. But her fear, it was real."

"Why did Krause think it was a joke?" Halliday asked.

"She claimed a stranger put a casserole in her oven and brought her dry cleaning back home. She said he left flowers next to her bed. A week or so earlier, she said someone had put a carton of milk in her fridge while she slept."

"That all sounds… insane," said Halliday.

"Yup, but some stalkers will do things that are bat-shit crazy," said Regan. "You can't imagine what these people will do to insert themselves into someone's life. I had a case once where the stalker got a job as a window cleaner so he could see into his victim's apartment. The night I was there I saw something that made me think Liv Reese was telling the truth."

"What was it?"

"While I was in her bedroom on the night Krause and I were called over there, I had a prickly feeling we were being watched. When everyone left the room, I turned off the lights and stayed behind. I saw a man holding binoculars in an apartment across the street," he said. "Liv Reese was definitely being watched. I know for sure because I saw him watching her."

"You told Krause?"

"He dismissed it as a creepy neighbor. Maybe if he'd taken her stalking complaints seriously then the murders wouldn't have happened."

Regan said that he'd seen Liv throw the flowers and chocolates in a trash can on the street after they drove away from her apartment. He'd driven around the block and gone back to collect them.

"The box of chocolates sent with the roses was an exclusive Belgian brand. Eight bucks a chocolate. All handmade. I took the box to the store hoping they could tell me who'd bought them. They insisted that someone had replaced their truffles with cheap imitations."

"Why would someone do that?"

Regan shrugged. "No idea, but Liv Reese claimed to have been drugged after eating one of the truffles. It was while she was drugged that she claimed someone came into her apartment. If the truffles delivered to her were laced with sedatives, then it would make sense for whoever sent them to switch them over when he was in the apartment to cover his tracks."

Halliday skimmed the forensics report from the double murder two years earlier.

"None of what you said, even if true, contradicts the possibility that she murdered her friends," she said, looking up from the report.

"True," said Regan. "But we never did get to the bottom of some of the other creepy things that went on before the murders."

"Such as?" Halliday asked.

"The dry cleaner said her clothes were collected by her boyfriend. When I asked him to describe the boyfriend, he said it was a man with light brown hair, tall and thin with a bump on his nose and a gap between his teeth," he said. "Marco Reggio didn't look a bit like that."

"Did you ever speak to the neighbor across the street? The one you thought was spying on the apartment?" Halliday asked.

"Krause chewed me out when I admitted that I'd looked into her stalking claims and that I thought there might be something to it. He insisted there was no stalker. He was certain Liv Reese had committed the murders. She was still unconscious in the hospital at that point, and he was biding his time for her to come out of the coma so he could interrogate her. He planned to get her to confess and charge her with the Decker-Reggio murders."

Regan added that he'd just earned his shield. It was his first gig in homicide and he had been told to defer to Krause as the more experienced detective.

"We had a big argument. Krause said that by looking into other lines of investigation, I was helping the defense build a case that Liv Reese didn't murder her friends."

A future defense team would get all the information gathered during the discovery process, including everything that Regan had turned up in his after-hours investigation.

"Krause said the defense would twist the information that I'd found to make the jury think there were other possible suspects. To create reasonable doubt," said Regan. "That's why we had a blowup, Krause and me. I resented his accusation that I was screwing up the case just because I wanted to make sure we arrested the right person. Krause stopped me from investigating further. He said it was our job to find the evidence to prove the Reese woman's guilt. Period. He didn't want any time wasted looking for other suspects."

"Yet Liv Reese was never charged," Halliday pointed out.

"The prosecutor refused to move forward with an indictment," said Regan. "She said Krause's case was all supposition, with little evidence. Meanwhile, I found out the neighbor who'd been watching her apartment with binoculars moved out the day before the murder. It was a short-term rental. He'd paid for a week of rent that he didn't use, and let me tell you, the rent didn't come cheap."

"Sounds like he wanted to get out in a hurry," said Halliday.

"Fortunately, he was a slob. He didn't bother to take out the trash. I found a dozen empty beer cans and a pile of take-out containers in the apartment when the janitor let me in. I took the beer cans and gave them to a friend at the forensics lab."

Regan took out a second file. He went through the papers one by one until he found the one he needed. It was a finger-print report. He held it up in the air so they could both see it.

"His name's Joe Chalmers," he said. "Long record. Breaking and entering. Car theft. One assault years ago. He was cashing welfare checks at the time of the murder. So how could he afford to rent the apartment opposite Liv Reese's place?"

"Someone else paid for it," said Halliday.

"I believe so."

"Did you track down Joe Chalmers?"

"He skipped town. Nobody knew where he'd gone."

"Maybe we should look for him again," Halliday suggested to Lavelle.

"Actually, when I heard you were interested in seeing the Decker-Reggio murder file, I looked him up," Regan said. "He's back in town. Living in public housing. I thought I'd check in on him sometime."

"Why wait?" said Lavelle, grabbing his jacket from the back of his chair as he stood up.

Chapter Forty-Four

Dr. Brenner's secretary leaves the reception desk to print an insurance form for a patient who's just arrived. I take advantage of her absence to slip out of the clinic and head to the nearest subway station, where I rush into a train car a moment before the doors close.

The late afternoon light is subdued and the street smells of fresh rain when I emerge from the subway steps onto the street and walk along the slick sidewalk toward my office.

This mysterious Ted was listed as my emergency contact in my file at Dr. Brenner's office. Incredibly, the address listed for him is the *Cultura* office.

Natalie's not sitting behind the reception desk when I go in. Instead there's a temp with cropped hair and platinum bangs. Her mascara has run and black stains have formed dark pools under her eyes. Track marks of tears run down her cheeks.

"Are you all right?" I ask.

She nods and shakes her head at the same time. Then she bursts into tears. "You'd better go in."

The office has been redecorated from understated classy neutrals to a brash color scheme of urban grays with touches of electric blue and lime green. The place looks more like a hotel lobby than an office.

Despite the upbeat decor, a sense of despair hangs over the place. In the middle of the office, a woman with corkscrew curls hugs another woman with long red hair. Their eyes are puffy. They've both been crying.

232

"I can't believe it," says the woman with red hair.

"Neither can I," says her friend as they embrace.

"What happened?" I ask.

Both women swallow hard like they're about to deliver bad news.

"Liv, you should sit down," says the woman with the curls.

"Why? What's wrong?"

My mind races as I try to think what could have happened to cause such despair. I look across the office into an expansive glass-walled meeting room, where staff sit around a boardroom table looking shell-shocked. Some hold their hands to their mouths. Others openly sob.

"What's happened?" Panic laces my voice.

"I can't put it into words because if I do, then it will be real... and I don't want it to be real," says the woman with the corkscrew hair.

Her friend with red hair takes my hand and lowers me onto a backless round sofa, like I'm an invalid. "This is so hard, Liv," she says, sitting next to me and resting our interlocked hands on her tartan skirt. I look into her despondent eyes in confusion and try to figure out how she knows my name.

"Ted is dead," she says, finally. Her freckled face puckers in sorrow. Fresh tears well in her eyes.

"Dead?" I respond weakly. They both burst into tears.

Their sadness is infectious. Tears stream down my cheeks and my chest is heavy with grief.

I don't know why I'm so emotional. After all, I don't actually know who Ted is, other than that Dr. Brenner seems to think he's my friend. I came to the office to find him.

My voice trembles. "Everyone must be in shock."

"We're devastated. We can't even imagine what you're going through. You've been through so much already, Liv. And now this..." Her voice drops off.

I'm hit by a sudden dizziness as her words reverberate in my head. Dr. Brenner also alluded to a trauma in my past. My body sways. Both women grab hold of me as if they're afraid I'll collapse.

"We should get her something to drink," one of them says to the other.

They help me to the office pantry, where someone pulls out a white chair for me at a matching table and someone else brings me a Coke.

"For the sugar," she says, pulling the aluminum tab with a hiss and handing me the cold can.

I take a few sips and set the can aside, watching colleagues console each other with drawn-out comforting hugs. Someone turns on an enormous television hanging on a wall in the pantry area. The electronic theme music of the afternoon news program blasts across the office.

"Police have released the name of the man who was murdered while he slept in a midtown apartment last night," says the newsreader. "He is Edward 'Ted' Cole, an executive at *Cultura Magazine*. Police say they have opened an investigation into his..."

The name echoes in my head as the TV blares. Ted is dead. That's why he didn't come with me to my appointment with Dr. Brenner.

Footage runs on the screen showing the words WAKE UP! written in blood on a window.

I have the same message on my wrist, just like the man who called me at that grim basement apartment earlier said when he made those vile accusations. He suggested that I murdered someone this morning. I gasp as I realize that "someone" must be Ted. Is it possible that I killed the very man that everyone in this office is mourning?

There's no way I could have killed him. I'm not violent. I faint at the sight of blood. It's ridiculous to even think I might have been responsible. But Ted is dead, and I have a big black hole in my memory and a slogan written on my skin that matches the one daubed at the crime scene.

Looking out the window, I try to absorb everything that's happened since I arrived at my office. Down on the street below, pedestrians crowd the sidewalks like pesky ants as they head home from work. It's a scene I've seen thousands of times before. This time it feels as if I'm watching it from another dimension.

The reflection of the red-haired woman in the tartan skirt appears in the window. "I'm so sorry for your loss, Liv," she says, standing behind me.

"Thank you," I answer without turning around.

"Even though you and Ted ended your engagement, it must be unbelievably painful. He always raved about how much talent you had, and how you worked your way up the ladder at the magazine," she stutters. "I guess I just want you to know that I'm here for you. We all are."

I'm shocked to learn that Ted and I were engaged. How could I not remember the man I was going to marry? "Why would someone kill him?" I ask.

She swings around to face the reception area.

"Looks like the police are here to find out," she says.

Chapter Forty-Five

Joe Chalmers was carrying home a six-pack of beer from the bus stop when the three detectives beelined toward him on the concrete expanse outside the public housing building where he lived with his girlfriend.

Lavelle and Halliday followed Regan toward Chalmers, striding in unison, their badges displayed on the waistbands of their suits. It was obvious that Chalmers immediately knew they were law enforcement. He was visibly torn between dropping the cans of Bud and bolting off, or staying put and talking to the police.

"He's going to run," Halliday said, reading his body language.

Chalmers's flight instinct, honed by years of being on the wrong side of the law, took over from his common sense. He dropped the beer with a thud and bolted toward the street, where a bus was pulling up.

Halliday, who was on the side closest to his escape route, sprinted after him. She chased him onto the grass, where he tripped over an exposed tree root and went flying.

"You okay there?" She approached the patch of grass where he was lying splayed on the ground and held out a hand to help him up. He looked at her outstretched hand skeptically.

"We can talk here or we can talk at the precinct," she said. "If we take you to the precinct, then we might as well charge you with failing to stop when requested by a police officer. I'm sure we'll think up a few other charges while we're at it. What's your preference?"

"I'll talk." He scrambled to his feet without her help. He had a gap between his two front teeth just the way the dry cleaner had described to Detective Regan two years earlier.

"What do you want to know?" he asked.

"Two years ago, you were living in an apartment that you couldn't possibly afford in Williamsburg," Halliday said. She recited the address. "What were you doing there?"

Halliday's eyes fixed on Lavelle for a second as she waited for Chalmers to answer. She didn't want the other detectives joining them and changing the dynamics. Lavelle nodded to let her know they'd give her space.

"I don't got to justify where I live," Chalmers said.

"Sure you do," said Halliday. "Especially when the neighbor you'd been spying on with binoculars turns up dead."

"I didn't have anything to do with that. I wasn't even living there when it happened. Left town a couple of days before." He slapped his hands together to wipe off the dirt from his fall.

"How did you know about the murders?" Halliday asked.

"Read it in the papers."

"I don't believe you," said Halliday. She reached for her handcuffs and snapped them open.

"Okay, okay. I'll tell you what I know," he said. "A dude paid me to live in that apartment for a couple of weeks. In return I had to do chores."

"What chores?"

"I had to drop off laundry. One time, I had to buy food from some fancy restaurant and heat it up in their oven. Another time I had to go inside in the middle of the night and put a carton of milk in the fridge. I didn't hurt anyone. I just did things to mess with the women living there."

"What was the point of messing with them?"

"Dunno. He never said. He just messaged me things to do. It was harmless stuff. Easiest money I ever made," he said. "I only went into the apartment a couple of times. I didn't break any laws."

"Other than breaking and entering. It wasn't your apartment," Halliday pointed out.

"Yeah, okay. But I didn't hurt anyone, or steal anything. He said if I did, I wouldn't get the rest of the money."

"How much were you paid?"

"Two grand up front. I was supposed to get another three at the end. Never got it."

"Because you skipped town?" Halliday asked.

"Yeah."

"Who hired you?"

"Some guy. Met him at a bar. He gave me a burner phone. We communicated by text after that," he said. "He messaged me tasks. Instructions. I texted him back when they were completed."

"What instructions did he give you?"

"The things I already told you. One time I had to leave flowers and chocolates by the front door. Then he texted me half an hour later and told me to go into the apartment and leave more flowers by her bed and replace the chocolates in the box with new ones. He'd put something in the chocolates to make her fall asleep and he wanted them all replaced."

"Did he explain why he wanted you to do these things?" Halliday asked.

"He said he wanted to scare her." Chalmers laughed nervously. "Well, he scared her all right. I'd watch her looking out the windows, trying to figure out whether she was going nuts."

"How did you get in and out of the apartment?" Halliday asked.

"He gave me keys. Told me to dress like a plumber and act like I belonged. That way nobody would be the wiser. It worked perfectly."

"If you didn't do anything violent, like you claim, why did you skip town?"

"He called me with one final task."

"What was it?" Halliday asked.

"He wanted me to kill them."

"Kill who?"

"The hot blonde who lived in the apartment and the guy she was sleeping with when her roommate was at work. Dark-haired guy. Looked Italian. He wanted them both dead. Promised to pay me another five grand."

"What did you tell him?"

"I said no," Chalmers said. "Murder is hard-core. I don't do stuff like that. He said he'd find someone else. A few days later he told me to meet at a warehouse at Hunts Point to get the rest of my cash. I didn't turn up."

"Why not?"

"It stunk. I worried he'd try to make sure I kept my mouth shut. Permanently. So I did a disappearing act."

"Who set you up with this guy?"

"Dude I knew used to give me jobs. Debt collection, mostly. He set up the meet. Turned out to be a bad move on his part."

"Why?"

"Because he's dead."

"How did he die?"

He shrugged. "Heard he was stabbed. Body was found floating in the East River. When I found out, I figured it was the man at the bar who did it, or someone he paid to cover his tracks for him. I made a good decision to get out of town. I've kept a low profile ever since. More than two years now on the straight and narrow."

"What did the man who hired you look like?"

He shrugged. "No idea. He sat next to me in a crowded bar. Told me to keep looking straight ahead while he slid over the phone. All I saw were his hands. No tattoos. No wedding ring. Nicely trimmed nails. Looked like he took care of himself. Dude didn't drink either," he said. "I thought that was weird. Who asks to meet at a bar and doesn't order a drink?"

When Halliday indicated she was done, Lavelle approached, holding the pack of beer that Chalmers had ditched. A couple of cans were dented, but they were otherwise intact.

"Not sure if I did you a favor by rescuing your beer," Lavelle said, tossing the box to Chalmers. "So here's what happens next. Detective Regan will take you to the precinct where you'll provide him with a sworn statement."

Chalmers breathed hard with a mixture of fear and relief as he nodded. He stepped forward to follow Regan when Lavelle slammed his palm hard against Chalmers's chest.

"If you disappear again, then me and Detective Halliday over here will personally look for you. We'll haul your ass back and we'll throw the book at you so hard your hair will be snow-white when you get out of the slammer."

As they climbed back into their car, Lavelle asked Halliday if she believed Chalmers's story.

"Why lie about something like that?" asked Halliday, starting the engine. "He has nothing to gain and everything to lose."

She pulled the car out into steady traffic. They drove in silence for a while, contemplating how Chalmers's information potentially changed the complexion of the case.

Halliday finally spoke. "Ted Cole's fiancée, Elisabeth, told us that he rented that apartment as a safe house for Liv Reese. He believed Amy and Marco's killer was coming after her."

"Why would the killer bother getting rid of Liv Reese, two years later?" Lavelle said. "Especially since she never remembered what happened."

"The killer might not know that," said Halliday, looking over her shoulder as she changed lanes. "Even if the killer knew she'd never remembered what happened that day, imagine the stress of knowing an eyewitness's memory could return any time. Now that really is a motive for murder."

"Where are you going with this, Halliday?"

"Jack, I think the killer is looking for Liv Reese. I think this whole thing is about tying off loose ends from the Decker–Reggio murders. Liv Reese is the biggest loose end of all. We need to find her before he does."

Chapter Forty-Six

The *Cultura Magazine* meeting room is like a fishbowl for all the privacy it offers. The police officers must quickly realize that everyone in the office is surreptitiously watching them through the glass walls because somebody lowers the internal privacy shade so we can't see inside.

An HR manager emerges from the meeting room and walks to the middle of the office as if she's about to make an announcement. Everyone drifts over to listen.

"The police are here, as you've all no doubt noticed. They've asked for everyone to stay back to be questioned. Detectives will be here shortly. Once they arrive, they'll split up and talk to us individually. They've asked that nobody leave until they've been questioned."

Everyone scatters as they wait to be summoned for their interview with the police. A telephone rings somewhere near me. My heart rate goes up with each successive ring. I grip my hands into fists until my knuckles are white and my nails cut into my palms.

The phone stops ringing as abruptly as it began.

"Liv. Liv."

My name is being called out by a disembodied voice behind a white partition.

"Liv, there's a call for you," says a man with John Lennon glasses, holding up a desk phone.

"Hello?" I press the phone receiver hard against my ear.

"Liv, it's me," says the same muffled voice I heard on the phone at the basement apartment.

"What do you want?"

"The cops in your office are going to arrest you once they know you're there. The net is tightening around you. I can help you, Liv."

"How?" I ask suspiciously.

"Your memory lapses. I'll tell you what happened last night. I'll tell you what you've forgotten."

"Why should I trust you?"

"Because Ted asked me to take care of you. I'm outside your building. Come down now and I'll explain everything."

"I need to think about it."

"You don't have time." His voice fades in and out as a police siren wails over the phone line. "Come down and I'll tell you what happened. I'll help you clear your name."

Car doors slam in the background.

"That noise you just heard are more cops," he tells me. "They're coming up to your office to look for you. Come down now, Liv. I'll wait for you outside the coffee place on the corner."

"I don't know." I'm torn between fear of this stranger and an overwhelming desire to hear what he knows about me.

He senses my desperation to find out the truth. "Write my phone number on your hand in case you can't find me," he orders. He dictates a cell phone number and tells me to write above it the words "Call for help."

"I'm waiting for you downstairs," he says. "Come down now. You don't have much time left until they come for you, Liv. Hurry." The call disconnects with a click.

Two police officers stand near the reception desk. Their casual stance doesn't fool anyone. It's obvious they've been posted to guard the office entrance.

Someone turns up the volume of the TV. Synthesized theme music blares, drawing everyone to the TV like moths to a flame. The evening news is about to begin.

"Police are investigating the brutal murder of a magazine executive, who was found stabbed to death this morning," the anchor says.

A photo of a smiling man with tawny hair and crinkled eyes appears on the screen. Everyone around me lets out an audible cry of shock at the sight of their colleague's photo on the news.

"Police are asking the public to call the hotline if they have details of the victim's whereabouts in the hours before he died. Police are particularly interested in finding a woman with long hair who was seen with the victim before his death."

The anchor pauses for a moment. "We've just obtained CCTV footage taken outside the building where the murder occurred. Our sources tell us the woman seen fleeing the scene is the prime suspect in this morning's murder."

Grainy security camera footage shows a woman with long hair in a loose plait emerging from a dark lane. I stare dumbfounded at the TV screen. The only difference between me and the woman on the TV is that her hair is incredibly long, whereas mine is cropped short. That woman is me. I was there last night when Ted Cole was murdered. I'm the police's prime suspect.

"Anyone who has seen this woman, or who has information on her whereabouts, should contact NYPD at the hotline…"

I'm barely conscious of the news anchor's voice reading out the hotline phone number as I glance furtively at the huddle of horrified magazine staff. Someone is bound to notice the resemblance between me and the police's prime suspect, despite our vastly different haircuts and the haziness of the image.

I need to get out of here. I can't go through the main doors. The cops standing near the reception desk will stop me.

Everyone returns to their desks when the news program moves to another story. I pick up a file and go into the photocopy room near the back of the office where the emergency door to the fire escape stairs is located. I turn on the copier and print off a ream of blank pages to cover the sound of me pushing open the fire escape door and shutting it behind me.

I race down the stairs, taking them two at a time, until I'm in a rear alley, trying to decide where to go now that I know I'm wanted for murder.

Chapter Forty-Seven

Two Days Earlier

Bang! Bang! Violent pounding rouses me from a deep sleep. There are three short bursts followed by a long knock that seems to go on for seconds after it's finished. *Baaaaang!!!*

I bolt upright, confused. Instead of my usual view of the flower-box window in the apartment across the street, I'm facing a cracked wall covered with writing.

The banging resumes, louder than before. This time the person knocking rattles a door handle and calls out my name.

I scramble up from the camping mattress. It's on the floor, which explains the ache in my lower back as I rise to my feet, disoriented and confused. Everything about this place is unfamiliar; the mattress, the odor of mildew seeping through the apartment. The newspaper clippings and paranoid writing slapped across the walls.

The apartment reverberates with another bang on the door. This time it's more of an open palm slap than a pounding fist. It sounds as if whoever is on the other side is about to give up.

"Liv. Please. Let me in," pleads a man with a British accent.

I'm wearing a sleeveless tight camisole and bikini underwear. Unsure of where my clothes are, I grab an oversized sweatshirt hanging off the closet handle and charge toward the front door.

"Who are you and what do you want?" I call out.

"Liv." His relief is audible. "I've been so worried about you. Please let me in. It's Ted."

I step toward the peephole. A man in jeans and a brown bomber jacket is on the other side, looking furtively over his shoulder.

"I don't know anyone called Ted." I clutch the collar of the sweatshirt.

"Yes, you do. You don't remember me, Liv, just like you don't remember the apartment where you woke up. There are a lot of things you don't remember. It's too complicated to explain through a door. Let me come in and I'll tell you everything."

I'm about to unlock the bolt when I see a Post-it note taped to the doorframe. It says: DON'T OPEN THE DOOR TO ANYONE!!! Underneath I've written: EXCEPT TED.

I look through the peephole again. He rubs the back of his neck anxiously. Something tells me I can trust this man with rumpled tawny hair and dimples denting his handsome cheeks.

I turn the bolt and let him into the apartment. He comes in and immediately locks the door behind him, looking through the peephole to make sure he wasn't followed.

"Liv, there's not a lot of time to explain," he says. "You're in danger. I've rented an apartment where you can stay until we figure out what to do. Grab some clothes. We need to leave quickly."

I barely hear him as my gaze takes in the dim mustard light of the apartment where I apparently slept last night. The old cracked leather sofa has stuffing coming out of the upholstery and the coffee table is covered with clutter and empty take-out cups of coffee. There are blister packs of medication strewn everywhere. I'm disgusted I spent the night in such a grimy place.

"Where am I? And who are you?" I ask.

The man puts his right hand into his jacket as if he's taking out a weapon. I instinctively flinch, afraid he's going to hurt me. He removes his hand slowly and produces a photo. It's the two of us with our arms around each other, laughing into the camera. I'm showing off a sparkling diamond ring on my finger.

"This was taken the day I proposed to you, Liv."

I'm speechless, transfixed by the expression of bliss on our faces. "Why don't I remember you?"

"It's a long story. I'll tell you everything. But first, I have to get you out of here, Liv."

He goes into the bedroom and pulls clothes off hangers, tossing them into a duffel bag. He throws jeans and a top in my direction and I dress quickly as he packs. Next to the camping mattress is a phone with a cracked screen. I stick it in the back pocket of my jeans and cover it with a long cardigan with big pockets.

He's in the living room, frantically rummaging through the clutter on the coffee table, when I come out of the bedroom, fully dressed in black-heeled ankle boots.

"Your journal, Liv. Where is it?"

"What journal?"

I stare in shock at the living room wall. "What the…"

The wall is covered with photos of Amy and Marco and a garbled mess of newspaper clippings. Arrows point in multiple directions between notes written directly on the wall.

"What is this?"

"I'll explain later. We need to get out of here. You're not safe. I'll come back tomorrow to get your journal and anything else you need."

He unlocks the door and opens it a fraction, sticking his head out to look down the corridor. We hurry down a dingy, airless corridor that smells of damp and greasy cooking fumes. Instead of taking the elevator, we sprint up the emergency stairs to ground level, where we come out into an alley at the rear of the building. I move toward the street, but he blocks my way with his arm.

"Wait." He steps out of the alley to check that the coast is clear.

He takes my arm and escorts me to a silver car parked farther down the street, which he unlocks with a remote-controlled key. He throws the duffel bag in the trunk and tells me to get into the backseat and lie low. He fires up the ignition before he even buckles up.

"Stay down, Liv." He glances back at me. "I'll explain everything at the safe house."

Chapter Forty-Eight

Streetlights cast a warm glow as Jack Lavelle parked his car opposite the Brooklyn building where Liv Reese and Amy Decker used to live.

Lavelle and Halliday leaned back in their car seats and watched the backlit silhouettes of the couple who now lived in the apartment move across the drawn window shades like shadow puppets as they cooked dinner. Below the kitchen windows, the street door to the building was shut and still in the evening gloom.

Liv Reese had arrived at that entrance in the early hours of the morning, firmly believing she still lived there. There was a good chance she'd return again if she fell asleep and woke without any memory of what had transpired over the past two years.

"It's as if she's living the same day over and over again," said Halliday. "She wakes every morning thinking her life is the way it was two years ago, before she was almost murdered."

"I'd feel bad for her if I didn't think she killed Ted Cole," Lavelle commented.

"Despite what Joe Chalmers told us?"

"I thought about it on the drive over," Lavelle said. "We're not investigating the Decker-Reggio murders. We're investigating the Ted Cole murder. We can't ignore that the evidence points to Liv Reese as Cole's killer."

"Maybe it only looks that way because we still know so little," Halliday said. Outside, a bearded hipster carrying a guitar case scrambled into a van that had stopped for him in the narrow car-lined street.

"It more than looks that way," said Lavelle. "Liv Reese's prints were found at the murder scene. The WAKE UP! sign on the window is exactly the type of message she writes to herself, according to the British social worker who taught her to write reminders on her hands as memory aids. Let's not forget the victim was Liv Reese's former fiancé. And he was about to get married."

"Not everyone murders their ex-fiancé just because they're getting married," said Halliday. "I didn't kill mine. In fact, I went to his wedding, danced with him and his bride. I even gave one of the speeches. The groom was blushing more than the bride by the time I was done!"

"You're not erratic, sleep deprived to the point of being psychotic, and your fingerprints aren't all over a murder scene," Lavelle pointed out.

After a tense moment of silence, he turned toward Halliday. "You don't really think that someone else murdered Ted Cole, do you?"

"All I'm saying is this case is like an iceberg. The more we find out, the more I realize that we're only seeing a fraction of what's there," she answered. "I'd like to know a heck of a lot more before I slap cuffs on anyone."

Time dragged on. Lavelle tapped his fingers restlessly on the steering wheel as they watched Liv Reese's old apartment building.

"It's the waiting that kills me," Halliday muttered, stifling a yawn.

"It comes with the job. Along with the two P's."

"What's the two P's?" Halliday asked.

"Patience and persistence."

"It was the same when I was in the military. We'd wait for days, even weeks, for a Taliban cell to break cover. When they did, half the time another unit would get the action, or everything would be over in minutes."

"Sounds like you miss it?"

"We all hated it while we were there. Couldn't wait to get home. We literally counted the days. But once we were home, we all felt a loss. We missed being around each other. I guess we missed the military life as well. I even missed the damn reveille. Imagine missing being woken by a bugle at dawn each morning!" She laughed dryly.

"It must have been tough to return to civilian life."

"Others had it worse."

"Like your friend. The one who died?" Lavelle asked.

"Him among others. Veterans have a suicide rate more than twice that of civilians."

"How did you get yourself on track?"

"I joined the NYPD," answered Halliday, hoping that would end that line of discussion. She was loath to talk about the dark days she'd experienced when she was first discharged. Regret mixed with relief was a potent combination. There was guilt, too, at leaving behind local translators and assets whose lives would always be at risk if the Taliban ever so much as suspected they'd helped the US military.

Halliday had fought hard for one of her informants in particular to be moved stateside. He was Emad, a medical student whose brother was in the Taliban. Emad had risked his life to bring her valuable intel on plans to bomb a humanitarian convoy. Her efforts to get Emad out had come to nothing other than her being ordered to redeploy two weeks ahead of schedule. It had taken a long time for her to come to terms with her abrupt departure from Afghanistan, leaving Emad and others in the lurch without being able to tell them that she'd failed them. For a while, the guilt had eaten into her so deep that it had almost overwhelmed her.

"Being a cop gave me purpose. It's the ones who can't find a purpose that get into trouble."

Halliday quickly changed the subject. "I'll let you in on a secret. I'm a little afraid of you, Jack," she joked. "In fact, I think most of the detectives at the precinct feel the same way."

"You don't strike me as the kind of person who's afraid of anything."

"Okay. Let's say I'm intimidated by you, not afraid," she clarified. "You have the highest solve rate of any detective in the city. You prefer to work alone. You turn down promotions routinely. It's considered a monumental feat to get you to attend Thursday night drinks."

"I signed up to be a homicide detective. Not a pencil pusher with a fancy title, even if they do get more money. As for the rest, I'm picky when it comes to partners. Eventually, the captain gave up and allowed me to work alone."

"You didn't answer my question about drinks night."

"My son sleeps over most Thursday nights. I get little enough time with him as it is." Lavelle turned on the car radio.

They listened in silence as Alicia Keys sang about dreams being made in concrete jungles to the faint orchestra of clattering pots and pans and cutlery scraping against plates drifting down from apartments along the street. Halliday felt a stab of hunger. Dinner, she told herself, would have to wait until later.

"I'm betting Al's not coming back," she said.

"That's the rumor."

"The precinct rumor mill is more accurate than the evening news," Halliday observed. "I'm guessing the captain partnered us up on this case because he wants you to vet me?"

"The captain wants to know how you think, and most importantly how you act under pressure. He also wants to know if you're a team player. Al's a great detective. His will be big shoes to fill."

"What are you going to tell the captain about me?" Halliday asked.

"It's too early to say, although so far I'm impressed."

"Even though we disagree over whether Liv Reese should be our prime suspect in this case?"

"Especially because we disagree," he said. "I prefer to work with people who aren't afraid to speak up. There are too many people who self-censor because they're afraid they'll rile people up or say something that goes against the consensus. I'm not like that. I value open, well-reasoned debate. I think it makes us better detectives."

Farther down the street, a man arriving home from work pushed a garbage can to the curb. Lavelle watched him with rapt attention.

"Look at both sides of the street," he told Halliday. "What does it tell you?"

Halliday looked around. Cans lined the curbs on both sides of the street.

"Tomorrow must be trash day."

"Now ask yourself, what were the two things missing from the Ted Cole murder scene?" Lavelle asked.

"The murder weapon and… Liv Reese."

"Exactly," said Lavelle. "Rosco messaged me while we were heading over here to say the search team still hasn't found the murder weapon near the crime scene. It occurs to me there's a possibility that Liv Reese might have tossed the weapon when she was here early this morning. The garbage cans along this street are going to be collected first thing tomorrow morning. I'd feel a heck of a lot better if I knew what was in them."

"You want to search every can on the street?"

"Not the whole street. But I sure would like to poke about in the trash over there." Lavelle pointed to a row of cans near the entrance to Liv Reese's old building.

He unclipped his seat belt. "Come on, Detective," he said, swinging open his car door. "It'll be fun. This is the glamorous part of detective work they don't show on TV."

Chapter Forty-Nine

Lavelle popped the trunk and removed a package containing disposable overalls, masks, and gloves, as well as a roll of giant extra-thick trash bags in case they needed to transport trash to the precinct to sort through.

"Are you seriously telling me you keep a trash collection kit in your car, just in case?" Halliday asked in amazement. "You must have been a boy scout as a kid."

"If you've ever had to stand in a Dumpster with garbage up to your neck, ruining a brand-new five-hundred-dollar suit, then you'll understand the value of being prepared."

"So you do this a lot?" Halliday asked dryly.

"Garbage is a window to a person's soul. A bit like their internet browsing history, but a whole lot smellier," he said, ripping open the packaging and removing a white plastic set of coveralls. "It's not the first time I've gone through trash and it won't be the last. In fact, I'd say it's an occupational hazard."

He took off his shoes before stepping into the coveralls and pulling them up over his charcoal suit. He put his shoes back on and donned a pair of thick rubber gloves. Halliday was ripping open her plastic pouch to get changed when they both heard high heels tapping purposefully along the street behind them.

A woman in an overcoat with extremely long dark hair was walking nonchalantly toward Liv Reese's building. The woman bore more than a passing resemblance to their suspect.

"It's not her. She's too tall," whispered Halliday, as the woman came closer. The woman took the stairs to the top of the stoop and rifled around in her purse for her keys to open the street door of the building.

"Follow behind her and go inside. Interview the neighbors. Ask if anyone saw anything. Tell them to call nine-one-one if Liv Reese turns up again."

There were fourteen apartments on four floors. Halliday took the stairs down to the basement and worked her way up to each apartment floor by floor.

Only half the people living in the building were home. None recognized the photo she showed them of Liv Reese leaving the crime scene early that morning.

On her way back down the stairs, Halliday stopped at an apartment on the third floor where she'd heard a baby crying earlier. Nobody had answered when she'd knocked on her way up. She knocked again, three loud taps.

A woman carrying a sleeping infant in a baby sling opened the door. She held a spatula in her right hand. Halliday introduced herself and showed the woman the photo of Liv Reese.

"Have you seen this woman around recently?" she asked.

"Not recently," said the woman.

"But you do know her?" Halliday pressed.

"Sure, she lived here with Amy a few years back. Her name's Viv, or Liv. Something like that."

"It's Liv," Halliday said. "You actually knew her?"

"I knew Amy better," said the woman, inviting Halliday into her apartment. She returned to the stove and flipped an omelet she was in the middle of cooking.

"We used to have a block party once a year on the rooftop. Amy and I were on the committee. She was a great gal. Her roommate was more introspective. Don't get me wrong, she seemed nice enough. I never thought it was right, all that stuff people said about her afterward."

"What did people say about her?"

"That she killed Amy and that boyfriend of hers and then pretended she'd been attacked."

"You don't think that's what happened?"

"I never thought she did it."

"Why?" Halliday asked.

"She didn't strike me as a killer."

"Lots of killers don't strike people as killers. Until they kill," Halliday countered.

"Maybe." She shrugged. "But I never thought she did it."

"Have you seen Liv around lately?"

"No," she said. "You're not the first person to ask either."

"What do you mean?"

"I took the baby and Lance for a long walk last week. Lance's our rescue dog." She gestured toward a dog with German shepherd coloring and floppy Labrador ears sleeping in a basket. "When we went out, I noticed a man sitting in a car. He was still there when we got back. I was struggling to get the stroller up the stairs. He got out of the car and carried the stroller up to the top of the stoop. Then he asked me if I'd seen his cousin. He showed me a photo of Liv."

"Are you sure it was her?"

"Absolutely. I recognized her instantly."

"What did you tell him?"

"I said I didn't know who she was."

"Why did you lie?"

"I didn't buy the cousin business."

"You didn't happen to get his plate number? Or remember the model of his car, or the color?" Halliday asked.

The woman closed her eyes as if trying to remember. "I'd like to say it was dark blue. It was a standard four-door sedan, that I remember. Not sure of the make."

"What about the man? Did he give you a name? Do you remember how he looked?"

"I was too busy with the baby and the dog to get a good look at him."

"Would you remember him if you saw him again?"

"I doubt it." She shrugged. "I'm pretty awful with faces."

When Halliday returned to the car, Lavelle was stepping out of the disposable coveralls.

"How did it go?" she asked.

"Better than expected."

He lifted up his trunk. Halliday expected to find it filled with garbage for sorting at the precinct. Instead, lying on the carpeted floor of the trunk were two clear plastic evidence bags. Both were neatly labeled. Lavelle held up the first bag. It contained a white T-shirt stained with blood.

"But that's not all," he said, as if he was a late-night TV salesman. He handed Halliday the second bag. Inside was a stainless steel knife coated in blood.

"The murder weapon?"

"I'd say so. The lab will tell us for sure. It was wrapped in the T-shirt and tossed into the trash. I've asked for a warrant for Liv Reese's arrest."

"Looks like you were right. She did do it after all," said Halliday, opening the passenger door and getting in.

"It's confirmation bias, Darcy," he said, sliding into the driver's seat.

"What do you mean?"

"People naturally look for evidence to support their preconceived views. You thought Liv Reese might not have done it. You were looking for reasons to prove your point."

"Not at all," said Halliday. "I simply hadn't made up my mind yet. Unlike you, Jack."

"I was just following the evidence," he said, turning on the engine. "We're out of here. We'll drop off the knife at forensics. Then we have to head straight to the precinct to put out a wildfire."

"What wildfire?"

Lavelle told Halliday that while she was going door-to-door, Rosco called to tell him the captain had leaked the CCTV footage showing Liv Reese leaving the crime scene.

"He figured that if the media ran the surveillance footage it would speed things up. The footage ran on the evening news.

Now the phones are running off the hook at the precinct. We're getting hundreds of calls with supposed sightings of Liv Reese all over the city. She's like the new Yeti."

"Ninety-nine percent of them will be bogus," Halliday groaned. "We'll spend the next week chasing dead ends."

"That's not the worst of it," said Lavelle. "Liv Reese was at the *Cultura* offices when our people turned up to search Ted Cole's office and question the staff. She must have seen herself in the CCTV footage on the news. She bolted out of there like she was being chased by the devil. Liv Reese is on the run."

Chapter Fifty

Escalators go up and down in endless loops as I join the back of a line at the Amtrak ticket office at Penn Station. It's impossible to hear myself think over the noisy announcements on the sound system.

I find myself weighing the pros and cons of each route. Deciding which train I'll take feels like the most important decision of my life now that I know I'm a fugitive.

I killed a man last night. At least that's what the police think. Not without reason, I might add. Millions of people will have seen the same news report showing CCTV footage of me fleeing the scene of Ted Cole's murder. It's only a matter of time until someone realizes that woman is me and alerts the cops.

I overheard enough whispered conversations during my visit to the *Cultura* offices to collect scraps of information on Ted Cole. I gather he worked at *Cultura*'s sister magazine in London before he was transferred to New York earlier in the year to lead the commercial team.

The redheaded woman in the tartan skirt at the office said that I was once engaged to marry him.

I can hardly believe that I was in love with a man I can't remember. Ted Cole is as unfamiliar to me as the random stranger standing in front of me in the Amtrak ticket line.

--

"I'd like an economy seat on tonight's train to Miami," I say when I reach the front of the line.

I pay with cash. I have no idea why I'm carrying so much cash, but I guess I'm lucky I have it. Without this money, I'd be destitute. My phone and wallet are missing, but it doesn't seem to matter much now that I'm on the run.

"The train leaves in an hour and fifteen," the man says, printing my ticket and pushing it toward me. "We recommend you head over to the platform at least forty-five minutes before the train is due to roll in."

Ticket in hand, I pause as Ted Cole's pixelated face flashes on a giant screen hanging on a pillar in the concourse. I take a moment to watch the news break flashing on the screen. Until a few hours ago, I didn't know Ted existed, let alone that we were once in love. A deep sadness washes over me as I stare at his crinkling eyes. Mom always told me to marry a man who smiles with his eyes.

A high-pitched squeak breaks into my thoughts. A cleaner in a blue coverall stops his cleaning cart to empty a trash bag and replace it. He works quickly with a practiced air, like he's been doing this all his life.

The nightly ritual of the station winding down for the night provides a mundane normalcy to this otherwise surreal day. I'm still coming to grips with everything that has happened since I woke on the subway train this afternoon.

I stifle an exhausted yawn. Dr. Brenner told me I forget things whenever I go to sleep. I can't allow myself to sleep no matter how tired I feel right now.

Since I have nothing else to do, I head to the assigned platform for my train, where I lean against a vending machine and watch a procession of people feed coins into a slot to select snacks. I distract myself trying to guess what snack each person will choose.

After a while, a woman gets up from a bench and I take her seat. An announcement tells us the Miami train is running ten minutes behind schedule. Everyone groans.

My body feels drained and my eyes are heavy. I force myself to stay alert by focusing on the rhythm of a train departing on a platform somewhere behind me. The clatter as it builds up speed morphs into a chant: *Stay Awake. Stay Awake. Stay Awake. Stay Awake.* I repeat it to myself as I stare at the tracks, waiting for my train to pull in.

The train tracks hypnotize me with their perfect symmetry. Exhaustion overwhelms me. My eyes close and I drift off.

A loud voice startles me awake.

"Excuse me, ma'am."

I snap open my eyes and stare into the concerned face of a train conductor leaning toward me.

"Ma'am, this platform is closed."

"Platform? Closed?"

I look down in confusion. I'm clutching a train ticket to Miami.

The conductor peers at the ticket. "Ma'am, the Miami train left a half hour ago. You slept through it."

I look at him blankly. I have no idea why I'd be taking a train to Miami. I close my eyes again, convinced I must be dreaming.

"Ma'am, I have to ask you to leave."

I flinch at his booming voice and immediately snap open my eyes again. I'm not dreaming. It's late at night and I'm on an empty train platform. I don't have the faintest idea how I got here. The last thing I remember is answering the phone at my desk in the office. It was daytime then.

"Did I black out or something?"

"You missed your train. You must have fallen asleep. The next train to Miami doesn't leave until morning. You'll have to find somewhere to stay for the night."

"Somewhere to stay... for the night?"

"Yes, ma'am. You can't stay here. We're closing the platform. You have to leave."

I stumble to my feet and take the escalator up to the concourse. I'm so woozy and confused that it feels as if the ground under my feet is turning to quicksand as I walk. Nothing makes sense. I'm about to head to the subway to go home to my apartment in Brooklyn when I notice writing covering my hands and arms. It looks as if I've been vandalized while I slept.

Letters written under each knuckle spell out the words STAY AWAKE. Another message says: DON'T SLEEP! I FORGET EVERYTHING WHEN I FALL ASLEEP. A phone number under the words CALL FOR HELP is circled on my palm. It feels like a lifeline.

Near the escalators is a public phone. I feed coins from my pockets into the slot and dial the number written on my palm.

"Hello?"

"Liv! Where are you?" I strain to hear the muffled voice as a round of train departure announcements blare.

"I'm at Penn Station. I don't know what's going on." My voice rises in panic.

"Did you just wake up?" he asks, his voice barely audible under the deafening loudspeaker announcements.

"Yes. I must have fallen asleep waiting for a train." I yawn. The train station loudspeaker reverberates through my head. I shouldn't be here. "I need to go home."

"Liv, you can't go home. You're in danger."

"What danger?"

"It's a long story. I'll explain when I see you. Meet me at a bar called Nocturnal."

Chapter Fifty-One

Two Days Earlier

Ted swings open the front door and stands back to let me into the apartment. It's a modern one-bedroom with the sterile atmosphere of a hotel. It has an open-plan kitchen with stainless steel appliances and a white stone counter. The bedroom is furnished in blue-grays. There are satin sheets on the mattress and a sliding-door closet.

"Liv, I can't stress enough that you can't go out and you can't contact anyone. Do you understand?" Ted's tone is deadly serious as he locks and bolts the front door. "It's for your own protection. Nobody knows you're here. We have to keep it that way."

"Sure." I say it with conviction so he'll believe me. The cell phone that I slipped into my rear pocket presses into my flesh. It's my escape plan if I decide I don't trust him after all.

Ted opens the fridge and tells me to help myself to anything I need. He has filled the shelves with salads, yogurts, and fresh fruit. "You've been living off coffee for too long," he says, pouring orange juice into tall glasses and tossing in ice cubes.

He picks up our glasses and moves them to a coffee table in the living area. I curl up in the corner of a gray L-shaped leather sofa, sipping my drink while he paces nervously.

"Now would be a good time to tell me what's going on," I suggest.

He runs a hand through his tawny hair as if bracing himself for a difficult conversation. "I'll start at the beginning. Two years ago, Amy and Marco were murdered."

"You're lying." Nausea rises in my throat until rage takes over. "Actually, I'm not listening to this."

I get up and storm past him to the front door. It's locked. I turn around to demand he unlock the door when I see the headline of the newspaper clipping he's holding up in the air to show me. I snatch the newspaper from his hand and read in silent horror. The article says Amy and Marco were killed in a double homicide.

"This article says a third person was taken to the hospital with critical injuries. Who was it?" I ask quietly, still holding onto the clipping.

"It was you, Liv. You're lucky to be alive. There's a scar on your torso from the stab wound."

I lift up my top and am confronted by a jagged scar under my rib cage. Seeing the scar drives home the truth of what I've just read. Amy and Marco really are dead. I lower myself back onto the sofa, my body trembling with shock.

Ted sits next to me. He leans my head against his chest and puts his arms around me. His warm comforting embrace tugs at my heart. I feel as if I've come home.

"I'm so sorry, Liv. I hate having to tell you the same terrible news over and over again," he murmurs. "Each time it devastates you as if it's the first time you've heard it."

"Who killed them?"

"Nobody knows."

"I was there. I must have seen something?"

"You were almost killed yourself. When you woke from the coma, you didn't remember anything about the murder," he says. "Over time, snippets of images would flash in your head. You thought they were memories from the murder, but you were never sure."

Ted recounts how I once described a flashback of looking up from the floor and seeing Amy's pink kimono hanging on her bedroom door hook. Another time I woke in the middle of the night and immediately sketched a dotted medallion pattern that flashed in my head. I'd insisted that I'd seen it when I was stabbed.

"One time you had a memory of shoes covered in blood walking away from you. When you looked into it, you found out there were no bloody footprints at the scene. You must have imagined it," Ted tells me. "You also remembered a voice urging you to 'stay awake' and a siren in the background. Although those recollections came to you after you insisted on listening to a recording of the nine-one-one call in the hope that it would jog your memory."

Later, I think about the flashbacks Ted described as I hang my clothes in the closet in the bedroom and arrange my toiletries in a bathroom cupboard.

My last memory before waking this morning was answering my office phone. "This is Liv," I'd said into the receiver.

After that I remember nothing until Ted's pounding on the front door woke me this morning at that dingy basement apartment. I don't remember Amy and Marco's murders. I don't remember being stabbed, or being in the hospital. I don't remember Ted, or our engagement. Or any flashbacks of the murder. My life over the past two years is a blank.

"How did we meet?" I ask Ted later, sitting on a kitchen barstool as I watch him make sandwiches for lunch.

"We met when you moved to London," he says, cutting in half my lox and cream cheese bagel.

"I lived in London?"

"After Amy and Marco were killed, you moved to London and freelanced at *Cultura UK*. That's where I worked. We fell in love and got engaged."

I look at my hands. No rings. "Where's my engagement ring?"

"It didn't work out," he says, handing me a plate.

"Why? What happened to us?"

"I was offered a big promotion. It involved relocating to New York. You flatly refused to move back here. You were afraid the killer might come after you since you were the only witness. We tried to keep things going, but it gradually fizzled out," he says, pausing as if deliberating how much more to tell me. "To be fair, things weren't great before then."

"In what way?" I toy with my sandwich. My appetite has disappeared.

"You were consumed with finding out who killed Amy and Marco. It took over your life. You blamed yourself because you knew the killer was still free, and you believed that if you could only remember who it was, then the cops would arrest him, or her," he says.

"That's why we broke up?"

He lifts up my chin and looks deeply into my eyes. "I wanted to make a life with you, Liv. Get married. Have a family. You kept delaying it."

"Why?

"Your obsession with the past. Constantly trying to piece together what happened. Listening to the nine-one-one recording over and over again. Papering the walls of our flat with newspaper clippings. Amy and Marco's murders were all you ever talked about. It consumed you. Ultimately it consumed our relationship. It destroyed us."

He reaches for my hand and squeezes it gently. "Marco cheated on you, Liv. With your best friend. They betrayed you, and yet you couldn't let go. You blamed yourself for their deaths. You kept letting the past come between us." His voice is laced with raw pain. "You never gave us a chance."

"I wish I could go back and change things," I say, my eyes wet. "I feel like you and I could have been happy together."

"Yes," he says, shaking his head as if to break a spell. "It's too late now to turn back the clock. But it's not too late to help you. Something happened to you after we broke up, which has caused you to lose your memory. You never had any memory problems when we were together in London, but now you forget things on a daily basis. It makes you vulnerable, and it puts you in danger. That's why I arranged for you to see a doctor who specializes in amnesia. I want to help you get your life back on track."

He releases my hand. It makes me feel lost and alone, a reminder that whatever we had together is gone.

He notices that I've only taken a single bite of the bagel sandwich. "Eat up, Liv. You need to take care of yourself. Proper nutrition, and sleep. Lots of sleep."

He watches with grim satisfaction as I eat. "For as long as I've known you, you've suffered from severe insomnia. It gave you wild mood swings and made you paranoid and fatigued. Dr. Brenner says the insomnia may be a cause of your memory problems. That's why I want to make sure you get back into a healthy routine."

"Why are you helping me, Ted? If we've broken up?" I ask later, as we wash the dishes.

"Because I still care about you. I worry about you, Liv," he says, handing me a plate to dry with a dish towel.

He tells me that when he tracked me down at the basement apartment a couple of weeks ago, he saw that I'd put up all sorts of information about Amy and Marco's murders on the walls. Apparently when we were together in London, I kept files and drew diagrams on the wall where I listed leads and unanswered questions. In the past, he'd resented it. When he saw I was still doing it, he was more sympathetic.

"God knows how you'd come that far with your investigation, let alone managed to get from London to New York and rent an apartment all by yourself with your memory issues," he says. "It made me realize that finding out what happened to Amy and Marco might be a compulsion because deep down you *want* closure. You *want* to move on with your life. So I helped you with your investigation." He rubs the back of his neck. "Helping you turned out to be a mistake."

"Why?"

"We poked at a hornets' nest," he says. "That's why you're here."

"I don't understand."

"I asked the night doorman at your apartment building to keep an eye on you. He called me early this morning because he saw someone following you home in the middle of the night, and then hovering around on the street. I'm worried that my inquiries into Amy and Marco's murders might have alerted their killer that you're back. That's why I moved you here. To keep you safe."

Ted hands me another wet plate to wipe and checks the peephole in the front door. His nervousness astonishes me. He truly believes I'm in danger. I wonder how all the things he described could have happened without me remembering any of it.

"It feels as if I've woken from a deep sleep and the world has changed, except for me," I say sadly. "How long do I have to stay here for, Ted?"

"A few days. You saw Dr. Brenner almost two weeks ago. He's the medical expert I arranged for you to see. I took you to get scans at the hospital the other day. We have an appointment with Brenner tomorrow to get the results and a treatment plan. It's all written in your journal."

"My what?"

"You have a journal. We left it behind at your old apartment, along with your purse, in our rush to leave," he says. "I'll get it all tomorrow. You write everything that happens to you in your journal. It's become a proxy for your missing memory. It allows you to function somewhat normally, which is probably how you were able to get to New York from London. You write the key events of the day as they happen."

He hands me a piece of paper and a pen and suggests I write everything he's told me in longhand so I can add it to my journal when he brings it back tomorrow. "It's important you have a written history of what we've discussed in your own handwriting in case you fall asleep and wake in a panic."

He hands me a roll of cash that he said he found amid the clutter on the coffee table when he came to get me this morning. I put it in my jeans pocket. He makes me write his cell phone number on both palms so I'll notice it.

"In case of an emergency," he says.

Later, I'm staring at my long hair in the bathroom, wondering whether I should ask Ted to book me a haircut with my stylist, Stevie, when I hear a hushed phone conversation in the kitchen. He's talking to a woman.

From his side of the conversation, I can tell she's upset he's here with me. He placates her by promising to come over soon. I feel a twinge of jealousy.

"Liv, I need to go out for a while," he tells me. "Lock the door behind me."

Next to the door are Post-it notes with instructions like DON'T OPEN THE DOOR and DON'T TALK TO STRANGERS. He made me write the notes after I wrote the journal entry. He said it's better if the warning notes are in my own writing as I'll be more likely to obey the instructions.

I look through the peephole as I bolt the door shut. He hovers near the door until he hears the final click of the lock, then turns toward the elevator.

Picking up the remote control, I turn on the television and lie on the sofa. I drift off to the canned applause of a game show.

I'm woken by a phone ringing. I open my eyes to discover that I'm lying curled up on a sofa in a dark apartment that I don't recognize, looking out at a nighttime view I've never seen before.

Fluorescent lights blink at me from the living room windows as the phone rings. Through my dazed confusion, I gradually realize the ringing is coming from a phone in my back pocket.

"Hello?"

"Liv?" The voice is almost drowned out by the raucous noise of a bar in the background.

"Yes?"

"Amy needs your help."

"Where is she?"

"She's at a bar called Nocturnal. Write down the address."

There's no paper, so I write it on the back of my hand.

Chapter Fifty-Two

Halliday and Lavelle walked into a deafening hive of activity at the precinct. Half a dozen cops sat at a row of desks that had been pushed together to form a long line across the back wall of the Detective Bureau.

They'd been rounded up to take calls from the general public. The phones had been running hot ever since the security camera footage had been broadcast on the nightly news. That, along with the message written in the victim's blood on the window, had turned the murder into the biggest story on a slow news day.

Halliday slipped off her jacket and checked the messages on her desk. A thick package of crime scene photos had been sent by special delivery along with an initial report on the forensics that had already been processed. She gave it a cursory inspection. There wasn't anything there that she didn't already know.

Someone turned up the volume of the television on the wall. Halliday looked up, curious to see what the media was reporting.

"Police are looking for a woman who they suspect may have killed a British magazine executive during a romantic tryst," the anchor's voice blasted across the office. "The murderer is believed to have used the victim's own blood to write a chilling message on a window. Police have not yet released the name of the suspect. Our sources tell us that she may be the former fiancée of the murdered businessman, Ted Cole, who was stabbed to death last night...."

Lavelle muted the television and turned to the staff manning the hotline. "Any leads?"

"We have one guy who thinks the suspect is his long-lost sister who was abducted by aliens forty-nine years ago and kept in a cryogenic freezer on a spaceship," said one of the officers. "He says that's why her hair is so long."

"I just finished with a caller who's convinced the woman is a vampire. He claims to be a vampire slayer. He's offering his services at a discount."

"What's his rate?" asked Lavelle.

"Twenty bucks an hour. Plus tax," said the officer, shaking his head with disbelief.

"That is the going rate," said Lavelle dryly. "Did we get any tips that are actually worth chasing?"

"A hairdresser called earlier." A uniformed officer leaned back in his chair and handed a note to Halliday. "She said a woman with long hair arrived this morning without an appointment. The woman insisted on having her hair cut very short."

Halliday looked at the note. The hairdresser worked at a salon near the *Cultura* offices. Halliday called the hairdresser from her desk.

"She had very long dark hair down to her waist just like in the picture on the news," said the hairdresser, once Halliday had gone through the preliminaries. "Her behavior was weird, like she was zoned out. I thought she was drugged or on sedatives."

"What did she talk about while you were cutting her hair?"

"Nothing," said the hairdresser. "She daydreamed, mostly. When she came to the cash register to settle her bill, she panicked like she didn't know how she was going to pay. Then she patted down her clothes and found a big wad of cash in her jeans pocket. I mean a *huge* wad of cash. At least a thousand dollars. Probably more."

"Did she say or do anything else that seemed odd?"

"She had writing all over the back of her hands. Weird stuff. I remember seeing the words STAY AWAKE written on her knuckles. It reminded me of the WAKE UP! sign I saw on the news. That's why I called the hotline."

Based on the hairdresser's description, Halliday was sure the woman in question was Liv Reese. By the time she was done talking to the hairdresser, Lavelle was on the phone taking another tip.

"Who was that?" Halliday asked Lavelle as she passed his desk after he hung up.

"It was Liv Reese's doctor. His name is Brenner," he answered. "He said she turned up hours late for her appointment this afternoon."

"That's not exactly a crime," Halliday said.

"Ted Cole was supposed to have come *with her* to the appointment," said Lavelle. "Dr. Brenner was shocked when he saw on the news that Ted Cole had been murdered. He immediately called us."

"How does he know that Ted Cole was supposed to have accompanied her?"

"Because Cole set it up. He contacted Brenner through a mutual friend a couple of weeks ago to beg him to help an ex-girlfriend who was suffering from memory loss," Lavelle told her. "Ted Cole brought Liv Reese to Brenner for an initial appointment, and took her to the hospital to get brain scans. He was supposed to be there with her today to get the results."

"What kind of doctor is Brenner?"

"He's a neurologist. Apparently, he's a world leader at helping amnesiacs get their memories back," said Lavelle. "He said Liv Reese was very upset after her appointment this afternoon. He said she's likely very confused and disoriented. He thinks there's a good chance she'll reach out to a friend for help the next time she wakes without any memory."

"I'll go through the Decker-Reggio murder files and put together a list of people she might contact," Halliday offered.

"Good. By the way, the captain wants us to brief him as soon as he gets in."

The captain's interest in the case was at a fever pitch. It had risen over the course of the day along with the storm of media coverage.

Halliday went back to her desk to go through the files. The ringing of the hotline phones was so loud that eventually she took the document box to a vacant interview room so she could concentrate.

She spread the contents of the files in small piles along the table and wrote key names on the whiteboard. Halliday's phone rang while she was adding another name to the list.

"Detective Halliday," she said.

"It's Gene Tawalski here, from Eastern Island Cabs. We got a request to go over our GPS data. Turns out we had a car on the street in question a few minutes after three this morning. I just got off the phone with the driver. He picked up a woman."

"Did he describe her?"

"Long hair. He told me that she was out of it, but not in an addict-on-a-high sort of way. He said that she reminded him of his mom who has Alzheimer's. The woman was confused. She couldn't decide where she wanted to go. Halfway into the ride, she changed her mind. Asked to be dropped somewhere else."

"Where did he drop her off?"

"At a bar. It's called Nocturnal."

Chapter Fifty-Three

Laughter spills onto the street as the glass doors of Nocturnal are pushed open. A man and a woman step unsteadily onto the sidewalk, their arms drunkenly entangled. Their voices are decibels too loud for the hushed street. I slip past them into the riotous roar of the crowded bar.

I squeeze past a table of men in dress shirts and loosened ties as they raise their glasses and toss down their drinks in unison. The thud of empty glasses slamming onto a table hits me like an aftershock. I head toward the bar where I was instructed to wait.

"Hey, honey. I like your new look." The warm drunken voice in my ear is quickly followed by a hand snaking around my waist, pulling me in. "Come here." A ruddy-faced man leans in to kiss me with foul whiskey breath. Instead he kisses air as I evade his grasp and disappear into the crowd.

Hoots of laughter and shouted conversations assault me as I push through a tight crush of people. I'm hit by an eerie sense of déjà vu when I glimpse my flushed face in a triple paneled mirror behind the bar. It's as if I'm looking at an alternate version of myself in a parallel universe.

A bartender with dark hair and a goatee pours drinks from a beer tap nozzle. His shirt sleeves are pushed to his elbows, displaying a tattoo on his forearm.

I slide onto an empty barstool near the black-painted window facing the street. Looking into the mirror, I check to see if anyone is beelining toward me through the sea of drinkers. So far nobody seems to have noticed me, except the bartender.

He looks up and winks as he pours tequila into shot glasses, barely spilling a drop before adding a plate of lime wedges and crushed salt to the tray. A waitress picks up the tray and takes it to the table of businessmen.

"You're looking great tonight, Liv," the bartender says. "What can I get you?"

"I don't suppose you serve coffee!" I stifle a yawn, certain I must have imagined the bartender saying my name. "I need something to wake me up."

"How about an espresso martini?"

"Is it any good?"

"It must be. You drink a couple of them a night."

I'm about to tell him that's not possible, since I've never been here before, when he turns around and takes a bottle of vodka off a shelf. He pours a generous amount into a cocktail shaker before adding vermouth and other ingredients I can't identify in the murky light.

I stare into the swirling colors reflected on the stainless steel of the cocktail maker as he shakes it and pours the icy mixture into a frosted martini glass. He tosses on a couple of roasted coffee beans as decoration before sliding the glass across the bar to me.

"I know this is a weird question," I say, after paying him and taking a tentative sip. "I wanted to ask you if…"

"You've been here before?"

"How did you know I was going to ask you that?"

"Because every time you come here, you ask me the same question."

"I don't remember ever coming here before."

"That's because you have a problem with your memory." He gestures toward the writing on the backs of my hands. "That's why you write reminders on your hands."

The bartender abandons me midsentence to serve a customer farther along the bar. My eyes dart toward a large-screen television broadcasting the news.

When he's back, the bartender takes something from a drawer under the bar and hands it to me. It's a cell phone with a cracked screen.

"Why are you giving this to me?"

"It's your phone. Someone found it last night and handed it in to the cloakroom attendant. It eventually found its way to me."

"This phone isn't mine." I hold out the phone so he can take it back. "I've never seen it before in my life."

"Trust me, Liv. It's your phone. You just don't remember," the bartender says, making no effort to take it.

A silver-haired man gestures to the bartender that he wants a drink. "Turn it on. You'll see it's your phone. You use your thumbprint to unlock it instead of a code," the bartender says, moving away to pour the man a single malt.

I fiddle with the phone button to turn it on. As I do, my eyes catch sight of the TV again. A grainy photo of a woman is on the screen. I blink, certain I imagined it. When I look again, I know it's real. The woman on the TV screen is me.

Chapter Fifty-Four

I stare in astonishment at my face plastered on the evening news. "Police searching for woman suspected of murdering magazine executive," says a graphic below my photo.

I'm convincing myself the vodka must have been spiked to induce this hallucination when I glance in the mirror behind the bar and see the reflection of a patrol cop pushing open the art deco glass doors at the entrance. My stomach free-falls as more cops enter.

"Is there a nearby exit?" I ask the bartender, who has just finished serving his customer. I fan my hand in front of my face as if I'm about to faint. "I'm feeling claustrophobic. I need fresh air."

"I'll let you out through the back. Come with me."

I slip off the barstool and join the bartender at a STAFF ONLY door at the end of the timber counter. He pushes open the door with his shoulder and we enter a narrow dimly-lit corridor. It's much quieter than the bar, but I can still feel the vibrations of the music. The bartender unlocks a storeroom with a key from his pocket. He swings the door open to a small windowless room filled with supply boxes.

The door slams shut behind us after we enter. I swallow nervously as I realize that I'm trapped in here with him. The bartender rummages around in a metal locker, seemingly unaware of my sudden trepidation. He turns and throws something in my direction. I catch it in midair. It's a black leather jacket infused with men's aftershave.

"It's freezing outside. Put it on. You can give it back to me some other time," he tells me.

He unlocks another door, which he pushes wide open, letting in a cold draft of air. I step out into the night chill, shoving my hands in the pockets of the borrowed jacket to stay warm as he closes the door behind me.

Parked near the rear door is a white van with a navy Nocturnal logo on its side. I walk past the van and come out onto a street around the block from the bar. Curious to see what's happening with the police, I backtrack to the entrance.

Three police squad cars are parked on the curb; their siren lights rotate. I merge into a crowd of drinkers who are talking loudly on the sidewalk, speculating about why the police are there. The prevailing theory appears to be a drug bust.

"What's going on?" I ask someone who's just finished talking to a cop near the entrance.

"The police are looking for a murder suspect." He shoves a flyer at me. "Take it. I don't need it."

I read the notice as I shuffle through the crowd of bar patrons spilling across the sidewalk. It contains the same grainy photo I saw on the TV of a woman who looks just like me. It's impossible to read the writing under the photo until I'm near a streetlight.

"Police are asking the public to call the hotline number below if they have any information on the whereabouts of the woman in the photograph. Her name is Liv Reese. Her height is five foot six and she is described as…"

Electricity crackles inside my head. It goes faster and faster, mimicking my racing heartbeat. The police really are looking for me in connection to a murder.

It's ludicrous to think that I'd kill anyone. On the other hand, I know that I blacked out for a period of time because I have no recollection of anything that happened between the time I answered a phone call at my office on a sunny summer's day and the moment I woke on the Amtrak platform clutching a train ticket to Miami. There's obviously a missing gap of time that I can't account for. And if there's a missing gap of time then how can I be certain of anything?

I slip into the doorway of a Korean restaurant and scan my thumbprint on the cell phone the bartender gave me earlier. The phone unlocks. A series of voicemails and text message alerts immediately pops up on the screen.

They're from someone called Ted. I don't know anyone by that name. But when I listen to the first voicemail, it's apparent that Ted knows me.

"Liv, it's Ted. Where are you? You were supposed to stay in the apartment."

"Liv, it's Ted again. Please call me. It's urgent." He recites a cell phone number.

His messages get increasingly frantic.

Liv. I'm heading back to the apartment to see if you're there, reads one of his texts.

In the last voice message, he sounds almost resigned. "Liv, it's Ted. I'm guessing you fell asleep and don't remember me. You're probably asking yourself why some guy called Ted is calling you. Please check your emails. It will explain who I am and why you urgently need to call me. You are in danger, Liv. Read the email. Do it now and then call me!"

I follow his instructions and tap the email icon. The top message in my inbox is an email from Ted containing a photo of a journal entry written in my own handwriting.

A man called Ted woke me this morning. He pounded on the door of a basement apartment where I was sleeping on a camping mattress on the floor. I didn't know why I was in that apartment. I also didn't know who Ted was, even though he claimed to know me. It felt as if I'd woken to discover that I was living someone else's life.

Ted explained that I'm suffering from memory problems. I forget everything going back almost two and a half years, when Amy and Marco were murdered.

Yes, they were murdered.

I didn't believe it until Ted showed me a news article. He's since shown me other articles explaining what happened in horrifying detail. One article was illustrated with a photo of me on a stretcher with an oxygen mask over my face as paramedics lifted me into an ambulance. The article said I was taken to the hospital with life-threatening injuries. There's a scar on my torso from where I was stabbed. Ted says I've never remembered what happened because I was in a coma afterward. Once I recovered, I moved to London where we met and fell in love.

Things didn't work out. Ted moved to New York for work. I stayed behind. Apparently I was fine for a while, going about my life without any memory problems, although Ted says the underlying trauma of the murder left me with insomnia, and what he calls an unhealthy obsession with finding out what happened the day Amy and Marco were killed.

Sometime over the past few weeks, I began having memory problems. Ted only found out a couple of weeks ago when I turned up at a function out of the blue without remembering him. He said he's since taken me to a specialist who believes that my memory resets every time I wake up, taking me back to the day of the murder.

That's why I didn't recognize Ted this morning. That's why I didn't recognize the basement apartment where I was sleeping, even though I've apparently lived there for several weeks after renting it when I left London. That's why everything Ted tells me about the past two years feels as if it's happened to someone else.

Ted's moved me to this apartment to keep me safe. He made me write warnings on Post-it notes that he stuck next to the front door. They're to remind me not to go out. Ted's worried that Amy and Marco's murderer may come for me.

The letter goes on to explain the intricacies of my condition, Ted's and my rocky relationship, and the reasons for our breakup.

If the journal entry hadn't been written in my own handwriting, I wouldn't have believed a word of it.

I look up from my phone. Several cops are standing in a huddle by a patrol car down the street near the bar. I consider approaching them and telling them that I'm the woman they're looking for.

I take a step forward and then withdraw back into the shadowed doorway of the restaurant. I can't bring myself to do it. A crowd of bar-goers take videos of each other while they wait to be allowed back into Nocturnal. The last thing I want is to be handcuffed and shunted into a police car while dozens of people post videos of my arrest on social media. The public humiliation would be excruciating.

I do the next best thing. I dial the number of the police hotline printed on the flyer that I'm holding.

Chapter Fifty-Five

The siren lights from the patrol cars parked outside Nocturnal shone through the stippled glass, casting a purple haze across the sea of revelers as Darcy Halliday and Jack Lavelle pushed open the doors and entered the loud and stifling bar.

"She's changed her hairstyle." Halliday shouted to be heard over the explosion of noise as she spoke to a cop standing near a velvet rope inside the entrance.

"What do you mean?"

"We're not looking for a female suspect with long dark hair anymore. The photo on this notice and in the media is out of date. She cut her hair. We're looking for a woman with short hair. Tell your people."

Lavelle and Halliday split up. They moved through the crowds, showing patrons a digitally enhanced photo of what Liv Reese would look like with short hair.

"Have you seen this woman?" Halliday showed the photograph on her phone screen to a waitress clearing empty beer bottles from a ledge.

"Sure. She comes here a lot," the waitress yelled back.

"Has she been here tonight?"

"Beats me. Ask Harry. She always gravitates to his end of the bar. We think she has a crush on him."

Halliday waded into a tight knot of drinkers to get to the bar. "Watch it," she said when she was jostled by a drunk man passing her.

A bartender with a nose ring told her that Harry had gone to the storage room and would be back shortly. While she waited, Halliday talked to a few customers hunching over their drinks. They all shook their heads when she showed them the updated photograph of Liv Reese. Some of them appeared so drunk that Halliday doubted whether they'd have recognized photos of their own grandmothers.

A bartender with sleeves rolled up to his elbows came out of a STAFF ONLY door, carrying a cardboard box of chilled juices. He squatted down and packed the bottles into a fridge under the bar.

"What can I get you?" he asked Halliday when he stood up.

She held up her detective's shield and her phone with the photo of Liv Reese. "We're looking for this woman."

"Yeah, I know her. What do you want with her?"

"She's suspected of murder."

The bartender's head snapped up. "Liv? No way. She wouldn't hurt a fly. Sure, she has issues. She comes in here every night like it's the first time she's ever seen the place. I don't know how many times I've had the same conversation with her. But murder. Man, that's nuts."

"Ever seen her here with this guy?" Halliday swiped her phone to a photograph of Ted Cole.

"Sure. Liv was here with him a couple of nights ago. Nice guy. British. We had a long talk."

"About what?"

"Liv, of course."

"What about Liv?"

"He was worried people could take advantage of her because of her memory issues. Exploit her or lure her away. He said it would be like taking candy from a baby." He poured a whiskey sour and slid the glass over to a customer.

"When was she last here?" Halliday asked, gesturing to Lavelle to come over.

"She left a few minutes ago," said the bartender. "She was feeling claustrophobic and asked me to let her out through the back."

"So she's gone?"

Halliday looked at Lavelle incredulously as he joined her at the bar.

"Yeah," the bartender admitted.

"Any idea where she went?" Halliday asked.

"Maybe she went back to her apartment. She lives near here."

"Do you know where?"

His shrug was her answer. "There's a bodega across the street. Liv's a regular there. The delivery guy sometimes walks her home when she gets disoriented. They might know where you can find her."

Lavelle handed the bartender his card. "If you remember anything else, call us." He and Halliday turned to leave.

"Hang on," the bartender called out. He scrambled around in his wallet, searching for something. After a moment, he took out a business card and handed it victoriously to Halliday.

"Liv's friend Ted gave it to me," he said. "He'll help you find her."

"Thanks," said Halliday, looking down at Ted Cole's name and contact number embossed on the glossy *Cultura Magazine* business card. "Unfortunately, it's not much use to us."

"Why not?" asked the bartender, wiping a spill on the bar.

"Because Ted's the man who was killed overnight. Liv Reese is wanted for his murder."

Chapter Fifty-Six

I move deeper into the doorway as my call to the police hotline is answered.

"I'm calling with information on Liv Reese," I whisper nervously.

"Go ahead. What information do you have?" a man asks.

"I know where she is."

"How do you know where she is?" From his skeptical tone, he thinks I'm a crank caller.

"Because I *am* Liv Reese."

Silence follows as he digests my comment. "I'll transfer you to someone. Stay right there."

Hold music blasts for a few seconds. It cuts out when a woman's voice comes on the line. "This is Detective Halliday." It's hard to hear her over the background noise.

"My name is Liv Reese. I think you're looking for me."

"Liv?" she says after a pregnant pause. "We've been so worried about you." She sounds like she cares. My eyes prick with tears. "Are you okay?"

"I'm not sure. I don't remember things. Lots of things. It's very confusing."

"You must be feeling very alone."

"I am." My mouth trembles, this time from emotion more than the cold. "I saw on the TV that the police are looking for me. Why?"

"It's hard to explain on the phone. It's better if we talk in person."

I can see the entrance to Nocturnal clearly from the doorway of the Korean restaurant. Near the patrol cars, a slim woman with shoulder-length hair talks on the phone amid a huddle of police She's dressed in a dark suit with a teal shirt. I'm certain that she's Detective Halliday.

"Where are you, Liv?"

"I'm near a bar called Nocturnal," I say, watching closely for a reaction from the woman on the phone to confirm my suspicion.

The woman taps the shoulder of a man in a charcoal suit and gestures to him. Within seconds, there's a flurry of activity. Police spread out along the street. I enter the Korean restaurant in a panic and wait behind a bamboo partition near the cash register, pretending to study a take-out menu. I feel sick to my stomach with fear. I should hang up, but I stay on the line.

"There are a lot of police out here tonight," I comment.

"They're looking for you. Liv, tell me where you are. I'll come to you," Detective Halliday says. "We'll talk. Just the two of us."

"I need to think."

I'm about to hang up when she calls out urgently. "Liv, take down my personal phone number. Call me directly."

She dictates a cell phone number. I write it on the top of a take-out menu and stuff it in my jeans pocket.

"Liv, are you still there?"

I can tell that she's trying to keep me on the phone. Through the gaps in the bamboo partition, I see cops jogging along the street, looking for me. I hang up without saying anything.

A waitress comes out of the swinging doors of the kitchen to the front counter where I'm standing.

"Are you here to collect a take-out order?" she asks.

"No, I'm here to eat in."

The waitress escorts me to a row of empty tables. I opt for a table behind a rowdy party of twelve celebrating a birthday.

I sit there, hunched over a bowl of beef short rib soup, as I go through more messages on my phone.

I pay special attention to a voicemail and a text message that Ted sent me along with an attached photo of a sketch of a lily drawn out of tiny dots. In an accompanying message, Ted explains it's a fleur-de-lis, a symbol of French royalty, and a favorite of designers.

Ted says I drew the dotted picture after waking up one night when we were still together in London. I'd believed it was a flashback from the murder, although I had no idea what it meant. Ted says he made his own inquiries over the past few days to help me figure it out.

"The friend I contacted about the sketch just called me back," Ted says. "He's asked around and he has information on the design. I'm coming back now so we can discuss it. I think I know who killed Amy and Marco. It's time to involve the police."

Chapter Fifty-Seven

The night manager was deep-frying a fresh batch of jelly donuts for the late-night crowd when Halliday and Lavelle entered the bodega.

"Gimme a minute," he called out over the high-pitched spit of sizzling oil.

Halliday moved to the corner of the store to take a call coming through. She hoped it would be Liv Reese calling her back. It wasn't. It was her old army buddy Owen Jeffries.

"Darcy," said Jeffries. "I have the results of the writing analysis."

"What did you find?"

"It doesn't match any writing in our database at Langley."

Halliday deflated. It was another dead end.

"All that means," he added, "is that it wasn't written by a known terrorist, a convicted criminal, or anyone on our watch list. Our algorithm did provide some interesting insights, though."

"Like what?"

"The Post-it notes were not written by the person who wrote the message on the window. The Post-it notes were written by a left-hander. The words on the crime scene window were written by a right-hander."

"Liv Reese is left-handed," Halliday pointed out.

"Are you sure she's left-handed?"

"The forensics report in the Decker–Reggio murder files said the stab wounds were inflicted by a right-hander. It states categorically that Liv Reese was left-handed. Apparently, that discrepancy was a key reason why the prosecutors decided not to charge her, even though the investigating detective, a guy called Krause, was hell-bent on locking her up."

"Well, that is interesting." Jeffries was silent for a moment. "How tall is she?"

"About five six."

"In that case, it's very unlikely she wrote it," he said definitively.

"Why are you so certain?"

"According to the CIA algo, the person who wrote WAKE UP! on the window was somewhere between five foot nine and six foot three in height."

"How does your algorithm determine that?"

"It's based on machine learning," he said. "The angles of the letters, their shape, and the amount of ink, or in this case, blood, in specific areas of each letter indicate the direction where the hand pressure was coming from. That gives us a pretty good read of the person's height and hand preference."

The bodega manager lifted a metal drainer with the donuts out of the deep fryer as Halliday finished the call. She wondered how she'd break the news to Lavelle. His discovery of the likely murder weapon in the trash outside Liv Reese's old apartment had convinced her that Liv Reese had murdered Ted Cole. Jeffries's call turned that theory on its head.

"Sorry about the wait," said the manager.

Lavelle showed the manager his detective's shield and introduced Halliday, who'd joined him at the counter.

"We need an address for a customer. Her name is Liv Reese," he said, showing a couple of photos of her on his phone.

"That's the lady with the writing on her hands? I know her," the manager said. "She sure likes to drink caffeine drinks. Orders them by the box. Her address is in the delivery book."

He pulled a book out from under the cash register and flipped through the pages until he found her address. Liv Reese lived a couple of blocks away.

"Who was that on the phone?" Lavelle asked Halliday as they left the bodega.

"It was Owen, my buddy from the CIA. He ran the writing from the crime scene through their AI handwriting analysis system. It's one of the most sophisticated in the world. Their system says that Liv Reese did not write that slogan on the bedroom window." Halliday recounted everything that Jeffries told her.

Lavelle didn't look convinced. "I don't know how much stock I put in computer algorithms when there's so much hard and compelling evidence against her. She even disposed of the murder weapon," he said, opening the car door. "I have the warrant for Liv Reese's arrest. It was just emailed to me. Let's bring her in."

"We're going to arrest her?" Halliday asked, stopping in the middle of the sidewalk. "Despite what I just told you?"

"If she's innocent then she has nothing to worry about. I don't throw people into jail just to keep up my solve rates. But I'm not going to let her go on the say-so of a CIA algorithm."

"I'm not suggesting we let her go," said Halliday.

"Then what are you suggesting, Darcy?"

"We treat her as what she is. A potential witness. A possible suspect. But mostly a person going through a crisis. She doesn't have a memory anymore, Jack," said Halliday. "She must be terrified. We shouldn't amplify the terror by treating her like a criminal when the evidence is ambiguous, and now apparently contradictory."

"We'll bring her in for questioning and then we'll take it from there. You drive. I'll update the captain on the way." He threw Halliday the car keys.

Halliday parked halfway down the street from the building where Liv Reese now lived. When the backup team arrived, they all put on flak jackets and checked their weapons. Lavelle posted a few cops at the rear of the building. The other two came in with him and Halliday. They took the stairs down to the basement level.

Liv Reese's apartment was near the end of the corridor. Halliday and Lavelle both drew their weapons, pointing the barrels toward the ground as they each took a side of the front door.

"Police. Open up." Lavelle knocked on the door.

They pressed their backs to the wall and waited. There was no suggestion that Liv Reese had a gun, but the arrest operation would be carried out by the book. She didn't answer the first knock. Lavelle knocked again. There was still no response.

Rather than wait for a battering ram to be brought down, Lavelle took a small piece of wire from his pocket and jimmied the lock.

"Where did you learn how to do that?" Halliday whispered.

"An informant. Taught me everything he knew about breaking and entering." He pushed down the handle and swung open the door. Halliday went in first.

It took them less than half a minute to reach the conclusion that Liv Reese wasn't there. Someone turned on the living room light switch so they could see properly. The naked bulb dangling from the low ceiling was too weak to light up the room properly.

"It's because the walls are all painted black," said Halliday.

A noxious smell of wet paint indicated the walls had been painted recently. She stepped over an empty can of black paint and a roller brush on the floor. "Why paint the walls black?"

"So that nobody can see what's written on them," Lavelle said, picking up a loose piece of paper lying on the floor. It was a photograph of Marco Reggio. Tape on the corners of the page indicated it had originally been stuck to a wall.

Halliday found a pile of unused blister packs of NoDoz tablets on the coffee table. The British social worker hadn't been kidding when she said Liv Reese did anything she could to stop herself from falling asleep.

Halliday went into the galley kitchen and closed a partly open window with a loud thud. A bag of garbage slumped in the corner of the kitchen was filled with empty cans of caffeine drinks and a few used blister packs of medication to prevent sleep. On the fridge, the words STAY AWAKE were spelled out with colorful preschool letter magnets.

She swung open the fridge door. If trash was a window into a soul, as Lavelle had claimed, then refrigerators were equally revealing. Halliday had once found a packet of diamonds stuffed in a cabbage in a vegetable drawer, and an Uzi submachine gun in aluminum wrap under a frozen turkey in a freezer. She whistled in shock when she saw the contents of this fridge.

"Jack, take a look at this."

There was no food inside the fridge. It contained shelves of unopened caffeine drinks and cans of espresso coffee.

"She must be permanently wired if she's drinking this much caffeine all the time," Lavelle said. "No wonder she can't remember anything."

Halliday didn't respond. She was examining a stack of burned paper piled up in the kitchen sink. Among the scorched documents was the hard cover of a book embossed with the word "Journal." The social worker had told her that Liv Reese's journal was her lifeline. It appeared that lifeline was now a pile of ash.

"I'll get the crime scene team to come and process this place," Lavelle said, once they'd looked around properly. "Go home and get some sleep, Darcy."

"It's okay. I need to be up in case Liv Reese calls again," she said, stifling a yawn.

"You need to sleep. We both do. I'll head home as soon as the crime scene team arrives. Keep your phone on."

"I suppose she won't go far without any memory," Halliday said, making no effort to leave.

"She can't. The whole of NYPD is looking for her."

Patrol cars near the bus and train terminals were told to be on alert in case Liv Reese tried to skip town. There was also a car staking out her old apartment, and one outside the *Cultura* office building.

"We're waiting for a warrant to track her phone signal. It will be signed by a judge first thing in the morning. Once we have that, it should be easy to find her. Now go home and get some shut-eye, Darcy. In fact, take the car." Lavelle tossed Halliday the keys. "I'll take a cab home."

Chapter Fifty-Eight

Twenty-Four Hours Earlier

The stippled glass doors of the bar swing open as a couple drunkenly stumbles out. I step into the warmth, glad to be out of the cold. Loud music vibrates through my body as I push through crowds of drinkers, some bopping to music as they watch a live band perform a Lady Gaga cover.

Everything has passed in a haze since I was woken by a phone call from a stranger telling me that Amy was in trouble and needed me to meet her here. I came right away. I'd walk over burning coals for Amy.

Amy always sticks out in a crowd, but I don't see her anywhere. My eyes settle on a blond woman watching the band. She turns to talk to the man next to her. I see her face and rule her out. She's definitely not Amy. Behind the bar, a bartender with a dark goatee in a white shirt rolled to his elbows pours a tray full of beers. I head over to ask if he's seen Amy. She lights up rooms. Everyone notices her.

"How are you, Liv?" the bartender asks when he sees me.

I do a double take. I don't know how he knows my name since I'm pretty sure that I've never been here before. Amy and I have barhopped together plenty of times, but not here. This place is memorable with its distinctive atmospheric decor; it's both modern and vintage, with the triple-paneled art deco mirror behind the bar that harkens back to the prohibition era.

"What can I get you?"

"I'm looking for my friend Amy." I describe her. "Have you seen her?"

He hesitates uncertainly and then sadly shakes his head.

"Did she leave already?"

"Not exactly," he says awkwardly. "Er, does Ted know you're here?"

I ignore his question, assuming he's mixed me up with someone else. Instead I twist around to look for Amy, scrambling off the barstool when I notice another tall blond woman in the crowd listening to the band. "Actually, I think I see her."

I push through the crowd looking for the woman, who seems to have disappeared. I move in and out of knots of people dancing to the music until I'm dizzy from looking at so many faces. The room begins to spin. Afraid I might faint, I head into the restroom, its walls painted midnight blue. I put my phone on a ledge above a sink and splash my face with water to revive myself.

After I've turned off the tap, I realize I've washed off writing on my palm. All that's left are remnants of a phone number and a faded word that says "Ted." There's still writing on the back of my hands. Weird messages that say things like STAY AWAKE and DON'T TRUST ANYONE, as well as the address of this bar.

The restroom door opens, letting in a blast of loud music as several women trail inside and begin to fix their makeup in the mirrors. I leave abruptly. As I come out, I'm enveloped in a warm embrace.

"Liv. Thank God I found you."

Chapter Fifty-Nine

A waitress clears away my empty bowl. The Korean restaurant is emptying out. The police cars parked outside Nocturnal have disappeared. I have to assume the cops left when they didn't find me. It's time that I left, too.

Even though Detective Halliday pretended to empathize with me earlier on the phone, I don't trust cops. Now that I know they suspect me of murder, I trust them even less. I'm afraid they'll frame me for a crime I didn't commit. I have no way to prove my innocence. I know that I blacked out for an unknown period of time until the moment I woke on the train platform holding a ticket to Miami. I also know from the messages from Ted that I forget things every time I wake up.

Once I've paid my bill, I head into the street, uncertain where to go. A couple of cops stand near the entrance of Nocturnal. Thankfully, neither of them see me. I glance back over my shoulder for a split second and collide into someone with such force that the wind is knocked out of me.

"Oh, my gosh, Liv. Are you okay?"

The bright glare of a streetlight burns my eyes as I look up at the first familiar face I've seen since I woke on the Amtrak platform earlier tonight without any memory of how I got there. "Brett, what are you doing here?"

"I had dinner with some colleagues at a place down the street. Are you sure you're okay, Liv?" he asks. "You're shivering."

"It's freezing tonight." I rub my arms.

"My car is down the street. I'll give you a ride," he offers.

"I don't want to take you out of your way." I hesitate.

"It's my pleasure. You'll freeze to death if you stay out here. Look at you, your teeth are chattering," he says. "Come on. Let's get you out of here."

I lower my gaze to the ground and watch our feet step in unison as we walk toward his car. My short black boots and his custom-made gray shoes move in an identical rhythm. A police car slowly approaches, its rotating siren lights reflecting on our faces.

Something niggles at me as we walk. Something important. It must be my nerves rattled by the police car cruising past.

"Almost there," Brett reassures me.

His car beeps twice as he unlocks it. I get into the front passenger seat and clip in the seat belt. Halos hover around the streetlights as we drive to the end of the street and make a right turn.

"You look tired, Liv." He glances at me with concern.

"I'm exhausted. It feels as if I haven't slept for days."

I'm so drained that I lean my head against the window and close my eyes, trying to figure out what was nagging at me before. An image pops into my head of the unusual sketch Ted had texted me. It was a dotted fleur-de-lis pattern, a symbol of the French monarchy.

Ted said I drew the sketch one night, insisting it was connected to Amy and Marco's murder. I realize that I saw that dotted pattern again just now as we walked to the car. His expensive leather shoes had the same unique fleur-de-lis dotted medallion pattern by the toes.

I glance at Brett uncertainly as he steers the car through nighttime traffic. Someone calls his phone. He lets it go to voicemail, telling me ruefully that it's the hospital calling him by mistake. Irritation inflects his voice as he tells me they've yet again forgotten that he's not on call tonight.

I stare out the window, looking into the dark as I visualize that dotted lily pattern again. This time an image comes into my head like a flashback. I'm looking down at a dotted pattern on the toes of expensive oxblood-colored shoes a moment before a man standing behind me plunges a knife into me. I fall to my knees and collapse on the carpet watching those oxblood shoes walk away from me, out of Amy's bedroom. Her pink kimono on the hook of the bedroom door sways as the front door slams shut.

Fear surges through me as realization dawns. I'm too scared to move, too scared even to breathe as I register just how perilous my situation is. I'm in a car with Amy and Marco's killer.

Perhaps sensing that something is wrong, he turns his head to look at me as he drives. "Are you okay, Liv? You look very pale."

"Yeah. Just tired." It takes every ounce of self-control for me to pretend that I still don't know what's going on.

"Why don't you close your eyes and go to sleep. I'll wake you when we get there," he suggests, his voice tinged with concern. He presses his foot on the gas as we accelerate through an intersection.

I don't fall for his kindness. I know who he really is. I know that he killed Amy and Marco, and that he probably intends to kill me.

I stare at the words STAY AWAKE written on the backs of my hands under my knuckles. From Ted's phone messages that I went through at the Korean restaurant, I know that every time I fall asleep I forget everything that has happened since the day Amy and Marco were killed. I close my eyes and pretend to sleep, repeating *Stay Awake, Stay Awake, Stay Awake* over and over in my head like a primal scream.

Sometime later, the car engine falls silent. He unclips his seat belt and gets out, locking me inside. I hear his footsteps recede, followed by murmured voices interlaced with the rush of cars speeding past. I take the risk of opening my eyes to sneak a peek. He's a few yards from the car, his back is to me as he talks on the phone. I assume he's returning the call that came while we were driving.

Keeping an eye on his back, I take the cell phone and the Korean take-out menu from the pocket of my jeans. I quickly type in the phone number of the female detective that I scribbled on the take-out menu and share my location with her.

Help me, I text her.

I press Send, then turn the phone to silent and slip it back into my pocket. The take-out menu has fallen to the floor of the car, but it's too risky to retrieve it. I kick it under my seat and pretend to sleep with my forehead against the passenger window. The driver's door opens and the car heaves as he gets in.

He fires up the ignition and pulls the car back into traffic. I feel his eyes boring into me. He must be trying to figure out if I really am sleeping. I force myself to breathe slowly and steadily as he watches me. He gently pushes my bangs off my face.

"It's a damn shame you and that friend of yours had to start poking around in the past," he says to himself.

A while later, he puts on instrumental jazz. The mellow music contrasts starkly with the cold terror gripping me so tightly that every nerve is on edge. I open my eyes for a millisecond to see we're driving through an unlit industrial area lined with warehouses. Gravel crunches under the car tires. We bounce over several deep potholes. Then we stop.

Chapter Sixty

I stay frozen, pretending to sleep, after he stops the car. All my senses are focused on trying to figure out what's going on and where we are. I'm too afraid to open my eyes to see our location. I sense that he is watching me. I need him to think that I'm still asleep.

He leans toward me, his breath warm against my skin. I force myself to stay still. This time he doesn't touch my hair. He flips open the glove compartment and takes something out. I don't know what it is until I hear a series of metal clicks. It sounds like a gun being loaded with a magazine of bullets.

"Wake up, Liv." He shakes my shoulders roughly and unbuckles my seat belt.

If I have any chance of getting away from him, I have to let him believe that I've just woken and thus lost my memory again. I give an exaggerated yawn and rub my eyes with exhaustion. "Where are we?"

"We're here to meet Amy." It chills me to hear him say her name in light of everything I've learned tonight.

"Amy's here?" I play along.

"She's waiting for you." He glances at his wristwatch. "We're running late."

I scramble out of the car. My knees are so weak they almost buckle under me. He holds on to my upper arm with pretend solicitousness. His grip is tight. There's no way I can break free. I don't let on that it hurts. The longer I keep this charade going, the longer I'll stay alive.

302

A cold wind buffets us as we walk toward an abandoned warehouse. Our way forward is lit up by the beam of his flashlight.

"What are we doing here?"

"Remember, Amy got tickets to a new production of *Macbeth* set in a dystopian world. You know how much she loves avant-garde theater. Personally, I think it's a bore, but I don't like to disappoint her."

We step over puddles as we approach the derelict building. The windows are boarded up and defaced with spray-painted expletives and crude drawings.

"I hope the audience gets to sit this time," I say, going along with his charade. "Last time Amy took me to one of these avant-garde plays, it was at an old brewery. We had to stand the whole time. My feet were in agony by the end of the evening."

"I'm pretty sure this performance is seated," he says, escorting me around to the back of the building. "Amy will be annoyed that we're so late."

He kicks in a board on a basement window at the back of the building, ruining any pretense that we're here to watch a play. He shoves me roughly through the window opening. I groan as I land hard on a concrete floor in a dark storeroom.

Hundreds of plastic bucket chairs are piled in stacks of varying heights. Old metal filing cabinets litter the floor, some tipped on their sides. Others stand upright. Boxes are stacked in unstable towers. A mass of desks is shoved against a wall. There are swivel chairs, too, dozens of them arranged in untidy rows.

High-pitched squeaking startles me. Rats. He points the flashlight at a rodent scampering along a window frame. Picking up a dusty folder from a desk, he throws it like a Frisbee at the rat. It hits its mark. The animals scatter. It makes my skin crawl. He eases his grip on my upper arm as he throws another folder.

I take my chance. I pull away from him and dive behind a desk. From there I slide on my belly under stacks of chairs until I'm far away from him. A flashlight beam moves across the concrete floor as he looks for me. I stay where I am, crouching in a ball under a stack of chairs. I watch his legs move through the gaps between the piled-up furniture as he searches for me.

There's a box of old staplers on the floor next to me. I pick one up and throw it as hard as I can across the room. It bounces off a wall with a thump and he goes after the noise to look for me. I push a swivel chair in his direction. Its wheels clatter as it rolls toward him. I use the noise as cover to hide behind a row of metal filing cabinets.

"Stop playing games, Liv. This place is dangerous," he says. When I don't respond, he adds: "We're running late. Amy will be annoyed."

"Amy's dead," I call out, unsure why he feels the need to keep up the pretense.

Through a narrow gap between the filing cabinets, I watch his custom-made shoes as he paces around looking for me. His shoes have a dotted fleur-de-lis design identical to the one in the drawing that Ted texted me along with a message suggesting it was a key clue to the identity of Amy and Marco's killer.

"I know that you killed Amy and Marco," I blurt out. My voice echoes around the room.

He pauses midstep and then freezes, like a cobra waiting to strike. When he realizes that I'm not saying anything else, he knocks over a stack of chairs as he intensifies his search for my hiding place.

"I always knew your memory would come back. That's why I had to kill your ex last night and frame you as the killer. I figured when you were found with his body, they'd pin Amy and Marco's murders on you, too. It would get me off the hook for good. It was sloppy of me to turn my back and let you disappear with the knife, but it ends here and now," he says. "You'll never get out of here."

He pauses to listen for a response so he can figure out where I'm hiding. I cover my mouth to stifle the sound of my breathing.

"I told you I was bringing you to Amy. And I am. Just not in the way that you thought." He laughs. "If you come to me now, I'll make sure it doesn't hurt. Just the way it didn't hurt your ex last night. An injection of pentazocine in his hairline with a fine needle. He fell onto the bed and was sleeping like a baby when he died.

"Make it easy on yourself, Liv. It's only a matter of time until I find you."

Chapter Sixty-One

Twenty-Four Hours Earlier

It's the ceiling fan that wakes me, brushing my skin with a steady stream of cool air as it rattles above my head. I open my eyes and stare into a bluish haze that slowly morphs into someone else's bedroom.

The fan spins so fast I worry it might topple. The mattress is too firm. The satin sheets too slippery. The humming I heard in my sleep gets louder and more ominous until it crackles like a live electrical wire. The noise is coming from inside my head. It's my own private warning system and it's telling me that I'm in trouble. Big trouble.

I lie very still, my eyes shuttered by my lashes as I glance around the blue-gray bedroom trying to figure out where I am and how I got here. There's a bottle of white wine next to the bed. That surprises me. I don't like white wine and rarely drink it. On the carpet is a trail of women's clothes that I presume are mine. Just as I'm trying to figure out what's going on, the bedroom door is pushed open and someone comes into the room. His shadow reflects on the wall. It gets bigger as he gets closer until I recognize him.

"Brett?" I mutter, as if talking in my sleep.

"For fuck's sake, go to sleep," he says. "You're supposed to be sedated."

The cruelness of his tone terrifies me almost as much as his words. Sedated? I think to myself. Why would I be sedated? And then I know through the most primal core of my being that he intends to hurt me. My survival instincts kick in. I feign sleep so well that I'm almost dozing off as he squats down to check on me, touching me with a rubber-gloved hand.

He must be satisfied because he steps away and soon, I hear him humming in the kitchen as he opens a cabinet and takes something out. I turn my head to the side and gasp as I come face-to-face with a tawny-haired man sleeping next to me.

I pretend to sleep when Brett returns, letting out steady rhythmic breaths, all the while listening to the rustle of fabric as he strips clothes off the man next to me and drops them on the floor.

There's a squelching noise. The mattress shifts. I don't know what's going on until Brett puts the cold handle of a knife in my hand. It's wet and sticky. I smell blood. He arranges the sheets over both of us, practically tucking us in before disappearing into the bathroom.

Pipes groan and water splashes loudly. He's washing up. When I turn my head, I know instantly that the man next to me is dead.

Quickly, I get out of bed and pull on jeans and the woman's top lying on the carpet. I don't bother zipping up the jeans as I slide my feet into ankle boots, keeping one eye on the strip of light under the bathroom door to make sure he isn't coming out. The smell of bleach wafts into the bedroom through the crack under the bathroom door.

The knife has fallen off the bed onto a T-shirt lying on the floor. I grab the T-shirt, wrapping the knife in it, and head into the living area. With my free hand, I quietly unbolt the front door.

Hanging from a hook near the front door is a women's buttonless cardigan. I throw it over my arm as I creep out of the apartment and close the door softly behind me. A reflective light on the floor guides me to the stairwell in the dark. I take the stairs down to the basement, where I push open a door and find myself in an alley. I put on the cardigan and slide the

T-shirt–wrapped knife into a pocket to save as evidence as I walk toward a liquor store on the corner. I'm so terrified and confused that all I can think about is warning Amy before he gets to her.

I wave down a taxi and give him the address of our apartment in Brooklyn. I stare out of the cab window as halos blink around streetlights like they're sharing a secret. Lulled by the hum of the radio, I feel my eyes get heavy, and I drift off.

Chapter Sixty-Two

Wednesday 11:24 P.M.

Halliday was cruising around the block looking for a parking spot near her apartment building when a text message came through on her phone.

Help me, it said.

The phone number matched the number that Liv Reese had used to call the police information hotline earlier. She had also sent a tracking pin to allow Halliday to track her location. The tracking pin indicated that she was on the move, heading toward Queens.

Halliday called Lavelle's phone. There was no answer. She made a sharp turn and drove toward the location on the tracking map on her phone screen as she tried to get hold of Lavelle again. His phone went directly to voicemail. She assumed he was still waiting for the crime scene team at the basement apartment, where the phone signal was poor.

"Jack, it's Darcy. Liv Reese sent me a location tracking pin. I'm following it. She's heading to Queens. I think she's in trouble. Call me."

She called the precinct and spoke to Rosco, who was still going through CCTV footage, and told him the same thing.

"It could be a trap," he said dubiously.

"There's only one way to find out. I'm following her. Tell Jack. I'll keep you posted."

The location marker kept moving farther away on the navigation map as Halliday drove toward it. It moved along the grid to Queens and then headed toward Maspeth, where it turned into a labyrinth of side streets. Halliday estimated she was ten minutes away when Lavelle called.

She updated him on what had happened and her current location. As she spoke, the map showed that Liv Reese's car was driving through an industrial area of factories and warehouses.

"It's stopped," she said, when the tracker came to a sudden halt. "At an old storage warehouse. It's about five minutes away."

She gave him the address and asked him to get backup cars to meet her there. Halliday sped up. It was a bad sign that the tracking pin had stopped moving, especially in such a remote location. Nobody had any legitimate business in an old factory district so late at night.

Halliday turned into a narrow, unlit street lined with warehouses. The location marker for Liv Reese had stopped in a compound at the dead end of the street. She pulled to a stop while she was still out of view of the warehouse and radioed in her location. The dispatcher told her that backup was approximately ten minutes away.

She drew her weapon and entered the compound through a pedestrian gate that was bent and falling off its hinges. It rattled in the wind.

The asphalt parking area outside the warehouse was disintegrating and riddled with potholes. Most of the warehouse windows were boarded up. Some were defaced with graffiti.

A Lexus was parked in a delivery bay, the internal light still on. One of the car doors hadn't been closed properly. Halliday opened the door and looked around. A Korean restaurant menu with her phone number scribbled on top was on the floor under the front passenger's seat. Halliday moved behind a wall as she called in the plate number to Rosco.

"It's a leased car," he said after looking it up in the DMV database.

"Who does it belong to?"

"Don't know. It's a private company."

"Liv's location tracker is still on but it's not moving. She's somewhere in this compound. It doesn't look good," Halliday whispered.

"Hang tight. Backup will be there in under seven minutes."

Two loud bursts echoing from the warehouse drowned out his voice. "Shots fired," Halliday said. "I can't wait for backup."

Chapter Sixty-Three

Brett pushes over a stack of chairs and they collapse on the floor with a deafening crash. "The police are looking for you, Liv. They think you killed Ted. There's strong evidence this time."

"What evidence?" I call out stupidly. He immediately moves toward my side of the room while he talks.

"The message on the bedroom window, for starters," he says, bending down to look for me under a desk. "I wrote it after you disappeared with the knife. Then I went upstairs and waited until daybreak in a utility room. The elevator was packed with people when I left. Nobody noticed me. The police saw you leave, though, in the middle of the night. The CCTV footage of you fleeing after the murder has been running on the news all evening. Everyone believes you killed Ted Cole, especially the police. There's only one thing that links me to his murder."

"What is it?" I ask, again despite my better judgment.

"The knife," he answers. "While I was cleaning up, I discovered I nicked myself with the blade when I stabbed Ted. The knife has my blood on it. My DNA. When I came out of the bathroom after cleaning up with bleach, it was gone. You took the goddamn knife." He sighs impatiently. "I need to know where you put it, Liv. But, of course, you don't goddamn know what you did with it. Do you? You don't remember. Well, you're going to have to remember," he hisses.

Instead of responding, I crawl to a new hiding place, crouching under the legs of another stack of chairs. A filing cabinet hits the concrete floor with a loud crash. He pushes down another cabinet and kicks over a pile of boxes as he searches for me.

"Maybe I should leave you here and let you fall asleep," he calls out. "You'd wake up without knowing why you were here in the first place. That's if the rats don't gnaw you to death first."

I cover my mouth with my palm so he won't hear my shallow breathing as he stops talking and listens for a hint of where I'm hiding. He kicks a box like it's a hockey puck. It slides across the floor, hitting a brick wall. Rats squeal as they scatter. I grit my teeth as one of them runs over my leg.

"Liv, you have ten seconds to come out or I'm going to shoot," he calls out. "Ten, nine, eight…"

When he reaches the number four, he gives up counting and fires a gunshot into the wall. Another shot ricochets off a metal desk. I bite my lip to stop myself from screaming. I'm certain he fired the shot to elicit a scream so he'll know where I'm hiding.

He moves to the other side of the room, dragging desks out of the way. A shadow jumps into the basement through the window. It's so fast and so quiet that I decide that I imagined it.

He topples over a stack of chairs, slowly working his way across the basement toward me. I'm about to slide under a metal desk to hide somewhere else when a firm hand slaps over my mouth. I scream. No sound comes out. The hand presses against my mouth like a suction cup.

"I'm Detective Halliday," a voice whispers in my ear. "Liv, I need you to lie flat on the floor. Whatever happens, do not get up. Do not even move. No matter how scary it gets. Do you understand?"

I nod.

Chapter Sixty-Four

Halliday left Liv lying flat on the ground as she crouched low and crept on her toes in the darkness. Any noise she made was drowned out by filing cabinets and piles of boxes hitting the floor as he tore up the place in his desperate search.

Halliday used the darkness and the noise to her advantage. She stayed down as she navigated around the overturned office furniture, sticking to the darkest edges of the room so he wouldn't notice any movement. She needed the advantage of surprise. When he turned his back to topple over another set of chairs, she rose and pointed her gun at his torso in a two-handed grip.

"Police. Drop your weapon."

He whirled around to face her, his gun hanging by his side.

"Drop your weapon. Or I will shoot," she repeated.

He held the gun by his thigh, making no attempt to drop it. Halliday sensed from his body language that he'd decided to go for broke.

As he lifted up his hand to fire at her, she fired two shots in quick succession. The first hit his hand gripping the gun. The force of the bullet flung the weapon out of his grasp onto the floor. The second shot hit him in the right shoulder, causing him to cry out in agony.

He'd collapsed onto the floor when Halliday reached him. She pushed him onto his stomach and cuffed his good hand to the leg of a desk. His other hand was bleeding profusely, but she was not going to leave him unrestrained while his gun was still lying around somewhere.

Halliday gave him first aid as she radioed for ambulances and additional police support. The beam of her flashlight found his weapon lying under a chair. She left it there. There would be an investigation into her use of live fire. It was better if his gun was found by someone else.

Liv was still huddled under the desk when Halliday found her. "Are you okay?" she asked, reaching out her hand to pull Liv from her hiding place. "It's all over."

"He was going to kill me," said Liv. Her face was pale, and she trembled violently. Halliday could see that she was in shock.

"It's over, Liv," said Halliday, putting her arm around her. "You're safe now."

The whine of sirens cut through the sudden silence that had descended on the basement storeroom once the echo of gunshots had faded.

"That must be the ambulances. The paramedics will take care of you."

"And then what?" Liv asked. "Are you going to arrest me for murder?"

Police lights lit up the darkness outside. A convoy of cop cars and two ambulances pulled to a stop outside the warehouse. Doors opened and slammed shut, followed by the thump of footsteps as police and medics ran toward them in the dark.

"You'll go to the hospital to make sure you're okay. While you're there, we'll look at the evidence with a new set of eyes. Remember, I was in here with you. I heard him talking to you before I came through the window. I heard him confess. All of that helps us build a case against him. Either way, he kidnapped and almost killed you. He's going to go away for a very long time."

Halliday helped Liv climb out of the basement window where a police officer waited with a thermal blanket. He threw it over her shivering body as he took her to the front ambulance, its whirring siren lights painting the warehouse crimson.

Chapter Sixty-Five

"Halliday. Lavelle," the captain called out when he noticed the two detectives enter the office, single file. The glass Detective Bureau doors slammed shut behind them. "In my office. Now."

Lavelle leaned against the filing cabinet with his arms crossed. Halliday sat by the captain's desk while they waited for him to finish a phone call.

"Lavelle, you look like shit. Get rid of the stubble," the captain said when he'd hung up the phone. "That was the media team. They've scheduled a press briefing. You can't face TV cameras looking like a drunk, Jack."

"Not a drunk, just a hardworking detective too tired to shave this morning. We both had maybe two hours' sleep last night," Lavelle said, looking at Halliday for confirmation. "Anyway, I won't be addressing the media. Detective Halliday will do the talking."

The captain turned his attention to Halliday. She wore a dark blue suit with a pale pink shirt that matched her light makeup. Her chestnut hair was tied up in a tight ponytail. She looked fresh and focused.

"Jack says you did well."

"I held my own."

"You more than held your own," the captain said approvingly. "Now tell me. What evidence do we have against Brett Graham?"

316

Halliday handed him a preliminary report, which he flicked through as she spoke. "The lab's checking the Ted Cole murder weapon for Brett Graham's DNA. Apparently, he cut himself on the blade when he stabbed Cole."

Halliday's voice was hoarse. She'd been up most of the night fielding questions from internal investigators about the shooting. She'd been swabbed for gunshot residue and she'd had to write a detailed statement about what had happened at the warehouse. Her final statement was eight pages long.

Lavelle had stayed at the warehouse for most of the night while it was processed by investigators and the forensics team. He and Halliday had gone straight to the lab first thing in the morning to find out what evidence they had to build a case against Brett Graham.

"I see the Reese woman's prints are on the knife," the captain said, scanning the report. "That will complicate things in court."

They all knew it wouldn't be a cut-and-dry case, especially given Liv Reese's amnesia. It would be difficult to build a solid case on the testimony of a witness with documented memory problems.

"Any hard evidence that ties our suspect to the Cole murder?" the captain asked, handing the lab report back to Halliday.

"Microscopic chips of black paint were found at the murder scene," said Halliday. "The lab matched paint scraped from under Brett Graham's fingernails to the paint traces found at the murder scene. It also matches the black paint at Liv Reese's apartment, suggesting Brett Graham was at her apartment where he destroyed evidence by painting the walls and setting fire to her journal."

"He sure did everything he could to cover his tracks," the captain said. "That's a heck of a lot of effort to go to. He didn't even know Ted Cole. Why kill him?" the captain asked.

"To frame Liv Reese for the murder," said Lavelle. "He figured that once we charged Liv Reese for the Cole murder, we'd charge her with the Decker-Reggio murders as well, which had a similar MO. Then the case would be officially closed. He didn't want to live in fear that Liv Reese's memory might come back."

"Still, to kill a man just in case. I'm not sure if a jury would buy it," the captain said.

"Ted Cole was also helping Liv Reese find out who'd killed her friends," Halliday explained. "He was asking around about things that connected Graham to the Decker-Reggio murders. Graham found out and decided to remove Cole from the equation. Permanently. Framing Liv Reese was the cherry on top."

"What sorts of questions was Cole asking?"

Halliday told the captain how earlier that morning she had finally reached the designer who'd telephoned Cole when he was at the apartment of his fiancée, Elisabeth, on the night Cole was murdered. The designer said that Ted had asked him to make inquiries about a dotted fleur-de-lis sketch that Liv Reese had drawn after a flashback of Amy and Marco's murders.

"The designer reached out to an exclusive men's custom-made shoe store on Cole's behalf. The store is well-known for giving each client their own unique dotted medallion design. Brett Graham's design was a fleur-de-lis. It was on all his shoes."

Halliday showed the captain a copy of the sketch, as well as a photo of Graham's shoes from the previous night, which they'd taken into evidence. The captain whistled when she told him that the shoes cost over $1,500 a pair. Graham apparently owned more than a dozen pairs.

"When the owner of the shoe boutique heard that questions were being asked about Graham's unique shoe design, he contacted Graham as a curtesy to let him know," explained Halliday. "That's probably what tipped Graham off that Ted Cole, Liv Reese's ex, was asking questions about him."

On the way to brief the captain, the two detectives had stopped at the exclusive bespoke shoe store on Fifty-Seventh Street. The owner had shown Halliday and Lavelle photos of the shoes his artisans had made for Graham over the years. Among them was a pair of oxblood shoes that Amy had given Brett for his birthday before she died. Halliday suspected this was the pair he'd worn when he'd murdered Amy and Marco. That might explain Reese's flashback of shoes covered with blood that Detective Larry Regan had mentioned when they'd spoken to him earlier. At the time, Reese's recollection had been dismissed because there was no blood tracked on the carpet at the murder scene. Maybe the killer's shoes weren't covered in blood, they were simply the color of blood: oxblood, Halliday had suggested to Lavelle on the way back to the precinct.

"Liv Reese is awake again. Her doctors say she can talk to us," said Lavelle after checking a message on his phone. "We'd better head over to the hospital before she falls asleep again."

"Before you go, I'll need you to hand over your weapon, Detective Halliday," the captain told Halliday as she stood to leave. "It's only until the report on the shooting is submitted. You'll have plenty of time to catch up on paperwork over the next few days."

Halliday unclipped her service weapon from her holster, removed the ammunition clip, and put both down on his desk. She'd be on desk duty until the Internal Affairs investigation into the shooting was complete. From the way she'd been questioned the previous night, one of the key issues would be why she didn't shoot to kill. There had even been a suggestion that she might need extra sessions at the firing range to improve the accuracy of her shot.

Halliday told the investigators that she'd deliberately winged the suspect. They'd asked her why. She'd said she did it because she was a good enough shot to accurately disarm him without killing him. She preferred knowing he was in a prison cell rather than the grave.

"Being a desk jockey for a few days is actually good news," the captain said as he put her weapon and badge in a locked desk drawer.

"In what way?"

"It will give you time to prepare."

"Time to prepare for what?" Halliday asked.

"Your application. We have a permanent homicide detective position opening up. We're advertising it next week. You'd be our preferred candidate. That's if you decide to apply, of course. Maybe I'm being presumptuous, Detective Halliday. Maybe working homicides isn't your thing."

"I'll be putting in an application. Yes, I will," said Halliday before heading to the door.

"I'll need a referee to vouch for you," the captain called after her.

"You can put me down," said Lavelle, putting on his jacket and following Halliday out of the office.

Chapter Sixty-Six

Thursday 2:45 P.M.

Liv Reese was dozing in a hospital bed when Halliday and Lavelle entered her room, waiting near the window as the nurse checked her vital signs.

She stirred from the noise of the beeping heart monitor machine and slowly opened her eyes. Liv had been up half the night giving a sworn videotaped statement to Detective Tran about what had happened at the warehouse. Lavelle had insisted Tran take her statement before Liv went to sleep because of the possibility that she might wake with no memory of the events of the previous night.

"How're you feeling today?" the nurse asked, half-opening the venetian blinds. Streaks of daylight covered the hospital bed linen.

"Exhausted," Liv answered. The hospital gown she wore emphasized the pallor of her skin. Her hair was rumpled from sleep and her eyes were bleary as she blinked to adjust to the light. "What's the time?"

"It's after two," the nurse said, wrapping a Velcro blood pressure sleeve around Liv's upper arm. "You've been asleep since the doctor woke you at ten this morning to check on you."

Liv noticed Halliday and Lavelle standing near the venetian window shades. When the nurse was done, she plumped up Liv's pillows and blankets and pulled over the uneaten food tray before leaving the room.

"You're the detective from last night." Liv's gaze fixed on Halliday.

"You remember me?" Halliday asked, pulling out the visitor's chair and sitting down so they were at the same eye level.

"I remember everything that happened after I woke on the train platform last night. I remember the warehouse, the shooting, and the ambulance ride to the hospital. I especially remember you. You saved my life."

Halliday colored slightly from the depth of Liv Reese's gratitude. "So you're cured? No more memory problems?" she asked.

"The doctors say that if I sleep properly and I don't take caffeine and other stimulants to stay awake, then it's unlikely to happen again. But there's no guarantee."

"Getting your memory back is a big step in the right direction," said Halliday.

Liv Reese's face was downcast. "I suppose," she said with a sad shrug. "The doctors don't think I'll ever remember the period that I've forgotten. That means I'll always be missing two years of my life. I guess it's something that I'll have to come to terms with."

Liv picked up the remote control for the bed and pressed a button to raise the bed so she could sit up properly. "I wouldn't be here if it wasn't for you, Detective. I'd be dead for sure. There are no words to thank you for what you did. Risking your own life to save mine."

"You should thank yourself. You were smart enough to alert me by sharing your location," Halliday said. "I dread to think what would have happened if you hadn't been so quick-thinking."

"I was taking a risk, trusting you," said Liv. "I knew you suspected me of murder. It was all over the TV. I figured that worst-case scenario you'd track me down to arrest me for murder. It seemed like my only hope."

"We're not pursuing any murder charges against you. We believe that Brett Graham drugged and killed Ted Cole. He wrote the WAKE UP! message on the window to make it look as if you'd done it because you have that same message written on your hand. It was another link that tied you to the Cole murder," said Halliday.

"Why would he kill Ted Cole?"

"Ted was asking uncomfortable questions that could connect Brett back to the Decker-Reggio murders. Brett decided to kill Ted and frame you for his murder," said Lavelle.

The pathologist had found a needle mark in Ted Cole's hairline. Their theory was that Brett Graham injected Ted with a sedative from behind, most likely in the bedroom. Ted collapsed on the bed where he was stripped of his clothes and stabbed. It was set up to look like an assignation. The idea was that Liv would be found holding the bloodied murder weapon while sleeping alongside Ted's lifeless body in the morning.

"Brett must have met you at the bar, Nocturnal, and taken you back to the apartment Ted rented for you. We don't know why you went with him. Perhaps, knowing you had no memory, he pretended to take you to Amy. Either way, at some point he gave you white wine from a bottle he'd laced with sedatives."

"I hate white wine. I never take more than a sip," said Liv.

"He probably didn't notice that you'd drunk very little. He must have left you alone, thinking you were fast asleep from the wine. That must have been when you escaped."

"I ran away?" Liv shook her head as if hoping it would help her remember.

"You more than ran away," said Lavelle. "You ran away with the murder weapon."

"Why would I have done that?" Liv asked.

"Maybe it was to save an important piece of evidence. The knife may help us convict him."

At the precinct, Rosco and Tran were trawling through CCTV footage to find footage of Brett Graham sneaking out of the apartment building after spending the night in the utility room. Halliday was sure something would come up in the hundreds of hours of surveillance footage if they looked hard enough.

The crime scene team would go back to the apartment building that afternoon to look for fingerprints in the utility room where he'd hidden. Once the search warrant was signed, Halliday and Lavelle would lead a team searching Brett Graham's apartment. They intended to take his custom-made fleur-de-lis shoe collection as evidence so that the lab could test the shoes for blood splatter that connected to the Decker-Reggio murders. They hoped to charge him for the double murder as well.

"How did Brett track me down?" Liv asked.

"He must have seen you at the hospital when you came to get your brain scans," said Halliday, explaining that Ted had arranged for Liv to see a neurologist about her amnesia. "We know that Brett accessed your medical file on the day you had the scan. His hospital ID number appears in the data history. That's what the hospital administrator told us when we spoke to her earlier. That's probably how Brett got hold of your address."

"Is that how he knew that my memory was erased each time I went to sleep?"

"We believe so. That information was detailed in your medical records he accessed."

There was a fine line between answering Liv's questions and giving her an information overload that might traumatize her further. They'd spoken to Liv's doctor before they came in and he'd asked them to go gentle on her. She was still emotionally fragile.

"It's my fault that Ted Cole was killed," said Liv. "He died because he was helping me. I'm incredibly sad that I don't remember him."

Halliday was sorry that Liv's journal had been destroyed. The social worker had said the journal was a written account of Liv's life since she'd been treated for unexplained memory loss at the hospital in London. Brett had burned the journal, turning it into a pile of ashes. With the journal destroyed and Ted gone, there was nobody to fill in Liv's memory.

Halliday and Lavelle had theorized how the murder had gone down on the way over to the hospital. The way they figured it, in the hours before the Cole murder and possibly afterward as well, Brett Graham had gone to Liv's basement apartment and destroyed everything she and Ted Cole had found out about Amy and Marco's murders. He burned her journal and the newspaper clippings she'd collected. He painted the apartment walls black so that nobody would be able to decipher the theories and clues Liv had scribbled on the walls.

Liv's cell phone number had probably been written in her journal. He'd called her up and lured her to Nocturnal, which he knew from reading her journal was her regular haunt. He'd somehow tricked her into taking him back to the safe-house apartment. That's where he drugged her with wine and hid while waiting for Cole to return. It appeared from phone records that while he waited, he'd used the apartment phone to contact the cleaning service to send a cleaner in the morning. The phone number for the cleaning service was on the fridge. He must have intended for the cleaner to find Liv fast asleep with Ted's body in the morning.

"What happens to me now?" Liv asked.

"You'll be free to resume your life once you're discharged in a couple of days," said Lavelle.

"What life? Either I go back to London to live a life I don't remember, or I stay here in a life that has changed beyond recognition," she said, despondently.

"Or maybe you start fresh," said Halliday, rising from her seat. "Transitions are never easy. You'll get through this, Liv. Trust me."

"We'd better get going," said Lavelle, checking his phone messages. "The doctor says we can talk to Brett Graham."

"Brett's here? At the hospital?" Liv asked, visibly distressed at the thought they were under the same roof.

"He's in a different wing, handcuffed to a bed with a police guard," said Halliday. "I hear he finds it humiliating to be treated like a criminal at the hospital where he used to throw around his weight as a big-time surgeon. He'll have to get used to it. It'll be a lot worse when he's in prison."

She paused as a good-looking man with dark hair and a goatee entered the hospital room carrying a stunning gift basket of flowers and a large foil GET WELL balloon.

"I know you," said Liv, as the man reticently approached her hospital bed. Liv furrowed her brow as she tried to place him. "You're the bartender from last night."

"Yes. I'd like to think that we're also good friends, even though this is the first time you've actually remembered me," he said with a smile. He put the flower arrangement next to Liv's hospital bed.

"If we're friends, then you'd better tell me your name, so I remember it the next time we see each other," Liv said.

"I'm Harry," he said, reaching out to shake Liv's hand before sitting down on the chair next to her hospital bed.

Halliday and Lavelle left the room, closing the door gently behind them.

Acknowledgements

Stay Awake was written during the throes of the COVID-19 pandemic. That is to say that it was largely written in my car, which was the only quiet place I could find while homeschooling my kids during 270 days of lockdown in Melbourne, Australia. It was a structurally challenging novel to write for a variety of reasons, not least because it was written from the perspective of an amnesiac. So, in short, I chose the worst possible time to write it. Perhaps not surprisingly, I wrote myself into the occasional blind alley. I have my agent, David Gernert, and Ellen Coughtrey and Anna Worrall from the Gernert Company, to thank for helping me navigate myself out of those dead ends. I wish to extend my deepest appreciation to Charles Spicer for his invaluable advice and support, as well as to Jennifer Enderlin, Sarah Grill, and the rest of the fabulous team at St. Martin's and Macmillan.

To Ali Watts and Johannes Jakob at my Australian publisher, Penguin Random House Australia, as well as to my other international publishers and translators, I am enormously grateful for all your support. I'd like to extend my appreciation to Rebecca Gardner and the rights team at the Gernert Company, and all their co-agents, for getting my novels the widest possible audience across the world.

Stay Awake was also written during two deaths in the family: that of my husband's beloved mother and his older brother. May their memories be blessed.

To my husband and sons, thank you for all you do for me (and I am not just referring to the constant flow of cups of tea!).

Thank you also to my parents and my sister and brother. After *The Night Swim* was published, I received many messages that moved me greatly. Somehow these messages always managed to arrive just at the right moment, usually when I was going through an existential crisis and about to rip up the current manuscript. So a very special thanks to all the readers who reached out to me.

CANELOCRIME

Do you love crime fiction and are always on the lookout for brilliant authors?

Canelo Crime is home to some of the most exciting novels around. Thousands of readers are already enjoying our compulsive stories. Are you ready to find your new favourite writer?

Find out more and sign up to our newsletter at canelocrime.com

Praise for Tilly Bagshawe

'Who said hotel management wasn't glam? Honor Palmer would disagree, given the opulence that runs throughout this fun romp. *Do Not Disturb* is like *The OC* meets *Dynasty* – but with even more sex. What more could you wish for?'   *Heat*

'A rollicking romp of a read ... Bagshawe has come up with a corker'   *Glamour*

'A racy, pacy and very funny updating of Jilly Cooper set in the racing world on both sides of the Atlantic'
                                                                    Observer

'*The Horse Whisperer* and *National Velvet* meet Jackie Collins behind the barn'   *Publishers Weekly*

'Hums with sex and glamour – the 1980s blockbuster with an ironic, 21st-century twist ... *Adored* ... will lead the field'   *New Statesman*

'Fans of *The OC* will love this sex-scene-studded romp ... Excellent escapism'   *Cosmopolitan*

'*Adored* is total self-indulgent, escapist pleasure, I adored it!'   Sophie Kinsella

'*Adored* is an ambitious romp of a novel ... all the crucial ingredients are there – cads, gold-diggers, starlets, super-models and whores – in suitable slinky settings ... you'll find yourself getting wrapped up in the drama of Siena McMahon and her messed-up family'   *Heat*

'A grand tale of a young girl born into a Hollywood dynasty ... that is so much fun you won't be able to put it down'   *OK!*

Do Not Disturb

TILLY BAGSHAWE

An Orion paperback

First published in Great Britain in 2008
by Orion
This paperback edition published in 2009
by Orion Books Ltd,
Orion House, 5 Upper St Martin's Lane,
London WC2H 9EA

An Hachette Livre UK company

3 5 7 9 10 8 6 4

A CIP catalogue record for this book is available
from the British Library.

ISBN 978-0-7528-8453-0

Printed and bound in Great Britain by Clays Ltd, St Ives plc

The Orion Publishing Group's policy is to use papers that
are natural, renewable and recyclable products and
made from wood grown in sustainable forests. The logging
and manufacturing processes are expected to conform to
the environmental regulations of the country of origin.

www.orionbooks.co.uk

To my parents, Nick and Daphne Bagshawe.
Whenever I count my blessings, you're first on the list.

Acknowledgements

Thanks, as always, to everyone at Orion for putting up with me, and for the fantastic job you all do at turning my tatty manuscript into a finished and (if I do say so myself) rather gorgeous book. Special thanks to Lisa Milton, Kate Mills and Genevieve Pegg for all their patience and advice about the title, the universe and everything; and to Susan Lamb for convincing me to try something new.

To my agents and friends, Tif Loehnis and Luke Janklow. Also to everyone at Janklow & Nesbit, especially Tim Glister, Kirsty Gordon and Claire Dippel who have helped me so much this year with all sorts of things that are not their job, and whose cheerfulness and good humour are a huge part of why I love my agency.

Thanks to my family. To my husband Robin, our gorgeous children, Sefi, Zac and Theo, and to my brother and sisters for always being there for me. Finally I would like to thank my parents, to whom this book is dedicated, for teaching me to read and write, encouraging me in everything, and for loving me all my life. There are plenty of dysfunctional families in this story – but I'm happy to say not one of them bears the slightest resemblance to mine. I only hope I can give my own children a childhood half as magical as the one you gave us.

(P.S. Dad, don't read the book, there's too much sex in it.)
    Love
    Tills xx

The Major Players

HONOR PALMER	Heiress to the Palmer family fortune and the iconic Palmers Hotel. A society beauty with brains.
TINA PALMER	Honor's nymphomaniac younger sister. A Hollywood starlet.
TREY PALMER	Their elderly, Alzheimer's-riddled father.
LAURA PALMER	Their late mother.
LISE PALMER	Trey's latest gold-digging wifelette.
CALEB	Honor's faithful Boxer. A very naughty dog.
TERTIUS PALMER	Honor's legendary grandfather, the founder of Palmers Hotel.
DANNY CARLUCCI	Mafiosi. Boss of Massachussetts and sometime paramour of Tina Palmer.
DICK GRATE	Another of Tina's conquests. An 'adult entertainment' star, he lives up to his name.
JACOB FOSTER	Trey's distant cousin. A money-grubbing born-again Christian.
SAM BRANNAGAN	Honor Palmer's lawyer and friend.
LUCAS RUIZ	Hotel industry Wunderkind, a poor boy made good. Rampantly ambitious in business and in bed, Lucas is Ibiza's hottest export.
INES RUIZ	His struggling, downtrodden mother.
JOSE RUIZ	Her husband, Lucas's stepfather. A drunken bully.

PACO and DOMINGO RUIZ	Lucas's half brothers.
CARLA LEON	Lucas's lover-cum-mentor, a beneficent Mrs. Robinson.
PEPE LEON	Her doting husband.
BEN SLATER	Hedge fund millionaire, genius and all-round good guy. An Essex boy with a heart and wallet of gold.
EILEEN SLATER	His mum, a terrible cook.
KAREN and NIKKI SLATER	His sisters.
TAMMY	His devoted gem of a secretary.
SIAN DOYLE	Irish American beauty from Nowheresville New Jersey, an aspiring newspaper reporter.
SIMON DAVIS	Features Editor at the *News of the World*. Affectionately known to his staff as Satan.
BIANCA BATTISTA	Latin American supermodel. An angel inside and out.
DEVON CARTER	Fifty-something pillar of East Hampton Society, a successful lawyer and family man.
KARIS CARTER	His neurotic, fragile wife, a former model.
LOLA CARTER	Their drop-dead gorgeous, wild, red-headed daughter.
NICK CARTER	Their equally gorgeous, but spoiled and obnoxious son.
ALEX LOEB	East Hampton trust-fund brat, friend of Nick Carter.
ANTON TISCH	Billionaire businessman, hotelier and financier. An utterly ruthless control freak.
HEIDI	One of Anton's many exes, the mother of his daughter.

MITZI	Anton's German Shepherd dog, the only living thing he truly loves.
JULIA BRETT SADLER	Manager of the Tischen Cadogan, Anton's flagship London hotel.
PETRA KAMALSKI	Russian oligarch's daughter turned up-and-coming hotelier. Lucas Ruiz's sworn enemy, one of the few women impervious to his charms.
SASKIA KENNILWORTH	Slutty, Sloaney PR girl. Works for Anton in more ways than one.
MORTY SULLIVAN	Head of the East Hampton Planning Committee, courted by all would-be hotel builders.
WHIT HAMMOND	The last in a long line of lazy managers at Palmers.
ENRIQUE	Head Barman at Palmers. Part of the furniture, he has known Honor since childhood.
MIGUEL MUNOZ	Manager of The Britannia Hotel, Ibiza, and Lucas's first boss. A shit running a shit-hole.
PADDY MCGUIRE	Irish journalist and racing fanatic. A sweetheart.
MARTI GLUCKMAN	Clark Kent look-a-like internet entrepreneur.

Part One

Chapter One

'Over my dead body! D'you hear me? You'll take Palmers over my dead body, you scheming, greedy little—'

A fit of wheezing stopped Trey Palmer from finishing his sentence. But Honor, his eldest daughter, had already gotten the gist. Alzheimer's may have cruelly eaten away at his mental faculties, and old age ravaged his once enviable physique, but his bitterness was as razor sharp as ever.

'Mr. Palmer, please, don't upset yourself,' said the lawyer. Sam Brannagan had sat through more family disputes than he could remember, many of them in this very room. With its dark oak-paneled walls and reassuringly expensive soft furnishings it was all very old-school Bostonian – an appropriate setting for internecine warfare if ever there was one.

Watching the old man grapple with his oxygen mask while he glared at his hapless daughter, however, Sam didn't think he'd ever seen quite as much open hatred as he'd witnessed today. Looking around the room at the eager, greedy faces turned towards him, he felt intensely depressed.

Honor Palmer, who had convened today's meeting, was the only decent one among them. But even she was not exactly warm and cuddly. With her spiky, boyish hair, aquiline features and tiny, taut athlete's body, the newly minted Harvard Law graduate looked beautiful but forbidding. Everything about her, from her four-inch Louboutins and starkly formal black Prada pantsuit, to her low, authoritative voice and impressive grasp of the complex legal issues being discussed, betrayed a steeliness unusual in one so young. Especially a woman.

As for the rest of them – crowded into his office, huddled around the old man like sharks circling a wounded seal – they made his stomach churn.

There was Tina, Honor's younger sister, looking bored in the corner, glancing pointedly at her Chopard diamond watch. Also beautiful, but in a polar opposite way to her sister: blonde, blowsy and buxom were the three words that most readily sprang to mind. Tina looked like she'd picked up her wardrobe from Hookers-R-Us. Even at an important legal meeting like this, Boston's answer to Paris Hilton had shown up in a frayed denim skirt that barely covered her crotch and a pink man's shirt tied beneath her breasts to reveal a mind-boggling expanse of cleavage. From the look of distaste on her face as she listened to her father's phlegmy spluttering, it was clear she had no sympathy for him; nor did she seem remotely interested in her sister's attempts to save them all from financial ruin.

Even more see-through were the Fosters. Jacob, a distant cousin from Omaha, and his wife, had heard in the press about Trey's Alzheimer's and the threat to his empire and crawled out of the woodwork to see what they could scavenge. Both wore ostentatious crosses and proclaimed themselves loudly to be born-again Christians, but every reference to Trey's frozen bank accounts had them salivating like starving puppies. They'd spent most of today's meeting glowering disapprovingly at Lise, Trey's bimbo wifelette, whom they wrongly considered to be their key rival for the family inheritance.

Lise might give Lil' Kim a run for her money in the slutty dressing stakes, but, unlike the Fosters, she did at least have the advantage of being recognized by her husband. It was clear to Sam that neither Trey nor his daughters had ever set eyes on Cousin Jacob before in their lives.

On reflection, perhaps it was hardly surprising that they'd all shown up today. There was, after all, a lot at stake. The Palmers were one of the wealthiest, most prominent

4

families in Boston, and had been for three generations. Already rich when he emigrated from England, Trey's great-grandfather had multiplied the family fortune five-fold, becoming one of the first great American hoteliers. His first hotel, the Cranley in Boston's exclusive Newbury Street, made so much money that within a decade he'd opened two more: the King James Hotel in Manhattan, and the now legendary Palmers in East Hampton. By the time Trey's father, Tertius Palmer, came into his inheritance, the family's net worth was conservatively estimated to be over ten million dollars. And that was in the fifties. Heaven only knew what it translated to in today's money.

Like his father and grandfather before him, Tertius had been a naturally shrewd businessman. But whereas they had been expansionists, Tertius was a consolidator. Cashing in on the post-war real-estate boom, he sold the original two hotels for an outrageous profit, which he went on to invest very successfully in the equity markets. Having hired a raft of stockbrokers to manage his portfolio, he was free to focus his own energies exclusively on the one hotel he hadn't sold: Palmers. By the time of his death – the year before Honor was born – Palmers was widely considered to be the most exclusive, most desirable hotel in the world.

Honor and Tina grew up surrounded by reminders of its illustrious history. The hotel itself was like a second home to them. As little girls they could hardly contain themselves with excitement when, every summer, their mother Laura would help them pack their cases and they'd set off for three joyously long months of fun in East Hampton.

But when their mom died – Laura Palmer was killed in a car accident when her daughters were aged ten and eight respectively – everything changed. Trey, unable to admit his grief for fear it might overwhelm him, had cut himself off emotionally from everything that reminded him of his wife and their former life together. This included not only his children, who needed him more than ever, but also

Palmers. The hotel that had been the jewel in the Palmer family crown for half a century rapidly lost its premier status as Trey started spending less and less time there.

Now, some thirteen years later, it had become little more than another dime-a-dozen 'luxury' hotel, perhaps even a little shabbier than most of its rivals. If it hadn't been for the Palmer fortune propping it up, and for its still-legendary name, it would doubtless have closed years ago.

Honor took a deep breath to calm herself and gazed out of the window. She knew that what she was doing was right. Taking control of her dad's assets was the only way to save Palmers and what little was left of her once immense inheritance. But she still couldn't look Trey in the eye. Even after all these years, his dislike and distrust of her still hurt her very deeply.

Ironically, Brannagan's offices were on Newbury Street, almost directly opposite what had once been the Cranley hotel and was now a souped-up shopping mall. It was June, the schools had just got out for summer, and the place was busy. Students in shorts and varsity T-shirts stood around in groups laughing, sipping their frappuccinos in the courtyard cafe out front, while wealthy women hurried past them into the designer stores, no doubt looking for a bargain in the summer sales.

They all seemed to be having so much fun. For a fleeting moment, Honor wished she were down there too, frittering away her trust fund like she didn't have a care in the world. That was how Tina lived her life, after all, along with most of the other vacuous Boston rich kids they'd grown up with. So why not her?

But her stepmother's whining, wheedling voice soon dragged her back to reality.

'It's outrageous, Mr. Brannagan,' Lise was saying, doing her best to look hard done by, which wasn't easy given the twenty-odd carats of diamonds scattered generously about her person. 'Just because my baby is sick,' she placed a skinny, red-taloned hand on Trey's wizened leg, 'these vultures are trying to move in and take advantage.'

'Oh, please,' said Honor witheringly. Her voice was low and husky, making her seem even more masculine. 'Dad's nobody's "baby". And if anyone's the vulture here, it's you.'

Though officially her stepmother, Lise was actually only a couple of years Honor's senior. A former flight attendant with inflated Angelina Jolie lips and hair extensions that must weigh more than she did, she was the fourth bimbo Trey had married in the last twelve years, in the vain hope that one of them might bear him his longed-for son.

Ever since Honor and Tina's mom died, Trey had been obsessed with fathering a boy to take over Palmers and carry on the family name. Honor, who loved her father deeply and wanted desperately to please him, spent most of her teenage years trying everything she could think of to become the son he wanted. Not content with excelling at both academic work and overtly male sports like baseball and shooting, she started cutting her hair short and wearing boyish clothes in an attempt to make him happy. She even began starving herself: anything to stave off the arrival of puberty and the breasts she dreaded as unwanted, but irrefutable, symbols of her femininity.

But nothing was ever enough for Trey.

Unwilling to accept it was *he* who had the fertility problems, he'd refused to give up hope, foisting a series of ridiculously young stepmothers on his daughters. When each one failed to get pregnant, he simply divorced them in favor of a newer, younger model. But not before he'd been forced to pay out a small fortune in alimony.

After a while, Honor had become immune to these women. Lise was no better or worse than the others. But at twenty-seven, she sure wasn't with an elderly cripple like Trey because she loved him. To pretend she was was laughable.

'Dad's been declared incapable of managing his own affairs,' Honor continued matter of factly. 'That gives Mr. Brannagan, as his trustee, automatic power of attorney. The decision to put me in control of Palmers, and the rest of the family assets, was his and his alone. Right, Sam?'

The lawyer shifted uncomfortably in his seat. Was it just him, or was it getting awfully hot in here?

'So you're saying it means nothing that cousin Trey made it abundantly clear during his lifetime that he wanted Palmers to pass down the male line?' spluttered the Omaha cousin, sensing his hoped-for pay day slipping through his fingers.

'It's still his lifetime, Mr. Foster,' said Honor scathingly. 'He's not dead yet.'

'I've told you,' the cousin snapped back, 'it's Jacob.'

'Sorry,' said Honor, with heavy sarcasm. 'I'm afraid I was raised never to use first names with people I don't know from Adam.'

'Who's not dead?' Trey looked around him, bewildered. 'And who's Adam?'

Despite everything, it broke Honor's heart to see him so lost and confused. If the doctors were right, he might not remember who she was in a few months' time. Alzheimer's was a bitch of a disease.

'It's nothing for you to worry about, Mr. Palmer,' the lawyer interjected kindly. 'I can assure you that your daughter is acting in your best interests. She's very well qualified to take over the running of the business.'

Trey gave a short, derisory laugh. 'Well qualified? She's a woman, Mr. Brannagan,' he sneered. 'Evidently she's every bit as sly and conniving as the rest of her sex. But that hardly equips her to run the greatest hotel in the world.'

'But a dick and a pair of balls would equip her perfectly, right?' chimed in Tina. 'You're so pathetic.'

It was the first time she'd spoken since the meeting began and everyone turned to look at her. Cousin Jacob's wife

8

looked like she might be about to spontaneously combust with disapproval at the coarseness of her language.

'Don't get me wrong,' Tina continued, smiling at Brannagan. 'I really don't give a rat's ass what happens to Palmers. But if Honor wants to play the great white hope, I say we should let her. As long as I get my trust fund *and* my allowance, I'm easy.'

'Yes, we all know how easy you are,' said Honor furiously. It was bitchy, but she couldn't help it. Tina's devil-may-care wantonness had always provoked a mixture of revulsion and envy in Honor. She certainly didn't need it in her face today. 'And for your information, I'm not "playing" at anything. I'm only doing this because Dad's so ill.'

'Please,' said Tina, reaching down her bra to rearrange her breasts without a hint of embarrassment. 'That's bullshit and you know it. You've wanted to run Palmers since the day you were born.'

Honor was silent. It was true: she had always wanted Palmers.

But not like this.

From her earliest childhood, Honor Palmer knew she was different.

It wasn't just the envious way her little friends looked at her when the chauffeur would drop her and Tina off at kindergarten in the Bentley T-type. Or the photographers who frightened her by swarming around her mother and father whenever they went out to dinners or charity events. It was more than that. It was an awareness, reached very early, that the Palmer name she bore was not just a privilege but an immense responsibility.

She had never known her grandfather, and yet Tertius Palmer's presence seemed to be everywhere when she was growing up. His portrait hung in the entrance hall of the family's grand Boston townhouse. His books were on the shelves in the library. His heavy mahogany desk still dominated Honor's father's study. Even the gardens where she and Tina used to play, with their splendid formal maze and the willow walk along the banks of the Charles, had been designed and planted by Tertius.

Nowhere, however, was his spirit more alive than at Palmers. In the early days, before her mother died, Honor would spend every summer at the grand old Hamptons hotel, listening to stories of her grandfather and the wild and wonderful times he'd had there. To her child's eyes, Palmers was a wonderland. When she and Tina played mermaids in the pool, or had tricycle races along the endless polished parquet corridors, it was as if the outside world didn't exist.

The hotel guests, many of whom were elderly and had been coming for years, were remarkably tolerant of Trey's two boisterous little girls. Those who remembered Tertius were happy to pull Honor aside and tell her tall tales about the New Year's Eve party when her grandfather had danced with an Italian princess, or the day he'd landed a biplane on the hotel's croquet lawn.

Honor lapped up the romance of it all like a bear with a pot of honey. She wasn't the most attractive child – with her short hair, wire-rimmed glasses and skinny, matchstick legs, strangers often mistook her for a boy, and a nerdy boy at that. But at Palmers, she always felt like a princess. She was the chosen one, born to inherit and preserve all the excitement and magic that surrounded her. Because for Honor, above all, that's what Palmers *really* meant – magic.

Tina saw things differently, even back then. Two years younger than her sister, Cristina Maud Palmer was as blonde, blue-eyed and chubby cheeked as a Botticelli cherub, with a line in cuteness that would have put Shirley Temple out of business had she been born a generation earlier. Adults universally pronounced her 'adorable'. And she was, if pink hair ribbons, a frilly dress and an ability to sing 'How much is that doggie in the window?' were all you looked for in a child. But underneath the butter-wouldn't-melt exterior, a frighteningly detached, self-centered little person was forming.

Having learned early how to bend adults to her will, Tina pursued her own pleasure with all the ruthless determination of a general before battle. 'Pleasure' for Tina meant, very simply, the accumulation of things: toys, clothes, money, a puppy. Whatever the flavor of the month was, Tina Palmer would twirl and simper and cajole until it was hers.

Like Honor, she understood from an early age that her family was rich and important. But as far as Tina was concerned, that simply meant that she would grow up to have even more stuff, and live in even more luxury than she did now. Palmers was nothing more or less than another sign of that wealth. She had never understood Honor's sentimental obsession with the place and its history. As a child she longed for people to stop banging on about her boring, old, dead grandfather and bring her another ice-cream. Preferably with hot fudge sauce and a cherry on top.

Despite their differences, Honor and Tina had tolerated each other well enough in those early years. It was their mother's accident that changed things between them.

Honor still remembered the awful day as though it were yesterday. She'd been up in her room in Boston, playing an imagination game with her dolls, and had jumped out of her skin when Rita, the nanny, burst in. She was supposed to have grown out of the dolls and passed them on to Tina. But all Tina ever wanted to do was dress them up, and Honor felt sorry for them, discarded in her sister's toy box, never getting to go on any fun adventures any more. Her first thought was that Rita was mad she'd taken them back. She remembered feeling almost relieved to be told it was only her father wanting to see her downstairs.

Needless to say the relief was shortlived. The first thing

she saw when she walked into Trey's study was Tina sobbing hysterically on the couch. Honor remembered being shocked, because these clearly weren't her sister's usual crocodile tears. Something was very wrong.

Trey was making no move to comfort her. He just stood there, as gray and still as a granite statue in the middle of the room. 'Honor, there's been an accident.'

That was all he said at first. He wasn't crying. In all the weeks and months and years that followed, in fact, Honor never once saw him cry for the wife she knew he'd loved more than anything. But still, he seemed to be having difficulty getting his words out.

'Mommy's dead. She's not coming back.'

Clearly her father was not a subscriber to the 'break it to them gently' school of parenting. As an adult, Honor often wondered how many thousands of dollars in therapy that moment alone would have cost her, had she grown up to be the navel-gazing type. Thankfully, she hadn't. Because as awful as her mother's death was, far, far worse was to come.

Tammy. That was the name of their first stepmother. And what a fucking nightmare she was. Unlike the later models, she came from a respected Boston family, but her upbringing didn't seem to have prevented her from growing up into a class-A bitch. It was a year almost to the day since their mom's death and Trey had brought Tammy home like a trophy, beaming with a pride and happiness that Honor couldn't fathom.

'Honor, Tina, this is Tammy,' he said, kissing the strange woman on the lips. Honor, who was eleven at the time, thought she looked like a taller Snow White, with short black hair and porcelain-pale skin. But she wasn't kind and smiley like Mommy.

'She's going to be living with us from now on,' Trey continued. 'And we hope that pretty soon she's going to give you girls a little brother.'

We? Who was this *we?* Honor didn't hope for any such thing.

It was the first time she'd heard her father expressing a desire for a son. Over the next decade, that desire was to bloom into a full-grown obsession.

'Why?' Tina had asked, twirling her ringlets skeptically in the corner.

'Your daddy needs a boy so he can take over Palmers one day, honey,' simpered Tammy. 'And take care of you girls, too. That's what brothers do.'

'Daddy doesn't need a *boy*!' yelled Honor, pulling herself up to her full four foot nine, her jaw jutting in defiance. '*I'm* going to take over Palmers when *I* grow up. What do you know about it, anyway?'

'Honor.' Her father's voice was stern. 'Don't you dare speak to Tammy like that. Apologize at once.'

Honor had apologized. Not because she was remotely sorry. But because she couldn't bear for her father to be angry with her.

That night, she'd tried to talk to Tina about it. 'We have to do something to get rid of her,' she whispered, once the sound of their nanny's footsteps had finally died away.

'Like what?' Tina had her Winnie the Pooh flashlight on under the covers and was brushing her hair, admiring its shiny blondeness in the mirror with quiet satisfaction. Though only nine, she was already taller than Honor and much more physically developed, with tiny, nascent breasts of which she was inordinately proud. 'It's not up to us.'

'For goodness' sake,' hissed Honor, exasperated. 'Don't you understand how serious this is? She's horrible. She's a witch. And if she does have a baby boy, Daddy won't want us anymore.'

'I don't think he wants us now,' shrugged Tina, not missing a beat.

'Of course he wants us!' said Honor hotly. Although deep down she knew that the tears were pricking her eyes because her sister was right. Since their mom's death, Trey had been distant to the point of abuse. 'It's Tammy that's the problem. You know she's going to try and act like she's our mom. *And* I bet she'll try to take Palmers away. Her and her new baby.'

Sighing, Tina reluctantly switched off the flashlight and slipped the mirror under her bed. 'I wish you'd stop going on about Palmers. It's only a stupid hotel.'

Honor was so flabbergasted by this, she was temporarily speechless.

'And if she does try to act like our mom, we'll just ignore her. It's really not a big deal. Anyway, I'm tired. Let's go to sleep.'

Seething with frustration, Honor pulled her bedspread up to her shoulders and turned her head to the wall. There was no point pushing it any further. Clearly Tina had no understanding whatsoever of the dangers they were facing. As usual it would be up to her, Honor, to do something.

If a son was what their father wanted – and clearly it was – then that was what she'd have to become.

'Miss Palmer?'

Honor looked up with a start at the sound of Sam Brannagan's voice. For a moment she'd forgotten where she was.

'Shall we continue?'

'Yes, yes of course,' she said, smoothing the crease in her black pants as she got to her feet. This was no time for melancholy reflection. She needed to be in control.

'The fact is that while I appreciate all of you coming, there's really nothing left to discuss. The trustees have appointed me to manage Dad's affairs, including Palmers, and that's what I'm going to do. I had hoped,' she looked plaintively at Trey, 'to make you understand why I'm doing this, Daddy. Believe me, if there were any other way—'

'I'll change my will!' Trey shouted, the effort plunging

him back into another bout of coughing. Jacob Foster made a great show of passing him his oxygen mask, but the old man pushed him angrily away. 'You're a viper, Honor. A snake in my house!'

'Mrs. Palmer.' Seeing Honor struggling to suppress her emotions, the lawyer addressed himself calmly to Lise. 'For your husband's sake, I think you'd better take him home now. And that goes for the rest of you, too. All interested parties will be receiving copies of the documentation in due course. But this meeting is over.'

Slipping on her oversized Gucci sunglasses, Tina was the first to head for the door, without so much as a backward glance at Trey. 'Honor, call me,' she said brusquely. 'I wanna know when that money will hit my account.'

'This isn't over, you know,' said Jacob furiously, yanking his dumpy wife up out of her seat. 'Not by a long way. You'll be hearing from us again, Mr. Brannagan.'

Honor said nothing as they filed out of the room, but her heart was pounding. Harvard may have taught her how to deal with confrontation and take control of a hostile meeting, but it hadn't taught her not to feel sick to the stomach each time, especially when your adversary was your own father, whose mind had been taken over by dark, inexplicable shadows that made him distrust everything and everyone around him. He couldn't even trust his own senses any more, the poor bastard.

Lise was the last to go, leading the doddering Trey by the hand. Honor winced to see him so frail. She could only pray that, behind closed doors, his child-wife treated him with more kindness and compassion than she'd shown today. Somehow, she doubted it.

'I'll make you proud, Dad,' she heard herself calling after him, ashamed to hear her voice breaking with emotion. Why did she still need his approval so badly? 'I'll make Palmers great again. You'll see.'

Turning to look at her as the elevator doors opened,

Trey shook his head bitterly. He knew his periods of lucidity were getting rarer and rarer. But to be outwitted by his own daughter was more than his pride could bear.

'I hope God forgives you for this, Honor,' he muttered darkly. 'Because I never will.'

And stepping into the elevator with the rest of his so-called family, he was gone.

Chapter Two

'Lucas, stop – we can't! My husband might come any minute.'

Lucas Ruiz unzipped his jeans and pushed Señora Leon back against the living room wall, hitching up her skirt as he did so.

'Fuck your husband,' he growled. '*I'm* going to come any minute. And I intend to be inside you when I do.'

They were in the living room of the Leons' luxury villa in Ibiza. To Lucas's left, double height glass doors gave way to one of the most stunning panoramas on the island. Manicured gardens ran down the hillside, merging into olive groves that in turn blurred into the still, sparkling blue of the Mediterranean.

But Lucas was focused on a different view.

At forty-four, Carla Leon was twenty years his senior, but she still had a body designed for fucking. Her tits were round and high, and seemed to be straining now at the silk and lace of her bra as if willing him to release them. Her legs were long, but shapely, not like the twiggy twenty-something models at Pacha who seemed to think it sexy to starve themselves skeletal. Boy, did he hate that look. And even after three children her stomach was flat and toned, a testament to the long hours she spent each week in the gym.

Lucas was impressed. He liked a woman who took care of herself.

'Oh, God,' Carla moaned, closing her eyes and squeezing her muscles tightly around his dick as he powered into her, despite her earlier protests. 'That's so good.'

'Shhh,' he said, slipping a rough, warm hand over her mouth. 'Your husband, remember? Besides, I've hardly started.'

It was by no means the first time that he'd 'visited' Mrs. Leon. They'd first met five years ago, when he was still in his teens, and she and her husband were holidaying in Ibiza for the first time. Back then he was stuck working for that asshole Miguel, washing sheets and scrubbing toilets at the dreadful Hotel Britannia in San Antonio, the scummiest part of the island.

Even then, he already knew he was going to get out one day. One thing Lucas Ruiz had never been lacking was ambition. Nevertheless, it was Carla Leon who'd bought him his ticket to a new life, funding him through Hotel Management School in Switzerland.

This was the summer after his graduation, and he'd come back to see her to express his gratitude, the best way he knew how.

Staggering across the room with Carla's long legs wrapped around his waist, he laid her down on the pool table.

'Careful! Don't break it!' she gasped, arching her back and throwing her arms back behind her head so she could grip onto the corner pockets. Ignoring her, Lucas climbed on top of her, increasing the pace of his thrusts as he ripped at the lace of her bra with his teeth.

'You are so fucking sexy,' he breathed, his long black hair tickling her shoulders and neck now as he whispered in her ear. 'I'm gonna make you come so hard, you won't walk for a week.'

'Carla!' Pepe Leon's gruff, booming voice echoed through the house like the voice of God. '*Dónde está?*'

'Lucas!' Carla's eyes widened with panic. 'For God's sake, get out of here. Pepe's back.'

'I'm not going anywhere,' he said, his eyes lighting up like a mischievous schoolboy's. 'Not until you come for me, my lady.'

'Lucas!' she hissed. But at the same time she felt his hands slipping downwards beneath her bottom and his fingers probing her everywhere, rubbing and stroking as he pushed his huge cock deeper still inside her.

This was the sort of fuck that was worth losing your marriage for.

Gripping him tightly round the neck, like a drowning woman grasping for a buoy, her body exploded into shuddering orgasm. Moments later Lucas also came, biting down hard onto his forearm to muffle the sound of his own delight.

'What are you waiting for?' he whispered, grinning, once he'd finished. Leaping off the table he started pulling up his jeans with lightning speed. 'Don't you know your husband's home?'

Before Carla could catch her breath, he'd prized open the French doors, blown her a kiss, and sprinted off down the hillside like Carl Lewis.

She only just had time to do up her blouse and jump off the table herself before Pepe walked in.

'There you are, darling,' he said, kissing her on the cheek with the routine, absent-minded affection of the long-married. 'Did you have a good morning?'

'I did, thank you,' she said, glancing briefly out of the window. Thankfully Lucas was nowhere to be seen. 'I had a very enjoyable morning. Very enjoyable indeed.'

Lucas's birth had been a difficult one.

His mother Ines, at only sixteen and unmarried, had been left to cope with her delivery alone. Too frightened to go to hospital, she endured a long and terrifying labor in a remote olive grove close to the ramshackle farmworkers' cottage where she and Lucas's father Antonio were living.

Antonio had promised to be there for the birth. But of course when the time came he was too high on heroin to see straight, never mind deliver a baby. This was the seventies, at the dawn of the tourist explosion on Ibiza, and drug culture had descended on the once unspoiled island like a plague, bringing misery and destruction in its wake.

Lucas's father was only one of its many early victims. By the boy's first birthday he had disappeared from the scene completely. Ines presumed him dead, overdosed in a doorway somewhere, but she never knew for sure. In any case, within a year she was married, under intense pressure from her family, to a reclusive local farmer named Jose Ruiz.

Twice her age and a heavy drinker, Ruiz was not much of a husband. Nor did he have any interest in his young wife's brooding, withdrawn two-year-old son. The marriage was miserable from the start, but Ines nevertheless went on to produce three more sons in as many years. Lucas's earliest memories were of fighting with his brothers – for some reason they were always fighting – in the filthy two-roomed shack up in the hills that the Ruiz family called home.

They weren't happy memories. But as the years rolled by, they were to get worse. Jose's drinking spiralled into full-blown alcoholism, and shortly afterwards the beatings began. One day, an eight-year-old Lucas arrived home from school to find his stepfather passed out on the kitchen floor and his mother hunched over the dishes, crying, and trying to hide her split lip and swollen eye.

'Mama!' Running over to her he wrapped his arms around her waist, as fiercely protective as a little terrier. 'What happened? Did he hurt you, Mama?'

But Ines just shook her head angrily. 'Do your homework, Lucas,' she said, without looking up. 'Everything's fine now. Off you go.'

It was the moment that crystallized the boy's dislike of his stepfather into hatred. And it was also the first time he fully realized what it meant to be powerless. Those two feelings – hatred and powerlessness – became the driving forces of Lucas's adolescent years.

When Jose hit him there was physical pain, but Lucas rapidly learned to cope with that. It was the emotional torture of seeing his mother and little brothers being hurt that kept him awake at night, sobbing tears of frustration and rage. He knew what he had to do, of course: grow. Once he was big and strong enough to take on his stepfather physically, *then* he would know freedom. Then, and only then, he would know revenge.

He first started lifting weights at the age of ten. Not dumbbells, just any of the heavy detritus left strewn around the farm – tractor wheels, old crates of grain, rusting parts of long-abandoned harvesters. Though he was still short for his age, he rapidly saw a change in his build from wiry and athletic to stocky and strong. It was the first time any action of his had actually achieved something tangible. Before long he was hooked.

His longed-for day of reckoning didn't arrive for another five years, however. After a sudden growth spurt right after his fifteenth birthday, Lucas was finally able to look in the mirror and see a grown man staring back at him. Six foot tall, with an almost comically over-developed upper body, he was the sort of boy that anyone would think twice about picking a fight with. But it was the look in his eyes that really put the fear of God into would-be opponents. Underneath that wild, jet black mop of Jim Morrison hair, two darkly narrowed slits of liquid rage glinted murderously. All he needed now was an opportunity.

The next time Jose raised his fist to his wife, Lucas didn't just hit him. He beat him into bloody unconsciousness on the kitchen floor. Turning to his mother, flushed with triumph, he was horrified to find himself being screamed at.

'Lucas!' she yelled, tearing her hair, while his younger brothers looked on in awe. 'What have you done? You could have killed him!'

'And why shouldn't I kill him, Mama?' Lucas looked

21

baffled. 'After the way he treats you. The way he treats all of us.'

'He feeds us, Lucas,' said Ines, shaking her head. 'He clothes us. He puts a roof over our heads.'

'Barely,' spat Lucas, pulling at the peeling paper on the wall in disgust.

'Who's going to take care of us if your father can't work?'

'He's not *my* father,' said Lucas indignantly. He couldn't believe that they were having this conversation. Didn't his mother want to escape? Didn't she want to be free of him? 'And I can take care of us, Mama. I'll get work in town, in the hotels. I won't even drink away three quarters of my wages. How's that?'

'You don't understand!' said Ines. Wetting a tea towel she sank down to her knees and began mopping away the worst of the blood from Jose's face. 'You're still a child. You don't understand anything.'

She was right about that. He didn't understand.

Within twenty minutes, he'd thrown his few paltry possessions into a bag and was on the point of storming out. Jose remained motionless on the floor, although occasional soft moans indicated he *was* still alive – more was the pity.

'Mama,' said Lucas, hesitating at the last moment. 'Please. Come with me. Bring the boys. What do you have to stay for, for Christ's sake?'

He felt betrayed, bewildered, hurt beyond belief by her behavior. But he still loved her, and his brothers. If there was any chance at all to rescue them …

'*Querido*,' she whispered. There were tears in her eyes. 'I can't.'

It was the last time Lucas was to see her for four years.

The first twelve months were the worst. Lucas was used to poverty, but he wasn't used to having to sleep on the beach or in shop doorways. His first few jobs were all in the kitchens of cheap tourist cafes. The pay was third world, but the food was free, and a couple of the places even let him sleep on the floor behind the counter during the winter months.

The problem was that Lucas could never hold down a job for more than a few weeks. As soon as anyone crossed him – a temperamental cook, a demanding boss or a dissatisfied customer – he flew completely off the handle, settling disputes the only way he knew how: with his fists. Having worked so hard for it, it came as a shock to him to discover that his physical strength did not automatically translate to power and control. That sometimes it could lead him into situations beyond his control – situations that harmed him.

At sixteen, waking up cold and aching from yet another long night on the beach surrounded by junkies and hobos, he decided that his days of drifting were over. He needed a steady job, one that provided meals and accommodation as well as a wage.

By the end of that week he'd found one.

The kindest thing you could say about the Britannia Hotel in San Antonio was that it was a shit hole. Managed by a fat, ignorant sadist called Miguel Munoz, the place smelled constantly of disinfectant – it was that or vomit – and operated against a constant background white noise of electronic fruit machines, arguing couples and screaming children.

Lucas worked in the laundry room, which in some ways was a blessing as it kept him away from the loutish British and American guests, whom he soon came to loathe with a passion. But the work was tough, and often revolting, with sheets regularly covered in sick or worse. It made Lucas seethe that these rich foreigners – rich by his standards, anyway – flocked to his beautiful island in their droves, but when they got here, all they wanted to do was drink themselves into oblivion.

None of them made even the most cursory attempt to speak Spanish. They couldn't even be bothered to sample the cuisine, eschewing the delicious local tapas and fresh traditional dishes in favor of spaghetti bolognese or the ubiquitous 'chicken 'n' chips'.

But his time at the Britannia wasn't wasted. The hotel, like the rest of the dives in San Antonio, opened his eyes to a world of possibilities. If a fat slob like Miguel was making money hand over fist offering a service as atrocious as this – and he was, as he liked to remind his impoverished staff constantly – how much more money must there be in a decent, professionally run hotel?

Lucas had no intention of spending the rest of his life removing used condoms from other people's filthy bedding. He was going to get out of Ibiza. And he was going to get rich in the hotel business.

The first thing he needed, he rapidly realized, was an education. School had never felt like much of a priority during his hand-to-mouth childhood and the gaps in his basic learning were huge as a result. Undaunted, he enrolled himself in night school, and though he was often so tired after a day's work that he fell asleep in class, he nevertheless managed to complete his high school diploma within a year.

'I don't know what you're so happy about,' Miguel had taunted him the day he heard his results. 'What do you expect to do with that? Run ICI?'

But for once, Lucas didn't rise to the insult. Instead he quietly continued with his studies, focusing on the subjects that he knew would provide a passport to the better life he craved. To his own amazement and delight, he turned out to have a marked aptitude for languages. He'd already picked up a lot of English by osmosis from the tourists at the Britannia, and he rapidly added German, French and Italian to his repertoire. Not since he first started weight training as a kid had he experienced such a sense of achievement in such a short space of time. Slowly, like an early spring flower struggling up through the frost toward the sunlight, his confidence began to grow.

And languages were not his only talent. At school he'd been so withdrawn and moody, he'd barely noticed the lingering looks he got from girls in his class. But by seventeen he was well aware of the effect he had on the opposite sex, and the power it gave him.

Lucas's attitude to women was complicated. Having grown up watching his mother suffer, he felt protective toward most of the girls he slept with. His natural instinct was to like them. But his mother's example had taught him other things too: namely that women were weak, and not necessarily deserving of respect. These two conflicting beliefs, combined with his naturally awesome libido, made Lucas that rarest and yet, to many women, most desirable of males: a benevolent chauvinist pig: the sexual equivalent of a benign dictator.

Older women in particular found his combination of Latin good looks and macho sexual dynamism irresistible. Lucas made them feel beautiful, because that was truly how he saw them. But he refused to be controlled or tied down in any way.

Getting one of his wealthy, older lovers to fund his education was never something he consciously planned. And yet, when it happened, he felt quite happy to accept it as no more than his due.

As the months and years passed at the Britannia, his fantasy of one day owning his own hotel became more detailed and fully formed. His hotel would be the polar opposite of the Britannia: simple lines, an aura not just of luxury but of peace. In his mind he'd planned everything, right down to the linens and the table settings. It even had a name.

Luxe.

Not 'The Luxe' or 'Hotel Luxe'. Just the one word:

four letters to symbolize Lucas's vision. His little piece of heaven on earth.

He was describing the place to Carla Leon one Sunday afternoon five summers ago, after making love. The latest in his seemingly never-ending stream of Mrs. Robinsons, Lucas liked Mrs. Leon because she was adventurous and funny, and because she seemed to know so much about the educated, wider world that he yearned to be a part of.

'It sounds incredible, my darling,' she murmured, laying back against the mossy ground of the secluded woodland where he'd taken her. 'But you mustn't underestimate what you're going to need to make it happen.'

'You're talking about money?' said Lucas, sitting up and gazing moodily ahead of him. Why did everything always come down to that in the end?

'Not just money,' said Carla. 'The hotel trade is highly competitive. You need an education.'

'I'm getting one,' said Lucas proudly. 'I've told you that.'

Sitting up herself, gloriously naked, Carla leaned forward and began to stroke his bare back. Sometimes his strength frightened her. His muscles were so taut and bulging they looked like they might be about to erupt through his skin.

'It won't be enough,' she said gently. 'You need relevant qualifications. An MBA. The place you should really aim for is in Switzerland. The École Hôtelière in Lausanne. EHL. That's where all the top hoteliers train. Have you heard of it?'

'Of course,' said Lucas, who hadn't, but was too arrogant to admit it.

By the end of the week, he knew all there was to know about the school – courses, entry requirements, fees, foreign student visas. Carla was right. Lausanne was exactly where he needed to be. But getting there was going to be a daunting task.

The night she left with her husband for Madrid, Carla

made Lucas a promise: 'This time next year, if you've succeeded in passing all the international exams you need for entry, I'll fund your application.'

He neither thanked her, nor questioned her. He simply trusted in her word, and set about studying like he'd never done before, slaving over his books and sleeping with a copy of the EHL prospectus under his pillow, like a holy text. When at last he got his qualifications, with a month to spare before his 'year' was up, he called her.

They hadn't spoken since she'd left the previous summer. But Carla didn't sound remotely surprised to hear from him.

'Send me the application form, Lucas darling,' she told him. 'All you have to do is sign it. I'll take care of the rest.'

And so she had.

Lucas adored Lausanne. His courses were hard work, but nothing compared to the hell of the Britannia, and his ambition and drive carried him through the four years like adrenaline spurring on a marathon runner.

Most of his classmates were from wealthy, middle-class families, but to his surprise, Lucas found it easy to fit in. Social life at the EHL revolved around frat house parties and weekend ski trips, both of which he took in his stride. And of course, it didn't hurt that he was far and away the best looking guy on campus.

'Are you sure you haven't skied before?' Daniel, a buddy from his macroeconomics class, quizzed him suspiciously on their first trip to the mountains. 'You sure don't look like a beginner to me.'

They were in Murren, a tiny car-free hamlet burrowed into a mountainside in the Jungfrau valley. Home of the famous Downhill Club in the 1920s, it remained popular with British skiers looking for natural Alpine beauty, but without the ritz and pretension of the big resorts like St. Moritz or Courchevel, and was also favored by the local

Swiss. Lucas, who didn't know such storybook, Hansel and Gretel villages still existed, was utterly charmed.

'What can I say?' he grinned. Having just completed a tricky red run, he was feeling more than a little pleased with himself. 'I guess I'm a natural.'

'Right. A natural asshole,' the girl taking her skis off next to him muttered sourly, trudging up the hill to the restaurant to join the others.

Lucas had won over ninety-nine percent of his female classmates at Lausanne with his combination of humor, confidence and insanely good looks, but Petra Kamalski remained immune to his charms. The only serious challenger to his crown as EHL's top-performing student, she was just as beautiful as Lucas, although in a polar opposite way. In fact, with Petra, 'polar' was definitely the operative word: tall, reed-thin and as pale as the Snow Queen, she had cheekbones that could cut glass and the sort of ice-blue, Russian eyes that both mesmerized and terrified at the same time. Her long blue-black hair was always worn up in a high, tight chignon and her body, though clearly perfect, was hidden at all times beneath polo-neck sweaters and long governess-style skirts.

'What's her fucking problem?' Lucas asked Daniel, glaring after Petra as she strode up the hill in her ultra-expensive, fur-lined Prada ski suit.

'Don't take it personally,' said Daniel, slapping him on the back. 'That's just Petra. She hates anything with a penis.'

Although this was true, Petra's dislike of Lucas clearly ran deeper than generic froideur towards the opposite sex. In lectures she was constantly trying to trip him up, picking holes in all his arguments and doing her utmost to embarrass him in front of the professors. She'd even gone so far as to accuse him of plagiarizing one of her papers last semester – a serious allegation that, had she proved it, would have gotten Lucas kicked out. As it was, the authorities had ruled 'insufficient evidence', hardly the ringing endorsement of his honesty that Lucas had been hoping for. How come *Petra* had never been reprimanded for bringing the case maliciously, and stirring up trouble?

The answer to that one was simple: Petra's uncle was the oligarch Oleg Kamalski, a man rich enough to buy the whole of Lausanne, if not Switzerland, with his loose change. Old Oleg was not a man that anyone wanted to alienate – least of all an institution second only to Harvard Business School in squeezing cash out of its successful alumni.

For the rest of the ski trip, Lucas did his best to keep out of Petra's way. But it was hard. Not only were they sharing a chalet along with nine other classmates, but Murren was so minuscule it made Ibiza look like New York City, making it even harder to escape.

When the day of their departure finally dawned, Lucas wasn't sorry. He'd come back to Murren another time on his own, or at least without Petra, when he'd be able to relax. Checking out of the chalet, with only ten minutes to go before the train for Lauterbrunnen was due to leave, he suddenly discovered that his briefcase was missing.

'I don't understand it,' he said, spinning around in frustration. 'It's been under my bed the whole trip. Where can it possibly be?' Then, noticing Petra standing smugly in the lobby with the others, firmly clasping her own matching Chanel luggage, it dawned on him. 'You moved it, didn't you? What the hell have you done with it, you shit-stirring bitch?'

'My, my, we *are* paranoid,' she smirked. 'It's no good blaming others for your own disorganized habits. I don't know why you brought work up here with you anyway. I'm going to trounce you in management theory no matter how hard you cram.'

Lucas, who had never hit a woman, contemplated breaking his duck. But he knew that if he laid one finger on

Petra he *would* get kicked out. And he wasn't about to risk that for anything.

There was nothing for it but to stay behind and hunt. After three long hours, he found the case stuffed behind a pile of ski boots in the garage – damn that stupid woman. But by then it was too late to get a connection to Lausanne. He'd have to stay in the village another night – yet more wasted time and expense – and catch a train first thing in the morning.

With nothing else to do, he trudged up the snowy hill to the Regina Hotel and settled in for a long night at the bar. His plan was to stare into his whisky glass until a strategy for wiping Petra Kamalski off the face of the earth appeared before him. But after about fifteen minutes he found himself joined by a big blond Englishman about his own age who looked even more depressed than he did.

'Would you do me a huge favor?' the man asked, looking nervously about him. His accent was pure cockney, straight out of *Mary Poppins*, and deep enough to be menacing, had it not been for his 'gentle giant' aura. 'Would you pretend you know me?'

Even sitting on a bar stool, Lucas could see he was huge, at least six foot six and broader than a WWE wrestler. But his kind, slightly drooping eyes, freckles, and mop of surfer-blond hair were all more overgrown Labrador than killer Doberman. He was handsome, in an Iowa-farm-boy-meets-London-barrow-boy sort of a way. And right now he had a desperate, pleading look in his eye that not even a hardened cynic like Lucas could ignore.

'Sure,' he said, smiling. 'Why?'

Before the man could explain, three of the dullest-looking businessmen you could imagine – gray suits, center-parted hair, matching blue ties done up to strangulation point – walked into the bar and headed in his direction. Flinging his arms around Lucas in a bear hug, the stranger started loudly proclaiming his surprise and delight to see him.

'After all this time! Amazing!' he gushed enthusiastically. 'Fancy seeing you in Murren, of all places!'

The three Swiss stooges held back and hovered, looking baffled.

'This is Jimmy,' the man explained to them, gesturing towards a mutely smiling Lucas. 'We used to knock about together as boys. Haven't seen each other in ... ooo, how long has it been now, Jim?'

'Longer than I can remember,' said Lucas, who was rather enjoying himself.

The blond turned back to his companions. 'Look, d'you mind if we catch up for a bit? You guys go on to the fondu restaurant, and I'll, er ... I'll join you a bit later, yeah?'

'But ... but ... ' the first suit stammered, 'we are booking the table for four. Without you, we will be three.'

Jesus, thought Lucas. They couldn't have been any more Swiss if they'd been full of holes and gone 'cuckoo' on the hour.

'They'll understand at the restaurant. They know me there,' said the blond, reassuringly. 'Honestly, you lot go ahead and have a good time on me, all right? I'll catch up with you later.'

After more persuading in a similar vein, they finally waddled off, like three penguins skidding back out onto the polar ice. Only then did the blond breathe a sigh of relief and introduce himself.

'Thanks,' he said, pumping Lucas's hand like the arm of a slot machine. 'I'm Ben. Really, thanks so much. I swear to God, if I had to spend one more hour with those guys I'd have flung myself off the north face of the Eiger.'

'They did seem a little tightly wound,' conceded Lucas with a chuckle. 'I'm Lucas.'

'An honour and a joy to meet you, Lucas,' Ben grinned. 'Let me buy you a drink.'

Ben Slater, it turned out, ran a hedge fund in London and was in Switzerland wooing possible institutional investors.

The three stooges were all senior management from UBS, men almost exactly as powerful as they were dull.

'I know I ought to be over there with them, dunking my bread in the cheese and talking bond yield curves,' said Ben with a sigh. 'But I really can't face it. That fondu cheese is fucking disgusting anyway.'

Lucas laughed. 'I agree. Here's to bunking off.'

In the end, they got on so well that they both decided to stay on for a few more days, and this time actually enjoy the skiing. The staff at the Regina knew Ben well and were happy to move him into a larger two-bedroom suite so that he could share with Lucas. Better yet, he insisted on footing the bill for them both: 'Honestly, mate, my fund is paying. It's a corporate expense; you don't owe me a dickie bird,' and had been so persuasive that even the notoriously proud Lucas felt comfortable accepting.

Neither Ben nor Lucas were naturally big talkers, but over the course of numerous long piste-side lunches and evenings propping up the bar, they came to share pieces of their respective life stories, and discovered themselves to be somewhat kindred spirits. Ben had grown up in a happy family, unlike Lucas. But he had also been very poor, and had to work against the odds to shake off his background and achieve the professional success that he had. And there was something so impossibly good-hearted about him, so jovial and warm and open, one couldn't fail to be drawn to him. Having always hated Englishmen, especially cockneys since his string of bad experiences at the Britannia, Lucas was shocked to discover that the country could also occasionally turn out some genuinely charming people. Ben was the archetypal diamond in the rough, and from day one Lucas adored him.

For his part, Ben didn't think he'd ever met someone with as much energy and ambition and lust for life as Lucas. After the mind-numbing tedium of his business trip, being in Lucas's company was like being jolted back to life with a cattle prod – only funnier. They laughed all the time, about Petra, and Ben's hopeless love life, and the fat Swiss matrons in their bright pink jumpsuits, wiggling their hippo-like rear ends down the nursery slopes. By the time Lucas finally returned to Lausanne and Ben boarded his private jet back to London, both of them nursing hangovers worthy of a mention in the book of *Guinness World Records*, a lasting friendship had been forged. For a loner like Lucas, this was a seismic event in his life and, though they didn't see much of one another for the next few years, he never lost the feeling that in Ben he had gained a new brother.

Those carefree days in Murren with Ben felt like light years ago now. Jumping onto the bus for Ibiza Town, Lucas sank gratefully into a vacant seat and began to get his breath back. He flattered himself that he was still fit, but there was no doubt that the adrenaline involved in putting distance between himself and a potentially murderous, cuckolded husband took a lot more out of him than an hour on the treadmill.

Still, Carla was definitely worth it. She always had been. And a summer of exciting, extramarital sex was the very least he owed her after everything she'd done for him.

As the rickety blue bus wound its way down into town, he could see the tan-tiled roof of the guesthouse where he was staying. It wasn't the Ritz, but it was clean and the service was friendly. Certainly it was a world away from the dreaded Britannia.

He'd already come a long way. He knew he ought to feel happy, coming back home triumphant after graduating top in his MBA class. But in fact he felt more anxious than he had in Lausanne, before his finals. Part of it was nervousness about his upcoming interviews in London. He was applying for jobs at a number of hotels there, but the one he really wanted – a junior management position at the world-famous Tischen Cadogan in Chelsea – was going to be very hotly contested. Candidates with a lot more experience than he had were sure to be applying. And yet he knew, he just knew, that he could do a better job than any of them, if only he were given the chance.

But it wasn't just work that was bothering him. Yesterday he'd been to see his mother.

It was only the second time Lucas had been back since the day he'd stormed out aged fifteen. The first time was after he got accepted at EHL four years ago, and that had been so uncomfortable he'd been in no hurry to repeat the experience. He and his stepfather had hovered in the same room, barely acknowledging one another's presence, as awkward and stilted as teenage lovers at their first dance. Their mutual loathing hung in the air like the stench of rotting meat, but the only way to break the tension would have been through violence, a step neither man wanted to take.

It wasn't that Lucas didn't miss his mom and brothers, or that he'd stopped loving them. Far from it. But the pain of watching Ines wasting her life and continuing to take abuse from that monster Jose was more than he could bear. Instead he'd salved his conscience by writing and sending money. Even back in the Britannia days, when he could barely afford a stamp, he made sure to save something each week for his mother. Inevitably, though, the distance between them took its toll.

He hadn't realized quite how irrevocably his life had diverged from the rest of his family's until yesterday. Thankfully this time his stepfather was not around when Lucas turned up at the house. But that was all there was to be thankful for.

The house itself was even more dirty and dilapidated than he remembered it.

'Jesus, Mama,' he said, looking around him in horror at the grimy windows, crumbling woodwork and shoddy furniture. 'What did you do with the money I sent you last month?'

Ines shrugged. 'Your father took it. He had to pay some bills.'

Had to buy some more whisky, you mean, thought Lucas bitterly. The lines around his mother's mouth and etched in deep grooves along her forehead spoke of a lifetime of hardship – hardship that could have been avoided, if only she'd had the courage to come with him, to break away. She was only forty, but she looked twenty years older at least, and so fucking defeated, it made him want to scream.

'And what about Paco? He's earning, isn't he? Or Domingo. Why aren't they contributing?'

The two older boys were eighteen and twenty now and still lived at home. It was a disgrace that they'd let the place sink into such squalor.

Ines gave a short, bitter laugh. 'Your brothers? Since when do they help me? Paco's girlfriend is pregnant, nearly six months now. All his money goes to her.'

Lucas shook his head. Fucking idiot kid. How hard was it to use a condom?

'And Domingo, he's just like his father. Drinking.' Picking up an empty beer bottle from the table, she threw it onto the overflowing trash.

Sighing, Lucas rolled up his sleeves and set about tidying the place up. He'd wanted so badly to talk to his mom – really talk – about his life in Switzerland, and London and his plans for the future. But he realized now how futile that would be. There was nothing about his world or his friends that Ines would understand. Nothing at all. The education that had liberated him had also driven a wedge between the two of them that made communication impossible. He may as well have been talking Urdu.

By the time he left, the house was at least clean, and the flowers he'd brought his mother added a tiny touch of color and joy to the otherwise cheerless kitchen. That had made her smile, as had the rolled-up wadge of notes he'd pressed into her hand despite her protests, and made her promise to hide from Jose.

Even so, when they said their goodbyes Lucas drove straight down to the first dive-bar he could find and drank until he could hardly stand. He didn't think he'd ever felt so depressed in his life.

'Ibiza Town!' The bus driver's voice jolted him back into the present. 'Everybody off, please.'

Wearily, Lucas got to his feet and staggered down the steps into the harbor. It was gone two now, and the early afternoon sun beat down on his head remorselessly, re-awakening the hangover that his tryst with Carla had made him temporarily forget.

He'd go back to the guesthouse and sleep. And then tomorrow he'd look into booking himself onto an earlier flight to London.

Summer in Ibiza had seemed like a great idea when he was back in Lausanne. But now that he'd done his duty by the lovely Mrs. Leon, he realized there was nothing left here for him to stay for.

The Tischen Cadogan. That was the future.

And as far as Lucas Ruiz was concerned, the future was all that mattered.

Chapter Three

After an unpleasantly humid and muggy start to the summer, July brought a welcome still, dry heat into Boston that was already starting to turn the city's leaves a glorious pale gold. Like most college towns, Boston sank into a weird sort of suspended animation during the summer. The sedate flow of the Charles was no longer disturbed by rowdy rowing squads every morning, and America's gilded youth with their armfuls of books suddenly vanished into the ether, replaced by flocks of summer tourists who crawled all over Newbury Street with their cameras and fanny packs like so many heat-exhausted ants.

With the students gone, city gossip shifted from academic back-stabbing and faculty affairs to the comings and goings of the great old Boston families. Gossip, Honor had often thought, was Boston's lifeblood, and this past summer it had been her family's turn to provide the civic entertainment. Everyone who was anyone in Boston society had an opinion about Trey Palmer losing control of the family assets to his headstrong elder daughter. Most of them, Honor was all too uncomfortably aware, seemed to have decided that she was the villain of the piece.

'Do you still prefer to wait, Miss Palmer, or would you like to order an appetizer now?'

The waiter hovered awkwardly by Honor's table, waiting for a response. He looked barely old enough to have left high school, and seemed to suffer agonies of embarrassment every time she looked him in the eye. Beautiful women clearly made him nervous, poor kid.

'I guess I'll order,' she sighed, glancing again at the

understated, antique man's watch on her wrist. 'Fucking Tina,' she added under her breath.

She ought to have gotten used to her sister's lateness by now, but somehow it still pissed her off every time. How come she, with a vast business empire to run and a schedule so rammed with work it made the president's look lightweight, could manage to show up to lunch on time; but Tina, who appeared to do nothing but paint her nails all day and get her picture taken, was incapable of getting her shit together?

What made it worse was that they were meeting today at Tina's request. She was demanding an astronomical raise in her monthly allowance from the trust, which Honor had flatly refused to authorize. But Tina wasn't about to take no for an answer.

A commotion out on the restaurant terrace made Honor look up. A small gaggle of kids, college boys by the look of them, had pushed their way through the tables and were fighting with each other trying to get pictures on their cell phones, much to the annoyance of the al- fresco diners.

'Step back now, please.' A booming, male voice rang out through the melee. 'No pictures. Let Miss Palmer through.'

Honor put her head in her hands. Why did her sister always, *always* have to make a scene?

Dressed utterly inappropriately for the formal restaurant in a tiny pair of white shorts and pink vest top, Tina was strutting through the throng, accompanied by a suited black man not much smaller than a rhino.

'Hi,' she said breathlessly, reaching Honor's table at last, but sitting down only once she was sure that all eyes in the room were on her. 'Sorry about that. Ever since I hooked up with Danny I can't seem to go anywhere without, you know,' she waved regally at the gaggle of boys outside, 'all this shit.'

'Is Godzilla staying for lunch?' Honor asked frostily,

nodding at the black giant who stood looming over them, arms folded, like a sentinel. 'Because if so, you can eat on your own.'

'He's my security,' Tina pouted. 'I need him.'

Seeing Honor pushing her chair back to leave, she reluctantly relented.

'Oh, all right then. Mike,' she turned to the heavy, 'you'd better go wait in the car. I won't be long.'

Once he'd gone and the furore in the restaurant had finally died down, Honor let her have it: 'What the hell do you think you're playing at?' she hissed.

'What do you mean?' Tina feigned innocence. It wasn't a look that suited her.

'Turning up here looking like Cristina fucking Aguilera,' said Honor. 'Courting publicity like some cheap starlet. You promised me you'd cut it out, at least until I make some progress with Palmers. You *know* how conservative our clientele are – what's left of them,' she added ruefully. 'Everything this family does reflects on the business.'

'Blah, blah, blah,' said Tina, looking bored. 'Change the record, would you? Martini,' she added, barking at the waiter without looking up.

'*And* you're late,' said Honor. Her green cat's eyes were flashing with irritation, and her knuckles were white from where she'd been clenching her napkin so tightly. But other than that she betrayed no outward sign of her fraying patience. Unlike Tina, she had always preferred to keep her inner feelings private. Even at school, kids used to tease her that the 'C' of her initials – actually 'Constance' – stood for 'Control.'

'I'm late because people kept stopping me for pictures,' said Tina. 'And I'm not courting publicity, thank you very much. *I* can't help it if people find my life exciting, or think I'm a sex symbol or whatever, can I? That's the way life is when you're a famous actress.'

Honor bit her lip. The arrogance was breathtaking.

'Tina, you've done two commercials. That doesn't make you a famous actress.'

'It makes me an actress,' Tina shot back. 'And dating Danny's made me famous. Whether you like it or not.'

Ah yes. Danny.

Danny Carlucci, officially a local real-estate entrepreneur, was in fact a well known mafioso, tipped by those in the know as the likely future boss of Massachusetts. He was pushing sixty, heavily overweight, and already had a wife, two grown sons and a legion of grandchildren. He was also Tina Palmer's latest lover.

'We need to talk about that, too,' Honor whispered. 'It's got to stop.'

Tina's martini arrived at the same time as Honor's sparkling water. Taking their drinks they both ordered salads – Tina was on a diet and Honor seemed to have suddenly lost her appetite. It was a few minutes before either of them spoke again.

'I'm open to it. Breaking it off with Danny, I mean,' said Tina, taking the olive out of her drink and pulling it in and out of her mouth slowly, like a porn star.

'Really?' Honor was surprised. She hadn't expected her to give in so easily.

'Sure,' said Tina. 'If I can afford to, that is. Danny pays for a lot of my shit right now. And he's been talking about setting me up in my own place in LA. I really need to be there now, for my work.'

Oh, so *that* was the deal. Blackmail. She'd drop the mobster if Honor upped her cash. It was such vintage Tina, it actually made her smile.

'How much?'

Tina looked blank.

'How much for you to drop Danny and move to the West Coast?' Honor clarified.

'Well, LA's not cheap,' said Tina, downing the last of her cocktail and immediately scanning the room for the waiter to order another. 'And I'd have to live in Holmby Hills, obviously.'

'Oh, obviously,' said Honor, rolling her eyes. Holmby was by far the most expensive neighborhood in the city, out-pricing homes in next-door Beverly Hills by almost three to one. 'So. How much?'

'Forty-five a month,' said Tina.

Honor choked on her water. 'Forty-five thousand? Dollars?' she spluttered. 'A month? Jesus, Tina. Do you understand the financial hole Dad's gotten us into? Palmers is losing money every day. Every fucking day.'

'Fine.' Tina shrugged as her salad arrived and started attacking it with gusto. 'So I'll stick with Danny. He can pay. *Or* I'll move to New York. See what turns up there. I am willing to compromise you know, Honor. I don't know why you always make me out to be this, like, unreasonable bitch.'

A move to New York was Honor's absolute worst nightmare, and Tina knew it. It was bad enough having her sister all over the gossip columns in Boston. But at least Boston was insular, a tiny social world unto itself. Once Tina started flashing her underwear and flaunting her underworld sugar-daddies on the New York club scene, it was only a matter of time before the bad press went national.

Honor was flying out to the Hamptons herself next week, and when she did she wanted Tina to be as far away as possible. For the last month she'd been holed up with the accountants in Boston, poring over Palmers' depressing P&L and trying to figure out a plan of action. But the time had come to see the hotel's problems for herself. She was dreading it.

'Fine,' she said, waving at the waiter for the check, although she hadn't touched her own food. 'You win. I'll sign off on forty-five thousand.'

'Good.' Tina positively beamed with triumph.

'But I want you on a plane to LA by the end of the week. And the very first whisper I hear about you and that slimeball Carlucci …' Pushing back her chair, she got to her feet. 'The money stops like *that*.' She clicked her fingers for emphasis. 'Are we clear?'

'Sure,' said Tina. Having got what she wanted, she was more than willing to be accommodating. 'I'll get the check here, don't worry. And hey, good luck with the hotel next week, OK?'

'I don't need luck, Tina,' said Honor drily. 'At this point I need a miracle.'

And slipping on her sunglasses, she strode out of the restaurant.

Sitting in the back of a blacked-out limo five days later, Honor tried again to focus on the papers in front of her. On the top was a spreadsheet of all the Palmers staff and their monthly wages. Normally she was brilliant with figures, but today for some reason the numbers swirled around her head like the pink elephants in *Fantasia*, and she couldn't concentrate.

Giving up, she gazed out of the window instead. They were almost at Southhampton now, and she could still feel a faint echo of her childhood excitement as the familiar landmarks rolled past: The Boxfarm Inn; the roadside cherry stall that had been there since Honor was a tiny kid and which looked completely unchanged; the hollow tree where she and Tina used to play hide and seek.

Honor hadn't been back here in almost seven years, not since she first started college, and already she was regretting her long absence. Despite everything, the Hamptons still felt like home.

Not that today was likely to be much of a homecoming. Though she feigned indifference, the spiteful whispers about her 'conning' Trey out of Palmers and 'stealing' her inheritance had left her deeply wounded, and insecure about the reception she'd receive. She was also acutely aware that most of the industry shared her father's view that she was far too young and inexperienced to turn around the failing hotel. They'd written both her and Palmers off and beneath all the spiky bravado, Honor worried herself sick that they might be right.

She'd deliberately decided to show up unexpected a day early so that Whit Hammond, Palmers' dilettante manager for the past decade, wouldn't have a chance to get too prepared. However bad things had gotten at the hotel, she needed to see the reality, not the edited, Sunday-best version.

As always when there was a confrontation looming, she'd been horribly stressed last night. Twitching with nerves and frustration in her lonely kingsize bed, she'd tried to masturbate, but was so tightly wound she found she couldn't come. Thanks to her short hair and deliberately masculine dress sense, most people assumed she was either a lesbian or just not interested in sex. In fact her boyish look, like her punchy, aggressive personality, was only a disguise, armor she'd donned in her teens to protect her from her father's rejection and never quite learned how to take off. She yearned to be loved and desired, but sex was a game she simply didn't know how to play. The few lovers she'd had had all tended to be older men, fairly obvious father figures, but they never lasted for long. Her longest relationship, of eight months, had been with one of her professors at Harvard, a kind, bookish divorcee in his early fifties. Drawn by her fierce beauty and intelligence, he had done his best to coax her out of her shell as a lover, constantly assuring her of her beauty and gently offering his love. But Honor's insecurities were so huge – deep down she loathed the athletic, boy's body she went to such lengths to maintain, and she had about as much sexual confidence as a spotty teenager on a first date – that in the end he, too, gave up.

Sexual frustration added to the tension that snaked its way around her heart now, in the back of the limo, at the prospect of returning to Palmers. She was coming back, not just as Trey's daughter and Tertius's granddaughter, but as the boss. It was a strange and, at times, a terrifying feeling.

Thankfully, by the time the car swung into the grand, graveled forecourt, she'd pulled herself together sufficiently to make a suitably confident entrance. The hotel's timeless, half-timbered elegance was just as she remembered it. Originally built as a wealthy merchant's summer home in the late eighteenth century, Palmers had always exuded a sort of genteel restfulness, with its wraparound wooden porches and forests of trailing wisteria clinging to the ancient walls like barnacles. Most of the older homes in East Hampton were made of gray, weathered wood. But Palmers stood resplendently white, a single iridescent flake of snow amid the verdant green of her gardens.

To Honor, that pristine whiteness had always been a large part of the hotel's magic. But today she could see that the paint was not only fading but actually peeling away in places. Even worse, small nickel-sized pieces of facade had begun breaking off in chunks, and had been left lying scattered on the steps and front lawn like giant crumbs from a wedding cake. As for the gardens themselves, Tertius would be spinning in his grave to see how overgrown and neglected they'd become, with dead leaves blowing everywhere and weeds left to multiply unfettered amid his beloved English rose garden.

The place was a disgrace.

Striding grimly up the steps into the lobby, Honor threw the receptionist into a spin by demanding that the manager appear immediately.

'I'm afraid Mr. Hammond is, er, unavailable just now, Miss Palmer,' stammered the hapless girl. 'We weren't expecting you until tomorrow.'

'So I see,' said Honor, snapping the dead head off one of the wilted roses in the vase by the door, and staring pointedly at the overflowing wastepaper basket in the corner of the lobby. 'Where is he?'

'Well, I ...' the girl trailed off, blushing the color of an overripe beetroot. If she looked any more awkward she'd probably burst into flames. 'I'm not a hundred percent sure he'd want me to say.'

Honor's lips tightened. Resting both hands on the desk, she leaned forwards ominously. 'What's your name?'

The girl swallowed. She was older than Honor and a good foot taller, but she didn't think she'd ever felt quite so intimidated in her life. It was the deep, gravelly voice that did it.

'Betty,' she mumbled. 'Betty Miller.'

'OK, Betty,' said Honor. 'I'm going to ask you one more time. And either you tell me where Mr. Hammond is, or I fire you. Do you understand?'

The girl nodded miserably.

'So.' Removing her sunglasses, Honor smiled patiently. 'Where is he?'

'He's at the golf club,' whispered Betty. 'He's been there all morning.'

Guests who heard the screams and yells coming out of the manager's office a few hours later were sure that some of them must have warranted a reading on the Richter scale.

'But Miss Palmer, you're being completely unreasonable!' Whit Hammond could be heard shouting himself hoarse. 'I was entertaining guests. That's a legitimate part of my job. Perhaps if you knew a little more about the hotel business, or were willing to listen to wiser heads—'

But Honor hadn't let him get any further.

'Don't patronize me, you lazy son of a bitch,' she roared. 'I know enough about the hotel business to realize you've been ripping my family off for the last God knows how many years.' Leaning across the desk – this morning it had been his desk, but now it was most definitely hers – she brandished the rolled-up spreadsheets like a sword.

'Those numbers don't tell the whole story,' he spluttered lamely. 'It's a lot more complicated than that.'

Honor felt her upper lip curling with disdain. Whit personified everything that was wrong with Palmers: overweight, stubbornly complacent, his florid, ruddy cheeks criss-crossed with broken veins that spoke of a lifestyle of high living and neglecting his duties.

'You're right,' she said. 'The numbers are only half the story. The other half is shoddy housekeeping, poorly trained staff, a kitchen that would have us closed down in a heartbeat if anyone from Safety and Health saw it. This was the greatest hotel in America once, Mr. Hammond.'

'With respect, my dear,' he simpered, 'that was a long time ago. Things have moved on.'

'Yeah,' said Honor. 'They have. And now they're moving on again. You no longer have a job here. And I am *not* your *dear*.'

The decibel level had shot up still further at this point, with plenty of 'you can't do this's and 'you'll be hearing from my lawyer's thrown in for good measure. But within an hour the manager who only yesterday had been considered part of the furniture at Palmers, with a job for life, had packed his things into a couple of boxes and driven out of town like a spluttering, paunchy Jesse James.

By the end of the day, some twenty-five other staff had followed in his wake, fired with equal firmness and finality by a righteously indignant Honor. And there would be more to come. The era of the freeloader was well and truly over at Palmers, and anyone who didn't like it could lump it.

It was gone eight in the evening by the time Honor finally emerged from Whit's ex-office. She was shattered – she hadn't even had a chance to take her case up to her

46

suite and unpack, never mind eat or take a shower. Right now, though, the number one thing she needed was a drink.

Heading for the hotel bar through the lobby and the library with its roaring open fires and thickly comforting red velvet upholstery, she couldn't help but notice the way that staff scurried out of her way like terrified rats. Even the guests looked distinctly ill at ease. By the time she clambered up onto a bar stool and ordered her Scotch on the rocks she was starting to feel about as popular as Lady Macbeth.

'Tell me,' she turned to the middle-aged man sitting next to her. 'Can you see the blood on my hands? Or am I imagining things?'

'I'm sorry?' He looked perplexed, and she instantly regretted being so obtuse. Partly because he was probably a guest, and the last thing she could afford to do right now was alienate another paying customer, and partly because he was, she now realized, distinctly attractive, in a gravelly, distinguished, older-man sort of a way.

He was wearing a slightly threadbare tweed jacket and corduroy pants, giving him the air of a somewhat countrified Cary Grant. Until Honor had accosted him, he'd been reading Stephen Hawking's *A Brief History of Time*, which for some reason she found both surprising and endearing. Somehow it wasn't what you expected in East Hampton, or at least not in the Palmers bar.

'Never mind,' she said. 'I'm afraid I'm talking gibberish. It's been a long day.'

'Well.' Putting his book to one side the man smiled, revealing a row of slightly crooked teeth. Even those seemed to suit him. Perfect dentistry would have clashed with the whole academic, Indiana Jones vibe he had going on. He reminded her a bit of her Harvard professor, although perhaps not quite as gentle. 'Why don't you let me buy you that drink, and you can tell me about it.'

Honor waved her hand in protest, but he wasn't having any of it.

'A woman shouldn't drink alone,' he insisted. 'Especially not whisky.'

In another place, with another man, Honor would have taken umbrage at this sort of sexist pronouncement. As it was, she merely smiled, and offered him her hand. She hadn't the stomach for another battle this evening. 'Well, in that case, I'll accept the offer, thank you,' she said. 'I'm Honor Palmer.'

For some reason this nugget of information seemed to throw him off stride. For a moment he didn't say anything at all. When he did speak again, it was hardly the most articulate of responses.

'Honor Palmer. Good God.' He kept shaking his head, mumbling to himself like a lunatic. 'Honor Palmer. After all these years.'

'Er, have we met?' Now it was Honor's turn to look baffled. Just her luck that the only attractive man in the hotel should be a nut-job. It was turning out to be that kind of day.

'We have, yes,' said the man. He was smiling again now. 'But I don't expect you to remember. You must have been, oh, about eight at the time. Sitting on your mother's knee in the garden just out there. I'm Devon Carter,' he added belatedly.

Carter. Honor turned the name over and over in her mind, like an interesting pebble, searching for some clue to its meaning. Devon Carter. It did ring a bell. But she couldn't quite place it.

'My family's from Boston too, originally,' he explained. 'We've been coming out here in the summers for over a century, just like the Palmers – although sadly we never did quite as well in the Hamptons as your lot. My father and your grandfather were good friends.'

Honor clicked her fingers. 'Evelyn. Your dad was Evelyn Carter, right?'

Devon nodded. 'Exactly. Apparently our great grand-fathers used to play poker together back in Boston. My dad used to say that old man Palmer died owing his grandpa a fortune. But maybe that's apocryphal.'

Honor laughed. 'Well, if you've come looking for your money, Mr. Carter, I'm afraid you've come to the wrong place. Between my sister and this place,' she looked around her at the distinctly down-at-heel, half-empty bar, 'I'm pretty much cleaned out right now.'

'It's Devon,' he said, looking her directly in the eye in a way she found both flattering and disconcerting. 'And it isn't your money that interests me, Honor.'

Honor blushed. He was flirting with her! Men *never* flirted with her. At long last she felt herself letting go of some of her pent-up tension and starting to relax. It was nice. *He* was nice. At least, he seemed to be.

'Are you propositioning me?' she asked bluntly. She never had learned how to do the coy, eyelash-fluttering thing.

Devon grinned. He was looking less 'teacher' and more 'naughty schoolboy' by the second. 'If I am, then I'm afraid I shouldn't be,' he said. 'I'm probably old enough to be your father. And besides,' he stared deeply into the amber liquid in his own glass, 'I'm married.'

Honor couldn't help but notice that he said this last with all the enthusiasm of a man admitting to advanced-stage syphilis.

'You don't sound too happy about it,' she observed.

Devon shrugged. 'It is what it is.'

It was as if she'd inadvertently popped a balloon. All at once his mood had shifted from playful to serious. The next thing she knew he was looking at his watch and gathering up his coat, preparing to leave.

'Please, don't leave on my account,' she blurted, unable

49

to keep the disappointment out of her voice. 'I was only kidding about the proposition thing.'

'Look, sorry,' he said, pulling out a twenty-dollar note and leaving it on the bar beside the pretzels. 'It's not you. I have to get home, that's all. But it was a pleasure meeting you again, Honor. Really. Maybe next time you're in town we can catch up properly.'

'I'd like that,' she said. 'Actually, I'll be staying in town for a while, if you—'

But he'd already gone, hurtling out of the door like he had a fire to put out.

She seemed to be having this effect on people a lot today.

'What do you know about that guy?' she asked Enrique, the barman, after he'd gone.

Now in his sixties, Enrique had been running the bar at Palmers since before Honor was born. As one of the few staff who knew for sure his job was safe, he was more than happy to stop and chew the fat with her.

'Devon Carter? He's Mr. East Hampton,' he said. 'Or at least, he is for the summers. Comes out here every year with his family, sometimes for Easter too. He's on the planning committee, secretary of the golf club, part-time deacon over at St. Mark's ...'

'Jeez, OK, OK,' said Honor, frowning. 'I get the picture. He's Ned Flanders.'

'Not quite so God Squad,' chuckled Enrique, surprising Honor by getting the *Simpsons* reference. Somehow he didn't seem the type. 'But he's big on family values, yeah. Definitely not for you, my dear.'

'For me? Oh, don't be so silly,' said Honor, blushing again. 'Although, for what it's worth, I'll have you know I'm *huge* on family values. And I bet you my family's *much* more valuable than Devon – deacon-of-St.-Marks – Carter's.'

Enrique smiled and poured her another drink.

'It's good to have you back, Miss Palmer.'

'Thanks,' said Honor with a sigh. 'But I'm afraid you're the only person around here who thinks so.'

Chapter Four

Lucas tried to tune out the drunken ramblings of the stinking tramp sitting next to him on the tube as he re-read the article in yesterday's *Evening Standard*.

'What saddens me most,' says bubbly Heidi, her eyes brimming with tears, 'is that Carina's the innocent victim here. She's a four-year-old child that desperately needs help. How can her own father let her down like this?'

The paper had devoted two full pages to the interview and pictures of 'bubbly Heidi' explaining that she was now a trainee nursery school teacher – although looking at her brassy hair and short black skirt it came as no surprise to Lucas to learn that her previous occupation was 'exotic dancer.' It was in this incarnation that she'd met and become involved with the millionaire hotelier and hedge fund guru, Anton Tisch. The same Anton Tisch whose office Lucas was currently on his way to, for the third time in as many days.

'He makes himself out to be this kind, charitable man, like some sort of saint,' Heidi went on damningly. 'Yet he won't even provide basic medical care for his own kid. It's disgusting.'

If the story was accurate, Lucas was inclined to agree. Apparently, having fathered a daughter by this cretinous-looking young woman, Tisch had only agreed to pay basic maintenance for the child when forced to do so by court order. This, despite having, conservatively, eight hundred million-odd quid in the bank. Like so many of the Eastern European and Russian super-rich who'd washed up in London in recent years, the original source of Tisch's vast wealth remained an open question. Certainly he was known to have close links with Ilham Aliyev, president of Azerbaijan and ultimate controller of the Baku-Ceyhan pipeline responsible for piping a million gallons of oil a day into Western markets. Though no longer in the energy business – his passport described him as a 'fund manager and investor' – Tisch's money still reeked of Caspian crude.

When doctors had diagnosed his illegitimate daughter with severe autism a year ago, Heidi had gone back to her erstwhile lover asking for more money to pay for a nurse and to help fund a place for the little girl at special school. But Tisch had told her to take a running jump. Unable to raise the legal fees to fight him a second time, Heidi had sold her story to the tabloids instead.

Of course, it might not be true. To be honest, Lucas wanted to believe it wasn't; not least because it was depressing to learn that the man he hoped would soon be his employer was tighter than a mosquito's asshole and had about as much compassion as a Nazi concentration camp commandant. But something about *bubbly Heidi*'s face told him she was telling the truth. She might be a tart, but she didn't look like a liar.

'Embankment. This is Embankment.' The oddly soothing, automated woman's voice rang out through the speakers. 'Next stop, Westminster. Change here for Charing Cross and other mainline stations.'

Only one more stop, thank God. There were lots of things Lucas hated about London: the weather, the prices, the way strangers kept calling him 'mate.' But he reserved a specially vehement dislike for the filthy, overcrowded underground system. Normally he'd have walked the four-odd miles from the Cadogan, where he was staying, to Tisch's office overlooking the Thames. But despite the fact it was August, the rain today was torrential, and he couldn't afford to show up looking like a drowned rat.

He'd been to London before, to visit Ben, but never

for more than a few days, and he'd spent most of those trips too drunk to know his left from his right, never mind what city he was in. But having lived here now for nearly two months, he was having serious second thoughts. Why couldn't he have set his heart on a job somewhere warm and civilized, like Madrid or Rome? With his languages and starred MBA, he could have gone just about anywhere in Western Europe. Did he really *have* to pick this grayest, wettest, most astronomically expensive of cities, and surround himself with a nation of people he had long ago learned to loathe?

Unfortunately, the answer to that was yes. Lucas had made a decision years ago never to aim for anything less than the best. And in the world of luxury boutique hotels, the Tischen Cadogan was the best. No question.

Two weeks ago he'd moved out of the squalid bedsit he'd been renting in Tooting and checked himself in to the Cadogan. His room was the cheapest the hotel had to offer and was little more than twelve-foot square, but it had still cost him every penny of his remaining savings. Literally every penny. As of tomorrow morning, he had no idea how he was going to eat.

Still, it had been worth it. In the past two weeks he'd gotten to know the hotel's inner workings every bit as intimately as Julia Brett-Sadler, the Cadogan's bossy, school ma'am-ish manager did. He knew about the morale problems in the kitchen, and the Michelin-starred, megalomaniac chef who made his staff's life hell. He knew about the barman who regularly slipped free drinks to girls he was sleeping with. He knew about the maitre d's two-hundred-pounds-a-day coke habit.

If he was going to have any kind of a shot with Anton Tisch – a guy who wouldn't even give his own kid a break, apparently – Lucas knew he would have to be more informed and more impressive than everybody else. Of course, he first had to swing himself an appointment with the guy, something that so far was proving depressingly difficult.

Battling his way through the commuters at Westminster station, he finally emerged into the drizzle of the street. Storm clouds hung low in the sky like a thick, heavy blanket, blocking out so much light that it almost felt like night. Not even the gold-faced splendour of Big Ben or the intricately carved towers of the Palace of Westminster could lift the atmosphere of dreary depression lingering in the air. Clicking open his umbrella with a curse, Lucas made his way along the now-familiar route by the river, towards the Adelphi building where The Tischen Corporation had its offices.

'You 'ere again, mate?' The doorman seemed less than thrilled to see him. 'Don't give up easy, do you?'

'No,' said Lucas, pushing past him into the lobby. 'I don't. I'm here to see Mr. Tisch.' He smiled firmly at the Asian girl on the reception desk, who glowered back at him.

'Do you have an appointment?' she asked wearily. It was the third time she'd been through this charade this week, and the novelty was wearing thin.

'Yes,' lied Lucas. 'He's expecting me.'

The girl gave him a look that made it clear she knew he was bullshitting, but that at this point she really didn't care.

'Sixteenth floor,' she sighed, handing him a visitor's pass. 'Once you're up there, you're Rita's problem.'

Luckily for Lucas, Rita was much more amenable to his particular blend of Latin charm than the Thai harridan downstairs. Somewhere in the no-man's land between middle-aged and elderly, her sensible tweed suit and Miss Moneypenny manner hid a mischievous streak that Lucas was quick to pick up on. He guessed it was a long time since any good-looking young man had bothered to flirt with Rita. And it seemed he was right. No sooner had he started to banter with her than the floodgates opened.

'Darling.' Striding over to her desk, grinning from ear to ear, he kissed her hand while she laughingly attempted to get rid of another caller.

'Mr. Ruiz!' Switching off her headset she pulled her hand away and tried to look stern.

'I know what you're going to say,' said Lucas. 'We must stop meeting like this. People are going to start talking. But you know, all you have to do is let me see him. Just for five minutes. Then I'll be out of your hair for ever.'

'I've told you,' said the secretary, blushing like a giddy schoolgirl, 'it really isn't up to me. Mr. Tisch's diary is booked up months in advance. I can't just squeeze people in willy nilly. However charming they might be. I'd lose my job.'

'Ah, lovely Rita, surely not?' said Lucas. He'd perched on the corner of her desk now, close enough for her to smell his cologne. Really, he could be most distracting when he wanted to . . . 'No man in his right mind would let you go. Won't you at least let him know I'm here?'

'Well . . .' she said, her resolve already crumbling. 'All right. I'll buzz him. But I can tell you right now, he won't see you. He's having rather a bad day, I'm afraid.'

This turned out to be an understatement.

Inside his office, Anton reached for his open bottle of antacids and slipped another revolting, chalky pill into his mouth.

'No, I will not *calm down*, Roger,' he yelled into the phone. 'She's crucifying me. And that cunt of an editor's giving her a free pass to do it! There's more on the story in tomorrow's paper, apparently. When I think of how much fucking money I gave to their bloody Help a London Child appeal last year. I mean, where's the fucking loyalty, Roger, huh? Answer me that!'

Anton Tisch was one of life's winners. Having cleaned up in Azerbaijan in the mid nineties, he'd gotten out of the oil business while the getting was still good, before he found himself poisoned or shot, or shipped off to Siberia like so many of the Russians who'd gotten greedy and kept their fat fingers in the pie for too long. Diversifying into other industries, he had reinvented himself as a legitimate businessman. His hedge fund, Excelsior III, was now one of the largest and most profitable in Europe. His media empire stretched from Delhi to Vladivostok, and incorporated everything from online search engines to cable TV stations. And his hotel chain – the mighty Tischens – was among the most prestigious and well respected in a notoriously cut-throat and fickle business.

Dividing his time between his home in Mayfair – he'd had three exquisite Georgian mansions knocked together to create one of the largest privately owned residences in London – and his estate on the banks of Lake Geneva, Anton surrounded himself with every luxury that money could buy.

Of course, as for so many of the world's wealthiest men, it was the things money *couldn't* buy that kept him awake at night. Having grown up poor in an obscure village in rural East Germany, what Tisch craved more than anything was social acceptance among the English upper classes – to become part of the famously amorphous British 'Establishment.' But like so many wealthy foreigners before him, he was discovering the hard way that in England there were numerous doors that money alone could not unlock. Abramovich had won over the masses as Mr. Chelski when he bought and poured money into Chelsea football club. But Anton wasn't interested in being liked by lager louts and yobs. His social sights were set much higher.

His strategy – pouring funds very publicly into civic institutions and high-profile charities – was a good one. He wanted people to see him as a modern-day Carnegie: generous, philanthropic, paternalistic; in short, everything that the English aristocracy considered themselves, however misguidedly, to be. Eventually, the plan was for his good works to earn him a knighthood, the social equivalent of an access-all-areas backstage pass.

Only last month, his sources at Whitehall had been reassuring him that he was well on the way to achieving his coveted K. But that was before Heidi.

She wasn't the first girl to go to the papers with a story shredding his hard-earned reputation. A few years ago another ex, a journalist, had written a piece about Anton's sado-masochistic bedroom practices that had sent his social ambitions slithering back down the snake to square one.

He ought to have learned his lesson then. But even knowing the dangers he faced at the hands of the notoriously xenophobic British press – German-bashing still sold papers in England – his pathological dislike of women made it almost impossible for him to treat his lovers with the decency or generosity that might have kept them quiet. To Anton Tisch, women were possessions to be used and discarded. Any children he might accidentally have fathered along the way he viewed not so much as people, but as collateral damage.

'You know what I was doing last night, Roger?' he bellowed at his British lawyer, pacing like a cat between his desk and the floor-to-ceiling window overlooking the river. 'Cutting the ribbon on a brand new fucking dialysis machine at Great Ormond Street, that's what. But do they report on that? Do they fuck! No, they'd rather help that slag tell the world that I don't like children. It's libel, that's what it is. And she's not getting away with it.'

Slamming the phone down petulantly, he sat back down at his desk. The fact was he'd lose if he tried to sue the paper, or the girl, and he knew it. The picture Heidi painted might be one-sided, but it wasn't untrue. And even if it had been, dragging the thing out would only cause more damage to his good name. There really was nothing for it but to pay her off, and that was what was really driving him crazy: the thought that she was going to get the money she wanted after all. That she'd beaten him. She'd won.

Too restless and irritated to make another call, he idly picked up the piece of paper on the top of his in-tray. It was the CV for a man named Brent Dalgliesh, the candidate he'd decided to hire yesterday as deputy manager at the Cadogan.

With so many businesses under his control, a large part of Anton's time was taken up with delegation. The only areas he still focused on personally were his hedge fund, where he still made all the investment decisions himself, and his hotels.

Anton loved the hotel business every bit as passionately as Abramovich loved his football or Richard Branson his planes. In interviews, he often described the Tischens as his children, but few people realized quite how literally he meant it. His strategy had been simple and consistent from day one: he deliberately picked out locations with a dominant hotel already in place – Reid's in Madeira, The Post Ranch in Big Sur, Raffles in Singapore – and challenged them right on their doorstep. Always the last word in decadence and hip, Tischen hotels set out to make the old giants look like what they were: tired behemoths, long past their sell-by date.

The plan worked, time after time, but nowhere had he pulled it off with such spectacular success as in London, with the Cadogan. A stone's throw from both the Lanesborough and the Dorchester, Anton's gentleman's club-style hotel had out-earned both of those giants in only its second year. As one journalist had put it, in a piece that Anton had blown up, framed and hung on his office wall: 'With the Cadogan, the brilliant Mr. Tisch has out-Englished the English. A triumph of good taste.'

Looking at Brent's CV again now, Anton felt his irritation mounting. It was a stupid name for one thing. Made him sound like a shopping center, or a service station on the M25. As for the litany of achievements that had so impressed him yesterday: a first-class degree from the LSE, seven years at the Georges V in Paris, the Young Hotelier of the Year award – suddenly they all seemed cloyingly earnest and worthy. What kind of a resume-conscious suck-up became president of the student union, for God's sake?

It was at that moment that Rita buzzed his intercom.

'I'm sorry to disturb you, Mr. Tisch,' she said meekly. 'But there's a Mr. Lucas Ruiz here to see you. Again.'

Anton was about to snap at her that 'do not disturb' meant exactly that, when something made him think twice. This kid had been showing up like clockwork day after day, asking about the Cadogan job. He was fresh out of college and consequently ludicrously under-qualified. But he'd refused to take no for an answer, a trait that Anton greatly admired. He was also, according to the CV he'd insisted on leaving with Rita, quite brilliant academically.

Fuck it. He couldn't focus on work anyway, not with this Heidi shit hanging over his head. What harm would it do to see the boy?

'OK, Rita,' he said, ripping Brent's details into four neat pieces and dropping them into the trash can under the desk. 'Show him in.'

If Lucas was surprised to have been granted an audience, he didn't show it. Instead he burst into Anton's office, pushing his long hair out of his eyes and smiling, radiating confidence like a stadium floodlight.

'How do you do, Mr. Tisch?' he said, thrusting out his hand in greeting. 'Thank you for seeing me.'

He was a good-looking boy, and came across as much older and more self-assured than the twenty-four-year-old he claimed to be. Still, he hardly looked like a senior executive. Despite the suit and tie, there was a certain rock-star rebelliousness about him that was screaming to be let out. What with that and the flowing hair, he looked more like a drug dealer than a hotelier.

'I'm really not sure why I *am* seeing you,' said Anton, honestly.

Lucas scoured his face for clues as to his mood or character, anything he could use. But the great man was eerily expressionless, and much more waxy-faced than he appeared in pictures. Having never seen botox on a man before, Lucas made a mental note never, ever to try it. Tisch reminded him of the dead Lenin – only perhaps not quite so warm and cuddly. He was tall, with obviously dyed, chestnut-brown hair plastered to his head as though stuck on with glue, and was wearing what appeared to be some sort of naval uniform, a white jacket with blue stripes down the arms. Clearly he considered himself to be something of a natty dresser, but the overall effect was too Michael Jackson for Lucas's taste. He half expected to see fingerless leather gloves emerge from the military sleeves, or a black armband whipped out of the drawer.

'The position at the Cadogan is far beyond your experience and capabilities,' Anton went on. 'It's a world-class hotel. What on earth makes you think I'd hand any part of it over to an amateur?'

Lucas took a deep breath. 'With respect, sir, I think you already have. Julia Brett-Sadler couldn't run her own bath.'

Tisch raised an eyebrow and suppressed a smile. The boy was cocky as hell. But he liked that about him.

'All right, Lucas,' he said. 'You've got my attention. Let's hear what you have to say.'

And so Lucas told him. Calmly, dispassionately, he listed every problem, every failure he'd witnessed at the Cadogan in his last two weeks there as a guest. For each one he put forward his own solution, explaining concisely but meticulously just how he would do a better job than the current manager. When he'd finished, he sat back in his chair, cracked his knuckles with confident finality, and waited for Anton's response.

When it came, it was not at all what he expected.

'Do you have a problem with women, Mr. Ruiz?' Tisch's tone was as casual as if he'd been inquiring about the weather or the football results.

Lucas looked surprised. 'Not at all. I love women,' he said truthfully. 'But do I think they're better in the bedroom than the boardroom? Yes, sir, I do.'

Anton was warming to this kid more by the minute.

'You realize that's the sort of statement that can get you into a lot of hot water these days,' he said, without anger. 'There's no sexual discrimination in my hotels. In fact, the Tischens have a higher proportion of women in management positions than any other major chain.'

This was true. One of Anton's most successful weapons in countering the sexism claims made by ex-lovers was his excellent reputation as an equal opportunities employer. He'd learned long ago that it paid to have prominent, educated women on hand, whose job it was to make him sound decent and honourable.

Lucas shrugged. 'I wouldn't have a problem working for Julia if she were doing her job properly. Or if I didn't know I could do it better. But she isn't. And I could.'

Anton got to his feet. As a rule, he wasn't a man to make rash decisions. But every once in a while, he liked to act on instinct. And his instincts about the Ruiz boy were all good.

'I've heard what you said today, and I take those criticisms seriously, believe me,' he said. 'Nevertheless, Miss Brett-Sadler has done wonderful things with that hotel in the past two years. Things that you have yet to achieve, Mr. Ruiz. It would take a lot more than some internal politics to convince me to replace her.'

Lucas looked crestfallen.

'However,' Anton continued, 'the under-manager position is still open. And I'll admit, I'm tempted to give you a shot at it, if only to put your spectacular arrogance to the test.'

For once, Lucas was speechless. In fact, he was so frightened of jinxing things he could barely breathe. Still as a statue, he prayed for Anton to go on.

'Fuck it,' said Anton, cracking a smile for the first time that day. 'You're hired. I'm putting you on a three-month probation period. But if I'm not happy with your work I'll have you out of there in three minutes, believe me. Got that?'

'Absolutely,' said Lucas, springing to his feet. All he wanted now was to get the hell out of there before Tisch changed his mind. 'You won't regret this, sir. I promise.'

'I'd better not,' said Anton. 'Because if I do, Mr. Ruiz, it'll be you who suffers, not me.'

Despite the implied threat, Anton had a good feeling about Lucas, which only intensified once the boy had left his office, so happy he was practically skipping to the elevator. Julia *had* been getting a bit complacent over at the Cadogan. It was about time he shook her up a bit.

He had a feeling that appointing Lucas Ruiz to be her number two might put the cat amongst the pigeons most satisfactorily. He may not be able to teach Heidi a lesson – yet – but Julia was about to learn that it paid never to rest on your laurels when you worked for the great Anton Tisch.

Chapter Five

'Lola!' Karis Carter could feel her throat getting hoarse as she yelled up the stairs yet again for her daughter. 'Lola, get down here *right now*. We need those cases. Mo's loading the car.'

It was mid September, and the Carter family were finally, belatedly, leaving their summer home in the Hamptons and flying back to Boston. If Karis had had her way they'd have gone home at the end of August, like everybody else. East Hampton was like a ghost town in September, whereas in Boston the endless round of parties and charity 'dos' that were the center of Karis's existence was just beginning again. It was the best month to be there, and she'd missed it. All because of stupid, selfish Devon.

It was hard to pinpoint exactly when Devon and Karis Carter had grown apart. Certainly they'd loved each other once, back when Karis's modelling career was still thriving and Devon was an up-and-coming young lawyer, as handsome as he was brilliant. But those days were a lifetime ago now. The intervening years had brought them two children – Nicholas, now nineteen and his mother's favorite, and sixteen-year-old Lola – as well as enough money from both an inheritance and Devon's work to pay for two multi-million-dollar homes and the lifestyle to go with them. But in other ways they'd been less kind. Though still a handsome woman, Karis's youthful beauty had faded to a pale shadow of what it had once been. Having built not only her career but her self-esteem around her looks, aging took a terrible toll, not just on her but on her marriage. Insecure and pathologically demanding of attention, she pushed Devon's patience, not to mention his credit cards, to the limit.

Karis wasn't the only guilty party, however. As the years passed, familiarity with his wife seemed to breed contempt in Devon. He made no attempt to feign interest in her life, and was little better with his children, focusing instead on work and on the numerous social committees that earned him his reputation as a pillar of the community in both Boston and East Hampton. Though he pretended to find these extra-curricular commitments a burden, secretly Devon would rather die than lose the social prestige they brought him. Nevertheless, they were a contributor to the disintegration of his marriage – or at least, the disintegration of every part of it that had once brought him joy. Even so, neither he nor Karis had ever seriously contemplated divorce. They both had too much to lose for that.

'Lola!' Karis was really starting to lose her temper now. It was bad enough that Devon had spent the last four weeks coming up with one excuse after another to keep them in East Hampton. Not just bad, but odd. Normally he was the first to want to get back to Boston. And now Lola was doing all she could to ensure they missed the plane, all because she had a bee in her bonnet about going back to St. Mary's.

'Jeez, Mom. I'm coming!' came the exasperated cry from upstairs.

Standing in the middle of her bedroom, surrounded by a sea of open suitcases stuffed beyond bursting with clothes, paintbrushes, magazines and all the other detritus from a long, teenage summer, Lola Carter was in an even worse mood than her mother. Dressed head to toe in black – going back to St. Mary's felt like her own funeral, so why not? – she looked every inch the archetypal sullen teen: skirt so short you could see her underwear when she bent down, ripped pantyhose, thick black Suzi Quatro eye makeup and a silver skull and crossbones pendant the size of a fist swinging ominously against her chest. But not even the Morticia Adams get-up could conceal her striking beauty. With her thick, russet-red hair that flowed down her back like a river of molten copper, her long, slender legs and peaches-and-cream complexion, Lola looked like a taller, more willowy version of Lindsay Lohan. She'd been approached by scouts for model agencies more times than she could count. But (to her mother's private relief) the last thing Lola Carter was interested in was modelling. Her dream, what she longed for more than anything, was to be a fashion designer. And she'd do it too, one day. Whether her fucking father liked it or not.

'Whoa.' Nicholas, her elder brother and the bane of Lola's existence, stuck his head around the door. Like his sister, he was a great-looking kid, all dark hair and smouldering blue-gray eyes. Unlike her, he was also a card-carrying asshole.

Taking one look at Lola's nowhere-near-packed luggage, and the chaos strewn around her Gothic-themed bedroom, he smiled nastily. 'You are so dead when Mom sees this. The flight leaves in, like, two hours.'

'So?' said Lola, sitting down on the largest of her four bags in a hopeless attempt to get it to close. 'I'll miss the flight, then. Big whup. It's not like I actually care about going back.'

'You know they're gonna send you back to St. Mary's whatever you do, right?' said Nicholas, idly picking up a comb from his sister's dressing table and running it through his thick black hair. 'It's not like anywhere else will have you. And Dad'll drop dead before he lets you drop out.'

This, unfortunately, was true. Having been expelled from every other decent private school in Boston, St. Mary's Academy for Girls had been Devon and Karis's last hope for their wayward daughter. A generous donation to the new science building had helped the nuns to see past Lola's 'authority issues.' It had also ensured that they steered her away from the art programs she was desperate to enrol in, toward the more academic subjects that her father had his heart set on. As far as Devon was concerned, Lola's future was a place at Harvard Law and that was that. He didn't want to hear any more bullshit about goddamn fashion school.

'Don't you have some place to be?' Lola asked her brother wearily. 'Like downstairs blowing smoke up Mom's ass?'

'Very funny,' he sneered, 'but no.' There were few things Nicholas enjoyed more than watching his little sister fuck up. Sometimes his job as her self-appointed tormentor was just too easy. 'Unlike you, I don't have to go to college. I've already made a success of my life.'

'A success? Really? How do you figure that?' said Lola scathingly. 'So far steamingpileofBS dot com, or whatever it is you call it, hasn't earned you a red cent. Aw, *shit!*' With one last almighty tug, the zipper on her case finally pulled shut, only for the straining fabric to rip open immediately afterwards like a burst artery.

'My God, Lola, how many times do I have to spell it out for you?' said Nicholas, annoyed. He didn't appreciate having his business acumen questioned, especially not by his little sister. 'That's the new business model. It doesn't matter whether or not Enigma turns a profit in its first few years. This is the internet. It's all about volume.'

As founder and CEO of an inventions website he'd christened Enigma, Nicholas Carter saw himself as the next Steve Jobs. The fact that at almost twenty he still lived at home, and that his playboy lifestyle was funded a hundred percent by his besotted mother, did nothing to dampen his self belief. Or insufferable arrogance, depending on how you looked at it.

'Speaking of volume ...' Pushing the bedroom door open a little wider, he made a great show of cupping his hand to his ear. Devon was thundering up the stairs like a bull elephant on the charge. Seconds later he burst into the room, so mad you could practically see the steam coming out of his ears.

'What is your *problem*?' he yelled at his daughter. 'You knew what time we had to leave today.'

'Yeah,' Lola shot back. 'And *you* knew how much stuff I had to pack. What's the big deal, anyway? You guys go, and I'll catch the first flight out in the morning. I *am* almost seventeen you know, Dad. I am capable.'

'Capable?' Her father gave a short, derisive laugh. 'Do you think I was born yesterday? You've already missed two weeks of this semester. You aren't missing another one.'

And whose fault was that? thought Lola bitterly. You've been the one refusing to leave East Hampton on pain of death for, like, a month.

'You're getting on that flight, young lady,' said Devon, 'with or without your clothes, if I have to drag you on myself. You have two minutes. Two! And I don't know what you're looking so damned smug about.' He turned on Nicholas, who had been smirking quietly in the corner, enjoying the show, but who now looked distinctly put out to be included in his father's fury. 'You should be downstairs helping your mother.'

Elbowing past his son before he had a chance to defend himself, Devon stormed into his own bedroom and slammed the door.

He shouldn't be yelling at Nick. If anyone ought to be downstairs, helping to load the car, it was him. And he shouldn't be hiding out in here, either. But he was so goddamn stressed right now, if he didn't take a time out he was in serious danger of hitting somebody.

Devon didn't think he'd felt this bad, or this helpless, since he was a little boy and his mother had packed him off to summer camp despite his pleadings to be allowed to stay at home. He remembered pressing his face to the window of the train as it pulled away, his tears making two grimy rivers down the glass as he watched the platform and his mother's face slip into the distance and out of sight.

It was exactly the way he felt now, leaving Honor.

He was being ridiculous, of course. What the hell was he, sixteen? He'd only known the girl for a month or so, and their affair could still be counted in days. Plus he had work in Boston, commitments, a life. A big life, as it happened.

So why did going back there make him feel like someone had punched through his ribcage and ripped his heart out whole?

'I'll be in Boston myself in a month,' Honor had reassured him last night, after their poignant goodbye lovemaking session. 'We can hook up again then.'

Devon had taken her out on his boat for the afternoon, ostensibly for a business meeting, so they could be assured of privacy. So far their rendezvous had all taken place at Palmers, in Honor's private suite of rooms on the top floor. But he couldn't help feeling nervous there, and he wanted today to be perfect.

'*Hook up?*' He looked at her, aghast. 'God, Honor, is that all this is to you? Just sex?'

Wriggling out from under the white linen sheet, she sat up, pushing her spiky fringe out of her eyes. 'Of course not,' she said, horrified. 'You know it's not. Don't twist what I say.'

But the problem was, he didn't know it, not really. He didn't know anything with her. Looking at her smudged makeup and angular, jutting features, at once so aggressive and yet so vulnerable, he found himself fighting down the urge to pull her back on top of him and fuck her yet again until he was sure she loved him back. Karis was an attractive, desirable woman. But never, not even in the full flush of her youthful beauty, had his wife had the effect on him that Honor did.

The girl was such a mess of contradictions. It had taken

every ounce of his charm and negotiating skills to get her into bed in the first place. He'd had to lie through his teeth about the state of his marriage, insisting that he and Karis were 'as good as separated' before she would so much as kiss him. Part of him was surprised that such an obviously intelligent, tough young woman would fall for a line like that – but she had, hook, line and sinker, taking him at his word without any further probing. Beneath her carefully cultivated ball-breaker image – he'd seen the way that the staff at Palmers visibly quaked when Honor walked into the lobby – she was actually astonishingly naive and trusting, at least in romantic matters. She was also very inexperienced sexually. Their first night together was so dreadfully awkward that Devon started to wonder if he'd lost his touch, or misread her attraction for him. But after a few days, something seemed to shift. Years of bottled up loneliness and need and sexual frustration began pouring out of her like water breaking through a dam. All at once the clunked noses and fumbled gropings were replaced by a raw, unleashed sexual energy that utterly took his breath away. It was like making love to a generator.

The problem was that the moment sex was over, Honor would pull away from him completely, slipping back into tough-little-rich-girl mode. This left him feeling baffled and, if he was honest, more than a little rejected. She possessed a very masculine ability to compartmentalize her emotions and switch off at will, which drove him insane with frustration and insecurity. On the flip side, as much as he hated it, it was that same combination of sexual neediness and emotional independence, even detachment, that had him hooked, running back to her again and again for more punishment like some masochistic junkie.

'It's not easy for me either, you know,' said Honor, mollifying his wounded pride a little, though not enough, as she scrambled back into her clothes. 'You won't be living here again until next summer. That's a whole year away.'

'Nine months,' said Devon. 'We'll be back in June. But you mustn't think of it like that. We both have to focus on the next time we'll see each other.'

'Exactly,' said Honor, 'which is only a few weeks away, right? I'd make it sooner if I could, but you know I can't leave Palmers right now. I'm just beginning to get to grips with the problems here.'

'Fucking Palmers,' Devon grumbled, reluctantly getting out of bed himself and looking around the cabin for his underwear. Sometimes it felt like *she* was the one who was married, rather than him. Married to that blasted hotel of hers.

'Anyway,' she went on, ignoring him. 'You were the one banging on about East Hampton gossip and how dangerous it is, us seeing so much of each other here. You've got your "reputation" to think of, remember?'

She couldn't entirely keep the resentment out of her voice, although perversely Devon found this small hint of jealousy on her part more of a comfort than an annoyance.

Besides, it was true. He *had* begun to feel nervous. Apart from a few reckless one-night stands years ago, he had never been unfaithful to Karis, and he was finding the uncharted waters of betrayal difficult to navigate. Though he'd only been seeing Honor for a couple of weeks, there was no doubt in his mind that the affair was more than just a summer fling, which made things a lot more problematic. Truth be told, he'd become a somewhat vocal advocate of family values as he'd gotten older, using his deaconship at church as a platform to air his views. The slightest whisper of his relationship with Honor would be catastrophic for his reputation, both here and in Boston. He might be feeling like a love-struck teenager, but he was old enough and wise enough to know that no one liked a hypocrite. And why should they? Right now he wasn't even sure he liked himself.

'Come here.' Grabbing Honor's hand, he pulled her down onto his lap, burying his face in the hollow between her shoulder and neck and breathing in the scent of her. 'I know it's hard,' he whispered. 'Believe me, I wish we could stay on this boat for ever. Keep on sailing to where no one could find us. But we're both adults, right? We both know life isn't like that.'

Standing with his back against his bedroom door now, listening to the kids fighting and Karis barking at the chauffeur outside, he realized just how trite his words must have sounded. 'Life isn't like that'? What the hell was he, a fucking fortune cookie?

Life was what you made it. And right now Devon was in grave danger of making a serious mess of his.

'Karis!' Opening the sash window, he stuck his head outside. Even in September the gardens looked beautiful, a riot of scented blossoms and color. The yew hedges had been clipped and shaped with military precision, and the graveled driveway raked into a neatly furrowed semicircle giving the place an air of peaceful, ordered calm. If only he could regulate his family life and feelings so effortlessly.

'Oh, Devon, there you are.' Karis looked up at him, clearly irritated. 'I thought you were going to help Mo with the cases. He's almost finished now. Where's Lola?'

'She's nowhere near ready,' he said. Then, making a decision on the spur of the moment, added: 'Look, why don't you go ahead with Nicholas? I'll stay here, make sure Lola gets her act together, and we'll fly out first thing in the morning.'

Even behind her oversized Gucci shades he could see his wife's fury building. Not that he blamed her for that. Lola's behavior these past few weeks had been getting worse and worse. Today's stunt with the packing was the last straw.

'I thought we'd agreed,' she said wearily. 'No more excuses. If she isn't ready, she'll have to come as she is.'

'I know,' said Devon. 'But there are things she needs for school, honey. Trust me, Karis, I'm not gonna give her an easy ride. But it doesn't make sense for us all to have to wait around. What's one more day?'

In the end, too drained to fight about it any more, Karis gave in. Ten minutes later the Daimler containing her, Nicholas and a trunk full of Louis Vuitton pulled sedately out of the driveway. And Devon made a beeline back to his daughter's room.

The Led Zeppelin was deafening the moment he opened the door. Lola, nodding her head to the music, was sprawled across the bed, smoking a roll-up like she hadn't a care in the world.

'Looks like we're both still here,' she drawled, flicking ash into a used coffee cup on the bedside table as he walked in. 'Whatever happened to dragging me onto the plane yourself?'

'You can cut out the lip,' said Devon firmly, unplugging the stereo from the wall despite Lola's protests and pulling the cigarette out of her hand. 'I'm going out and I won't be back till late. Either you finish your packing and clean up this pig sty—' he picked up the coffee cup, frowning at the cigarette butts bobbing around in it like flotsam on a muddy pond – 'or I cut off your allowance till Christmas. Period.'

'Whatever,' said Lola, although inside her defiance was waning. St. Mary's was bad enough, but St. Mary's without an allowance would be hell on earth. 'Where are you going, anyway?'

'None of your business,' said Devon.

It was hard to tell which of them felt more relief when he finally left the house a few minutes later, slamming the front door behind him and zooming off in his BMW convertible. But one thing was for sure: wherever he was headed, he was in one hell of a hurry.

★

Anton Tisch buttered another piece of toast, cutting it carefully into four pieces before offering one of them to the slavering Great Dane that sat obediently at his feet.

'There you are, my Mitzi,' he cooed, bending his face so close to the dog's that their noses were almost touching. 'Who's my good girl?'

For the last six years, Mitzi had been Anton's constant companion, traveling back and forth from London to Geneva and reigning supreme as the undisputed queen of both his homes and his heart. Most people found his doting affection for the huge, intimidating-looking animal incongruous, even creepy. This was a man, after all, who couldn't seem to muster a shred of human sympathy for his own children, never mind business associates or social 'friends,' whom he routinely discarded with all the dispassionate ruthlessness of an executioner. Yet with Mitzi he was as adoring and besotted as any lover.

'The second post is here, Mr. Tisch.' A butler in full livery glided up to the table and set a neatly bound package down at his elbow. Anton made a point of keeping a full household staff in Mayfair – one must keep up appearances at all times – although in Geneva, where nobody cared how he'd made his fortune just as long as he *had* made it, he 'made do' with only a cook, driver and valet.

'Thank you, Gavin.' Idly, he began leafing through the stack of letters. 'That will be all.'

Annoyingly, there didn't appear to be anything from his New York lawyer. He was waiting on some documents that were supposed to have arrived by FedEx yesterday. As he was due to fly back to Switzerland later tonight, they'd be no use to him if they arrived in London tomorrow. It was all very aggravating.

Picking up his mobile he jabbed out a number.

'They're still not here,' he barked into the handset, so loudly that Mitzi jumped. 'What the fuck's going on?'

'Relax.' Josh Schwartz, one of Anton's many lawyers,

was used to his client's capricious moods. 'They'll show up. I'll get copies faxed to you in Geneva in the meantime. But listen, I have good news on a different front.'

'What?' Anton sounded distinctly nonplussed.

'I think I've finally dug up some dirt on Morty Sullivan.'

Anton sat up, interested. Now this *was* good news. Mortimer Sullivan was the dreadful old fossil who chaired the planning committee in East Hampton. For some years now, Anton had had his eye on the town as a perfect spot to open a new Tischen. The once-great Palmers had long since declined into mediocrity, and with Trey Palmer apparently on his last legs, usurped by his own utterly inexperienced daughter by all accounts, its position was looking more vulnerable than ever. The problem was that the town seemed to be run like the Palmer family's private fiefdom. Whenever Anton had found a suitable building to convert or plot to build on, he'd been denied permission to fart there by Sullivan and his small-minded, sycophantic cronies. Those guys didn't want *any* change at all, never mind some upstart European showing up to build one of his flashy hotels in their backyard. It was the same old story, and Anton was heartily sick of it.

'Tell me more,' he said, licking his lips with anticipation of the juicy gossip to come. 'Is it something we can use?'

'Hell, yeah.' Josh was actually laughing now. As far as Anton knew, his lawyer hadn't so much as broken a smile since his ex-wife's rottweiler of a divorce attorney got shot in the balls in a freak hunting accident. This must be good. 'It involves a twenty-two-year-old dancer called Danny. I'm looking at the polaroids right now. If this doesn't get the guy to back off, nothing will.'

Handing Mitzi the last quarter of toast, Anton hung up, smiling broadly. This business in the papers with Heidi had put him in a foul mood, but at last he felt it lifting. Yesterday's *Evening Standard* would be tomorrow's fish and chip wrapping anyway. People would forget about the story soon enough. Whereas the prospect of a new Tischen in the Hamptons? Now that was something lasting, something real.

Trey Palmer's daughter might not realize it yet. But her 'special relationship' with the East Hampton planning committee was about to come to an abrupt end. And not before time, either.

Waking up with a start, Honor looked at the time on the little electric clock by her bedside. It was ten fifteen.

'Fuuuck,' she groaned quietly to herself. How had that happened?

Admittedly she'd had a late and drunken night. She'd done a good job appearing together and in control on the boat, saying her goodbyes to Devon. But as soon as she got back to Palmers she'd headed straight for her suite and the drinks cabinet, and proceeded to take herself out on vodka, drinking into the small hours. The last thing she wanted was for him to realize how desperately she needed him and how much she dreaded his departure. They'd only been seeing each other a few weeks. She mustn't, mustn't, mustn't scare him off.

If Devon was confused by their blossoming relationship, Honor felt completely poleaxed by it. Part of her lived for the brief hours they spent together. But another, larger part was gripped by a permanent, cold panic. OK, so his marriage was a sham, but he was still married, and with children too. After all the lectures she'd given Tina, what the hell was she doing, playing fast and loose with her own reputation and, by extension, Palmers'? She knew she ought to break it off, for a myriad of reasons. But she'd been so lonely for so long, the thought of letting Devon go made her want to vomit. Subconsciously, she'd looked for father figures in the past. But in Devon she'd really, truly found one. He was so strong, so solid, so rock-like and reassuring. And sexually, he'd cracked her in a way that no one else ever had.

At some point during her drunken marathon last night, Honor couldn't recall exactly when, Tina had called. With her usual uncanny sense of bad timing, she'd picked this of all nights to moan about how hard her life in LA was without Danny.

'It's all right for you,' she whined. 'You're far too sensible ever to fall for a married man.' Tina made the word 'sensible' sound like the most pointed of insults. 'You don't know what it's like, knowing that person is out there, but that *you* can't have them. It's hell, Honor. *Hell.* You have no idea what I'm going through.'

It took a superhuman effort of will for Honor to keep her mouth shut about Devon, but somehow she managed it. Sharing any kind of sensitive information with her sister was tantamount to posting it on FaceBook. Tina had about as much discretion as a foghorn, as Honor knew to her cost.

Having finally managed to get Tina off the phone, it rang again almost immediately. This time it was Lise, bitching that she wasn't getting any help with the rapidly declining Trey.

'I'm on my own here with him twenty-four seven,' she complained. 'He can't even use the bathroom by himself anymore. It's disgusting.'

If she was looking for a sympathetic ear, she'd come to the wrong place.

'You married a guy old enough to be your father,' slurred Honor. 'What did you expect? Besides, he has two full-time nurses, Lise. No one's expecting you to play Florence Nightingale.'

'Like hell they aren't,' Lise snapped. 'Those nurses are lazy as shit. And what the hell happened to you and Tina, anyway? When was the last time either of you visited him?'

This was below the belt.

'He refuses to see me,' Honor mumbled, a knot of

confused emotion forming in the pit of her stomach like a tumour, even through her drunkenness. 'You know that. I'm trying to put things right at Palmers, for him more than anyone. I'm working flat out here.'

'Jesus, Honor, don't you get it?' Lise interrupted viciously. 'Your dad doesn't *care* about Palmers. The man's incontinent, OK? He's a retard.'

Honor had hung up at this point, and kicked up the alcohol consumption to a whole new level. Maybe it was losing her father that was making this thing with Devon so painfully important to her? She had in fact been back to Boston twice since taking over at Palmers, trips she could ill afford, but Trey had refused to let her onto the property. Back in East Hampton, she called three times a week, but not once had he allowed her to be put through. He'd told her in Sam Brannagan's office that he would never forgive her for taking control of his assets. So far, it looked as though he intended to be as good as his word.

Waking up this morning, Honor felt like someone had thrown the mother of all fourth of July parties inside her cranium. Scrabbling in the draw of her bedside table for some aspirin, she crammed three into her mouth without water before throwing off her covers and staggering into the shower.

Slowly, as the warm jets of water pounded onto her aching body, she started to feel more alive. Squirting a dollop of her favorite lemongrass shower gel into her palms, she began rubbing it all over her body, working up a lather that she massaged into her hair and face as well. She wanted to wash away all traces of last night, and was starting to enjoy the tingling sensation on her skin when suddenly, out of the corner of her eye she saw the shower curtain twitch.

There wasn't even time to panic. Ripping the rubbery fabric aside, still half-blinded by soap suds, she let out a blood-curdling shriek, launching herself on her would-be attacker with a well-placed kick to the groin.

'You fucker!' she yelled, kicking and punching and scratching blindly as adrenaline translated her fear into anger. 'You piece of shit!'

'Honor!' It took a second or two for Devon's voice to penetrate the fog in her brain. 'For God's sake stop, Honor. It's me.'

'Devon?' Opening her eyes at last, she saw him lying beneath her on the tiled bathroom floor, half shielding his face with one arm. 'What are you doing here? You should be on a plane to Boston.'

'Lola wasn't ready to go,' he panted. 'And neither was I. I had to see you again.'

Despite the searing pain in his balls from where she'd kicked him, the sight of her leaning over him naked, dripping and still slippery with soap suds was making him hard already. Reaching up around her neck he pulled her beautiful, elfin face down until the tip of their noses touched, then let his hands glide down the wet runway of her back to rest on her butt.

'You scared me,' she whispered, closing her eyes as she felt his fingers slipping around her hips and disappearing into the damp triangle of her pubic hair. So much for wrestling with her conscience. She could no more finish things with Devon than fly to the moon, and she knew it.

'Not half as much as you scared me.'

Unzipping his jeans, he freed his now rock-solid erection.

'You might have warned me you had a black belt in karate.'

Easing herself down onto his dick, Honor began rocking slowly back and forth, her hangover suddenly quite forgotten. Her face was pressed against his now, and she found herself doing something she never normally did: looking right into his eyes while he made love to her.

Before long, despite his best efforts at restraint, Devon felt his orgasm building.

'Oh, God,' he moaned, looking almost in pain as he bit into her shoulder and came deep inside her. 'Sorry. I'm sorry. I couldn't hold it. I ... shit, Honor, what's wrong?'

Opening his eyes he saw tears streaming down her face. Still inside her, he sat up and wrapped both arms around her.

'Shhhh,' he whispered, gently stroking her hair as her sobs became stronger and more violent. 'What is it, my darling? What's the matter? Did I hurt you?'

She shook her head, wiping the tears away almost angrily with the back of her hand.

'No,' she said. 'You were fine. You were lovely. You *are* lovely. I didn't ...' She was still struggling to get her breath, she'd been crying so hard, and was obviously having trouble getting the words out. 'I didn't want you to see it.'

'See what?' he said gently.

'How much I love you.' Biting down on her trembling lower lip, she looked like a lost and frightened little girl. Devon felt a surge of love and protectiveness flood over him, tinged with a slightly less noble feeling of triumph. 'How much I don't want you to go away from me. Ever.'

It all came out then: the feelings she'd tried so hard to hide from him yesterday, Tina's phone call, her deep, profound unhappiness about her father and his continued refusal to see her.

'It's OK, baby.' Holding her, he listened patiently while all the stress of the past months came pouring out.

'No,' Honor shook her head again. 'It's not. It's not OK, Devon. Palmers is a mess. I thought I could just come in here and fix everything, but I can't. It's going to take years, and the whole town's against me. They all think I ripped Dad off.'

'I'm sure that's not true,' said Devon, who knew that it was, but didn't want to hurt her. If anything the East

Hampton gossips were even more small-minded and belligerent than their Boston counterparts.

'It is true!' Honor wailed. 'And now you're leaving me, and I need you, and I don't *want* to need you; I don't want to need anyone.'

'Shhh.' He stopped her with a kiss. 'I need you too. I do. And I'm not leaving you. I have to go back home, but I'm gonna get out here to see you. Regularly.'

'But how?' Try as she might she couldn't seem to stop her bottom lip from wobbling again. What was she, six? 'You have a job. You have a wife, a family, a whole life in Boston. And I have Palmers. I can't leave.'

'I know,' he said. 'I know all that. But you just have to trust me. We'll find a way. I know your old man let you down, and you've had to learn to deal with everything, with Palmers and your sister and all this shit on your own. But those days are gone now, Honor. You have me. You'll always have me, I promise.'

He sounded so strong and so reassuring, she longed to believe him.

'Now get dressed, and get on the phone,' he said, pulling her up to her feet. 'Whatever you have in your diary today, cancel it.'

Honor was about to protest, but he held up his hand for silence, and for some reason she found herself complying.

'Tell people you have the flu. Tell them whatever you want,' he said. 'But for the next six hours, you're mine and mine alone.'

'OK,' she smiled. 'But we can't spend the whole time ... you know.'

'Fucking?' Devon laughed.

'I mean it,' said Honor. 'I really need your advice about Palmers. Legal advice. The surveyors handed in their structural report last night, and it's pretty grim reading.'

'You want to spend our last hours together going over a surveyors' report?' He looked at her incredulously, then

81

shook his head. 'You love me, but you love Palmers more, right?'

Honor gave him her very best, most adoring smile.

But she didn't correct him.

Chapter Six

'Are you sure you don't want me to stay a little longer?'

The girl loitering in the doorway of Lucas's flat fluttered her eyelashes and gave him the full force of the pouty, wide-eyed look that had made her the hottest model in London this season.

'Because I *really* don't mind.'

Lucas, wearing only a white towel tied around his waist, marveled again at her incredible body, shown off to perfection in a pair of skinny jeans and a tight white sweater, and felt his resolve fraying at the edges. They'd been shagging all afternoon, but he reckoned he had more than enough energy for a third round if she did.

But no, he mustn't. It was the big Christmas party at the Cadogan tonight. Julia was probably already furious that he wasn't at work right now – bossy, overbearing cow that she was.

'You're sweet, Georgie,' he said, rubbing a hand against his stubble and realizing belatedly that he needed a shave before tonight as well. 'But maybe next time, hey? Tonight's a big night for me.'

The girl shrugged and kissed him on the cheek. 'Your loss, Lucasito,' she said. Flicking her long, blond hair behind her, she skipped off down the stairs calling out: 'Oh, and merry Christmas!' over her shoulder as she disappeared from view.

'Thanks,' sighed Lucas to himself. Walking back into the flat, he shut the door behind him. 'Merry Christmas to you, too.'

He'd been in London for five months now, at the

Cadogan for four of them, and had already made a consider-able splash on the social scene. With his Heathcliff looks and moody confidence added to the intoxicating whiff of his dangerous, 'otherside of the tracks' background, he was an immediate hit with all the well-bred Chelsea heiresses, who'd taken to hanging around the hotel like groupies, hoping to get a crack at him. His job at the Cadogan gave him instant access to London's notoriously exclusive clubland, and to all outward appearances he appeared to have gained overnight acceptance amongst the city's bright young things. Night after night he could be seen squiring the most eligible girls to Annabel's and Tramp, and by day, in the rare hours when he wasn't working, he was a familiar figure in the West End, tearing around the streets of Soho on his Ducati motorbike like a Spanish James Dean.

But beneath the veneer of glamor, the reality was that he was still only a small step above broke. Anton paid him a fair wage at the Cadogan, and part-subsidized his bachelor pad on St. James's, which was a godsend. But the crowd that Lucas moved in, a mixture of trust-fund brats, city whiz-kids and old money aristocracy, all had disposable incomes to burn, and he was painfully aware of his own, inadequate funds as he tried to keep up. Most of the men in his circle knew that he was struggling and, already jeal-ous of his popularity with the It-girls and models that had swooned over *them* before Lucas showed up, responded by patronizing him socially. This, naturally, drove Lucas insane with rage, and he nursed his wounded pride like a stuck bull. If they'd openly challenged him, he'd have been able to hit back. But in typically British style, their exclusion of Lucas was far more subtle and insidious than that. So a group of Goldman bankers would happily share a table with him at a restaurant or club, and might even invite him to drinks parties. But when it came to shooting weekends at Blenheim or boys-only ski breaks to Verbier, Lucas only ever heard about it after the event. Not that he could have afforded to go anyway, but it would have been nice to be asked. In Lausanne, the European rich kids had accepted him without reservation. But British snobbery, he was beginning to discover, was of quite a different order. Outwardly, he pretended not to care about being snubbed. Inside, however, he was more determined than ever to beat the British bastards at their own game, and it wasn't long before he was living well beyond his means.

Despite these teething problems, he had grudgingly come to enjoy London. Though he still bitched about the weather and the cost of living (black cabs in particular were astronomical, although he couldn't seem to break himself of the habit), he had to admit that the city was magically transformed at Christmas time. Everywhere you went, shop windows were illuminated with brightly colored displays, and the old Victorian street lamps were adorned with mini Christmas trees, simply lit in white, that gave the darkening afternoons a cosy, Dickensian glow. From his bachelor pad Lucas could see the shoppers darting to and fro between Fortnum's and the Burlington Arcade, stocking up on presents and candies and every possible variety of ribbons, bows and rolls of shiny metallic paper to wrap them all up in. Though the promised snow had yet to materialize, the frost transformed the park every night into a gray-white wonderland, making Lucas's early-morning walk to work one of the highlights of his day.

Unfortunately, some days it was the *only* highlight. On top of the pressure of his unpaid credit card bills and ever-growing overdraft, recently his work at the Cadogan had become intensely stressful, too. More often than not, the stress took human form in the formidable, sturdy shape of Julia Brett-Sadler.

Relations between Lucas and his boss had begun as strained, then deteriorated steadily over the next few months to their current status of raging, open hostility.

Julia despised Lucas. She considered her new under-manager arrogant to the point of insubordination, and she wasn't the only one. Ever since he'd fucked some moron on the editorial desk at *Tatler* and managed to get himself named as London's fifth most elegible bachelor, he seemed to have become even more full of himself, treating the Cadogan like his own private fiefdom – although even Julia had to admit that, most of the time, he worked like a dog. Nevertheless, she was seething with Anton for appointing him in the first place without consulting her. Lucas was so under-qualified it was laughable. But instead of biding his time and trying to learn something constructive from more experienced professionals, like her, he'd blundered in like a bull in a china shop, deliberately fanning the flames of Julia's anger by wearing his contempt for her and the other senior staff firmly on his sleeve.

For his part, Lucas resented Julia for routinely dismissing all his suggestions for change or improvements at the hotel. It didn't occur to him that perhaps a constant stream of criticism and invective might not be the best way to win her over to his point of view. With any other woman he'd have been able to flirt his way out of trouble. But Julia was such a battleaxe, she'd never displayed so much as a hint of sexual interest in him. Though he wouldn't admit it, even to himself, this also annoyed Lucas intensely.

Unfortunately, however, she *was* his boss, for now anyway, and he couldn't afford to lose this job. Which meant that, whether he liked it or not, her word was law. He had no choice but to sit back and watch as, one by one, his ideas and projects got sidelined. It was beyond depressing.

He could have run to Anton about it, of course. But that would have made him look weak and immature and he knew it. Besides, Anton Tisch had more important things on his mind than the problems of one of his lowliest undermanagers.

No. It was up to Lucas to outsmart Julia. But so far, he'd got precisely nowhere.

Sighing, he loosened his towel and threw it down onto the sofa before wandering naked into the bathroom. Like the rest of the flat, it was decorated in classic bachelor style, with lots of black granite and chrome crammed into a small but elegantly masculine space. There was no bath tub, just a huge shower, and an ornate, oriental floor-to-ceiling mirror that Lucas looked in now, examining his reflection.

He was aware he was handsome – he wasn't blind – but he wasn't vain in the sense of being focused on his good looks. He merely acknowledged them as another fact of his existence, like being tall or good at languages. If anything, he had a tendency to be critical of himself physically, particularly if he felt his strength faltering as it had been recently. Since taking the Cadogan job, he hadn't had any free time to go to the gym. Mostly it was seventeen- or eighteen-hour days, squeezing in the girls in between. By the time he got home he hadn't an ounce of energy left for lifting weights.

Still, there was no time to worry about that now. The party officially kicked off in less than three hours' time. He'd better get a move on.

Over at the Cadogan, Julia was rushing around like a blue-arsed fly getting everything ready, and silently cursing Lucas.

'For God's sake, Matt,' she could be heard berating the poor head barman. 'People don't want to drink vodka out of a penis. Whose idea was this monstrosity?'

She pointed to an ice sculpture of cupid, three feet high, through which a steady trickle of neat vodka was already flowing, exiting via the frostily shriveled appendage.

'Lucas's,' said Matt, pulling out the order sheet like a shield. 'One vodka ice fountain, Cupid,' he read, adding, somewhat rashly, 'You signed off on it, Julia.'

'It's obscene,' she snapped. 'Get it out of here. And find me another ice fountain within the next hour. Something that doesn't piss on people.'

This really was the last straw. Against her better judge-ment, she'd allowed herself to be browbeaten into letting Lucas organize tonight's event, a vitally important evening for the hotel. From what she'd seen so far today – burlesque pole dancers, pornographic ice sculptures, some ludicrously overpriced DJ who'd cheerily told her a few minutes ago that he'd spent the past four months in Belmarsh for drug offenses – he seemed to have decided to turn the place into a brothel for the night.

Right on cue Lucas, looking even more devastating than usual in a bespoke Ozwald Boateng suit (still unpaid for) and blue silk shirt, sauntered into the bar.

'Sorry I'm late, Julia,' he said, with a casual insouciance that made her want to strangle him. 'Something came up.'

'Your dick, I shouldn't wonder,' she shot back furiously. Lucas almost laughed, but then wisely thought better of it. 'What on earth were you *thinking*, Lucas?' Julia looked around her, gesticulating at the semi-naked women writh-ing around on poles behind them, practising their 'routine.' 'We're a traditional, conservative hotel. I have the leader of the Tory party and his wife coming tonight!' she added, tearing at her hair in exasperation.

'From what I hear, he's quite a fan of dancing girls,' said Lucas. But one look at Julia's face told him flippancy was not going to score him any points. 'Look, it's edgy, I grant you,' he admitted.

'Edgy?' Julia looked apopleptic.

'Trust me,' said Lucas. 'It's what this place needs. People are going to love it.'

'People are going to be offended!' she shouted at him. 'How stupid *are* you? This isn't Ibiza. It's SW bloody three. We've got national press in here taking pictures, and you want to have the Dowager Duchess of Devonshire sucking vodka out of a baby's dick?'

'It'd sell some papers, that's for sure,' he laughed.

But Julia was implacable. 'This isn't a game', she hissed.

'You'd better pray I'm wrong about how tonight goes down. Because whatever little boys' club you think you have going on with Anton, trust me, all Tisch really cares about is reputation.'

This was undoubtedly true. Anton was the most rampant social climber Lucas had ever met, and he'd met a few. He wasn't even going to be at the party tonight, after receiving a last-minute invitation from the Duke of York to join him at the opera. Tisch wouldn't have missed the chance to rub shoulders with royalty for his own mother's funeral, never mind the Cadogan's Christmas drinks.

'You think you can drag this hotel's name into the mud and live to tell the tale?' Julia gave a short, derisive grunt of a laugh and shook her head pityingly. 'Maybe you are as dumb as you look.'

Infuriatingly, Lucas couldn't think of a comeback and could only stand and watch as she stormed off.

Bitch.

'Matt, get me a whisky, straight up,' he said, taking a seat at the bar for a moment. The drink appeared and he downed it in one gulp, shivering slightly as the amber liquid burned his throat and chest. He'd tried to act cool in front of Julia. But the truth was he was riddled with doubt himself about whether tonight's gamble would pay off. He'd been so full of confidence when he organized it all. So blindly certain that a genuinely hip, cutting-edge event aimed at younger clientele would catapult the Cadogan out of her safety zone as a classy, well-run boutique and into something truly iconic: the hotel synonymous with Cool Britannia, *the* place to be seen in London.

But maybe Julia was right. Maybe it did all look like a tacky, vulgar publicity stunt in the cold light of day?

She was certainly right about one thing. If it wasn't a success, his days at the Cadogan weren't just numbered. They were over. And what would he do with his growing collection of red bills then?

★

By ten thirty, the bar was heaving.

Flitting from group to group, glad-handing and flashing his teeth like the big bad wolf, Lucas still wasn't sure if things were actually going well. Everyone was congratulating him, naturally, but he knew better than to trust in that. These people were so fake, they'd say whatever they thought you wanted to hear to your face. Still, it was a relief that they had at least shown up.

Whatever he might privately think of the 'in-crowd' who hung out at the Cadogan, it was Lucas's job to court them and keep them coming back for more. There was no doubt that the movers and shakers crammed into the bar and lobby tonight were a PR man's wet dream. Actors, rock stars, politicians, artists, aristos, they were all mingling like old friends, their inhibitions broken by a free flow of cocktails that was costing the hotel a small fortune.

'Lucas, isn't it?'

Feeling a tap on his shoulder, Lucas spun around. He knew he recognized the strident, pushy little blonde from somewhere, but he couldn't quite place her. Part of the problem was that so many of these London socialites looked identical, with their expensive honey highlights, year-round St. Tropez tans and Luella Bartley accessories. He'd seen countless women like them in Ibiza – spoiled, rude and vacuous, not one of them had treated him with respect when he was a lowly laundry boy. But now that he could provide or deny access to the hottest venue in London, he couldn't beat them off with a stick.

'Don't you remember me?' the girl cocked her head to one side like a hurt puppy and pushed her surgically inflated lips forward in a theatrical pout. 'Caroline. Caroline Hambling. We met at Oscar's Halloween bash at Momo's.'

'Oh, yes, of course,' he said, unconvincingly. 'I'm so glad you could make it. Are you enjoying the party?'

'It's OK.' She shrugged, in the manner of a person whose

name was on the guest list at every A-list social event in town. 'There aren't enough sexy boys, though. Naughty Lucas!' She wagged her finger at him flirtatiously. 'You didn't want any competition, did you? Well, your wicked plan has worked, my darling. You've got my full, undivided attention.'

Lucas smiled thinly. He mustn't be rude to guests. But did she really think she was sexy, this girl, with her braying British accent and her pearls and her address book full of Hugos and Jeremys?

Thankfully he only had to endure a few minutes of listening to what a marvelous time she'd had at the Billionaire's Club in Sardinia last summer – 'Don't you think Flavio's a *hoot*?' – before he spotted a familiar, burly figure fighting his way through the throng toward him.

'Fuck me,' Ben panted, finally arriving at Lucas's side. 'How many people did you invite, mate? 'Ave you seen that bar? It'll be bloody New Year's Eve before you get served over there.'

Oddly, Lucas and Ben hadn't seen much more of each other since Lucas moved to London than they had done when he was in Switzerland. Both of them were so busy at work, there never seemed enough time to get the beers in. But they spoke regularly, and Ben wouldn't have missed tonight's extravaganza for anything.

'Caroline,' Lucas grinned, 'meet my friend Ben. Ben, Caroline.'

'Hello.' Ben turned to face the girl, smiling broadly. With his huge frame covered in a thick Aran sweater and his face even browner and more freckled than usual after a business trip to Asia, he looked more like a surf bum, or possibly a trawlerman, than a city high flier. 'So,' he asked brightly, 'how d'you know Lucas then?'

Caroline, who was not a fan of cockney accents, or fisherman's sweaters, gave a little shudder of distaste. 'We met at a party,' she said frostily. 'Actually, er, I've just seen someone I need to have a word with. Will you excuse me?'

'Blimey,' said Ben, frowning as she shimmied off. 'That was quick. Was it something I said?'

'More likely something you didn't say,' said Lucas. 'Like your last name, perhaps?'

Had Caroline realized that the working-class lug with the appalling dress sense was in fact Ben Slater, founder, owner and CEO of the most profitable hedge fund in the UK, Lucas had little doubt that her bra would have spontaneously unhooked on the spot.

'Forget it,' said Ben. 'If that's all she's interested in, I'm not bothered.'

When they'd first met, in Murren, and Ben had told Lucas what he did for a living, Lucas hadn't thought much of it. It was only after he arrived in London that he began to piece together quite how successful, not to mention rich, his friend really was. You'd never know it to look at him, or even to stay in his flat which, though comfortable, was hardly a billionaire's lair. But his Stellar Fund was one of the top three hedge funds in Europe.

Most of the playboys and grandees who hung out at the Cadogan had their heads so far up their asses it was painful, bragging about their funds and their yachts and their mistresses like so many yapping dogs. But Ben, who could have bought out the lot of them and still have change for a G4 or twenty, was ultra low-key about his wealth. Sometimes, Lucas thought, he was actually embarrassed about it. Certainly he blushed like a virgin whenever anybody complimented him on his skills as an investor, or when the papers referred to him as 'Fund God Slater.'

In many ways – most ways – the two boys were very different. While Lucas slept around shamelessly with the apparently endless stream of models who threw themselves at him, especially since the *Tatler* thing, Ben was a hopeless romantic. He was forever bemoaning the fact that he couldn't seem to find a nice, decent girl who would see past his money and love him for himself alone.

'This place looks the bollocks, by the way,' he said admiringly, changing the subject as he found his arms full of one of the writhing burlesque dancers. 'Julia must be pleased with the turnout.'

'You'd think so, wouldn't you?' said Lucas bitterly, shooing the girl away. 'Actually she's done nothing but bitch at me all evening. Apparently the whole thing is vulgar and tasteless.'

'Well, Tisch is gonna love your arse, whatever she says,' said Ben. 'I just spoke to a mate of mine from the *Daily Mail*, that bloke collapsed by the bar.' He pointed to a slumped figure on the other side of the room. 'He says they're doing a huge write-up tomorrow. Best Christmas do he's ever been to, he said, and believe me he's been to a few.'

'I don't doubt it,' said Lucas. 'But enough about my career prospects. You just rescued me from Caroline, the most appalling woman in London, and one good turn deserves another. Let's get you laid, my friend.'

Ben laughed, and held up his hand. 'Uh, no, no thanks,' he said. 'I prefer to let these things happen naturally.'

But Lucas had already dived into the crowd like a harpoon fisherman. Within a minute he was back, hand in hand with a stunning Brazilian in a yellow mini-skirt so tiny it might have started life as a napkin.

'Kiki was asking to meet you,' he grinned at Ben, ignoring his pleading eyes and head shake and shoving the girl forward. 'She's *fascinated* by the hedge fund business. Aren't you, sweetheart?'

The girl nodded blankly and smiled at Ben. Clearly her English was not the best.

'Hello, Kiki.' Ben shook her hand awkwardly, looking daggers at Lucas. Part of him envied his friend's seemingly limitless sexual confidence. But he could never treat sex as a sport, the way that Lucas did. What was he supposed to say to this girl who couldn't understand a word he said and only wanted to sleep with him because Lucas had told her he was richer than the Aga Khan?

'Look, I'm sorry but I'm not staying,' he said, slipping his coat back on despite Lucas's protests and the girl's disappointed pout. 'I've got a big meeting in the morning. I need my beauty sleep.'

Lucas sighed as he watched him go. What was the point of being rich and successful if you never used it to get women? Or to buy yourself a decent wardrobe? Tomorrow, he decided, he'd go round to Ben's apartment and burn that awful sweater.

'He leaving?' Kiki looked up at Lucas, bewildered. She might not be the sharpest knife in the drawer, but she had the little-girl-lost thing down pat. And by God she was sexy.

'Don't you worry about him, sweetheart,' said Lucas. Figuring Slater's loss may as well be his gain, he slipped a warm hand under the sliver of yellow fabric that passed for a skirt. 'I'll take care of you. Come on. Let's find ourselves a drink.'

Chapter Seven

The next morning, hung over, late for work and stuck in a hideous jam on the Embankment, Ben leaned on the horn of his bright red Mini Cooper and swore at no one in particular.

'Fucking traffic!' he yelled, regretting it as the throbbing pain in his temples immediately kicked up a notch. 'What's the bleeding hold up?'

Normally he prided himself on being a pretty even-tempered guy. With billions of pounds of other people's money under management, he had learned early on how to deal with stress and compartmentalize his life. But this morning's meeting was important.

Success had come so quickly to Ben – he'd only founded his fund five years ago, and never in his wildest dreams imagined it would grow as fast as it had. It would have been easy to lose perspective and start believing in his own hype. He'd seen it happen to countless others in the hedge fund business: Anton Tisch, Dan Frazer, Dante Capellini. They'd all turned into right self-important tossers. Ben remembered Capellini from his days as a trader at Lehman, not so long ago. He'd actually been a fun bloke back then. These days he swanned about with bodyguards and private jets, giving press conferences about his political beliefs like bloody Bono. It was sad, really.

He could only imagine that none of his competitors came from a family like his. If his mum, never mind his sisters, ever turned on the telly and saw him wearing wraparound sunglasses, pontificating about world peace – my God, he'd never hear the end of it!

The Slaters were Essex to the core and about as close as a family could be. Ben was the youngest, and the only boy, but despite those two facts he'd never been spoiled or molly-coddled as a child. He and his two sisters, Karen and Nikki, grew up in a pokey little terraced house on Canvey Island. His mum and dad still lived on the island, although these days 'home' was a sprawling single-story mansion that Ben had bought for them, complete with five-car garage and an outdoor Jacuzzi they never used but were inordinately proud of nonetheless. Karen, married to a local hairdresser she'd been dating since she was fifteen, was ten miles away. And Nikki, also married with two kids, lived not much further in Chingford where she had her own beauty salon, Faces. All three of the Slater kids went home every other Sunday for a family lunch, and treated one another's houses and lives as an extension of their own.

They were all proud of Ben's success, if a little bewildered by the scale of it. But the Slater parents were every bit as impressed with Nikki's salon as they were with his multi-billion-dollar fund. As a result, Ben's feet had remained firmly on the ground, and he'd never been allowed to let either the pressure or the adulation go to his head.

After fifteen infuriating minutes at a complete standstill, the cars in front of him finally started to move, and soon the high-rises of Canon Street began looming into view through the chill December mist. Turning left onto King William Street, he swung the Mini at breakneck speed onto the parking ramp and down into the subterranean gloom of the Stellar Inc. garage.

'Morning, Mr. Slater.' Jerry, the parking attendant, was chirpy as ever. 'You're later than usual. Big night, was it?' He winked knowingly.

'I wish,' said Ben, with feeling, rubbing his aching head. Annoyingly, having told Lucas he wasn't interested, he'd been plagued with erotic dreams last night about the Brazilian girl. 'Are the Daiwa guys here yet?'

This morning's meeting was with some Japanese institutional investors. If there was one group of people you really did *not* want to be late for, it was the Japanese.

'Fraid so,' said Jerry. 'They got here about fifteen minutes ago.'

'Bollocks.'

Not bothering to wait for the elevator, Ben bounded up the steps two at a time, picking up his morning bundle of press clippings from the front desk without breaking stride. He'd just closed the door to his office and was hastily putting on one of the silk ties he kept in his desk drawer, whilst simultaneously hunting for some aspirin, when his phone went off.

Seeing 'Mum' flashing insistently, he hit 'busy' and stuck his head round the door of his PA's office.

'Morning, Tam. Are they in the conference room?'

'They are.' Tammy, his utterly devoted secretary of the past three years and a fellow Essex native flashed him a smile. 'You look like shit, by the way.'

'Thanks,' said Ben. 'I know.'

'I gave them tea and biscuits five minutes ago,' said Tammy. 'But your mum's on line one and I think you'd better talk to her before you go in there. You forgot your nan's birthday, apparently.' She raised a disapproving eyebrow. 'She's not happy about it.'

Ben groaned. That was all he needed. Jabbing the flashing red button on Tammy's phone he reluctantly picked up the receiver.

'Hello, Mum.'

Tammy giggled as he held the phone away from his ear, shielding himself from the rising maternal decibel level. When Mrs. Slater lost her rag, she really lost it.

'Yeah, I know, I'm sorry,' he pleaded, once he could get a word in edgeways. 'Yes, she does deserve better at ninety-one. I'll make it up to her, honest. I'll come over there tonight, drop off her present myself, how's that? No

97

'... yes, I *do* care, Mum, I'm just late for a meeting. Look, I've gotta go. I'll call you later, yeah?'

Handing Tammy the phone, he dashed off down the corridor, clutching his aching head and still struggling to straighten the knot on his tie. He looked more like a schoolboy late for class than the CEO of one of the biggest funds in Europe.

What a bloody awful start to the day.

Pushing open the double doors of the conference room, he wondered briefly whether Lucas was feeling as rough and hung over as he was. If there were any justice in this world, he ought to be.

In fact, at that precise moment, Lucas was feeling more than a little pleased with himself.

Though he, too, was late for work, he reckoned that even Julia would probably cut him a little slack today. Slicing his way through the traffic on Piccadilly on his beloved Ducati racing bike like a hot knife through butter, he allowed memories of his epic lovemaking session with the Brazilian girl to drift back to him, interspersed with flashbacks from last night's triumphant party.

His gamble had really paid off. Even the Tory leader's wife, a famously po-faced killjoy, had weaved over to him at the end of the night to say how much she'd enjoyed herself. There was bound to be a big write-up in the *Standard*'s society pages tonight, which would hopefully start a trickle-down effect of positive press for the Cadogan. Anton couldn't fail to be impressed.

Parking his bike in one of the public stands opposite the hotel – to his fury, he had been denied a parking space in the Cadogan's forecourt, where Julia's mint-green Porsche was already glinting smugly in the sunshine – he sauntered into the lobby, grinning from ear to ear.

'What time do you call this?'

Derek, the flamingly gay head receptionist, fancied

Lucas madly and liked to demonstrate his devotion through confrontational flirting. Happily this was a game that Lucas also enjoyed playing.

'Shut it, Shirley,' he said, with a wink that reduced Derek to jelly. 'I think I earned my extra hour in bed.'

'That's as maybe,' said Derek, recovering his composure. 'But you'll wish you'd set your alarm clock when I tell you who you missed this morning.'

'Who?' Lucas, rifling through his post, was only half listening.

'Only Anton the Almighty,' said Derek archly.

Instantly Lucas looked up. 'Tisch? He was here?'

Derek nodded. 'Holed up with Julia for almost forty minutes,' he said. 'And when they came out of her office, I heard him tell her ... hmm, no, I'm not sure I should tell you. I wouldn't want to ruin your morning.'

'Spill it, sweetheart,' said Lucas, 'before I get behind that desk and beat it out of you.'

Derek flushed with pleasure. But when he spoke again, he looked serious.

'Well,' he said, 'I heard Anton tell Julia she'd done an amazing job with the party, and the whole Moulin Rouge thing. And she just said, "Thank you," that she'd decided it was time to revitalize our stuffy, conservative image. She never even mentioned your name.'

'*Conyo*,' Lucas murmured under his breath. The bitch knew damn well he'd probably be late this morning and had deliberately arranged the meeting with Anton without him. How dare she take the credit for his idea and hard work? How dare she?

'Where is she?' he asked murderously.

'Still in her office, I think,' said Derek. 'Don't go doing anything silly now, Lucas,' he added, as Lucas stormed down the corridor. But it was too late for that.

'You fucking liar!' Bursting into the manager's office like a comet of fury, he slammed the door behind him.

'Good morning, Lucas,' said Julia calmly, not looking up from her PC screen. 'Nice of you to join us at last.'

'You told Anton the party was your idea,' he yelled.

Slowly and deliberately, she right-clicked her mouse, minimizing the spreadsheet she was looking at, and sat back in her chair, looking at him.

'I did no such thing,' she said. 'Anton had heard good reports and came by to congratulate us. I merely thanked him and said that I was as pleased with how things had gone as he was.'

'Bullshit!' Lucas exploded. 'You took the credit for *my* party.'

'It wasn't *your* party,' said Julia acidly. 'The entire hotel worked their arses off to make last night the success it was. As I remember, you couldn't even be bothered to show up until a couple of hours before kick off. It was a team effort.'

Lucas looked so furious, she half expected to see steam coming out of his ears. Enjoying herself, she threw petrol on the flames by adding patronizingly: 'There's no *I* in team you know, Lucas. You'd do well to remember that if you want to succeed in the hotel business.'

'Yeah, well, there's an *I* in bitch,' he said, throwing the last remnants of professional caution to the wind. 'I'm going over to Tisch's office right now, and I'm going to tell him exactly what a lying piece of work you are. Fuck you, Julia. You had nothing to do with that party and you know it.'

'On the contrary,' said Julia. 'I'm the manager. I had everything to do with it.'

'You were trying to talk me out of it till the last second!' Lucas spluttered. 'I'm going to make sure Anton knows it.'

'Be my guest,' she said, with a maddeningly nonchalant shrug. 'You'll only end up looking like more of a spoiled child than you do already. Oh, and that little tirade of yours?'

She glanced up to the corner above the window, where a tiny CCTV camera was swiveling ominously. When the hell had she had that installed? 'It's all on tape. I'm sure Mr. Tisch will find your professional conduct gripping viewing when I bike it over to him later. Close the door on your way out, would you, please?'

Cursing both Julia and himself for apparently playing right into her hands, he hurried out of her office, through the lobby and back into the crisp December air, crossing the road to where his bike was parked. Just as he was reaching for his helmet, his mobile rang.

'Ruiz,' he barked.

'Ah, Mr. Roooo-eeeez. I've pinned you down at laaaarst.'

The nasal, droning voice of his bank manager felt like lead pouring into Lucas's heart. That was all he needed.

'Hello, Mr. Chorley.' He tried to sound upbeat. 'Listen, I know I owe you a call. But I'm right in the middle of something at the moment. Do you think I could call you back?'

'You owe us a lot more than a call, Mr. Roooo-eeez,' said the manager darkly. 'Are you aware of your last month's overdraft charges?'

'Er, yes, yes, I am,' blustered Lucas.

'Because you're now seven thousand pounds over your authorized limit,' whined the man from Natwest. 'I'm afraid you've left me with no choice but to put a temporary freeze on your accounts.'

Lucas's heart tightened. He hadn't realized that things had got quite that bad. Then again, he had so many un-opened bank statements and angry red bills piled up on the floor of his apartment, it was starting to look like a recycling facility.

'I'm sure there's no need for that,' he said, battling to keep the fear out of his voice. 'I can raise seven thousand pounds pretty easily.' Running a hand over the gleaming body of his beloved Ducati, he realized with a pang that he'd have to sell her. 'It's more of a cash flow problem than anything else.'

'I hope so, Mr. Roooo-eeez, for your sake.' The voice on the other end of the line sounded unconvinced. 'Nevertheless, I'm freezing your accounts until the funds arrive.'

Deciding it was useless to try to negotiate further, Lucas hung up, angrily ramming his phone back into his inside jacket pocket.

'Fucking jobsworth,' he muttered darkly. But he could only deal with one problem at a time. Pulling on his helmet and straddling the powerful bike – God, he'd miss her; what a tragedy she had to go – he started the engine. If he didn't get to Anton before Julia did, his standing with the boss would definitely take a serious nosedive. The hideous thought struck him that he might even lose his job. Please God, no. Then old misery-guts Chorley really would have his nuts in a vise.

Tearing along the Embankment at breakneck speed, the roar of his engine audible from the South Bank, he arrived at Tisch's offices within ten minutes. Leaving his bike illegally parked out front, he darted inside.

'I need to see Anton ... Mr. Tisch,' he panted. 'It's urgent.'

His old enemy the receptionist smiled maliciously. 'Tough luck,' she said. 'He's not here.'

Lucas frowned. 'Well, where is he?'

At first the girl said nothing. But Lucas shot her a look so threatening, she eventually capitulated.

'He's on his way to City Airport,' she pouted. 'He's flying to Geneva this morning. You won't catch him,' she yelled after Lucas's disappearing back as he raced outside. But the electric doors were already closing and he didn't hear her.

When he arrived at City it took all his powers of persuasion to get security to allow him onto the airfield where

Tisch's private jet was parked. But finally, after flashing his Cadogan ID, his passport and his best, most winning smile to the girl on the desk, he was ushered through.

Anton, apparently, was already on board while the technicians made some final checks to the plane.

'Where d'you think you're going?'

The burly bodyguard at the foot of the stairs leading up into the cabin barred Lucas's way.

'My name is Lucas Ruiz. I need to talk to Mr. Tisch before he leaves. It's urgent.'

'I dare say it is,' said the heavy. 'But I don't care if your name's Jesus fucking Christ. You're not going aboard and that's that.'

'If you'd just let him know I'm here,' said Lucas, nodding towards the walkie talkie on the man's belt, 'I'm sure he'll agree to see me.'

'Read my lips,' said the guard. 'Piss. Off.'

It wasn't perhaps the wisest of moves, but desperate times called for desperate measures and, catching him by surprise, Lucas landed a swift upper cut right under the man's jaw. Like most hired muscle, he was so unused to being challenged he seemed completely unprepared for it, staggering backwards uselessly and giving Lucas a crucial few seconds in which to land two more punches followed by a sharp knee to the groin. Leaving the unfortunate guard writhing on the tarmac, Lucas straightened his tie, smoothed down his collar and darted up the steps and into the cabin.

Inside, Anton was sitting on a couch in his reading glasses with a sea of papers spread out in front of him. He looked first surprised and then annoyed to see Lucas.

'What the hell?' he spluttered. 'Who let you on board?'

'Your security was kind enough to let me pass,' said Lucas, his voice drowning out the groans from outside. 'I apologize for disturbing you, Mr. Tisch. I know you must be busy.'

'I am,' said Anton coolly. 'Very.'

Just then the pilot opened the door to the cabin. Ignoring Lucas, he addressed himself directly to his boss.

'We're ready to go, sir. Shall I close the doors?'

'Yes.' Anton turned to Lucas. 'If you want to talk, Mr. Ruiz, I suggest you strap yourself in.'

Taking a seat, Lucas did as he was told. Looking out of the window as they taxied toward the runway, he could see the security guard on his feet now, still bent double with pain, talking frantically into his walkie talkie. Too late now, asshole.

Moments later they were airborne. The plane gave a series of little shudders as they climbed through the cloud cover, before settling into a steady purr as they achieved altitude.

'So.' Anton was the first to speak. 'What's all this about? It had better be good, Lucas. I don't appreciate having my time wasted.'

Lucas felt his stomach churning with nerves. All the Mission Impossible stuff had kept his adrenaline pumping. But now that he was actually here, face to face with Anton, he had no idea how to begin. Julia's words about him looking like a spoiled child were ringing in his ears. But it was too late to turn back now.

'It's about last night,' he began. And he proceeded to explain not only the battles he'd had with Julia over the Christmas party but the whole history of hostility and resentment between them, and their opposing views about the right direction for the Cadogan.

'I understand that she's the manager. And that she has more experience than I do. But I know I'm right about this,' he said, winding up his long, impassioned speech. 'We have to keep evolving to stay ahead of the competition. That's what last night was all about. And that was *my* vision. Not hers.'

Anton, who'd kept his arms crossed and his head down

while Lucas was talking, now looked up at him. He wasn't remotely interested in the micro-political struggles at the Cadogan. But he *was* interested in Lucas. It hadn't escaped his notice what a name the boy had made for himself since coming to London, not easy for a broke outsider with no contacts, no title, and nothing but his good looks and confidence to recommend him. Anton himself had been trying for years to gain acceptance to the British establishment, but Lucas seemed to pick up friends in high places with the same ease and inevitability that other newly arrived foreigners picked up a cold. He clearly had a natural genius for PR, which was a very valuable asset in the hotel business, and was being wasted at the Cadogan. Despite his poker face, Anton had in fact been delighted by the buzz generated by last night's party. Something about Lucas's direct, fiery gaze convinced him that the kid was telling the truth, that it really had been his idea all along.

That Julia had been less than honest earlier didn't surprise him. To be fair, he'd have done the same had he been in her shoes. She was sick to death of the battles with her under-manager, and Anton didn't blame her. Though Lucas didn't know it, she'd already been on the phone to him this morning, complaining that Lucas's insubordination had now gone beyond all appropriate professional boundaries and that she had evidence of this on tape. She wanted him fired.

If it had been anyone else, Anton wouldn't have hesitated. But Lucas's talent for self promotion was too good to be jettisoned over some petty squabble. And no one could deny the boy had balls.

'Have you ever heard of a hotel called Palmers?' he asked him.

Lucas looked bemused. This was a bit of a non-sequitur.

'Palmers, in the Hamptons? Of course,' he said. 'It's a legend. Probably the most prestigious family-owned hotel in the world.'

'Used to be,' said Anton. He handed Lucas a spreadsheet from the pile in front of him. 'These are last year's numbers. Take a look.'

Lucas's eyes scanned down the page, his almost photographic memory taking in the relevant points on the P&L at once.

'Yeah, well. That's not good. How did you get hold of these?' He handed the paper back.

'Never mind that,' said Anton brusquely. 'The point is that Palmers is on its last legs. I've decided to build my next Tischen in East Hampton, just a couple of streets away. It's going to be called the Herrick.'

'Great,' said Lucas, unsure what any of this had to do with him. 'But listen, about the Cadogan—'

Anton held up his hand for silence.

'For Christ's sake, boy, stop whinging about all that before I change my mind. Clearly that hotel isn't big enough for the two of you, and there's not a snowball's chance in hell I'm letting Julia Brett-Sadler go. You can consider yourself fired from the Cadogan, Lucas.'

'But Mr. Tisch—'

'As of right now,' said Anton firmly.

Gulping, Lucas ran a hand through his thick mop of curls, trying desperately not to show how crushed he was. He was far too proud to beg for his job – it wouldn't have made a difference anyway – but what the fuck was he going to tell his bank manager now?

Noticing the gesture, Anton added: 'Oh yes, your hair. That'll have to go. From now on I want you clean shaven and preppier than a Gap model at a loafer-wearers' convention. Got it?'

'Not really,' said Lucas. 'I thought you just said I was fired.'

'From the Cadogan, you are.' Anton smiled. 'In a few short months you've shown yourself to be completely incapable of compromise, taking direction or working within a team. I'm not surprised Julia's sick to death of you.'

Lucas's face fell.

'But you've also shown yourself to be an innovator and a risk taker,' Anton went on, 'with a quite masterful grasp of the media. Those are skills I can use.'

Blindsided with relief, and not having the first idea what to say to this, Lucas wisely said nothing.

'What I need at the Herrick is youth, energy and above all some real momentum in the press,' said Anton. 'Palmers may not be the giant it once was. But old names like that don't die out overnight, especially not in a closed, elitist society like the Hamptons. I've been reduced to blackmailing the planning committee just to get the damn project off the ground,' he said bitterly. 'None of the locals will rest until they've run us out of town, and we haven't even begun construction yet. I need someone out there who doesn't shy away from confrontation, but who can also be charming in the right quarters. You'll be project manager-cum-foreman for the first year at least, then take over as manager once she's up and running. What do you think? Are you up to it?'

Slowly, grindingly slowly, the full import of what Anton was saying began to sink in to Lucas's brain.

'D'you mean … you want to hire me as the manager?' he stammered.

'Ah. You don't think you're ready.' Sensing his hesitation like a shark smelling blood, Anton snapped shut the folder of documents with a sigh. 'Well, perhaps you're right. You are less than a year out of school, after all. It's a big step.'

'No, no.' Lucas shot to his feet like he'd just been shocked with a cattle prod. 'I'm ready. Of course I'm ready. When do you want me to start?'

'Soon,' said Anton. 'As you're here now, you can spend the next month in Geneva learning the ropes of the project. Then it'll take a few weeks to sort out your visa, etc … But I'll want you on the ground by February, latest.'

Lucas grinned. Anton Tisch might be a bastard to the rest of the world, but he was rapidly turning into Lucas's own personal guardian angel.

'Palmers has been in a lot of trouble for years,' he went on. 'But their real weak spot right now is Honor Palmer, old man Trey's daughter. She's taken over as manager with no prior experience in the hotel trade, and the locals all hate her for pulling a fast one on her father, seizing control of his assets against his wishes.'

'I'm not surprised,' said Lucas. 'Grasping bitch.'

'What I want *you* to do,' said Anton, 'is to get that message out there nationally, and even internationally. Once people stop seeing Honor and Palmers as the underdog, they'll be a lot more accepting of us. I've done this many times now and I can tell you, building a world-class hotel is only half the battle. You have to win over the local hearts and minds too. We don't want to be the Big Bad Corporate Wolf.'

Lucas's heart was pumping nineteen to the dozen. He wasn't worried about turning the PR tide against Honor. That should be a piece of cake. But to be responsible for building and managing a Tischen hotel in such a prestigious location? A rival to the great Palmers, no less? That was more than a dream. It was the wildest, most ridiculous fantasy. And it was about to come true.

Sensing his excitement, Anton smiled, and dropped the heavy bundle of paperwork in Lucas's lap.

'Merry Christmas,' he said drily. 'Oh, and Lucas? I'm serious about the haircut. I'm not having my hotel run by Leo bloody Sayer.'

Chapter Eight

Honor glanced up at the ominous, bruise-gray storm clouds gathering over the ocean and stepped up her pace a notch. It was a typical drab, windy January morning and apart from her devoted Boxer Caleb jumping excitedly at her heels, the beach was deserted. That suited Honor just fine. She preferred to be alone when she ran. It helped her to think.

Right now she had a lot to think about. Ignoring the ache in her thighs as the lactic acid streamed through her muscles, she made a sharp left and began pounding her way over the bumpy dunes, trying to sort her various problems into some sort of order.

First, as always, there was Palmers. The first whisper she'd heard about a new Tischen hotel being built right on her doorstep had come via Devon, back in October. She'd been worried, of course, but had somehow convinced herself that this was a problem to be faced in the distant future, long after she'd restored Palmers to its former glory. She never imagined that things would move as fast as they had. Less than twelve weeks later and the old houses on the proposed Herrick site had already been demolished, with a forbidding chainlink fence erected around the resultant vast plot of muddy earth. Even if they only built on half that space, it would be twice the size of Palmers.

At first Honor was pissed at Devon for failing to do anything to stop the development.

'You're on the damn planning committee, aren't you?' she'd yelled at him in bed, after a particularly unsatisfactory bout of lovemaking. They saw each other so rarely these days – one snatched weekend in three, if they were lucky – that the pressure for everything to be perfect when they did meet hung over them like a death sentence. Her desire for him was as strong as ever, but the wave of sexual confidence that had swept her away in the early months was already subsiding, and all her natural insecurities were creeping back. 'Can't you do something?'

'Like what?' Devon, equally frustrated by the sex, sounded exasperated. 'I told you, Tisch clearly has some dirt on Mort Sullivan. The guy did a total U-turn overnight, and he's got enough influence on the other members to swing the thing his way, whatever I say or do.'

'But there must be something … an appeal, maybe?' Sitting up in bed, Honor ran her fingers through her hair. Devon reached up and started stroking her back, trying to calm her.

'On what grounds? You don't want the competition? Look,' he added more gently, 'the planning decision's been made. Trying to fight it will be a waste of your time and money, believe me. But that doesn't mean there's nothing you can do. You can turn Palmers around, just like you planned. And you can beat Anton Tisch at his own game.'

His words came back to her now as the cold wind whipped against her face. He was right, of course. It was pathetic how frightened she was of a little competition. Her grandfather Tertius had seen off more rivals than he could count in his thirty years at Palmers' helm. And here she was, after only a few months, running scared at the first whiff of a threat. Then again, in her grandfather's day, Palmers hadn't been falling apart at the seams. Among the myriad problems that the surveyors' report had thrown up last year, two were particularly serious. They needed a new roof, and the entire building would have to be rewired.

'If you only had the funds to fix one of those things, which would you fix?' Honor, ever the pragmatist, had asked the surveyor.

'I'd fix my bank account,' he said grimly. 'You really can't cut corners here, Miss Palmer. These are essential repairs, and they'll cost you a lot more in the long term if you don't deal with them now.'

Which was all very well. But it would be at least a year, assuming she got her bookings back up to year-round capacity (and how the fuck was she going to manage that?) before she could begin to afford such a major refurb. In the end, deciding that a working roof really was a genuine essential, she'd begun only minor repairs to the wiring. She figured if she got the roof fixed by May, and got enough bookings over her first summer season in June through August, at a push she might be able to rewire before the following summer, when the Herrick would be up and running. But she still tossed and turned in bed each night praying that she'd made the right decision. What if something really went haywire, and she woke one morning to find the building being consumed by an electrical fire? At least if the roof had still leaked, it might have doused the flames. Oh God! Why did Anton bloody Tisch have to crawl out of the woodwork now?

Reaching the top of the dunes, she began the long descent back toward the shore. Caleb had run so far ahead he was little more than a speck in the distance, but there was no way he'd hear her above the breaking waves if she whistled for him now. A gift from Devon, the rescue dog was affectionate and loyal to a fault, but obedience had never been his forte – something else that Honor loved about him.

If it hadn't been for Caleb, she'd probably have had a nervous breakdown over Christmas. Desperately lonely without Devon – she couldn't even call him over the holiday season; it was too risky with his family around – it felt like one thing after another had conspired to dampen her festive spirits.

First there was the situation with her father, which only

seemed to get worse as the weeks passed. He was still refusing to see or talk to Honor, but she knew from the few family friends who visited that his Alzheimer's was in full, raging swing now, and he probably wouldn't know who she was even if he *did* take her calls. Devon had promised her he'd check up on the old man while he was in town, to make sure Lise wasn't abusing him. She wasn't, but the picture he painted to Honor was still pretty grim: Trey rarely acknowledged his wife at all, and spent long periods each week in a state of total regression, even to the point of sucking his thumb and asking repeatedly for his mother. Honor's desperation was made worse by the fact that relations between her and her stepmother were at an all-time low.

'You know, you're very good at telling everyone else what to do,' Lise had told her angrily during a Christmas eve phone call that had deteriorated, as usual, into a slanging match. 'But I'm the one that's here with him every day. You can't even be bothered to make it home for Christmas.'

'It's not a question of being bothered,' Honor shot back angrily. 'What's the point of me being in the house if Dad won't see me? Besides, Christmas is a crazy time at the hotel. I can't just abandon ship.'

In fact Palmers was depressingly empty of guests over the holiday. True, East Hampton was primarily a summer resort, but another winter like this one would finish them. The real reason she hadn't gone back to Boston for the holidays was that she couldn't bear the thought of running into Devon there with Karis and the kids. From the beginning he'd assured her repeatedly that his marriage was one of convenience, and that both he and Karis stayed in it for the children. Honor told herself she believed him, but going to Boston would mean putting that trust to the test, a thought that filled her with a lot more fear than it ought to have done. But after what Devon had told her about her father, she realized that she would have to bite the bullet soon and force her way in to see Trey, whether he liked it or not. After all, as long as she didn't leave the house, she *couldn't* run into Karis Carter, could she? She had a two-day trip penciled in for the end of the month, and was absolutely dreading it.

She was at the end of the beach now, in the flat, scrubby area where the sand petered out and the bracken and spiky grass began. A narrow, winding path led from here up to the road and a two-mile flat jog back to Palmers. Caleb, for once, had decided to stop and wait for his mistress and Honor spent a few seconds patting and praising him while she caught her breath, before sinking down onto the grass for her sit-ups.

Ever since she'd turned thirteen she'd been obsessive about staying in shape and maintaining her lithe, boyish figure. At first, exercise was a weapon in the losing battle against puberty. But once she grew up and realized that not only could she not become a boy, but her father probably wouldn't love her even if she did, the focus of her workouts changed. Now they were all about control, about power. As though if she could keep her own body in check, she stood a chance at doing the same with the rest of her life. Or something.

As she jack-knifed into a series of painful-looking crunches, her mind wandered to Tina, who was supposed to be joining her on her upcoming visit to their father. Although relieved her sister's relationship with the awful Danny was at an end, Tina's move to LA had not meant the end to all the gossip that Honor had hoped for. No sooner was she out of one inflammatory relationship than she had launched herself headlong into another, this time with a nineteen-year-old toy-boy model and sometime porn star who rejoiced in the name of Dick Grate. Really, you couldn't make up Tina's life if you tried. She and Dick seemed to spend an inordinate amount of time making out (or worse) in public places, and had generally succeeded in establishing themselves as Hollywood's most-watched 'It' couple. Rarely did a week go by without some compromising picture or other making its way into *US Weekly* or the *National Enquirer*. It didn't help that, if anything, Dick actually looked even younger than he was – like an overgrown schoolboy out on a date with his buxom math teacher.

Tina, however, refused to see any problem with the relationship.

'You're just jealous,' she said breezily when Honor tackled her about it before Christmas, insisting it was doing harm to both the family's reputation and Palmers'. 'Dick's single, I'm single, so what? It's not my fault you never get laid and waste your life stuck in that mausoleum of a hotel.'

To add insult to injury, she'd positively insisted on bringing the infamous Dick back to Boston with her in a few weeks as well, which meant Honor was going to have to meet him.

'You don't understand the passion we have for each other,' Tina explained to a by-now nauseous Honor. 'We can't be apart at all, not even for one night. Anyway, Dad's not gonna care, is he? He won't know who *we* are, never mind Dickie.'

This was true. But it didn't make Honor feel any better.

'C'mon boy.' Bouncing back up onto her feet, she dragged Caleb by his collar up the steep path to the road. Normally she treated this last stretch of her morning run as a cool down. But just thinking about Tina and Dickie made her so mad, she found herself sprinting faster than ever, her soles pummeling away at the tarmac as if they had some sort of personal vendetta. By the time she rounded the corner into Palmers' driveway she was dripping with sweat, and even in the chilly January air her cheeks were flushed redder than a Russian doll's.

'Miss Palmer?' The girl on reception was new and even more nervous of Honor than the rest of the staff. Her voice sounded positively querulous, and Honor found herself battling down irritation. As long as people did their jobs properly, they had nothing to fear from her. She hated when they cowered like she was Saddam Hussein or something.

'What is it, Agnes?' she snapped, unclipping Caleb from his leash and shooing him out into the gardens.

'You have a visitor,' mumbled the girl. 'He's waiting in the parlor. I lit the fire for him.'

'Well, who is it?' said Honor. 'Can they wait fifteen minutes? I need to take a shower.'

'Erm, I'm not sure.' The girl looked properly panicked now, as if she'd just been asked to explain quantum theory, or translate the Koran into Urdu. 'It's Mr. Carter. He seemed . . . he looked . . . I think it might be important,' she blurted.

Typical. Devon showed up to surprise her for the first time in almost a month, and she looked like something the cat had dragged in. Torn between running into his arms right away and disappearing upstairs to at least wash the sweat out of her hair, the decision was taken out of her hands when Devon appeared in the lobby.

'I need to talk to you,' he said stiffly. He couldn't risk showing any affection in front of Agnes. 'Can we talk in private?'

'Of course,' said Honor, matching his businesslike tone, although inside her heart was pounding. 'Come on up to my rooms. We can talk there.'

Only when the door of her suite was safely closed behind them did she reach up and put her arms around him. Kissing him softly on the mouth, before he had a chance to say anything, she breathed in the comforting man-smell of his body, a combination of aftershave, sweat and the starch from his shirt, and felt herself relaxing like a stretched spring.

Her euphoria, however, was short lived.

Pulling away, Devon looked her in the eye. She could tell at once that something was wrong.

'What?' she said. Oh, please, please let him not have come to finish things between them. Anything but that. 'What is it?'

'Honor, I'm so sorry,' he began. She felt the bile rising up in her throat. He *had* come to dump her! But he didn't even love Karis. Why? Why would he leave her, why now?

'Your father passed away this morning.'

She stood there staring at him blankly. After what felt like an age, she eventually managed a strangled 'I'm sorry?'

'It was very peaceful,' said Devon. 'I was with him when it happened, purely by chance. I stopped in to see him on my way to work and Lise told me he'd taken a turn for the worse last night. The doctor was with him, but I don't think there was anything he could have done.'

'Lise didn't call me,' said Honor. She was still staring straight ahead, like a zombie. 'No one called me.'

'I asked her not to,' said Devon. 'My pilot brought me straight down here. I thought ... I don't know. I didn't want you to hear over the phone. And I figured you could use a shoulder to cry on.'

'But ... I'm coming to see him,' Honor whispered. 'This month. I booked my flight.'

With infinite tenderness, Devon pulled her to him, wrapping his arms tightly around her.

'I'm sorry, sweetheart,' he said. 'I really am sorry.'

Trey Palmer's funeral was a circus.

A stream of black-clad bimbos, like aging ghosts of Christmases past, filed into St. Stephen's Cathedral and proceeded to argue loudly about which of them should have precedence in the seating arrangements. They were fighting for space with all the great and the good of Boston:

hoteliers, captains of industry and their wives, and old family friends like the Carters, most of whom hadn't laid eyes on Trey for a good twenty years. Then there was the press, none of whom Honor could recall inviting, but who seemed nevertheless to have turned out in spectacular force to see the old man off.

'Did you ask these people to show up?' Honor hissed at Lise after one particularly insensitive photographer had shoved a lens within inches of her face.

'Of course not,' Lise snapped back. Her skintight Dolce & Gabbana mini-dress, though black, was possibly the most un-funereal item of clothing Honor had ever seen, and the red soles of her sky-high Louboutin stilettos undoubtedly said more about her true feelings than anything else she was wearing. 'Tina's the one who can't take a shit unless it's on film.'

Of course. Tina. Sharing the front row with her sister, stepmother and of course the ubiquitous Dick, she was, as usual, reveling in the attention in a bright red trouser suit and more diamonds than a De Beers advertisement.

'I look on today as a celebration of my dad's life,' Honor overheard her earnestly explaining to a reporter behind them. 'He would have hated to see all this black. It's so depressing.'

What was truly depressing, of course, was the hypocrisy. In private, Tina had made no effort to hide her elation that the final chunk of her trust fund would at last be made available to her. All she wanted to talk about was selling the house, and how quickly they could come to a financial agreement with Lise.

Admittedly, Trey had been a pretty awful father. Even so, her sister's utter lack of compassion shocked Honor to the core. Especially when she herself was struggling with feelings of guilt for not having visited him enough, and regret that his last lucid memory of her was having Palmers wrenched out of his control. She desperately wanted someone to confide in, to unburden herself to, but Devon was with his family, as usual, and as unavailable to her as if he'd been on the moon.

Looking across at him now, she felt her frustration mounting. Poring over his hymnal, looking every inch the upstanding family man, he was pointing something out to his daughter. Karis, elegant in floor-length black, stood dutifully beside him, with their son Nicholas on her other side. Honor knew it was wrong to feel jealous. What right did she have to resent his family? But she couldn't help it. Despite his protestations to the contrary, looking at them now she could easily believe he and Karis were exactly what they seemed: a strong, loving unit, shored up against the hard times by twenty-five years of marriage, two children and a whole life built together.

There were days, mostly when she was alone and exhausted at Palmers, when she thought she wanted nothing more than to marry Devon. As though being his wife would complete her, and give her the security and unconditional love she'd craved ever since her mom died. But at other times, the nagging doubts she'd harbored from the beginning of the affair grew louder and harder to ignore. Both his kids were adults now – it wasn't as if they were nine. Surely, if he really loved her, he'd find the courage to call it quits with Karis and make a commitment to her?

He often talked about their future together, as if it were a fact. But whenever she pressed him on timing, or mentioned the dreaded 'd' word – divorce – he became defensive and shut the conversation down.

The service dragged on for what seemed like an age. The priest read out a eulogy that bore so little resemblance to her father it almost made Honor wonder whether she'd accidentally wandered into the wrong church, and Tina read a Rudyard Kipling poem in a faux-sentimental voice that she thought made her sound like a serious actress, but that made Honor want to throw up.

Afterwards there was some general milling about outside, although thankfully the weather was so arctic that no one wanted to linger long. Honor shivered in her black mink coat, gracefully accepting condolences from people she barely knew, and pretending not to notice the disapproving whispers and sly, condemning looks from mourners and onlookers alike. Even the priest had been distinctly chilly towards her. What *was* it with people in this town? You'd have thought by now they'd have found somebody else to hate. Not that it was much better in East Hampton, where to Honor's sensitive ears the snide whispers sounded almost deafening. Was she never to be forgiven for trying to save her family from financial ruin, and her father from himself?

She was wondering at what point it would be reasonable to slip away – there were still a ton of papers to be gone through at the townhouse and nobody else was volunteering to deal with them – when she felt a hand on her shoulder.

'Hey.' Devon smiled at her and she tried not to melt. In his dark suit and black cashmere coat he looked even more handsome and distinguished than usual, the gray flecks at his temples highlighting his dark eyes as they searched hers for a response. 'How're you holding up?'

'How am I holding up?' She mimicked his formal tone, her misery making her lash out, despite herself. 'Why, thank you for asking, Mr. Carter. I'm just peachy. And how are you and your wife? You all looked nice and cozy together in church.'

Devon grabbed her arm, lowering his voice to a whisper. 'That's not fair. It killed me seeing you across the aisle, all alone, not being able to hold you. You know it's you I want to be with.'

'Do I?' snapped Honor, breaking free of his grip. 'You were holding her hand. I saw you.'

'Christ, Honor.' He shook his head. 'It's a funeral. How do you want me to act?'

'I don't know,' she said miserably. 'I don't know and I don't care. Just leave me alone, OK?'

Alone in the safety of her blacked-out limo a few minutes later, she thought she'd want to cry, but instead she just lay back against the headrest and closed her eyes, exhausted. Forcing Devon out of her mind, she groaned at the thought of how much work still had to be done here before she could get back to Palmers. Trey's personal effects were in a hopelessly disorganized state. In some ways it was a good thing to be overloaded. It kept her from dwelling on her grief and guilt, and blocked out the worst of the loneliness. And yet she felt herself teetering on an emotional precipice. Yesterday, sorting through some old files, she'd come across a black and white snapshot of her mother and to her horror had found herself dissolving into wracking, uncontrollable sobs.

Never much of a one for introspection, she found it impossible to untangle her conflicting emotions. All she knew for sure was that her father's death had crystallized something in her. Once her tears subsided, she could feel the grief hardening in her veins into something more solid: determination.

Her father had died disappointed in her, believing that she'd not only stolen Palmers from him, but that she was incapable of making the hotel a success. Now, more than ever, she had to prove him wrong.

Tina and Lise could fight over the house and the trust if they wanted to. But for Honor, Palmers was all that mattered. It was, in some indefinable way, all that was left of her family. She wasn't about to let anyone take that away from her.

Anton Tisch had obviously written her off, just like her father. He wouldn't be opening his hotel next door if he didn't think Palmers was finished. But he was wrong, just as Trey had been wrong. She knew she had a mountain to climb, but she was damn well going to climb it.

She'd show them, all those vultures today who'd looked down their noses, judging her. She'd show them all.

Chapter Nine

Crawling along the Long Island Expressway in the back of the Hamptons Jitney bus, Lucas seethed quietly to himself.

As if arriving in America, a country he loathed almost as much as Britain, during a February cold snap weren't bad enough, he'd landed at La Guardia to find that not only had his suitcase been lost in transit, but the driver who was supposed to pick him up had had an accident on the Sunrise Highway, and he'd be forced to take the bus.

Ironically, from the moment Anton had offered him the managership of the Herrick, his life seemed to have become one giant stress after another. Admittedly, telling Julia she could stick her job at the Cadogan up her ass had been fun. But from then on in it had all been downhill.

Tisch had insisted that Lucas should be on site in the Hamptons by February at the latest to begin the building works, and he'd made it – just. It was a tall order, leaving him only a few weeks to organize his visa, move out of his London flat, sell his bike, settle his debts and find himself a place to live in East Hampton until the Herrick was ready. But he couldn't afford to cut corners on the time frame Anton had given him. He was expected to have the hotel built by next Christmas, including all landscaping, open in the spring, and have generated enough positive buzz to have the place heaving with celebrity guests by the following summer. That gave him only sixteen months to, as Anton put it, wipe Palmers off the map. All he had today was a bare patch of earth and a missing suitcase.

But the epic task that lay ahead of him wasn't the only depressing thought on Lucas's mind. There was also his family. Guilty because he'd barely been in touch since moving to London, he decided on a whim to fly out to Ibiza for Christmas. It was a mistake. Things at home were as bad as they'd ever been. The farmer who rented out his miserable little cottage to Lucas's mother and her waster husband had finally gotten tired of waiting for his rent and kicked them out. It wasn't until Lucas showed up at the doorstep on Christmas eve, weighed down with gifts, that he learned they were gone. The new tenant told him they were now living in a so-called 'studio apartment', which turned out to be little more than a squalid, one-room bedsit in the dodgy part of Santa Eulalia.

'Your brothers had to leave,' Ines told Lucas when he finally tracked her down, inhaling deeply on one of the hand-rolled cigarettes she seemed to smoke constantly these days. 'No room.' She looked around the tiny living quarters and shrugged hopelessly. Jose, drunk as usual, was snoring loudly on the sofa-bed in the corner.

Lucas had done his best to improve things. Apart from emptying his meagre savings account and giving it all to his mother in cash, he'd tried to inject some Christmas spirit into the gloomy little apartment, rigging up a garish artificial tree in the middle of the room and dashing off around the island on Christmas morning to round up his good-for-nothing brothers for an enormous, if somewhat stilted, family lunch. But in three days, there was only so much he could do. He had to be back in Geneva for a strategy meeting with Anton on the twenty-seventh.

Staring out of the grimy window of the bus now, he watched the rain pounding its steely needles onto the drab, flat landscape on either side of the freeway and tried to push thoughts of his mother from his mind. How he hated America. His loathing had begun years ago, at the Britannia, but this was the first opportunity he'd had to observe Americans on their home turf, and so far, they'd done little to reverse his prejudices.

The guy at the immigration desk was a power-hungry asshole, questioning Lucas for almost thirty minutes, though he could plainly see that all his papers were in order, before finally stamping his visa as if he were performing a personal favor. Then there was baggage claim, where the United staff first lost his luggage and then, when Lucas complained, began playing what was clearly a favorite game of theirs, entitled something along the lines of 'Let's-see-who-could-give-less-of-a-shit?' They were really quite competitive at it.

The last straw had been the bus driver, a man so grossly overweight he looked like he might well have eaten his previous load of passengers, and who smelled like he hadn't washed this year. Having refused to help Lucas with his one remaining bag, this gem of a human being then claimed to have 'no idea' how long the bus might take to reach its destination – despite the fact that all he'd done for the past twelve years was make the mind-numbing journey back and forth from the airport to the Hamptons fifteen times a week.

Dickhead.

But the thing that really got under Lucas's skin was the fact that so many of the lowliest positions at the airport – rubbish sweepers, toilet attendants and the like – seemed to be filled almost exclusively by Hispanics. He'd only been in the country three hours, and already he was starting to feel like a second-class citizen.

Instinctively, he lifted his hand to run it through his hair, something he always did when he felt agitated, only to be surprised yet again to find his trademark mop of curls gone, replaced with the preppy short back and sides Anton had demanded. Numerous girls back in Europe had assured him they loved the new look, but Lucas couldn't get used to it. Every time he looked in the mirror, he did a double take when he saw a clean-shaven drone staring back at him. All he needed was a college tie and some veneers and he could be a fucking CNN newsreader.

'Thz Bridgehammon,' mumbled the driver, which Lucas interpreted by looking at the road signs as: 'This is Bridgehampton.' Great. He could already speak moron.

How many fucking Hamptons were there, anyway? The road had become single lane some time ago, but it seemed to stretch on for ever, through a bunch of dull clapboard towns that all looked as drearily empty and sodden as the next. He thought he saw a sign saying 'East Hampton, ten miles,' but that must have been a good fifteen miles ago by his reckoning.

Finally, three long hours after leaving the airport, they reached the edge of town. A few minutes later the Jitney pulled over in a lay-by beside what looked like the main village green, and Lucas gratefully climbed out of his cramped seat.

Outside the rain had turned to sleet. Even so, it felt great to breathe fresh air after the muggy confines of the bus. The guy sitting next to him must have eaten enough garlic last night to sustain a small town's worth of Italians. Holding his small case over his head in lieu of an umbrella, Lucas sprinted across the green toward the nearest available shelter, a coffee shop, shaking the freezing droplets off himself like a wet dog as he staggered inside.

'Wow. You look *cold*.'

It was hardly the most insightful of opening lines. But one look at the waitress's small but perfectly formed body, all Latin curves and breasts heaving enticingly beneath her tight cashmere sweater, helped him see past her conversational deficiencies.

'Do I?' said Lucas, grinning. 'Well, you look phenomenally sexy.'

The girl laughed nervously. 'Er, thanks. I guess.' She blushed. 'You're pretty direct, aren't you?'

Lucas shrugged. 'I find it saves time.' Taking off his coat, he rubbed his hands together for warmth before offering one to the girl to shake. 'I'm Lucas Ruiz.'

'Desiree,' said the girl, shaking his hand, still somewhat warily. He was a divine-looking man. Different too – not at all like the bland, all-American Ralph Lauren-model types she was used to seeing in East Hampton. This one was more Antonio Banderas, perhaps crossed with a young Warren Beatty. And that deep, soulful Spanish accent was to die for. Even so, the way he looked at her made her feel naked and vulnerable. It was nice and disconcerting at the same time.

'Can I get you something to drink?' she asked, pulling herself together.

'Desiree,' said Lucas, rolling the word over his tongue like he was tasting an exquisite wine. 'Beautiful name. Very appropriate.'

She blushed again, deeper this time.

'I think I *will* have a drink, thank you Desiree,' he said, enjoying the effect he was having on her. 'Hot chocolate, please. With as much cream as you can manage on the top.'

He was the only customer in the cafe – in fact, looking outside through the rain-splattered window, he and his fellow Jitney passengers appeared to be the only people in the entire town – and his drink wasn't long in coming.

'The place looks dead,' he said, nodding toward the window and the empty village green beyond as he sipped gratefully at the creamy chocolate. 'Is it always like this?'

'June, July and August you can't move. It's a zoo,' said Desiree, pulling her thick dark hair back into a pony tail and tying it with a cheap elastic band. 'But off season, yeah, it's pretty quiet. I actually prefer it this way.'

'Really?' Lucas looked surprised. 'Why? Aren't you bored?'

'Sometimes,' she shrugged. 'But, you know, I read. I paint. There's more to life than party party party.'

'There is?' He was so deadpan, it made her laugh. She was finally beginning to relax.

He'd have liked to stay here chatting her up and gorging himself on hot chocolate for the rest of the day, but sadly it wasn't an option. Thanks to all the delays and fuck-ups at La Guardia, he was already late for his meeting at the Herrick with the site manager and a bunch of potential contractors and architects, all bidding for the work. He should ask her for directions and get going.

'Tell me,' he asked casually, 'have you heard much about the new hotel opening up here? I gather it's going to be a big deal.'

'So they say,' said Desiree. 'Everyone's talking about it: the Herrick, it's called. They're building just a couple of blocks away from Palmers. All the local bigwigs are up in arms.'

'They are?' Lucas sipped at his drink, avoiding her eye. 'But surely another big hotel means more jobs, more local business, more money. I'd have thought people would be pleased.'

Desiree laughed. 'You obviously don't know much about East Hampton. People here already have enough money. They like to keep things the way they are: traditional. From what I hear the Herrick's going to be anything but that. According to Honor Palmer, the building's going to be a hideous modern glass thing, designed by some trendy Manhattan architect. A real eyesore, so they say.'

'Is that so?' muttered Lucas angrily. How dare Honor act like she had inside information! He hadn't even definitively picked an architect yet, although the design would be modernist. He wondered what other lies she'd been spreading, and whether the whole town was already poisoned against him.

Perhaps he was foolish to have expected anything less. With so much to do in London before he left, he'd put off reading the fat file Anton had given him on Honor until he got on the plane. It was quite an eye-opener. Born with a silver spoon in her mouth, she'd evidently decided that one wasn't enough. This girl wanted the entire cutlery set, wrenching control of her old man's assets while he was dying of Alzheimer's.

What kind of a bitch did that to her own father?

'Personally, I think this German guy, whatever his name is, is wasting his money.' Oblivious of Lucas's stony face, Desiree trundled on. 'Palmers may be a bit run down, but it's an institution. I can't see how some faceless newcomer can compete with it. Especially not one run by a college kid with no experience.'

'A college kid?' spluttered Lucas, unable to keep up his pretence of detachment any longer. 'Is that what Honor Palmer's been saying?'

'Well … yes.' Desiree looked baffled.

'Who the fuck is she to talk?' roared Lucas. 'This time last year she was still at Harvard fucking Business School!'

'Hey, look, what do I know?' Realizing she'd offended him in some way she kicked herself about it. Having gotten over her initial nerves, she'd decided Lucas was properly gorgeous. 'Do you want another drink?'

'No,' he snapped, dropping a ten on the table and getting up to leave. 'I don't.' Looking up at her confused, apologetic face he relented. 'Look, sorry,' he said. 'It isn't you I'm mad at, sweetheart. But I do have to get going. Do you think you could direct me to the site of this new hotel, the Herrick?'

'Sure,' she said, relieved to be back in his good books, and praying silently that he'd ask for her number before he left. 'Make a right into the center of town, away from the beach. You'll see Palmers about six blocks down; you can't miss it. Five hundred yards further on and you're there. But there's nothing to see,' she added. 'It's just a big, muddy hole.'

'Thank you,' said Lucas, pulling open the cafe door so that a chill blast of air hit the both of them.

'Wait!' Desiree heard herself calling after him. She couldn't just let him leave. 'You never said what you were doing in town. If you're staying for a while I could show you around a bit. You know. If you'd like,' she finished lamely, her cheeks turning from pink to maroon with embarrassment. It was a long time since she'd had to make the running with a guy, and she was clearly out of practice.

Lucas smiled. 'I'd like that,' he said. 'And as it happens, I *am* staying for a while.'

'Oh?'

'Yeah,' he grinned. 'I'm the college kid with no experience who'll be managing the big glass eyesore. The one the German guy is wasting his money on.'

And with a wink he disappeared into the rainstorm, leaving Desiree staring wordlessly after him.

By the time Lucas reached Palmers he was freezing once again, having trudged through the rain like a hobo for almost twenty minutes without passing another soul. But despite the cold, and his intense curiosity to check out the competition, he decided against going inside. Honor, he knew, was still away in Boston, dealing with her late father's affairs, but he didn't want to risk encountering any of her staff until he both looked and felt on top of his game. Right now, nothing could have been further from the truth.

From the outside, though, he was encouraged. It was hardly the all-American idyll he'd been expecting. Beneath the solid gray blanket of clouds the whitewashed wooden structure looked bleak and forbidding, and the entire upper stories were covered with an ugly latticework of scaffolding. Leaping from bar to bar like so many human squirrels, a motley crew of grumbling workers were busy stripping tiles off the roof, hurling them to the ground where they joined a growing pile of shattered debris, littering up what must once have been a heavenly formal rose garden. All that noise and mess must be driving Honor's guests crazy.

Walking round to the side of the hotel, he peered through an original sash window (very nice) into the main drawing room, and his spirits were further lifted to see that the bar and sitting areas were almost empty. The few guests that were in residence looked like the sort of permanent fixtures that all the old-name hotels relied on off-season. There was one old man with close-cropped hair and a graying moustache, sitting bolt upright on one of the overstuffed sofas – ex-military, Lucas would put money on it – and two overweight matrons, conservatively dressed in tweeds and pearls, sharing a pot of tea by the roaring, baronial fire. All three were probably too old and deaf to hear the roof works. No wonder Honor had been doing her best to slag off him and the Herrick. If this was the level of occupancy she was reduced to, she must be absolutely terrified at the prospect of competition. Structurally, the place looked to be on its last legs.

On the other hand, pressing his nose to the window pane like Tiny Tim looking at the rich folks' Christmas feast, Lucas caught glimpses of what had once made Palmers the greatest hotel in the world. Yes, the furnishings were threadbare, and the antique English furniture scratched and battered round the edges. There was even a visible hole in the exquisite Persian rug. But the room gave off such a welcoming, old-world warmth and charm, it seemed to draw one in anyway. It was an old truism that money and class don't always go together, but Palmers was living proof of its veracity. You could quite see how its understated ambience had been a magnet to all that old, protestant, Connecticut money. Mayflower money. If he hadn't come here with the express purpose of destroying the place, and its eponymous owner, he might even have felt sorry to see such a once-great giant brought so low.

But he had. And anyway, he'd never been much of a one for sentimental musings. Turning away, he trudged back to the road. Honor clearly intended to play dirty with him, but little Miss Privileged was about to meet her match. No woman was going to outsmart Lucas, not Julia Brett-Sadler, and certainly not an inexperienced trust-fund brat like Honor Palmer.

He was enjoying himself, mentally embellishing his plan to nuke his would-be rival out of the water with a few well-placed bombs in the New York press when, turning a corner, he stopped dead in his tracks, his confident defiance deflating on the spot like an old man's erection.

'Fuck . . .' he whispered out loud.

He knew there wouldn't be a lot to see. But somehow the quagmire in front of him, stretching across acres like an abandoned, rain-swept battlefield, was far more depressing in reality than it had been in imagination. A few beams and pieces of tape had been laid on the ground as markers and in the far right-hand corner of the plot was a single twelve-by-twelve-foot hole, filling up with rainwater. But that was it. That was what he had ten months to transform into a five-star resort, and another six to have it heaving with celebrities. It wasn't possible, surely?

Set back a few yards from the hole, an aluminum trailer mounted on concrete breeze blocks contained a temporary office, in which one man – one! Lucas had been expecting to meet at least five contractors and architects – was sitting behind a formica desk, tapping away in a desultory, one-fingered manner at his keyboard.

'Hey, buddy. You look cold,' the guy said, looking up but not moving from his seat as Lucas squelched in. Lacking Desiree's unique advantages – this man was fat, bald and had sweat patches under his arms the size of small dinner plates – there was nothing to mitigate the banal stupidity of the comment. Lucas exploded.

'*Cold?*' he snarled. 'No shit I'm *cold*, Sherlock. It's about minus nine out there, which you'd know if you bothered to get up off your fat backside and actually do some fucking work. Where the fuck is everybody else?'

The man opened his mouth to speak, but Lucas was on a roll.

'The building works are supposed to be finished by Christmas. *Finished!*'

'Well, that ain't happening,' tittered the fat man, ill advisedly.

'Where are the contractors?' Lucas was apoplectic. 'Our meeting was at two.'

The fat man nodded, and started shuffling the papers on his desk in a distinctly nervous manner. 'Ah, about that. What I understood from Tisch's office ... it was never, like, a definite meeting for today. I wasn't sure exactly when you'd be arriving.'

'Bullshit!' bellowed Lucas. 'I faxed you my flight details myself, weeks ago. All you had to do was pull together one lousy meeting, and you haven't even done that.' Grabbing a plastic chair from the back of the trailer, he dragged it noisily over to the desk and sat down. 'Get them all on the phone, right now. Maybe we can salvage a conference call.'

The foreman looked apologetically at the basic plastic handset in front of him. 'Sorry, man,' he said. 'We ain't set up for conference calls and shit.'

Lucas looked as though he might be about to commit murder.

'Come on, lighten up a little,' said the foreman defensively. 'This ain't Manhattan, you know. No one round this neck of the woods is high tech.'

Slamming both fists down on the desk, Lucas leaned right across it until his face was millimeters from the man's nose. With one easy movement, he swept the computer keyboard, monitor and several stacks of paper onto the floor.

'You're fired,' he said quietly, but with such menace that the foreman shivered, his fat arms wobbling like a shaken jelly. 'Get the fuck out of here, and don't come back.'

Backing away from Lucas like a startled crab, clearly

anticipating imminent physical violence, the foreman made a few half-hearted protests as he gathered up the remnants of his files.

'I don't know who you think you are, b-b-buddy,' he stammered, once safely within reach of the trailer door. 'But I work for the Tischen Group, not you. I gotta contract.'

Picking up a heavy brass paperweight, Lucas raised it purposefully above his head. The 'debating' part of the conversation had come to an end.

Taking the hint, the fat man waddled out of the door. Lucas watched his gleaming bald pate from the trailer window as he climbed into his Ford pick-up and sped away, no doubt in the direction of the nearest employment lawyer or union representative. Only once he'd gone did Lucas sink back down into his chair, pick up the 1980s-throwback telephone, and call Anton.

As usual he was unavailable – 'traveling' was all his uptight Swiss secretary would divulge – so Lucas left a message, briefly outlining the events of the last half hour. There was no point going into detail. Tisch would either back him or he wouldn't.

Either way, all the ebullience he'd felt earlier outside Palmers had now deserted him utterly. The next year seemed to stretch ahead of him like a life sentence, stuck in this dreary, drizzly small town trying to build a hotel from ground zero – a hotel that ninety percent of the local populace had already decided they despised, thanks to Honor fucking Palmer.

He'd felt from the beginning that landing the Herrick job was too good to be true.

Looked like he was right. It was.

'Fuck, Caleb, what is wrong with you?'

Hopping into the bathroom, Honor turned on the shower and wrinkled her nose at the smell as she rinsed the dog shit off her bare foot.

Three weeks after Lucas's arrival in town, she had finally made it back to East Hampton herself, having handed what was left of the tangled web of Trey's affairs to Sam Brannagan, the family lawyer.

'I've done my best, Sam,' she told him wearily, unloading an entire trunkload of papers from the back of her hire car. 'Most of the personal stuff is filed, but I really can't give it any more time now. I have to get back to Palmers.'

Sam thought how tired and stressed she looked. He hadn't seen her since that ghastly meeting in his office last summer, and she'd been tiny enough then, but now her collar bones jutted visibly through her white cotton shirt and her sludge-gray size-zero pants hung off her hips like dirty ship's sails. Running Palmers must be taking more out of her than she'd anticipated.

In fact, her wasted appearance had more to do with grief and stress about her dead-end relationship with Devon than it did with anxiety over Palmers, although she was itching to get back, especially since word had reached her that the future manager of the new Tischen was in town and had moved into a little cottage by the beach. It was now two days since her return and, rather to her annoyance, she had yet to meet the elusive Mr. Ruiz. To be honest, she'd rather expected him to stop by Palmers and make an appointment to see *her*. As the new kid on the block, sent here for the express purpose of putting her out of business, she figured the responsibility of a courtesy call lay firmly with him. But maddeningly he'd made no effort to get in touch, and Honor certainly wasn't about to.

Though she forced herself to keep confident about Palmers' future, she was still hopelessly unprepared for the coming summer season. So much of her energy had been devoted to getting the structural problems under control without causing too much disruption to her few, precious off-season guests, that she'd barely had time to begin her much-needed PR drive. Nervous about promoting Palmers' renaissance, in case the media used it as an excuse to rehash the twisted allegations about her 'betraying' her father, she'd hoped for the first few months that if she kept her head down, the bad press would eventually fizzle out. But it hadn't. Thanks to the growing media interest in Tina and Dick, and Lise's shameless attempts to add to her already whopping inheritance with interviews in glossy magazines, looking as grief-stricken as she could in Atelier Versace and vintage Tiffany emeralds, the Palmer family soap opera looked set to run and run, with Honor unfairly cast in the role of resident villainess.

After the funeral, she'd decided to adopt a different tack, pulling up the names of every guest to stay at Palmers over the last decade, and placing personal calls to each of them, urging them to think about returning this summer and offering them significantly discounted rates. It was a risky strategy that could easily have smacked of desperation had she not handled each phone call with the delicate balance of confidence and humility that such a task required. It had also taken weeks to plough through the list. But it seemed to have paid off. Once people heard Honor in person, they sensed immediately that she bore no resemblance to the money-hungry monster portrayed by the gossip press. Flattered by the personal attention, and tempted by the low rates, they began, slowly – painfully slowly – to call back and start booking.

The rising summer numbers were wonderful, a real shot in the arm, but they'd come at a cost. With the reduced rates, they would barely cover costs, and she'd be forced to put off the major electrical work for at least another few months. In the meantime, she'd done her best to start discrediting her soon-to-be rival, emphasizing Lucas's lack of experience and Anton Tisch's penchant for Blade Runner-esque architecture, knowing how much that would piss off the arch-conservative Hamptonites. Slowly, the tide of local opinion was beginning to turn in her favor, but who knew how long that would last? Now that Lucas was here in person, he was bound to start returning fire.

'You're a rescue dog, you know,' said Honor, trying to look stern at the sweetly snub-nosed boxer sticking his curious head round the door, and failing miserably. 'I rescued you. That means you *owe* me. So what's with all the crapping indoors, huh?'

Caleb responded by thumping his stumpy tail loudly against the tiles a few times, before running around in an excited circle and finally launching himself at his mistress with such force he almost knocked her flying.

'Oh, all right, all right,' Honor laughed, submitting happily to his enthusiastic licks as she perched on the side of the bath and began drying her foot with a fluffy hand towel. 'I'll take you for another run. Just give me a minute to throw some clothes on, OK?'

It would take more than a dog-poo-stained carpet, or Lucas Ruiz's pointed radio silence, to dampen Honor's spirits today. Devon had called last night to tell her he was coming out early for Easter, 'officially' so that he could deal with some local politics or other and attend a bunch of committee meetings, but actually as an excuse to spend some quality time with Honor before Karis and the kids flew out for the holiday weekend. For ten glorious days, Honor would have him all to herself, the longest they'd ever spent together. And it hadn't come a moment too soon.

She'd only seen him for one snatched, unsatisfactory night in a New Jersey motel since the day she'd let him have it with both barrels at her father's funeral. Perhaps that *had* been a bit unfair, she could see with hindsight. But somehow watching him play the dutiful husband to Karis had been a thousand times worse than just knowing he did it when she wasn't there. The fact she'd been burying her dad at the time probably hadn't helped her tolerance levels much either.

They spoke on the phone daily, but it wasn't the same. Despite her long years of practice at it, extended periods of celibacy weren't Honor's forte and tended to make her stress levels rocket. A few more days and she'd be able to stake her claim as the world masturbation champion. Forget 'Mistress of her Domain'. These days she was just a mistress of frustration – or a frustrated mistress. Devon wasn't gonna know what hit him when he walked through that door tonight.

Pulling on her running shorts and sneakers, she looked out of the window while Caleb went demented with excitement, hurling himself at the front door to her suite like a canine battering ram. March storm clouds were gathering, but they looked high enough in the sky that there was a good chance they'd blow over. A run would do her good, warm her up for the marathon fucking session she fully intended on having later.

'Come on then, you moron,' she said, ruffling Caleb's ears affectionately as she grabbed his leash from the coffee table. 'Let's go.'

Stuck in his caravan on the building site, Lucas was rapidly losing the will to live.

Three weeks he'd been here now – three weeks, one day and two hours, to be precise – and he didn't think he'd had more than forty hours' sleep since his plane landed. He had bags under his eyes the size of Louis Vuitton trunks, and his voice had taken on the hoarse, gravelly Serge Gainsbourg edge it always got when he was chronically overtired, exacerbated in this instance by hours spent screaming down the phone at everyone from architects to lawyers to building suppliers.

To Lucas's amazement, Anton had been sanguine to the point of nonchalance about his depressing report from the front line, and completely relaxed that he'd summarily fired the foreman.

'It's always the way,' he commented blithely. 'When you've been in this business as long as I have, my boy, very little that construction companies do, or don't do, will surprise you. Now that you're out there things will kick up a notch.'

A *notch*? Did the man have no idea what they were up against?

Naturally workaholic, Lucas went into overdrive, spurred on by his terror of failure and his fury at the steady stream of negative campaigning that had been spewing out of the Palmers camp for months. It turned out that it wasn't only the locals that Honor had poisoned. Seemingly she'd been busy as a bee, bad-mouthing Anton and the Tischen chain generally, as well as Lucas personally, in a whole bunch of lifestyle magazines, including the influential *World Traveler*. He couldn't imagine how Anton had missed it. But then again, he'd missed it too. There simply hadn't been enough hours in the day to keep track of everything before he left Europe, and there still weren't. But from now on, he'd be all over that bitch like a rash.

By day, he spent hour after hour glued to the phone in the pokey little trailer, hiring site managers, contractors and engineers, most of whom he didn't even have time to meet before they showed up for work. It was risky, he knew, using cheap, anonymous labor like that, choosing builders purely because they were available and gave him the lowest quote. But his only hope of meeting Anton's targets was to flood the place with more workers than an episode of *Extreme Makeover: Home Edition*, and pray that they worked as fast. Already the site was crawling with men like an enormous muddy anthill, while Julian, the stressed-out architect's assistant who did most of his boss's work, yelled at them ineffectually through a loudhailer, waving his drawings in the bitter March wind like a surrender flag.

At night, Lucas spent long hours doing press searches on the internet, perched on a packing case in the twee little beach cottage his moron of a relocation agent had rented for him – what did she think he was, a fucking Munchkin? The ceilings were so low he hit his head everywhere, and the place had more pink and lace than Liberace's bedroom. Though he was desperate for sleep, he knew he had to think of ways to hit back at Palmers. If Honor was to be believed, every senator, film star and pop artist in her little black book had committed to taking suites at Palmers for the summer. If he read one more puff piece about the hotel's 'astonishing revival' he was going to throw up.

Then, this morning, his annoyance level had shot up still further when the expensive new multi-line phone system he'd had installed in the trailer had died on him, right in the middle of a crucial conversation with Dean Roberts, his head architect and the hapless Julian's boss.

'Fucking motherfucker, son of a motherfucking beetch!' he yelled. Switching on his new state-of-the-art US cell phone to try and call Dean back, the words 'no service' flashed in cheerful neon pink across the LCD screen. The guy in the T-mobile store had warned him that reception locally was erratic and suggested that 'if all else fails' he could try the beach.

Sighing heavily, Lucas grabbed the keys to his rented Ford pick-up. It was a fucking farce, trying to get anything done in this stinking country.

In the car he turned up the Van Halen full blast and opened all the windows to keep himself from nodding off. Not even his anger could stop the tiredness lapping at his body like a rising tide, and for once he was grateful for the light drizzle of rain blowing into the car and pricking his cheeks, keeping him awake. He had to go home and sleep tonight, no matter what.

Pulling into the almost deserted beach parking lot a few minutes later, he turned off the ignition, pulled out his phone and looked again for the slightest flickering of a bar to indicate he had reception.

Nothing. If he lost any more time because of this, he'd sue T-fucking-mobile . . .

Swearing under his breath he grabbed an umbrella from the back seat and got out, slamming the driver's door and pulling his sweater more tightly around him against the bitter, wet wind as he set off toward the shore. It was easier to get fucking network coverage up a hill in Ibiza than it was on Long Island. Fucking ridiculous.

He must have trudged half a mile along the sand before his phone finally sputtered into life. Quickly punching in Dean's direct line, he cupped his hand against his ear to block out the roar of the ocean behind him.

'Look, darling, I don't care if he's in a meeting,' he shouted into the mouthpiece at the unfortunate receptionist. 'I've spent the past hour trying to get hold of him. I'm shivering my ass off on a fucking freezing beach here. I can assure you, he wants to take this call.'

The next thing he heard was some tinny hold music, followed by an ominous rumble of thunder and two dramatic flashes of sheet lightning. He barely had time to open his umbrella before the heavens opened and a veritable monsoon of water began pounding down onto the beach.

'Shit, shit shit.' There were some dunes about fifty feet away that would have offered him some protection beyond the feeble respite afforded by the umbrella. He contemplated making a dash for it, but decided it wasn't worth the risk of losing his precious signal again.

'I'm putting you back on hold for just a moment, Mr. Ruiz,' the girl's voice drifted back to him through the din of the storm. 'Mr. Roberts will be with you very shortly.'

'No!' Lucas shouted. 'Don't put me on—' But it was too late. The whiny refrain of 'Greensleeves' had already started up and the rain, if anything, was intensifying.

'Excuse me?'

Lucas jumped a mile when someone tapped him on the back. Spinning around, his adrenaline pumping, his fear soon turned to annoyance: it was just a kid. Dressed in running shorts and a thin vest, the tiny, androgenous figure was soaked to the bone.

'Have you seen . . .' it panted, 'a dog? He ran into the surf ten minutes ago and I'm worried he might have . . . it's so rough out there.'

On closer inspection, Lucas could see that 'it' was in fact a 'she', and not a child but a very short young woman. Despite her tiny build, there was something unnervingly mannish about her. Her hips were thrust forward, and she squared her shoulders with subconscious aggression when she spoke to him, in a low, husky voice that also seemed quite at odds with her doll-like frame. The only touches of femininity were the brilliant green eyes, like violent slits of storm-wet grass, and the perfect smoothness of her skin.

'He's a Boxer, about yay high.' She held her hand up to the level of her waist, looking up at him pleadingly. 'He's brown and white, with a—'

'No,' said Lucas, cutting her off. 'Sorry. I haven't seen anything.'

He knew he was being rude. But Dean would be on the line any moment, and he needed to concentrate. If he didn't hire this guy today, and get him and his men out here by next week, he risked losing more precious months of development time. The last thing he had the time for was to go running round the beach on a wild goose chase, because some dippy girl was too stupid to control her dog.

'Look, please, he might be drowning. Would you mind helping me look for him?' The desperation in her voice was palpable.

Her arms, Lucas noticed, were thin and muscly, like a sprinter's, and her chest was so flat he could have ironed his shirt on it. Why *did* women do that to themselves? Exercise away all their curves like that? Didn't they realize how unsexy it looked?

'I wouldn't normally ask,' the girl went on. 'But there's

no one else around and it's such a huge area to cover.' She gazed forlornly along the sodden beach in both directions. There were tears in her eyes. 'And he can't swim, you see. He thinks he can. But he's such a dumb dog ...'

'Look.' Lucas held up his phone bad temperedly. 'I'm on an important call here, OK? If you can't control your dog you shouldn't take him out. Ah, Dean. Sorry about that. I'm having a few technical problems I'm afraid.' He turned away from her as the project manager finally picked up the line. 'Where were we?'

Jogging along the sand a few minutes later, calling Caleb's name into the wind, Honor let her anger distract her from the awful worry. What a vile, rude, arrogant man! Not only had he refused to help her look for poor Caleb, but he hadn't even offered her shelter under his huge umbrella! What sort of a jerk-off stood there in the dry making phone calls when a woman was practically drowning right in front of him? And when a dog might be dying, for God's sake, struggling for breath in those huge, punishing waves?

OK, so he was a good-looking jerk-off. Why was it that handsome, rich men always figured they could get away with anything? That the rules of good manners that lesser mortals lived by didn't apply to them?

Assholes like Mr. Olivier Martinez lookalike were ten a penny in Boston. Honor could totally picture this guy's life: probably some stinking rich investment banker, down at his beach house for a few days and pissed because of the shitty weather, used to taking out his bad moods on his wife or his secretary or whichever other of his minions happened to be around.

Bozo.

Fucking vain, spoiled ...

Breaking away from her indignant thoughts, her heart suddenly soared as a very wet, very tired and somewhat sheepish-looking Caleb came ambling across the wet sand in her direction. Thank God he was OK.

'There you are! You bad boy.' She grinned.

Stopping a few feet in front of her, Caleb sat down sedately and started wagging his tail, a picture of obedience all of a sudden.

'Oh, don't you give me that,' said Honor, sinking to her knees while she clipped on his leash and hugged him, pressing her face against his sodden fur. She felt quite choked with emotion. What would she have done if she'd lost him? 'You are such a pain in the ass. But you can make it up to me by keeping your eyes peeled for an asshole on a cell phone, OK? If either of us sees him, I want you to kill. Got it? *Kill*! You think you can do that?'

Cocking his head to one side, the dog looked at her blankly.

'Never mind,' said Honor, shivering as she stroked his head lovingly. Now that he was back safe, she was suddenly feeling the cold. 'I'm wiped out, anyway. Let's go home.'

Later that night, wrapped up in a cashmere blanket and bedsocks and clutching a hot water bottle to her chest, she told Devon all about her encounter with the rude man on the beach.

'I mean, he just *stood* there,' she raged between sneezes. 'It was the biggest umbrella I've ever seen in my life, and he left me standing there like a drowned rat. He'd have let Caleb drown.'

'Shhh.' Devon handed her the hot whisky toddy he'd had ordered up from the Palmers bar. 'Save your voice, honey. The main thing is that you found Caleb and you both got home safe.' He frowned. 'I don't like that you were out there half dressed in this awful weather. You need to take better care of yourself, Honor.'

Honor sipped the whisky and smiled. Sometimes it annoyed her when Devon talked down to her like a little girl. But tonight it felt comforting to be babied. Having never had that reassurance from her own father, it was a huge part of her attraction to him, and she knew it.

'Why?' she teased him. 'Don't you like the idea of another man seeing me in a wet T-shirt?'

Taking off his jacket and loosening his tie, Devon climbed up onto the bed. Removing the drink from her hand, he put it down gently on the bedside table and pinned her arms back against the pillows, bringing his face right down to hers.

'No,' he said gruffly. 'I don't.'

Kissing her, tasting the whisky and lemon in her mouth, feeling the tiny but firm apples of her breasts rising up to meet his hands as he moved them slowly down over her body, he felt a wave of desire and possessiveness wash over him.

Being away from her for so long had been hard, stuck in Boston with Karis and her incessant demands for attention. Though he'd told Honor he no longer made love with his wife, this wasn't strictly true. Sex was infrequent and, from Devon's perspective, perfunctory. In his own mind sharing the marital bed wasn't really a betrayal of Honor, more something he kept from her out of consideration, because it would hurt her. But Karis would have smelled a rat if he'd switched their love life off completely – he daren't risk it.

It did make him feel a little weird, though. When he was at home in Boston, his life continued much the same as it always had. He loved Honor and he missed her, missed her mind, her body, her touch, everything. And yet when he was away, there were days when his relationship with her felt almost like a dream. Karis, the kids, the office – they were reality. It was becoming easier to compartmentalize his affair, to switch it off mentally, when he needed to.

'I need you,' Honor whispered. Shrugging off her blanket and sliding down the bed beneath him, she opened her legs and wrapped them tightly around his waist, like a baby monkey clinging to its parent.

'And I you,' said Devon. Easing himself out of his pants he slipped inside her, as urgent and hungry as a virgin schoolboy. 'Christ, Honor, I've missed you. So much.'

Arching her back, Honor gently rocked him back and forth inside her, closing her eyes the better to lose herself in his movements and the musky, masculine smell of him she'd been dreaming of for so many long weeks.

Finally, gloriously, the frustrations and annoyances of her day began to melt away like the last of the winter snow dissolving in the spring sunshine.

Caleb was OK. Palmers was improving, albeit at a snail's pace. And now her darling Devon was back in her arms, where he belonged. It would take more than one arrogant prick with a cell phone to spoil that.

Chapter Ten

Two weeks later, Lola Carter looked at her reflection in the bathroom mirror and sighed loudly. After a sleepless night, interspersed with some heavy bouts of sobbing, her face was so puffy she looked like she was having an allergic reaction.

'Fuck you, Bryan Sutton,' she said, splashing freezing water onto her skin. The shock made her gasp for breath, but she had to do something to snap herself out of this funk. The bastard *so* wasn't worth it.

Bryan was supposed to have flown out with her from Boston to the Hamptons this weekend. He was the one thing that would have made her mom's tedious birthday drinks party bearable. But now ... now it was all ruined.

OK, so he loved himself a bit. High-school quarterbacks always did. And Lola did have a worrying habit of falling for the best looking, most popular guys around, rather than the nice, decent boys. (Being packed off to St. Mary's by her parents had done nothing to dampen her social life. Everyone knew that boys hung around all-girls' schools like flies on shit.) But Bryan also had a sensitive, loving side – or at least, she'd thought he had, before she caught him red handed with that slut Lorna Mantoni.

'No more high-school jerks,' she told her reflection sternly, slathering on a big dollop of moisturizer and willing herself to feel better. In an hour's time she'd have to play the dutiful daughter in front of two hundred of her parents' dullest East Hampton friends, so she had to get her shit together.

From now on, she would only date college guys. Period.

Someone from Harvard College or the Law School even. That should at least make her dad happy.

Things between Lola and her father were still not good. Devon might have won the battle to enroll her in St. Mary's and steamroll her into taking a bunch of science courses that bored her to tears, but Lola still hadn't given up her dreams of becoming a designer. They rowed about her future constantly.

Unbeknownst to Devon, she'd already made formal applications to a bunch of fashion schools and sent them off in secret. Man, was he was going to go ape-shit when he found out. But so far she'd done a good job of hiding all the brochures and paperwork. And at least breaking up with Bryan would score her a few advance points in her dad's good books. Devon had hated him from day one.

Wrapping her green toweling robe around her shoulders, she padded back into her bedroom and opened the blind. It was only half past five, but the sky was already getting dark. Right now it was the sort of bruise-blue color that Lola loved. She'd tried many times to capture it in a silk dye – how great would it be to have a full-length evening gown that color? – but had never quite gotten it right.

'Knock, knock?'

Karis, immaculate in a white Givenchy jacket and navy flared trousers, slipped into her room carrying a tray laden with smoked salmon and scrambled eggs on toast, Lola's all-time favorite snack.

'I thought you might be hungry,' she said, smiling, setting down the tray on the end of the bed. 'How're you feeling, honey?'

Both Lola's parents had been in bizarrely good moods lately. Her dad had been practically skipping around the house since she arrived, chipper as a lottery winner – and that was before he heard about Bryan. And her mom, who could normally be counted on to get drunk and depressed on her own birthdays, seemed giddy with excitement about tonight's party. Especially since the guy who was building some big new hotel in town, this Spanish dude everyone was talking about, had agreed to come. Personally, Lola couldn't see the big deal. It wasn't like the guy was Rod Stewart or anything. But this was the first social engagement he'd accepted since coming to East Hampton, and her mom clearly viewed it as a major coup.

'I'm fine.' Lola took a suspicious bite of the toast. 'Do I have a terminal illness that no one's told me about?'

'What? Of course not.' Karis looked shocked. 'Why would you say a thing like that?'

Lola smiled. Her mother could be terribly literal sometimes.

'I was kidding.' The eggs were delicious. Sitting down cross-legged on the bed she set about demolishing them in earnest. 'You're being awfully nice to me, that's all.'

'Well, you've just been through a break-up. I know how tough that can be.'

Had she O.D-ed on Doctor Phil or something? All this concern was seriously out of character.

'But I do have some news that'll cheer you up,' Karis beamed. 'Guess who's just turned up downstairs?'

'Brad Pitt?' said Lola hopefully.

'Better,' said her mother. 'Nicky. He managed to get a flight out after all. Isn't that terrific?'

'Mmmm.' Lola nodded through a mouthful of toast and rolled her eyes sarcastically. 'Terrific.'

Great. Just when she'd thought her weekend couldn't get any worse, her dip-shit brother had to show up. He was bound to give her a hard time about Bryan, in between sucking up to their mom like a leech.

'Who else is coming?'

'Oh, everyone!' gushed Karis. 'Well, everyone who's anyone, let's put it that way. Lucas Ruiz, as I told you ...'

'Yeah, yeah, yeah,' said Lola, bored. 'And?'

'Oh, darling,' Karis waved her hand distractedly, 'I don't

know. Do you really want me to list them all? The Sullivans, the Meyers, Antonia Dickinson, Reverend Jameson and his wife.'

Lola took another big bite of toast. 'Anyone under the age of, like, ninety?'

'Don't be cheeky,' said Karis on autopilot. 'Honor Palmer's coming. She's young, and rather fun.'

'I guess,' said Lola.

She'd liked Honor the few times they'd met last summer. The girl didn't take any shit from anyone.

'Hey,' her eyes lit up mischievously, 'd'you think Honor and this Lucas guy will have a big cat-fight at the table? She must hate him, right, setting up shop so close to Palmers?' Scraping up the last of the eggy crumbs, she pushed her empty plate to one side.

Karis shrugged. 'I don't see why she should. Competition's a healthy thing in business. But I imagine she's as curious about him as the rest of us.'

'Who's "us"?' said Lola. 'I'm not curious. *At all.*'

She loved her mom, but she felt sorry for anyone whose life was so boring that they considered meeting a hotel manager to be a major event. The most *she* hoped for from this evening's party was that it would take her mind off Bryan for an hour or so. Plus it was a chance to get dressed up, and she'd had precious few of those since her incarceration at St. Mary's.

'Suit yourself,' said Karis, not unkindly, smoothing down the creases in her pants as she got up to leave. 'But tonight is my birthday, and it's a celebration, OK? Don't let some idiot boy ruin it for you, or the rest of us.'

'Don't worry, Mom,' said Lola with feeling. 'I won't. I've practically forgotten all about him already.'

Two hours later, Lucas was sitting in his parked truck in the Carters' driveway, tilting the rear-view mirror while he adjusted the knot on his tie.

149

'Give me a second, OK?' he asked the impatient-looking valet hovering by the open driver's door.

He could have strangled Lucy, his PA, for accepting tonight's invitation on his behalf. She'd only been working for him a week, and he needed the help desperately, but one more fuck-up like this and she'd be out on her ear.

East Hampton was a small town and Lucas had already heard the whispers – that the local hostesses were starting to take offense at his refusal to accept social invitations. He'd even overheard a conversation in the newsagent yesterday in which one woman had described him to her friend as a 'recluse.'

What did these people want from him, for God's sake? Couldn't they see that he had a fucking mountain to climb at the Herrick? That in the few, snatched hours he got to spend away from work, all he wanted to do was sleep? Or perhaps, if he was feeling really adventurous, crack open a beer and collapse on his couch in Liberace Cottage in front of a decent porno?

Thankfully, things had finally started speeding up on-site. The foundations were in, and three days ago Lucas had watched gleefully as the first steel load-bearing beams sprang up out of the ground like a phoenix rising from the ashes. Yesterday he'd made a rare trip into Manhattan for a presentation at Dean Roberts' office, where he saw a computer-generated mock-up of the enormous, curved, ecclesiastical arc of glass that was to form the core of the Herrick's facade. Personally Lucas thought it quite beautiful, like the bow of a ship. But if the general whispers he'd picked up from the locals so far were anything to go by, he expected most of them would disagree. Anything that wasn't eighteenth-century weatherboard counted as a 'hideous modern monstrosity' in their book. He was sure to be dragged over the coals tonight, with every neighborhood busybody and their wife grilling him about the building works. Frankly, he could have done without it.

The only silver lining to tonight's cloud was the prospect of at last meeting Honor Palmer in the flesh. When he'd first arrived, he'd confidently expected her to turn up at the site and introduce herself, out of curiosity if nothing else. But no, Her Majesty had maintained an infuriating regal lack of interest from the start. Well, screw her. When the interview he'd just done with American *Vogue* came out next month, she'd have to sit up and take notice. By a great stroke of luck, an old friend of Lucas's from Ibiza days was deputy features editor there now, and had been happy to do a straightforward promo piece on the Herrick as the new, hip hotel in the Hamptons. Miss High and Mighty Palmer was about to discover that the power of the press worked both ways.

'Sir.' Somehow the valet managed to make the word sound like an insult. 'We do have people waiting behind you. Perhaps you could take care of that inside?' He glanced disdainfully at Lucas's tie.

Climbing down from the truck's cab, Lucas towered over him like a brooding, Spanish Goliath. 'Listen to me, you snooty little shit.' The valet swallowed nervously. 'If I want to take a moment to fix my tie, then that's what I'm going to do. Would you tell *those* gentlemen to hurry it up?' He gestured to the pair of grumbling old buffers in the Bentley Continental behind him. 'I don't think so. And you know why not? Because they're white, that's why. And I am Spanish.'

'Sir, I can assure you that's not the case,' the valet mumbled, backing away as Lucas drew even closer. 'Your being Hispanic ...'

'I am *not* Hispanic!' Lucas roared. 'I'm Spanish. Not that I'd expect you to know the difference. Maybe you think *I* should be the one in that uniform. Huh? Is that it?' He grabbed at the guy's lapels, but then abruptly released him. 'Ah, forget it,' he muttered, straightening his tie again for good measure. 'You're not worth it.'

Ignoring the open-mouthed stares of the other arriving guests, he walked calmly up the steps to the house – or 'estate' as people here pretentiously insisted on calling every decent-sized property. In fairness, the Carter place was almost grand enough to warrant the title. Not that it was ostentatious or in any way flash. Quite the opposite. Everything about the house reeked of old money, from the understated white clapboard facade to the original Victorian gas lamps lining the driveway. Even the family's cars were distinctly low key – a Jeep Cherokee and a BMW convertible that had seen better days – compared to the Ferraris, Bentleys and Aston Martins littering the driveway. Devon Carter could clearly have afforded a fleet of Ferraris if he wanted them. But that was the point. He didn't.

As he walked through the front door, a maid relieved Lucas of his coat and led him down an apparently endless corridor towards a crescendoing buzz of voices at the rear of the house. Four years at the École Hôtelière had given Lucas an expert eye for interiors, and he appraised Mrs. Carter's decor as he ambled along: simple and uncluttered, with lots of white wood and enormous bunches of freesias everywhere, it was exactly what he would have expected in a wealthy Boston family's vacation home. A little too feminine for his personal taste, perhaps. But undeniably classy.

'The party's in the drawing room, through there on your left,' the maid informed him, a little frostily Lucas felt, before walking off. He watched her go, an ugly girl with drooping shoulders and spots struggling to break through her thick makeup. He wondered what had possessed Devon Carter to employ her, before the thought struck him that it was probably Mrs. Carter who made the hiring decisions at home. No doubt she didn't want some poppet in a maid's uniform making her look bad.

'You must be Lucas!' Right on cue, the drawing room door swung open and a very pretty, only marginally over-the-hill blonde opened her arms wide, greeting him like an old friend and kissing him on both cheeks in the European fashion.

'Mrs. Carter,' he smiled. If she weren't so uptight, he decided, she could be quite sexy. 'Thank you so much for inviting me. I must say, it was unexpected.'

Though hardly short of social invitations – they'd been falling from the sky like unwanted confetti since the week he arrived – the last person Lucas had expected to hear from was the wife of Devon Carter. Devon had been by far the most vocal of the Herrick's many opponents on the planning committee, and was a paid-up member of the Palmers' Old Guard, Modernism-Is-Evil squad.

'Unexpected? Goodness me, what nonsense!' Karis let out a tinkling little laugh. 'You're the hottest ticket in town, Mr. Ruiz, don't you know that? Our very own international man of mystery. Although,' she wagged her finger at him teasingly, 'I'm afraid there are quite a few people here to-night who want to have a word with you about that glass ... *thing* you're building.'

Here we go, thought Lucas. The barbed comments were starting already. On second thoughts, he *was* going to fire Lucy for putting him through this.

'I'm afraid I'm strictly off duty tonight, Mrs. Carter. No talking shop.'

'Please,' Karis squeezed his hand. 'Call me Karis. You'll make me feel old otherwise.'

'Karis.' He repeated the word in his slow, knee-weakening Spanish accent, throwing in a wink for good measure that made his hostess glow with pleasure.

'Let the poor fellow catch his breath, darling, before you start haranguing him.'

'Devon, there you are. This is—' Spinning around, Karis looked thoroughly put out at the interruption.

'I know who he is,' said Devon.

The man who stepped forward to shake Lucas's hand

was older than he'd pictured him and much more distinguished, with graying hair and the sort of deep voice and firm grip one associated with captains of industry or senior military officers. He was good-looking, if you liked the whole silver-fox, roué senator thing, but stiffer than a day-old corpse. And his superior, snobbish, noblesse oblige manner was instantly off-putting.

'How are you finding East Hampton?' He smiled, ostensibly in welcome, though it came off as patronizing. The Boston accent didn't help, either. It was pure JFK. Lucas found himself wondering whether it were genuine or had been deliberately acquired, and decided probably the latter. Either way it made him sound like he had the mother of all sticks up his ass.

'I'm still finding my feet,' said Lucas, adding jokingly, 'To be honest, I feel like a bit of a circus freak tonight. People keep staring. Are they always like this?'

Devon frowned defensively. 'Like what? It's natural for people to be curious,' he said. 'You're making dramatic changes to both the look and the spirit of their town. Or at least you will be.'

'I'm building a hotel, Mr. Carter,' said Lucas wearily. 'Not turning East Hampton into Las Vegas.'

'Hmmm.' Devon sounded unconvinced. 'I'd say the jury was still out on that one. But let's canvas some other opinions, shall we? Morty!'

Before Lucas could protest, his host started waving to a doddery, white-haired man with a pronounced stoop, who dutifully shuffled over.

'This is Morty Sullivan, chairman of our planning committee, among many other things,' he said brightly. 'I believe he's rather a friend of your boss. Morty, meet Lucas Ruiz.'

Shit. This must be the guy Anton had blackmailed to get the Herrick project off the ground. According to the files Lucas had read, he was only fifty-two, but he looked decades older, poor bastard. As for him and Anton being 'friends', he presumed this was Devon's idea of a joke. A pretty cruel one, judging by the old man's terror-stricken face.

Morty shook Lucas's hand with all the enthusiasm of someone greeting the Grim Reaper. 'How do you do?' he asked querulously.

'Mr. Sullivan.' Lucas nodded respectfully in return. He felt genuinely bad for the guy. Devon, on the other hand, seemed to be reveling in the awkwardness of the moment. Evidently he was not only pompous, but spiteful.

Lucas spent the next half hour being thrust like a ritual sacrifice in front of the various great and good burghers of the town, smiling until his jaw ached, and defending the Herrick, or trying to, until his head throbbed. Devon stood beside him through each encounter, his smug, paternalistic smile seeming to suggest that he was doing Lucas a great favor by introducing him into 'polite' Hamptons society. Which was ironic, seeing as the one thing these people were self-evidently *not*, was polite.

'Glass is one thing, Mr. Ruiz,' a withered crone dressed head to toe in black Chanel, like a crow, conceded grudgingly. 'But is all the steel really necessary? That's what I'd like to know.'

'Has your employer ever *been* to the Hamptons?' The crow's equally ancient friend was keen to join the conversation, closing her bony, arthritic fingers around Lucas's arm like a vise while she harangued him. 'Perhaps if he actually saw the town he was defacing ...'

'It wouldn't make a difference, Sheila.' The crow talked through Lucas as though he were invisible. 'He's *German*. None of these Europeans – no offense, Mr. Ruiz – none of them really understand the American concept of class. I may disapprove of the way Honor threw over her poor father, but there'll never be another Palmers in this town. It's as simple as that.'

Lucas longed to tell the pair of them to stick their ignorant, racist opinions where the monkey stuck his nuts, but for once he restrained himself, escaping instead to the far side of the room and sinking gratefully down into an empty space on one of the couches. Some kind soul handed him a fresh martini, which he downed in a single gulp.

Beside him, a dark-haired boy was talking animatedly on his cell phone. Jumping off the call with a loud and self-important 'ciao, ciao,' he turned to Lucas.

'Nick Carter,' he said, pumping Lucas's hand vigorously. 'And you must be Lucas. Welcome.'

'Thanks,' said Lucas warily. It was hard to put his finger on it, but there was something about the boy, a certain arrogance, that he instantly disliked. He reminded Lucas of every spoiled, cocky rich-kid playboy who used to prop up the bar at the Cadogan: handsome, certainly, although in quite a different way from his father. Devon might be stiffer than a porn star's cock, but he was masculine to the nth degree. This boy, on the other hand, was metrosexual to the point of foppishness – slicked back hair, doused with enough Gucci Envy to stop a train, manicured nails, a mouth full of enamel veneers. He clearly hadn't done a day's real work in his life.

Just then, Lucas was distracted from his musings by the appearance of a bombshell of a redhead.

'Aren't you going to introduce me?' She addressed herself to Nick, who looked up at her disdainfully.

'Sure,' he grunted. 'Lucas, this is my kid sister, Lola.'

'Hell*ola*,' drawled Lucas. At long last the evening was starting to look up.

She was wearing exactly the sort of outfit he usually hated: a long gypsy skirt that swished like a mermaid's tail when she walked, and some sort of peasant smock shirt with a gilet thrown over the top. But on her, it worked. And unless he was hallucinating – unlikely after only one martini, though God knew he was tired enough – he could have sworn he saw her give him a distinctly lascivious wink.

For her part, Lola's pulse had taken off like a rocket – holy crap, was this guy *hot!* – but she made a titanic effort to play it cool, not wanting to betray any sort of weakness in front of her brother. No wonder all her mom's friends had gotten so excited over Lucas. The words 'hotel manager' had conjured up an image in her mind of a balding middle-aged bore with a paunch and a polyester suit. Who could have guessed East Hampton's public enemy number one would turn out to be such a love god?

On the other side of the room, Devon could feel the tension coiling around his arteries like a slowly squeezing fist. Honor, who'd arrived late and very obviously tipsy five minutes ago, was making a spectacle of herself flirting with one of the waiters. Itching to go over and confront her, he had to wait almost ten more minutes until Karis was safely engrossed in conversation with one of her girlfriends before he made his move.

Weaving his way through the crowd, he surprised her, grabbing her by the arm and pulling her to one side.

'What's wrong with you?' he hissed. 'Are you drunk?'

'No,' Honor lied, staring back at him defiantly.

She'd been dreading this evening's party for weeks, and had only agreed to come because Devon insisted that everyone else would be there and it might look suspicious if she didn't. She'd been seeing him for nearly nine months now, and had exchanged brief pleasantries with Karis on numerous occasions, both here and in Boston. But she'd never set foot in his family home, nor had she ever expressed the remotest desire to do so. As soon as she walked through the door, she knew it had been a mistake to come. Smiling family photographs in gilt frames littered every surface and fought for space on every wall. In panic, Honor had retreated at once to the bathroom, but in there it was even worse. Finger paintings that Nick and Lola had done in nursery school were proudly stuck up next to snapshots of Karis from her modeling days. No one could deny she looked utterly ravishing in those pictures. Nor could Honor close her eyes to the look of love, and quite genuine happiness, on Devon's face as, over the years, the camera caught the two of them together. If their marriage was a sham now, it had not always been that way. Just being in the house felt like a grave intrusion. Who was she to fantasize about marrying Devon and breaking up this once-happy home?

What made it sicker was that this was Karis's birthday party. Here she was, a mistress, attending the birthday party of her lover's wife. Now that she was actually in the house, the wrongness of it hit her like an iron bar in the face. Suddenly, she deeply regretted having opted for the blatantly raunchy, micro-short, black Dolce & Gabbana dress that clung to her athlete's body now like tar. She'd thought it might boost her confidence to look sexy for once, especially in front of her 'rival', Karis, and had even gone to town with the makeup, buying some vampy bright red lipstick especially for the occasion. But now she just felt foolish. Not only was she behaving like Tina, but she was dressing like her, too. Who had she become? Horribly ashamed, and feeling more out of place and insecure than ever, she'd over-compensated by drinking far too much. No wonder Devon was in a foul mood with her.

'We agreed we'd keep it low key and act natural,' he hissed in a stage whisper. 'And you turn up in ... *that*,' he looked at her dress reprovingly, 'and start throwing your-self at every single man in the room. Even the goddamn serving staff.'

'Bullshit,' slurred Honor. 'I'm not throwing myself at anyone.'

But she knew he was right. She *had* been flirting, trying to get his attention. How pathetic was that?

'I can't help it if guys want me. Anyway, whadda you care? You've been all over your wife like a cheap suit the whole night. Everywhere I turn I see pictures of the two of you.'

Devon sighed. So that's what this was all about.

'It's her birthday party, Honor. And this is our home. What do you want me to do? I'm *married*.'

'I know you're *married*,' she snapped back at him, downing her drink and immediately grabbing another from a passing waiter, glaring at Devon when he prized it firmly out of her hand. 'But maybe you shouldn't be, seeing as, according to you, you can't stand the sight of each other. Or maybe that's bullshit, huh, Devon? Maybe your marriage is ticking along just fine.'

'It isn't,' he said firmly.

'Prove it!' hissed Honor.

'What are you saying?' whispered Devon angrily. 'You want me to get a divorce? Is that what you want?'

'Yes!' said Honor, loud enough for people to turn and look.

'Keep your voice down, for Christ's sake,' pleaded Devon, putting on a fixed smile for their newfound audience. He waited a few minutes for the interest to die down, then dragged Honor out into the corridor.

'You want me to leave Karis?' He was surprised to find himself trembling as he asked the question. 'Are you sure about that?'

'Yes. No,' said Honor miserably. 'I don't know. Maybe. I just ... I hate this. Sharing you.' She bit her lower lip, and Devon's heart softened. Suddenly she looked ridiculously young. 'It was so perfect until your family came out.'

There were tears in her eyes, and for a brief moment he felt a stab of guilt. He knew he loved Honor. That wasn't the issue. But divorce? Well, that was a whole other ball game, one he wasn't sure he had the stomach for. Even saying the word out loud made him nauseous.

'Honor, sweetheart. There's nothing real between me and Karis,' he assured her, looking around nervously for witnesses as he stroked her hair. 'Our relationship is like ...'

'A business arrangement,' Honor sighed, leaning into him. 'I know. You told me.'

'It's the truth.'

'Devon? Honor?' They both jumped as Karis materialized in the hallway like a ghost, her head cocked curiously to one side. How long had she been lurking there?

'What are you two doing, skulking out here on your own?'

Honor's heart was pounding so violently she thought she might be about to black out, but thankfully Devon kept his cool.

'Honor was feeling a bit emotional. About her father,' he said. 'We were just having a little chat about things.'

'Oh.' Karis did her best to look sympathetic. But really, it was a bit much to hog the host at his wife's birthday party, especially as Trey Palmer died months ago. Couldn't Honor have found someone else to snivel on? When Karis's own father had died last year, she'd pulled off a charity ball in Boston for fifteen hundred people the very next week. Life had to go on, after all.

'Well, if she's all right now, perhaps I could borrow you for a bit, darling?' she scolded. 'Lola's been monopolizing poor Lucas for ages, and I still have so many people to introduce him to. In fact, Honor,' she said brightly, 'you haven't met him yet, have you? Come with me.'

'Oh, no, thanks.' Honor blanched. She'd been hugely curious to meet Lucas for weeks, but after the gut-wrenching conversation she'd just had with Devon, not to mention the umpteen vodka and tonics she'd ill-advisedly stowed away for dutch courage, she suddenly couldn't face it. 'I'm, er ... I don't feel terribly well. I think I might head home, actually.'

'Don't be so silly,' said Karis bossily, dragging her back into the drawing room despite her protests. 'The two of you *must* meet. You'll have so much to talk about.'

Meanwhile Lucas, annoyed because the lovely Lola had wandered off somewhere and he'd got stuck listening to her ridiculous, fantasist brother bang on about his internet business – snore – was at last making his escape to the bathroom when he saw Karis Carter thundering down the corridor towards him like a heat-seeking missile.

'Speak of the devil!' she squealed. She had a girl manacled to her hand like a death-row prisoner. With a sinking feeling, Lucas realized he recognized her.

'Lucas, it's my pleasure to introduce Miss Honor Palmer,' said Karis, patently thrilled to have effected the introduction that everyone in town had been waiting so long to see. 'Honor, this is Lucas Ruiz. Your nemesis,' she added dramatically.

'*You*? *You're* Honor Palmer?' For once Lucas was lost for words.

'Last time I checked,' said Honor witheringly.

If it hadn't been for those distinct, slanting emerald eyes, and ridiculously jutting cheekbones, he wouldn't have recognized the stunning creature in front of him as the bedraggled, flat-chested child-woman from the beach. The transformation was so dramatic, he had trouble stopping himself from staring. Even without the va va voom dress, and spiky, S&M stilettos, with her short slicked-back hair and predatory expression, she had a violent, traffic-stopping sexual presence that he wondered how on earth he could have missed before. He must have been more distracted than he'd thought.

'Have you two already met?' Devon, appearing at Honor's other side, eyed Lucas suspiciously. He had a natural distrust of younger, more attractive men.

'Unfortunately, yes.' Honor glared at Lucas, who glared back.

OK, so she was fuckable, but she was still macho as hell, exactly the sort of strident, pushy American woman he loathed. A man in woman's clothing, this time anyway. Give him Lola Carter's soft, curvaceous femininity any day of the week.

'It turns out Mr. Ruiz is the rude man from the beach. The one I told you about the other night.'

Devon shot Honor a warning look, but she missed it completely.

Lucas, being a much older hand at adultery, caught it at once.

Well, well, well. Mr. Up-His-Own-Ass Carter and Honor Butter-Wouldn't-Melt Palmer were sleeping together. He'd put money on it.

'You *know*.' Honor was annoyed now, willing Devon to remember. 'The asshole who wouldn't help me find Caleb? I *told* you.'

'I was on a business call,' Lucas shrugged, not looking remotely apologetic. 'It wasn't a good time for me.'

'Not a good time? My dog was drowning, and I was soaked to the bone!' Honor spluttered with drunken rage. 'You didn't even offer me your umbrella, you selfish, self important ...'

'Honor, please. Don't upset yourself.' Devon gave her another meaningful 'for God's sake, shut up' look, but it was too late. The wheels in Karis's head had belatedly begun whirring into life. She turned to Honor.

'I'm sorry,' she said. 'But did you just say you told Devon about this the other night?'

'Uh huh,' said Honor. Then, finally realizing the minefield she'd inadvertently wandered into, she blushed crimson and tried to back track. 'Well, kind of. I ... well, I er ...' she stammered.

Karis looked accusingly at her husband. 'But didn't you tell me this morning that you hadn't seen Honor since the funeral? I'm sure you did.'

Devon went white.

Lucas, meanwhile, was starting to enjoy himself. It was fun watching the smug, self-righteous wasp Carter squirming on his wife's line like a maggot.

'I meant I hadn't seen her *properly*,' blustered Devon.

He might be a raging hypocrite but he had nerve, Lucas would give him that. He looked Karis right in the eye when he spoke to her.

'We did run into one another at the coffee shop the other day, though. Very briefly.'

'The other *night*.' Honor corrected him hurriedly. 'Remember? It was in the evening. Like I said.'

'That's right,' said Devon, nodding his agreement. 'And you told me about what happened at the beach earlier in the day.'

Nice save, thought Lucas, although it pained him to admire anything about Honor, however fleetingly. This was the woman who'd betrayed her own father, after all, not to mention all the lies she'd spread about him in the press. She was the enemy, and he couldn't afford to forget it.

'I must say,' said Devon, turning on Lucas in a blatant attempt to deflect the heat away from himself. 'It did sound as though you acted somewhat less than chivalrously.'

'Oh?' said Karis, falling for the switcheroo and transferring her attention to Lucas like an obedient puppy. 'What happened?'

Lucas despaired. The woman obviously had the attention span of a gnat, and the insight to match. How could she not see what her husband was up to? He and his girlfriend had just given themselves away right in front of her!

'Nothing,' he said brusquely. 'Nothing happened. Miss Palmer here was unable to control her pet, that's all. Which is hardly my fault.'

Devon's relief at having put Karis off the scent began to fade when he looked at Honor's face. She was clearly about to launch into a full-scale row with Lucas, and was more than drunk enough to let more indiscretions slip.

'Come on, darling.' Grabbing a very reluctant Karis's hand – she enjoyed a good melodrama – he dragged her away. 'This is between Lucas and Honor. I think we should let the pair of them talk in private.'

As soon as they'd gone, Honor jumped right back on the offensive.

'So,' she glowered at Lucas. 'Leaving a girl to catch hypothermia while you take care of yourself – that's considered acceptable behavior in Spain, is it? Very gentlemanly, I must say.'

'Oh, on the contrary,' said Lucas suavely. He wasn't going to give her the satisfaction of rising to the bait. 'Spanish men consider it of great importance to show courtesy towards women. But then *our* women would not go out running half dressed with their nipples showing through their T-shirts, pestering men who were trying to work.'

'They'd be back home in the kitchen baking cakes, I suppose?' said Honor, coloring. Had her nipples really been showing?

'That's right,' he said, smiling. It was so easy to wind her up. 'Or making themselves beautiful for their husband's return. Spanish women know how to be feminine.'

'You're a fucking dinosaur,' said Honor contemptuously. 'I'm gonna enjoy wiping the floor with you next year. How're your pre-bookings coming along, by the way?'

'Very well, thank you,' lied Lucas. But Honor saw the way the smug smile had died on his lips.

'Really?' she said. 'I'm real curious to know what big names you've managed to convince to spend their vacation under the stars on your building site.'

'We'll be built by Christmas, and open for business by this time next year,' said Lucas, with a confidence he wished to God he actually felt. 'So please, try not to worry your pretty little head about our clientele. In any case, we won't be going after the Zimmer frame market – we'll leave that for you over at Palmers. Assuming your rickety old building hasn't given up the ghost before then, of course.'

'Fuck you,' snarled Honor.

OK, so it wasn't the most sophisticated of comebacks, but after so many cocktails it was the best she could manage. At least it came from the heart.

Lucas took a step forwards, until he was so close that Honor could smell the faint lemony musk of his aftershave. For the first time she got a sense of how powerfully built he was. On the beach she'd focused on his face, then his rudeness – she'd kind of bypassed his body. But now she could see he must be twice Devon's size, at least; a real meathead. How appropriate.

'You'd like that, wouldn't you?' he whispered.

'Like what?'

'To fuck me,' said Lucas, deadpan.

Honor tried to laugh in his face, but he was making her so nervous it came out as a sort of weird yelp.

Stretching out his hand, Lucas slowly traced a line down her bare forearm with his finger, making the rows of downy hair stand on end, like a swathe of ripened corn.

'Sorry to disappoint you,' he smiled, 'but I'm not attracted to ball-breakers. You'd do better to stick with your Sugar-Daddy Carter.'

Honor felt her stomach lurch. Belatedly, she pushed him away. 'What do you mean?' she asked, sharply. 'What do you mean by that? Devon's a family friend. Nothing more.'

'Whatever you say,' said Lucas.

'Listen!' fumed Honor. But before she could say another word, Lucas turned on his heel and strode off down the corridor.

Waiting at the front door for the maid to arrive with his coat, he felt a tap on the back.

'Hey, you.' It was Lola, looking even sexier than she had earlier, now that her eye makeup was smudged and her long red hair slightly tousled, presumably from dancing up a storm. 'Sneaking off without saying goodbye? That's not very polite.'

Lucas smiled. 'Sorry. Things were getting a little heated in there between Honor and me. I figured it was best I left.'

'Best for who?' pouted Lola. The next minute the maid had materialized with Lucas's coat. Seconds later the valet drew up outside with his truck.

Vaulting up into the driver's seat, he wound down the window. 'I'm sure we'll see each other around,' he said. It wouldn't do to sound too keen.

Wordlessly, Lola walked over and, leaning in through the window, kissed him lingeringly on the lips. Lucas felt his dick harden and his resolve soften, but she pulled away before he had a chance to do something he'd regret.

'I leave for Boston in the morning,' she said, heading back toward the house. 'But I'll be back in the summer. Just in case you were wondering.'

Driving home along the beach, Lucas let his mind wander back over the evening. Meeting Lola had been the high point, definitely. But it was his fight with Honor that really stuck with him. There was no doubt he'd come off better than she had – and yet the encounter had left him with an oddly bitter taste in his mouth.

How could she be attracted to that pompous old fossil, Carter? He didn't know why, but the thought of Honor and Devon in bed together made his blood boil.

On the other hand, an affair was a potential Achilles heel for Honor, one he might be able to use to his advantage in the future.

Perhaps he wouldn't fire Lucy after all.

Chapter Eleven

It was June, fourteen months after Karis Carter's birthday party, and forty-five miles away Sian Doyle was packing for her eagerly anticipated summer job at Palmers. Holding up two bikinis, one pink and tiny, the other blue and even tinier, she waved them questioningly in front of her best friend.

'So? C'mon Taneesha. Which one?'

'I dunno.' Stretching her long ebony legs out in front of her, Taneesha wiggled her newly painted toes luxuriantly. 'Both?'

She should have known when she agreed to help Sian pack for the Hamptons that it would take an entire afternoon, and that every single decision would have to be debated, right down to the panties and socks. 'It's not like they take up much room. Your case is practically empty. Anyway, forget about swimwear. Have you *seen* this guy?' Holding a copy of *Vogue* open at a double-page spread about the newly opened Herrick, she flashed a picture of Lucas, shirtless and in drawstring linen pants on the beach, staring moodily out to sea. 'Marlon Brando eat your heart out!'

'Yes, I've seen it,' said Sian. 'It's my magazine. But Neesh, seriously. Which one? I have a ton of reading to bring, remember?' She gestured to the wall behind her, on which a wobbly set of Ikea shelves groaned under the weight of more books than the Bergen County Library: *Journalism Today; Media Studies in the New York Area; 'Missing in Action': A war reporter's story.* 'Only half the space is for clothes.'

Taneesha sighed. Sian had been obsessed with becoming a reporter ever since watching *Superman* at the age of eight. In fact, the two girls had seen the movie together, having been inseparable best friends since second grade. Competitive as hell, in everything from sport to academic studies to boys, they remained closer than close. If it hadn't been for their all-too-obvious physical differences (Taneesha was black, with the body of a sprinter and beaded plaits streaming down her back like the jeweled tail of a kite, while Sian was so pale she was practically translucent) they might almost have been sisters.

'You know, you're not gonna have time to read half that shit,' said Taneesha, who couldn't see the point of taking a semester's worth of reading material on a working vacation to the Hamptons. 'Hotel work is hard. Trust me, I know. I've been there.'

Sian rolled her eyes. 'Three weekends washing dishes at the W hardly makes you the world's expert.'

Ignoring her, Taneesha began reading aloud from Lucas's interview. 'Listen to this: *With his movie-star good looks, Anton Tisch's achingly hip Spanish protégé is shaking up the stuffy denizens of East Hampton. As the manager of the newest and coolest Tischen hotel, the Herrick, I meet him in mid preparation for the much-hyped June 10th opening party.* Hey, June tenth, that's tonight. Too bad you won't be there in time.'

'Yeah,' laughed Sian, plumping for the blue bikini and flinging it into her bag. 'If only I were in town, I'm sure I'd be *top* of their guest list.'

'*Lucas Ruiz has some fighting words for his local rival, Honor Palmer, owner/manager of the legendary Palmers,*' Taneesha winked at Sian, '*that has itself undergone a dramatic revival over the past year. "I've chosen not to respond to the many false, malicious and in some cases outright libelous claims that Miss Palmer has made about me personally, Mr. Tisch and our hotel over the past few months," Lucas tells me. "I have the privilege to be the manager of what I truly believe to be the greatest hotel, not just in America, but in the world. That's been a tough reality* for Honor Palmer to accept, especially given the murky circumstances surrounding her takeover of Palmers." What murky circumstances?'

'Some people say she pulled a fast one on her father,' said Sian, who'd followed the story vaguely but without much interest. 'I'm not sure exactly.'

'"A broken family is a heavy price to pay if your business then doesn't make it,"' read Taneesha, finishing Lucas's quote. '"Palmers is doing better now than in recent years, but obviously our presence here is challenging for them, and Miss Palmer has chosen to take that challenge personally. In my view, that's a reflection of her lack of experience in the industry. The market will dictate which of us succeeds. I certainly know who my money's on."'

'Well,' said Sian firmly. 'I don't care if Honor strangled her old man with a clothes line. Palmers has a great guest list this summer, whatever Mr. Herrick Hot Shot says. And I'm going to be there, mingling with the stars.'

As far as Sian was concerned, spending a whole summer working at Palmers was the opportunity of a lifetime. For one thing, it would enable her to save enough money to prove to her dad that she was serious about going to college next year to take some media studies courses. Her parents were good people, and Sian loved them both, but they were small-town, blue-collar stock to the core. Her mom's idea of an exotic getaway was a trip to the Jersey shore, and her dad couldn't see the point in getting educated beyond high school, especially not for a girl.

'There's plenty of jobs going right here in Lymington,' he was fond of reminding his daughter, whenever the subject of college came up. 'Whaddaya wanna go and land yourself with ten tons of debt for, when you could be saving right now?'

It didn't help Sian's cause that her older brother Seamus had left school last year and gone straight to work in a local bar.

'Making great money, I might add,' as her dad liked to say. '*And* he's a man. You're a girl, Sian-y, and a beautiful one at that. You'll be married before you can say kiss-my-ass, so what's the difference with all this "media studies", you know?'

Sian tried not to take it personally. For her, a career as a reporter meant a passport to an exciting, adventurous life, and an escape from Bergen County. But as no one else in her family felt the slightest need or desire to escape Bergen county, this was a tough concept for them to grasp.

That was the second, wonderful thing about her summer job. Working at Palmers would bring her into contact with people who *did* grasp that concept, with both hands. Successful, traveled, educated, connected people. East Hampton might be less than fifty miles away from Bergen County. But it was a different world, and one in which Sian, at least, could see a raft of possibilities.

'You know,' said Taneesha at last, putting down the magazine and examining the chosen blue bikini more closely. 'You ain't gonna have much time for sunbathing, girl. You do realize that?'

'Whatever. You're just jealous,' said Sian, sticking her tongue out playfully as she chucked book after book into the case. Not having time to sunbathe might be a blessing anyway. Despite her father's assurances to the contrary, Sian was by no means sure she was pretty, and the idea of baring her figure on a public beach made her flesh creep. Very tall and skinny, with long deer-like legs but no breasts to speak of and the sort of white-girl's butt that could slip into a pair of jeans without undoing them at the waist, she was extremely self-conscious about her body. Her face she grudgingly deemed OK, with its long, slender nose and huge, widely set brown eyes. But as for the rest of her, she was more than happy to keep it covered.

Deciding that her toenails were dry enough to risk a ginger walk across the carpet, Taneesha hobbled over to the bedroom window. Outside, a warm wind was blowing and, though it was only early June, summer was already in full swing. Groups of kids eight to ten strong were loitering on the street corners, the boys wannabe gangstas, with their pants hanging off them and hoodies pulled low, while the girls looked like extras from a Jay Z video. Trainee hookers, basically.

It was good that Sian wanted something better for herself. Secretly, Taneesha wanted it too.

'I tell you when I will be jealous,' she said, pulling her head back into the room. 'When you land yourself a rich, sugar-daddy boyfriend from one of the stuck-up Palmers guests.'

'I don't want a boyfriend, Neesh,' said Sian seriously. 'I want to network.'

'Oh, yeah, I can picture you networking right now,' Taneesha teased her. 'There you are in your skimpy little maid's uniform, just happen to be bending over the bed while you're changing some billionaire music producer's sheets . . .'

'Taneesha!'

'. . . and then wham, bam, you *network* that sucker till he can't walk no more!'

Taneesha laughed as a barrage of missiles – bras and panties mostly – came flying at her from the bed.

'If I did get with anyone up there,' said Sian, once she'd run out of ammo, 'and I'm not saying I'm going to, it wouldn't be a guest at Palmers.'

'Oh? Who would it be, then? Lucas, the Herrick Hunk?'

'Not my type,' said Sian haughtily.

'Please,' said Taneesha. 'He's everybody's type.'

'Not mine,' said Sian, adding jokingly. 'Not rich enough.'

Taneesha shrugged her shoulders. 'You're gonna be too tired to date, anyway. Hot guys like that don't usually go for exhausted hotel maids with big bags under their eyes.'

'Is that so?' said Sian, her ears pricking up as always at this hint of a challenge. 'Well, a hundred dollars says by the time I get home in September I'll have *at least* one millionaire notch on my bedpost. How's that?'

'*Soooo* competitive.' Taneesha shook her head in mock disapproval.

'You know it.' Sian grinned back. 'So what, do we have a bet? Or are you scared to put your money where your mouth is?'

'Oh, we have a bet, girl.' Laughing, Taneesha shook her hand. 'We have a bet all right.'

Meanwhile, at Palmers, Honor was also sitting on her bed surrounded by a sea of clothes, as she tried to settle on an outfit for tonight's party at the Herrick.

Naturally uncomfortable in dresses and skirts, she longed to wear a trouser suit, but she didn't want to be the only person dressed for a business meeting if everyone else was in full-on party gear. Lucas's VIP guest list remained shrouded in secrecy, but if the hotel's clientele since April was anything to go by – tonight was the official launch party, but the hotel had in fact been up and running for two months – there would be enough Young Hollywood and MTV types in hotpants and tassels to make her Armani suit look ridiculous.

Not that she was contemplating the hotpants and tassels look. As much as she wanted to wow the hateful Lucas and his guests, she had her own guests to think about. Lucas had once bitchily referred to Palmers clientele as the 'Zimmer frame' set, and whilst that might not be strictly true, they were certainly a lot older and more conservative than the racy Herrick crowd. If Palmers was to survive the onslaught from the new Tischen, their only hope was to play to their core strengths, and keep sweet with the old money families. And that meant dressing demurely, whatever P Diddy and his entourage might be doing.

Turning away from the depressing pile of clothes, she took a moment to look at the pictures lining the wall of her bedroom suite, and felt her spirits lifting. Directly above the headboard was a series of old, black and white shots of Palmers in the twenties and thirties, at the beginning of its heyday. Her grandfather was in most of them, looking young and dapper in his dark suit and waistcoat, with the polished orb of his signature gold pocket watch hanging from a chain at his chest. The shots were almost always of groups, formally dressed men and women with daringly short hair and long strings of pearls, lounging around on the croquet lawn, or ambling down the graveled paths of the rose walk. Behind them rose Palmers like a great white ship, her doors and windows flung welcomingly open in what seemed to be a permanent summer. The rocking chairs and love-seat swing on the porch were still there today – Honor had had them restored the first month she arrived – but the couples sitting in them in those old pictures came from an era so totally and utterly gone, they were as alien as martians. Occasionally, Honor spotted her grandmother in some of the shots, dark haired and tiny, just like she was, invariably hiding toward the back of these jolly groups, content to let Tertius shine. Or perhaps she wasn't content? Perhaps she hated playing second fiddle to his larger-than-life personality, and all the long nights he spent away from her, entertaining guests, throwing himself heart and soul and body into his beloved hotel? It was never easy for the partners.

To the right of the bed, another wall was devoted to before and after shots of Honor's own, brief tenure. The week she arrived and fired the useless Whit Hammond, she'd taken hundreds of photographs as evidence of his negligence, and the surveyors had taken thousands more: broken windows, leaking pipes, crumbling plaster, gardens so full of mess and rust and debris they looked more like a mad old lady's backyard than the grounds of a great hotel.

But lovingly, piece by piece, Honor had put the only true home she'd ever known back together. Rotten boards were replaced by new ones, but all in the same reclaimed oak of the originals, and limed in the age-old way before being whitewashed. She could have saved a fortune using newer, cheaper materials, but Honor looked on restoring Palmers as akin to life-saving surgery. Better to wait and do the thing properly than patch the old girl up with half measures. To Honor, the 'after' pictures on her bedroom wall – of the painstakingly crafted new roof, the riotously flowering gardens, the restored sash windows sparkling anew in the ocean-reflected sunlight – were all the vindication she needed that her policy had been the right one, however her accountants might bitch about it.

She'd already confounded both them and her critics by pulling Palmers back from the brink of bankruptcy against all the odds. Even *Vogue*, whose reporter was clearly in Lucas's pocket, not to mention his bed, had conceded that Honor had worked wonders with the hotel. Despite Lucas's barbed comments, most people had now forgiven her for 'stealing' the place from Trey when they saw what a great job she'd done of restoring it to the jewel in East Hampton's crown. Its formerly faded, crumbling walls and weatherboarding now gleamed white like a sun-baked bone, and the tangled mess of weeds in the rose garden and lavender walk had been ruthlessly stripped away, transforming the grounds into a riot of color and scent in white and pink and deep, bruised purple. Inside, the new staff kept the hotel silently running like a well-oiled machine, as unobtrusive and low key as civil servants, and the decor, though still a little dated, was now more chic than shabby. Staying at Palmers felt like staying at the comfortable but well appointed home of one's very smartest friends, which was exactly the ambience of welcoming luxury that Honor had been aiming for.

Thanks to these improvements, and her dogged behind-the-scenes wooing of guests old and new, she'd achieved excellent occupancy rates. Though not as flash or media friendly as Lucas's, her summer bookings were nevertheless very impressive, and included a smattering of European royalty as well as a number of senators, Fortune 500 CEOs and heavyweight opinion-makers. As for the locals, confronted first by the vast, incongruous steel and glass reality of the Herrick, and then by its rowdy, vulgar rap-star guests, they had practically stampeded to align themselves with Honor and the Palmers camp, welcoming her back into the fold and vowing to help in any way they could to drive the unwanted foreign newcomer out of business.

But for all the good news – her return as East Hampton's prodigal daughter, her overbooked summer and Christmas seasons, her pride in the physical transformation she'd wrought at Palmers – Honor knew how fragile the hotel's 'revival' really was. She'd need at least another year as good as this one if she was going to be able to afford to finish the vital electrical work and other refurbishments she hoped for. And with Lucas baying like a bloodhound at her heels, backed by apparently limitless money from Anton Tisch and beloved by all media, that was by no means a certainty. Palmers had class and charm, but the Herrick had four swimming pools, a movie theatre, helipad, state-of-the-art gym and a three-Michelin-starred chef for starters. Maybe that was what the new, shallow, celebrity-obsessed America really wanted? All mod cons, hold the tradition.

Turning back to the clothes littering the bed, she settled on a gray brushed-silk, high-necked midi dress and suede kitten heels. Pulling them on, she moved over to her dressing table, where her very basic makeup kit – concealer, powder and a swipe of bronzer for the cheeks – was laid out waiting. Thank God Devon would be there tonight, for moral support. For once he'd be without Karis, who'd cried off this morning with a migraine, so she might actually be able to talk to him.

The early, unsettled days of their relationship were over now, and Honor felt quietly confident in his love and much more able to bear the long separations that she had been so distraught about in the beginning. She still occasionally daydreamed about marriage and children, but it had ceased to be an active topic of conversation between them, and they'd settled into the comfortable, cautious routine of long-term lovers.

She knew he wouldn't be demonstrative with her tonight at the Herrick, or anywhere in public. But she'd learned to read his briefly flashed smiles or winks of encouragement, and to cherish these little signals of their secret bond without pushing him for more. Just knowing he was there this evening would help make Lucas's arrogance and constant baiting more bearable.

Ugh. Lucas. Dabbing a blob of Vaseline onto her lips and eyelids, she tried to push the image of his self-satisfied, handsome face from her mind. She was used to him taking pot shots at her in the press, but that last *Vogue* piece had really pissed her off. Palmers had been in business in East Hampton for the better part of a century. Who the fuck was he, two months after opening his doors, to imply that they were finished? Over the past year, the personal animosity between Honor and Lucas had grown like a particularly virulent cancer, fueled by the public PR battle and the social tensions locally. Although the official line was that everybody in the Hamptons hated Lucas and his ghastly hotel and sided with Honor, at least half of the local population (the female half) were unwilling to erase him completely from their address books. You didn't tell Brad Pitt you were washing your hair, however appallingly he may have treated poor Jennifer Aniston. Lucas was quite simply too sexy to be blackballed, which meant he and Honor still ran into one another occasionally at dinner parties and events. More often than not, such meetings resulted in fireworks.

But tonight would have to be different. However much she loathed him, this was a very public event, and Honor knew she must keep a lid on her temper. Hopefully Devon could help her with that as well.

Over at the Herrick, Anton Tisch carefully unwrapped another Rococo Belgian chocolate and, leaning down, placed it lovingly into the open mouth of his Great Dane, Mitzi.

'Good girl,' he cooed, bending his face low over the dog's like a doting parent. 'Who's my precious baby girl, hmmm?'

He was sprawled out on the day-bed in the newly finished Daria suite (named after his mother), watching one of the home-made pornos he'd brought with him from Geneva. One of the many advantages of having one's own plane was being able to bring 'sensitive' items of baggage – including tapes from the library that he liked to think of as a sort of virtual harem – without some underling from airport security rifling through them.

Out in the grounds, the launch party was already in full swing. Anton had flown out to the States especially to be here, and soon he'd have to put in an appearance. Not yet, though. Not until he'd come. Petting his beloved dog with his left hand, his right was thrust down his suit pants, rhythmically rubbing his throbbing erection.

God, it felt good. He was pretty close now.

An enthusiastic amateur film-maker, over the last ten years Anton had built up an extensive video collection of himself having sex with a variety of different women. A true obsessive compulsive, he'd catalogued the footage alphabetically by the girls' first names: the long shelf in his Geneva screening room ran all the way from Abigail to Zoe. Today he was enjoying some old footage of Heidi, the bitch who'd done so much to damage his reputation by selling her story to the *Evening Standard*.

Looking back at it now, sex with Heidi had actually been

pretty average. Despite being an exotic dancer back then, she'd always been disappointingly prissy in bed, reluctant even to let him do her from behind and absolutely vetoing anal. Nonetheless, watching the film now still gave him a powerful erotic thrill. As with all the other lovers he filmed, Anton had assured Heidi that he'd destroyed the tapes years ago. Knowing that, without her knowledge, he could access her naked body whenever he felt like it – rewinding and freezing the frame on her spread legs and open, inviting cunt whenever he wanted to, for his own private pleasure – felt like a sort of mental rape. Rubbing his groin faster and faster, he felt his excitement building, as much from the sensation of revenge as from the titillation of the images themselves.

'Yeaaah,' he moaned, snarling at the screen as he finally came, his left hand gripping involuntarily tighter onto Mitzi's collar while his right hand cupped his twitching balls. 'Fuck you, you fucking whore.'

Grabbing a couple of Kleenex from the box by his side, he gave himself a perfunctory wipe and zipped up his pants. Then, turning off the flat-screen TV, he ruffled Mitzi's fur and got to his feet.

'Daddy won't be long,' he cooed, dropping another chocolate into the dog's slavering mouth, and heading for the door.

Once outside, he strolled around the grounds of his new hotel, watching the growing crowd with quiet satisfaction. He'd been right to hire Lucas. The boy had done a fantastic job under difficult circumstances and today's launch party was the culmination of sixteen months of effort. It was the sort of glorious, early summer's day that could make even the most lackluster of gardens look beautiful, and the Herrick's grounds were anything but lackluster. An exquisite Japanese water garden, complete with Koi pond and a twenty-five-foot waterfall dominated the landscape, adding to the overall air of tranquillity and peacefulness.

There were no garish flowers here, none of the riotous candy pink blossoms so ubiquitous elsewhere in the Hamptons at this time of year. Instead, the Herrick designers had gone for a consciously muted palette of greens and whites, offset with softly winding paths of gray slate, and the occasional smooth, black granite sculpture. It was a restfulness that mirrored the clean lines of the hotel itself, with its curved glass frontage, which glinted and gleamed in the sunlight now like the over-polished windshield of a new car.

Yes, it was modernist. Very. But only a dyed-in-the-wool philistine could deny its serene beauty. Certainly it had exceeded Anton's own expectations. He'd seen thousands of pictures during construction, but they were nothing compared to its beauty in the flesh.

Despite his satisfaction, he felt tired. Having flown into New York yesterday afternoon, he hadn't gotten out to East Hampton until nearly ten at night, but had insisted on meeting all the staff personally, then getting a two-hour run-down from Lucas on the plans for the launch party before he finally went to bed.

'More champagne, sir?' A pretty uniformed waitress offered him a flute of Cristal from a glinting silver tray.

'Thank you.' Stifling a yawn, he swapped his empty glass for a full one. Across the lawn he could see Lucas, surrounded by a gaggle of journalists. Since the *Vogue* article on the Herrick's rivalry with Palmers – *Five-Star Wars* they'd called it, which Anton thought was rather good – media interest in both the hotel and Lucas personally had risen exponentially. This was good for business, of course, and was exactly what he had hoped for when he hired Lucas. But now that it was actually happening, ironically, he found it annoying. Lucas was getting all the press attention, not to mention his dick sucked by the prettiest girls, while he, the owner and inspiration behind the Herrick, seemed to be practically invisible. There must be more than five hundred people here, many of them genuine A-listers, yet still the hacks swarmed around Lucas as if he were the big draw.

The guest list was certainly impressive. Billy Joel had shown up with his new, very young wife; as had the Seinfelds, and even Martha Stewart, who normally turned down all invitations that were even semi-public. But the biggest coup of all had undoubtedly been getting Magnus Haakenson, the Danish action star and Hollywood's latest Next-Big-Thing, not just to come to the party but to book himself and his entourage into the hotel for a four-night stay. Honor Palmer must surely be crying into her cocktail over that one.

Honor, in fact, had yet to hear the bad news about Magnus. No sooner had she stepped out of her limo and wandered into the gardens than the paparazzi swooped like vultures, their flashbulbs popping.

'Miss Palmer. We weren't sure we'd see you here.' A reporter Honor vaguely recognized from the *New York Times* diary pages popped up at her side.

'But of course I'm here, John,' she smiled serenely, hoping her gray dress wasn't washing her out too much. 'It's a beautiful evening, there's free champagne. What's not to love?'

'What about the comments Lucas Ruiz made about you in last month's *Vogue*? You're not offended?'

Honor waved her hand regally, as if swatting away a fly. 'I don't have time to read fashion magazines I'm afraid,' she lied. She'd read Lucas's poisonous quotes so many times now she could recite them backwards in Hungarian. 'I'm far too busy running the best hotel in America. Ah, Billy. How are you?'

More bulbs flashed as she strolled over to a waving Billy Joel, greeting him warmly with a kiss on both cheeks.

A few feet away, Devon was chatting to the chairman of the golf club. When he saw Honor, he shot her a furtive smile, which she returned equally cautiously. They both knew they'd have to be careful today. Lucas would be even more confident on his home turf and he'd be watching Honor like a hawk. One slip and he'd pounce on her like a rattlesnake.

Rather to Honor's surprise, since his original barbed comment at Karis Carter's birthday drinks last year, Lucas had made no further hints about her relationship with Devon, either to her face or, heaven forbid, in print. She was starting to think she must have misheard him that night, or somehow misinterpreted what he'd said. She had been very drunk, after all, and it was deeply uncharacteristic of Lucas to let her off the hook about anything, never mind something as potentially explosive as her and Devon's affair.

But her palms still started to sweat uncomfortably when she saw Lucas cutting through the crowd and making a beeline for Devon. What was he up to? Whatever it was, it couldn't be good. If only she were close enough to overhear what they were saying.

'Devon. Michael. Welcome.' In his white linen suit and pale pink shirt, Lucas looked like more of a Miami playboy than ever, his teeth shining white and predatory against his deeply tanned skin when he smiled. 'I trust you're both having a good time?'

'Indeed,' said Devon stiffly.

'If you'll excuse me.' Mike Malone, the chairman of the golf club, gave Lucas the sort of look he normally reserved for things found stuck to the bottom of his shoe. 'I'd better go and join my wife. She gets awfully antsy if I desert her for too long.'

Rude son-of-a-bitch, thought Lucas. The only thing that made Lucille Malone antsy was when the marrow-sized vibrator that she used to compensate for her husband's inadequacies ran out of batteries.

Though he feigned indifference, it really got under his

skin the way the locals continued to look down on him socially. Whether it was because he was Spanish, or working class, or simply because his name wasn't Palmer, he didn't know. But it bugged the crap out of him.

'You must be pleased with today's turn out,' said Devon.

Privately, like his friend Mike, Devon also considered Lucas to be little better than a third-rate Dago waiter who'd gotten lucky. And he was livid about the vicious things he'd said about Honor in that dreadful, one-sided interview. But unlike Malone, he knew how to be diplomatic.

'I *am* pleased,' said Lucas. 'And Anton's thrilled. I hope, now that we're up and running, we'll be seen to have answered some of our critics. She's beautiful, no?' He pointed behind him to the cathedral-like splendor of the Herrick's facade, its glass glinting in the sunlight and sending rays ricocheting off the Gucci sunglasses of the partygoers.

Devon smiled patronizingly. 'If you like that sort of thing, I suppose.'

'You don't?' Lucas maintained a stiff smile, but inside he was seething. Why couldn't these people give credit where it was so clearly due?

'Perhaps it's a cultural difference,' said Devon, unwittingly adding insult to injury. 'Our concept of beauty is rather different from yours and Mr. Tisch's, I suspect. It's a question of what one grew up with. What one was born to, if you like.'

Lucas didn't like. Who did this asshole think he was, the Prince of fucking Wales?

'How's Lola doing?' he asked, delighted to see a cloud of distrust and disapproval fall immediately over Devon's face. 'I was hoping she might be here today.'

Lucas and Lola had enjoyed a brief fling last summer, much to Devon's fury, but it had fizzled out once she returned to Boston. The last thing Devon wanted was a re-run this year. Quite apart from his social unsuitability,

Lucas was far too old for her and a well-known playboy. She should be meeting eligible boys her own age.

'She's in the city this weekend,' said Devon tersely. 'Staying with friends. Why?'

'Oh, no reason. She's a terrific girl, that's all,' said Lucas, twisting the knife. 'You must be proud.'

'I am,' said Devon, with a grimace worthy of someone undergoing root canal surgery without anesthetic. 'I'd hate to see her get hurt, or throw away her future ...'

'On someone like me?' Lucas smiled sweetly.

'I was going to say, over a relationship that can't possibly go anywhere.'

'Not all relationships have to "go" somewhere, do they?' said Lucas. 'I mean, if someone were married, say, and had a long-term mistress on the side, that arrangement might work very well for everybody, without it having to "go" anywhere. Don't you think?'

Devon's eyes narrowed. Was that a veiled reference to him and Honor?

'Lola's still only eighteen,' he said gruffly. 'You know very well that it's inappropriate, Lucas.'

Lucas shrugged calmly. 'Perhaps you're right. Perhaps I *do* need someone a little more worldly. Miss Palmer, perhaps? She's single.'

'Honor?' Devon's teeth ground audibly. 'Don't be preposterous.'

Lucas laughed. 'Please. I didn't mean *Honor*,' he said scathingly. 'I wouldn't fuck that bull dyke with somebody else's dick. No, I'm talking about the other Miss Palmer. The sexy one. Over there.'

Devon spun around. Oh Christ, poor Honor. That was all she needed.

Tina, in her trademark cut-off denim hotpants and boots, her newly augmented breasts covered only by the tiniest of waistcoats – no shirt – was fawning over Anton like a groupie at a rock concert.

'Wow, Mr. Tisch, I gotta hand it to you. This place is *awesome*,' she gushed. 'How on earth d'you get it built so fast?'

Anton smiled and sucked in his paunch as the paps began snapping the two of them together.

'Please. It's Anton,' he purred. 'And you know, when you've built as many hotels as I have, these things become rather second nature, Miss Palmer.'

'Call me Tina,' said Tina, resting one red-taloned hand on his arm and leaning even further forward, the better to show off her jaw-dropping cleavage.

She'd decided to come out to the Hamptons on a whim. Well, sort of a whim. Having finally broken up with Dick Grate, she'd been caught in bed with the CEO of Paramount a few days ago by the guy's deeply unimpressed wife, and it had all gotten a little ugly. The old battleaxe had too much to lose to expose her husband publicly, but she'd sure as hell gotten her pound of flesh in private. When Mr. Paramount suggested that Tina might like to skip town for a month or so while the marital heat died down – adding weight to his suggestion with the two hundred grand's worth of Neil Lane diamonds that dangled from her wrists now – she simply hadn't the heart to refuse him.

Besides, having seen the amount of press Honor and Palmers had been getting recently (though why anyone should be interested in a tedious old hotel, Tina had *no* idea), she was itching to get in on the action. She was still a part owner of Palmers, after all. And the Herrick's opening party was *the* hottest ticket in New York this weekend.

Having finally managed to extricate herself from her conversation with yet another journo, Honor seized her chance to casually wander over to Devon.

'Have you seen who's here?' he whispered, kissing her on both cheeks.

'You mean Magnus Haakenson? Yeah, I saw,' she

whispered back. 'If Lucas got any smugger about it he'd disappear up his own asshole.'

'Really, darling,' Devon frowned, 'your language is appalling. But I wasn't talking about Magnus. Look over there.' He nodded towards Tina.

Honor went white. There was her sister, looking cheaper than chips as usual, all over Anton Tisch like shrink wrap. 'Oh. My. God,' she whispered. 'What the hell is she doing here?'

'Sizing up her next victim, by the look of it,' said Devon.

'Don't joke.' Honor shuddered.

'I'm not joking,' said Devon. 'Tisch has everything your sister looks for in a man, after all. Money. Money,' he counted them off on his fingers, 'and, oh yes, money. If he weren't such a thoroughly unpleasant piece of work, I might even feel sorry for the guy. Uh oh.' Stepping back from Honor, he smiled over her head and started waving enthusiastically into the middle distance. 'It's Don Hammond from the church council. I'd better go.'

No sooner had he scuttled off than Honor felt a tap on her back. Expecting another journalist, she fixed on her best PR smile, but replaced it with a glare when she found herself face to face with Lucas.

'I must say, I'm half surprised you made it,' he gloated. 'It can't have been easy for you.' He waved at the swarming sea of VIPs triumphantly.

'On the contrary,' said Honor, 'it's a welcome distraction. We've been *so* busy at Palmers, I haven't had a second to relax. Besides, there's nothing I like better than helping your boss to waste his money. How much did all this cost, anyway?' She gestured around her at the free-flowing champagne and the hundreds of open mouths devouring Russian caviar blinis that must have cost at least twenty dollars a pop, as if they were Oreos.

'Looks like your sister's asking Anton the very same

question as we speak,' said Lucas. Tina was flirting so outrageously now, her back arched and her improbable chest thrust forward like an exploding airbag, that Honor couldn't help but blush for her.

'Ah. Listen.' Grinning, Lucas cupped his hand to his ear as Kanye West's 'Gold Digger' came thumping through the state-of-the-art, outdoor Bose speakers. 'They're playing her song.'

Honor shot him a look of purest hatred. Lucas noticed again what incredible, Kryptonite-green eyes she had, and how they looked even more striking when lit up with anger, as they were now. Shame about the rest of her. At least she was wearing a dress, a welcome change from all those gruesomely butch pantsuits and boxy jackets, but even today's brushed gray silk number was conservative enough for an off-duty nun. Why did she go to such lengths to hide herself? He wasn't into scrawny girls, but even he had to grudgingly admit that Honor had good legs and a lovely tapered waist, so small that his fingertips could probably meet around it, in the unlikely event that he ever got to touch her. What a waste, covering them up like that.

Her sister might be soft on the outside, but you could tell at a glance that Tina was hard as nails beneath all that womanly display of flesh. Honor, Lucas imagined, was the reverse. He wouldn't be at all surprised to find that her 'fuck you' exterior masked a heart of pure marshmallow. There was a woman in there somewhere, he was sure of it. She just needed a real man to bring her out – not a crusty old fart like Devon Carter.

'That *Vogue* interview you did was a crock of shit, by the way,' said Honor, anxious to steer the conversation away from Tina.

Lucas shrugged. 'After all the libelous things you've said about me and my hotel, you're hardly in a position to throw stones.'

'Please,' sneered Honor. 'It's Tisch's hotel, not yours. You're just a paid employee. The way you talk about it, anyone would think you'd designed the place yourself and built it brick by brick.'

Now it was Lucas's turn to look daggers. He was well aware that he was only the Herrick's manager, while Honor owned Palmers outright. He tried not to let this difference in status rattle him. After all, by any objective standards he was incredibly lucky to have climbed so far at such an early stage in his career. And yet it did rankle that his dream of owning his own hotel – his Luxe – remained years away, while Honor had had Palmers handed to her on a plate. Or rather, she'd snatched the plate out of her own father's hands while the poor bastard was too incapacitated to stop her.

'May I interrupt?'

A smiling, middle-aged woman in wide-leg sailor trousers and a blue blouse with a huge, pussycat bow at the neck inserted herself between Honor and Lucas, handing each of them a business card. 'Megan Grier, *Talk Today*. I'm a producer at NPR,' she chirruped. 'I'd really love to get the two of you on my show. That Five-Star Wars thing in *Vogue* was terrific,' she smiled at Lucas. 'Exactly the sort of real-life story we're looking for.'

'No thanks,' said Honor, tersely. These radio talk-show hosts were all sweetness and light when they met you, but as soon as they got you on air, live, they ripped into you with all the balance and compassion of a great white shark in a dolphin sanctuary. 'I know your show, and I don't feel it fits with Palmers' profile.'

'Which is what, exactly?' said Lucas, still smarting from the 'paid employee' jibe. 'Stuffy, over the hill, small-minded?'

Before Honor could think of a comeback, he'd turned his most flirtatious smile on Miss Grier. 'I'd love to come on. It'd be great publicity for the Herrick, and I'd be happy to explain to your listeners exactly how we've eclipsed Palmers as the hotel of choice in East Hampton.'

'Terrific,' said Megan, returning Lucas's smile. 'But we would really need a debate. I'm afraid you'd both have to be there to make it work.'

She looked at Honor, who was busy choking on her martini olive. Eclipsed Palmers indeed!

'That's a shame,' said Lucas to Megan, shaking his head. 'It seems Miss Palmer is too frightened to put her money where her mouth is. She's used to being the biggest fish in this particular little pond, you see, and now she feels out of her depth.'

Honor knew it was childish, that she shouldn't rise to his schoolboy taunting. But something about his revoltingly handsome, cocky, chauvinistic face pushed her over the edge.

'Fine,' she spluttered, dislodging the offending olive at last from her oesophaegus. 'I'm game, Miss Grier. Name the day.'

A few minutes later, after Lucas had disappeared to attend to his other guests, Tina popped up beside Honor, smiling from ear to ear like a simpleton.

'Boo!' she giggled. 'Why the long face?'

'Hmm,' said Honor. 'Well now, let me see. I'm at a party to celebrate the launch of a hotel whose sole purpose is to put *our* hotel out of business. I'm being harassed by the most objectionable, arrogant, sexist asshole ever to walk the face of the earth – with whom I now have to do battle on live fucking radio, by the way, with a host who clearly wants to jump his bones. And to cap it all off, my publicity-whore sister shows up, without a word of warning, and starts prostituting herself to the very man who has spent the last year and a half doing his utmost to destroy what's left of our family.'

'Jeez,' Tina rolled her eyes. 'Lighten up, would you? Are you on your period or something?'

188

'What are you doing here, T?' Honor's voice rose in exasperation. 'And what were you thinking, flirting with Anton Tisch like that? Don't you have any fucking shame?'

'Shame?' Tina looked blank. 'About what? Anyway, I wasn't flirting with him. We were talking, that's all. He's a very interesting guy.'

'He's trying to ruin us!'

'Oh, fiddlesticks. Stop being so melodramatic,' said Tina dismissively. 'He's a hotelier and he opened a hotel here. So what?' She looked around her admiringly. 'I actually quite like it. I might book in myself, if Anton'll give me a decent rate.'

'You will *not*!' said Honor furiously.

'I was joking.' Tina looked at her like she had a screw loose. 'You know, joke? Ha ha? Of course I'll be staying at Palmers. It's free. Who knows, I might even hang around for a while. Things are a lot more interesting around here than they used to be.'

Honor followed her gaze some thirty-odd feet away, to where Lucas and Anton stood huddled deep in conversation.

'Now *that* is a good-looking man,' sighed Tina, whistling through her teeth.

'You are kidding me. Right?' said Honor. 'Lucas? Have you read the things he's been saying about me and Dad in the press?'

'Yeah,' said Tina absently, still drooling like a puppy. 'He can be pretty harsh, I guess. But then so can you.'

'Promise me you won't go near him.' Honor grabbed her by the arm. 'Near either of them, in fact.'

'Are you serious?' said Tina.

Honor didn't reply, but the painful tightness of her grip spoke volumes.

'OK fine, jeez. I'll leave them alone,' said Tina. 'But personally I think you're missing a trick. I could be, like, a honey trap.' Her eyes widened mischievously. 'If I got

Lucas into bed, I could pump him for insider secrets. I could be a double agent!'

'This isn't a game,' snapped Honor, and stalked off.

Across the garden, Anton was listening while Lucas filled him in about the NPR talk show. Though his face gave nothing away, he was irritated. Here was yet another example of Lucas rushing to take credit and plaudits without bothering to first clear it with him. It hadn't occurred to him to suggest that Anton himself might have been a more appropriate guest for Miss Grier.

Still, no matter. It was more good PR for the hotel, and there would be time enough to teach the boy a lesson in humility later. Right now another idea was crystalizing in the recesses of his mind, one for which he would need Lucas's help.

'What do you know about the sister?' he asked, interrupting Lucas mid-rant about Honor, and how she was running scared over at Palmers.

'Tina?' Lucas smiled. 'Yeah. I noticed the two of you getting cozy earlier. As far as I know, she's single. She was hooked up with some teenage kid called Big Dick or something, but that's all over, apparently.'

'I'm not attracted to her, you idiot,' snapped Anton, his annoyance beginning to show despite himself. 'I'm wondering how we might use her to our advantage.'

'Use her?' Lucas frowned. 'What do you mean?'

'Well, the elder girl's obviously frigid. I doubt we're going to unearth many skeletons in *her* closet.'

'Actually, I'm not so sure,' said Lucas. 'Honor's a hardnosed bitch, but I suspect she's not as squeaky clean as she makes out.' He lowered his voice to a stage whisper. 'I'm pretty sure she's having an affair with Devon Carter.'

'Really?' said Anton, quietly storing this golden nugget of gossip for use later, like a spider stowing away a captured fly. 'Interesting. Well, be that as it may, it's Tina I'm more concerned with right now. She's a loose cannon. I want you to get close to her.'

'Me?' Lucas frowned. 'To be honest with you, she's not really my type.'

Anton laughed mirthlessly. 'I don't give a shit if she's your *type*. I'm a businessman, not a fucking dating agency. I want Palmers out of business by this time next year.'

'Of course,' said Lucas, hurriedly. Anton seemed very touchy all of a sudden. 'So do I. But how will getting close to Tina help?'

Anton, so lost in his own vitriol, didn't seem to hear him.

'I want that little cunt Honor Palmer bankrupt,' he spat. 'I want her penniless and scrounging at my feet, like a stray fucking bitch. Understand?'

Lucas suppressed a shiver. He was no fan of Honor's, but Anton's unbridled hatred was disturbing. It seemed to have exploded out of nowhere like a bizarre, splenetic volcano. Then again, what did he expect? Clearly Tisch hadn't got to the top of his game by being Mr. Nice Guy. If he was going to play in the big league himself one day, he was gonna have to learn to toughen up.

'OK,' he said. 'I'll work on Tina.'

Anton wandered back inside, and for the first time all evening, Lucas found himself alone. Looking around, his eyes rested on Honor, who was chatting to some local bigwigs over at the oyster bar. He knew she was worried about the prospect of their radio showdown, and about the Herrick's burgeoning profile in general. But watching her throw her head back and laugh, glad handing his guests like she hadn't a care in the world, you'd never have guessed it.

She might be an heiress with no experience in the hotel business, but despite what he'd told umpteen reporters, she was also a consummate professional, and she'd fight for Palmers to the death.

Squeezing her out of business was going to be no mean feat.

Chapter Twelve

Ben Slater fumbled with his mouse, desperately trying to shut his screen down before his secretary, Tammy, could see what he was up to. But he was too late.

'I saw you stuck on that bloody stupid geography quiz again,' she said, laying a stack of mail down in front of him and somehow managing to look disapproving without once glancing at either him or the computer. 'If you've really got nothing else to do, why don't you piss off home and let the rest of us do the same? It's a nice day out there.' She nodded towards the window, through which the July sun could indeed be seen glinting off the polished chrome and glass of the Natwest tower. 'I could be down the lido with my kids having a Mr. Whippy.'

'It is my company, you know,' Ben defended himself sheepishly, maximizing the boring window of spreadsheets he'd been looking at before. If there was one thing Tammy excelled at it was making him feel guilty. 'Anyway,' he lied, 'I haven't been on it that long.'

The geography quiz – a borderless line drawing of Europe where you had to fill in all the countries from memory – was the latest email craze sweeping the city, and it was horribly addictive. Some of the guys in the back office had got all forty-three countries in less than a minute. Ben's personal best was a less than impressive thirty-five which, despite his protestations to the contrary, had in fact taken him most of the morning.

While Tammy tut-tutted back to her own desk, Ben gave the numbers in front of him another desultory glance. It was no good. He couldn't concentrate.

There had been a time, not so long ago, when he'd loved this business. The thrill of building up his fund from nothing, of venturing forth into the jungle of the financial markets every day and outwitting his competitors – he was sure he used to enjoy it. He couldn't pin point when, exactly, the excitement had faded. But faded it definitely had. Recently he'd been unable to shake the feeling that there really must be more to life than the endless accumulation of wealth.

He'd tried to talk about it with his sister Karen last weekend when he'd gone down to Essex to visit her and the kids. But if he was looking for sympathy, he'd come to the wrong place.

'You're a bit young for a mid-life crisis, Benny,' she laughed, stirring a saucepan of spaghetti hoops with one hand and scooping dried formula milk into the baby's bottle with the other. 'If you're that bored you're welcome to stay with us and get stuck in to Darren's dirty nappies. Yesterday he did four poos in an hour. Four! *And* one of 'em went all over his new car seat. Jim was up scraping the last of it off at six this morning, before he went to work. The 'ole car smells of shit now, apparently.'

Ben rolled his eyes. 'What a lovely picture of domestic bliss you do paint, Karen. I think I'll pass.'

'Hey, don't knock it till you've tried it,' said his sister. 'I'm not the one who thinks her life ain't got no purpose. It's about time you got married, Benny boy, and had a couple of kids. Then you wouldn't have time to sit around moping, staring up your own arse all day like the Dalai bleeding Lama.'

God bless Karen. She certainly had a way with words. But deep down, Ben realized she also had a point. He would have loved nothing more than to find a nice girl and settle down. But for some reason, Miss Right was proving aggravatingly elusive. The last two girls he'd dated had both seemed sweet enough when he met them, but both turned out to be after more than just his personality, demanding jewellery and expensive holidays almost as soon as he'd got them into bed.

'What do you *mean* you're not going to St. Tropez this year?' Mischa, the last one, had berated him a few weeks ago, after he changed his holiday plans at the last minute. 'Everyone's going. What's the point in us dating for the summer if all you want to do is stay in London and work?'

'We don't have to stay in London,' said Ben reasonably. 'We could go anywhere. Provence. Tuscany. Maybe even Cornwall.'

'*Cornwall*?' Her face implied that this was tantamount to suggesting they vacation in a sewage treatment plant.

'What?' Ben looked baffled. 'Cornwall's gorgeous in the summer. I just can't be bothered with the whole scene-y bullshit in St. Tropez, you know. Or Sardinia, or any of that wank. I'd much rather go somewhere quiet. With you.'

That was the last he saw of Mischa. Two days later she'd dropped him for a derivatives trader from Lehman.

Depressed, Ben had called Lucas. Neither of them had had much time to chat since Lucas moved to America, but their bond remained as close as ever, and as soon as Lucas picked up the line, it was straight back to the same old banter.

'Well, of course she dumped you!' he laughed heartily when Ben explained what had happened. 'Cornwall? Jesus Christ, how old are you? Sixty?'

'Not you too,' said Ben. He sounded genuinely put out. 'What the fuck's wrong with Cornwall? St. Tropez's a shit hole, especially in July. You know that.'

'So, come out to the Hamptons,' said Lucas. 'Come and stay at my hotel. It is, as you would say, the bees' bollocks.'

'Oh. *Your* hotel, is it now?' Ben teased him. 'Don't let Herr Tisch hear you say that. He'll have you straight off to the Gestapo before you can say sauerkraut.'

'Very funny,' said Lucas drily. Honor's 'paid employee'

comment still rankled. He didn't need the same shit from his friends.

'Oh, come on, I'm only kidding,' said Ben, sensing his shift in tone. 'I've been reading all about you. There was a massive article about your launch party in *W*. It looked bloody brilliant. Cheers for the invite, by the way.'

'You should have come,' said Lucas.

'I wanted to. Honest,' said Ben. 'But work was insane last month. Your boss's fund is doing so fucking well right now, the rest of us are having to scramble to keep up.'

Lucas found it hard to picture Ben 'genius' Slater scrambling to keep up with anyone, but he let it go, returning instead to the subject at hand. 'I'm serious,' he said. 'Why don't you come out? You wouldn't even have to bring a girl. The Herrick's crawling with them.'

'Yeah,' said Ben. 'I can just imagine the kind of birds you have propping up your bar. They're hardly likely to be wife material, are they?'

'Careful,' said Lucas. 'You're in danger of getting vertigo on that high horse of yours, my friend. Look, I've got to go. But think about it. You'd have fun here, I promise you. I'll save you a room, just in case.'

That conversation had been a week ago, and Ben hadn't thought much of it since. But now, with nothing better to do, he idly opened Outlook and clicked open Lucas's contact details again.

Fuck it. Why not take a holiday?

Tammy was right. He was only spinning his wheels in the office anyway. Every other fucker and his wife in the fund business had taken July off. Why should Ben be the only schmuck stuck at work?

'Tam,' he said, buzzing the intercom next to his monitor. 'Get me a flight to New York tonight, would you, darling? I'm taking a couple of weeks off.'

'Great!' she said, enthusiastically. 'Does that mean I get a break 'n' all?'

'No, it bloody doesn't,' said Ben. 'You've already had twice your holiday allowance this year, you cheeky cow. Someone's gotta keep this place going.'

'I could 'ave you for sex discrimination, talking to me like that,' said Tammy. But she was smiling broadly. Like everyone else who worked for him, she thought Ben was the best boss in the world. If anyone deserved some time away, it was him.

Honor looked at her brushed-steel Philippe Patek watch – a birthday present from Devon – and felt her irritation building. Where the fuck was Lucas?

She was sitting in the lobby of an NPR satellite radio station, freezing her ass off thanks to a broken air-con fan that was belting out arctic temperatures into a room roughly big enough to house a hamster. The radio station's offices, in the attic of a grand old Victorian building on Bleeker and Broadway, were an attempt at 'old world' style that veered dangerously towards just plain 'old.' The couch Honor was sitting on had once been white, but decades of spilled coffee and clammy, newsprint-covered hands had turned it into the sort of amorphous, overboiled cabbage color of old ladies' panties. This, combined with the peeling paint on the walls, a vase full of dead lilies by the door, and selection of tattered, four-year-old magazines lying forlornly on the antique coffee table gave the place a down-at-heel air that was distinctly depressing.

Shivering in her city shorts and vest – outside, temperatures were in the mid nineties with the off-the-scale humidity that Manhattan summers seemed to specialize in – Honor wondered for the umpteenth time what the hell she was doing here. She'd had four weeks since the Herrick party in which to cancel today's live, on-air head-to-head with Lucas. But she remained genuinely torn about it. On the one hand, it would surely be more dignified to rise above the fray and let the interest in the Herrick burn itself out naturally. But on the other, as much as she loathed him with every breath in her body, even Honor had to admit that Lucas was proving to be a master of spin. He'd already painted Palmers very effectively as the Herrick's poorer, shabbier cousin, not to mention the damage he'd done by insinuation to her own reputation. Leaving him to run rampant in the press, unchallenged, was a very risky strategy.

'Would you like to come through, Miss Palmer?' Megan Grier's assistant, a young man so camp he could have made the Olympic gay team, popped his perfectly groomed head into the waiting room. Clearly he was more used to the air-con malfunctions than Honor and was swaddled from head to toe in more cashmere than a Jewish princess's baby. 'Mr. Ruiz isn't here yet,' he said, plainly disappointed. 'But we can go ahead and sound-check you. Save ourselves some time later.'

'Sure,' said Honor, hoping it would be warmer in the studio.

It wasn't.

After making polite small-talk with Megan, she was offered a hard plastic seat on the other side of a console covered in more switches than the Starship Enterprise, and told to put on some headphones.

'Let me know if you get any feedback,' said the gay assistant. 'Just start talking in your regular voice. You can say anything you like, doesn't matter.'

'Lucas Ruiz makes my flesh crawl,' said Honor, smiling. 'How was that?'

'Very clear.' The deep, familiar male voice from behind her sounded distinctly amused. 'No feedback at all, was there, Megan?'

Lucas, looking disheveled and unshaven, marched straight over to their host and kissed her on both cheeks, before taking his seat next to Honor with an infuriatingly cocky grin. With his creased shirt and baggy jeans, he looked more like an Abercrombie model after a hard night's partying than a professional hotel manager. Honor could clearly smell the stale alcohol on his breath.

'You're late,' she hissed.

'I know,' he whispered back. 'I got held up.'

In fact he'd been 'held up' since six o'clock last night by Cassandra, an old acquaintance from Ibiza days whose husband worked on Wall Street, but was conveniently away on business for a few days. It was rare that he got an excuse to spend a night in the city, and he'd certainly taken full advantage of his chance to play hookey. Apart from a couple of one-night stands with frustrated Hamptons housewives, Lucas's sex life had been pretty barren of late. Running into Cassie again had been a chance too good to pass up, even with today's head-to-head with Honor looming. Although with hindsight, perhaps the second bottle of bourbon hadn't been the smartest idea in the world.

'My guests today are Honor Palmer and Lucas Ruiz.'

Before they could exchange any further pleasantries, Megan was already into her introductory spiel and the green 'off-air' bulb had switched to a threatening red.

'For those of you who are new to this story, they are the protagonists at the heart of what's being dubbed the Five-Star Wars, a battle for supremacy between two great Hamptons hotels: the world famous Palmers, and the new architecturally acclaimed Tischen hotel, the Herrick. Honor, Lucas. Welcome.'

'Thanks Megan,' they choroused in unison.

'It's a pleasure to be here,' added Lucas.

'Perhaps we could start with you, Lucas,' Megan purred.

Honor noticed with rising alarm the way she dipped her head and fluttered her eyelashes coquettishly when speaking to him. She obviously still fancied the pants off him. What kind of a one-sided savaging had she let herself in for?

'What was behind the decision to open a rival hotel so close to a great name like Palmers?'

'Well, of course, that was Anton Tisch's decision, not mine,' said Lucas smoothly. 'I'm merely the humble manager.'

He looked pointedly at Honor, who rolled her eyes. Lucas didn't even know how to spell humble.

'But without wanting to speak for Anton . . .'

' . . . you're going to.' Honor couldn't resist.

'I was going to say,' said Lucas, stiffly, 'that while we both think Palmers has a rich and wonderful history, the hotel business has changed profoundly since its heyday. Today's guests expect more. They aren't prepared to put up with sub-standard service for the privilege of staying somewhere well known.'

'There's nothing sub-standard about our service,' Honor shot back testily.

'You see, this is part of the problem,' said Lucas. 'Miss Palmer has chosen to take personal offense where none was meant. Opening a Tischen in East Hampton was a purely a rational business decision, aimed at meeting the changing needs of the luxury hotel market.'

'What I take offense at,' said Honor furiously, 'is Mr. Ruiz's repeated implication to journalists that I cynically manipulated my father's illness for personal gain by taking over the running of Palmers. What you said in your *Vogue* interview in May was an out and out lie.'

Lucas shrugged. 'Not according to your father it wasn't. He was quoted only months before he passed as saying that you had "robbed him blind." I believe those were his exact words. He also went on record, saying "my daughter is dead to me." I'd say that was pretty clear, wouldn't you?' Leaning back in his chair he looked Honor right in the eye and gave his knuckles an audibly satisfying crack.

Fifteen love to Lucas.

Winded with pain, Honor took a few seconds to respond.

When she'd taken over at Palmers, she'd deliberately avoided reading the press reports, knowing how misinformed and poisonous they were bound to be. Having to hear Trey's confused, hurtful words for the first time now, on live radio, and from the mouth of her sworn enemy, was like taking a sucker punch to the stomach. For one hideous moment she thought she might be about to cry. But with an effort, she pulled herself together.

'He was ill,' she said finally, her voice barely a whisper. 'He didn't know his own mind when he said those things.'

In that instant she looked so small and pale and vulnerable, even Lucas felt a stab of guilt. But Megan wasn't about to let him dwell on it.

'Lucas, you can understand, presumably, why Honor would feel emotional about her father, and a hotel that has been synonymous with her family name for over five decades?' said Megan.

'Of course,' said Lucas. 'But, you see, this is another difference between us. Being a woman, and naturally more emotional—'

'Oh, because all women are over-emotional I suppose?' interrupted Honor angrily.

'No,' said Lucas patiently. 'I'm not talking about women in general, I'm talking about you.' He addressed her directly. 'You were born into the sort of wealthy, privileged background most people, people like me, can only dream about. You've never had to work to get where you are. That sense of ... entitlement ... is that the right word in English?' he asked Megan coyly.

'It could be,' said the host.

'Well, it's reflected in your attitude to business, to competition.'

'How?' said Honor. 'That's an outrageous accusation!'

'Well, let's take your guest list,' said Lucas. 'Talk about elitist. Tell me, are people without titles actually permitted to book into Palmers?'

200

From that point on the interview degenerated into little more than a slanging match, albeit one that made for damned good radio. Honor accused Lucas of sexism, narcissism, and of cynically playing his 'poor Spanish farm boy made good' card, to try to glean public sympathy, when all he was *really* doing was buying and bribing his way into a community that didn't want him with Anton Tisch's limitless money, and doing his best to bully her out of business.

Lucas hit back that Honor was not just a snob but a racist, who was terrified of competition. 'Name one black guest staying at Palmers today,' he challenged her. 'Just one!'

By the time Megan had finished her summing up and thanks, and the light had once more switched from red to green, Honor had already ripped off her headphones and was storming furiously towards the elevator lobby.

'Hey, come on.' Reaching her right before the doors opened, Lucas put a restraining hand on her shoulder. 'Don't be a bad sport. Admit it, you kind of had fun in there. Like a little terrier with a bone.' He shook his head from side to side and made growling noises, but Honor looked far from amused.

'This may be a game to you, Lucas,' she said, still shivering in her skinny vest. 'But it's my life. My family. Although obviously "family" isn't a concept that means much to a guy like you.'

The smile died on Lucas's lips. Wedging his body in the door, he stopped the elevator doors closing.

'You know nothing about my family,' he said, glaring at her with eyes that were suddenly quite murderous. 'You know nothing about the real world at all, you spoiled little beetch.' As always, when he was angry, his Spanish accent became more pronounced. 'My mother has lived hand to mouth all her life.'

'Spare me the sob story,' said Honor coldly. 'Sell that

shit to one of your bimbos who's stupid enough to buy it.'

'Maybe I'll try your sister,' said Lucas nastily. 'I don't doubt she's stupid, but at least she looks like a fucking woman.'

'What's that supposed to mean?' said Honor, feeling herself blushing. She was still horribly sensitive about her physical appearance.

'It means I wouldn't be surprised to find you've got a bigger dick than your boyfriend,' said Lucas, twisting the knife. 'Maybe you should think about Karis Carter and her kids before you go preaching to other people about family values.'

The blood drained from Honor's face. 'You know what? I'm getting tired of your fucking insinuations. If you have something to say about me and Devon, why don't you come right out and say it?'

'Because I don't have to,' said Lucas. 'That's why. Because you know. And I know.'

Stepping back, he allowed the the elevator doors to creak slowly shut.

Back at Palmers, Sian Doyle was examining her reflection in the grimy, cracked mirror of the communal staff bathroom.

'Shit,' she sighed. The shadows under her eyes were as deep purple as overripe plums and her complexion, pale at the best of times, was so washed out with exhaustion that she looked as white as one of the hotel sheets that she seemed to spend her life washing.

Delving into her makeup bag for some concealer – screw Touche Eclat, she needed fucking industrial-strength whitewash to cover those eye bags – she set about trying to make herself look presentable. Tonight she was going to her first Hamptons house party with Rhiannon, another girl from work. It wouldn't do to turn up looking like something out of the *Night of the Living Dead*.

Though it pained her to admit it, Taneesha had been dead right about the drudgery of hotel work. Working at Palmers had sounded glamorous on paper, but the reality was endless, mindless hours spent stripping and making beds, carrying loads of laundry so heavy that she'd developed permanent lower back-ache, and scrubbing out other people's filthy bathrooms. For such rich and supposedly upper-class people, the Palmers guests had some pretty disgusting habits.

Most nights she finished work too shattered to even think about going out. On the rare evenings she forced herself to make the effort, she usually regretted it once she saw the prices in the upscale East Hampton bars. Three bucks for a Diet Coke! How could anyone afford to live here? As for networking, so far the closest she'd come to rubbing shoulders with any celebrities was glimpsing Princess Mette-Marit of Norway across a crowded breakfast room and picking up wet towels from Tina Palmer's bathroom floor. Hardly the sort of life-changing interaction she'd been hoping for.

Washing her hands, she began foraging for a clean towel amongst the dirty heap by the shower. Man, this bathroom was a tip. Palmers itself was idyllic, its polished oak floors and candlelit corridors overflowing with vases of lilies and jasmine and dog rose, but the staff quarters, tucked away behind the garages at the rear of the hotel (right next to the garbage cans – nice) were horribly cramped. Segregated by sex, the girls slept three to a room, with two rooms sharing a single, poky bathroom. An ancient and very temperamental shower took up most of the space, leaving only one tiny wall-mounted cupboard for toiletries. Needless to say this didn't go far between six teenage girls, and the overspill of makeup, tampons and other feminine detritus littered every available surface, including the floor.

'Borrowing' Maxine's eyeliner and mascara (her own had mysteriously gone missing days ago) Sian finished her makeup and, untying her hair from the tight bun she always wore at work, ran back into her bedroom to get changed.

Hmmm. What to wear?

The party was at some big-shot investment banker's house, one of the many ten-million-plus beach properties that Sian rode past every weekend on her bike rides. The actual owners were a couple in their sixties, but tonight's bash was being thrown by their son, a waste-of-space playboy called Alex Loeb. At least, Sian imagined him to be a waste of space. Like ninety percent of the girls going tonight, she'd never met him. But Rhiannon assured her there was an open-door policy for all passable-looking females under twenty-five. Even washed out and exhausted as she was, Sian figured she still just about fitted into that category.

Rummaging through her meager options – she hadn't bought many clothes, and half of what she had was either dirty or totally inappropriate – she pulled out a short, red cocktail dress and her one pair of high-heeled shoes. They were beige suede and fraying at the toe, and didn't really go with the dress, but as the only alternative were flat brown open-toed sandals, it couldn't be helped. Pulling the dress up over her non-existent hips, she slipped on the heels, spraying herself liberally with Rive Gauche and tipping her head upside down to give her long, dark hair a little more volume. Then she pulled open the wardrobe door and took a final, self-appraising look in the full-length mirror.

Not Angelina Jolie, perhaps. But not bad. A passable Lois Lane, anyway. And in Sian's book, that was more than good enough.

Nick Carter straightened his Hermès tie, brushed the telltale traces of powder from the tip of his nose and headed back downstairs to rejoin the party. If you could call this tedious collection of nobodies a party.

He'd known Alex Loeb all his life, in the way that the

kids of all the rich Hamptons families knew one another – that is to say, socially and superficially, but with no real connection beyond a mutual desire to party at their parents' expense. Alex was the better part of a decade Nick's senior, but their paths still crossed every summer. Devon Carter's son could be relied upon to turn up at social events with at least two or three top-notch women on his arm; and Alex – in previous summers, anyway – had a reputation for throwing the wildest, most extravagant parties in a town where 'though-shalt-indulge-thyself' was considered the eleventh commandment.

Unfortunately though, so far tonight's effort had been distinctly lackluster.

Naomi Campbell was supposed to be here, with Puffy, and the entourage of less famous (but *much* prettier) models that followed her everywhere. But of course, she'd failed to show, and she wasn't the only one. Alex had invited a bunch of the other big names in town – including Mariah Carey, Formula One star Luca Fattorini and George Hambly, the hot Hollywood sci-fi director – none of whom had put in an appearance. Besides a smattering of B-list actors and the usual crowd of anorexic Manhattan model-wannabes, tonight's guests were the same, tired old group of East Hampton hangers-on that Nick rubbed shoulders with every year. Even the coke that had cost him a small fortune to procure ('the hottest shit to come out of Colombia this year' according to his dealer) had been disappointing.

'There you are.' His sister Lola accosted him at the bottom of the stairs, looking as nonplussed as he was. 'Have you seen Lucas yet?'

Having gone to the effort of dolling herself up in her new A-line Marc Jacobs mini – the neon, emerald green of the dress made her russet mane of hair stand out even more than usual, and showed off her long, tanned legs to perfection – bloody Lucas had decided to add his name to the long list of no-shows.

'For the last time, no,' said Nick, rolling his eyes. 'He's obviously not coming. He must have decided to stay in New York for another night.'

Like everybody else in town, the Carter kids had tuned into this afternoon's NPR interview, and heard Honor and Lucas ripping into one another like rabid dogs in the latest installment of the local soap opera. Thanks to the absence of all the promised celebrities, the radio clash was becoming the evening's number-one topic of conversation.

'He wouldn't do that,' said Lola. 'You know how paranoid he is about spending time away from the hotel.'

'Yeah, like you know him so well,' said Nick snidely. 'You haven't laid eyes on the guy since last summer.'

Annoyingly, this was true. Lola had been staying with friends in Maine for the early part of the summer, and had only got out to East Hampton ten days ago. Having perfected her tan and lost seven pounds in preparation for seeing him again, she was itching to accidentally-on-purpose bump into Lucas and wow him with her new, more mature look. Devon, who'd been furious about their fling last year, had insisted that she break off all contact with him when she went back to Boston. Reluctantly, Lola had complied – there was no point fighting *every* battle, and she wanted to hold back her big guns for the inevitable fight about her going to fashion school. But her dad couldn't keep tabs on her twenty-four seven now she was here. Sooner or later, her path and Lucas's were bound to cross, and when they did, she had every intention of re-seducing him.

'Oh my God.' Belatedly clocking her brother's wildly dilating pupils, she eyed him suspiciously. 'Are you high?'

'No,' Nick lied.

'You're supposed to be the designated driver,' Lola yelled at him. 'I *always* have to drive; it's not fucking fair.'

'I am not high,' he insisted, in as self-righteous a tone as he could muster. 'So don't go squealing to Mom and Dad that I am, all right? I can drive.'

'Hmm.' Lola sounded unconvinced. 'Well, let's go then, while you still can. This party blows.'

Lucas clearly wasn't coming, and some nerd had just put Billy Joel on the sound system. It seemed as good a time to leave as any.

For once in his life, Nick was inclined to agree with his sister. But just at that moment, a gorgeous girl in a microscopic red dress sashayed into the room. She had the shy, coltish look of a genuine ingénue – obviously new in town – and was clinging tightly to the arm of her dumpy blonde girlfriend.

'Actually,' he said, grinning wolfishly, 'I think I might stick around a little longer.'

Lola followed his gaze toward the red dress girl.

'Hey, don't be an asshole, OK?' she said. 'Leave her alone. She seems sweet.'

She knew her brother's reputation with women, and she also knew it was well deserved. One look at this girl's Pay-Less shoes and plastic evening purse gave her away as a blue collar out-of-towner, no doubt here for casual work over the summer. If she was looking for a rich, handsome prince to carry her off to his tower, she'd picked the wrong guy in Nicholas.

'I'm not sure "sweet" is the word I'd use,' said Nick, ignoring Lola and making a beeline for the girl. In his eagerness to introduce himself, he pushed straight past the chunky blonde.

'Hi.' Grabbing the pretty one's hand he kissed it ostentatiously. 'I'm Nick Carter. What's your name, angel?'

Sian's eyes narrowed. The boy was male-model goodlooking. Everything about him, from his couture jacket and platinum cufflinks to his manicured nails and immaculate dentistry spoke of serious wealth. But she didn't appreciate the presumptuous endearment from someone she'd never met before. Nor did she approve of the way he'd just blanked Rhiannon like she didn't exist.

'My name is Sian,' she said coolly, retrieving her hand. 'And I'm not your angel.'

'Not yet,' said Nick, not missing a beat. The cheap clothes and makeup hadn't escaped his attention either. It was a safe bet a trailer-trash hottie like that would be easily dazzled by his money, if not his charm. 'But play your cards right and you could be. Ever been for a ride in a Porsche?'

Sian cringed. Oh my God. Did he really just say that out loud?

'Why, no, suh.' She put on her best Black Mammy voice and widened her eyes in faux amazement. 'I is just a poor, ignorant girl from the farm, suh. I ain't *never* been in no aut-o-mo-bile. I jus' walks ever where, in my bare feet. Ain't that right, Rhiannon?'

She turned to her friend, who dissolved into fits of giggles. Nick looked furious. He despised being made fun of, especially in public, and especially by women.

'Hey. Your loss, sweetheart,' he said, turning on his heel and stalking back over to Lola. 'Let's go,' he said grumpily, grabbing her arm.

'Uh uh, no way,' she said, wriggling free. She'd watched the whole exchange, and was cheered to see a girl standing up to her Casanova brother for once. 'Just because you crashed and burned. I wanna go meet her.'

'She's a bitch,' snarled Nick. 'I'm leaving, so if you want a ride you'd better come now.'

'I'll take a taxi,' said Lola firmly.

'I promised Mom I'd have you back by one,' he said petulantly. Devon and Karis were up in the city for the weekend and had left Nick in charge, so he felt free to throw his weight around. 'It's quarter of now.'

'Breath one word to Mom and I'll tell her you were coked out of your mind,' said Lola. 'I'm staying.'

Nick thought about it for a moment. Their mom always took his side over Lola's. But Devon was bound to ask questions if Lola really did start squealing. It wasn't worth the aggro.

'Fine.' He pouted. 'Do what you like. But I'm telling you, you're wasting your time. She's just an ignorant redneck slut.'

By this time Sian had wandered out into the garden. It took Lola a minute or two to track her down, leaning against the summerhouse and looking more than a little out of place. Her friend had disappeared somewhere, and she was on her own. 'I'm sorry about Nick,' said Lola, proffering her hand. 'That was great, the way you kicked him to the kerb in there. I'm Lola, by the way.'

'Sian.' They shook hands. 'You know that guy?'

Lola, she decided, was absolutely stunning, a pre-botox Nicole Kidman with curves, and her green dress the most divine item of clothing she'd ever laid eyes on. Suddenly struck by an awful possibility, she blurted, 'Oh, God, you're not his date, are you? Honestly, I swear to God, he came on to me.'

'His date? Eeugh. No.' Lola looked suitably disgusted. 'He's my brother, I'm ashamed to say. For some unfathomable reason, girls normally fall at his feet. I get a kick watching his ego take a battering every once in a while.'

'Oh!' Sian laughed. 'Well, glad I could help.' Other than their shared, Hilfiger model gorgeousness, Nick and Lola didn't seem very likely siblings. He was an Olympic-level prick, but there was something exciting and mischievous about his sister that Sian found herself instantly warming to.

'So, where are you working?' asked Lola.

'Palmers,' said Sian. 'How did you know I was working?'

Lola blushed and hoped she hadn't just been rude. 'Oh, no reason. Just a guess. I haven't seen you around before. How d'you like it? I bet Honor's fun to work for, isn't she? Have you met anyone famous yet?'

Sian shook her head. 'I wish. All I do is wash sheets. I see Honor Palmer in the lobby sometimes, but that's about it. Why, d'you know her, too?'

'Everyone in East Hampton knows her,' said Lola matter of factly. 'She's a friend of my parents. Sort of.'

There was a general commotion as someone emerged from the house. Turning to look, Lola felt her heart skip a beat.

'Whoah,' said Sian. She recognized Lucas immediately from his *Vogue* picture. 'So the camera really doesn't lie. He's seriously attractive, isn't he?'

'Hands off,' said Lola, only half jokingly. 'I saw him first.'

Catching her eye, Lucas grinned. In that green dress – if you could call it a dress, it was so wonderfully short – she looked even more voluptuously sexy than he remembered her. Ignoring the other girls who'd formed an admiring circle around him, he headed in her direction.

'Miss Carter.' He gave her a look that made Lola's stomach flip over like a pancake. 'Long time no see, baby. Where have you been hiding all summer?'

'*Me* hiding?' she said playfully. 'Oh, that's cute, coming from you. What are you, like, half bat or something? You sleep all day and work all night?'

Lucas smiled. He liked girls to challenge him, as long as they ultimately recognized who was boss. Lola's feistiness, tempered as it was with a healthy dose of adoration, was exactly the sort he appreciated. She wasn't a rabid man-hater like Honor.

'This is Sian.' Lola indicated the beanpole brunette beside her.

'Hi,' said Lucas, without averting his gaze from Lola's for so much as a split second.

Rude asshole, thought Sian. I'm glad I work for Honor and not for him.

Having no desire to play gooseberry, she took the hint

and disappeared back inside, leaving the two of them alone.

Casually resting one hand on Lola's bare shoulder, Lucas started caressing her smooth skin with the ball of his thumb.

'I've thought a lot about you, you know,' he said. 'Since last time.'

'Is that so?' Lola raised one eyebrow archly.

She was determined to play it cool. She knew he fancied her, but she also knew that deep down he considered her to be too young for him – just a kid. This time around, she was determined to prove him wrong.

'Yes,' he murmured. 'It is. I've missed you.'

He was so close now that she could feel the warmth of his breath on her collarbone, and his voice had collapsed into a soft, husky whisper. The next thing she knew, his lips had parted, as if to kiss her, and she instinctively closed her eyes and stood up on tip-toes to respond. But after two long seconds, the kiss failed to materialize. Opening her eyes, she saw to her fury that he had in fact stepped back, and was waving to someone about fifty feet away.

'Sorry, sweetheart,' he said, kissing her briskly on top of the head. 'Hold that thought.' And just like that he disappeared to join his friend, leaving her standing there like an idiot.

The arrogant bastard! How could he embarrass her like that?

In fact, Lucas was every bit as reluctant to break off their encounter as she was. As well as wanting her physically, he loved the idea of pissing off Devon Carter by rekindling his affair with Lola. That'd teach the stuffed shirt to look down his patrician, American nose at *him*. But the guy waving at him was the head of A&R at Sony, an important guest at the Herrick. He couldn't simply ignore the man.

After the requisite five minutes of small talk, he turned to look for Lola again, but she'd gone.

'Damn it,' he muttered under his breath, wandering back to the house in search of her. Moments later he felt a female arm snake around his waist.

'What's wrong, baby?' its owner purred. 'Lost something?'

Tina Palmer must have only just arrived. In a full-length, tight black, sequined dress and Marilyn Monroe makeup, she was overdressed enough to look borderline ridiculous. But there was still something very sexy about her, if you liked the whole brazen, brassy, Anna Nicole vibe.

As a rule, Lucas didn't. But Anton had told him to get close to Tina, and this was his chance. Besides, flirting with her was bound to enrage Honor, and that alone made it worth the effort.

'No, no,' he said, responding to her wandering arm with a sly squeeze of his own. 'I'm a little tired, that's all.'

'Worn out from making mincemeat out of my poor sister, I imagine,' said Tina.

Underneath his tux, Lucas could feel her fingers already starting to slip inside the waistband of his pants. Talk about a fast mover.

'I heard the show. But don't worry.' She smiled lasciviously. 'I don't bear grudges. Anyway, Honor can take care of herself.'

'Indeed she can,' said Lucas bitterly. 'Listen.' Pulling a business card out of his jacket pocket, he scrawled his cellphone number on the back and handed it to her. 'I have to get back to the hotel now, I'm afraid. Business.'

'Business?' Tina pouted. 'At this time of night?'

'I'm afraid so,' said Lucas. In fact, the only 'business' he had right now was to catch up with Lola Carter before she gave up on him completely. But he wasn't about to tell that to Tina. 'But please do give me a call, OK?' Lowering his arm he allowed his hand to wander appreciatively over her ample buttocks. 'I'd love to ... you know. Some time.'

Tina slipped the card into her Versace evening bag.

'Don't you worry, Mr. Ruiz,' she smiled knowingly. 'You'll be hearing from me again. You can bet on it.'

Five minutes later, Lucas finally caught up with Lola as she was climbing into a cab.

'Hey!' he called after her. 'Where are you going?'

'Home,' she said frostily. 'Like you care.'

'Scoot over,' said Lucas. Ignoring her scowl, he opened the door and shoved her further along the back seat, then climbed in himself, shutting the door behind him. 'Woodcock Lane, please,' he instructed the driver firmly.

'I don't want to talk to you,' said Lola, turning her head away and staring out of the window in a sulk.

Lucas responded by putting his hand on her thigh. 'I think you do.'

'Well, I don't,' said Lola, unconvincingly. The downy hairs on her legs were already prickling upwards at his touch. 'I saw you giving Tina slut-bitch Palmer the come-on back there.'

'Slut-bitch? Dear me.' Lucas leaned in closer. Lola still wasn't looking at him, but she could hear the smile in his voice. 'That's not a very nice way to talk about a family friend, is it?'

'It's not funny!' she snapped, spinning round to face him. 'If it's Tina you want, why don't you go back there and fuck her? Stop wasting my time.'

'If it were Tina I wanted,' he said, edging his hand northwards, 'I would. But it isn't. It's you.'

'But I saw—'

'You saw me giving her my card,' said Lucas. 'That was business. Believe it or not, I thought she might be able to help me build bridges with her sister.'

Lola didn't believe it. '*You* want to build bridges with *Honor*?' she laughed. 'I'd say that was gonna be a tall order after today's massacre on NPR, wouldn't you?'

Lucas shrugged. He didn't want to talk about Honor. He wanted to get this gorgeous, desirable, desiring girl back into bed. Ideally her daddy's bed. Devon was away for the weekend, and Lucas couldn't think of any sweeter revenge for the condescending way he'd treated him than to take the guy's daughter between his own, starched Ralph Lauren sheets.

'Lola.' Murmuring softly into her hair, he finally allowed his wandering hand to slip beneath the silky fabric of her panties.

At first she jumped. But then her breathing slowed audibly and she leaned into him, her lips parting silently but tellingly at his touch.

The battle was won.

'Lovely Lola,' he whispered. 'I've missed you, little one. It's you that I want, I promise you. Only you.'

Chapter Thirteen

'Relax. Let go of your arm.'

Honor's fingers were so stiff they felt fossilized as the masseur pulled at each of them in turn.

'I am relaxed,' she insisted, through clenched teeth. 'This is as relaxed as I get.'

'If you'll forgive me for saying so, Miss Palmer, that's the problem,' said the masseur, giving up on the fingers and pinning her forearm behind her back instead in a vain attempt to loosen up the latticework of knotted muscles across her shoulder blades. 'You ought to be having a massage *daily*, not once a year.'

'Daily, huh?' said Honor, wincing with pain as his fingers kneaded her sore flesh. 'Sounds nice. Maybe next lifetime, Gerard.'

This was the first time she'd taken advantage of the newly refurbished spa facilities at Palmers, complete with Moroccan plunge baths and a traditional hammam. Even now, mid-massage and surrounded by burning incense sticks, with some ghastly, jangly, zen-like muzak wafting through the speakers, she couldn't stop herself focusing on the cracked tiles in the floor that needed fixing (already!) and wondering whether or not it would make more economic sense to split these large treatment rooms into two and hire more staff.

That was the thing about running a hotel. You could never switch off. Or, at least, Honor couldn't.

Having said all that, this new masseur that she'd poached from the Georges V in Paris was doing a damn good job, and she could feel waves of tension leaving her body as his rough hands worked their magic.

It was two weeks since her now infamous radio head-to-head with Lucas, and Honor was still seething about it. She didn't know what bothered her more: his comments about her father, his implied threat to expose her affair with Devon or the way he'd insulted her about her looks. His 'bigger dick than your boyfriend' comment now played over and over in her head whenever she was alone, like a whining, insistent child, demanding to be heard. How dare he imply she was less of a woman than Tina? Stung more than she cared to admit, she'd stopped by Barneys on her way back from the studio and splurged horribly on some floaty Marc Jacob dresses and a clinging, peach-colored pencil skirt for work. As soon as she got back to Palmers, still fired up, she'd thrown open her closet, pulled out thousands of dollars-worth of pin-striped suits in her trademark black and gray and flung them unceremoniously into the trash.

The next day she'd almost had a panic attack, waking up to find she had nothing to wear but dresses. Plumping for a deep maroon empire-line sundress because it was simple and long enough to wear with flats, she could feel the stares of the Palmers staff burning into her back like lasers the moment she came downstairs and bolted into her office, blushing furiously.

Desperate for male affirmation, she waited hopefully for Devon to make some positive comment on her new look. He was meeting her that morning to help her plan the next steps in her PR war with Lucas. But when he arrived, he was so enraged about Lucas's public rekindling of his relationship with Lola – after the Loeb party, the pair of them were the talk of East Hampton – he barely seemed to notice Honor's existence, never mind her wardrobe.

'I always knew he was a playboy, but even I didn't have him down as a pedophile,' he ranted, pacing the office like a hungry cat. 'I've put my foot down and stopped all Lola's allowance until she agrees to stop seeing him. But that child is so damned stubborn.'

'Can't think where she gets it from,' said Honor, raising an eyebrow. It had taken all her tact and patience to persuade him that playing the enraged Lord Capulet in all of this would only heighten the drama for Lola and fan the flames of her attraction.

'Come on, honey,' she said gently. 'You remember what it was like to be eighteen and in love.'

'I most certainly do not,' said Devon. 'When I was Lola's age I was a hundred percent focused on my studies. And I respected my parents' wishes like God's law.' He shook his head sadly. 'I just don't know where Karis and I went wrong with those kids . . .'

Honor thought back to their conversation now, as Gerard worked his magic. She was fond of Devon's tearaway daughter and shared his concerns about Lola getting mixed up with Lucas. But she also knew that the heavy-handed approach would be counterproductive. She loved Devon dearly, but even she felt he overdid the whole 'Victorian father' thing at times – especially given that he himself was hardly the saintly family man he pretended to be.

In truth, Lola's welfare wasn't her only concern. She also had a firm eye on safeguarding her own secrets. Not wanting to panic Devon – he was already skittish enough about their affair – she hadn't told him about Lucas's implied threat at the radio station. But for the last two weeks she'd been a nervous wreck, waiting for him to spill the beans, either to Lola or – even worse – the press.

So far, though, it hadn't happened. God knows why, but he had decided to keep his own counsel. The last thing Honor wanted was for Devon to wade in now, shouting the odds about him and Lola, and pissing Lucas off so much he changed his mind.

Increasing the pressure of his thumbs, Gerard started kneading Honor's glutes mercilessly. Breathing through the pain, she tried not to focus on the fact that this was probably the closest she'd come to a sexual experience all week.

Deception, like so many life skills, seemed to get better with practice, and the longer her affair with Devon continued, the more imaginative and resourceful they both became in finding ways and excuses to meet one another. The anguish and anxiety of those first few months together seemed like a lifetime ago now. But the flipside was that the wild, uncontrollable passion of their early days had also gone, replaced by something calmer and steadier, something Honor told herself she much preferred, but that at the same time left her with a bitter aftertaste of sexual frustration that she found increasingly hard to shake.

On the rare occasions when she voiced that frustration to Devon, he was dismissive. 'I'm fifty-three, baby,' he'd say with a shrug. 'Even if we lived together twenty-four seven, I wouldn't want to do it all the time. I'm just not at that stage in my life anymore.'

He always seemed surprised when this nugget of information failed to comfort Honor.

Few people around her knew Honor well enough to notice how bad-tempered and strung out this dwindling of her sex life was making her. Unfortunately Tina, who'd moved into a suite at Palmers for the season, was one of the few.

The tension that had been growing between the sisters for weeks had come to a head this morning over breakfast.

'You know your problem?' Tina asked loudly. 'You need to get laid. *That's* your problem.'

They were in the middle of the Palmers dining room, a light, oak-panelled former ballroom filled with tables dressed with white linen cloths and offset by gleaming silver jugs overflowing with white-scented stocks, lilies and michaelmas daisies. Around them, the great and the good were busily tucking into their buttermilk pancakes and fresh-fruit compotes, pretending not to listen.

When they sat down, Honor had made the mistake of

making a critical remark about Tina's ultra-low-cut, ass-hugger jeans; that was one snide comment too far. Tina was sick to death of her big sister's assumption that her dress sense, love life, or indeed any aspect of her life, was any of her goddamned business; while Honor resented the fact that while *she* worked her fingers to the bone trying to keep Palmers going, Tina seemed content to spend her days swanning around the pool in a series of ever raunchier bikinis, and her evenings flirting with every rich or powerful man who crossed her path. Including the hated Lucas.

'Keep your voice down,' said Honor.

'No. Why should I?' Tina was on a roll. 'You're so up-tight right now, you could be sponsored by Feminax.'

'Jesus, T, *stop* it,' Honor hissed, blushing despite herself. 'People are staring.'

'Get over yourself. If they're staring, it's at me, not you,' said Tina, flicking back her perfectly coiffed blonde hair. Even at this time of the morning, she looked every inch the sex bomb in the J-Lo jeans Honor had so objected to and a skintight, hand-embroidered Fred Segal tee. Honor, by contrast, sported deep shadows under her eyes after a series of late nights, and looked thoroughly washed out by the slate-gray halterneck top and skirt that had seemed so ethereal and womanly on the rail at Barneys. She could have used a year of sleep, or at the very least an IV of coffee.

'Seriously,' said Tina, pushing the point, although she did mercifully lower the volume a little. 'When did you last have sex?'

'None of your business,' snapped Honor, adding reck-lessly: 'Recently, OK?'

She hated it when Tina was right. Luckily it didn't hap-pen that often.

'Recently? Really?' Tina frowned, surprised. 'With who?' Then, clapping her hand over her mouth in an exaggerated rendition of surprise, she gasped, 'Oh my God!' Clearly her acting style owed a lot to the reruns of *Melrose Place* she watched endlessly on TV. 'It's Lucas, isn't it?'

'What's Lucas?' said Honor testily. 'What are you talking about?'

'This whole feud between the two of you,' said Tina, with the look of someone who's just solved a particularly troublesome crossword clue. 'It's gotten you all fired up. Underneath all that hostility, you're hot for him, aren't you? You slept with him in New York! Admit it!'

'I will not admit any such thing,' said Honor. 'We did *not* sleep together and I do *not* find him even remotely attractive. Nor would you if you knew him like I do.'

'Bullshit,' said Tina, warming to her theme. 'OK, so maybe *you* want him, but *he's* not biting, and that's what's driving you crazy. Huh?' She was laughing by this point. 'C'mon. Am I getting warmer?'

'No, you are not getting warmer!' said Honor furiously. 'You are fucking arctic, is what you are. How can you say that to me? Do you know ... do you even have any conception of how hard I've worked to re-establish this place?'

She waved her arm around the packed breakfast room, where fifty pairs of eyes turned guiltily away and back to their breakfasts.

'I don't mind competition, as long as it's a fair fight. But that ... *man*.' She spat out the word with disgust. 'The lies he's told about our family! And it's not just that. He's sexist. He's arrogant. He's common as muck. I wouldn't sleep with Lucas Ruiz if he was the last man on this earth, and if you can't see that then you're even more stupid than you look in those ridiculous pants.'

'Wow.' Tina shook her head slowly. It was fun to have Honor on the back foot for once. 'Talk about protesting too much.'

*

'Miss Palmer.'

The masseur's voice brought Honor back to the present with a jolt.

'If you'd like to turn over, I can begin work on your abs.'

'Oh, yeah. Sure, Gerard,' she groaned.

He was holding up a towel as a makeshift screen and modestly averting his eyes to allow her to flip over without having to show her breasts. A big, stocky, heavy-featured guy – the giggling gaggle of beauticians at the spa had already nicknamed him Gerard Depardieu – he was not at all Honor's usual type. But to her horror, she found herself fantasizing that he would drop the towel, climb on top of her and fuck all the tension out of her frustrated body, right then and there.

Damn Tina.

And damn fucking Devon.

Why was he never there when she needed him?

Ben Slater picked his way along the beach, trying desperately to suck in his flabby stomach and wishing he'd taken Tammy's advice and booked himself a few hours on a sunbed before he flew out here. As far as he could tell, the average age of the blokes staying at the Herrick was about nineteen and a half, and most of them looked like professional surfers, tanned and buff and with ridiculously macho names like Chip or Chuck and a body mass index somewhere in the minus numbers.

And that was just the white guys.

Ben's skin, by contrast, hadn't seen daylight since his Easter ski trip to Val D'Isère, and then it was only his face and forearms that had caught the sun, leaving lingering tidemarks at his neck and elbows that only accentuated his general pallor elsewhere. He felt like an unpleasantly overgrown larvae that had crawled out from under a rock and was putting all the beautiful people off their lunches – or would be, if any of them ate anything.

Strolling by the beach volleyball nets, he smiled tentatively at a Cindy Crawford lookalike in a Special K red bikini. She was limbering up on the sand before her match, like her girlfriends, arching her body in a sort of yoga-meets-porn way that seemed to Ben to be positively begging for attention. Yet she returned his smile with a 'fuck off' look so frosty, he almost felt like he'd molested her.

He'd mentioned this phenomenon to Lucas last night.

'American girls are weird,' he said, taking a philosophical sip of his third beer at the Herrick's Japanese-themed bar. 'Every time you try to start a normal conversation with them, they shoot you down. But five minutes later and there they are hanging off every word of some bragging wanker in a Ferrari telling them how much his last year's bonus was in every bloody currency. What's that about?'

Lucas laughed. 'You have to be forceful here,' he said. 'The girls don't understand the whole reticent, understated British thing. If you're successful, they expect you to shout it from the rooftops.'

'I'm not reticent,' said Ben indignantly. 'I'm completely bloody up for it! I just don't like talking about money, that's all. It's naff. Aren't these birds interested in anything else?'

'Sure,' said Lucas, waving to a pair of Playboy-perfect blonde twins giggling at the other end of the bar. 'Fame. And enormous dicks.'

Ben stared down at his beer morosely. 'Great. Well, I'm fucked then, aren't I?'

'Or not,' said Lucas drily, 'as the case may be.'

'It's all right for you,' Ben grumbled. 'You've got the lovely Lola. You don't need to flirt around.'

When Lucas had told him over the phone that he was dating a teenager, Ben's disapproval was palpable. But now that he'd met Lola, he felt confident she was mature enough to hold her own. She was feisty and funny, a good match for Lucas. He liked her a lot.

'I've told you,' said Lucas, downing the remnants of his

own drink and ordering another, 'Lola and I aren't serious. It's just a casual, summer thing.'

Ben frowned. 'I hope she sees it that way, mate.'

Lucas hoped so too, especially as Anton was on his case again about getting intimate with Tina Palmer. The Herrick was going great guns, but Anton clearly considered Palmers' continued survival as some sort of personal affront – a chink in the formerly foolproof Tischen business plan. He wouldn't be happy until the great old hotel was on its knees, and he remained weirdly convinced that Tina held the key to its downfall.

Privately, Lucas wasn't sure what pulling Tina was going to achieve, besides winding up Honor and appeasing his boss. Still, he could think of worse assignments. And Lola had been getting a bit clingy recently. It was probably time he rocked the boat a little.

Continuing his walk along the beach, Ben's thoughts turned back to Lola. It was obvious she worshipped the ground Lucas walked on, just like every other woman he'd dated. But beneath all the teenage tearaway bravado, she was actually a sweet kid. He hoped she wasn't going to get too badly burned.

The further he got along the public beach, the more the crowds began to thin. It was another gloriously hot day, with the sun bouncing off the ocean like so many fireflies, and a cloudless, kingfisher-blue sky. But despite the undeniable natural beauty of the place, there was something about the Hamptons that Ben didn't really like. It was all a bit too precious and dolls' house-y for his taste. A bit twee, his mum would have called it, and he was inclined to agree.

The Herrick itself was an impressive building, and with an objective eye he could see that the architects and interior designers had fulfilled their brief thoughtfully and with flair. All that glass gave it incredible light on every level, and the myriad fountains and water features, simple bamboo and teak furniture, and pervasive oriental scent of lotus flowers was undeniably calming. But, though he wouldn't dream of saying as much to Lucas, he still felt the hotel lacked soul.

Palmers, on the other hand, was much more his cup of tea. Classy, welcoming, but not over-the-top cutesy, he could quite see why it had such a unique reputation, and the building itself was gorgeous, as stately as any southern gentleman's estate with its wood porches, stone fireplaces and wisteria-clad white walls. He was approaching its private beach club now, with its striking blue and white striped sun umbrellas and the waiters all dressed in white, except for the dark blue piping on their blazers. They looked like they'd just come from Henley Regatta. More English than the English, but then New Yorkers all seemed to love that.

Ben knew about Lucas's feud with Honor, of course. The whole world seemed to know about it by now. Lucas would have his guts for garters if he caught him now, sticking his head over the fence to get a better look at his arch rival's grounds. But his curiosity got the better of him, and a few moments later, he was very glad it had.

There, standing by the poolside amongst the snoozing, elderly guests, picking up dirty towels, was a girl with the most incredible legs Ben had ever seen. Without thinking, he started looking for a gap in the rickety wooden fence and, finally finding an appropriately weak-looking spot, set about clambering over it towards her.

'Er, excuse me. Can I help you?'

The skinny, effete, and very obviously gay head waiter who accosted Ben looked as though he could happily have replaced the word 'help' with 'castrate.'

'This is private property.'

'I know,' said Ben, blushing. He had one leg inside the Palmers compound and the other stuck awkwardly through the slats of the fence – not the most dignified of positions for one of the wealthiest, most successful financiers of his generation. 'Sorry. I, er ... I'm meeting someone here actually,' he blushed. 'For lunch.'

'Oh?' The waiter looked unimpressed. His right eyebrow had taken on a life of its own, disappearing up somewhere dangerously near the line of his toupée, and his thin, neatly groomed moustache twitched with irritation. 'And who might that be? *Sir.*'

'It's, erm ...' For some reason Ben's mind had gone completely blank. Shaking his back foot as hard as he could, trying to pull it free, he willed himself to conjure up a name – any name. But it wasn't happening. 'It's, er ... it's her!'

He pointed at the long-legged pool attendant. Just then, his foot suddenly burst free from the fencing, sending him flying, face first, into the sand.

'*Sian?*' The waiter was fast approaching the end of his tether. 'Sian is working at the moment, sir, as you can see. She doesn't have a lunch date with anyone. Now, who are you? And why are you trying to break into this hotel?'

Sian, who'd spent a thoroughly dull morning carrying piles of towels back and forth from the beach to the laundry room, was watching the commotion by the fence with amusement. Rico, her boss, was a total bitch. He was obviously letting the poor blond guy have it. Now that he stood up she could see the intruder was enormous, twice Rico's size at least. It was a bit like watching Pooh getting a dressing down from Piglet.

'Miss Doyle. Come over here, please. Hurry up.'

Rico clicked his fingers imperiously, a favorite habit, and began hopping from foot to foot like an impatient hobbit.

Sian dropped her pile of towels and did as she was told.

'Do you know this gentleman?' he asked. A vein on his forehead was throbbing visibly. He looked seriously ticked off.

Sian looked up at the blond guy. He had freckles and kind of a bashed-up face, but there was definitely something attractive about him. She'd never seen him before in her life. But something about his urgent, pleading, wide-eyed stare made her decide to play along.

'Sure,' she said, scanning his face again for clues. 'He's my, er ... he's my ...'

'Doctor,' blurted Ben.

'Yes.' Sian grinned at him. 'Exactly. Thank you. He's my doctor. How are you doing, Doctor ...?'

'Slater.' Ben grinned back, dusting the sand off himself and offering his hand to his still-skeptical inquisitor. 'I'm Doctor Benjamin Slater. Sian ... Miss Doyle, is a patient of mine.'

'I see,' said Rico witheringly. 'Well, perhaps next time – doctor,' he looked Ben's garish surf shorts and vest combo up and down, allowing his eyes to linger on his paunch with ill-concealed disgust, 'you'd do us the courtesy of using the front entrance like everybody else. *And* of picking a more convenient time for your ... consultations. Sian is on the clock now, as I said. She has a lot to do.'

Reluctantly taking this as her cue, Sian turned to go.

'No!' said Ben, grabbing her arm. He'd got this far after all. He may as well see it through. 'You don't understand. I'm afraid it's very important. An emergency, in fact. I have to speak with her ... with Miss Doyle ... right away.'

'You're saying this is a medical emergency?' said Rico. He couldn't have looked more scathing if he'd tried.

'Exactly,' said Ben, turning from pink to scarlet at this second lie. 'An emergency.'

Sian smiled. Cute. Definitely cute. And the Lock Stock cockney accent was to die for.

Rico wasn't convinced for a moment, but decided he was tired of his part in this charade. He'd have words with Sian about it later. In the meantime, one of them needed to get back to work.

'Make it quick,' he snapped. 'Very quick.' And with a meaningful glare at Ben, he turned on his perfectly polished heel and stormed off.

'So.' Sian cocked her head to one side, curiously. 'What's wrong with me, Doctor Slater? I must confess I'm dying to know.'

Close up she was even more stunning than she had been from forty meters away. With her pale skin and straight, silky brown hair she looked so ... strokeable. And the white, shirt-dress uniform she was wearing made her legs look even more endless than they had from the other side of the fence.

'There is nothing at all wrong with you,' said Ben dreamily. 'You're perfect. That's the problem.'

Now it was Sian's turn to blush. 'Who are you?'

'Oh, fuck, shit, sorry. I'm Ben. Ben Slater,' he babbled nervously. 'That is my actual name. I'm not a doctor. Obviously. That was a bit of a fib. I just wanted to think of something to get rid of Elton John.' He nodded towards Rico, who was still eyeing the two of them suspiciously from the outdoor bar. 'And it was the first thing that popped into my head.'

'Genius,' Sian teased him. 'He *totally* bought it.'

For a long, awkward moment, silence fell between them.

Oh, bollocks bollocks bollocks, thought Ben. Why was he such a lame-o with women? Why couldn't the right words just flow for him, like they did for Lucas?

'Look,' he said eventually, screwing up the courage from somewhere. 'I'm crap at chatting up girls. Especially American ones.'

'How many have you tried to chat up?' Sian looked amused.

'Oh, God, loads,' said Ben, unthinking. Then noticing her grin broaden, he tried to undo the damage. 'I mean, not literally *loads*. Some. You know, one or two. Shit.'

Sian laughed. 'And are we really that different than British girls?'

'Fuck, yeah. You're all bananas,' said Ben. 'I mean, not you personally. You're not bananas. You're gorgeous.

227

When I saw you from the beach just now, I sort of ... found myself coming over here, and yeah, sure, then I made a bit of a tit of myself, but the thing is, what I was wondering was, if you're not busy, you know, which you probably are, obviously ...'

'I'd love to go out with you,' said Sian.

Ben did a double take. 'Really? 'Cause American girls never fancy me.'

'Is that so?' she laughed again. He was such a dork, but it worked for him. 'And you so suave and smooth and all? Incredible.'

Rico was advancing towards them again, and this time he'd brought reinforcements. Ben decided to quit while he was ahead.

'What time d'you get off tonight?' he whispered.

'Six,' said Sian.

'Great. I'll pick you up outside the front of Palmers at seven.'

Watching Ben vault back over the fence, cleanly this time, and run off down the public beach, Rico turned to Sian.

'You seem to have made a miraculous recovery, Miss Doyle,' he said archly.

'You know what, Rico?' she beamed. 'I think I have.'

After the long, boring summer she'd had, a date with a handsome stranger was just what the doctor ordered.

Standing outside Palmers a few hours later in the one good suit he'd brought with him from London, clutching a wilting bunch of roses, Ben was sweating buckets.

What if she thought better of it and didn't show up? He could hardly blame her. She was stupidly far out of his league anyway, plus he'd behaved like a complete fucking fruit loop this afternoon. If she had any sense, she was probably on the phone to her lawyer right now, sorting out a restraining order.

Then again, sometimes it paid to aim high and have a crack at a woman out of your league. Look at Billy Joel and Christie Brinkley. They used to live in the Hamptons when they were married, before Christie jacked him in for a bloke that didn't need to wear stilts to kiss her. But then *that* bloke ran off with a teenage intern. Or something. Come to think of it, maybe Billy and Christie weren't such a great example …

'Hi.'

His internal ramblings were interrupted by Sian, who emerged from the front door of the hotel in jeans and a cute yellow daisy-print sweater. Ben didn't think he'd ever been so pleased to see anyone.

'Are those for me?' She nodded toward the flowers.

'No, actually,' said Ben, deadpan, 'they're for Sir Elton. I thought we ought to kiss and make up, you know. After this afternoon. Is he around?'

Sian giggled, and Ben felt his confidence rising. If he couldn't be Brad Pitt, he could at least be funny.

'You look amazing,' he said truthfully, kissing her on both cheeks.

'Thanks,' she smiled. 'I'm absolutely famished. Shall we eat?'

He took her to a tiny out-of-town place, where there was no menu to choose from, just a different set meal every night. The concierge at the Herrick, a local boy, had told him about it this afternoon after he'd vetoed all Lucas's suggestions – the Almond, Tierra Mar and the like – as being far too flash for a first date. It was more like a farmhouse kitchen than a restaurant, with mismatched tables covered with ancient, threadbare squares of gingham cotton trimmed with red ribbon, and the only lighting coming from cheap church candles wedged willy-nilly into old wine bottles. Sian loved it.

Afterwards they drove back into town, where Lucas had invited Ben to join him at the launch party of a new club.

'We don't have to go if you don't want to,' said Ben, struggling to keep his eyes on the road rather than Sian's tiny but perfect daisy-covered chest. 'My friend Lucas has put us on the guest list, but it'll probably be a bit of a scene.'

'Lucas?' Sian's ears pricked up. 'You don't mean Lucas Ruiz, by any chance?'

'Yeeees,' said Ben warily. 'Why? Do you know him?'

Please God let her not have already fallen for Lucas, he thought. Oh fuck. Maybe she'd even slept with him? That'd be just his luck.

'Not really.' Sian sounded reassuringly unimpressed. 'He's dating a really nice girl ...'

'Lola, I know,' said Ben. 'She's lovely. Not as gorgeous as you, mind you.'

'Yeah, right,' Sian laughed. 'Anyway, the one time I met your friend he looked right through me like I didn't exist. Which I guess to a guy in his position, I don't,' she added philosophically. 'I don't know. To be honest, I didn't much care for him. Are the two of you very close?'

Ben thought about it for a moment. 'We are, actually,' he said. 'I've known him a long time. But we're very different. I won't deny Lucas can be a wanker when he puts his mind to it. He does love himself a bit.'

'A bit?' said Sian.

'But there's a good bloke lurking under all the bullshit,' Ben qualified. 'Honestly. He's a seriously loyal friend. And he sees through a lot more of the pretentiousness around him than he lets on. I guess in the hotel business you have to make nice with everyone.'

'Maybe,' said Sian. 'Then again, he hasn't been too shy in making enemies around here. Anyway, let's not talk about Lucas.' Reaching over, she rested her hand on Ben's thigh and smiled at him encouragingly. 'It's boring.'

'Fine by me,' Ben grinned. 'I don't even know a Lucas. Lucas who?'

Inside the Omega club, Lucas sat at the bar, rubbing his throbbing temples. How could people come to these places for fun? The music was merciless, pounding techno crap, the sort of violent, tuneless rant beloved only of neo-Nazi teenagers and the clinically deaf, and the cramped subterranean bar was heaving with more hot, sweaty, overexcited people than a Baptist church on Easter Sunday.

To make matters worse, Lola had been stuck to his side all night like fucking Teflon. At least, she had been until a few moments ago, when he'd finally snapped at her to give him some space, and she'd disappeared off to the ladies' in a strop. It was funny: when she wasn't being insecure and needy, he was genuinely fond of her. But the cocky, devil-may-care party girl he'd had so much fun with last year seemed to have gone for good this time round. It was only a couple of weeks since Alex Loeb's party, but she'd already started referring to him as her 'boyfriend' – a warning sign if ever there was one – and quizzing him boringly about his movements whenever they weren't together. Sooner or later, he thought gloomily, something was gonna have to give.

Catching sight of Ben hovering tentatively in the doorway, his eyes lit up.

'Slater! Over here!' he shouted through the din, waving wildly like someone bringing in a plane to land.

'Blimey,' said Ben, once he'd finally battled his way through the crowds to Lucas's side. 'I think my eardrums might have just shattered. Is it legal to play music this loud?'

'I wouldn't call it music,' grumbled Lucas. 'Drink?'

'Er, no, I'm all right. I'm driving,' said Ben. 'I dare say Sian would like one, though. Angel?'

He stepped aside to reveal his date.

'Just a white wine spritzer please,' said Sian, turning to Lucas. 'We've met, actually. At that awful party out at the Loeb place. I was chatting with Lola. I think it was the night you guys got together. Remember?'

'Sure,' said Lucas, who plainly didn't. 'Hi.'

Sian felt her mood darken. God, he was rude, too self-obsessed even to follow this monosyllabic response with a 'good to see you again' or 'how are you?' What did Ben see in him?

'Sian and I just had the most incredible dinner,' said Ben, oblivious of the tension between them. 'That place your concierge recommended was the bollocks, wasn't it, babe?'

'Hmm,' said Sian moodily, still pissed about Lucas.

Lucas glanced at Ben and, clocking the puppy-dog eyes he was giving Sian, immediately found himself feeling protective. Who was this girl, anyway? Now he came to think of it he *did* dimly remember her from Alex's party: skinny, no tits, those cheap Bridge and Tunnel clothes – a real Polyester Polly. She was in another shocking outfit to-night. What was that flowery sweater all about? No doubt about it, a girl that poor was bound to be after Ben for his money.

'Sian? Is that you?' Lola, back from the bathroom at last, was still looking a little red-eyed. But it didn't detract from her overall gorgeousness in a tight, chocolate brown Roland Mouret dress and vertiginous calfskin boots. 'Oh my God. *You're* Ben's big hot date! That's so funny.'

Sian looked teasingly at Ben. 'Your "big hot date"?'

'I didn't say you were big,' he mumbled.

'This is *soooo* great,' said Lola excitedly, grabbing Sian's hand. 'You should have heard him waxing lyrical about you this afternoon. Lucas and I were practically at barf-point, weren't we, sweetie?'

Lucas gave a bored grunt that could have meant any-thing, and Sian noticed how Lola's face fell. Boy, did this man have tickets on himself.

'Well, anyway,' said Lola, making an effort to hold it together in public, 'it's great to see you again. We must make sure we swap numbers this time. We should get together.'

'Sure,' said Sian, pulling out her cell phone. 'Let's do it now. In case we're too drunk later.'

While the two girls punched digits into their handsets and set about catching up on a fortnight's worth of East Hampton gossip, Lucas pulled Ben quietly aside.

'You can do a lot better, you know, mate,' he said.

Ben just laughed. 'As if!'

'I'm serious,' said Lucas. 'Are you sure you trust this girl?'

'Yes, of course,' Ben frowned. 'Why shouldn't I trust her?'

Lucas shrugged. 'It's just a feeling I get with her.'

Part of him, he realized uncomfortably, didn't like Sian because she reminded him too much of himself in his younger days. Despite the cheap clothes, you could smell the ambition on her, and she wasn't stupid either. For a hotel maid, she'd already done well getting herself invited to the local rich kids' parties, and had obviously come to the Hamptons on the make.

'Well, Lola obviously likes her,' said Ben, nodding toward the two girls, who were huddled together in a corner, nattering like old friends.

'Lola's a terrible judge of character,' said Lucas.

'Which explains why she's dating you, I suppose?' Ben didn't miss a beat.

Lucas grinned. 'Touché. Look, I'm only trying to watch your back, that's all. You'd do the same for me.'

'Thanks,' said Ben. 'But I'm a big boy now. I can cope. Anyway,' his chest swelled as he looked over at Sian. 'I think she's bloody gorgeous.'

Just then Esther Canadas, the Spanish supermodel, sauntered into the VIP section of the club. With the briefest of 'excuse me's to Ben and not a word to Lola, Lucas took off like a rocket launcher in her direction.

'You shouldn't take it personally,' said Ben, watching Lola's face crumple. 'It's just work to him. I'm sure he'd much rather be at home, tucked up in bed with you.'

'Well, why isn't he, then?' said Lola bitterly.

'I agree,' said Sian firmly. Why was Ben making excuses for him? 'It's totally disrespectful. Look at him.'

Ben had to admit that Lucas wasn't doing his own case much good, with one arm around Canadas and the other coiled around the rather ampler waist of a newly arrived Tina Palmer. The pirate grin, unbuttoned shirt and cigar clamped between his teeth completed the picture. If this was work, it was hard to imagine what he must look like at play.

'Fuck this. I'm leaving,' said Lola, kissing first Ben and then Sian on the cheeks. She was doing her best to look angry and brave, but it was pretty obvious she was suffering. 'Call me, OK?'

Once she'd gone, Sian turned accusingly to Ben. 'And you still figure he's a good guy?'

'He can be,' said Ben awkwardly. 'Not always. Look, I thought we agreed not to talk about him. You wanna get out of here too?'

Standing up on tiptoes, Sian kissed him softly on the lips. Being so tall she usually had to stoop to kiss guys, so the whole tiptoes thing made a nice change.

'Yes, please,' she said. 'I thought you'd never ask.'

Later that night, Honor sat slumped over the coffee table in the living room of her private suite at Palmers, catching up on paperwork. Why was it that no matter how many bills she paid or letters she answered, her 'to-do' pile seemed to grow by the hour, like an out-of-control weed?

Rubbing her eyes sleepily, she looked at the grandfather clock against the wall, a relic from Tertius's days. Shit. It was almost two a.m., and she had a breakfast meeting with the new head chef at seven tomorrow. She'd better turn in.

On top of the pile of ripped and discarded envelopes lay one addressed to Tina that she'd opened by mistake. It was a note from one of the trustees, upbraiding her for over-spending her July allowance to the tune of almost twenty grand. Twenty grand! On what, for fuck's sake? The girl slept till four, and barely set foot outside of Palmers (where everything went on her never-paid tab) from one week to the next.

Pulling on her old, coffee-stained robe over her sweat-pants and T-shirt, Honor grabbed the letter and slipped out into the hall. Tina's rooms were at the other end of the corridor. It was too late for a confrontation tonight, and after such a long day she didn't have the stomach for it anyway. But if she slipped it under the door, they could at least talk about it first thing tomorrow – whatever Tina's idea of 'first thing' turned out to be.

As she drew nearer, she was surprised to see the door to the suite ajar and music – loud, thumping rock music – coming from inside.

'Tina?' she called through the din. No answer. Pushing the door open, she marched over to the stereo and ripped the plug out of the socket. Typical Tina. They'd be in-undated with complaints tomorrow. People didn't pay a thousand bucks a night to have their sleep shattered by Van Halen at two in the morning.

Wearily, she opened the door to the bedroom. Though how anyone could be sleeping through that racket, unless they were drunk out of their mind of course, which was always a possibility with Tina ...

But the bed was empty. Judging by the wildly disheveled sheets, it didn't look as if it had been that way for long.

'Tina? Are you in there?' Peering into the ensuite bath-room, still clasping the trustee's letter, the question died on her lips. For there, laying back in the bubble-filled jacuzzi, with his arms spread wide and a look of rapture on his face, was Lucas.

'You?' Honor exploded. 'What the hell are you doing here?'

Lucas's only response was a beatific smile. Two seconds later, Tina popped up from under the water, sleek and glistening as an otter.

'Hey, baby.' Lucas pulled her naked, bubble-smeared body towards him as she opened her eyes. 'I think your sister would like a word.'

'My sister?' Turning around, Tina at least had the decency to look a smidgen shame-faced. Unlike Lucas, who had stood up, naked as the day he was born and apparently completely unperturbed by Honor's presence, and was making no effort whatsoever to find himself a towel.

'Made you look,' he laughed, catching Honor's involuntarily glance at his dick.

'Oh, grow up!' she snapped.

Lucas walked past her into the bedroom and she slammed the door shut behind him, before turning her fury on Tina.

'How could you?' she hissed, keeping her voice down so as not to give Lucas the satisfaction of eavesdropping. 'Lucas?'

'Look, I'm sorry, OK?' Tina climbed out of the tub, still dripping, and wrapped herself in a toweling robe. 'We were both at this new club tonight. I guess we both had a bit to drink,' she giggled. 'What can I say? One thing led to another. Does it have to be a big deal?'

'Yes, it has to be a big deal,' said Honor, tearing at her hair in frustration. Catching sight of herself in the mirror she noticed for the first time how awful she looked: tired, with greasy hair and the sort of sallow, spotty complexion commonly associated with heroin addicts. It was typical that the first time she'd seen Lucas since New York should be the one day she'd chosen to wear a shapeless pair of sweatpants, rather than the feminine clothes she'd been wafting around in like an idiot for weeks, hoping to bump into him. 'Did you tell him anything?'

'About what?' Tina looked baffled.

'About Palmers, of course,' said Honor. 'Did he ask you anything? I don't know, about our bookings rate or … or the electrical problems?'

'Are you for real?' Tina's nanosecond of remorse was apparently over. 'He was fucking me, Honor,' she said witheringly. 'You know, that thing you don't do anymore, where the man puts his penis inside the woman's vagina?'

'Oh, Jesus, enough.' Honor put her hands over her ears. 'I don't wanna know.'

'You are so fucking obsessed with this stupid hotel!' yelled Tina. 'You really think that's what we were doing? Talking about Palmers?'

'So he wasn't pumping you for information?' Honor looked skeptical. 'Well, I guess maybe he wouldn't, not the first time …'

'He was pumping me all right,' said Tina, tipping her head upside down and shaking out her wet hair like a dog. 'But it wasn't information he was after. Hey. Where are you going?'

Honor had stormed into the bedroom, but it seemed Lucas had already made a swift exit.

'I'm going to catch up with him,' she yelled. 'Give the bastard a piece of my mind.'

'You'll only make a fool of yourself,' Tina called after her. 'It was a one-night stand Honor, for God's sake. We're both adults. Get over it!'

But Honor was already gone.

After sprinting down three flights of stairs, she finally caught up with Lucas in the deserted lobby, fumbling in his jeans pocket for his car keys.

'Ah,' he said sarcastically, seeing her enraged, diminutive figure heading in his direction. 'If it isn't Aurora, goddess of the dawn. You know, if you can't afford soap powder,' he glanced disdainfully at the coffee stains on her dressing gown, 'you're more than welcome to pop by the Herrick any time and use our laundry facilities. Really. Any time. Mi Casa, su casa.'

'Ha ha,' said Honor, pulling the filthy robe more tightly around her and wishing that she'd bothered to wash her hair this morning. But Devon never noticed, so there hadn't seemed much point. Lucas, of course, was looking god-like despite the lateness of the hour, his enormous, bronzed biceps clearly visible in a short-sleeved Abercrombie T-shirt and his preppy haircut offset by a dark shadow of distinctly rock 'n' roll stubble. It was tough getting the upper hand over a living slab of testosterone while looking like something the cat sicked up oneself, but Honor was determined to give it her best shot.

'My sister might not be the sharpest tool in the box,' she said, 'but you needn't think I can't see right through you.'

'I'm not sure we should be talking about 'tools' and 'boxes' where your sister's concerned,' quipped Lucas. 'But I'm happy to hear you have me figured out, Miss Palmer. In that case, you have nothing to worry about, do you?'

'And you can quit with the "Miss Palmer" bullshit,' said Honor. 'I don't need your fake respect. And I'm not worried. I'm disgusted. Apart from anything else, how could you do this to poor Lola?'

For the first time, Lucas's fixed face of arrogant amusement slipped. He looked annoyed. 'You are a piece of work, you know that?' he told her. 'Lecturing *me* on fidelity? And on hurting Lola's feelings?'

'She's crazy about you,' said Honor. 'Fuck knows why, but she is. Of all the women you could have picked to screw around with in this town ... why'd you have to pick her? She's just a child.'

'She's not a child,' said Lucas hotly. 'Besides, if you're so fucking concerned about her welfare, maybe you should

238

think twice about sleeping with her father and screwing up her parents' marriage.'

'I . . . I . . .' Honor spluttered. There was no point denying the affair with Devon, but at the same time she didn't want to have to defend it to Lucas. 'I'm not screwing up their marriage. It's already screwed up. It has been for years.'

'Please!' He laughed in her face. 'Is that what he told you? Talk about a cliché.'

'It's the truth,' said Honor furiously. 'You know nothing about it.'

'Are you sure about that?' asked Lucas. 'Don't you think Lola ever talks to me about her parents, her home life?'

Honor could feel her blood pressure rising. She didn't like the turn the conversation was taking.

'Karis and Devon tolerate each other for the kids' sake,' she said firmly. 'That's it.'

'They still share a bed,' said Lucas.

'Crap,' said Honor. But inside she could feel her stomach lurching, like someone had just cut the elevator cable. Devon had sworn to her that he and Karis had slept apart for years. 'Anyway, we're not talking about my relationship.' She jumped back on the offensive. 'We're talking about you and Lola.'

Lucas gave her a pitying look.

It was weird. He hated Honor. Despised everything she stood for. But at the same time it drove him nuts to think of her being pawed by that arthritic hypocrite Devon Carter. Couldn't she see what a lying toerag the man was?

'Listen, sweetheart,' he said, opening the night-door leading out into the parking lot and striding towards his car, so Honor was forced to follow him outside barefoot. 'I like Lola a lot. She's a sweet kid. Why else do you think I've kept your sordid little liaison with her daddy a secret? It certainly wasn't to protect *you*.'

Honor hadn't thought about it that way before, but she supposed it did make sense. Still, if she expected her to be grateful just because he'd kept his mouth shut, he could forget it.

'Well, if you care about her so much,' she snapped, 'what were you doing upstairs in *my* hot tub with my sister?'

'I was getting a blow job,' said Lucas matter of factly.

Honor was grateful he couldn't see her rising color in the darkness.

'And as long as you don't go spilling your guts to lover-boy, Lola will never know about it, and never get hurt. Deal?'

Honor glared at him. 'You're a bastard, Lucas Ruiz,' she hissed. 'A selfish, manipulative bastard.'

'Yeah? Well, you're a bitch,' said Lucas, climbing into his car and slamming the driver's door firmly behind him. 'Lola's not my wife, OK? It's a summer fling, nothing more and nothing less.' Revving the engine loudly he jerked the car forward. Honor had to jump out of the way to avoid being run over.

Lolling his handsome head out of the window, Lucas delivered his parting shot.

'Seriously, sweetheart,' he said, 'you should look at your own messed-up love life before you start throwing stones at mine. Karis Carter still loves her husband. And she still sleeps with him. Whatever bullshit he's been feeding you.'

Only once he'd driven off, leaving Honor standing alone in the gravel driveway, did she realize she was shivering. Not from the cold night air. But from hideous, crawling, paralyzing doubt.

Devon was her rock, her anchor of truth and goodness. He was her safety net.

She told herself that Lucas was just being spiteful. But if she really believed that, why did she feel like the ground had just opened up beneath her feet? Like she was falling, falling so far and so fast and so hard that she knew, once she hit the ground, she'd never be able to get up again?

Chapter Fourteen

Ben slipped both hands under the small of Sian's naked back, and slowly dragged them down the bed until he was cupping the two firm, warm globes of her bottom.

'Don't worry, Miss Doyle. This won't hurt a bit,' he whispered, bringing his mouth so close to her ear that his breath tickled as he eased himself back inside her. 'You can trust me. I'm a doctor.'

It was the morning of his last full day in the Hamptons, and he and Sian were in his bed at the Herrick, savoring each precious minute they had left in each other's company. Tonight Lucas was throwing him a farewell party on the beach. But right now all he cared about was Sian.

Letting out a noise that was half laugh, half moan, she arched her hips against him. She loved the size and scale and weight of him, the way his back and shoulders seemed to go on for miles when she ran her fingertips across them. Being so tall, she rarely got to feel fragile or feminine. But Ben made her feel tiny, like a precious china doll. It was liberating.

Their lovemaking had been intense from the beginning. It was only two weeks since Ben had stumbled, quite literally, into her life. But already Sian found it hard to imagine being without him, or to remember clearly how independent and complete and happy she'd felt before they met.

The irony was, he was the absolute antithesis of her type. She'd always been drawn to sophisticated, educated, urbane guys – Clark Kents. Admittedly, Ben had vaguely hinted that he had a financial job back in England, so he must have been to college, but she found his life back home impossible to picture. To her, the boy she had come, in a frighteningly short time, to love, seemed to be a classic of the beach-bum genre complete with scruffy hair, a worrying penchant for loud, vulgar Hawaian print shorts and a wickedly irreverent sense of humor. Best of all, he loved her. She could feel his passion in the tightening of each muscle across his back as he made love to her, as though his body were one giant engine designed for the sole purpose of pleasing her. And please her he did, more than she could have believed possible.

'Mmmmm,' she moaned, feeling her climax build as he brought one hand back across her hip and stomach and allowed his thumb to explore downwards into the welcoming softness of her pubic hair. Finding her clitoris, he began stroking it gently, the lightness of his touch in sharp, delicious contrast to the quickening rhythm of his thrusts. 'That is *sooooo* good.'

'I love you,' he murmured, half into her ear and half into the pillow as he came, and Sian's own orgasm immediately followed. 'God, I fucking love you!'

He rolled over onto his side, propping himself up on his elbow. To his amazement, he saw she was crying.

'Hey. What's wrong?' Gently, he stroked the damp tendrils of hair back from her face.

'What's wrong?' asked Sian, her watery eyes widening and her bottom lip wobbling with emotion. 'How can you ask me that? You know what's wrong. You're leaving.'

Ben sat up and ran his hands through his hair. 'Please understand,' he said. 'I don't want to go. I have to. I have a business to run. If I don't get back to London, that bloody Kraut Tisch is gonna swipe this deal right out from under me.'

In all honesty, he should have flown back to the office a week ago, as soon as he heard that Excelsior, Anton's fund, was moving in on one of his biggest institutional investors.

Sian was the only reason he'd stayed. But he couldn't put things off indefinitely.

Sian looked at him blankly. She didn't understand, not really. 'Hedge fund', 'fund of funds', 'fixed income,' 'return performance': they were all just meaningless words to her. Meaningless and boring.

'It doesn't mean things have to end between us,' said Ben, resting a comforting hand on the flat expanse of her belly. 'That's why God invented aeroplanes. And it definitely doesn't mean I don't love you.'

'I know that,' she said, sounding utterly unconvinced.

Pulling her to him, Ben wrapped his arms around her and squeezed her so tightly Sian worried about breaking a rib. But it was a good feeling, to be straight-jacketed against the comforting warmth of his chest. She felt safe, the way she had as a little girl when her father held her in his arms.

And yet, at the same time, she knew the security was an illusion. Soon Ben would be gone, back to his real life, and the fantasy of their summer romance together would fade into a milky, nostalgic haze.

He'd forget her. She knew he would.

'I promise you,' he said solemnly. 'I won't be gone for ever. But for now, let's just try to enjoy today, OK? I want tonight's party to be fun. For both of us.'

'Me too,' said Sian, doing her best to sound positive and brave. If this was to be the last night they spent together, she didn't want to waste it crying. There'd be time enough for that later.

Over at Lucas's beach cottage, he and Lola were also in bed.

'What do you mean you can't?' Kneeling over her with an erection the size of a baguette, Lucas playfully tried to prize her legs apart. 'You're a woman. Women can always do it. We're the ones that have to come up with the goods.'

'I know,' Lola smiled, idly stroking his dick with her fingertips but keeping her thighs firmly clamped together. 'And I can see you've come up with the goods fabulously, sweetie, as always. But if I don't get home before my mom realizes I'm gone, I'm dead meat. So are you, I might add. My dad'll be round here with a rusty pair of garden shears before you can say coitus interruptus.'

The thought of Devon advancing towards his genitals with a sharp implement was enough to dampen even Lucas's ardour. Feeling himself wilting, he reluctantly climbed off Lola and slumped back against the pillows.

'I guess twice will have to do,' he said grumpily, staring at the ceiling.

Actually, what he really needed was not more sex but an extra hour of sleep. But there was no chance of that. His mind was racing.

His hot-tub shenanigans with Tina Palmer, and the run-in with Honor, had left a bitter taste in his mouth that still lingered now, weeks later. At the time, he'd gone on the offensive with Honor, turning the heat onto her and Devon. But the truth was he did feel guilty about sleeping with Tina. Lola was part of that guilt, although he stood by his belief that what she didn't know wouldn't hurt her. In any case she'd be back at school in Boston within a week, and would no doubt soon forget all about him, like she did last year. What bothered him the most was a general sense of unease that he had somehow let *himself* down, and in the process allowed himself to become Anton Tisch's puppet.

At first he'd been as keen as Anton to play dirty with Honor, if it meant wiping Palmers off the map. But as time went on, he found himself navigating increasingly murky moral waters.

He still wasn't sure what seducing Tina Palmer had achieved other than forming an illicit, pseudo-friendship between the two of them – what Anton called a 'bond.' During the last two weeks he'd encouraged Lucas to use this bond to arrange introductions for Tina with some of his business associates, including a guest at the Herrick by the name of Toby Candelle. All Lucas knew about Candelle was that he was a personal friend of Anton's, was unusually obsessive about privacy and anonymity, and was well connected in the movie business. In any case, Tina had seemed perfectly happy to entertain the guy, and a few days later Anton had shown his pleasure by offering Lucas an unsolicited pay rise.

Taking advantage of his upbeat mood, Lucas had decided to risk asking him for a favor. For months now, he'd felt guilty about spilling the beans to his boss over Honor and Devon's affair at the Herrick's launch party. Now he wanted an assurance that Tisch wouldn't go public with the information, so he could keep his side of the deal he'd struck with Honor.

Anton seemed taken aback by the request, but agreed to do as Lucas asked. 'If it's really that important to you, of course I'll keep schtum,' he said. 'Consider it forgotten.'

And Lucas had. But still the miasma of guilt hanging over him failed to lift. He heartily wished he'd never got tangled up with either of the Palmer sisters.

'Have you seen my cell?'

Lola, washed and dressed, and with her damp, bracken-red hair tied back in a loose bun, emerged from the bathroom looking harassed. Even in yesterday's old T-shirt and jeans, after a sleepless night and without so much as a scrap of makeup on, she was edible. Still, Lucas reflected with a pang, she did look terribly young. With that smattering of sun-freckles across the bridge of her nose and the pink fluffy shoulder bag she took everywhere that wouldn't have been out of place on an elementary school cloakroom peg, she combined her sexiness with an innocence that could be quite disconcerting at times.

Maybe Honor was right.

Maybe he shouldn't be fucking with her.

'On the couch, in the living room,' he said. 'Right there, beside the white cushion.'

Shoving the phone into her purse, Lola pulled out her car keys and skipped over to the bed to give him a goodbye kiss. To her surprise, he grabbed her and pulled her face down to his, kissing her back with much more tenderness than usual.

'What was that for?' She smiled.

'Nothing,' he said, smiling back.

He was relieved she was going back to Boston. But at the same time, he knew he'd miss her. Since his one-night stand with Tina, guilt had made him start treating Lola more kindly. As a result, the clinginess that had so irritated him earlier in the summer had disappeared. Their last two weeks together had been almost as much fun as the old days.

'Don't forget it's Ben's party tonight,' he said, dragging himself out of bed, too.

'I'm hardly likely to forget,' said Lola. 'I feel so bad for poor Sian. She's really cut up about him leaving.'

'Hmm,' said Lucas grumpily. 'So she says.'

It niggled him that Lola had become so tight with the scrawny little maid from Palmers. Quite apart from suspecting Sian of being a gold-digger, he was pretty sure that she was one of the loudest voices warning Lola off him. The sooner she pissed off back to nowheresville, the better.

'What's that supposed to mean?' said Lola.

'Nothing. Just that she'll get over it,' said Lucas, who didn't want a fight. 'She'll be leaving herself soon enough.'

'Yeah, I guess.' Lola ran her fingers absently through his short, preppy hair as he sat on the edge of the bed. 'At least she won her bet.'

Lucas yawned. 'What bet?'

'Her girlfriend from home bet her a hundred bucks she couldn't land herself a millionaire in the Hamptons,' said

Lola, getting up to go. 'Hey, it was just a joke,' she added hastily, seeing Lucas's face darken and his forehead knot into a disapproving frown. 'Sian adores Ben. You know that. She couldn't care less whether he's loaded or not.'

Like so many people born into money, Lucas reflected, Lola underestimated its importance to those born without it. Her loyalty to her new best friend was endearing, but it was also naive.

'I gotta run.' She kissed him. 'Say a prayer that Mom and Dad are still in bed when I get back.'

'I'm praying, I'm praying,' said Lucas, as she shot out of the front door, slamming it behind her.

The mental picture of Devon and Karis entwined in one another's arms made him turn his thoughts once again to Honor.

Lola wasn't alone in her naivety. Even a tough cookie like Honor could be blind where love was concerned. She seemed to have swallowed Devon Carter's lies whole, like a credulous bait-hungry fish.

Feeling inexplicably irritated all of a sudden, he rolled over, pulled the duvet up over his head, and tried once again to fall back to sleep. What did he care about Honor's love life anyway? Or Ben's, for that matter?

Right now he had more than enough problems managing his own.

It was already nearly noon in London when the courier arrived at Anton's Mayfair mansion.

'Package for Mr. Tisch,' he grunted through his motorcycle helmet visor, thrusting a clipboard under the butler's nose. 'Sign 'ere.'

William, Anton's long-suffering butler and head of all the domestic staff in London, scrawled something across the paper and took the parcel. The boss had been hopping up and down like a cat on hot coals all morning, waiting for it. He'd better take it straight in.

'Ah, at last. There you are.' Anton, still in his silk Turnbull & Asser dressing gown, was pacing around his study. 'Give that to me.'

He'd been up since six, trying to woo a US pension fund's finance director into investing in Excelsior, and between that and looking over the third quarter figures for the Tischens, he hadn't had a second to dress. His hair, usually meticulously smoothed down, was sticking up on one side at an oddly jaunty angle, quite at odds with his humorless face, and making his dodgy dye job look even more obvious.

William handed over the package with a polite little bow, although inside he was seething. Tisch thought he was so properly English, but he still hadn't mastered the use of 'please' or 'thank you.' One of these days someone would strangle him with that damned tasseled dressing-gown cord.

'You may go now.'

Fumbling in the desk drawer for a letter opener, Anton didn't even bother to look up.

Once the butler was gone, and he'd found the little silver Asprey's dagger, he ripped open the package and triumphantly pulled out a VHS tape. With one press of a button on his universal remote, the door to the study locked, the lights dimmed and metal black-out blinds began closing automatically over all the windows. A second button made the two faux Chipperfield bookcases swoosh to one side, and an enormous flat-screen plasma TV emerged from the recess in the wall behind them. Anton took a childish delight in these James Bond touches, although on this occasion the effect was rather spoiled when he realized he would have to walk across the room and load the tape manually into the VCR.

Just as he was doing so, the phone rang.

'Tisch,' he answered, brusquely.

'Anton, I'm sorry to disturb you,' came the whining voice on the other end. 'It's Jordy here.'

Jordy McKenzie was the new editor of the *New York Post*. A former gossip columnist, he'd first crossed paths with Anton years ago when, desperate to make rent, he'd accepted a bribe not to run a negative story about one of his political friends. It was a mistake Anton had never let him forget.

When he decided to leak the story of Honor Palmer's affair with Devon Carter, it was Jordy who Anton turned to. Partly because he knew he'd be too scared to refuse, and partly because a New York paper was the natural place for a piece about Hamptons gossip. Having the *Post* lead the story would also add credibility to the idea that Lucas was behind the leak, as they'd covered a number of Herrick-related tidbits in the past, so would be assumed to have a relationship with him.

Anton had been casting around for a while for a way to get rid of Lucas – ever since the boy had started taking sole credit for the Herrick's success and mouthing off in interviews as if he owned the place. He could simply have sacked him, of course, but that would have been too easy, not to mention lacking in all the elements of revenge that Anton found fun. Teaching Lucas a real lesson required something more ... imaginative. Ironically, it was Lucas himself who'd finally drawn Anton's attention to his Achilles heel, by pleading with him not to spill the beans about Honor and Devon. He had in fact forgotten all about about their suspected affair, but now set about gathering hard evidence of Lucas's suspicions with a firm of top-notch New Jersey PIs. Now he was at last ready to break the story that would not only shatter Honor's reputation at a crucial point in the year – by making herself and her family synonymous with Palmers and its revival, she'd ensured that any negative personal publicity would have a huge knock-on effect to the hotel's image – but would also create the perfect excuse to fire Lucas, by outing him publicly as the 'mole' behind it.

'Listen, Anton,' said Jordy, doing his best to sound firm. 'I've been having second thoughts about this. Tina Palmer's a well-known name, but her sister? Outside of the Hamptons, Honor Palmer's nobody very much. Who cares if she's banging some married guy?'

'I do,' said Anton coldly. 'So will Palmers' clients, and the entire US hotel industry.'

'So run it in an industry paper,' said Jordy. 'This isn't news.'

'I've told you,' said Anton, his voice rising. 'That's not good enough. I don't want her compromised, I want her ruined. It has to be the *Post*.'

While he spoke, the plasma screen in front of him flickered into life as the video at last began to play. Glancing up, his eyes widened. The quality and clarity of the images was extraordinary. It took a lot to shock Anton, but this tape had almost done it.

'Look, Jordy,' he said soothingly. He must be careful not to be all stick and no carrot. It wouldn't do to alienate a now-powerful editor completely. 'Something else is about to break that will make this story very newsworthy indeed.'

The editor sighed. 'I suppose it's too much to hope that you might tell me what that something is?'

'I can't – yet,' said Anton. 'You're going to have to trust me and run with what you've got for now. But you won't regret it.'

The flipside of this promise – the threat that if he didn't run the story, he *would* regret it – hung on the line between them like a cloud. In the end, with no realistic choice, Jordy reluctantly agreed.

'I can't run it for at least a week,' he said petulantly. 'And if something really big comes up in the meantime, I may have to push it back further.' He had no idea what this poor Palmer girl had done to upset Anton Tisch so badly. But she was soon going to regret it, whatever it was.

'Of course,' said Anton, happy to be conciliatory now that he'd got his way. 'I leave that up to you.'

Settling himself down on his antique Chesterfield couch, he lay back to enjoy the rest of the show, confident in the knowledge that, in a matter of days, millions of eager internet users would be doing exactly the same thing.

'I thought you said it was gonna be a quiet barbecue. Just a few friends, remember?'

Ben stared in dismay at the champagne-swilling hordes, crowded onto the Herrick's private beach like sardines. He barely recognized any of them.

'I lied.' Lucas grinned. 'You didn't seriously think I'd send you back to rainy old London without a proper send-off?'

As usual, Lucas had put together a spectacular party in record time. Admittedly, nature had provided an ideal setting. The sun, which was just beginning to set, glowed the rich red of theatre curtains, its light just soft enough to allow the outdoor candles and shimmering crystal champagne flutes to dance and sparkle like so many fireflies. But the music (six barefoot flautists dressed as nymphs), food (mouthwatering sashimi and miniature, individually garnished blueberry cream pies) and dancers (a Hawaian, fire-eating troupe) were all courtesy of Lucas.

Ben was touched that he'd gone to so much effort. But nothing Lucas had laid on could distract him from Sian. She was luminous tonight, paddling in the surf with Lola, her long gypsy skirt wet at the bottom and her dark hair flying around in the wind like gossamer. He still hadn't figured out the practicalities of how to keep the relationship going after tomorrow. Long-distance romance was a killer, he knew that, but he was determined to make it work. The alternative – walking away and letting her go – was as impossible to him now as stopping breathing.

'I tell you what, mate,' he said to Lucas, unable to tear

his eyes off the girls as they splashed each other and giggled in the water like the teenagers they were. 'We are both seriously lucky.'

'Hmm.' Lucas sounded bored.

'What's the score with you and Lola, then?' asked Ben. 'Are you gonna keep seeing her after she goes back to Boston?'

Lucas gave him a questioning look. 'Of course not,' he said bluntly. 'How could I? She's going back to school, and I'm going back to work. It was only a summer romance, you know. I don't know why everyone's so keen to marry us off.'

Ben shrugged. 'Fair enough. I suppose I'm so happy with Sian, I want everyone else to have what we have. You know what I mean?'

Lucas cleared his throat. 'About that,' he said. 'Are you quite sure ... how can I put this? Are you *sure* you have what you think you have?'

Ben sighed. He was starting to get seriously tired of Lucas's negativity on this subject. 'Don't you ever stop? I love her, all right? And she loves me. Be happy for me.'

Lucas looked pained. 'I would,' he said. 'If I really believed that, I would be happy for you. But I heard something else today ...'

'What?' said Ben, biting back his anger. He didn't want to fall out with Lucas tonight, after all the trouble he'd gone to. 'What did you hear?'

'Lola told me that Sian had a bet. With a girlfriend from back home.'

'So?'

'Apparently,' Lucas took a deep breath, 'she bet this friend a hundred bucks that she'd land herself a rich man out here before the end of the season.'

'That's bullshit,' said Ben, his face draining of color. 'Sian would never do a thing like that. She doesn't have a materialistic bone in her body.'

'OK.' Lucas held out his hands in innocence. 'If you say so.'

'I do say so,' said Ben crossly. 'You don't know her.'

'Do *you*?' asked Lucas. 'You only met the girl two weeks ago. What do you really know about her? Look, I'm sorry,' he added, sensing he'd already ruined his friend's evening. 'I don't want to see you get hurt.'

'Crap,' said Ben bitterly. 'You just can't stand it that for once *I'm* the guy who's happy with a terrific woman, while you're still ...'

'What?' Lucas's eyes narrowed. 'I'm still what?'

'Lost,' snapped Ben. 'Lost, lonely and fucking insecure, all right?'

To be honest he didn't really know what he was saying. He simply wanted to lash out at Lucas. To pay him back for what he'd said, for trying to make him doubt the best thing that had happened to him since ... well, ever, really.

'If you don't believe me,' said Lucas angrily, 'ask her yourself.' And with that he stalked off, but not before adding under his breath: 'Of course, she'll probably lie to you.' He knew he was being spiteful and childish. But Ben's last comment had really ticked him off. Lost, indeed! He wasn't *lost*. He knew exactly where he was going. Unlike some people he could mention.

Sian, meanwhile, was happily oblivious to the unfolding drama. Chasing Lola up and down the surf, she was hampered by her now completely drenched skirt, which clung to her legs like shrinkwrap as she tried to splash water over her friend's way-too-perfectly blowdried hair. She'd promised Ben to try to enjoy tonight, and it was a promise she meant to stick by.

'You look like a newsreader!' she yelled into the waves. 'Come back here! You look like Diane freakin' Sawyer! I'm trying to *help* you!'

Lola squealed and started running back toward the beach. Sian made an ill-timed lunge as she came past and lost her footing, collapsing into the water in fits of giggles.

Wiping the salt water from her eyes and pushing back her dripping hair, she looked up to find Ben standing over her. 'Hey, babe. What's going on?' she spluttered. 'Are you having fun?'

His body loomed in front of the fading sun, so his features were mostly in shadow. It wasn't until he spoke that she realized something was wrong.

'Not really,' he said. His voice sounded strangled.

Struggling unsteadily to her feet – her clothes weighed a ton and the sand beneath her was uneven in the current – Sian put one hand on his arm to steady herself.

'Ben? What is it? What's wrong?'

'Am I a bet?' he asked.

'What?' She looked genuinely baffled. 'A bet? What are you talking about?'

'Did you make a bet with your friend before you came out here? About getting a rich guy to sleep with you?'

Sian felt her stomach drop to the floor and her heart start pounding. She'd murder Lola. 'Who told you that?' she asked warily.

'Never mind who told me it!' Ben exploded.

Sian shrank back. She'd never seen him this mad. Never seen him mad at all, come to think of it.

'Jesus Christ.' Shaking his head angrily he prized away her hand. 'It's bloody true, isn't it?'

'No!' said Sian. 'Well, yes, *technically* it is true. But it's not what you think. You seriously believe that's what you and me has been about? That bet was a joke. It was nothing. Anyway, you're not that rich, are you?' She tried to make a joke of it. 'You've got holes in your socks and your business is something to do with hedges. That hardly makes you Bill Gates.'

But Ben wasn't listening. He'd already turned away and started storming through the shallows back toward the beach and the rest of the party. Sian tried to run after him, but her skirt dragged her down into the water like concrete with every step.

'This is crazy!' she yelled after him. 'For God's sake, Ben. You asked *me* out, remember? It's not like I made a play for you. Ben!'

Having made dry land, Ben ran up the beach, brushing past bewildered party goers, staring into space and muttering like a crazy man.

'Hey.' Lucas grabbed his arm as he shot past. 'Wanna talk about it?' He nodded toward Sian, who was scrambling inelegantly out of the water now, dripping and screaming like something out of *The Kraken Wakes*. 'I was right, wasn't I?'

'Fuck you,' said Ben. He looked so desolate in that moment, Lucas almost felt guilty. But it was better he found out now, before his heart got really trampled on. 'Fuck you, and fuck your stupid party.'

By the time Sian reached the spot where they'd been standing, Ben was gone.

'Where is he?' she panted, turning on Lucas. 'What did you say to him?'

Lola, who'd just caught sight of the commotion, came over to join them. Sian spun round to face her, shaking her head in disbelief.

'You told Lucas about my bet with Taneesha,' she panted. 'It was a *joke*, for God's sake.'

'I know it was,' said Lola vehemently. Now both girls were glaring at Lucas. 'I totally told him that. Why? What's happened?'

'Your shit-stirring boyfriend here told Ben I was a gold-digger,' said Sian. 'That's what happened.' For the first time, she began to feel the cold. Her whole body had started to shudder.

'Lucas?' Lola looked at him furiously. 'Tell me you didn't.'

'I'm sorry,' he shrugged, not looking anything of the

sort. 'Ben's a friend of mine. I don't like seeing him being taken advantage of.'

'For God's sake. Sian's not taking advantage of him,' said Lola indignantly. But Sian waved for her to stop.

'Forget it,' she said. In the last two minutes she'd gone from shock, to fear, to nausea. But right now all she felt was anger. 'If that's what Ben chooses to think of me, he can shove this relationship up his ass.'

'But, sweetie, you can explain to him,' said Lola. 'Tell him it's all a big misunderstanding.'

'No,' said Sian firmly. 'Why should I have to explain anything to him?'

She might not be as beautiful, or as smart or as rich as all the rest of them. But she had her pride. If Ben Slater was going to take the word of an asshole like Lucas over hers, he could take a running jump.

Peeling off her sodden skirt and T-shirt, so she was down to her chocolate-brown string bikini, she bundled the wet clothes under her arm and stormed into the hotel in search of a towel. Lola was about to follow her, but Lucas held her back.

'Leave it,' he said. 'It's for the best.'

'The best?' she scowled at him. 'How'd you figure that?'

Catching the flash of anger in her eyes, Lucas felt his dick start to harden. He wished she'd pluck up the courage to challenge him more often. It was no fun dominating someone who never fought back.

'Let's go to bed,' he said, pulling her tightly against his chest.

'What? No!' Lola squealed indignantly. 'I don't want to go to bed with you. You're a horrible man. How could you do that to poor Sian?'

But a few seconds later she was melting into his kiss, just as Lucas knew she would – sisterhood was no match for raw desire.

'Come on,' he said, leading her by the hand. 'If it's meant to be, they'll sort it out between them. Let's not let it ruin our night.'

'Well,' said Lola, weakening as she followed him inside, 'OK, but I'm not staying long. I have to go and find Sian and apologize. If I'd known you were gonna do something this dumb, I'd never have told you.'

'Yeah, yeah,' said Lucas, not listening. 'Whatever.'

Chapter Fifteen

A week later, strolling down Main Street with a spring in her step, Honor was lost in her own, contented thoughts.

It was a Sunday morning, bright and clear but markedly cooler than the days preceding it. September seemed to have crept up on East Hampton and dealt a guillotine blow to summer. All at once, the most stressful and yet in many ways most rewarding summer of Honor's life was over, blown away on the first of the cool fall winds. Tourists had begun oozing out of town like pus from a lanced boil, taking with them their frenetic, New York energy, and once again, the calmer daily rhythms of the full-time locals reasserted themselves, reclaiming the town along with a smattering of older, wiser vacationers who'd sensibly put off their holiday until after the high-season crush.

Palmers was still at ninety-five percent occupancy, a very respectable rate for the time of year, particularly given the effort certain people had gone to to drum them out of town altogether. Honor knew she couldn't afford to rest on her laurels, but she did allow herself to savour the sensation of relief, and not a little pride, that she'd successfully sailed her tired, rickety ship through such stormy waters. It was a good feeling.

She hoped her dad was up there somewhere, watching. And that maybe, at long last, he was proud of her too.

The pressure was lifting in other parts of her life as well. Though she felt guilty admitting it, she was actually relieved to have an enforced break from Devon, who'd flown back to Boston with his family four days ago. They'd had an almighty row a few weeks ago, after Honor had challenged him about whether or not he still slept with Karis.

'Of course not,' he'd replied, heartbeat-quick. 'Why on earth would you think that?'

'Oh, I don't know,' said Honor bitterly, her fear and insecurity morphing into anger. 'Because your daughter says you do? Because she's been telling Lucas all about your fucking healthy marital sex life?'

Devon, who was also fearful – although in his case, it was a fear of being caught out – had fought fire with fire, yelling himself hoarse at Honor for being so 'fucking naive' as to listen to Lucas's poison. 'You trust that little Spanish shit's word over mine?' he roared. 'How stupid are you?'

They'd made it up, and afterwards made love with more passion than they had done in years. But an indefinable tension still hung in the air between them, and for once Honor had been glad to see him go. She still loved him, and of course she trusted him above Lucas; why wouldn't she? But even so, the prospect of a couple of weeks of peace to sort out her own feelings was a welcome one.

Speaking of peace, the icing on the cake for Honor's newfound sense of zen had been Tina's departure last night. Officially, she'd dragged her perfectly rounded ass back to LA for work, although in reality it was more a case of swapping one round of parties for another. The Hamptons was, to quote Tina, 'dull as shit' in the fall. Having Palmers to herself again was nothing short of joyous for Honor. All she had to do now was steer clear of Lucas, and finally get around to fixing those fucking electrics – thankfully, the surveyors' dread prophecies had failed to come to pass and they'd got through the summer season without incident – and then life could settle back to something approaching normal.

'Morning, Nate!' Jogging past the pharmacy, she waved cheerily at the owner, whom she'd known since she was a kid. Oddly, he didn't wave back, but scurried inside his store without even acknowledging her.

Oh well. He must not have seen her. He was getting on a bit, after all.

But as she made her way further along Main Street, her sense of unease grew. At first she thought she was being paranoid. But no. People were definitely looking at her strangely. When she stopped into the bakery to pick up her walnut loaf, a regular Sunday morning treat, you could actually hear the conversations shut down, replaced by a silence so thick you could eat it with a spoon.

Her last stop was the newsagent. Scooping up her usual Sunday paper from the pile on the floor, she smiled at the normally friendly woman at the counter. 'Hey Nancy,' she began. 'I don't mean to sound weird, but do I smell funny to you? Or have I got spinach stuck in my teeth? People keep staring at me like I just climbed out of a UFO or something.'

The newsagent, a kind, motherly woman in her fifties with round cheeks like a chipmunk, blushed scarlet.

'You haven't seen it, then?' she whispered.

'Seen what?' Honor looked blank.

'Oh dear.' Looking dreadfully flustered, Nancy handed her a copy of *US Weekly*. 'It's pages six and seven.'

Honor flipped open the tabloid.

'Oh, God,' she said, feeling suddenly dizzy. 'Dear God, no.'

The only fractional mercy was that the editor had deemed it inappropriate to show Tina fully naked and had strategically blacked out the most sexually graphic parts of each of the four pictures. Nevertheless, it was pretty clear what was happening from the visuals alone – although anyone in any doubt could also refer to the text: *Socialite Starlet in Coke-fuelled Orgy*, proclaimed the headline.

Tina Palmer, aspiring actress and daughter of one of America's most privileged families, was this morning revealed as a class-A drug abuser, willing to sell her depraved sexual services for money. Along with two other high-class prostitutes, our shocking pictures show the heiress:

- Engaging in intimate lesbian acts as part of her 'performance'
- Videoing herself and others during a series of graphic sexual encounters
- Snorting cocaine herself, then offering it to ANOTHER woman.

Honor felt the bile rising up in her throat. The sex shots, weirdly, she could deal with. It was the pictures of her sister crouched over another girl's naked body, snorting a long white line of coke off her back, that made her want to vomit. She knew that Tina liked to party and had seen her smoke the odd joint. But that was enough cocaine to stop a train. She'd truly had no idea her sister had a drug problem.

'I'm afraid there's more,' said Nancy, not unkindly, bringing a chair around for Honor and helping her to sit down into it. 'It's in the *Post*.'

Honor took the paper with her heart in her mouth. At first glance she couldn't even tell what the piece was about. But then she noticed a small picture of herself and Devon standing together, raising champagne glasses. It could have been taken at any number of this summer's parties, and in itself was hardly very incriminating. Unfortunately, the article that ran with it most certainly was.

Tina Palmer's publicity-shy elder sister Honor, owner-manager of Palmers hotel, has been carrying on an illicit affair with a MARRIED multi-millionaire for the past TWO YEARS! the writer drooled salaciously. *Devon Carter, a respected Boston lawyer and father of two, who has been happily married to former model Karis Carter for over two decades ...*

'Could I get a glass of water?' asked Honor, unable to read on. Her eyes were blurring, as though she had a migraine coming on. But it was going to take a lot more than a couple of Nurofen to erase this particular pain.

'Sure, honey,' said Nancy, bustling off to get one. A couple more customers wandered in, but much to Honor's relief she shooed them out of the store and locked the front door behind them.

'There you go.' She handed a tumbler to Honor, who was still staring into space looking shell-shocked. 'I thought it was very unfair, that second article,' she said kindly. 'It's always the poor woman that gets the blame in these things. I expect he strung you along, did he, my dear?'

'Hmm?' said Honor absently. Her mind was racing, but she was not yet fully capable of speech.

How had the press gotten wind of her and Devon? As for Tina ... those pictures. Who'd taken them? And where? Surely it couldn't be a coincidence that the two stories should break on the very same weekend? It was a coup, a carefully orchestrated coup, that's what it was, designed to finish her and Palmers for good. And it had blindsided her completely.

'Did you know?' Nancy was talking again. 'About Tina taking drugs?'

'No,' said Honor vehemently, finding her voice at last. 'No, I didn't. I hadn't the faintest notion that she was ... no.'

And that was another thing. If the *US Weekly* shots were genuine, this was more than simply a PR disaster. Tina was in serious trouble. She needed help.

'Look, I'm sorry,' she mumbled, getting to her feet. 'Thank you, and everything. You've been really kind. But I have to go.'

She staggered out of the store in a daze, like a survivor emerging from the wreckage after a plane crash. Come to think of it, that was exactly what it felt like: she'd been flying high, cruising at forty thousand feet without a care in the world, and then – BAM! – someone had fired a rocket launcher and blown both her wings off.

Except it wasn't just 'someone.' It was someone in

particular. And it didn't take Einstein to figure out who.

She had no idea how she made it back to Palmers. But somehow she found herself there, having battled her way through the first few reporters who'd begun to gather outside. Finally reaching the safety of her office, she bolted the door, only to turn and see some joker with a camera trying to open the window.

'Fuck off!' she yelled at him, but not before he'd got a good three shots of her advancing towards him, screaming and open-mouthed – not her best angle. 'Get off this property before I call the cops!'

Closing the heavy wooden shutters with a thud, she sank down into the chair at her desk, put her head in her hands and tried to will her muddled, panicked thoughts into some sort of order. She'd already instructed the hotel staff on her way in to keep the press out at all costs, and to try to make life as normal as possible for the guests. Anyone who said so much as 'boo' to a reporter could consider themselves fired. She'd also had the receptionist call the local chief of police, who'd promised to get some men there within twenty minutes.

So far so good. But what now?

She longed to talk to Devon. Just hearing his strong, capable voice would reassure her. He always seemed to know what to do, and was far calmer in a crisis than she was. But punching out his mobile number for a second time, she found it was still switched off.

Where the hell was he? And why hadn't he called *her*? Surely he'd heard the news by now. God knows everybody else had.

Right on cue, her phone let out the annoying series of beeps that meant she had a new text. It was from him.

Sit tight, it read. *I'm denying and so should you. If they had proof they'd have printed it. Delete this. Don't call me. D.*

Despite herself, Honor felt her heart sinking. It was hardly the warmest of notes. Not so much as a 'love' or an 'xxx', never mind a 'how are you doing?' But maybe that was too much to ask under the circumstances? He was probably having a nightmare his end too, besieged by these bloodhounds just like she was, dying to talk his way out of trouble with Karis at the same time.

His advice to deny the story made her feel distinctly uneasy. What if he was wrong, and the paper did have proof? Then again, she could hardly admit to the affair if he denied it. That would land him right in the shit. If his marriage to Karis ended, it had to be his doing, not hers.

Pushing thoughts of Devon aside for a moment, she turned her attention to Tina. Clearly, the two of them badly needed to talk. But when she dialed her sister's number, she was greeted by a recorded message of Tina's voice, chirpily informing her that she'd be 'back real soon!' and inviting Honor to leave her number.

Hanging up, Honor banged her fist on the desk in frustration. What was she supposed to do now? Go outside and make a statement? But saying what? Sit here and do nothing until all the reporters gave up and went home?

She was tempted to call Lucas. Obviously he was the one behind this whole nightmare, the fucking Judas. He'd sworn to her on his honour that he wouldn't tell a soul about her and Devon. So much for his word. She strongly suspected the pictures of Tina had also been taken at the Herrick – she recognized the minimalist decor in the background. What had he done, she wondered? Rigged up cameras and lured her in there, somehow? Was it possible for a person to sink that low, just to promote their hotel? A hotel that they didn't even own?

But before she had a chance to try Lucas's number, her direct landline started ringing. Without thinking, she jumped on it.

'Hello?'

'Why did you pick that up?'

It was Sam Brannagan, her attorney from Boston. Not

even Devon's voice whispering sweet nothings could have sounded more reassuring to her at that moment.

'From now on do not pick up any calls unless you can see the caller ID flashing. And turn off your cell. Got it?'

'Sam! Oh my God, thank God it's you.' The relief in her voice was palpable. Words started tumbling out of her mouth in one long, continuous exhale. 'Have you seen all this shit? What am I going to do? Can I sue the paper? I know who leaked the stories, if that helps.'

'You can only sue if it isn't true,' said Sam. 'I'm afraid Tina's pictures rather speak for themselves, although there is a question of invasion of privacy. But what about you and Mr. Carter? Is what was printed accurate?'

There was a pause while Honor considered her answer. 'Sort of. I mean, it's sensationalized.'

'But you have been having an affair?'

The lawyer's tone was matter of fact. He was her lawyer, not her priest, after all. But somehow he still managed to make her feel guilty, like a kid caught with her fingers in her mom's purse. She wondered if Devon's instructions to deny everything applied to attorneys too?

'Look,' she mumbled, deciding on balance that Sam could be trusted to keep a secret. 'We do ... have something together. But I don't think the papers have proof.'

'Hmm,' Sam sounded skeptical. 'I wouldn't bank on that if I were you. But let's not worry about it now. The main thing is not to panic, or say anything you might regret later. I'm already at the airport, so I should be with you by early afternoon, tops.'

'Thank you,' said Honor weakly.

'Do you think you can stay inside and away from the press until then?'

'Sure,' she shrugged. 'Where am I gonna go?'

'Good.' Sam sounded satisfied with this response. 'Oh, and there is one other thing you need to be aware of. Have you checked your email in the last twenty minutes?'

'No.' Honor shuddered, her heart racing. The nausea that had subsided when she first heard his voice on the line was suddenly back with a vengeance.

'I sent you a link,' said Sam calmly. 'It appears that the *US Weekly* pictures aren't actually photos at all, they're stills from a video. Someone has released the rest of it anonymously on the net.'

Honor groaned.

'Yeah,' said Sam. 'It's not pretty.'

'Please tell me *that's* not legal,' said Honor. 'Taping a person without their consent, invading privacy, profiting from illegal footage, I don't know.'

'It's a gray area,' admitted Sam. 'But we can talk about that when I get there. Have you spoken to Tina yet? Do you know how this happened, exactly?'

Honor shook her head but said nothing. While he was speaking she'd opened her inbox and downloaded the video clip.

'Honor?' His voice sounded miles away. 'Honor, are you still there?'

'Barely,' she replied, at last.

The tape was horrific. It made *One Night in Paris* look like *The Sound of Music*.

'Have you and Tina spoken?' Sam asked again.

'No, not yet,' said Honor. 'But I'm a hundred percent certain how this tape happened. Lucas Ruiz set her up.'

'All right. Well, just sit tight,' said Sam, kindly.

He'd always liked Honor. Having an affair with a married moralizer like Devon Carter might not have been her smartest move ever, but she didn't deserve this shit storm. Especially not after she'd worked so hard to turn the family business around. He suspected these twin scandals, but particularly Tina's tape, would be a death blow for Palmers. But he tried to keep his tone optimistic, for Honor's sake.

'I'll be there as soon as I can,' he told her. 'And remember: you don't talk to anyone until I get there. That's my job.'

While Honor was holed up at Palmers, a steady trickle of reporters had been gathering at Lucas's beach cottage. When he hadn't shown up by eleven thirty, most gave up and dragged their equipment up the hill to set up camp outside the Herrick. This was lucky for Lucas who, by the time he finally arrived home at noon, had the sort of hangover that could stop a train.

'Can I help you?' The small group of stragglers who'd decided to wait it out at the cottage looked up excitedly when he rolled up, unshaven and looking distinctly the worse for wear. 'Are you guys waiting for me?'

He'd spent last night with Becca, a barmaid from Bridge-hampton, and thoroughly enjoyed himself. But boy, had she put him through his paces! Not since Carla Leon had he been with such a voraciously sexually demanding woman. Becca also had the alcohol tolerance of a hippo. Fuck knew how many vodka shots they'd got through at the bar, and that was before they moved on to the tequila at her place. Lucas had barely managed to crawl out of her bed an hour ago, still feeling like a rat's ass. But when he left, she was already out on the terrace, doing yoga and drinking some hideous green sludge, looking fresh as a fucking daisy. It was actually kinda depressing. He must be getting old.

'Is it true you set the whole thing up?'

'Who's the guy in the video, Lucas? Is he a friend of yours?'

Before he could even unlatch the gate, Lucas found himself surrounded by people and beset by a barrage of questions that made his head spin.

'How well do you know Tina Palmer?'

'What about her sister's affair? Any comment on that?'

'I have no idea what you're talking about,' he said truthfully, elbowing his way to the front door. 'Now, if you'll all please excuse me, I have an urgent date with my espresso machine.'

'It's a bit late to plead ignorance, buddy!' one of the hacks shouted after him, prompting snorts of laughter from his colleagues. Lucas firmly closed the door in their faces, doing his best to look confident. But inside, he could feel the anxiety building in his veins like a pulmonary embolism. What the hell were these people *doing* here?

The first thing he noticed was his answer machine flashing furiously on the desk.

'You have NINE messages,' it announced, with its usual automated lack of concern.

The first, from Lola, was terse, tearful and to the point.

'Fuck you!' she sobbed. 'You're a fucking asshole and I hope you fucking die!'

Nice.

The second and third were both from newspapers, asking for comments and indicating they'd be prepared to pay handsomely for an exclusive interview about Tina Palmer – what the fuck did they think he knew about Tina? – but neither spelled out what all this was actually about. He was on the point of checking the fourth message when the phone rang and, like an idiot, he picked it up.

'Lucas? Thank God. Where have you been? Your cell's been switched off.'

It was Guy Harrington, the PR who'd been helping him orchestrate the media war with Palmers over the summer.

'Sorry,' said Lucas wearily. 'I was kinda tied up last night. But look, what the hell is going on? There are reporters at my house. My ex-girlfriend wants to kill me. Has this got something to do with Tina Palmer?'

Guy laughed mirthlessly. 'Do you have cable?'

'Sure,' said Lucas.

'Turn on E! Entertainment. Right now.'

After a brief hunt for the remote, Lucas did as he was asked. Silently, he listened to the 'breaking-news' report on the Tina Palmer sex-and-drugs tape scandal.

'And this tape was shot at the Herrick?' he asked Guy,

268

once he'd gotten the gist. 'That's why they want to talk to me? As the manager?'

'Lucas, this is me you're talking to.' Guy sounded weary. 'Don't bullshit me, OK? You set this up.'

For a second, Lucas was too flabbergasted even to defend himself.

'Jesus.' The PR seemed irritated by his silence. 'There's not much point being coy about it. Anton Tisch admitted the whole thing in his statement a half hour ago.'

'What do you mean *admitted*?' said Lucas, angrily. 'Admitted what? I'm telling you, Guy, this is complete fucking news to me. How can Anton admit something on my behalf? Something that I haven't even done? My God. I would never—'

'Oh come on,' said Guy. 'You hate the Palmer sisters. Everybody knows that. How could hidden cameras have been rigged up in *your* hotel without you knowing about it?'

'I have no idea,' said Lucas truthfully.

'You introduced Tina to this guy Candelle, right?'

'Toby Candelle? *He's* the guy in the video?'

'Lucas.' Guy's exasperation was building. 'You introduced them!'

'Only because Anton asked me to!' said Lucas vehemently. 'I don't even know the man. I've met him twice and that's the God's honest truth.'

'Uh huh. And Honor's affair with Devon Carter? Devon Carter, whose kid you're dating?'

'Was dating,' said Lucas.

'I suppose you're gonna tell me you knew nothing about *that*, either?'

Lucas ran his hands through his hair. He could see it must look bad.

'I knew they were having an affair,' he admitted. 'But I never told any—'

The words died on his lips as he remembered the one

person he *had* told. And how that person had sworn to him, sworn on his honor, that the story would never see daylight.

'That must be why Lola left that message,' he muttered to himself. 'She thinks it was me.' Slowly, horribly slowly, the pieces of the puzzle were starting to fall into place. Tisch had set him up.

'Who ran the Honor/Devon story? Which paper?' he asked.

Guy didn't reply.

'Look, humor me, OK?' said Lucas. He knew Guy didn't believe him, but he didn't care. All he wanted right now was the information.

'The *Post*. A paper whose entire features desk claims to be on first-name terms with you,' said Guy. 'The networks only picked up the story this morning, after Tina Palmer's home vid got released on the net. Or at least parts of it did. The rest's gonna be Pay-per-view from Monday, apparently. Not that you know anything about that either, right?'

Lucas hung up at this point. If his own PR didn't believe him, the conversation was pointless.

What if no one else believed him either?

The Tina story was still running on E! but he switched the TV off. He needed to think. Picking up the phone again, he dialed Anton's number in Geneva.

'I'm sorry, but Mr. Tisch is unavailable at present,' barked his rottweiler Swiss PA.

If it were Monday, Lucas could have called dear old Rita in London, but the business office would be shut up like a clam today.

'Ask him to call me back,' he snapped. 'It's urgent.'

But he was already starting to get the sinking feeling that Anton had no intention of calling him back. Now or ever. He'd made a pre-emptive strike against the Palmer sisters. And he'd deliberately set Lucas up to carry the can.

His next call was to the Herrick.

'Ah, Debs, thank God it's you,' he said, relieved that the competent head receptionist had picked up the phone and not one of the useless temps. 'I need you to keep calm and keep the press out until I get there. I'm in a bit of a jam here right now, but I hope to be with you soon.'

'Lucas—' She tried to interrupt him, but he ignored her.

'These fucking hacks are everywhere. But once I figure out a way to get past them, I'll come straight to the hotel—'

'Lucas!' She spoke louder this time. 'Look, I'm really sorry. I hate to be the one to tell you this. But we've had instructions from Mr. Tisch himself this morning not to allow you back into the building.' Her voice dropped to a whisper. 'I shouldn't even be talking to you now. If anyone heard me, I could lose my job.'

'Debs, that's ridiculous,' he laughed. 'You must have misunderstood. I had nothing to do with these stories. Mr. Tisch knows that better than anyone,' he added, bitterly. 'Now listen, I'm still your manager, OK? And I'm telling you, as your manager—'

'I'm sorry, Lucas.' The poor girl sounded near to tears. 'But I don't think you *are* my manager anymore. I have to go.' And to his utter amazement, she hung up on him.

His heart was beating at a mile a minute and his brain, still foggy from alcohol, sex and an almost complete lack of sleep, struggled to keep pace. He'd have liked to call a lawyer, but he didn't have one. Weirdly, he found his thoughts turning to Ibiza, and his mother, eking out her pitiful existence in that squalid one-room flat. He'd promised to come back one day and rescue her. Promised to build his own hotels, his Luxes, and make enough money that she would never need to work or worry or go hungry ever again.

How was he going to keep that promise now?

If he really had been fired from the Herrick – and it was starting to look that way – what then? People would think he was some kind of Rick Solomon-type asshole. He'd be branded a pervert and a blackmailer. No one in the luxury hotel world would touch him. Not if Anton made this stick.

But why? It didn't make sense. Whichever way he flipped it, he couldn't figure out why Tisch would want to do this to him. What had he ever done to deserve it?

Meanwhile, in London, Ben was lying in bed in his London apartment, morosely chomping his way through a family-sized tub of rum and raisin ice-cream, and idly flicking through the channels on Sky, when he stumbled upon E! News and caught the tail end of the Tina Palmer story.

Since he'd got back to England he'd sunk into something close to real depression. Sian hadn't called since his leaving party, and neither had he called her. He was still furious with her about the bet. But it didn't stop him missing her so badly it felt like a physical pain in his gut. He didn't think he'd ever been so miserable in his life.

He still dragged himself into the office every day, ploughing through his workload on autopilot. With Tisch's Excelsior fund snapping at his heels like a tiger shark, he really didn't have any choice. But as soon as he got home he unplugged every phone in the flat and crawled straight into bed, then proceeded to spend the rest of his evening watching trash TV and drinking beer until he eventually passed out in a sea of crisp crumbs and used mini-roll wrappers.

But the footage of Tina was enough to rouse him from his stupor. When the presenter mentioned Lucas's name he leaped off the bed, plugged his bedside phone back into its socket and immediately called Lucas at home.

The answerphone picked up: 'Hi,' said the recording, in Lucas's distinct Spanish accent. 'You have reached Lucas Ruiz. Leave a message.'

'Mate, it's me,' said Ben. 'If you're there, pick up.'

'Ben?' There was a click as he came on the line. Even in that one short syllable of greeting, Ben could hear the strain in his voice.

'Yeah. You all right?'

'Not really,' said Lucas. 'You've seen it?'

'I'm watching it now,' said Ben. 'Shit.' He almost dropped the phone. 'Anton just came on. D'you want me to turn it up so you can hear what he's saying?'

'Yes,' said Lucas shakily. 'They're on a commercial break here.'

Retrieving the remote from beneath an empty Doritos packet, Ben turned the volume up to high.

Tisch was being interviewed on the lawn of his Geneva mansion. Lake Geneva shimmered in front of him, and behind him stood the gothic splendor of his palatial pile, bordered on either side with perfectly symmetrical formal gardens.

Neat freak, thought Ben. But it was an impressive display of wealth. And it looked every bit as old-money and conservative as Anton could have hoped.

'Bloody hell,' he said, genuinely shocked. 'What's he done to his face? He looks like one of the Thunderbirds. His lips are the only things that move.'

'Shhhh,' said Lucas. 'I want to hear.'

'All I can do is apologize to both the Misses Palmer for this grave intrusion into their privacy,' Anton was saying smoothly, with barely a hint of his native German accent lacing his clipped, RP vowels. 'The individual responsible for leaking these stories is no longer in the employ of the Tischen Group, and I am looking into what legal measures, if any, are open to us at this time.'

'Legal measures!' spluttered Lucas. 'This is insane. He wants to fire me *and* sue me? I haven't done anything!'

'Quiet,' said Ben. 'Listen first, fight back later.'

'I can only imagine the anguish of both the Palmer and

273

Carter families,' Anton went on, glancing at his manicured nails while he spoke, like a cat examining its bloody claws after a kill. 'And I would like to extend my sympathies to all concerned. That's all I have to say at this point.'

The camera panned out as he strolled back into the chateau, affording an even more glorious view of the estate. Then they cut back to the studio, where a presenter was trawling through archive footage of Tina Palmer with various former boyfriends in the absence of any further actual news.

'Is that it? Is that all he said?' On the other end of the line Lucas's voice sounded hollow, as if he'd been winded.

'That's it,' said Ben.

A long silence followed, broken in the end by Ben.

'You didn't really set her up, did you?'

'Of course I didn't!' Lucas was practically shouting. 'I would never do a thing like that.'

'All right, all right,' said Ben. 'I didn't think so. But I had to ask. 'Cause, you know, you did sleep with her.'

'So did half of East Hampton,' said Lucas reasonably.

'Yeah. But they didn't do it 'cause their bosses told them to,' said Ben. 'And they're not trying to put her sister out of business.'

'Maybe not,' said Lucas. 'But it wasn't me. It was Anton, obviously. He's setting me up.'

'Why would he do that?' asked Ben.

'I don't know!' Lucas sounded close to tears. 'I should never have told him about Honor's affair with Carter.'

'Whoa, whoa, whoa,' said Ben. 'Did you say Carter? Honor's been sleeping with Lola's wanker brother?'

'Try father,' said Lucas.

'*Devon?*' Ben laughed. 'No! Are you serious?'

'It's been going on for years,' said Lucas, 'since before I moved out here. I mentioned it to Anton in passing, ages ago, mind you. I know I shouldn't have, but it was before me and Lola got together, and he promised me he wouldn't say anything. But now it's all over the papers, and Lola thinks it was me who blabbed, of course, because I'm being blamed for this stupid sex tape … Christ, it's a mess. Doesn't she know me better? I mean, I would never betray her like that. Not deliberately.'

Ben couldn't help but think that screwing Tina Palmer rated pretty high on the betrayal scale, but he didn't say anything. Lucas was already being punished enough for what he'd done, as well as for quite a few things that he hadn't, apparently.

'What am I going to do?' he wailed. 'I'm innocent, but I can't prove it. Anton's crucifying me.'

'Come here,' said Ben. 'Come to London.'

He hadn't spoken to Lucas since telling him to go fuck himself at his leaving party last month. But their friendship ran far too deep to let one silly spat come between them now. If Lucas was in trouble, Ben wanted to help. Besides, maybe focusing on Lucas's problems might help take his mind off Sian for a nanosecond.

'There's nothing left for you in East Hampton,' he said bluntly. 'You need to lie low for a bit and let the dust settle. You can stay with me.'

'Thanks,' said Lucas. He was so touched by the offer, he felt quite choked. 'But you don't need me getting under your feet.'

'Bollocks,' said Ben. 'If you really wanna know, I could use the company. I'm turning into a right lard arse sat here on my own moping about Sian. Pretty soon they'll be winching me out of the window with a crane.'

Lucas laughed. 'I'm sorry about Sian,' he said sincerely. 'Maybe I shouldn't have gotten involved.'

'Forget it,' said Ben. 'This business with Anton is much more important. I doubt he'll sue you, though, whatever he says. If you're right and he did set you up—'

'Of course I'm right,' said Lucas indignantly. 'There's no "if" about it.'

'Well, *if* he did, the last thing he'll want to do is go to court. Besides, he's a typical Kraut, isn't he? All mouth and no trousers.'

Lucas laughed. He'd missed Ben's pearls of cockney wisdom.

'Of course, your job's fucked.'

'Thanks for that,' said Lucas drily.

'If you want my advice, tell anyone who asks that you had nothing to do with it. Then get yourself to JFK pronto and disappear. I can book you on a flight right now if you like.'

Listening to Ben start up his laptop thousands of miles away, Lucas was shocked to find himself blinking away tears. He hadn't cried since the day he'd left home, at fourteen. But with his world crashing around his ears, Ben's stalwart friendship moved him more than he could put into words.

'Thanks,' he said, reining in his emotions with an enormous effort. 'I owe you one.'

'Don't mention it, mate,' said Ben cheerfully. 'That's what friends are for.'

By four o'clock Honor was back in her office at Palmers, having made a brief statement to the press. Sam Brannagan's flight got delayed, and she couldn't keep them waiting indefinitely. At least, not without looking like she'd gone into hiding, which was the last thing she wanted people to think.

Even so, a large group of reporters was still hanging around outside the gates, hoping for something juicier than the terse two-liner Honor had given them, blaming Lucas for orchestrating a smear campaign against her family and denying the affair, as Devon had asked her to.

Ideally, she'd like to have made a joint statement with Tina and presented a united family front. But typically her sister, having not deigned to return any of Honor's calls, had gone ahead with her own press conference in the Beverly Hills Hotel, which Honor had watched on TV along with everybody else.

It was quite a performance. Dressed in a demure cream pencil skirt and chocolate brown jacket, her hair swept up under a silk Louis Vuitton headscarf, Tina had channeled Grace Kelly for all she was worth. Putting on a faltering, little-girl-ish voice, while her nervous fingers fiddled constantly with a boulder-sized Tiffany solitaire on her ring finger (was she engaged?), she had evidently mastered the Princess Diana gaze (half shy, half coquettish, guaranteed to reduce grown men to dribbling idiots from twenty paces). Peppering her public apology with charged words like 'betrayal' and 'entrapment,' she somehow managed to turn the tables and shift her own role from vixen to victim. By the end of it even Honor was starting to feel sorry for her.

Unfortunately, not all of the guests at Palmers felt the same way. Four families had already cut their stays short and checked out, disgruntled to find their relaxing vacation hijacked and themselves thrust into the eye of a breaking media storm. When not fielding calls from the press, Honor spent most of the hours waiting for Sam desperately trying to convince her fall and winter bookings not to cancel.

'C'mon Danny, you can't do this to me,' she pleaded, squeezing a runner stress ball with her left hand whilst trying to type a begging email with her right.

'I'm sorry, sweetheart. No choice.' Danny McGee, an old family friend and Republican senator, was explaining that he would no longer be able to spend Christmas at Palmers. 'I just can't be seen to be endorsing drug taking, in any way. This is purely about Tina and that awful tape, you understand. It's not about you and Devon.'

'There is no me and Devon,' said Honor, grateful that he couldn't see her blushes over the phone. Unlike Tina, she was a terrible liar. But it hadn't made any difference.

'What you do in your private life is your own business,' said Danny. 'But it's different for me. I'm a public figure, and Palmers is indelibly linked in the public mind with you and Tina. I'm sorry, angel, really I am, but I can't swing it.'

When the knock finally came on her office door, Honor jumped, dropping the phone with a clatter as Betty ushered in a harassed-looking Sam Brannagan.

'Why did you make a statement?' were his first, accusatory words. 'I *told* you not to talk to anyone. And certainly not to lie to anyone. Can't you see that's gonna make things worse?'

'Worse?' Honor let out a hollow laugh. 'How could they be worse? Anyway, relax. People are far more interested in Tina's bedroom antics than mine. Devon and I agreed to stick to our story, and let it all blow over.'

'Yeah, well,' said Sam, 'it looks like your story got a little unstuck.'

'What do you mean?' Honor's eyes narrowed.

'I mean, lover boy admitted the whole thing.' Sam threw his arms wide in a dramatic I-told-you-so. 'I heard him myself on the radio on the way from the airport.'

Honor shook her head in disbelief. 'That's not possible. He wouldn't do that. Not without warning me.'

'Well, he did,' said Sam bluntly. 'Half an hour ago.'

Poor girl. Underneath her whole tough, feminist facade, she was still terribly young. Devon Carter had pulled the oldest Indian rope trick in the book and she'd fallen for it, hook line and sinker.

The guy was a walking cliché. All that drivel he spouted about family values; it was only a matter of time before he got caught with his pants down. Sam only wished that it hadn't been with Honor. She could have done so much better.

'Like I say, I only heard it,' he said, more gently. 'I haven't seen the footage yet. But apparently he went the

278

whole nine yards, standing outside the family home with his wife, looking suitably contrite. He said some bullshit about how much he regretted what happened, blah, blah, blah.'

'He said he regretted it?'

Bent forwards, clutching her stomach as though she'd just been punched, Honor's body language gave away her anguish more clearly than any words. Sam's heart went out to her.

'He asked for privacy for him and Karis, so they could rebuild their marriage,' he went on. 'Basically, he painted you as Monica to his Bill. The decent man led astray. I'm sorry, Honor. I did warn you.'

Walking across the room to the window, Honor cracked the blinds open a fraction and peered outside. The rhododendrums were in full bloom, heavy with blossoms that looked ready to drop into the gathering carpet of russet-red leaves already littering the lawn. Between the blanket of fall leaves and the copper-yellow light of the early autumn sun, the whole garden glowed as peacefully golden as a sepia photograph. Only the noisy gaggle of cameramen shattered the idyll. Forced by the local cops into a compact group in front of the hedge, their long lenses jutted out viciously like weapons, and their ugly, furry boom mikes protruded into the still afternoon air like giant mechanical bulrushes.

Honor closed the blind. She felt sick.

She didn't want to believe what Sam had just told her. That Devon would cynically and deliberately sell her down the river, saving his own reputation without a shred of concern for hers. But she did believe it. Most bizarrely of all, it didn't even surprise her, not really. On some deeper level, it all rang horribly true.

'He said he was going to deny it,' she said, turning back around.

Sam shrugged. 'He lied.'

They both jumped when Honor's cell phone started jumping up and down on the desk, buzzing like a demented insect. Picking it up, her eyes widened.

'Oh my God. It's him.' She held the flashing screen aloft. 'Should I answer it?'

'No!' said Sam. But she couldn't help herself.

'You've got a nerve, you lying son of a bitch,' she began furiously. 'How dare you call me? How *dare you*? You're not talking your way out of this one, asshole.'

But when she heard the faltering female voice on the other end of the line, her bravado deserted her.

'I didn't have your number. But I figured my dad would,' said Lola. 'So I'm using his phone.'

'Listen, Lola ...' Honor began. She had no idea what to say, but felt that she had to say something. 'I ... Your dad and I—'

'Save it,' said Lola, cutting her dead. 'I'm not interested in anything you have to say. I'm only calling because I thought you ought to know what you've done. We're in the hospital.'

'What? What hospital? Why?' She hated herself for caring, but she couldn't help it. 'Is Devon ... your dad ... is he OK?'

'Dad?' said Lola witheringly. 'Oh, he's fine. He's just peachy. It's my mom who's fucked up. You remember my mom? The woman whose life you just ran over with a bulldozer?'

Honor winced.

'After that sick charade Dad put her through for the TV cameras, she totally flipped out. She locked herself in the bathroom and took an overdose.'

'No!' It was more of a gasp than a word, and it was out of Honor's mouth before she had time to think.

'Yeah,' said Lola. Even through her anger, Honor could hear she was fighting back the tears. 'She emptied a fucking bottle of paracetamol down her throat, and Dad had to break the door down. So if anything happens to her, it's on your conscience, you heartless bitch. I hope you're happy.'

And she hung up, leaving Honor shaking, phone in hand, and looking about as far from happy as it was humanly possible to be.

Part Two

Chapter Sixteen

Lola Carter pulled her trenchcoat more tightly around her and struggled vainly with her crappy Boots umbrella as the rain started to kick in in earnest.

She loved London, even though it had rained pretty much ceaselessly since she'd moved here in January. The same week that her father's affair had hit the press, and her home life had come crumbling down around her ears, she'd discovered she'd been offered a place at the prestigious Central Saint Martins College of Art and Design, to study Fashion. At the time she'd been too distraught to give the idea much thought. It felt like years since she'd filled in the application, along with a slew of others, behind her father's disapproving back, and her long-cherished dreams of becoming a designer seemed frivolous and stupid when she thought about what her poor mom was going through. But as the weeks rolled by and the tension at home went from bad to utterly unbearable, escaping Boston began to look like a more and more attractive possibility.

It was now March and officially spring, but the monsoon season seemed far from over. If anything it was getting colder. Lola could feel the wet tips of her toes growing numb through her loafers as she sploshed along the King's Road, jumping in and out of puddles like a naughty five-year-old.

So much had happened in the last six months, good and bad, that in a way it felt appropriate to be in this strange, sodden city, starting again. Already the events of last summer felt so distant, they might as well have been someone else's life.

Devon's affair with Honor had changed everything. Initially, one of the worst things was knowing it was Lucas who'd exposed it. Despite the way he'd blown hot and cold with her over the summer, Lola had left East Hampton still nursing a serious soft spot for him. She knew he didn't love her. But she had thought he at least liked and respected her. The idea that a man she'd willingly shared her dreams and fears and body with, could throw a nail bomb of pain into her family like that ... it shook her.

For one thing, it meant she must be a pretty terrible judge of character. She'd honestly thought Lucas was a good guy at heart, but he'd turned out to be a snake of the lowest order. As for Honor, who she'd come to look up to almost as an elder sister, she was even worse: a lying, calculating bitch. And her father? Even now Lola couldn't really get her head around it. Sure, she and her dad had never gotten along, even before this bombshell. But deep down she'd always believed that he, too, was a decent, honorable, upstanding man. That he practiced the strict morality he preached, not just to her and her brother, but to the world at large. Underneath all the teenage tantrums, she'd respected him. But now that respect was shredded.

It was harrowing, having to stand by uselessly while her mom crumbled like a stale piece of wedding cake. Her parents might never have been the Waltons, but they'd depended on one another, and trusted each other, for the better part of thirty years. The affair had blown her mother's world apart.

Lola could still remember feeling sick to her stomach in the hospital, watching her dad hold her mom's hand as they waited for her to come round after the overdose, playing the concerned husband, when he was the one who put her there in the first place. It was gross. All he seemed to care about was how things looked.

Even so, both he and Nick, who wasn't normally known

for dramatic displays of emotion, burst into tears of relief when Karis finally came to. But not Lola. She couldn't. She just felt numb inside.

On the drive home, she wouldn't even look at her father. For the next month, while Karis recuperated in hospital, the only time Lola agreed to be anywhere near him was during visiting hours, and that was purely for her mother's sake. At home the two of them rattled around like strangers, Lola having refused point blank to contemplate retaking her SATs at St. Mary's.

'The doctor says Mom can come home next weekend,' said Devon one gloomy Sunday night, forcing the cheeriness into his voice. 'I thought mabe you and I could throw her a welcome home party, now that Nick's gone back to LA.'

He was sitting on a red damask couch at one end of their enormous Boston living room whilst his daughter, coiled like a snake into a rattan armchair at the other end, refused to look up from *Harper's Bazaar*.

'Do what you like,' she snapped, still not looking up. 'I won't be here.'

'Oh?' said Devon, trying hard to mask his annoyance. 'And why's that?'

'I've been offered a place at fashion school. In London,' said Lola nonchalantly. 'I've decided to take it.'

'I see,' said Devon.

'My course doesn't start until the new year, but I've booked a flight out on Friday to start looking at apartments and get the lie of the land.'

He looked across at her determined, defiant face. A month ago he'd have slapped her down for talking back to him like that and sent her back to St. Mary's with a flea in her ear. But everything was different now. The contempt in her eyes burned so brightly it frightened him. If he tried to lay the law down now, she'd bolt. Then he'd have lost her for good.

'What's the name of the college?' he asked, playing for time.

'St Martin's,' said Lola truculently, flipping the pages of her magazine with unnecessary violence and keeping her eyes down. 'Like you care.'

'Well,' said Devon, projecting a calm that he was far from feeling, 'you're not moving to England on your own. I'm sorry, but you're far too young for that.'

'I'm eighteen,' Lola shot back at him, looking him in the eye at last. 'Plenty of kids younger than me leave home. Besides, I'm not asking you, I'm telling you. I'm going, whether you like it or not.'

Wisely, Devon had decided to let the conversation lie at this point. For all her fighting talk, she would of course need him to fund her studies, not to mention her accommodation, if she wanted to go. But keeping her in Boston as an economic prisoner would be the surest way to drive a permanent wedge between them. Morally, she had him over a barrel and they both knew it. The affair had robbed him utterly of his authority as a father. As much as he disliked it, he realized that if he was to have a chance at winning Lola's forgiveness, and earning back her love, he'd have to let her go.

In the end, he'd agreed to rent her an apartment in Chelsea, on condition that she roomed with a friend. Both he and Karis had hoped she'd pick one of the daughters of the many respectable old Boston families that they knew socially. But Lola had other ideas.

'But darling,' Devon had tried to reason with her, watching her bent over the sewing machine in the kitchen one November evening, lost in concentration as she restitched one of Karis's skirts. Despite Devon's best efforts to encourage her to eat, Karis had been losing weight at an alarming rate since she came home and most of her clothes hung off her now like rags on a skeleton. 'A girl like Sian would be so far out of her depth in a cosmopolitan city like London. How do you think she'd afford the rent?'

Lola shrugged, biting off a stray thread with her front teeth. 'We can subsidize her. 'Until she finds a job.'

'We'? thought Devon. Who the hell was 'we'? He was on the point of demurring, but thought better of it. The daughter of some blue-collar New Jersey oik might not be ideal company for Lola, but at least the two girls would be safe together. And if agreeing to fund Sian meant Lola moved even an inch towards a reconciliation with him, he figured it was a price worth paying.

Ever since Karis had come back home, he'd begun to feel like a stranger in his own house. His wife drifted aimlessly from room to room like a zombie; his son had hightailed it back to LA as fast as his legs could carry him; and his daughter looked at him like something that had crawled out from under a rock every time he walked through a door.

He did regret the affair. Part of him still missed Honor and the thrill of youthfulness and excitement that being with her had given him. But for the first time the enormity of what he'd done to Karis really hit home. Underneath all the bickering and social climbing, he now realized, she still loved him. The damage to his reputation, much as it pained him, wasn't half as bad as the crushing guilt he felt watching her struggling to rebuild her life and carry on as normal while inside she was clearly still in a million shattered pieces. The other day he'd watched her from their bedroom window, chatting happily to one of the gardeners as she planted out bulbs for the spring. But as soon as the man left, she'd dropped her head into her hands, and he'd watched helplessly as her frail shoulders began to shake with sobs. Tears had come to his own eyes then. He wanted desperately to make things right. But the affair and all the ensuing publicity had left him so far adrift, he had no idea where to start.

Part of him hoped that with Lola abroad and Nick back in LA, things might get easier at home. But whether they did or didn't, he knew he had little choice but to let his headstrong daughter go.

Turning into Tite Street now, Lola closed down her umbrella – the stupid thing was practically useless against such a pounding torrent anyway – and fumbled in her purse for the front door keys. The flat Devon had rented comprised the ground and first floors of a white stucco-fronted Victorian house, overlooking pretty, communal square gardens. Through the bay window at the front, Lola could see Sian slumped over her PC at the kitchen table, and banged on the glass to get her attention.

'Can't find my keys!' she yelled, lifting up her purse and rattling it to illustrate the point. 'Can you let me in?'

A few seconds later Sian was at the door. Barefoot and in sweatpants she had a long, chunky-knit cardigan pulled tightly around her and her hair scraped back in an elastic band. She looked tired.

'Have you been to sleep yet?' asked Lola.

After months of interviews Sian had finally landed herself a job at the *News of the World*, but it was mostly nightshifts copy-editing, which didn't pay her enough to cover the rent. Lola was always telling her not to worry – 'my guilty asshole father can pay' – but Sian had no intention of freeloading, and was still trying to write and pitch freelance articles during the day to top up her meager salary. Unfortunately, this didn't leave her a lot of time for sleep. In the last week she'd started sporting full-on panda eyes, which didn't do much for her already pasty, sun-deprived complexion.

'Not yet.' She shook her head. 'Nice swim?'

'It's unbelievable!' Lola laughed, shaking out her wet hair and peeling off her coat and shoes. Her socks were so wet she had to wring them out on the porch like used flannels before she could come in.

'Well, maybe the rain agrees with you,' said Sian. 'You certainly look a lot more cheerful.' Padding back into the kitchen she flicked on the kettle to make them some tea. Both the girls had taken to drinking Earl Grey and eating chocolate digestive biscuits when they got home from work, a ritual that made them feel marvelously English and Mary Poppins-ish, especially when the storms set in. 'Did Ego call?'

'Ego' was the nickname Sian had given Lola's latest boyfriend, Igor, a revoltingly chiseled Russian in the year above her at college. A part-time model, he was also a full-time jerk, although it had taken Lola until yesterday, when he dumped her by text message, to see it.

'No.' Lola shoved the last biscuit from the open packet into her mouth before greedily ripping open a new one.

It never ceased to amaze Sian how a girl who ate like a Sumo Wrestler, and whose idea of exercise was stretching for the TV remote, kept such a sickeningly perfect body. Not to mention her flawless, alabaster complexion.

'He didn't call, and I don't give a shit,' she said, spraying biscuit crumbs across the table with happy abandon. 'Asshole. His designs were all lame Vivienne Westwood rip-offs anyway. He can fuck-right-off-ski.'

Sian set about making the tea, opening and closing cupboards and hunting for the quaint flowery teapot they'd picked up at Portobello market. Man, she was exhausted. Even getting out the china and tea bags felt like a monumental effort today.

She was pleased Lola was over Ego, and tried not to envy her friend's uncanny ability to bounce back from heartbreak like a human Tigger. Since they'd come to London Lola had gotten through boyfriends like other people got through toilet roll. She never mentioned Lucas, not once, and seemed to have succeeded in blocking out the painful events of last summer completely, by diving head-first into her new life at fashion school.

How Sian wished she could do the same. She was fed up of being the Eeyore in their partnership, moping and brooding and worn out all the time. But she wasn't like Lola. She didn't have the supreme confidence, born of lifelong wealth and serious, supermodel beauty, that protected Lola like a magic cloak from whatever stones life might throw at her.

Not that life was treating Sian too shabbily at the moment. Being offered the chance to come to London was a miracle for a girl like her. She still remembered getting Lola's phone call, back home in Lymington. Looking back, it was like the opening scene from a movie: her mom in the kitchen, making dinner, her dad and brother sprawled on the couch in the living room, Budweisers in hand, engrossed in the final minutes of the game. And Sian herself, running down the stairs screaming with excitement, holding the phone in front of her like a talisman, begging her parents to let her go.

'I can pay my own way,' she pleaded. 'I've got almost three thousand dollars saved up now. And I'll find work as soon as I get there, I swear.'

'I thought that money was for college?' said her mom. 'How long have you been telling us about wanting to get more education?'

'This is *London*, Mom,' Sian explained patiently. 'It *is* an education. Anyway, you and Dad always wanted me to start work right after high school. So now I will.'

'We meant work here,' said her father. 'In Lymington. Not halfway across the world with some heiress kid we've never even met.'

They'd taken some persuading. To her parents, moving to London was equivalent to saying you wanted to spend a year on the international space station, or join the submarine corps. It was something they couldn't picture, and consequently feared.

'Soon as you get homesick, you get right on the next

plane,' her mom said tearfully at the departure gate. 'There won't be no "I told you sos". You just come on home, all right, honey?'

'Sure, Mom,' said Sian. 'Of course I will.'

But inside she was rolling her eyes. Like she was gonna be homesick! For what? Burgers at Dino's on a Friday night? Hanging out at the mall?

Yet to her surprise, she found she *did* miss home, almost from the moment she landed in England. Two solid months of waitressing at a greasy spoon cafe in Earl's Court probably hadn't helped. But even now that she'd finally landed a job on a Sunday tabloid, her dream for as long as she could remember, there was still a feeling of restless unhappiness she couldn't seem to shake.

She hesitated to attribute this to Ben, who she soon discovered was some kind of micro-celebrity in England, a sort of Richard Branson mini-me. Like most eighteen-year-old girls, she found the financial pages deathly dull, useful only as cat litter, or possibly to start a fire. But Ben's name cropped up in the *Financial Times* with such regularity, it was impossible not to take a morbid interest. Seeing his name in print was like picking at an emotional scab – disgusting, painful, and yet weirdly addictive. It wasn't long before she found herself actively scanning the hedge fund articles, looking for a mention or a picture.

He'd told her when they met that he worked in finance, so she'd assumed he was reasonably well off. To stay at the Herrick he'd have had to be. But despite Lucas's assumptions to the contrary, she'd actually had no idea Ben was a fully paid-up member of the super-rich. In some ways she supposed it explained his sensitivity over the whole bet thing. Explained it, but didn't excuse it. Even after six months the pain of their parting was still raw and the wound to her pride still stung like acid every time she thought of him. Which, these days, was pathetically often.

'You know,' said Lola, pouring herself a second cup

of tea, into which she heaped three towering teaspoons of sugar, 'breaking up with Igor does leave me with one problem.'

'It does?' Sian looked disbelieving.

'Kind of. It means I'm gonna be dateless for the Burnstein wedding.'

Araminta 'Minty' Burnstein was the daughter of family friends from Boston. Her wedding to some random shipping heir or other promised to be one of the grandest seen in New York since Liza Minnelli's. Lola had had mixed feelings about going. She hadn't been back to the States or seen her parents since Christmas, but she knew from Nick, who'd spent the holiday at home, that things there were still treading-on-eggshells tense. Minty's wedding would be the first big social event her mom had attended since her dad's affair with Honor became public. Lola wasn't sure she could bear to watch the forced, brittle smiles of people trying to pretend nothing had happened. And what if her mom broke down?

On the other hand it looked set to be an *awesome* party. And Lola Carter had always been an awesome party kind of a girl.

'Wanna be my date?'

Sian choked on her tea, spraying hot liquid and biscuit crumbs all over her copy.

'Me?' she said, cleaning up the mess as best she could with a tea towel. 'You don't want me cramping your style. Anyway, it's not for another ten days. You'll have guys lining up by then.'

'Probably,' said Lola, not bothering to deny it. 'But I really don't wanna bring some guy I barely know. Not to this. And I don't want to go alone, either. I need someone to carry the bucket for me if my dad starts playing the devoted husband and I have to puke halfway through the vows.'

'As glamorous as that sounds,' said Sian, 'I really can't.'

'Why not?' Lola looked crushed.

'I can't afford the plane ticket, never mind a hotel,' said Sian simply. 'Anyway, I ought to be working.'

'You're always working, sweetie,' said Lola. 'It's only one weekend. You could see your mom and dad afterwards,' she added, by way of further incentive.

Sian rubbed her tired eyes, and to her horror found she was on the verge of tears. She tried not to dwell on it too much, but she missed home and Taneesha like crazy.

'I can't afford it, Lo,' she said again. 'And please, don't tell me your dad will pay, OK? We've been through all that a million times.'

Leaning across the table, Lola grabbed her hand. 'I know you don't believe in taking handouts,' she said. 'That's cool. But I already paid for Igor's ticket. It's transferable but it's not refundable. If you don't come, I'm literally gonna have to throw it in the trash.'

'Really?' Sian looked skeptical.

'Yes, really,' said Lola, sensing her resolve weakening. 'Absolutely. And I have a double room at the Four Seasons, also bought and paid for. We can share the bed, have our own girlie slumber party. Oh come *on*! It'll be so much fun.'

Sian wavered. Oh, what the hell.

'All right,' she said, grinning. It really would be wonderful to see her folks. 'Count me in.'

'Yay!' Leaping to her feet, Lola clapped her hands and whooped around the table in an impromptu victory dance. 'Fuck you, Igor. New York, here we come!'

Chapter Seventeen

'I'm sorry, sir, but the captain has switched on the "fasten seatbelts" sign. I'm going to have to ask you to buckle up.'

Lucas opened one eye lazily and looked up at the stewardess. She was young and pretty, but her looks were ruined by the drag queen makeup that airlines seemed to insist upon nowadays – thick brown lip-liner filled in with pink shimmer gloss, too-dark foundation that stopped with an abrupt tide-mark at the jaw line and mascara so thickly caked it was a wonder the poor girl could open her eyelids at all. Combined with her severely pulled-back hair and starched orange and white uniform, the overall look was more dental hygienist than sex siren.

Pity. He could have done with the distraction.

'How long till we land?' he asked, running a hand through his thick curls. One of the few good things about his ignominious firing from the Herrick was that he no longer had to keep the hated Matt Lauer buzz-cut, and could revert to his favored disheveled look. For the flight back to Ibiza he was wearing battered jeans and a faded blue, open shirt with a string of worry beads underneath. No one would have recognized him as the preppy, East Hampton playboy of six months ago.

'Not long now, sir,' said the girl. 'You on 'oliday?'

She was eager to engage this gorgeous man in conversation for as long as she could, and hoped fervently that he might ask her for her number before they landed. Sadly for her, Lucas was in no mood for chit chat.

'No,' he said grumpily, clicking his belt buckle closed

and gazing stonily out of the grimy plastic window. 'I'm going home.'

He'd tried to tell himself that coming back to Ibiza was nothing to be ashamed of. That he was here to visit his mother and brothers, to help out, to do the right thing. But it wasn't working. The truth was he was coming back with his tail between his legs, because he'd failed. And because he'd reached a point where he honestly felt he had nowhere else to go.

Since leaving the Herrick under such a massive cloud last September, his mood had swung violently between deep troughs of self-pity, and murderous, obsessive hatred of Anton, whose weirdly impassive, botoxed face had begun to haunt his dreams. Sometimes it would appear, unbidden, during his waking hours too: after every failed job interview, when door after door was slammed in his face at hotels from Rome to Paris to London. Overnight, Lucas had gone from being the industry's wunderkind to persona non grata. Even the family-run boutiques seemed to have banded together against him. It was as though they were all part of an exclusive private members' club, from which Anton had had Lucas black-balled.

His name was now synonymous with Tina Palmer's infamous sex tape. He could protest his innocence until he was blue in the face, or pay a fortune to have lawyers do it for him, but his reputation was already shot. By October, the clip of Tina snorting coke at the Herrick was the single most downloaded item on the web. By Christmas *Palmer-Gate* had outsold 1 *Night in Paris* by almost three to one. The fact that Lucas could prove that he had never received a cent of its proceeds was apparently immaterial. As manager, he was technically responsible for everything that went on at his hotel. His dismissal from the Herrick was quite legal.

Meanwhile, Anton had been careful to ensure that *he* emerged from the whole sordid affair looking whiter than white. No money from the Pay-per-view could be traced to his accounts either, and his 'friend' Toby Candelle, now a minor celebrity in his own right as Tina's co-star, flat out denied ever having met or spoken to him, which meant it was their word against Lucas's. Two against one. How much had Anton had to fork out to secure that little shit's loyalty? Lucas wondered bitterly. A lot more than thirty pieces of silver, that was for sure.

Ironically, the only person who had ended up doing well out of the tape was Tina herself, Anton's intended victim. She was cautioned over the drug taking, but never charged. And as no one else was stepping forward to take responsibility for the footage, she ended up winning retrospective ownership to the rights herself. When she announced she'd be donating all the proceeds to Guatemalan orphans, Angelina Jolie-style, her media rehabilitation was complete. All of a sudden America couldn't get enough of Tina Palmer.

Lucas, on the other hand, was very far from being forgiven. After over five months of job hunting, he had yet to get so much as a sniff of interest from any of the top-tier hotels in Europe. (He'd already given up on the US, where the press had shat on him so hard, employers could smell him before he walked in the door.) Unless he found something soon, he'd be forced to slide right back down the ladder and take a junior management position in some anonymous chain somewhere. How the mighty had fallen. Then two days ago, to add insult to injury, he'd been skimming through *Hotel World* on the way home to Ben's flat – financial necessity had turned his two-week stay into a semi-permanent arrangement, and the boys were now flatmates – when he saw a double-page spread on the Herrick's new manager.

He recognized her instantly. Her once black hair was now super short and dyed platinum, and her snow-white skin had gained some artificial color over the years. But the cruel, ice-blue eyes were just the same, as was the permanent man-hating sneer that hung over her angular, Slavic beauty like a shroud.

Petra Kamalski.

Surely it couldn't be a coincidence that Anton had hired his old enemy and rival from Lausanne days to be his replacement? It must be his idea of a sick last laugh – a metaphorical kick in Lucas's ribs when he was down. If so, it had worked. When he saw Petra's picture, he felt sick to the stomach.

According to the article, a sycophantic wank-fest obviously written by one of Anton's pet journos, Petra had returned to Moscow after graduating from EHL. Lucas had always assumed she'd shove her MBA in a drawer, marry some other ludicrously wealthy trust-fund bratski, and go off to make Damian babies in a palace somewhere. She didn't need to work, after all. But it seemed he'd misjudged her ambition. After working her way up at the notoriously political Ritz Carlton Group, she'd gone on to become number two at the Palace, the grandest hotel in St. Petersburg. That, in itself, was impressive less than four years out of college. But to go from there to the Herrick was almost as big a quantum career leap as it had been for him, leaving the Cadogan two years ago. She must have made quite an impression on Anton. Or maybe he just recognized a kindred spirit. Lucas couldn't think of anyone who'd make a more perfect bride to Tisch's Frankenstein.

The plane finally landed in Ibiza, and Lucas followed his sheep-like fellow passengers down to baggage reclaim. He made no effort to hide his disdain for the Easter holiday tourists huddled around the lone, rickety conveyor belt. Fat women, squeezed into Bermuda shorts designed to make their ample backsides look even more bovine, stood beside their already drunk husbands – most of them had been stuck into the Boddingtons since before they'd left Gatwick – while their unruly kids jumped on and off other people's luggage, swarming around arrivals in their Man United replica kits like so many red ants.

His own bag, as usual, was practically the last to arrive, which did little to alleviate his foul mood. And when he finally struggled out to the taxi rank, a pixie-like American woman barged past him and shamelessly stole his cab.

'Sorry,' she said, not looking anything of the sort as she flashed him a mouthful of porcelain veneers and chucked her Louis Vuitton tote onto the back seat. 'I'm in a real rush.'

Lucas yelled obscenities after her as the cab sped away. With her scrawny little body, spiky hair and outrageous sense of entitlement, she reminded him of Honor Palmer.

He'd thought about Honor a lot since he'd left America.

'Why don't you call her and apologize?' Ben suggested innocently at Christmas, after Lucas had brought her name up yet again in conversation. 'Put the past behind you.'

'Apologize?' Lucas looked amazed. 'Why the fuck should *I* apologize to *her*?'

'Because you feel bad?' offered Ben. 'Because if you hadn't slept with Tina, and set her up with that guy, and spilled the beans to Anton about Honor and Devon's affair, none of this shit would have happened?'

'That's crap,' said Lucas hotly. 'Firstly, I didn't know the Tina thing was a set-up.'

Ben raised an eyebrow. 'Oh, come on. You must have had your suspicions. Why did you think Anton frog-marched you into bed with her? And why would he go to so much trouble to arrange introductions for a woman he barely knew?'

Lucas scowled. Ben's perceptiveness could be quite annoying at times.

It was true, of course. He had smelled a rat. He simply hadn't cared enough to dig any deeper. Nor had it crossed his mind that *he* might be the one at risk. But he wasn't sure he was ready to admit that to himself yet, never mind Ben.

'Honor has no one to blame but herself,' he said firmly. 'She shouldn't have been screwing around with someone else's husband. Especially not one old enough to be her father,' he added with disgust. 'She deserved to get caught.'

Ben laughed. 'Talk about the pot calling the kettle black! What are you now? The patron saint of fidelity? How many older, married women have you banged in your time?'

Lucas looked sulkily at his shoes and said nothing.

'For fuck's sake, call the woman and straighten things out,' said Ben. 'You know you want to.'

But Lucas was adamant he did *not* want to. Honor was a hostile, self-important cow. *His* life was the one in ruins. Why should he call her?

Despite his loudly proclaimed indifference, he found himself keeping an eye out for references to Honor and Palmers in the press. In the same *Hotel World* article where he'd read about Petra's appointment, the journalist claimed that Palmers had been losing market share to the Herrick at a consistent rate since last summer, and that their bookings for the coming season were at an all-time low. Of course, it might not be true. The writer was clearly a Tisch stooge, and Honor, as usual, had been 'unavailable for comment' and so couldn't confirm or deny the rumors. Since the scandal had broken, she'd become a virtual recluse, leaving it to Tina to bask in notoriety in the pages of the gossip magazines.

Staring out of the window at the scrubby palm trees, battered by the recent gales, and the squat, low-rise apartment buildings that had sprung up like toadstools along the main road from the airport, Lucas felt sad. Every time he came back, this part of the island seemed to have gotten uglier. Soon he'd be in his mother's dingy apartment, doling out what little money he had left like Santa Claus, all the while knowing it would almost certainly be wasted on booze by his stepfather, or sucked into the black hole of the family's debts.

He closed his eyes and let his head flop back against the soft plastic of the headrest. He felt bone weary, but was too wound up to sleep. Instead, as usual, he allowed a picture of Anton's smug, smiling face to float into his consciousness. It wasn't long before he felt his simmering rage bubble up to boiling point.

Some twelve hours later, at just after midnight, he staggered blindly out of a dive bar onto the filthy sidewalk.

'And don't come back, asshole!' the owner shouted after him in Spanish. 'You're lucky my bouncer had the night off. Next time, he'll break both your arms, tough guy.'

Lucas didn't bother to shout back, partly because he wasn't at all sure he could string a sentence together, but mostly because he knew the guy was right. He had been an asshole, picking a fight with two of the patrons over some bullshit politics or other, purely because they were American.

In his defense, it had been one hell of a rough day. He'd arrived at the apartment to find that his mother, at the age of forty-one, was pregnant again – heavily pregnant – a fact she'd omitted to mention in any of their phone conversations of the past six months. Quite apart from the head-fuck of being about to have a baby brother or sister he was old enough to have fathered himself, Ines's pregnancy was yet another financial and emotional pressure thrust onto his already overloaded shoulders. He couldn't deal with it.

In the end they'd had a titanic row about it, with an incoherently drunk Jose and Tito, the only one of Lucas's waster brothers not in prison, both throwing in their two cents' worth, adding fuel to the fire.

'Take it!' he finally snapped, emptying his wallet and pockets of every last note and coin and flinging them hopelessly onto the floor at his mother's feet. 'It doesn't matter what I make; it'll never be enough, will it, Mama? There's always another mouth to feed, another fucking bailiff at the door. You're your own worst enemy.'

He stormed out with the sound of Ines's sobs and his stepfather's slurred abuse still ringing in his ears. Heading straight for San Antonio, he walked into the cheapest bar he could find and set about the important task of drinking himself into oblivion.

Finding himself hurled out onto the street, the cool night air hit him in the face with sobering force. Ibiza in March could be quite cold, and Lucas found himself shivering in just a shirt and jeans. Slinging his one small bag over his shoulder, he set off in the direction of Plaza della Playa, where he hoped one of the cheaper, off-season B&Bs might give him a room, even at this time of night. It was far too cold to sleep on the beach, even warmed from within with whisky as he was.

Without thinking, he turned a corner and found himself standing at the foot of the front steps to the Britannia, the ghastly dive where he'd worked as a teenage no-hoper all those years ago. Looking at the place, it might have been yesterday. Nothing had changed, from the dingy facade with its depressing, peeling paint to the stench of pine disinfectant that wafted out of the lobby and into the street like chemical warfare.

The smell made him retch. And yet some strange impulse seemed to draw him up the steps. Putting one blind foot in front of the other, he soon found himself standing, swaying like a reed in the breeze, in the middle of the deserted reception area.

'Well, well, well.'

The taunting, malevolent voice was accompanied by a slow hand clap. Lucas turned unsteadily around.

'If it isn't the prodigal son returned.'

Miguel, the manager, emerged from the shadows like

a fat, bald genie of the lamp. His face was markedly more lined than when Lucas had last seen him, and his grotesque, wobbling beer belly now protruded a further inch or two from beneath his straining, food-splattered T-shirt. But otherwise he was the same sneering bully he'd always been. Lucas had assumed that even a deadbeat like Miguel would have moved on to pastures new by now. But apparently not.

He looked his old boss up and down as if he had scabies. 'Miguel. What an unpleasant surprise.'

'So tell me.' The manager eased his spreading thighs down into the one threadbare sofa shoved against the wall in reception, and threw his arms wide with exaggerated bonhomie. 'Just how exactly *do* you move from managing a famous Tischen Hotel to flogging home-made porn on the internet? Is that the sort of savvy career move they teach you at EHL?'

But Lucas wasn't playing along.

'You know,' he said, wrinkling his nose in distaste. 'Something smells rotten in here. You'd have thought disinfectant this strong would wipe out all the vermin.' Sniffing pointedly, he looked Miguel right in the eye. 'But I guess not. Will you excuse me? I'm afraid I have to go outside and vomit.'

The poisonous smile melted from Miguel's face.

'Sticks and stones, Ruiz!' he shouted, waddling after Lucas's retreating back like a venomous toad. 'Say what you like about me, but at least I have a hotel to run. You were so full of it when you left, swanning off to Lausanne. Remember your *Luxe*?' he jeered. 'You were going to blow the hotel world wide open. Show us all how it was done. Ha!'

With an effort, Lucas kept walking. What on earth had possessed him to come back to this shit hole?

'But of course, you've come crawling back. Just like I said you would,' Miguel called after him, struggling up from the sofa to follow Lucas out. 'Staying with that junkie slut mother of yours, are you? No wonder you got tangled up with Tina Palmer.' He laughed, a horrible, wet, gurgling sound, like someone drowning in phlegm. 'They say boys are always attracted to girls that remind them of their mamas.'

Lucas had reached the bottom of the steps now and was standing in the plaza. Only one desultory pizza place was still open, its few patrons glued to the big screen above the bar, where Sky Sports was screening a welter-weight boxing match. Miguel was a couple of steps above Lucas, but was short enough to still be at his eye level. Which meant that when Lucas turned around and launched his first punch, a wild swing directed straight at his opponent's nose, Miguel had plenty of time to see it coming. Luckily for him, after so much booze, Lucas's reflexes were not what they otherwise might have been.

Ducking to avoid the blow, Miguel swiftly hit back, landing one of his own right hooks in the pit of Lucas's stomach – this was no time for Queensberry rules – winding him just long enough to land a second blow across the top of his jaw. Jolted, Lucas staggered backwards. Having grown up taking beatings from a powerhouse like Jose, Miguel's feeble efforts were little more than bee stings. But, like bee stings, they were irritating. And the more irritated Lucas got, the less he seemed able to make his tired, drunken body do what he asked it to.

The punters in the pizzeria had turned their attention from the dull televised fight to the much more exciting live action. But it was a bit like watching a small child baiting a bear: Lucas had all the strength, but apparently no idea what to do with it.

Letting out a great, bloodcurdling roar of frustration and rage, he ran head first at the steps like a charging bull. For a split second, Miguel panicked – jammed between solid stone stairs and two hundred pounds of lean, angry muscle, there was nowhere to go. But to his great relief, Lucas lost his footing just at the crucial moment. With a collective, audible gasp, the pizzeria diners watched as his head slammed down onto the bottom step with a sickening, audible crunch.

'Not so high and mighty now, are we?' snarled Miguel, swinging his fat leg back and launching a kick at Lucas's head as if it were a football.

A semi-conscious Lucas merely groaned. Then he lay back as slowly, pixel by pixel, the world faded to black.

When he next opened his eyes, the first thing he was aware of was the drill that seemed to be soaring through his skull and into the soft tissue of his brain. He'd never known a headache like it.

'Where am I?' he groaned, trying to sit up, but instantly regretting it as a wave of nausea slammed into him and he sank back down onto the bed.

'You're in the Euro Clinic Eivissa,' said the middle-aged woman who seemed to have materialized out of the ether.

'The German hospital?' said Lucas, weakly.

'Yes. You were lucky. A German lady at the Plaza Pizzeria called an ambulance for you. The rest of them would have left you there to bleed to death, or freeze.'

Typical. Just his luck to be rescued by a bloody German.

'What happened?' asked the woman.

Fractured memories of Miguel's malevolent face came floating back to him, interspersed with images of his pregnant mother, Anton and, bizarrely, Honor. What was she doing right now? he wondered. This very second?

He still kept a mental picture of her from that first day on the beach, before he knew who she was, when he'd been so unforgivably rude and refused to help her. What was it about Honor that always seemed to bring out the absolute worst in him?

'Lucas?' The woman's voice was back.

How did she know his name? He must have had his driver's licence on him when they brought him in. He couldn't imagine any of his credit cards were left.

'Do you know who did this to you? The German lady said it seemed as though you knew the other man. The two of you were talking . . .'

'No,' Lucas shook his head. 'She must be mistaken. I can't remember anything. Sorry.'

He didn't want to go after Miguel. What was the point? At the end of the day, everything he'd taunted him with was true. Maybe, in a twisted way, he'd done him a favor? Maybe it had to come to this – waking up alone, broke, and bloodied in a strange hospital – for him to finally see the light?

He'd left Ibiza with a dream – to build his Luxe. But somewhere along the way he'd lost sight of it.

Being made manager of the Herrick so young had gone to his head. He'd gotten sucked into this stupid war with Honor Palmer, jumping whenever Anton said jump, like a performing monkey, desperate to hold on to his status as the US hotel world's next big thing. And he'd sacrificed his morals and his judgment in the process.

His vanity, he now realized, had hurt a lot of people. Some of them, like Devon Carter, might have deserved to suffer. But others – Karis, Lola, even to a lesser extent the Palmer sisters – they'd all been collateral damage. The person he'd hurt the most though, ultimately, was himself. It was *his* dreams that had come to nothing. His future that had folded before his eyes, like a house of cards.

He still hated Anton for double-crossing him. And he was still determined to get his revenge. But he would no longer let his hatred consume him. From now on he would focus his energies on something positive.

Tomorrow, Lucas would sit down and rewrite his business plan.

Screw finding a job.

The next time he saw Miguel Munoz, he'd be the owner – not the manager; not, as Honor had once goaded him, 'a paid employee;' but the *owner* – of the best boutique hotel in the world.

'Luxe,' he whispered, under his breath. Even saying the word out loud revived him.

'What was that?' The nurse pricked up her ears. 'Have you remembered something?'

'Yes,' said Lucas, with a smile. 'Yes. As a matter of fact, I have.'

Chapter Eighteen

Honor checked her hair in the elevator mirror and fiddled nervously with her silver and topaz cufflinks. Officially you weren't supposed to wear white to a wedding other than your own, but she hoped her wide-cut Marni trouser-suit would count as oatmeal. Maybe the white rule didn't apply to pants anyway? Or maybe pants were just a total 'no-no' at a wedding? Oh shit, what if they were? If only she weren't so damned nervous.

The Burnstein wedding was the first big social event she'd agreed to attend since last year's scandals. Her first instinct, when the stiff white invitation had landed in her in-tray at Palmers, was to decline, the same way she'd declined everything else she'd been invited to since her affair and Tina's tape were made public. But a series of things had made her change her mind. Firstly, the Burnsteins and the Palmers had been friends for generations. Honor had been mates with Arabella, Minty's elder sister, since grade school in Boston, and had known the bride since the day she was born. Secondly, Billy Malone, her ex-professor, ex-lover and dear friend had been staying with her at Palmers the week the invitation arrived, and had read her the riot act about chickening out.

'Listen, Howard Hughes,' he told her sternly. 'This whole recluse schtick has gotta stop. If you're not careful you'll wind up sleeping in an oxygen chamber and telling people that your cats are like your children. Go to the damn wedding, OK?'

But the deciding factor was when yet another old friend from Boston had called to assure her that Devon and Karis

Carter, who also knew the Burnsteins, would be in Asia that weekend and would categorically *not* be going.

Even so, she thought, wondering if the flash of aquamarine Manolo heel visible beneath the hem of her flared pants was too much, today was gonna be an ordeal. All the questions, the curiosity veiled as sympathy, the stares ... She was dreading it.

Since the very public end of her love affair with Devon, Honor's self-confidence had been at an all-time low. She could understand him wanting to protect his family. After all, she'd devoted all *her* energies to trying to protect Palmers from the fallout (for all the good it did her). Even she could see that saving a hotel was hardly on a par with saving a marriage.

But nothing had prepared her for the brutal way he had simply exorcised her from his life, overnight. Once the worst of the storm had died down, she'd waited for him to make contact. She wasn't expecting hearts and flowers. A simple 'how are you coping?' would have sufficed. 'Sorry,' would have been even better. But what she got was deafening silence.

Because of all the furore about Tina, the story of their affair wasn't allowed to die a natural death in the media. Every time Tina did another interview (which was every other week – the girl knew how to milk a story) Honor and Devon's names would get dragged up again. Honor felt helpless. Her life, her private heartbreak, was being served up as the glacé cherry on the top of Tina's self-made soap-opera-sundae, for people to pick over at their leisure.

To make matters worse, article after article started appearing painting Honor as the scarlet woman, the manipulative home-wrecker. Anyone would have thought she'd drugged Devon, clubbed him over the head and dragged him into bed to rape him.

Not once did he defend her, or lift a finger to contradict this impression in the press. Not once did he call. When the chips were down, he'd abandoned her and their relationship without a backward glance. And Honor didn't see him for dust.

Now, six months later, she was over the heartbreak. Mostly. But she was still left with the nagging doubt that comes from having trusted, deeply, and been so terribly let down. She'd always considered herself to be a good judge of character. But clearly she'd been kidding herself. When it mattered the most, none of her so-called instincts had been worth a dime.

Which was a shame, because right now she needed those instincts more than ever. Things at Palmers were going from bad to worse, and she had no idea how to turn the tide. When the Herrick had first opened, she'd gambled on survival by differentiation, and played the 'old-money, conservative' card for all it was worth. Up until the scandals broke, it had worked. But now her strategy had turned around to bite her. Palmers' guests were the last people on earth to be attracted by notoriety. These were the sort of people who packed their kids off to rehab after one puff of a joint. As for sexual liberalism, most of them viewed even marital relations with distaste, never mind four-in-a-bed lesbian orgies and S&M shows caught on film. With her core client base leaving in droves, Honor had no choice but to change tack and go after the younger, hipper crowd more typically drawn to the Herrick. But to those people, Palmers was the last word in stuffy. It was a classic lose-lose situation.

The elevator came to a stop with a worryingly sudden jolt. But after a few nerve-wracking seconds the doors glided open and Honor stepped out into the hallway.

On the sixty-fifth floor of number thirty, Rockefeller Plaza, the Rainbow Room restaurant with its incredible views, sky-high ceilings and revolving dance floor was the epitome of classic New York chic. It was unashamedly old-fashioned – more Rat Pack than *Sex and the City* – but then

Honor would happily take Sinatra over Carrie Bradshaw any day. Clearly the Burnsteins felt the same way.

On a good day you could see every square inch of Manhattan from up here. But today the March clouds hung low and heavy over the city, and what would have been the view was smothered in mist.

Honor sighed. What a shame.

'I'd offer you a glass of champagne, ma'am.' An elderly waiter in white tie appeared at her side. 'But I'm afraid the service is about to start. Perhaps you'd like to slip in quietly at the back?'

He was a kind man, with that part-of-the-furniture air about him common to staff in grand old restaurants. Honor suspected he'd worked here his whole life.

'Heavens. I thought I was early,' she said. Glancing at her watch she realized belatedly that it had stopped. Damned antiques. 'I can't believe I'm late for a wedding! Maybe I should just wait it out. I'd hate to cause a scene.'

'Wait it out? You mean, miss the ceremony?' The old man looked horrified. 'Nonsense, my dear, we can't have that. Come with me. I'll slip you in there without a fuss.'

Inside the anteroom-cum-makeshift-chapel, Lola was suffering from a serious attack of the giggles.

'Kick me!' she hissed at Sian, her mouth twitching at the corners. 'Pinch me. Do something. I'm gonna lose it in a minute, I swear.'

But Sian wasn't faring much better herself. She was too busy biting back her own mirth to help Lola. The service was so unutterably, cringe-makingly naff, it could have been sponsored by Philadelphia cheese. She wasn't sure what she'd expected from a high-society New York wedding. But it definitely wasn't this.

First, the bride had arrived in a dress so over-the-top wide it couldn't fit through the specially built rose archway. After much po-faced pushing and tugging, she was forced to reverse while the arch was dismantled, with the organist gallantly playing 'Here Comes the Bride' throughout the entire five-minute charade.

'Whoever designed that dress should be shot,' Lola whispered in Sian's ear, as poor Minty, flushed as red as the roses in her bouquet, finally made it to the altar. 'She looks like a poodle that swallowed a hand grenade.'

That comment marked the start of the girls' giggling fit. But it was the vows that really finished them off. Both bride and groom had written their own.

'I love you like the stars love the moon,' intoned Stavros, the groom, who at least had the decency to look embarrassed as he said it. Minty, by contrast, gushed so enthusiastically through her own efforts, she had the entire chapel wincing: '*I* am you. *You* are me. *We* are one,' she bleated.

'She sounds like a frikkin' perfume commercial,' giggled Sian.

'Smells like one too,' said Lola. 'The poor rabbi must be about to pass out. Death by Eternity asphyxiation. I bet that's a medical first.'

Quite apart from the hilarity value, Lola was glad she'd decided to come, and even gladder that she was here with Sian and not Igor the Ego. Nick had bailed at the last minute, an added bonus – apparently the world of global e-commerce would grind to a shuddering halt if he took one weekend off – but her parents had braved the gossips and made it. Sitting two rows ahead of her and Sian, Lola could see that they were actually holding hands, which made her feel strangely but deeply happy. Having said that, her dad looked anxious. He'd lost weight, and hair. The last six months had clearly taken their toll on him, not that he didn't deserve it. But her mom seemed much, much better than she had the last time Lola was home. She was no longer skeletal, but attractively slender, and her cheeks had finally regained some of their former color and glow. It was good to see.

'Hey.' Sian leaned over and whispered in her ear. 'Check it out. Two o'clock. Superman can't keep his eyes off you.'

Lola glanced across the aisle to her right. A tall guy, she guessed in his early twenties, with a shock of jet-black hair and glasses that were indeed *fully* Christopher Reeve, flashed her a fifty-megawatt smile, which she returned.

'He's cute,' said Sian, nudging her in the ribs.

'He is, isn't he?' said Lola, grinning from ear to ear. This wedding kept getting better and better. 'Sold to the girl who hasn't got laid in a week.'

'A *week*?' said Sian, more loudly than she'd intended to, so she had to try to turn it into a cough when people turned around and glared at her. 'Jesus. I haven't had it since last summer. Oh my God. Speaking of last summer . . .'

'What?' said Lola.

'All right, now don't freak out.' Sian laid a restraining hand on her arm in anticipation. 'But Honor Palmer just walked in.'

'No!' Lola went white and her lips pursed in fury. 'She wouldn't dare!'

For the second time, scores of people spun around to look, as Lola raised her voice in indignation. One of them was Devon, who began by scowling at his daughter, but whose frown rapidly morphed into a look of purest panic as he caught sight of Honor, hovering at the back of the room like a ghost.

Lola looked round too and gave Honor a murderous stare. But she needn't have bothered. Honor could see nothing but Devon.

This couldn't be happening.

How could he be here? *How?* He was supposed to be in Asia.

Regaining his composure, Devon looked away, leaving her staring at his broad tuxedo-clad back. He seemed to have developed a sudden intense fascination with the ceremony, which had reached the stage of exchanging rings. Only his stiffened shoulders and the tightness of his arm muscles as he gripped Karis's hand gave away his inner emotional maelstrom.

Meanwhile, Honor's own stomach was flipping cartwheels. If only she could sneak away! But the double doors had been firmly closed behind her, and opening them now would only cause more of a scene. There was nothing for it but to wait it out.

After what felt like an eternity, Stavros was finally invited to kiss his bride, and the vast, lacy meringue that was the new Mrs. Minty Pavlos swayed back down the aisle and out into the lobby. Bolting out of her seat, Honor tried to dash after her. But to her dismay, she found herself being collared by Arabella, the matron of honour, before she could make her escape.

'Oh, Hon, I'm *so* glad you made it. But my gosh, haven't you gotten thin,' she said, hugging Honor tightly.

'I know.' Honor tried to smile. 'It's been a stressful year.'

'Well, sure,' said Arabella understandingly. 'I was so sorry to hear about your dad. And, you know ... that other business.'

'Thanks.' Honor looked longingly toward the exit, but now it was clogged with departing guests. Thankfully, Devon and Karis seemed to have already made their own escape.

'You bitch!'

Honor jumped as Lola, a vision of red-headed righteous indignation, stormed over and physically shoved her back against the wall.

'What on earth ... ? How dare you!' said Arabella, stepping between them. 'What do you think you're doing? This is my sister's wedding, not a bar brawl.'

'I'm not talking to you,' hissed Lola rudely, lunging at Honor again. Her russet curls, which moments ago had been pinned into an intricately formal up-do, now broke free of their restraints and started tumbling down over her shoulders like lava. In a short, green taffeta dress, and no jewellery other than an exquisite pair of emerald and diamond drop earrings that swung wildly now as she flung herself forwards, she looked scary but stunning. Somehow she also seemed much older than Honor remembered her. The innocent little girl of last summer, the kid that Honor had worried about Lucas Ruiz corrupting, had morphed into a fully fledged young woman.

'Lola, listen to me. I didn't know your parents were coming,' she explained. 'I was assured they were in Asia. Otherwise I would never have accepted the invitation.'

'Yeah, right!' spat Lola. 'You fucking liar.'

Arabella Burnstein was a strong woman, but even she was having trouble containing the wildcat Lola as she scratched and clawed to get at Honor. She was very grateful when Sian arrived to help.

'Look, I'm sorry.' A visibly shaken Honor was close to tears. 'I'll go, OK? I'll just go.'

'You'll do nothing of the sort,' said Arabella firmly. 'You're a guest here – *my* guest – and I'll be mortally offended if you don't stay for the reception. You haven't done anything wrong, Honor.' She glared defiantly at Lola.

'Like hell she hasn't!' Lola yelled back. 'She's done nothing but wrong. Bitch!'

Sian finally managed to pull her away, steering her out into the lobby and on toward the bar before things got really out of hand.

'Honestly, Bels,' said Honor, once they'd gone. She was still shaking with shock. 'I don't feel comfortable. I'd rather go.'

'Listen,' said Arabella kindly, 'if you leave now, it'd be tantamount to admitting that you *are* the marriage-wrecker he's made you out to be. Devon was the one who broke his vows, honey, not you. Let him leave if he wants to.'

'But … I'll have to see him. At dinner. And Lola won't let it go. I don't want to ruin Minty's big day.'

'Don't worry about Lola. I'll sort her out. I'll even throw her out if I have to. And you won't have to see Devon at all if you don't want to. There's over a thousand people in that reception, and I happen to know for a fact that your table is about as far from his as it could be.'

Honor looked doubtful.

'Come on,' said Arabella, taking her hand. Apart from a couple of stragglers, they were the last ones left in the chapel. 'You have to come out of hiding sometime. It may as well be now. I'm going to have Johnny fix you a big, fuck-off martini, and then we're walking into that ballroom with our heads held high. OK?'

Honor nodded miserably.

'Good,' said Arabella. She'd make a great White House Chief of Staff. Or head coach at a fat camp. 'Follow me.'

The service itself may have been more farce than fabulous, but the reception was quite another matter. Having safely deposited Lola at the bar in the care of two ushers (unsurprisingly, they were more than happy to devote the rest of their evening to keeping an eye on a show-stopping redhead while she got stuck in to the hard liquor), Sian set off into the throng to star-spot.

Not even at Palmers had she seen so many famous, wealthy people gathered in one room. Socialites, actresses, politicians, fashion designers: everyone was there. Sophia Coppola was loitering glamorously in one corner while in the other the Clintons were chatting with old friends. And not ten feet away stood Lola's long-time role model, Donna Karan, outshining beauties half her age in a simple midnight-blue column dress that clung to her curves like a mud-wrap.

By the time dinner was served, Sian's brain was groaning with names and snippets of overheard conversation. If only she had her notebook with her! Still, with any luck she'd be able to remember enough to put together a witty diary piece that she could pitch to the *Daily Mail* when she got back to London. The Brits pretended to be uninterested in the New York social scene. Since Bush came to power, you could smell the anti-Americanism in London like an over-ripe gorgonzola. But beneath the veneer of disapproval, editors still fell over themselves for insider pieces like this. Especially if they had a decent celebrity angle.

Taking her seat, Sian looked around in vain for Lola at the bar, but she appeared to have vanished.

'Hello.'

She looked up to find Superman had taken the seat next to her.

'Is your friend not staying for dinner?' He gestured forlornly to the empty place opposite Lola's name tag.

'She's supposed to be,' Sian shrugged. 'She's having a micro crisis tonight. Family trouble. I left her at the bar earlier, but she seems to have gone awol.'

His face fell. It was so cute, Sian had to laugh. He looked about two years old.

'I wouldn't worry too much,' she said kindly. 'She'll turn up eventually. If it makes you feel any better, she already told me she thinks you're cute.'

'She did?' The pout evaporated and his face lit up again like a firework.

Obviously, he wasn't much of a liar. Which would make a refreshing change from the two-faced dickheads Lola usually went out with. Sian liked him at once.

'Scouts' honor,' she assured him. 'She likes you. But for now you're gonna have to make do with me, I'm afraid. Sian Doyle.' She thrust out her hand.

'I'm so sorry,' he stammered. 'How rude of me not to introduce myself.' His accent was educated, but deep enough to save it from sounding effeminate. 'I'm Marti. Gluckman. Really, I feel awful. I don't normally behave like a—'

'Goofy teenager?' offered Sian.

'Was I really that bad?' Marti blushed even deeper.

'Fraid so.'

'It's just that your friend is so ... mesmerizing,' he said dreamily.

'So I'm regularly told,' said Sian.

'I couldn't find her after the service, but a guy told me her name. So I ran around every table in here trying to find where she was sitting. Which is more exercise than I've done in years, by the way. Have you seen how many people there are? Goddamn freeloaders.'

Sian laughed.

'Anyway, I finally found her, and I had to beg this weird Armenian guy to switch places with me – I don't know, his English wasn't the best. I think he thought I wanted to sleep with him later or something, but anyway, he moved. But *now*,' he sighed heavily, finally drawing a breath, 'she's not here. Although, obviously,' he added hastily, 'it's terrific to have met you. Sian Doyle.'

Despite this less than auspicious start to the conversation, the two of them were soon chatting away like old friends. Only when Marti nipped off to the loo did Sian realize she'd been completely ignoring the girl sitting on her other side.

'Hi,' she said, turning around, and realizing for the first time that the girl was actually supermodel stunning. Her thick black hair glugged like molasses down her bare back, the only flesh visible in the floor-length, fire-hydrant red dress she was wearing and her skin was that gorgeous, smooth, milk-chocolate color unique to South American women. Combined with her voluptuous figure, wide-set, nut-brown eyes and perfect, naturally full lips, she looked every bit the storybook Inca princess.

Sian was all set to start hating her, but infuriatingly she turned out to be perfectly charming.

'I would have introduced myself earlier,' she said, smiling

319

shyly, 'but you and your boyfriend seemed a bit, you know ... engrossed. I didn't want to put my foot in it.'

'Oh,' Sian laughed, 'he's not my boyfriend. We just met, actually. He wants to put the moves on my friend, but she's already hooked up with a Mr. Jack Daniels, so the poor guy got stuck with me.'

'Really?' said the girl. 'Well, he looked like he was having a great time to me. My name's Bianca, by the way.'

'And I'm Sian,' said Sian. 'So, are you a friend of the bride or the groom?'

'Neither,' said Bianca, lighting up a Marlboro red and inhaling deeply, then blowing the smoke out through her rounded lips in a perfect 'o'. Whoever said smoking was a dirty, unsexy habit had obviously never seen Bianca do it. 'My boyfriend's a friend of Stavros's. An acquaintance, really. We were supposed to come together, but he had some work crisis as usual, so here I am, alone. Again. I know *nobody*.'

'Me neither,' said Sian, recrossing her legs and moving her chair closer to her new friend. 'Lola, the girl I mentioned to you – her family know the Burnsteins. I'm just tagging along for the ride.'

'Well, in that case, we should stick together,' Bianca beamed.

For such a beautiful girl, she really was disarmingly nice.

Marti's trip to the bathroom seemed to have taken a turn for the permanent. For the rest of dinner the two girls chatted away happily, taking the piss out of the more outrageous fashion victims swanning around the room like over-dressed matchsticks. After that, they told each other their own potted histories. Bianca, surprise surprise, was a model, and split her time between New York and London. Sian's life felt so dull by comparison, she skipped most of it, and instead told her new friend about her friendship with Lola, and the background to the earlier drama in the chapel with Honor Palmer.

'So,' she finished finally, wolfing down the last crumb of her meltingly delicious pecan dessert, 'when Lola saw Honor here today, you can imagine. She totally flipped.'

'I'm not surprised,' said Bianca with feeling. 'What a cheek, turning up like that! I've never met the girl, but I've heard a lot about her – most of it bad. But she is very beautiful,' she added, looking across the room to the top table, where Honor was throwing her head back and laughing at some joke of the bride's.

In her simple trouser-suit, Honor was underdressed for the occasion, but somehow the plainness of her outfit only served to emphasize her unique face with its beautiful, hawk-like features.

'I can quite see why your friend's father fell for her,' said Bianca.

She's not half as beautiful as you, thought Sian.

Honor seemed to have taken Arabella's advice to heart and decided to enjoy herself, despite Lola's histrionics. Unlike Devon who, Sian noticed, was sitting next to Karis at the opposite end of the dance floor, looking about as cheerful as a prisoner awaiting the firing squad.

'My boyfriend actually knows her a little bit,' said Bianca.

'Honor?' Sian, still looking at Lola's parents, was only half tuned in.

'Yeah. He ran into her in the Hamptons last summer. A few times I think.'

'Really?' said Sian. 'How funny. I was working out there myself last summer. At Palmers. Small world, huh?'

Bianca nodded. 'My boyfriend stayed at the other hotel, not Palmers. You know, the new one.'

'The Herrick,' said Sian.

'That's it. His best friend used to run it.' Bianca took a long sip of champagne. 'He doesn't anymore, but that's a whole other story.'

Sian felt her blood run cold. 'You mean Lucas? Lucas Ruiz is your boyfriend's best friend?'

'Uh huh,' said Bianca. 'A lot of people didn't want to know Lucas after he got fired. But Ben's never had a bad word to say about him. He's really loyal like that.'

'Oh yeah,' said Sian bitterly, as a creeping nausea rose up from her belly. 'Ben Slater's loyal all right. As long as you're a guy.'

Bianca's eyes widened. 'You know Ben?'

Sian kicked herself. Why couldn't she have kept her mouth shut?

'Er, yes,' she admitted. 'I used to know him. We dated actually.'

'You *did*?' Bianca looked suitably surprised. 'Ben never mentioned he was seeing someone out there.'

'Well, it wasn't serious,' said Sian hastily. 'Honestly. It was like, five minutes. It was nothing.'

She had no desire to open up a conversation about Ben. Bianca was lovely. But it still hurt to think that she'd been traded in for someone so incomparably stunning – and that Ben hadn't even deemed their relationship important enough to mention to his new girlfriend. All at once she felt her confidence oozing away, like air from a slow-punctured balloon.

Gluing on a fake smile for Bianca's benefit, she gave herself a stern talking to. So Ben had moved on. Well, of course he had. Big deal. That was hardly news. It had been six months after all, and they'd dated for only a couple of weeks. Besides, what did she care what he did, or who he was with? He'd accused her of being a gold-digger, let's not forget, and taken the word of a try-hard like Lucas Ruiz over hers. According to Bianca, he and Lucas were still thick as thieves. Who needed him?

'Look, let's not talk about Ben, OK?' she said. 'I'd much rather hear more about modeling. Are the agents really as sleazy as people say they are?'

Bianca smiled. She was evidently as keen to drop the subject as Sian was.

'Honey,' she said conspiratorially, 'you have no idea.'

Meanwhile, in a janitor's closet hidden away next to the ladies' room, Lola Carter was straddling Marti, arching her back and squeezing her muscles tightly around his dick as she came.

'Shhhhh,' he laughed, cupping one hand over her mouth to stifle her full-volume moans. 'Someone'll hear us.'

Marti had been feeling marginally guilty about taking advantage of a girl he'd only just met, and who was clearly very, very drunk. But after Lola had torn his clothes off and leaped on him like a starving animal, his concerns had alleviated considerably. Gazing rapturously at her flushed, happy, post-orgasmic face, he decided she was clearly a young lady who knew exactly what she wanted.

Pushing aside a pile of stacked chairs, sending them flying to the ground with an almighty clatter, she sprawled out on her back and spread her legs wider, grabbing hold of his butt and pulling him hungrily inside her.

'Your turn now,' she grinned.

With her red hair spreading around her like a halo, and her green dress pulled down to the waist to reveal the two large orbs of her breasts, as plump and ripe as grapefruits, she was a vision of desirability. Marti was justly proud of himself for having held on this long, but he didn't have an ounce more restraint in him. Closing his eyes he gave himself up to the slippery, needy warmth of her body and came, driving himself so hard into her that she slipped along the linoleum floor and clunked her skull against the back wall of the closet.

'Ow,' she giggled, rubbing her head as she finally, reluctantly squirmed out from underneath him.

'Sorry,' said Marti. Leaning down he tenderly kissed the bump on her forehead.

Lola smiled. Watching him putting his pants back on, pulling up his zipper and trying to straighten out his disheveled hair, she felt bizarrely affectionate towards him. She didn't make a habit of one-night stands, never mind dragging guys she bumped into outside the ladies' room into dark corners and ravishing them. But the combination of the Jack Daniels, being blindsided by Honor, and Marti's deadly attractiveness seemed to have brought on a bout of temporary insanity.

'You probably think I'm a real slut now, right?' she said, straightening her own dress and scrabbling around in the semi-darkness for her shoes.

'What do you mean "think"?' said Marti. 'I know you are. I have first-hand evidence.'

Lola gasped. He wasn't serious, was he? But she relaxed as she felt his arm snake around her waist. The next thing she knew he was kissing her passionately on the mouth.

'It's a compliment,' he whispered, coming up for air. 'I'm a big fan of sluts. The biggest. You have no idea.'

Lola laughed, a deep, full-bodied cackle. Life was so freaky. Only an hour ago she'd been sobbing into her drink, swearing off men for evermore. And now here she was, half naked in a broom closet with a total stranger, so happy she felt like she was walking on air.

Stavros's ushers had finally abandoned her at the bar at eleven. Even pretty girls got boring when they wouldn't quit crying. Meanwhile, her parents seemed to have forgotten she was even here – neither of them had come over to say hello. Sian was off mingling and having a good time, and fucking Honor Palmer was so deeply embedded with the bride's family, Lola couldn't have got near her, even if she'd been sober enough to try it. Which she wasn't. If she hadn't been so desperate for a pee, she'd probably be slumped over the bar where the ushers had left her. But Cupid, fate and a weak bladder had conspired to bring her and Marti together. And now he'd rescued her from her misery, just like the real Superman.

'Listen,' he said, opening the cupboard door a crack to check the coast was clear. They could hear the Hora, the traditional Jewish wedding dance, in full swing next door. 'I don't know about you, but I'm kind of weddinged out. I don't suppose you want to sneak back to my place?'

'Definitely not,' said Lola teasingly. 'My mom told me never to go with strangers. You could be an axe murderer, for all I know.'

'Me? No way,' said Marti, squeezing her hand. 'I'm a terrible coward. Faint at the first sight of blood. I'm more of the poisoning, smother-you-with-a-pillow type.'

Lola giggled.

'So're you coming, or not?'

'Yes please,' she said, kissing him again.

He wasn't as good-looking as Lucas, or even Igor. But he was fifty times funnier, and nicer. Suddenly she longed to be waking up with him tomorrow, eating bagels in bed like an old married couple. Sian would be OK to find her own way back to the hotel.

Marti took her hand and was just about to slip out into the lobby, when raised voices made them both slink back. Lola felt her heart jump into her mouth, and squeezed his hand even tighter. She recognized the voices. It was her father and Honor Palmer.

'Because I miss you,' Devon was saying. 'That's why. Hell, Honor, can't we even talk to each other anymore?'

'No.' Honor sounded furious. 'We can't. You have some fucking nerve, Devon Carter. Just leave me the fuck alone, OK?'

Grabbing her by the hand, Devon dragged her down the side corridor directly toward the closet where Lola was hiding.

'Get back!' Lola hissed at Marti. He did as he was told, pulling the door almost completely closed, but leaving a crack so Lola could still see what was happening.

Honor, jacketless now, looked so tiny in her aqua shirt and pants she could almost have been a child. She'd always been skinny, but Lola could see now that she'd lost even more weight. Her collar bones visibly jutted out, like a human rack of lamb.

'I know you're angry.' Devon's voice was smooth and conciliatory. 'You have every right to be.'

'Don't tell me about my rights,' Honor snapped, freeing herself from his grip and backing away. 'Or my feelings. You threw me to the fucking wolves!'

'That's not fair,' said Devon. 'I couldn't control what the press were writing. You think it didn't hurt me, too, seeing them lay into you like that?'

'I'm sure you were devastated,' said Honor, witheringly.

'I was, sweetheart. Truly I was.'

Lola winced at the endearment. *Sweetheart*? But painful as it was to listen to, wild horses couldn't have torn her away from that door.

'So devastated, you forgot my number?' Clearly Honor was in no mood to let him off the hook. 'Not one call from you, Devon, in all this time. Not one shred of concern. You let those bastards paint me as the marriage-wrecker, while you sailed off into the sunset with Karis on your little boat of so-called regret. You make me sick.'

'I hardly sailed off into the sunset.' Devon laughed bitterly. 'Life at home has been hell, complete hell. Karis has me under surveillance night and day. I'm trapped. But I don't love her, Honor. I love you.'

Lola gripped Marti's hand so tightly her nails were in danger of drawing blood. He could feel her breathing stop dead.

'After the overdose, I couldn't risk pushing her any farther. For me to defend you in the press, contact you, even mention your name – don't you see? It might have pushed her over the edge. She had me by the balls, sweetheart.'

'What balls?' said Honor.

'Damn right,' Lola whispered indignantly from the closet. Up until now it had been easy to believe what she read in the papers and blame Honor for everything. But suddenly, for the first time, she wondered if maybe her father was the true villain of the piece. A few hours ago, he'd been holding her mom's hand in the chapel, playing the contrite husband. But now here he was, telling his mistress it was *her* he really loved. He was so two-faced, it made Lola's blood curdle.

'Darling, listen to me.' Stepping forwards, Devon laid a hand on Honor's shoulder. 'I think we're over the worst. Tonight, when Karis realized you were here, she was OK about it.'

Honor's eyebrows shot up. *'What?'*

'I mean, she wasn't thrilled, obviously,' Devon conceded. 'But, you know, she didn't insist we go home. She didn't try and confront you.'

'She didn't have to,' Honor shivered. 'Lola did that for her. Not that I blame her, poor kid. After everything we've put her through ...'

'You're not listening.' Devon grabbed her hands.

Despite herself, Honor let him. She hated the fact that the warmth of his palms wrapped around her own still felt so comforting.

'A few months ago Karis would have been in pieces,' he said. 'But today, she didn't even cry. I think this whole mental instability of hers – this depression or whatever it is – I think it's gonna pass. And when it does ...'

'When it does, what?' said Honor.

Bending down, Devon kissed her softly on the neck. 'Well,' he whispered, 'we can carry on where we left off.'

For a second, Honor stood there, stock still, while he nuzzled into her. Then, like someone snapping out of hypnosis, her head whiplashed up and she pushed him away.

'Karis isn't mentally unstable,' she said, ignoring his

frantic hand signals and making no effort to keep her voice down. 'I am. Or at least I was. For ever trusting you in the first place. *My marriage is a sham. We haven't slept together in years*. Jesus. How could I have fallen for that old cliché?'

She was a brilliant mimic, and had his hectoring tone down to a tee. It gave Lola goose pimples to hear her. Was that really what her dad had told her, to get her into bed? Suddenly, Lola could believe it. All his protestations of love and regret to her mother had been a crock of shit too.

'It might be a cliché,' said Devon, doing his best to sound wounded. 'But it happens to be true. Karis and I haven't shared a bed in years.'

'Bullshit!' said Honor and Lola simultaneously. Luckily, Honor's roar of rage drowned out Lola's furiously hissed whisper.

'Lola told Lucas she had to put earplugs in at home to block out the sound of you guys making love through her bedroom wall,' said Honor. 'Lucas told me all about it.'

'And you believe Lucas Ruiz over me?' said Devon, indignantly.

'I didn't at the time,' said Honor. 'I loved you, God help me. But now? Now I'd believe Osama Bin Laden over you, Devon.'

'But Lucas was the one who exposed us! If it weren't for that little shit, we'd still be together.'

'Well, in that case, he did me a favor,' said Honor. 'I'll have to write and thank him.'

And turning on her heel, she stormed off.

Only once Devon had gone too and he was sure they were alone again, did Marti speak.

'You OK?' he asked Lola, pushing open the closet door and stepping out into the light. But one look at her tear-streaked face told him the answer.

'Not really.' She shook her head miserably. 'Let's just get out of here.'

*

Honor was already downstairs, scanning the deserted streets in vain for a cab. Above her the night sky, its natural blackness stained by the dim orange glow of the city's light pollution, rumbled ominously. At first the rain fell in slow, heavy drips that burst like water balloons on the sidewalk. But it wasn't long before the ponderous early splashes had turned into a full-scale torrent that left her soaked to the bone.

The rain was so cold it made her gasp. But at the same time, it was exactly the physical shock she needed. Soon she was laughing out loud as she skipped about in the puddles. Maybe she really *was* losing it.

She'd expected to feel pain after her conversation with Devon. Or shock, or disillusionment, or regret. Something bad, anyway.

But in fact, the overwhelming sensation was relief. It was as if some terrible, heavy weight had been lifted from her shoulders. But when it was set down in front of her, she could see that it wasn't a boulder at all. It was nothing but a tiny, insignificant pebble all along.

Falling in love was incredible. But falling *out* of love, she now realized, could be even better.

At last the scales had fallen from her eyes completely. She had herself back. And for the first time in years – probably since before her mother died – she felt truly, deeply content.

Chapter Nineteen

A year to the day after the Burnstein wedding, Lucas stood in the newly finished lobby of his new hotel, Luxe Ibiza, feeling like Lazarus risen from the ashes. All the new building smells still lingered: varnish mingled with sawdust and drying paint, overlayed by the scent of freshly laid turf which wafted in through the open French windows. Lucas inhaled joyously.

In a few weeks, all these smells would be gone, replaced by the ubiquitous aroma of calming lavender. Lucas had already received the first shipment of scented Dyptique candles from Paris – expensive but worth it – and the midnight-blue gas lamps that would burn essential oils of lavender and cedarwood in each suite should arrive in the morning. A local artisan glass blower had made the lamps for next to nothing, with his brother throwing in the hand-pressed oils at an even more outrageously knocked-down price. They should have asked more. Lucas would happily have paid them. Local, natural products were at the core of the Luxe ethos, and he was quite prepared to pay a premium to get the ambience of his new hotel pitch-perfect.

Connor Armstrong, his Irish partner and financial backer, was a pompous, preening prick of a man and a pain in Lucas's ass on many levels. But at least he knew better than to try to tinker with Lucas's artistic vision. The twelve bedroom suites and two guest studios were all furnished with low, unfussy teak beds, decked out in old-fashioned starched white linen. Lucas was allergic to those stupid little decorative cushions so beloved of other luxury hotels, and to beds piled high with enough pillows to give people neck ache. At Luxe, nothing was extraneous. Flower arrangements were simple and fresh, with lots of greenery. Artwork was minimal and calming, mostly local landscapes, mixed up with the odd interesting antique map or illustrated page from an old book. Every room had an open fire, the pine logs carefully chosen for their scent and crackle, and was well stocked with books to suit every taste and inclination. There were no televisions, no ghastly piped muzak, nothing to remind his guests that only a few miles below them, at the bottom of a hill scattered with olive trees, was the neon, drug-fuelled buzz of Europe's most infamous party island.

Stepping through the open windows into a central court-yard garden overhung with faded pink roses, Lucas offered up a little prayer of thanks. Sometimes he still found it hard to believe that he'd actually made it this far, that his fantasy had at last taken solid, physical shape. Two weeks from now they'd be open for business.

He could still remember the phone call he'd made to Ben last June, the day that Connor had agreed to back him.

'I've done it!' he panted breathlessly, leaning against the plastic wall of a phone box in Santa Eulalia.

'You have? That's great!' said Ben, who had no idea what he was talking about but didn't want to burst his bubble by asking. He'd only heard from Lucas twice since he'd gone back to Ibiza. The first time he'd been drunk out of his mind, rambling incoherently about Anton and Petra and the great injustices of the world. The second time he was sober as a judge, but also deeply depressed. He'd insisted that he was going to turn his life around, and that he wouldn't call Ben again until he had. That was six weeks ago, and he'd been as good as his word, not even leaving a number or address where a worried Ben could get in touch with him.

'I've got a backer for Luxe,' said Lucas excitedly.

It took Ben a moment to remember what Luxe was: the

fantasy hotel that Lucas had been banging on about ever since they first met in Murren, all those years ago.

'Wow,' said Ben. 'Who?'

'A guy called Connor Armstrong,' said Lucas. 'You remember him, right? He used to drink at the Cadogan sometimes. Irish. Bit of a twat.'

More than a bit, thought Ben, but all he said was, 'Sure, I remember.'

Connor was exactly the sort of smug, self-important tosser that gave bankers a bad name; a man who considered it a great joke to harass his secretaries, or tell the minimum-wage Pakistani janitor in his office how much he'd spent on dinner the night before. He wore too much aftershave, spoke too loudly on his mobile phone and affected a nause-ating mid-Atlantic accent that made him sound like a local radio DJ from Hemel Hempstead trying to be cool.

'I didn't know he was in the hotel business.'

'He isn't,' said Lucas. 'Well, he is now, but he wasn't. He's in property. He made some canny deals in Marbella; villas, condos, tourist apartments, that sort of thing. He's done well.'

'I don't doubt it,' said Ben truthfully. The assholes always did.

'Anyway, now he wants something in Ibiza. I told him about my ideas for Luxe, and he was sold.'

'That's terrific,' said Ben. 'How d'you convince him?'

Lucas made a grunt that seemed to imply he didn't understand the question. 'I didn't have to *convince* him,' he said. 'He knows any hotel of mine will be the coolest thing to happen on this island since Manumission. Why wouldn't he want in?'

Ben smiled, but said nothing. It was a relief to hear some of the old Ruiz arrogance making a comeback. Without it, Lucas just wasn't Lucas.

As it turned out, it wasn't just idle boasting. From the beginning, there was a buzz of excitement on the island about the Luxe project that gave Lucas an incredible frisson and fuelled his already rampant ambition. The name alone seemed to have a sort of magic to it, generating hype and anticipation even before the first brick had been laid. Leveraging off that magic for all he was worth, Lucas worked inhuman hours to get the thing off the ground, whirling like a dervish from supplier to supplier and breathing down the necks of his builders like a jealous lover.

Knowing that Petra Kamalski had replaced him at the Herrick only added to his sense of inner urgency. It wasn't enough to build a great hotel. Luxe had to be *the* greatest, the boutique David that would one day bring down the Goliath Tischen brand, and with it both Petra and her scheming two-faced bastard of a boss. As far as Lucas was concerned, Ibiza was just the beginning. Once he'd achieved success here, he could tweak the concept, ironing out any early glitches or issues, then roll his Luxes out across Europe and, eventually, America and Asia too.

Unfortunately, Connor turned out to be rather less of a big thinker. From the beginning he'd moaned on like an old woman about 'risk.' And that was just on the Ibiza project.

'It's too remote,' he whined, the first time Lucas drove him up to the site he'd found, high up in the hills close to where he was born. He'd chosen it because land was still relatively cheap up here, and the views were nothing short of spectacular.

'No one's gonna want to hike all the way up here,' said Connor gloomily. 'They'll need a chopper just to get to the clubs at night.'

'Fine,' said Lucas stubbornly. 'We'll build a helipad.'

A screaming match ensued, but Lucas eventually got his way. His raw energy and natural flair, combined with Connor's cash and contacts, acted like rocket fuel, propelling the building work forward at a frightening speed despite Connor's 'cup half empty' attitude and almost ceaseless nay-saying. Lucas acted as architect, project manager and PR chief rolled into one. Having had every detail of the plans in his head since he was a teenager, he was damned if he was going to pay some outsider to come and tinker with them, wasting money and time on sketches and pie charts.

He'd also learned a number of lessons from building the Herrick. All the construction workers on the Luxe site, down to the lowliest plumber's assistant, had their pay tied firmly to deadlines. The result was that now, a mere ten months after construction began, the hotel was finished. And a fucking work of art she was too.

'Fuck you, Anton Tisch!' Yelling at the top of his lungs, Lucas listened as his voice ricocheted off the walls and steep hillside in a volley of echoes. With the contractors finished, paid and sent home, he had the place entirely to himself – king, at long last, of his castle.

'Fuck you, Petra!' he roared, sending a second ripple of sound off in pursuit of the first. 'I'm back! Lucas Ruiz is *fucking back!*'

Annoyingly, he was interrupted mid-shout by a buzz from his inside jacket pocket.

'Yes?' he barked grumpily into his battered old Motorola. But seconds later the annoyance was gone, and his face suffused by a broad grin.

'That's wonderful! How long are you here?' he asked, picking up a stray pebble and hurling it high into the air, then watching it fall out of sight into the depths of the valley below.

'Tonight then. At seven.' He laughed, shaking his head as he hung up the phone.

Well *that* was a turn up for the books. It looked as though his already glorious day was about to get even better.

Bounding up the gravel path a few hours later, clutching a chilled bottle of Moët and a fistful of wild daisies he'd picked on the way, Lucas rapped loudly on the front door with his fist.

God it felt strange to be here! The last time he'd been in this garden – three years ago now, although it felt like thirty – he'd been running the other way, taking off down the hill like a bat out of hell before old man Leon could get his hands on him. He remembered his feelings so clearly: the panic and adrenaline, mingled with the joyous rush of the great sex he'd just had, and an overwhelming urge to burst into laughter. Nothing had seemed very serious to him then. Now, he thought with a pang, everything did.

But his gloomy thoughts were banished the next moment as the door swung open and he found himself face to face with a gloriously naked Carla.

'Querido,' she breathed huskily. 'Flowers, for me? You shouldn't have.'

Gazing in unashamed admiration at her body, he wondered if she'd had any work done since he last saw her. If she had, then her surgeon deserved a medal of honor. She must be, what, forty-seven now? But her skin showed no signs of crepiness and her breasts, as brown and full as coconuts, the tiny pale pink nipples standing to attention to greet him, were as firm and high as ever. Her dark hair had been cut shorter and dyed a striking, deep red, but it suited her. And her bush, he noticed with delight and amazement, had been trimmed and shaped by some extortionate pubic topiarist into the shape of a heart, and dyed to match the hair on her head. In nothing but a pair of red Louboutin stilettos and a diamond choker, she looked like every schoolboy's fantasy, with only a few faint fans of lines around her eyes and lips to indicate middle age.

Dumping the bottle and flowers unceremoniously on the floor, Lucas gathered her up in his arms without a word and carried her straight up the stairs.

'That way,' she giggled, pointing to a door at the end of the corridor as he burst into bathrooms and offices, looking for a bed. Following her directions, he carried her to

335

what he assumed must be the marital bedroom and laid her gently down on the black satin counterpane.

'Very Ozzy Osbourne,' he said, clocking the deep red velvet curtains and vast, black onyx sculpture of a panther at the foot of the bed. 'I wouldn't have thought old Pepe had it in him.'

'That's Rex,' said Carla, nodding at the panther as she fumbled with the buttons on Lucas's fly. 'He's supposed to protect me from intruders when Pepe's away. Symbolically, obviously.'

'Well, he's doing a pretty lousy job,' said Lucas, freeing his rock-hard erection at last and boring into her like a freight train.

Carla gasped at the force of him. He hadn't even taken his shoes off, so desperate was he to get inside her. Though it was over quickly, she was gratified that he hadn't lost any of his skill or generosity as a lover, going down on her afterwards for a languorous twenty minutes until she had come twice herself. Pepe went down on her occasionally, usually on Valentine's day or their anniversary, but he always made her feel as though he were bestowing some hugely irksome favor. With Lucas, she felt like an ice-cream that he was taking his sweet time to enjoy. It was pure heaven.

Afterwards they showered together, dressed and went downstairs to the kitchen, where Carla put together a simple supper of cold meats, salad and a perfect Spanish omelette, washed down with plenty of chilled Chablis. As it was still so warm they ate out on the terrace, drinking in each other's company, the heady scent of bougainvillea, and the beauty of the view, which looked even more lovely in the milky moonlight than it did by day.

'You have to come up and see her before you leave.' Lucas, who'd talked about nothing but Luxe since they'd rolled out of bed, was still waxing lyrical. 'You were the one who made her possible, after all. If it hadn't been for you, for your inspiration and help and support—'

'You'd have made it anyway,' said Carla, pouring herself a third glass of wine. 'No, don't shake your head at me, Lucas. You were the most ambitious man I'd ever met back then. I suppose you still are now,' she added dreamily.

Lucas's face darkened. 'My ambitions have changed,' he said grimly. 'It's not only about personal success anymore.'

'Oh?' Carla looked at him questioningly. His features had set hard and the veins on the back of his hand, she noticed, stood up like swollen tree roots as he clenched the stem of his wine glass. 'What is it about, then?'

A muscle in Lucas's temple twitched involuntarily. 'Revenge,' he said quietly. 'It's about revenge.'

He told her the whole story, of how Anton had set him up and blackened his name throughout the industry.

'It wasn't enough to get rid of me at the Herrick,' he said bitterly, stabbing at the remnants of the omelette on his plate with a fork. 'He wanted me bankrupt, ruined. He tried to take away everything I've ever worked for.'

'Why would he do that?' asked Carla rationally.

'How the fuck do I know?' said Lucas, getting increasingly irate. 'Because he's a fucking psychopath. He even tracked down Petra fucking Kamalski and hired her as my replacement.'

'The girl from EHL?' Carla remembered Lucas's passionate rages about Petra from years ago. Privately, she'd always thought his hatred of Petra was at least partly fuelled by sexism. Much as she adored him, Lucas had always been pretty unreconstructed when it came to women in the workplace, particularly women who threatened to outperform him. But she wisely kept her thoughts to herself.

'Yeah, can you believe it?' said Lucas furiously. 'He pulled her out of the Ritz in Moscow, *hugely* over-promoted her.'

'Look who's talking,' teased Carla gently.

'That was different,' snapped Lucas. Clearly, he wasn't in the mood for banter. 'Look, I'm sorry,' he said. 'I don't mean to take it out on you. But you don't understand. Anton's evil and so is that bitch.'

Getting to his feet, he wandered over to the edge of the terrace. Below him, the olive groves glowed an eerie white-gray in the moonlight, and beyond them the calm waters of the Mediterranean stretched out like a giant sheet of silver foil. Coming up behind him, Carla slipped her arms around his waist and pressed her lithe, soft body against his. She could feel the tension coiled inside him like a mattress spring about to snap.

'Be careful,' she whispered softly. 'Tisch is a very powerful man, and not just in the hotel world. From what I've read he has a lot of contacts in Russia still, and those guys don't mess around. You might end up with Polonium 210 slipped into your tea.'

Turning around, Lucas kissed her tenderly on the forehead.

'Don't worry,' he smiled. 'I don't drink tea.'

But Carla did worry. It was wonderful to see him bouncing back after all he'd been through, and she didn't doubt he would make a roaring success of his new hotel. But he was still so headstrong and stubborn, and now he was determined to make an enemy of one of the most powerful men in the world. She only hoped he'd come to his senses before Tisch decided to finish the job he'd started, and wipe Lucas off the map once and for all.

Chapter Twenty

Essex in the autumn could really be quite beautiful, thought Ben, putting his foot down and pushing his trusty Mini Cooper to a chassis-rattling sixty miles per hour. As soon as you turned off the M11 it was all wooded lanes and half-timbered thatched cottages, their chimneys smoking a welcome amid the chill wind and the swirling, golden tumble of autumn leaves. Everyone associated the county with dumb blondes and blank, faceless suburban towns. Both of which existed, of course – his own parents lived in probably the blankest, most faceless of them all. But there was a lot more to Essex than bimbos and council housing.

Maybe one day he'd move down here with a young family of his own. Buy somewhere rural. Have ... pigs. Or something.

Or maybe not.

A lot had changed in Ben's life in a few short years. His fund, Stellar, had had its third rough quarter on the trot, which was bizarre, given their investment performance had held steady in a very dicey market. But for some mysterious reason, his investors kept redeeming their shares and jumping ship to Excelsior, Anton Tisch's fund. Three years ago, Ben had been almost neck and neck with Anton at around the five billion mark, but now Excelsior was the clear market leader, hoovering up the Russian money flooding into London at a rate that none of its rival funds could compete with. It was depressing.

Today, though, business woes were the last thing on Ben's mind. He was driving home for the weekend, which ought to have been relaxing, if it weren't for the fact that he knew he'd get a grilling about his love life. The moment he walked through the door, his mum and sisters were bound to strike up their familiar refrain – the one that sounded like a train gaining momentum and was about as difficult to stop: Marry Bianca, Marry Bianca, Marry Bianca.

Grinding the gear stick belatedly up into fifth – no wonder his poor car sounded so wheezy – he wondered again how he might try to change the subject. Last time his dad had taken pity on him and dragged him down the pub to watch the football, but Ben doubted he'd be so lucky again today. Apparently Dad got a right ear-bashing about it afterwards. Ben could just picture his poor father, trying in vain to defend himself from three screaming Slater women, all intent on frog-marching their precious boy to the altar.

The problem was, he really didn't have an answer for their biggest question: *why* didn't he propose? Bianca was wonderful, a real gem. Beautiful, smart, devoted, funny – he couldn't think of a single thing about her that he'd change. She'd moved into his Kensington flat a year ago after a year and a half of dating, and to this day had yet to get on his nerves, which was quite a feat. Even more amazingly, she seemed to be suffering from some sort of rare glaucoma that blinded her to his own all-too-obvious faults: the midnight crisp-eating, the hopeless fashion sense, the complete inability to put the loo seat down after having a pee. All this on top of the fact that he was no Brad Pitt, whereas Bianca could give Angelina a run for her money any day of the week.

She loved him. And in his own way, Ben loved her back. But the idea of marriage still made his blood run cold, which was something he couldn't explain to himself, never mind his matrimony-crazed mother.

Passing Thorney Bay, he felt a wave of nostalgia wash over him. He used to come here sometimes as a kid, looking at the lights from the caravan park across the water and dreaming of making it big amid the even brighter lights of London.

By all objective standards, Canvey Island was a dump: rampant unemployment, blocks of flats and cheap-as-chips housing that must have looked awful even before the decades of neglect, sea wind and graffiti had worn them down. Nothing to do but hang out at the waterfront drinking miniature bottles of Baileys and trying to get off with girls. But Ben had happy memories of the place. It would always be special to him.

'Blimey. At last. What time d'you call this?' Nikki, the younger of his two sisters, came running out as he pulled the Mini into the forecourt of his parents' house. 'Mum's going spare. She 'ad dinner ready quarter of an hour ago.'

With her short-cropped peroxide hair and uncompromisingly tight stonewashed jeans, Nikki had never fully grown out of her Roxette phase. But she was very pretty in an eighties throwback, Essex sort of a way. And she took good care of her body, which was more than Ben could say for himself right now.

'You've put on weight,' she said cheerfully as he climbed out of the car. 'Lard arse.'

'Fuck off,' he responded, kissing her and linking arms as they walked up to the house.

'Where's Bianca?'

Ben sighed wearily. 'I told you. She's in New York, on a job. She does work you know.'

Like all successful models, Bianca traveled a lot. Though he didn't like to admit it, Ben suspected that her long absences might be part of the reason that they got on so well when they were together. Any relationship comprised of a series of joyous reunions strung together was going to seem fresher and more passionate than one based on the predictability of daily routine. More passionate than marriage, in other words.

'What if she meets another bloke out there?' Nikki raised

an eyebrow in warning. 'Someone who ain't afraid to make an honest woman out of her?'

They hadn't even got indoors yet, and already she was off on one.

'She meets loads of blokes, all the time,' said Ben, 'and most of them look like Freddy bloody Lundberg. What can I say?' he shrugged. 'I guess she must have a thing for lard-arsed commitmentphobes. Hello, Mum.'

He bent down to kiss his mother, who looked adorably furious in her apron with a wooden spoon in hand. Dear old Mum, she did love her props. They all knew that 'dinner,' whatever it was, would have come straight out of a Findus packet and that the only kitchen implement she'd actually have used was a fork for piercing the film lid several times. But Eileen Slater was not a woman to let insignificant details like that spoil her sense of occasion.

'You're late, Benny. No Bianca?' She made a great theatrical show of hunting for his missing girlfriend, as if he might have hidden her in a pocket. But her son was so big, and she was so small, it was like watching a penguin trying to see around an iceberg.

Ben rolled his eyes to heaven.

This was going to be a long afternoon.

Lunch passed predictably enough. Ben fielded the questions and accusations as best he could, in between mouthfuls of Birdseye Sunday Special: incinerated strips of roast beef, smothered with gravy so thick it almost certainly qualified as a solid, which he soaked up with floury roast potatoes and three Yorkshire puds, earning himself a reproachful 'steady on, Geoff Capes' from Nikki.

By the time the Iceland trifle arrived in all its quivering, gelatinous, artificially colored glory, conversation had mercifully turned to other matters.

''Ere, look at this.' Ben's dad shuffled over to the sofa to retrieve the travel supplement from one of the Sunday papers. 'That's your mate, isn't it? El Spic-o.'

Like everyone of his generation from Canvey Island, Rog Slater peppered his speech with racist, sexist and generally politically incorrect references. But you wouldn't find a kinder man in England, and Ben had long ago ceased to be offended.

'His name's Lucas, Dad,' he said, patiently. 'And yeah, that's his new hotel. Looks brilliant, doesn't it?'

It was only a little over a year since Luxe Ibiza had opened her doors, to rave reviews in travel supplements all across Europe. Never one to let the grass grow under his feet, Lucas had already capitalized on his early success and launched the second hotel in his franchise, a chi-chi urban boutique in Paris.

The article was a double-page spread of the sumptuous new Luxe, a tiny townhouse off the Boulevard St. Germain. So discreet it was practically invisible from the outside, inside it was an oasis of luxurious tranquillity, with the sort of minimalist, less-is-more glamor that only Lucas could pull off. In contrast to the white walls of his Ibiza flagship, he'd opted for a warmer decor of claret-red velvets and deep-green baize, though it was still lit exclusively by candlelight. To Ben's untrained eye it looked part spa, part bordello and part eighteenth-century salon. The pictures were out of this world.

'Let me see.' Karen, his other sister, snatched the paper off him and spread it open on the dining table so her husband could look too. 'Oooo,' she cooed. 'Very nice. D'you think you could get us mates rates, Benny?'

Ben laughed. None of his family could resist a bargain.

'Dunno,' he said. 'I can certainly try.'

Although back in semi-regular touch, he hadn't actually seen Lucas since the launch party for the Ibiza hotel last summer. It was a great night, not least because Lucas and Bianca had hit it off famously.

Wrapped around Ben like a wood nymph in a pale green, chiffon wisp of a dress, she'd proclaimed herself to

343

be a fully paid-up fan of the Luxe 'aura,' complimenting Lucas on everything from the canapés to the candle-lit rock pools.

'They look so natural, like the garden of Eden. Hey, maybe Ben and I should go skinny dipping later? This is Ibiza, after all.'

Ben blushed and mumbled something suitably English about not wanting to frighten the horses. After she'd gone, Lucas drew him aside.

'Stunning girl,' he said approvingly. 'Congratulations. You see? I told you you could do better than that anemic little maid from Palmers, didn't I?'

Ben could recall that comment now as if it were yesterday, could still feel the way it had sent his stomach lurching like a free-falling elevator. Even now, thoughts of Sian still bothered him. It bothered him that they bothered him.

'You finished, darling?'

His mum's voice brought him back to the present with a jolt.

'Yes, thanks,' he said, handing her his empty trifle bowl. 'It was really delicious.'

Eileen blushed, as happy with the compliment as if she'd made the dessert herself from scratch, and handed him a mug of his favorite PG Tips, with two bourbon biscuits for dunking. 'Take those through to the lounge, if you like,' she said.

The family decamped en masse to the enormous living room, sinking themselves into the various super-sized World of Leather sofas and continuing to ooh and aah over Lucas's new Paris hotel. The rest of the Sunday papers were still on the dinner table and Ben hung back, having caught sight of the lurid red print of the *News of the World* at the top of the pile. Flipping the pages idly, he wondered if Sian would have a byline in this week.

Ever since she'd graduated to the features desk at the

infamous Sunday gossip rag, Ben had become a regular reader.

Bianca couldn't understand it.

'But it's such a horrible paper,' she pointed out each week, when he guiltily handed over his eighty-five pence to the newsagent. 'All they do is prey on people, trying to break up marriages and wreck families. Why on earth do you buy it?'

'Good football coverage,' was his stock, lame excuse. He felt bad lying, but there was no point in rocking the boat with B by telling her Sian was a columnist. Since Bianca had actually met Sian two years ago, at that New York wedding – what sort of sick celestial sadist had sat his girlfriend next to his ex, for God's sake? – she'd had a face to put with the name, and as a result had always maintained a slightly anxious curiosity about her and Ben's relationship.

There was no way he could excuse his interest in Sian's writing without sounding suspect. And he couldn't very well tell the truth: that reading her pieces gave him a strange sensation – part pride, part nostalgia, part something else he couldn't quite put his finger on – that had become weirdly addictive. Putting his personal feelings aside, she was a terrific writer. He loved her unique brand of acerbic wit, and often found himself laughing out loud at things she'd written, taking the piss out of some fat-cat politician in the withering, deadpan voice he remembered so well from their brief summer together.

He still regretted the way things had ended between them. With hindsight, he could see he'd overreacted. What the hell had he been thinking, taking love-life advice from *Lucas* of all people? Lucas, who wouldn't know true love if it bit him in the arse and whistled Dixie? It was like asking Donald Trump for a lesson in humility. He'd like to have had the chance to say sorry, at least. But the moment for apologies had long since passed. Sian probably wouldn't even remember him. And anyway, he had Bianca now.

Even so, he'd lost count of the times he'd sat in front of his screen at work, struggling to compose a suitably casual email, congratulating her on her writing and just saying hello. But he always lost his nerve before he pressed send.

'Ben!' Nikki crept up behind him and made him jump. Why were all the women in his family cursed with voices that sounded like pneumatic drills boring into bedrock? 'What are you doing hiding in here? We all want to talk to you about Bianca. You needn't think you're off the hook.'

'Heaven forbid,' muttered Ben, shutting the paper like a guilty teenager caught fingering a porno mag and walking into the other room to face the inevitable music.

Chapter Twenty-one

A few days later, in a restaurant overlooking the Seine, Lucas leaned back in the comfort of his padded Louis XIV chair and inhaled deeply and luxuriantly on a Gitane. His temporary move to Paris had provided a perfect excuse to take up smoking again. In fact, without his pack a day of lethally strong French cigarettes, he doubted he would have made it through the stress of the last two months.

Hotel construction was always hell, but French contractors were a unique breed of nightmare. The union regulations here made Ibiza look like a walk in the park, and the local officials took more bribes in a week than your average banana republic dictator saw in a year. But somehow, after untold sleepless nights and near misses, they'd pulled the thing off. Luxe Paris was open for business.

Come to think of it, 'they' was probably pushing it. In Ibiza, Connor had shown a token interest in proceedings, but he'd been against the Paris hotel from the start, leaving Lucas to carry the can completely solo. Not that he minded. He preferred to work alone, and was finding Armstrong's worry-wort tendencies increasingly annoying. The business was taking off faster than either of them had imagined, and global interest in the Luxe brand was already building at a satisfyingly robust pace. But while Lucas sprinted to meet these challenges full of optimism and energy, Connor had hung back in the shadows like a nervous old woman, muttering about the dangers of over-extending and the importance of sticking to the business plan.

If it carried on much longer, Lucas would have to start scouting around for a new backer, although buying Connor out wouldn't be easy. But for now, sadly, they were still in this together, and he struggled to hide his irritation over lunch, as Connor regaled him with one self-aggrandizing anecdote after another. Christ, the man could bore for Ireland.

'Do you enjoy your meal, messieurs?'

The shy, very young waitress serving them blushed as she presented their bill. Lucas, for one, welcomed the interruption to Connor's interminable monologue and smiled at her warmly. But Connor was annoyed.

'I've had better,' he said gracelessly. 'But don't worry, love. I always tip pretty waitresses, no matter how crap the chef.' He winked and, pulling out a wad of hundred-euro notes, allowed one to flutter down on to the table like a falling leaf, as if to indicate how little it meant to a man as rich as himself.

'Oh, non, non, monsieur.' The girl shook her head. '*C'est trop*. Is far too much. I bring you change.'

'It's nothing,' leered Connor. Reaching around, he groped her ass so blatantly the poor creature jumped a mile. 'Now take it and skedaddle, all right, gorgeous? Before I get carried away.'

Lucas felt his fists twitching. Jerk. It was all he could do not to lean over the table and slam Connor's boorish features down on the wood so hard his nose would break. But he managed to restrain himself. Until he had another partner lined up, he needed Connor.

'So,' Connor smiled, unaware anything was wrong. 'The Herrick's been nominated in the Relais Chateaux rankings. D'you see that? Apparently it's a two-horse race between them and the Post Ranch for the number one spot. I bet your mate Anton's chuffed.'

Lucas inhaled even more deeply on his cigarette and struggled to keep his temper. To Connor, his rivalry with Anton and Petra had always been a big joke. But this was one subject about which Lucas would never see the funny side.

'When are *we* gonna get that kind of recognition, eh?' Connor delighted in pushing his buttons.

'When you bung me enough money to buy off the judging panel, you clueless fuckwit,' was what he wanted to say. But he settled for a more straightforward lie.

'I'm not interested in the Herrick,' he said stubbing out his cigarette so violently that it snapped in two. 'They're welcome to their five minutes of fame. Relais Chateaux don't know their arse from their elbow, anyway.'

In fact, ever since the nominations were published last week, Lucas had been consumed with a rage so violent he could barely sleep. Not that he wasn't enjoying his own fair share of recognition: if Anton was the industry's god, and Petra its queen bee, then Lucas was without doubt its favorite prodigal son. Word was spreading that Luxe Ibiza and now Luxe Paris were *the* hot new vacation destinations in Europe, and with only fifteen rooms apiece, competition for prime season bookings was fierce. The Ibiza hotel's waiting list already read like a Who's Who of the European A-List, and Lucas had no doubts that even the notoriously sleepy Relais Chateaux would catch on to their success eventually.

But with the Herrick up for the number one spot, his own success suddenly lost all its sweetness. Nor had it escaped his notice that all but one of the names in the top five were American hotels. Conquering Europe was no longer enough. He had to claw his way back into the US market, and blow Anton Tisch out of the water for good.

As much as it preoccupied him, returning to the States remained a frightening prospect. Anton had seen to it that his name remained mud in the US industry. Going back would be tough, no question. He couldn't afford to fail a second time.

'I tell you what,' said Connor, still determined to get a

rise out of Lucas before their meal was done. 'That Ruski bint's no slouch in the looks department. I'd do her over Honor Palmer any day. Here, take a look.'

Reaching into his briefcase, he handed Lucas a copy of the latest *Robb Report*, open at a three-page feature on the Tischen Group. In the section devoted to the Herrick was a small side bar mentioning Palmers, with an accompanying headshot of Honor. Set beside it was a much bigger picture of Petra, Rosa Kleb-like as ever in a severe black suit, standing in front of the Herrick. She had her arms spread wide in a 'Look at me! This is all mine!' pose, and her thin Slavic lips were wrenched up at the corners in a stiff attempt at a smile. If she was trying to look welcoming, she failed miserably. She looked like Jack Nicholson's Joker, only creepier, and with Myra Hindley hair. How Connor, or indeed anyone, could fancy her was quite beyond Lucas.

To the right of her picture, she'd given a quote about Anton ('my mentor') that was so grovelingly sycophantic, Lucas had to look away. His eyes were drawn instead to the small picture of Honor.

What a change! Although it was only a head shot, she looked unrecognizable from the boyish, spiky-haired virago he remembered. In a pale lemon silk blouse, with her dark hair now grown out almost to her shoulders and cut in soft, feathery layers around her face, she was suddenly all woman. The razor-sharp cheekbones were as unforgivingly beautiful as ever, but the light tan and smattering of freckles she'd acquired over the summer made them somehow less regal and forbidding. And was that a pearl necklace she was wearing? The last time Lucas had seen Honor she might just about have stretched to a signet ring, but otherwise had an allergy to jewellery almost as strong as her aversion to makeup and feminine clothes. Had it not been for those narrowed, emerald green cat's eyes, battle-ready as ever, he wouldn't have believed it was the same girl.

Her new look wasn't the only thing that drew his

attention. He'd always suspected there was a vulnerability lurking behind Honor's bravado. Now, in this picture, he could actually see it for the first time. There was something bravely tragic about her, like the Polish cavalrymen charging hopelessly on horseback against the incoming German tanks; or the brave Southern soldiers making their doomed stand against the Yankees at Gettysburg. It was a miracle Palmers hadn't folded by now, battered by scandals, then drowned by the tidal wave of the Herrick's success. But it hadn't – not yet, anyway. Somehow, like a lone, desperate shipwreck survivor, Honor had managed to keep the place alive. He found himself wanting to reach into the page and rescue her, and wished more than anything that she didn't still believe that he was the one who'd betrayed her and Tina.

Staring at the tiny picture of her face, thousands of miles away, he suddenly had a revelation. It wasn't only Palmers Honor was fighting for. It was the whole way of life that the hotel represented. A quieter, gentler, more decent way of life. A way of life that the likes of Anton and Petra and Connor Armstrong didn't understand. He hadn't understood it either, back in his own Herrick days. But he did now. The irony was that in a way, it was the same magic that he was trying to create with his Luxes, albeit in a different vein. A magic that the global chains like Ritz Carlton and Tischen were intent on destroying, no matter what the cost.

'You all right?' Connor's Americanized drawl broke his concentration. 'You've gone all comatose on me.'

'I'm fine,' snapped Lucas. 'I'm reading.'

Against his better judgment, he turned back to Petra's interview.

I really can't claim much credit for our success this year, she told the reporter. *Anton Tisch is a genius. His hotels sell themselves.*

Jesus. She had her forked tongue so far up Anton's anus you could probably see it when he opened his mouth.

My only real challenge was to rebuild our reputation and rela-tionships locally, she went on. *I don't want to remind people of the way my predecessor behaved*, she said, reminding people. *That's not what the Tischen family is all about. But I think the trust is slowly coming back. I know Honor Palmer. We get on well.*

Lucas choked on his espresso at that. Everybody in the business knew that Honor and Petra loathed one another.

'Oh, I nearly forgot,' said Connor, retrieving his maga-zine before Lucas sprayed coffee all over it. 'Before I go, I want to talk to you about that interview in *The Times*.'

'What about it?' said Lucas.

'I've changed my mind. I don't think you should do it.'

Lucas pulled out another Gitane and lit it. 'Sorry,' he said. 'Too late. I spoke to the journalist this morning.'

After the flurry of interest in Luxe Paris, a writer for the London *Times* had asked for a no-holds-barred interview with Lucas. They were going for the rags to riches angle, focusing on his impoverished childhood. But Lucas had dropped heavy, enticing hints that he also wanted to dis-cuss his 'feud' with Anton Tisch, and it was this aspect that worried Connor.

'For fock's sake,' he growled. 'Why didn't you discuss it with me first? You know how litigious Tisch is. Please tell me you didn't bang on about your ridiculous conspiracy theory, and Anton being out to get you.'

'It's not a conspiracy theory,' snapped Lucas, losing his cool. 'It's a fact. That bastard set me up and he's been out to destroy me ever since. Why do you think he hired Petra as my replacement?'

'Because she's good?' said Connor. 'Because he wanted to get his leg over? I don't fucking know. So what did you say?'

Lucas took another long drag on his cigarette.

'I may have mentioned my intention to open a Luxe in

America. And I may *possibly* have said that it would piss all over the Herrick when we do open.'

'What! *Why?*' spluttered Connor, his florid face turning an even deeper shade of puce. 'We've discussed this, Lucas. I am not going to be bullied into over-extending our franchise just because you've got a bee in your bonnet about Anton bloody Tisch. The US was never in the business plan. We are not opening there, and that's final. You'll have to call the journalist and retract it.'

Lucas shrugged. 'Fine. I'll call him.'

He had no intention of doing any such thing, but he didn't have the energy to debate the issue with Connor. In any case, there was no point. Today's lunch had crystallized his decision once and for all: he needed a new partner. Connor Armstrong had served his purpose, but he didn't have the vision to carry the Luxe brand to the next, glorious stage in its future. And he was a dickhead.

There was a global conference coming up in the new year, in Vegas. He'd scout around for a suitable new backer there. In the meantime, he had enough work on his plate in Europe to last him a lifetime, not to mention the small matter of finding a suitable site for Luxe America.

As he'd told the *Times* journalist only a few hours ago, East Hampton had a good ring to it. After all, the town was crying out for at least one *really* world-class hotel ...

A few days after Lucas's lunch in Paris, Honor ducked into the East Hampton market, grateful for the blast of warm air that enveloped her as she slipped through the automatic doors.

'Good grief, it's cold out there!' She smiled at the checkout girl, who smiled back. 'Can you believe it's still only October?'

'Gonna be minus four tonight, they said on the radio,' said the girl. 'Better wrap up warm.'

Honor shivered at the thought. Minus four! With the

electrics at Palmers now on their very last legs – 'borrowed time' was how the last engineer to inspect the system had described it – she'd been trying to use the central heating as little as possible in the public areas, relying instead on open fires. Happily, the guests all much preferred this arrangement, but if this cold snap continued she'd need more than pine logs to keep out the chill.

Unfortunately, time wasn't the only thing that Honor had borrowed recently, in her increasingly desperate attempts to shore up the hotel. The scandals of three years ago had hit the business hard, and she was now remortgaged up to the hilt. New hotels like the Herrick could get away with a high guest turnover, and expected to see different faces around the poolside every season. But Palmers relied on her regulars, families who returned to the hotel like clockwork every summer and Christmas. When they started defecting, as they did in droves after Tina's sex tape, Palmers' profits went into freefall. Thanks to a relentless and bravely fought rearguard action, Honor had managed gradually to claw some of these deserters back. But it was a long and arduous process, and in the meantime Anton was pouring money into the Herrick like Croesus, funding ever more indulgent facilities – an olympic-size mud bath was his latest folly – making it harder and harder for her or anyone to compete. How could Palmers *not* look tired and shabby, when up the hill Petra was offering diamond-dust facials and eight-handed massages in his and hers Polynesian love-pools, whatever the hell they were?

Things had been tough for Honor on the personal front too. Her affair with Devon, not to mention Tina's sex and drugs 'shame,' had shaken sleepy East Hampton to its judgmental, Republican core. Only now, three years later, was Honor finally beginning to be accepted again.

A number of circumstances had conspired to help ease her back into the social fold. Firstly, Devon had rented out his Hamptons summer home and decamped to Boston for good, so he and Karis weren't around to remind people of what had happened. Last Honor heard, they were still together and (outwardly at least) happy. They'd even bought a new place on Martha's Vineyard, where Devon was apparently already busy reinventing himself as a local politician and general all-round good guy. Good luck to him. Thankfully, his wannabe-Kennedy fantasies weren't Honor's problem anymore.

Secondly, Palmers was visibly struggling, and everybody loved an underdog, particularly a home-grown one. Thirdly, and perhaps most importantly from Honor's point of view, there was the Petra factor.

Whatever she might have told the *Robb Report*, the Herrick's new manager was in fact universally loathed by the locals. Many of the older generation were simply anti-Russian: the 'poor Ron Reagan would be spinning in his grave,' 'once a commie, always a commie' brigade. But even the younger, more broad-minded Hamptonites rapidly took against Petra's frosty, regal bearing, not to mention her complete disregard for the local community and its wishes.

She'd made things worse at one of the few local events she deigned to attend – a charity auction on behalf of the Make A Wish foundation – by refusing to join Honor in auctioning herself off to local businessmen as a double date.

'Come along, Ms. Kamalski.' Walt Cannon, the rotund, sweet-natured former mayor who was organizing the event tried to egg her on. 'It's only a bit of fun. And remember, it's all for the kids in the end.'

'I've already made a donation,' said Petra haughtily. 'A generous one, I might add. I'm afraid prostituting myself to men I don't know is not my idea of fun, Mr. Cannon. I'll leave that sort of thing to Miss Palmer.'

From that remark on, it was open war between Honor and Petra, and the town knew whose side it was on. With

355

the Wicked Witch of the West instaled up the street, it was inevitable that Honor would eventually be reinstated as Dorothy, albeit a morally tainted one. Her new, more feminine style helped too. It was so much easier to feel protective towards a woman who looked like a woman, and not a KD Lang-alike who might pull a jack-knife on you at any moment.

Unfortunately, it would take a lot more than local goodwill to save Palmers. Honor could no longer afford to keep topping up the hotel's coffers from the family trust, especially not now that she had interest to pay on the whopping new mortgage. Lise, her wicked step-monster, had successfully sued Trey's estate last year for a bigger payout, swanning off to the Bahamas with her new tennis instructor boyfriend and a chunk of Honor and Tina's inheritance. The judge must have fallen for her sob story. Either that or her gravity-defying new boob job, which Lise had displayed in court to great effect in a low-cut Roland Mouret dress (black, of course. She was mourning, after all).

Anyway, the point was that the black widow had won. Meanwhile, Tina was still spending what was left of the family money like water, despite the fact that she was now earning millions in her own right. The dubious celebrity she'd earned from the sex tape had translated into modeling and endorsement deals up the wazoo. Only in America, right? But none of that money made its way to Palmers.

To make matters worse, no sooner had the money started rolling in than Tina got herself hooked up with a pseudo-religious group called The Path. A bunch of former hippies and con artists, they were happy to relieve her of the 'burden' of her wealth in return for 'speerchal' enlightenment, LA style. So while Tina continued to pay extortionate rent on a Holmby Hills penthouse she never used, she now spent most of her time at one of The Path's 'Wellness Centers' in Santa Fe.

The last time Honor had called her there, she'd been stoned out of her mind.

'You know,' she mumbled drowsily down the phone, 'you really need to reconnect to your well.'

'My *well*?' Honor sighed.

'Sure. Your energy well. We all have a pool of positive energy deep within us that we draw on, that we need to grow. Like flowers,' Tina added helpfully. 'I'm sensing a lot of negativity from you right now, Honor. Your well is drying up.'

'Listen, Tomasina Cruise,' said Honor. 'The only well drying up around here is the Bank of America well. That's looking pretty fucking parched right now. We have to talk about your spending, T. How much money are you giving these wackos, exactly?'

'Spiritual growth can't be measured in dollars and cents,' said Tina, in the new, serene voice she'd affected recently that she thought projected inner peace, and Honor thought made her sound retarded.

'I couldn't agree more,' she said robustly. 'So go ask your guru for your money back. What does he need it for? More incense sticks?'

But she may as well have been speaking Martian. Tina wouldn't give an inch. Nor did she give a rat's ass about Honor's problems bailing out Palmers.

Turning into the organic produce aisle, Honor threw a few essentials into her shopping cart – milk, wholewheat bread, recycled toilet paper. Suddenly seized by a very non-organic craving for Oreo cookies, she was about to make a U-turn to the junk-food section when she overheard something that made her stop in her tracks.

'If he does open here, I'm definitely applying.'

Honor recognized the voice of the Herrick's maitre d'.

'Careful,' said his friend. 'Walls have ears. I wouldn't put it past Petra to have bugs in the supermarket. KGBitch.'

They both laughed.

'But I wouldn't bank on Lucas being any easier a boss. All the old staff say he could be a real hard ass when he ran the Herrick.'

'He was never as bad as Kamalski,' said the maitre d'. 'He only yelled at you when you'd fucked up. I can handle that. Besides, it'd be worth a few ear-bashings to work at Luxe. Those hotels are gonna be the new Tischens, you mark my words.'

Honor, who was marking his words, edged closer to the shelf, moving aside some packets of lentils so she could hear them more clearly without being seen.

Surely Lucas couldn't be planning to open a Luxe *here*?

No, no. It was a European brand. And East Hampton would be the last place Lucas would want to return to. Wouldn't it? They must be mistaken.

'Well, if you go, I'm going,' said the maitre d's friend. 'I can't take much more of that snake pit. I've even thought about moving to Palmers.'

The maitre d' laughed. 'Forget it. They'll be bust in six months.'

Honor flushed red. Was that what everyone thought? That they were finished already?

'We'll just have to hope Ruiz doesn't lose his nerve,' the maitre d' went on. 'I don't mind admitting, *I* wouldn't wanna take Petra on head to head. The woman scares the living shit out of me.'

They moved on toward the cash register at that point, out of Honor's earshot. She was itching to follow them, but there was no way to do it without being spotted. And as soon as they saw her, they'd clam up, so there was no point.

Grabbing a packet of Oreos on autopilot, her mind raced as she ran over the significance of what she'd just heard.

Of course, it was only gossip. But she knew from experience that hotel gossip was usually accurate. And they'd both sounded horribly specific about the details.

Lucas was planning to open another Luxe here, in the Hamptons.

She tried to imagine worse news. But short of nuclear war, a direct meteorite hit on Palmers or Devon Carter being elected president, she couldn't think of anything.

How could he? After what he'd done to her, betraying her in the worst way possible, how could he have the balls to even contemplate showing his face in this town, never mind setting up shop here with one of his damn stupid, overhyped Luxes? God, how she hated that name. It sounded like a fricking soap.

Like everyone else in the business, Honor had read reams of copy about Lucas's famed comeback. Unlike everybody else, however, her heart wasn't remotely warmed by his rags to riches story. What kind of Karma was it that allowed assholes like him to bounce back from ruin like a fairground skittle, while decent, hardworking people like her got to sit in a shower of shit that never seemed to end?

If there was a God, she decided, he was definitely a man.

As for the whole Luxe 'phenomenon,' she couldn't see what all the fuss was about. A bunch of candles and lavender oil, and a few velvet cushions. That was the big concept, as far as she could tell. Big hairy wow. Like no one had ever done boudoir chic before.

'Are you OK?' the girl at the checkout looked concerned, and Honor realized with embarrassment that she'd been mumbling out loud.

'Sorry,' she said. 'I'm fine. Just tired.'

The two Herrick workers had gone, and she was once again the only customer in the store. Listening to the lonely 'beep, beep' of the scanner as her items passed through it one by one, she thought about Lucas. In her mind, his handsome, arrogant face was laughing at her.

'*You* couldn't beat Anton Tisch,' he seemed to be saying. 'But I'm gonna show you how it's done.'

Outside, weighed down with groceries, she drew her chunky-knit cardigan more tightly around her against the bitter wind.

She couldn't let him have the last laugh. Not this time. She'd have to come up with some sort of plan.

A week later, Anton arrived back in London in excellent spirits.

He'd spent the last week at St. Hubert's, an exclusive private clinic in Switzerland, having his botox secretly touched up, and was highly satisfied with the results. St. Hubert's 'no TV, internet or phones' policy was a pain in the ass, but the cosmetic surgeons there were such artists, it was worth the inconvenience once a year.

Marching through terminal three at Heathrow while his chauffeur struggled on ahead with the luggage, he allowed himself a small smile of satisfaction. Life was pretty damn good right now. Excelsior had had a fantastic write-up in last week's *Wall Street Journal* – the European Super-Fund, they were calling it now, much to his delight. Ben Slater's Stellar Fund had barely rated a two-line name check.

It particularly amused him how no one in the City could fathom how he'd managed to poach quite so many of Stellar's clients over the past eighteen months. As if it weren't patently obvious. He might have gone out of his way to distance himself socially from the Azerbaijani oligarchs to whom he owed most of his vast fortune. But that didn't mean he was above accepting their money. They were all the same, these Slavs and Russians and Central Asians: sheep. Born followers. Not like the Germans or the British, or even the Americans. Now that a select few of them had come into such phenomenal personal wealth, they were still following one another blindly, investing in the same funds, the same cities, the same yachts, the same property deals. All Anton had to do was to massage a few of his old contacts and land one or two big fish for Excelsior, and the rest of them had jumped on the gravy train like lambs to the slaughter.

But the fund's performance wasn't the only reason Anton had to celebrate. The share price of his Tischen Hotel Group had gone up sixteen points on the news that the Herrick had been nominated for the coveted number one spot in the Relais Chateaux rankings. And he had the incomparable Ms. Kamalski to thank for that.

When Petra had first contacted him after he'd fired Lucas, suggesting herself for the Herrick managership, he'd thrown her CV in the trash along with all the others. But a few days later she had the good sense to email a second version – this time with a photograph – and at once his interest was piqued. Something about her stark cheekbones and cold, predatory eyes spoke to him. She looked simultaneously sexual and frigid, controlled, but with the promise of raging passions bubbling beneath the skin. His original intention was to fly her to Geneva, string her along until he got her into bed, then get rid of her. But from the moment he saw her in the flesh and their eyes locked, everything changed. He recognized a kindred spirit.

For one thing, she hadn't needed the slightest encouragement to sleep with him. She agreed immediately to his request that they have the interview at his home, then showed up for it wearing nothing but a trenchcoat and patent black stilettos. Thinking about that afternoon now, as his limo surged smoothly out of the airport onto the M25, he felt his cock start to harden. After almost three years, he still wanted her constantly.

From that very first time, sex with Petra had been a revelation. Insatiable, athletic, submissive yet strong, she was like the missing piece of the jigsaw that Anton had been searching for his whole life. In the past he'd had to pay girls to do the depraved things he wanted. With Petra, he was begged for more. He only had to look at her wildly dilating pupils, or her nipples, hard as frozen berries, arched longingly towards him, to realize her excitement was every bit as real and intense as his own.

Not only was she a world-class fuck, she was an astonishingly gifted hotelier. Lucas had gotten the Herrick off to a flying start, but Petra took those early seeds of success and multiplied them a hundredfold. She'd broadened their guest list, from the New York-centric music-business types that Lucas had exclusively gone for, to the new super-rich from across the globe and she was also a genius at schmoozing stuffy industry types like the buffoons at Relais Chateaux. The locals might not like her, but who cared? The time when Anton had needed their support was long since past. When Petra had confided to him one night in bed that her main motivation in applying for the job had been to put one over on Lucas – the two of them were lifelong enemies, apparently – Anton's admiration for her became complete. He admired people who pursued their vendettas to the end, who didn't get distracted or allow the passage of time to smother their righteous indignation. Petra was a woman after his own heart.

'Your tea, sir.'

Gavin, the butler Anton always brought with him when traveling, handed him a bone china cup brimming with piping hot Earl Grey. Anton had had his entire fleet of cars fitted with tea-making facilities, along with the standard plasma screens and state-of-the art phone system. He took the cup wordlessly and settled down to peruse the last week's papers to see what he'd missed while he'd been stuck at St. Huberts.

Two minutes later, he let out a roar so loud it sent his driver skidding all over the road, and promptly spilled scalding tea down his Turnbull & Asser silk shirt.

'Sheiße!' he roared, pulling the wet fabric away from his skin, but not before a spreading red burn had formed across his chest and stomach like a birthmark. 'The little shit.'

Lucas, it appeared, had taken advantage of his absence

to give an interview to the London *Times*. And it wasn't pretty.

The Tischens have become a victim of their own success,' he was quoted as saying, in response to a question about whether he saw himself as being in competition with Anton. *'When a brand explodes to that degree, it soon becomes corporate and faceless, like every other global five-star chain. Mr. Tisch doesn't like the word 'chain' but that's what his hotels have become. And I should know. I ran one of them.'*

White-lipped with rage, Anton read on.

'Luxe offers something very different. Personal. Unique. So in that sense, no, I don't see us as competing, not directly anyway. Once we open in the Hamptons, I guess some people might choose to see it that way. But that's not my view.'

'Get Petra on the phone,' Anton barked at Gavin.

'She won't be up, sir,' he stammered timidly, shrinking back in his seat like a mouse before a rattlesnake. 'It's not even six on the East Coast yet.'

'Don't tell me what fucking time it is, you stupid fuck,' bellowed Anton. 'Just get her on the line.'

Already his buoyant mood of a few minutes ago had evaporated completely. Fuck Lucas. Who the hell did he think he was dealing with?

When Anton killed off an enemy, he expected them to stay dead, and he saw Lucas's revival of fortunes as a personal affront. He'd been too busy with the fund in recent months to take any further, concrete action against him. But he saw now that that had been a mistake. He'd given Lucas an inch and he'd taken a mile, threatening to open a new Luxe in the Hamptons, of all the outrageous ...

'About time.' Petra's sleepy voice ricocheted around the limo in surround sound. 'Where the hell have you been all week?'

'Never mind that,' snapped Anton. He wasn't about to admit his surgical sabbatical to anyone, least of all the woman he was sleeping with. 'I just read Lucas's interview.

He claims he's setting up shop in East Hampton. Why didn't you tell me about this before?'

'How was I supposed to tell you?' Petra snapped back. 'By carrier pigeon? I've left you about a hundred messages; you never returned a single one. I haven't even been able to make a statement to the press. Where *were* you?'

'Don't challenge me,' said Anton.

He sounded angry, but Petra could sense the lust simmering underneath. Their role play was always the same: she was the petulant schoolgirl, he the disciplinarian teacher. But Anton never seemed to tire of it.

'Speak to me like that again and I'll spank you,' he said.

Gavin the butler blushed scarlet and stared firmly out of the window.

'Apologize.'

'Sorry,' purred Petra meekly.

In the back of the car, Anton's hard-on was now clearly visible through the twill of his suit pants. How he wished Petra were here in the quivering, pliant flesh, and not on the other end of a phone line. But she wasn't. And they had business to discuss.

'So,' he said. 'Our friend Mr. Ruiz has crawled out from under his stone while I've been gone, has he?'

'It's pathetic,' said Petra, her voice dripping with vitriol. 'He opens two paltry hotels in Europe – Luxe Paris is so small it's practically a guest house – and already he thinks he's Rande Gerber. He's a joke.'

Anton didn't find the prospect of a Hamptons Luxe remotely amusing. But neither was he intimidated. Being forced to crush Lucas a second time was an unwanted irritation – like finding a cockroach you thought you'd killed still wriggling on the bottom of your shoe. But it was hardly a serious concern.

'Lucas is all talk,' said Petra. 'He always has been. He clearly hasn't found a site for this mythical new Luxe yet, or he'd have been boasting about that too.'

'And he's not going to find one,' growled Anton menacingly.

'To be honest,' said Petra, 'that stuck-up bitch Honor Palmer worries me far more than Lucas does.'

Honor's dislike of Petra was as nothing compared to the boiling hatred that Petra harbored for her local rival. Not since Lucas had threatened to eclipse her at college had she felt so threatened and, at the same time, so irrationally resentful of another human being. She despised everything about Honor, from her deep growling voice with its faint Bostonian twang, to her tiny doll-like body, to the easy way with which she seemed to wrap all the local snobs around her little finger. People treated her like aristocracy, and Petra like some low-life immigrant, when in reality Petra's family were far older, grander and richer than the Palmers. Honor was also routinely described in the press as 'cute' and even 'beautiful', which incensed Petra, who considered her own physical charms outshone Honor's like the sun outshone a candle, and was fiercely jealous of her reputation as the hospitality industry's great Russian beauty.

'Honor?' Anton sounded amazed. 'Don't be ridiculous. She's no threat to us. I've seen Holiday Inns in Des Moines with better occupancy rates than Palmers.'

'Hmm,' said Petra skeptically. 'Maybe.'

Now that Palmers was clearly on its way out, Anton was perfectly content to watch the old hotel die a slow, lingering death. Cancer, as long as it was terminal, was as good a way to finish off a rival as the firing squad. But Petra remained much more antsy. As long as Palmers was standing and open for business, and as long as that poisonous dwarf Honor Palmer hung around like a bad smell, playing the town sweetheart, she would never feel completely secure, no matter how many Relais Chateaux accolades they won.

'You mustn't fret so much, darling,' said Anton, reading her mind. 'The locals can huff and puff for Honor as much as they like. They won't blow our house down. And nor will Lucas. We'll see to that.'

The limo eased to a halt outside his Mayfair mansion, and Anton hung up and hurried inside, leaving Gavin and the driver to manage his cases.

His week away had been rejuvenating. But now there was work to be done. This time around, he'd make damn sure he finished off Lucas Ruiz for good.

Chapter Twenty-two

A few miles north of Mayfair, in the grounds of another mansion in St. John's Wood, Sian Doyle crouched uncomfortably in the bushes, trying to calculate exactly how many minutes she had left before her bladder gave out and she was forced to pee right here in the rhododendrons.

She wouldn't have minded so much if it weren't for Keith, the lecherous photographer crouched beside her. Watching her take her pants down would be the closest thing he'd come to a sexual experience since high school (with something that didn't take batteries or need blowing up with a foot pump).

There were days when Sian loved working at the *News of the World*. Like this Monday, after one of her pieces ran, and Simon Davis the features editor told her it was 'only slightly crap' – praise indeed from a man known affectionately to the rest of the desk as Satan. His wife had once berated a man for calling Simon a cunt, on the grounds that it was an insult to women's genitalia.

But Monday's praise already felt like a distant memory. Today was Thursday, and Sian was on the worst of all possible assignments – a stakeout. After the crappy pay (she was pretty sure trash collectors made more than her per week) and even crappier hours (whoever scheduled her shifts had clearly been raised in a cave, by bats), stakeouts were the worst part of her job.

This was the third day running she'd spent with Keith, knee deep in foliage at the house of Sir Jago Wells, a Tory grandee whom the paper suspected of having an affair with a stewardess. In thirty-six hours of mind-numbing surveillance they'd only seen the man twice, for a total of about sixteen seconds. Both times he'd been alone, hurrying to and from his Jaguar with a sheaf of papers under his arm. Given that Sir Jago must weigh about the same as a smallish hippo, but with a markedly less attractive face, the absence of a girlfriend failed to surprise Sian as much as it did her editor.

'It's incredible he convinced *one* woman to shag him, never mind two,' she'd told a seriously unimpressed Simon an hour ago. 'He makes Jabba the Hut look like George Clooney.'

But Satan wasn't in the mood for jokes. If she and Keith didn't have the goods on his desk by the end of their shift tomorrow, they could both 'sling their 'ook,' as he so poetically put it.

Sian was under no illusions. He meant it. No pictures, no tearful interview with the wife: no job.

'At this rate you're gonna 'ave to sleep wiv 'im yourself, love,' said Keith, licking his lips.

Sian looked at him witheringly.

'What?' He tried to look innocent. 'It'd make a lovely picture.'

He had so many pimples on his face, they outnumbered the patches of clear skin, and his round, owlish glasses were so grimy it was a wonder he could see anything at all. Sian's mind wandered bitterly to Paddy, her boyfriend, who was on assignment in Dubai for the *Telegraph*. He was probably yukking it up with some billionaire sheikh and his harem right now, having a fabulous time. Paddy was an Irish racing journalist, whose assignments always seemed to involve being sent to hot countries and/or luxury hospitality tents at race courses, swilling Guinness and eating strawberries until his stomach exploded, while Sian's were all about bushes, perverts and outdoor urinating. It wasn't fair.

'Why don't you quit the *Screws* and get yourself a proper

job?' he'd asked her in bed the other morning, after another of her hour-long moan-a-thons. 'Show most editors a pretty face and a bit of leg and you're in like Flynn. My boss'd snap you up in a heartbeat. I can see the interview now.' He fluttered his eyelashes coquettishly and put on his best Renée Zellweger voice: 'You had me at *hello*.'

'Oh, shut up,' said Sian, laughing and hitting him with a pillow.

Paddy had an uncanny ability to see the funny side in almost any situation, and to get others to do the same. Skinny as anything, with merry, dancing gray eyes and the same classically Irish coloring as she had – pale skin made even paler by his shock of black hair – he habitually looked as though he'd spent the previous night sleeping under a hedge. Not handsome, but definitely attractive in a roguish, new-romantic kind of way, he was as much her best friend as her lover. People often commented that they looked like brother and sister, which annoyed Paddy so much that Sian had never dared to tell him she sometimes felt that way, too.

Given that they were in the same profession, it was ironic that they hadn't in fact met through work, but through Lola's boyfriend, Marti. He and Paddy had been friends for years, since Paddy's days as an intern on the *New York Post*. Marti brought him round to the girls' flat one night for dinner, and the rest, as they say, was history.

Sian liked being part of a couple, if only to give her something to talk about with Lola, who'd been blissfully loved-up with Marti ever since the Burnstein wedding. The two of them had been clocking up the air miles flitting back and forth from New York to London to see each other, and they were still revoltingly besotted.

Last year, against Sian's advice, they'd decided to go into business together, with the newly graduated Lola designing evening gowns and Marti selling them online, through one of his many successful internet shopping sites.

Happily, Sian's fears about the wisdom of mixing business with pleasure had proved groundless. Their love remained as strong as ever and Marti was now in London almost full time. Trading under the name of Marla Fashions (as in Marti and Lola – sick-making, right?) the fledgling venture was already having remarkable early success. Only last month a famous British soap actress had worn one of Lola's designs to the National Television Awards, and since then orders had been up a staggering three hundred percent.

Sian was happy for her. She deserved her success. But there were times when her own life – job, relationship, bank balance, you name it – looked pretty pathetic by comparison.

Today, squatting on her aching haunches next to the most irritating sex pest on Fleet Street, was definitely one of those times. Swatting away a midge, she shifted uncomfortably from foot to foot. Her right leg was starting to get pins and needles from all the crouching.

'Pass me one of your boxes, would you?' she whispered to Keith. 'If I don't sit down soon I'm gonna fall down.'

Silence.

'Keith?'

Looking over her shoulder, Sian saw to her horror that her so-called partner was sprinting away through the trees as fast as his pudgy little legs could carry him. Moments later she realized why. Two burly men in overalls materialized out of thin air, grabbed hold of her roughly, and pinned her arms behind her back.

'Let go of me!' she screamed, kicking her legs uselessly like a captured cartoon character as they frog-marched her to the front of the house. 'Get off! This is assault!'

'No, it's not, love,' said the larger of the men. 'It's a citizen's arrest. You're trespassing. And you're nicked. So be a good girl and sit quietly until the old bill gets here. All right?'

Two hours later, stuck in a cell in Swiss Cottage police station, Sian racked her brains trying to think whom else she could call.

Simon, her editor, who only hours ago had been plaguing her non-stop with phone calls, had mysteriously disappeared in her hour of need. Probably holed up with the paper's lawyers somewhere figuring out how best to throw her to the wolves without getting his own hands dirty. Lola would have been her next call. She was a grand master at talking herself out of trouble. But unfortunately she was on vacation in Hawaii with Marti and totally incommunicado. Paddy was in Dubai.

She was rapidly running out of options.

'No one's given me a lawyer, you know,' she shouted through the door to the duty sergeant. 'I'm entitled to a lawyer. And a phone call. I know my rights. I'm an American citizen!' she added, more than a touch desperately.

'This is a north London nick, love, not *NYPD Blue*,' said the sergeant, brilliantly managing to roll his eyes without looking up from his *Sun* crossword. 'The DI'll get round to you as soon as he can. In the meantime, there's a pay phone in the corner there, and a paper if you're bored. You can ring whoever you like.'

Feeling slightly deflated – partly because she had no one to call, and partly because being arrested was a lot more dramatic on TV – Sian picked up the copy of the *Daily Express* lying on the formica table in her cell, and gave it a desultory glance. Sod's law decreed that the first thing she saw, slapped across the society pages, was a bloody great picture of Ben and Bianca.

It wasn't the first time she'd seen them pictured together, of course. Being so show-stoppingly stunning, Bianca was a natural favorite with the picture editors, and since becoming the new 'face' of Marks & Spencer her profile in the UK had shot up even further. She and Ben were rapidly becoming an It-couple to rival Posh and Becks.

Sian wished she could just ignore them, but working for a tabloid made it doubly hard. It was three years since she'd last seen Ben in person. But she'd never forgotten the humiliation of that day, at his leaving party, when he'd walked out on her in front of all those people. Even now, thinking back to it made her flush with embarrassment.

Why did she even care anymore? All that stuff had happened eons ago, back in another life when she was a lowly maid from Butt-Fuck-Nowhere, New Jersey. Now she was a reporter for a national newspaper, living abroad, with a nice boyfriend and an awesome apartment. She'd moved on, hadn't she? Who gave a shit what Ben self-righteous Slater did, or who he did it with?

'Know 'im, do you?'

The duty sergeant, who was actually a kind man, came in with a cup of tea he'd made for her. They certainly didn't do *that* on *NYPD Blue*.

'Not really,' said Sian. 'I used to. He's a jerk,' she added, taking the tea gratefully.

'He's a rich jerk, though, isn't he?' said the sergeant.

Sian shrugged.

'Listen, love. A word to the wise,' he said. 'If *I* had a rich mate like that, I'd get him on the blower, sharpish.'

'You want me to call Ben?' Sian translated. She was getting quite adroit at deciphering cockneyisms these days. 'Why would I do that? I told you, he's a jerk.'

They were alone in the cell, but the sergeant still looked around him and lowered his voice before he spoke again.

'The DI hasn't been in to see you yet because he's still interviewing Sir Jago,' he whispered. 'If the shouting's anything to go by, I'd say the old git wants to make an example of you and your paper. You 'eard from your editor yet?'

Sian shook her head nervously.

'No. I thought not,' said the sergeant. 'They're hanging you out to dry, love. You need a decent brief and you need him right now. The bloke they're sending you from legal aid is a muppet. Couldn't argue 'is way out of a paper bag.'

'But ... but ... you don't understand,' stammered Sian. 'I can't call Ben. Certainly not to ask him for a favor. Uh uh, no way. I'd rather die.'

The sergeant shrugged. 'Up to you, love. Of course, I don't know the bloke. But if it were me, I'd swallow my pride. I'd say you need all the help you can get.'

He returned to his desk, leaving Sian pacing the room, willing herself to think of someone, *anyone* else she knew in England who could help her. Surely somebody here owed her one? Or simply cared enough to get involved?

But try as she might, she couldn't dredge up a name and panic was starting to get the better of her. Sir Jago Wells was an important man. What if he pulled enough strings to have her sent to prison? Or deported? That would be even worse. The thought of going back to her old life in New Jersey filled her with dread. She couldn't do it.

Her hand shook as she punched out the number for Directory Enquiries.

'London, please,' she told the operator. 'It's a company called Stellar, in the City, EC1 I think. Yeah. You can put me straight through.'

Honor watched as the last few passengers from the United LA flight straggled into the arrivals hall at JFK. Still no sign of Tina. Please, please let her not have missed the fucking plane. Not today.

But no. Miraculously, there she was, floating through the double doors in a flouncy gypsy skirt and waist-length beads like a top-heavy Joni Mitchell, flashing a two-fingered peace sign to the ubiquitous paparazzi.

'Hey.' Drifting over to Honor, she enveloped her in a photo-friendly hug. 'Sorry it took so long. I had some trouble with one of the customs guys.'

'I'm not surprised,' said Honor, reeling from the overpowering smell of marijuana on her sister's clothes and hair. 'How'd you talk your way out of that one?'

Tina flashed her a wicked smile. 'I didn't need to talk.'

Honor felt almost relieved. Evidently her Mother Theresa of Topanga makeover didn't run *that* deep.

'Thanks for coming,' she said, pulling out of the airport onto the Expressway twenty minutes later once the paps had finally let them leave, and swerving into the fast lane as soon as she got a chance. 'I appreciate it.'

They were on their way back to Palmers. Honor had arranged a dinner with a possible investor tonight, an Australian hotelier called Baz Murray, who was looking to link his small chain with a high-visibility brand in the US. He'd specifically asked to meet both sisters together. Evidently the Australian public were a lot more relaxed about sex scandals than their American counterparts, and it was the Palmer family connection that really interested him. Honor had put a call in to Tina with low hopes, but to her simultaneous amazement, relief and terror, Tina had agreed to fly in for the meeting.

Petra had done her best to scupper things by throwing an impromptu celebrity birthday party at the Herrick tonight, and inviting Murray along. How she knew he was in town was anybody's guess, but as the woman had more spies in the hospitality industry than the CIA, it was more of an annoyance than a surprise. In any case, to Honor's great delight, Baz had turned her down, earning himself untold brownie points in Honor's book. As long as Tina didn't say or do anything too outrageous over drinks, things were looking good. God knew they needed a cash injection, and fast.

'You are, er ... you are gonna change before dinner, right?' Honor asked, glancing at Tina's gaping peasant blouse disapprovingly.

'You can talk,' said Tina, shooting her a look that was more pissed than peace.

It was a fair point. Honor had been in such a rush this morning, she was still in her workout clothes: a pair of Juicy velour sweat pants and a blue Nike vest top that clung to her small sweaty frame so tightly that her nipples were clearly visible. Shit. What if they showed up in the pictures those photographers had just snapped at the airport? They were bound to, weren't they, circled in the bloody *National Enquirer*? That was all she needed.

'So,' said Tina, changing the subject. 'I heard about Lucas coming back to East Hampton. What do you think? Is he serious?'

Honor bit her lip. How could Tina talk about Lucas's plans as if they were nothing more than an interesting tidbit of local gossip? Had she forgotten that it was Lucas who'd tried to ruin them in the first place? And who'd damn near succeeded?

But she had to try and stay on her sister's good side, at least until tomorrow. Of course, if it weren't for Tina's feckless spending, they wouldn't *need* to suck up to an outside investor. But that was beside the point now.

'I doubt it,' she said, with admirable calm. 'He's probably just shooting his mouth off as usual. Trying to eke out the publicity for Luxe Paris. But we'll see.'

For the rest of the journey, she steered the conversation towards safer topics, where they were bound to agree, like Lise, and what a bitch she was, and their dreadful, money-grubbing cousin Jacob Foster.

'Did you see that interview he did with *US Weekly* about me discovering Jesus?' ranted Tina indignantly. 'As if my spirituality could be confined by one religion. And as if that freak show even knows me!'

By the time they reached the windswept outskirts of East Hampton, they were back on amicable terms.

'That's funny,' said Tina idly, watching a fire truck thunder through the dreary landscape of marshland and empty holiday homes, and saying a tiny prayer of thanks that this

375

place was Honor's life and not hers. 'That's the second fire engine to pass us in the last five minutes.'

'Probably got a call to come deal with the smoke blowing out of Petra Kamalski's ass,' muttered Honor.

They both laughed.

But a few minutes later, their smiles disappeared. Nearing Palmers, a huge, gray mushroom cloud of smoke loomed in front of them. Soon it had all but filled the windscreen, plunging the road ahead into darkness like a solar eclipse. Honor slowed the car. Moments later a cop emerged out of the gloom, waving at her to stop.

Winding down the window, she was immediately hit in the face by a gust of acrid smoke so strong it made her eyes water. This must be quite some fire.

'I'm sorry, ma'am, I'm gonna have to ask you to turn around,' said the cop. Honor didn't recognize him. He was young and obviously new in town, and he had the intent, nervous look of someone seriously out of his depth.

'No, no,' she said, nodding at the road in front of her. 'You don't understand. We have to get through. My hotel's down there.'

'You mean Palmers?' said the young man. He'd obviously mistaken her for a guest. 'I'm afraid that's where the fire is coming from, ma'am. There's no need to panic,' he added, seeing Honor's face drain of color and her hands start to shake. 'Everyone's been evacuated safely. We're only talking property damage.'

Honor shot out of the car. Pushing past the cop, she ran blindly through the makeshift roadblock and into the smoke.

'Miss. Miss!' he yelled ineffectually after her. 'You mustn't go down there!'

'Leave her.' Tina got out of the car more slowly and stared toward the beach in disbelief. She'd never seen smoke like it. 'Trust me, officer. My sister can take care of herself.'

A couple of the young cop's colleagues, alerted by the shouting, ran after Honor. But years of training meant she was fitter than all of them, and was easily able to shake them off in the maze of sandy alleyways and back-lanes that led to the rear of the Palmers complex.

Down on the beach, a gathering crowd stared in horrified silence at the inferno, held back by more police, as well as the natural barrier of smoke and heat. Like a zombie Honor joined them, unable to speak or move as a third fire truck pulled up and its occupants began pumping yet more water at the blaze.

She didn't know why they bothered. It was clearly too late. Rushing around like red-suited termites, the firemen reminded her of desperate parents, trying to give mouth to mouth to an already-dead baby. *Her* baby. Next to the thirty-foot flames, which roared and leaped and licked the sky like the forked tongues of some giant lizard, their puny jets of water and foam were as ineffectual as water pistols in a volcano. Palmers was already a charred skeleton. The fire had eaten her alive, like a flesh-eating virus.

'Hey. Hey, you! What are you doing?'

One of the spectators, a middle-aged man watching the drama with his family, shouted out as Honor slipped through the police lines and ran kamikaze-like toward the hotel.

She couldn't hear the man, or anything other than the wild beating of her own heart. All she knew was that some force outside herself was pulling her forwards, oblivious of the searing heat and choking fumes that poured down her throat and into her lungs like poison. Closing her eyes, she stumbled blindly on.

'Over there!' The man grabbed hold of one of the firefighters and pointed. 'Some crazy girl just ran into the building. Look!'

'Where?' yelled the fireman.

'Over there!'

Within seconds, he and two of his buddies were inside. Thankfully, Honor hadn't made it more than a few feet into what used to be the kitchens, so they spotted her almost at once. Dragging her outside, disoriented and barely conscious, they handed her over to the waiting paramedics.

'Shit. It's Honor Palmer,' Honor could hear one of them saying.

'Miss Palmer?' asked a second voice. 'Honor, can you hear us?'

But before she could tell them that she could, the voices, and everything else, had gone.

Chapter Twenty-three

The next six weeks were the worst of Honor's life.

Confined against her will to a recuperation ward in South Hampton hospital ('I assure you, Miss Palmer,' said Dr. Reeves, her consultant, firmly, 'if I catch you trying to discharge yourself one more time I'll have you committed. Do you understand the damage you've done to your lungs?') she spent the bulk of her days having increasingly circular, frustrating conversations with the insurance agents, who were determined to link what happened to the hotel's sub-standard wiring, despite hard forensic evidence that it had not been an electrical fire.

'Why do you keep asking me these questions?' she complained, for the hundredth time. 'The police report was clear; it was arson.'

'Our investigators have yet to determine that,' said the charmless girl sent to interview her. She couldn't have been much over twenty-one, but had already developed the hardened, cynical manner common amongst her profession. She was dressed all in black, like a particularly unsympathetic funeral director. 'And even if they do, the fact that you failed to bring your electrical wiring up to code, despite repeated warnings, may well prejudice your claim even if it *was* arson. Which we dispute,' she added with a smile that made Honor want to rip the clipboard out of her hands and ram it down her scrawny, heartless throat.

Thankfully the police were more sympathetic, although their sympathy had yet to translate into progress.

A few days after the fire, an earnest cop had shown up by her bedside, armed with a long print-out of questions.

'Do you have any enemies, Miss Palmer?' he began gently. 'I know it's difficult. But can you think of anyone who might want to cause you or your family harm?'

Honor laughed bitterly. 'How long have you got, detective?'

The cops seemed quite certain that the fire had been set deliberately, and it wasn't a case of some careless guest forgetting to stub out their cigarette. But despite a list of possible suspects as long as the East Hampton telephone directory – disgruntled former employees, business rivals, embittered lovers – there were actually very few people that Honor could imagine going to such extreme, criminal lengths to hurt her. She thought briefly of Karis Carter, but quickly dismissed the idea as ridiculous. If Karis were the crazed, vengeful type, she'd have acted long before now. Who else? Her greedy cousins, the Fosters, were too stupid, not to mention gutless. Lise wouldn't have had the energy, or the foresight to start a fire. Besides, she was so plastic she'd probably be terrified of melting, like the wicked witch that she was.

There was a suggestion that Tina's former mafia connections might have had something to do with it, but as far as Honor could tell, this was a theory based more on a lack of any other leads than on anything more concrete. Not even the policeman who'd suggested it seemed particularly convinced.

Honor had had to be physically restrained by two nurses when the cop informed her that her insurance company had hinted to the police that she herself should not be considered above suspicion.

'They simply asked us not to formally close any avenue of inquiry at this stage,' explained the hapless officer. 'To be fair to them, it's no secret that your business was in some trouble financially at the time the fire occurred.'

'So what?' Honor was practically foaming at the mouth. 'You think I torched my own hotel? Palmers was my life!

There were *people* in there, for Christ's sake. Guests, staff. Friends of mine. It's a miracle nobody lost their life.'

As with previous tragedies in her life – her mother's death, the feud with Trey, being abandoned by Devon – the worst part for Honor was the feeling of utter helplessness. It wasn't just Palmers that had burned to the ground that day. All her hopes for the future had perished with it.

Tina finally stopped by the hospital for a visit a week after Honor was admitted. She'd been too busy partying up a storm in Manhattan to come back any sooner.

'So what'll you do?' she asked, devouring the bunch of seedless grapes she'd brought for Honor whilst flicking through a gossip magazine. 'Go back to Boston?'

Secretly, Tina was rather enjoying all the drama. The Palmers fire was the most fun she'd had since the sex tape came out. Talk show producers were once again beating down her door for interviews and photographers tailed her whenever she went out for coffee. It was fabulous! Plus, with Honor incapacitated in hospital, it fell to *her* to show the world just how the devastated (but plucky) Palmer sisters were coping with the tragedy. No one could turn a sob story into TV gold better than Tina.

'I guess I will go back to Boston. For now,' said Honor, wincing as the nurse changed one of the dressings on her arm. As well as serious smoke inhalation, she'd suffered extensive burning to her arms and hands, and had already undergone one skin graft. She'd never known pain like it. 'But as soon as I've screwed my goddamn money out of these insurance leeches, I'm coming back. I'm gonna rebuild Palmers just as she was. Brick by brick.'

'Really?' Tina put down the magazine and looked at her skeptically. 'You don't think maybe the fire was a sign? You know, like, time to move on? Open a new chapter in your life? Just think of all the things you could do with that insurance money.'

'Like what?'

'I don't know,' shrugged Tina. 'Whatever you want. Move to Paris. Buy a fuck-off yacht. Give it to charity. Who cares?'

Honor looked horrified. 'The only thing it's a sign of,' she said grimly, 'is that someone's determined to run us out of town. But they picked the wrong family to mess with. Palmers will be back, and it'll be bigger and better than ever.'

Tina wasn't the only one who felt her sister's obsession with rebuilding the hotel might be a sign of mental instability.

'She won't let it go,' she told Dr. Reeves. 'I'm actually worried about her. She's turning into a fucking fruit loop.'

'I wouldn't quite put it that way,' said the doctor. But he was also concerned about his patient's state of mind. So far Honor had been unable to give the psychiatric team any explanation for *why* she'd run into a blazing building on the brink of collapse, when she already knew there was nobody left inside. She denied being suicidal and claimed her mind had simply gone blank. But combined with her frequent outbursts of temper, and repeated attempts to check herself out of hospital long before she'd made a full recovery, these delusional fantasies about reopening Palmers as early as next year were a real cause for concern. Anyone could see it wasn't going to happen.

At long last, one crisp, late November morning, Honor's release day dawned. She still wore bandages on her arms, and it would be two more weeks before she could risk taking a proper shower. But otherwise, save for a lack of exercise, she was in good health, and Dr. Reeves had run out of excuses to force more rest on her.

'I suppose there's nothing I can do to get you to go somewhere peaceful and continue your recuperation?' he asked.

He'd stopped by her room to formally discharge her, and

was dismayed to find Honor hopping about impatiently, re-checking her long-completed packing. She was itching to get on the phone to her lawyer and see what could be done to pressurize the insurers, but she didn't dare turn on her cell phone in front of Dr. Reeves, in case he ordered her back to bed again. Secretly she was terrified that the horrible girl agent was right and she *had* voided her insurance by putting off that electrical work. Then she'd be ruined, and it would all be her own fault.

'Nope,' she said, trying to sound cheerful. 'There's nothing you can say. So don't even try.'

Watching his patient fidgeting, the doctor smiled. She'd gained a little weight during her stay, but it suited her. In a coral pink cashmere dress that clung to her like a second skin, you couldn't miss the fact that her small apple breasts had swelled into grapefruits, and the cheeks that had looked so sunken and hollow when she was first admitted were now fuller and rounded with health. When she'd first arrived in her scorched sweatpants, she looked so skinny and angular, making love to her would have been like sticking your dick into a fistful of thistles. This new, softer, smiling Honor was really much more alluring.

'Your friend's here to collect you, by the way,' he said, signing the requisite papers and dragging his thoughts back to the professional matters at hand. 'And you're to make sure he carries your case. None of your feminist nonsense today, all right? You're not to even *think* of over-exerting yourself.'

'Friend?' Honor looked puzzled. 'What friend?'

She hadn't asked anybody to pick her up, other than the car service that was coming to take her to the airport for her three o'clock flight to Boston.

'Hello, Honor.'

She spun around. For a moment she thought the good doctor must have slipped something into her water and she was hallucinating. For there, leaning against the doorway looking lean and tanned in a blue open-necked shirt, with his raven curls so long they were almost at his shoulders, stood Lucas.

'We're good now, thanks, doc,' he said, shaking the doctor's hand as he ushered him out. Honor could see that in his other hand he held a small bouquet of peonies, her favorite flowers, although Lucas couldn't have known that.

'I'll take care of her from here.'

'Make sure you do,' said the doctor, jovially. 'She's a handful this one.' And with a last smile at Honor, he was gone.

Annoyingly, for the crucial first few seconds, Honor was too gobsmacked to get a single word out. But inside her mind was racing.

What the hell was Lucas doing here, looking like a rock star just back from a relaxing break in the Maldives, while she looked pale and pasty and ... in fact, screw all that, what the hell was he doing here, period?

'I'm calling security,' she spluttered.

'Now that's not very welcoming, is it?' said Lucas, his upper lip curling in amusement. 'Aren't you at least going to put these in some water first?'

'No.' Snatching the peonies, Honor flung them on the bed. 'Thank you,' she added, automatically. 'In case you hadn't noticed, I'm leaving. Right now. I have a plane to catch.'

Ignoring Dr. Reeves' express instructions, she picked up her heavy case and began struggling toward the door. But Lucas was too quick for her. Placing a firm but gentle hand on her shoulder, he prized the suitcase easily from her grip.

'You heard the doctor,' he said bossily. 'You're not to lift anything. I'll do it. Nice dress, by the way. And the long hair's a big improvement.'

Honor erupted. 'What the fuck do you think you're

384

playing at?' she demanded. 'If you came to gloat, consider it done already, OK? Get the hell out of my face.'

'Why would I come to gloat?'

He cocked his head to one side like a confused puppy. If Honor didn't know what a scheming, self-obsessed bastard he was, she might almost have found it endearing. As it was, his feigned innocence only fanned the flames of her fury.

'Because my hotel is gone,' she said, her eyes welling up with tears despite herself. 'Because you've got what you wanted at last.'

Lucas put down the case. 'This is not what I wanted,' he said quietly.

'Yeah. Right. Whatever,' said Honor.

'Maybe it was once, years ago. But not anymore.' He looked up, willing her to believe him, but she glared implacably back. 'I was in town anyway, scouting out possible sites for my new Luxe—'

'Bully for you,' said Honor bitterly.

'I knew about the fire, obviously, but it wasn't until I got here that I realized you'd been hurt. As soon as I heard, I came straight to the hospital. I wanted to say how sorry I was, and to see if there was anything I could do. You know, to help.'

'There is,' said Honor, deadpan. 'Drop dead.'

Lucas sighed. Her feminine makeover clearly didn't extend to her personality, or her language.

'Do you really think I could ever forgive you, after what you did to me? Not to mention Tina?'

'Oh, come on.' Lucas's voice was rising with exasperation. 'Haven't you figured it out yet? Your sister's tape was nothing to do with me. It was Anton. He set her up. He set us *both* up, can't you see that?'

'No,' said Honor stubbornly. 'I can't.'

Lucas had been the enemy for so long, the idea of casting him in any other role was almost frightening. She must hold on to her anger, or she'd be lost.

385

'So what about leaking that story on me and Devon?' she challenged him. 'You're gonna tell me that was Anton too, I suppose?'

'Yes,' said Lucas calmly. 'It was. Jesus. You'll be accusing me of starting that fucking fire next.'

Honor narrowed her eyes. 'Did you?'

'No!'

Not sure what to think anymore, she sank down onto the bed. All this arguing was beginning to tire her out.

'You know, for a smart woman you can be incredibly stupid at times,' said Lucas. 'Granted, I may have said some unpleasant things about you in the press when the Herrick first launched—'

'*May have?*' Honor looked at him, incredulous.

'Hey, you weren't whiter than white either, you know,' Lucas reminded her. 'So up yourself, so fucking self-righteous. My God! Anyone would think you had a divine right to the East Hampton market. You said some terrible things about me back then, too.'

Honor simmered furiously but didn't say anything. She supposed he might be very, very slightly right on that one.

'I told you I'd keep my mouth shut about you and Carter, and I did. I wouldn't have put Lola through all that crap on purpose.'

'Right. Because you cared so much about Lola,' Honor shot back. 'I could tell that the night I caught you in my hot tub with my sister's head between your legs. That guy, I thought, is *all* about his girlfriend. Talk about loyalty. You were quite the gentleman.'

'You know what?' Lucas sprang angrily to his feet. 'Believe what you want.'

He was through trying to convince her. He'd actually come here to bury the hatchet. Because he'd thought about her almost every day since he'd left. Because when he heard she might be seriously hurt, he felt like someone had kicked him hard in the stomach and wouldn't stop. But there was no point offering an olive branch to Honor. All she wanted to do was beat him round the head with it.

'I have a hotel to build,' he said, storming out.

'Oh yeah?' Honor yelled after his retreating back as he disappeared down the corridor. 'Well, guess what? So do I! Asshole. You haven't heard the last of Palmers yet, you hear me?'

But Lucas was already gone.

Three thousand miles away in London, Sian sat at the table at Nobu, a fixed grin glued to her face, conjuring up mental images of the various tortures she would inflict on Lola later for suggesting tonight's dinner.

What in heaven's name had possessed her to come?

There were six of them at the table: herself and Paddy, who seemed to be having a high old time swapping football stories with the boys and getting drunk on sake; Lola and Marti who, as usual, spent most of dinner gazing gooily into one another's eyes like a couple of half-wits; and Ben and Bianca.

The dinner was intended as a 'thank you' to Ben for saving her ass after the whole Sir Jago Mills disaster. Once she'd finally plucked up the courage to call him, he'd swung into bat for her brilliantly, organizing a hot-shot lawyer within an hour and calling her editor himself, threatening to take private legal action if the paper so much as *thought* about making Sian a scapegoat and denying responsibility.

Thanks to his strong-arm tactics, she'd got away with just a warning from the police. But Simon, her editor, didn't take kindly to being threatened. After three weeks of being given dead-end stories about Thames Water or runaway guinea pigs, Sian took the hint and resigned from the *News of the World*. She was now back to freelancing again, and absolutely hating it.

'In a way, it must be liberating, though, isn't it?' asked Bianca, taking another sip of her vodka, lime and soda, the models' drink of choice. 'Being able to write what you want. Set your own agenda.'

She had no makeup on, her hair in a pony tail and was wearing a simple white vest top and jeans. But despite this every man, and most of the women in the room, were mesmerized by her, craning their necks to catch every word that fell from her goddess-like lips.

Sian tried hard not to be jealous, but she was only human.

'Kind of,' she said. 'But you never really set your own agenda. Editors always get to call the tune, whether you're freelance or in-house. That's the nature of the business.'

'What are you on about, now?' said Paddy, wrapping a long, skinny arm around her shoulders and kissing her tenderly on the top of the head. 'Not work, I hope. We're supposed to be having fun, babes. Remember?'

Ben, who couldn't help but notice the kiss and the affectionately proprietorial arm, felt a knot forming in his stomach. He really must pull himself together and grow up.

When Sian had called him from the police station that day, his elation was hard to describe. He'd thought about her so often since they'd parted, and wanted to make amends for so long for his idiotic behavior in America. But, of course, he'd been too chicken shit to make the first move. Then, out of the blue came her lovely sing-song voice on his line, not only calling him, but actually needing his help. It was the perfect chance to put things right. And he had done. At least, he thought he had.

So why was it still so awkward between them? If she really had forgiven and forgotten, why did she still avoid his gaze whenever he looked at her? And why, despite immediately taking to Paddy, did Ben find himself suffering repeated, strong urges to strangle the guy with his own shoelaces every time he touched her?

'What you need is one really good story, to make your

name,' said Bianca to Sian. 'Something all the papers'll be queuing up to buy.'

'Yeah,' said Lola, picking up a sliver of raw scallop with her chopsticks and dropping it adoringly into Marti's mouth. 'A scoop.'

What I need is a boob job, thought Sian, looking miserably from Lola's ample cleavage to Bianca's, then down at her own flat-as-a-pancake chest. She'd made an effort tonight too, in a flowing red dress from Top Shop and the patent black leather boots that Paddy called her Fuck-Me-Specials. She had been feeling quite pleased with her look, until first Lola and then Bianca rocked up looking like Lindsay Lohan and Angelina Jolie respectively. No wonder Ben kept giving her that weird look. He must be thanking his lucky stars he'd traded her in when he did. Talk about an upgrade.

'Thinking of good stories,' said Marti, tearing himself away from Lola for a nanosecond, 'did any of you guys read about the fire at Palmers hotel? I heard a rumor that Honor Palmer might have done it herself, for the insurance.'

'No way,' Lola shook her head vehemently. Though still not Honor's biggest fan, ever since she'd eavesdropped on the conversation with her father at Minty Burnstein's wedding, she'd stopped viewing her as the scarlet woman. Instead, she'd redirected her anger equally between her old man, for his rank hypocrisy, and Lucas, for his vindictiveness in going to the press about the affair. 'Honor may be many things but she's not an arsonist. That hotel was her life. There's no way she'd torch it. Not in a million years.'

'Well, someone doesn't like her,' said Marti. 'It was almost certainly arson.'

'Maybe it was Lucas,' said Lola, only half joking, raising an eyebrow at Ben. 'He hates her guts. And he's certainly vicious enough.'

'I don't think so,' said Ben mildly. He understood Lola's hostility – after the shoddy way Lucas had treated her, he could hardly blame her – but she was wrong about this. 'He doesn't hate Honor. Not deep down. And he's got better things to do with his time than run around starting fires.'

'Oh, of course it wasn't *Lucas*!' laughed Bianca, who didn't know his history with either Lola or Sian and had always got on well with him. 'He's a sweetheart, isn't he, Ben? He wouldn't hurt a fly.'

The two other girls caught each other's eyes and giggled.

'If Lucas has a vendetta against anyone, it's Anton Tisch,' said Ben, chasing a sliver of tuna around his plate with a chopstick he had no idea how to use. He hated Japanese food anyway. Bloody rip-off. 'And may the force be with him, I say. That man has single-handedly blown a hole in my business the size of the Grand Fucking Canyon.'

'Aww,' said Sian archly. 'Down to your last five hundred mill, are you? Poor diddums.'

Ben blushed, and she instantly regretted being so flippant.

'Well *I* think Tisch is dreadful,' said Bianca loyally. If she'd picked up on the awkwardness between Sian and Ben, she didn't show it. 'He makes himself out to be this charitable, caring guy, but he treats women like shit. And what he did to poor Lucas was unforgivable.'

This was a bridge too far for Lola.

'Poor Lucas? Are you kidding me? The guy entrapped a woman into making a porno in his hotel, then released the video on the internet! Not to mention what he did to me and my family. I'm sorry, Bianca, but he deserved to get fired, and then some.'

Realizing belatedly that she'd stepped on a landmine, Bianca shut up.

'Lucas has always said Anton was behind that tape,' said Ben bravely. He knew that both Sian and Lola would happily order Lucas's head on a plate if it were on the menu, but felt an obligation to try to stick up for a mate.

'Yeah, well. He would, wouldn't he?' said Lola. 'Anyway, can we not talk about that asshole? I'm trying to enjoy my meal.'

'Hear hear,' said Marti.

For a few minutes the conversation drifted onto other matters, chiefly fashion, and whether Bianca could be prevailed upon to consider wearing one of Lola's designs to a big fashion-week party. But Sian's mind was still stuck on the previous topic.

'It is interesting about Tisch, though,' she piped up after a while.

'What is?' said Paddy, not really listening. 'Does anybody else think this black cod tastes like shit?'

'Well, he's this mystery figure, isn't he?' said Sian, ignoring him. 'He has a public image, like Bianca said, and it's all good, even though people actually know a lot of the bad stuff.'

'Like him not paying child support,' said Bianca angrily.

'Exactly,' said Sian. 'Why hasn't that damaged him?'

'It has, to a point,' said Ben. 'But he's rich as Croesus, and famously litigious. The media are afraid of him, I reckon. Plus he's so bloody secretive, I doubt his own mother really knows him. But I agree, there are plenty of things about him that don't add up.'

'Like?' asked Sian.

'Well, like how the hell he keeps persuading my clients to leave Stellar, for a start. And why he went after Lucas the way he did. I mean, without opening up the whole Lucas debate again, what significance is a little guy like him to a global player like Anton? It's like a blue whale hunting down a lone pilot fish. It don't make sense.'

'*Doesn't* make sense, darling, not don't,' Bianca corrected him.

Sian tried not to feel pleased when Ben shot her a dirty look in return.

'Maybe that's your scoop, babes?' said Paddy to Sian.

'Dig up some proper dirt on Anton Tisch and every paper in the land will want to hire you.'

'I'll write you a cheque myself if you nail his slippery German arse,' added Ben with feeling. 'But it won't be easy.'

'Thanks,' said Sian sarcastically, 'but I don't want your money.'

Ben bit his lip. Note to self: must remember to rip out tongue when I get home.

'Shhhh now, Siany, don't upset him or he might not pay for dinner,' said Paddy, in a stage whisper that made everyone laugh. 'Heaven knows none of the rest of us can afford this place.'

After dinner Ben and Bianca drove straight home, while Marti and Paddy decided to walk into Soho together and find a late-night bar, leaving Sian and Lola to share a cab.

'This feels just like the old days,' said Lola, kicking off her Jimmy Choos and putting her bare feet up on the fold-out seat in front of her. 'You and me, cabbing it home together. Before the boys came on the scene.'

Sian smiled.

'You know, Ben really is such a nice guy,' Lola went on blithely. 'He hasn't changed a bit. Fuck knows what he sees in Lucas, but I guess he's entitled to one fatal flaw. Bianca's sweet too, don't you think?'

It hadn't occurred to her that, after three years, Sian might still be harboring any romantic feelings towards Ben, especially now that she seemed so settled and happy with Paddy.

'I guess,' said Sian, without a shred of enthusiasm. 'Yeah, she's OK.'

In fact she wasn't thinking about Bianca, or even Ben. (Though later, in bed, she'd spend several hours torturing herself by picturing the two of them making love.) Right now, her head was full of Anton Tisch. There were too many things about him that didn't smell right. For the first time in months, she felt her journalistic curiosity stirring groggily back into life.

Tomorrow, she'd do a little digging. She wouldn't spend too long on it; maybe a couple of hours on Google. There was probably nothing in it, after all. But she didn't have much else on. And who knew? Maybe it'd be worth a look.

Chapter Twenty-four

The 2.7-billion-dollar Wynn Las Vegas was the most expensive hotel and casino ever built, anywhere in the world. Nine-foot floor-to-ceiling windows in each of its two thousand seven hundred bedrooms, looked down over a spectacular view of the strip. Guests could choose between twenty different in-house restaurants, shop in the hotel's full-scale designer mall, or indulge themselves at the spa or on the world-famous golf course. They could even buy themselves a Ferrari to tour around town at the dealership downstairs.

Like all the big Vegas hotels – the monsters, as Trey Palmer used to call them – the Wynn aimed to provide a world so complete that once you stepped inside its glass doors, you'd never want to leave.

But Honor did want to leave. The hotel, the city, the conference. If only she'd remembered to pack her ruby slippers.

This January's conference at the Wynn was the IHA's biggest ever. Some sixteen hundred hoteliers from all over the globe were attending, as well as academics, journalists, investors, chefs, construction companies – anybody who was anybody in the hospitality industry.

Right now, as Honor was all too acutely aware, she was officially 'nobody' in the hospitality industry. With the police still no nearer solving the Palmers arson riddle – they'd interviewed Danny Carlucci and his cronies numerous times, but hadn't been able to pin so much as a parking ticket on any of them – her insurance money remained stuck in offshore permafrost. Realizing that it might be years, if ever, before she saw a penny of her claim, she'd decided to throw all her energies into plan B: finding a private investor to fund the rebuilding.

The first thing she did was recontact Baz Murray, the Australian magnate who'd been so keen on an alliance with Palmers a few months ago, before disaster struck. But having been a guest there when it caught fire, and narrowly avoided being burned to crisp himself, he'd understandably lost his enthusiasm for the place.

Which was what brought her to Vegas, armed with high hopes and the Powerpoint presentation she'd spent her entire Christmas vacation putting together, which included a fabulous set of computer-generated architect's images of what the 'new' Palmers might look like.

At first she'd wanted to recreate the place *exactly* as it had been, down to the last bent nail and crooked door frame. But she soon realized that idea owed more to nostalgia than good business sense. Tina was right about one thing. The fire *had* provided her with an opportunity. An opportunity to start again, without any of the structural problems that had had her eating through money like a biblical plague of locusts, and without the ghosts of her father and grandfather watching her every move disapprovingly from the rafters.

The 'new' Palmers would be Honor's creation – a chance to make her own, unique mark on her family history. She would maintain the period charm, of course. The sense of history and tradition that had become synonymous with her family name. But shabby chic would make way for real chic; down at heel, faded gentility would be replaced by a more confident, assured, quietly monied ambience. There would be none of the vulgarity and bling of the Herrick. And none of the spa-like hippyishness of Luxe. Palmers would once again become a bastion of understated American wealth and privilege. No one knew how to create that better than Honor.

On the plane ride up to Vegas, she must have looked at her own presentation twenty times, awash with confidence and excitement. How could investors *not* buy in to her vision, backed as it was by a brand name far too enduring to be destroyed by any fire? Soon, everyone would be talking about the new Palmers, and how it had risen like a phoenix from the ashes of the old.

But the minute she checked in at the Wynn, her chutzpah deserted her. The sheer scale of the place made Palmers seem like a doll's house, one of a million little white clapboard nothings viewed from a passing plane, a mere dot on the landscape. And the first few days of the conference had done nothing to lessen her sense of insignificance. Almost all the seminars were 'big picture' stuff, with titles like: 'Globalization, Branding and Expansion' or 'Debt Restructuring in the High Interest Era'. There was no opportunity for the sort of face-to-face schmoozing that Honor needed to do if she was going to bag herself a suitable backer. Even if there had been, she seemed to be the only person here with business on the brain. Everyone else, from the grandest CEOs to the lowliest MBA students, seemed to want to spend their free time at the roulette tables and/or checking out the local strip joints. Even the women.

Star spotting was the other leisure activity of choice, and the Wynn was like a physical incarnation of the pages of *People* magazine. Honor had no interest in celebrities, and avoided casino floors much as she would the gates of hell, but even she had already clocked Ben Affleck and Nick Lachey wandering around in the lobby. She'd even shared an elevator with Lisa Marie Presley, much good it did her.

She couldn't remember feeling so out of place anywhere since at the age of twelve, her father had forcibly enrolled her in ballet school in Boston, hoping to knock the tomboy out of her. She'd spent every class sulking in the corner in jeans and Doc Marten boots, while the other girls pirouetted around her in their fluffy pink netting and organza.

Unfortunately, sulking wasn't an option now. Not if she wanted to rebuild Palmers. As much as she hated Vegas, she had to get involved.

Today was day four, and so far the only approach she'd had was from the odious Bruce Austin, a big cheese over at Hilton. He'd sidled up to her during the lunch break, wrapped an unwanted arm tightly around her waist and suggested with a wink that she might like to give him her presentation 'in private ... if you know what I mean.'

'Thanks, Bruce,' she'd replied stiffly, trying not to stare at the way his beer belly was bursting through the buttons of his shirt at the bottom, or the sweat patches the size of dinner plates under his arms. 'But if it's all the same to you, I'd rather choke to death on my own vomit.'

She was desperate, but she wasn't that desperate.

It was evening now, and all the seminars were over. Honor headed for the largest of the Wynn's numerous cocktail bars, sorely in need of a drink. Plonking herself down on an empty stool, she tried to blot out memories of the day. As if Brace's clumsy come-on hadn't been bad enough, the afternoon lecture turned out to be a two-hour drone-a-thon from the owner of a Swiss group of motels. It was so boring, she'd actually nodded off in the middle of it and slipped ignominiously from her seat onto the floor. She was woken not by the fall, but by the deafening laughter of the delegates around her. Not her finest hour.

'Scotch on the rocks, please. Better make it a double.'

'You got it.'

The barman, a wannabe actor with the same perfect features and toothpaste smile as all the other staff at the Wynn, jumped to her request. She had to admit, the service here was excellent. When the drink arrived she took a big, thirsty gulp, but regretted it when she felt the alcohol scorch her throat. Soon she was coughing and spluttering like a TB victim. At the very moment she expelled a mouthful of amber liquid through both nose and mouth across the polished top of the bar, like a whisky sneeze, Petra Kamalski sauntered into the bar with a bunch of Tischen Group acolytes, all of them male.

Great. That was all she needed.

'Honor.' Smiling evilly, Petra walked towards her. In a bright red Chanel suit and matching ruby heels and lipstick, with her peroxide hair gleaming on the top of her head like a tight white helmet, she reminded Honor of a toy soldier, so much so that she half expected her to click her heels together and salute at any moment, possibly shouting 'Sieg Heil!'

'What a surprise to see you here. Reliving old times, are we?'

'Get lost, Petra,' said Honor, wishing that her eyes and nose weren't still running like faucets from the burning liquor.

'Now, now,' chided Petra. 'There's no need to snap. You seem stressed, my dear.' She was clearly enjoying herself. 'Perhaps you'd like a cigarette? Although I'm sure Mr. Wynn would appreciate it if you remembered to put it out in an ashtray when you're done.'

With an effort, Honor smiled thinly and let this not-so-veiled reference to the Palmers fire pass.

'Hey, boys,' Petra called over her shoulder to her gaggle of groupies. 'Can anyone offer Honor Palmer a light?'

Much sniggering broke out. One wag tossed Petra a lighter, which she made a great show of flicking open and waving the naked flame under Honor's nose.

'No? Not a smoker?'

Honor ignored her and turned back to what was left of her drink. But Petra wasn't done yet. Her hatred of Honor ran so deep, she couldn't rest until she'd got her to rise to the bait.

'Come on,' she said. 'I was only kidding. You shouldn't be sitting here, drinking alone. Why don't you come and join us?'

'I'll pass,' said Honor, coolly.

'Are you sure?' said Petra. 'We're all headed back to my room. Apparently they have one of your sister's movies available upstairs, on the X channel. I've heard it's very good. Can't I tempt you?'

Her posse watched Honor for her reaction like a drooling pack of hyenas. But they were disappointed. Tightening her grip around her glass, she took a moment to compose herself. Much as she'd love to leap on Petra like a wildcat and scratch her malicious, ice-blue eyes out, she knew she was outnumbered, and that a scene was exactly what the vicious cow was hoping for. Why give her the satisfaction?

'Sorry,' she said, draining the rest of her drink and leaving a twenty-dollar note on the bar. 'Not for me. But hey, you kids have fun. Every dollar that movie makes goes to Unicef. I'm sure they'll be grateful for your contribution.'

Only once she reached the sixteenth floor, and the safe privacy of her own room, did she allow herself to react. Shutting the door behind her, she turned the TV up and screamed at the top of her lungs for a full minute.

'Bitch!' she yelled. 'Fucking Russian slut, whore, BIIIIITCH!'

Then, peeling off her sweater, white pants and underwear, she jumped naked onto the over-sized bed and began pummelling her fists into the pillows in frustration.

Finally, exhausted but feeling a whole lot better, she slipped into the nude Calvin Klein camisole and panties that served as her nightwear, opened the minibar and pulled out four miniature bottles of Jack Daniels. It wasn't malt, but it would have to do.

Stretching her legs and wiggling her toes luxuriantly in the thick pile of the carpet, she turned down the volume on the TV, flipped channels to Seinfeld and began the long process of drinking herself into a stress-free oblivion.

*

Across town at McCarran International Airport, Lucas's evening was proving to be anything but stress free.

Thanks to a French air traffic controllers' strike that had brought Charles De Gaul to a grinding halt, he was already three days late for the conference. But now it transpired that the stupid fuckers at Air France had sent his bags, including his laptop, to Milwaukee or Mogadishu, or some other place beginning with M that sure as hell wasn't Las Vegas. Between this and the thundering headache that had gripped his skull 40,000 feet over Colorado and clung on like an asylum seeker to an undercarriage ever since, it was safe to say he was not in the warmest of moods.

He'd had a shit Christmas, working constantly, and battling ever more bitterly with Connor, his so-called partner. The crux came when Lucas had drawn down on a bank loan to pay for an expensive plot of land in the Hamptons, about a mile further along the beach from the Herrick, on which he intended to build his new hotel, tentatively, and more than a little grandly, entitled Luxe America.

Connor had hit the roof, showering Lucas with more expletives than Ozzy Osbourne with a stubbed toe: 'Fucking Spic!' 'No fucking restraint!' 'Greedy, ignorant, paella-eating peasant!'

It amused Lucas when people's racism and prejudices emerged in anger or drink, like so much scum floating up to the surface. In Connor's case, the tirade had provided him with the excuse he needed to break away and look for a new, better-capitalized partner. For all Connor's protestations about not wanting out of the business, they both knew they couldn't go on as they were.

His biggest problem was finding the time to hunt for such a person. Rushing around like a blue-arsed fly between the East Hampton building site and his two existing hotels, he barely had time to sleep, never mind network.

Standing in the arrivals hall, searching in vain for a sign with his name on it among the many placards being waved around, he wished fervently he were back in Paris. He much preferred it there to Ibiza, where he'd installed a very competent local guy called Alessandro as interim manager. The city itself was astonishingly beautiful, of course. Lucas had never been much of a culture vulture, but Notre Dame blew him away, and the Louvre was a labyrinthine world of its own that he never seemed to tire of. But it was the women who really had him hooked. French girls had a natural sexual confidence that was *so* much more attractive than the brash sluttishness of their Ibizan counterparts, all tits, tan and tassles. It was something like the difference between Honor and Tina Palmer. To this day, he regretted having had sex with the Ibiza Palmer sister, and not the Parisienne. But he wasn't about to lose sleep over it. It was Honor's loss.

After fruitlessly scanning every single sign, and finally running out of people to scream at, he filed a complaint with the airline and made his way, bagless, to the taxi rank.

'The Wynn,' he snapped bad-temperedly at the driver, then felt guilty when he saw a crucifix and rosary beads hanging from the rear-view mirror, along with pictures of the man's kids. The poor guy was only trying to make a living, after all. He didn't deserve to have his head bitten off.

He spent most of the forty-five-minute journey checking his Blackberry for emails – thank God he'd kept *that* in his pocket, and not in his bag, or he really would have been screwed. Only in the last few minutes of the ride did he put it away and focus his attention on the insane display of lights that signalled the approaching city.

Despite his exhaustion, he was horny. Sandrine, an exotic dancer from the Crazy Horse, who he'd been dating on and off back in Paris, sent him a couple of x-rated texts that had helped to push the whole lost-baggage drama to the back of his mind. One of the perks of his insanely hectic travel schedule was being able to have three totally separate, con-current sex lives – in Ibiza, Paris and the States – without fear of discovery, jealousy, or tedious female tantrums of the kind that Lucas previously had an uncanny knack of attracting. Emotional women bored him to tears. Happily, Sandrine wasn't remotely given to that sort of nonsense. He had no doubt she'd be screwing half the fourteenth arondissement while he was away, a mental picture that, combined with her graphic texts and the prospect of the many libidinous pleasures awaiting him in Vegas, made his dick begin to harden in his pants.

He wondered how complicated it would be to get hold of a hooker once he got to his room. Not very, he imag-ined. Although it wouldn't do his reputation much good if anyone at the IHA conference saw him paying for sex. To many people in the US, he remained indelibly connected to Tina Palmer, sex, drugs and videotapes, an image he needed to change if he was going to make Luxe America a success. Being caught calling dial-a-vagina would be a major PR disaster.

When they got to the Wynn, he headed straight for check-in.

'You're in room 1606, Mr. Ruiz,' the blonde at the desk told him brightly, 'on the sixteenth floor. Is there anything else I can help you with at this time?'

'Actually, yes,' quipped Lucas. 'You could you find my fucking bag for me. I think it might be in Maryland. Or Munich. One of the two.'

The girl looked at him blankly. Like most Vegas girls, she had the body of a goddess and the face of an angel, but the eyes of a retarded rabbit. Lucas suspected her IQ was somewhere around the level of a floret of broccoli. A small floret.

'Never mind,' he said wearily. 'I'll see myself up.'

On his way to the elevators – there were banks of them; the place was so huge it felt like the Pentagon – he stuck his head into the cocktail bar off the lobby, but withdrew it again instantly when he caught sight of Petra. It was the first glimpse he'd had of her in the flesh since Lausanne days, although he'd seen her picture countless times in the trade press. Somehow photographs failed to capture her aura of chilly, brittle malevolence that Lucas remembered so well. Her hairstyle and dress sense might have changed, but she hadn't.

Having said that, from the brief glimpse he'd caught of her, she seemed to be the worse for drink, which was distinctly out of character. Or perhaps in Petra's case, he should say the better for drink. The alcohol had evidently loosened her up a bit. Her red stilettos had been kicked off and at least one button of her crisply severe white blouse had popped open at the top. No doubt Connor would have found this sexy, thought Lucas with a shudder. He was welcome to her.

Desperate to get away, he slipped into the waiting elevator. All he wanted right now was some room service, his bed and possibly a decent porno – if he could keep his eyes open long enough.

'Oooo! Turn *off*, you stupid thing!'

Honor, blind drunk, stabbed away at the TV remote with rising annoyance, before realizing that it was actually her cell phone she was jabbing.

'Crap. Where is it?' she mumbled, staggering around the room looking under cushions and sweeping aside the minibar detritus that lay strewn across the floor: empty bottles, beer cans and boxes of peanuts were everywhere. She'd even eaten the cheese and onion Pringles, which she hated, on the assumption that the more food she ingested to mop up the booze, the better.

Giving up, she ripped the TV cord out of the wall, sending sparks flying and a sharp, stabbing pain shooting up her arm before the entire room plunged into darkness.

'Fuuuuck,' she whispered. 'Goddamnit.'

At least the TV was off. Ty from *Extreme Makeover* had really been starting to get on her nerves. Why did he have to shout the whole time? Opening the minibar fridge provided a sliver of light, enough to see that she'd somehow managed to get through an entire tray full of ice and consequently had none left for the two remaining miniature bottles of vodka. Remembering vaguely that she'd seen a sign saying 'ice' near the elevators, she got unsteadily to her feet and padded out into the corridor.

The lights were off out here too. She must have shorted the entire floor – oops! Only the dim glow from the emergency floor lighting enabled her to get her bearings. On the plus side this meant she could run to the ice box under cover of semi-darkness, fill up her glass and nip back to her room without anybody noticing she'd forgotten to put a robe on over her underwear. Double oops!

Finding the ice box was the easy part. Making her way back to her room – what number was it again? – without spilling the precious contents of her crystal tumbler proved to be a lot tougher.

Finally swaying to a halt outside her door, she reached for the key-card in her pocket. Except there wasn't any pocket. Or any key-card.

'Shit.' She stared blankly at the impassive wooden door, its key slot blinking red as if taunting her. Seconds later, she let out a wail of horror as the lights came back on. All of a sudden, the full force of her predicament was brought home to her: she was locked out of her room, as good as naked, standing in a public corridor in glaringly unflattering platinum-bright light.

Where the fuck did she go from here?

'Can I help you?'

Honor froze. The voice came from behind her, but she didn't dare to look.

It couldn't be him. Could it?

'Forgot our key, did we?'

Lucas tried not to laugh, but it was impossible. She was just standing there, stock still, like a two-year-old playing hide and seek who thinks that by not moving and covering her own eyes, she can somehow make herself invisible. It was awfully cute.

The last time he'd seen her was in the hospital, when he'd brought her flowers to try to make peace and she'd thrown them back in his face. Then, the weeks of bed rest and stodgy food had given her body a certain softness at the edges. But it was all gone now. Her figure was leaner than ever – too lean, actually. She couldn't weigh more than a hundred pounds, and five pounds of that was her newly long hair. Even so, in that truly minuscule underwear, her tiny, boyish body was displayed to highly alluring effect.

And what a treat to have caught her in such a humiliating, compromising position! For once in her life, Little Miss Prim and Proper was going to have to be polite to him. In fact, if she wanted his help, she was going to have to do more than that. She was going to have to grovel.

Apparently, however, she didn't want his help.

'Go away.' Turning around reluctantly she glared at him, as if he were somehow responsible for her predicament. 'I'm fine.'

Her nude camisole was sheer enough for him to make out the dark berries of her nipples beneath the fabric. It stopped about an inch above her g-string panties, allowing the faintest of glimpses of flat, toned belly, which was almost more tantalizing than the barely covered triangle of pubic hair below. But it was the brazen aggression in her eyes that really did it for him. How he longed to screw all that poor-little-rich-girl rage right out of her.

'Oh, well, if you're fine,' he shrugged, feigning a nonchalance he knew would drive her crazy, 'I'll go then. I was going to suggest you came to my room to borrow a robe.

But if you'd rather go down to the front desk on your own ... like that ...'

He gave her the sort of look a hungry lion gives a gazelle. Honor blushed, and belatedly tried to cover her breasts with her hands.

'Be my guest.' He started to walk away.

Honor was torn. Blast him! Why couldn't it have been someone else, anyone else, who came to her aid?

The way he'd looked at her just now had sent her pulse racing – something she put down to shock, possibly combined with extreme drunkenness. It may have *felt* like desire. But it definitely wasn't. It couldn't be, because she was absolutely, categorically *not* attracted to Lucas. God no. She'd rather sleep with George Bush.

On the other hand, a robe would seriously come in handy right now. The alternative – going down to the lobby in her underwear – would mean public humiliation on a scale that would dwarf today's earlier litany of indignities. She couldn't do it.

'Wait!' she shouted after Lucas's retreating back.

Slowly, infinitely slowly, he turned around. 'Yes?'

You bastard, thought Honor. You're loving every minute of this.

'I will borrow your robe,' she mumbled, gracelessly.

'Oh, you *will*, will you?' said Lucas. 'Well, I'm not so sure anymore. I mean, you haven't asked very nicely. What's the magic word?'

Honor gritted her teeth. 'I hate you,' she muttered murderously.

'Sorry?' said Lucas. 'I didn't quite catch that.'

'*Please*,' said Honor. 'OK? *Please*. *Please* may I borrow your robe?'

'Of course you may.' Lucas's grin broadened. 'See? That wasn't so hard, was it?'

The corridors at the Wynn were longer than most East Hampton streets, and it seemed to take an age before they reached Lucas's room, especially as he insisted on ambling along deliberately slowly, prolonging her agony. But at last they got there. As soon as he slipped his card in the door, Honor darted inside like a fish, making straight for the bathroom. She emerged moments later wrapped in an enormous toweling robe, her hands lost somewhere inside the cavernous sleeves, so that only her feet and tiny, doll-like head were visible.

Lucas burst out laughing. 'Help me, Obi-Wan Kenobi! You're my only hope!'

'Ha, ha,' said Honor mirthlessly. She started for the door, but he stepped in front of her, barring her way.

'What do you think you're doing?' She was angry, but for some reason her voice emerged all high-pitched and strangled. Reaching over her head, Lucas pulled the bathroom door shut behind her, pinning her between it and his body.

'I'm doing exactly what you want me to,' he said. And before she could respond, he'd slipped a hand inside her robe and started caressing the bare skin on her shoulder.

For a split second Honor closed her eyes, as an erotic charge shot through her body. Then she stiffened.

'Fuck off!' she said, pushing him away. 'You make me sick. You think you can ... you can ...' Fuck. Why had she drunk so much? She longed to come out with some witheringly acerbic put-down, but all she could do was blather like a cretin. 'Oh, just fuck off, all right?'

'No,' he said, pulling her close again. 'It's not all right. Not until you listen.'

'And why should I listen to you?' said Honor, not bothering to try to push him off again as it clearly wasn't going to work and the effort was making her feel dizzy. 'Give me one good reason.'

'Because,' said Lucas, 'you're wrong about me. You always have been, since that first day on the beach.'

'You reckon?' Honor's cat's eyes narrowed distrustfully.

407

She wished the smell of his aftershave weren't quite so distracting.

'I had nothing to do with your sister's tape,' said Lucas, looking her right in the eye. 'And it wasn't me who leaked your affair to the papers. I swear to you, Honor, on my mother's life. I didn't do it.'

Once again she felt torn. She didn't know what to believe. He *looked* like he was telling the truth, he really did. But then consummate liars knew how to pull off that trick, right?

'It was Anton,' said Lucas, his voice dropping to the low, husky whisper that seemed to make every woman but Honor melt. 'Why can't you believe that? What are you so scared of? Admitting you were wrong?'

'Scared?' Honor bridled defensively. 'I'm not scared.'

But in that moment, she realized that she was. Horribly scared. Scared of forgiving him. Scared that if she stopped hating him, even for a moment, she might feel something else. Something beyond her control.

'Let's just say for a minute that you're right – that it was Anton,' she said. The fear seemed to be helping sober her up. 'That still doesn't let you off the hook. *You* introduced Tina to that guy.'

'I did,' said Lucas. 'But only because Anton told me to. Look, he told me to do a lot of stuff that I regret now, OK? But, you know, he was my boss. I didn't realize he had this whole hidden agenda.'

'Hmm.' Honor looked up at him, willing her anger not to desert her. 'So, do you always jump like a monkey when the organ grinder says jump?'

'I don't know,' said Lucas. Pushing his knee forward between Honor's legs, he brought his face so close to hers she could feel the heat of his breath on her cheeks. 'Do you always lash out at men when you want them?'

'I don't want you …' she stammered. But he stopped her with a kiss so passionate she could barely breathe, let alone speak. Closing her eyes, she gave in to the sensation, allowing her senses at last to overwhelm her. Before she knew it she was kissing him back, tentatively at first but then hungrily, her desire escalating in response to his.

Staggering toward the bed, kissing and grabbing and scratching at one another like two wild animals, they finally collapsed on top of it. Honor's robe was already on the floor, and Lucas had somehow managed to scramble out of his jeans as he wrestled her beneath him.

'I meant what I said,' Honor panted, gasping as he ripped off her cami-top, tearing the thin silk as his hands grasped hungrily for her breasts. 'I still hate you. You're arrogant ... you're ...' It was hard to get the words out while being manhandled by someone with a body weight roughly three times your own. 'You're sexist. And boorish. And ... rude.'

'Yeah, well, I hate you too,' growled Lucas, struggling out of his boxer shorts and nudging her legs wider with his knees. 'You're a snob. You're horribly spoiled ...' He kissed her again, delighted and amazed by the strength of her response, and the way her tongue darted into his mouth like a slippery bullet. 'Pushy American bitch,' he said, pinning her arms down on the mattress with all his weight so she was spread like a butterfly on a pinboard. 'Stop trying to take the lead.'

Looking down, Honor saw his ramrod-straight erection jutting up towards her belly like a fence post, and felt a curious mixture of excitement and dread. Devon had been big, but not that big, and obviously Lucas was far more sexually experienced than she was. He had her arms pinned, so she had to draw one leg up in order to touch his dick with her foot, gently rubbing up and down the shaft with the smooth skin of her instep. Lucas closed his eyes and moaned, moving one hand down to guide himself inside her. But Honor was too quick for him. With a boldness that surprised her as much as it did him, she seized her chance, wriggling free and flipping herself round like a gymnast so that she was on top of him, and their positions were reversed. At least this way she would have some control over how deep he went.

Lucas groaned as she slipped his cock inside her. Part of him wanted to pull away and teach her who was boss. But the other part felt so fucking fantastic, as her tight muscles clenched and released him in a perfect, slowly accelerating rhythm, wild horses couldn't have got him to move. Closing his eyes, he reached up and ran his hands down her bare back, letting his fingers curl around the nape of her neck and run over each of her ribs in turn.

'You're too thin,' he said.

Honor opened her eyes for a moment and looked at him. She was about to tell him she didn't need his approval of her weight, or anything, but to her surprise she saw that there was genuine concern in his eyes. So she decided to be honest instead.

'I know. It's stress,' she said, shrugging. 'When it's bad, I can't eat.'

For the next two hours, they fucked like a pair of hormonally crazed stoats. Now that he'd finally gotten her into bed, Lucas realized just how much he'd been wanting her, and for how long. Sexually, she was a revelation, wilder than even he had imagined, and far more skilful in bed than her blow-up-doll sister. Her physical fitness and stamina were quite awesome. Honor's body might look fragile but, making love to her, Lucas discovered it was anything but. She was pure muscle. And as for her flexibility ... not even the rhythmic gymnast he'd dated in Ibiza last summer could compare. The woman had rubber bones.

For Honor, the experience was equally powerful, but in different ways. Lucas had broken her defenses and allowed years of sexual and emotional frustration to come tumbling out. Yes, he was a good lover – he ought to be, after all the practice he'd had – but it wasn't just that. Tonight was the first time Honor had had sex since Devon. It had reached the point where she'd gone without it for so long, she'd convinced herself that she didn't need it. That she was happy to let Palmers be her life, lover, family, everything. But Lucas's touch had changed all that. Like an H-bomb exploding through her body, blasting away all the fear and the pain and the loneliness, he'd reduced her to her most primitive, animal self. The delight she felt with him inside her was indescribable.

At last they collapsed side by side on the sheets like two sweat-soaked marathon runners.

'If I ask you something,' said Honor, staring at the ceiling, once she'd regained enough breath to speak, 'do you promise to give me a truthful answer?'

Turning onto his side, Lucas propped himself up on an elbow and looked at her. She looked like she'd been swimming. Her hair glistened with sweat like dewy grass and all her makeup was smudged off. Above anything else, she looked incredibly young. He didn't think he'd ever wanted another human being so much.

'Of course,' he whispered seriously. 'I'll never lie to you.'

'Am I better in bed than Tina?'

The question was so unexpected, Lucas burst out laughing.

'Sorry,' he said, seeing Honor looking crestfallen. 'I'm sorry. I've just never heard you sound so insecure before.' Her face fell further, and he quickly added: 'Of course. Of course you're better. Jesus, Honor, your sister ... she was ... it was nothing.'

'Nothing, sexually? Or nothing ...'

'Nothing, nothing. Nothing sexually, nothing emotionally. Nothing to me,' he said fervently. 'Nothing like you.'

Apparently satisfied, Honor fell silent.

'So, can I ask *you* something?' said Lucas eventually.

'Oh, yeah, you were great too,' Honor murmured, half

asleep already. 'Much better than Devon and everything.'

Lucas laughed. 'I know *that*,' he said, without a hint of irony.

'Oh, you do, do you?' said Honor, sitting up. She'd forgotten just how infuriatingly arrogant he could be. 'So what's your question, then?'

'Do you believe me? About Anton, and all the shit that happened that summer?'

Honor nodded slowly. 'I think I believed you at the hospital,' she admitted. 'I thought about what you said a lot, afterwards, and it all made sense. I just couldn't process it then. It was too soon, after the fire, losing Palmers.' She shook her head, fighting back tears. 'It was like I was at emotional ground zero. I didn't want to have to think about anything else. I didn't have the energy.'

'I understand,' said Lucas softly. 'Believe me. I do.'

Nestling against each other in the silk sheets like two sleepy, satisfied cats in the sun, they reveled in each other's warmth and the luxury of their surroundings.

'Isn't it great, being in someone else's hotel for a change?' said Lucas, dialing room service and ordering up a bottle of vintage champagne and a large bowl of french fries for Honor. 'If I owned this place I'd be stressing about every crack in the ceiling right now.'

'Me too!' laughed Honor. 'I thought I was the only person neurotic enough to do that sort of thing.'

'God, no. I don't think anyone in this business can switch off,' said Lucas. 'Not if they're any good at it anyway.'

The fries arrived, as hot and salty and greasy as Lucas could have wished for, and he was encouraged to see Honor tucking into them with undisguised relish, in between gulps of ice-cold champagne.

'Sorry,' she mumbled, her mouth full, blushing as she wiped away a trickle of vegetable oil with the back of her hand. 'I guess I worked up an appetite.'

'Good.' Grinning, Lucas slid beneath the covers like a

torpedo and began kissing her between her thighs, gently parting her pubic hair with his fingers. 'Let's get you a bit hungrier and then we can order more.'

'Honor gasped and giggled, her legs spontaneously opening wider as his tongue darted across her clitoris. She came embarrassingly quickly.

'Hey. What's wrong?' Emerging from beneath the sheets, Lucas was horrified to see she was crying.

'Nothing,' she sobbed. 'That was just ... so nice.'

Pulling her against him, Lucas stroked her long, tangled mane of hair as she lay on his chest. 'It was nice for me too,' he said, gruffly. 'Better than nice. Christ, I've wanted you for so long.'

Slowly, as the long hours of the night rolled by, he told her about everything he'd been through since leaving the Herrick: his long, desperate job search in London: the street brawl with his old boss in Ibiza that marked the low point for his battered self-esteem; the chance meeting with Connor Armstrong that changed his fortunes.

'Every day, when I walk into my hotel in Paris, or onto the virgin site in East Hampton, I pinch myself. I still can't believe this is my life.'

'Lucky you,' said Honor bitterly. 'Every time *I* walk onto that charred patch of earth that used to be Palmers, I pinch myself too. I can't believe this is *my* life. But it is.'

Lucas kissed the top of her head tenderly. 'I'm so sorry.'

'Hey, I don't want your pity, OK?' said Honor, suddenly tense again. He could feel the latticework of muscles in her back and shoulders tightening up, one after the other, like a subcutaneous Mexican wave. 'Palmers isn't done yet, whatever people might think. I'm gonna rebuild.'

Lucas didn't say anything, scared of putting his foot in it again. Privately he thought she hadn't a snowball's chance in hell of convincing anyone to fund her little pipe dream. Not with the Herrick riding high less than two blocks away, and now his new Luxe hot on its heels. Being a boutique, and modest in scale, he hoped to have the place built and open within a year, assuming he found a new, supportive partner.

'How are things with you and Petra?' he said, steering the conversation back to their mutual enemies.

Honor rolled her eyes. 'Dreadful. That bitch has been out to get me from day one,' she said, wriggling around in an effort to get comfortable in the heat of Lucas's arms. 'She's even worse than you were.'

'Thanks a lot,' said Lucas.

He told her about his own long-running feud with Petra, and his theory that Anton hired her as a deliberate, final slap in the face to him.

'If I were you, I'd have fought back,' said Honor. 'Set the record straight in the media about all this stuff. Or, failing that, gone round to the bastard's house with a baseball bat.'

'I've thought about it,' said Lucas, 'believe me. In the early days I thought of little else. But then I realized: there's no better revenge than success. Anton wanted to crush me, and he failed. Now I'm an owner, just like him. And I'm setting up shop right in his backyard. If I know the man at all, that's causing him more pain right now than a baseball bat ever could. I'll bet Petra's choking on her vodka too,' he chuckled quietly. 'Come to think of it, maybe she only drinks blood?'

He looked across at Honor to check whether she was laughing, and was annoyed to see that she'd fallen asleep. But he couldn't stay angry for long. Curled up in the fetal position with her back toward him, her truculent, hawk-like features softened in repose, hair falling across her apple breasts like Eve, she was already murmuring in her dreams. She looked so innocent and child-like, he wished he had a camera handy to capture the image so he could tease her with it in the morning.

Watching her sleep beside him, her breathing becoming deeper and slower with each passing second, he felt stupidly, deliriously happy. For a moment, he let himself indulge in a little White Knight fantasy. He imagined himself somehow finding her the backer she needed, and helping her to rebuild her beloved Palmers. He pictured her slavishly grateful to him for saving her ass, offering to do 'anything, anything at all' to thank him; while Petra struggled on foot down the Long Island Expressway's breakdown lane, dragging her suitcases behind her like a hobo.

Laughing at his own hubris, he pulled the sheet up over Honor and himself and flicked off the bedside lamp. Life, unfortunately, rarely turned out like one's fantasies. But one thing he intended to make sure of: this time next year, Luxe America would be a reality.

As for helping Honor, he'd just have to see what came up.

The first thing Honor was aware of when she woke was the glaring, blinding sunlight pouring in through the floor-to-ceiling windows. The second was the fact that she was not in her own bed. And the third was that someone seemed to be busy sawing through her skull with a hacksaw.

Groaning, she sat up, shielding her eyes from the light and trying to get her bearings. The next thing she knew Lucas, fresh from the shower and wearing only a blue towel wrapped toga-style around his snake hips, was looming over her like a gladiator.

'Good morning,' he said brightly, chuckling at her all-too-evident hangover. 'Feeling a little the worse for wear, are we, darling?'

Immediately, Honor felt her hackles rising. One night together did not make her his darling. Her brain was still foggy with sleep, but she knew she must have let her guard down horribly, a thought that left her gripped by a stomach-churning fear. But before she could say anything,

Lucas had kissed her on the top of her head (patronizing!) and launched into a monologue about his own plans for the day.

'As soon as I've called the lost baggage morons at the airport, I need to get going,' he said, dropping his towel without a hint of embarrassment while he rummaged around in his suitcase for underwear and a shirt. 'I have a meeting with a possible new partner at one over at the Venetian. Oh, that reminds me. Be an angel and call down to housekeeping, would you? Ask them to bring my blue suit up. They must have pressed it by now.'

Honor's mouth opened and closed furiously, but no words came out. Who did he think she was? His little Geisha?

Slowly, through the molasses-thick fog of her brain, the events of last night began falling into place. She felt sick. The sex had been amazing, no doubt about that. She still felt sore between her legs, and every muscle in her body ached after her energetic performance. Even now, with her head throbbing and stomach churning like a washing machine on spin, the memory of his touch excited her to a ridiculous degree.

But that was the problem. OK, so he fucked like Mick Jagger. And OK, so he *hadn't* betrayed her and Tina, like she thought. But he was still Lucas. Still one of the most arrogant chauvinist pigs to walk the planet. If not *the* most arrogant. Still the guy who, after one fuck, expected her to run wifely errands for him. Who assumed automatically that his stupid meetings were more important than hers.

Watching him pull his Calvins on over his perfect, tennis player's ass, she began to justify her anger in her own mind: he'd taken advantage of her in a vulnerable moment. She'd been drunk out of her head. She didn't know what she was doing.

But the real truth was, she was frightened. She'd opened up to Lucas last night, both literally and metaphorically, in a way she'd never done before with any man, not even Devon. She'd allowed him to see her vulnerability, her weakness, her need. That gave him power over her. Power she was now desperate to claw back.

'Get your own suit,' she snapped, wrapping the sheet around her body and heading for the shower. 'I'm busy too, you know.'

Still giddy with the rapture of last night, Lucas misjudged her mood completely. Running after her, he grabbed the corner of the sheet and whipped it off.

'Call housekeeping,' he grinned. 'Now. Before I put you over my knee.'

Somehow she looked even more gorgeous this morning, all crumpled and grumpy and still warm from bed. He made a clumsy lunge for her breasts and was taken aback when she first ducked, then lashed out at him like a rattlesnake, only narrowly missing landing a karate chop right on his balls.

'Whoah!' Backing away, he frowned, confused. 'What's the matter?'

'What's the matter?' said Honor. 'Are you kidding me? Get your own fucking suit! I have meetings of my own today which, thanks to you, I'm now late for. I was supposed to be having breakfast with Fred Gillespie at nine.'

Gillespie had been a big name in hotels in San Francisco and Seattle back in the sixties, around the time Trey took over at Palmers, and was still respected. He was something of an unofficial godfather to Honor. She hoped he might be interested in funding her rebuild, or at least loaning her some seed capital until the insurance money came through, so she could make a start.

'What time is it, anyway?' she snapped.

'Eleven,' said Lucas sulkily.

'Why didn't you wake me?'

'Because I didn't know you had a meeting, did I?' he yelled. 'Jesus, Honor. I'm not psychic.'

This was just great. Fucking American women and their fucking career bullshit. You never knew where you stood from one day to the next. Last night Honor had practically begged him to be the big, strong, macho man, and if her orgasms were anything to go by, she'd loved every minute of it. But this morning he seemed to have woken up with Germaine fucking Greer.

Well, if she wanted to pick a fight, he knew how to play that game.

'I can't believe you're seriously comparing sitting around drinking tea with some old Harvard club friend of your father's with my investor meeting,' he said.

'Fred's a serious investor,' Honor insisted.

'In what?' snapped Lucas. 'Scorched earth? You don't *have* a hotel for him to invest in, Honor. Wake up! Palmers is gone.'

For a moment she looked so wounded he regretted losing his temper.

'Look, I didn't mean that, OK?' He took a step toward her.

'Oh, sure you did,' said Honor, storming into the bathroom and slamming and locking the door behind her.

'Honor.' He banged on the door, gently at first, but when she didn't respond his knocks became louder and more irritated. 'Stop being such a spoiled child. I'm sorry if I hurt your feelings. I shouldn't have. But you have to face reality. Palmers *is* gone. I wish that weren't the case, but getting angry about it doesn't change the facts. And I *do* have a global business to run. Now, if that makes you jealous—'

'Jealous?' She took the bait. The door flew open. 'You think I'm jealous? Of *you*?'

Pushing past him, she grabbed her torn underwear from the bed and yanked it back on. Then, picking up the robe from the floor, she pulled it tightly around her tiny frame. Fuck the shower. She'd have one in her own room.

'Not in this lifetime, sweetheart,' she snarled. '*Global business* indeed! You have two hotels, Lucas. Two. And neither one of them can hold a candle to mine.'

Lucas snorted derisively. 'Rather an unfortunate turn of phrase, don't you think? Seeing as someone *did* hold a candle to yours?'

Honor walked to the door. 'Last night was a mistake.'

'At last,' said Lucas. 'Something we agree on.'

Down at reception, the desk clerk was very understanding about Honor's lost key, producing a new one in seconds and insisting on sending a bell boy up with her to make sure it worked properly. At last, alone in her room, she sat down on the bed and tried to banish the barrage of negative thoughts bombarding her brain.

It was odd. She'd done everything in her power this morning to push Lucas away. And yet part of her was crushed when he'd agreed so readily that their sleeping together was a mistake.

Down the hall, lying on his bed, Lucas wondered how it was possible to want to strangle someone and make love to them at the same time.

But neither of them put their thoughts into words. Instead, true to form, they got ready for their respective days ahead and pretended that they didn't care.

Chapter Twenty-five

Sian walked along the Strand, clapping her gloved hands together against the bitter, late-January cold.

'Why are you doing this?' she asked herself out loud, her breath shooting out in little warm clouds with each word. 'You've lost your mind, girl. You've totally lost your mind.'

Anyone watching her mumble as she weaved through the choking traffic would probably have agreed with this assessment of her mental health, although perhaps for different reasons. Sian's concern stemmed not from the fact that she was talking to herself, but from the fact that she was on her way to Ben's office. And that she was going there to ask for money.

He didn't know she was coming, which sort of made it both better and worse. Better, because it had spared her the impossible task of trying to explain everything on the phone beforehand (tricky, when every time she started dialing his number she had to rush to the loo to be sick with nerves). But worse, because it opened up the shameful possibility of him being too busy to see her.

She tried to encourage herself that he was the one who'd suggested she look into Anton Tisch in the first place. At least, she thought it was his suggestion – she'd drunk so much at that excruciating 'triple-date' dinner, she could barely remember her own name the next morning, so she couldn't be sure – and she hadn't seen or heard from Ben since.

But what if it was just a throwaway remark about Tisch? Something he'd said to be polite and show an interest in what she did for a living? Sian still tended to think of him as the tall, awkward, British beach bum who fell through Palmers' fence to ask her out – they used to joke that he'd literally fallen at her feet. But in reality, he had never been that guy. He was a seriously rich, successful businessman. An important man. Naturally he had better things to do than run around the globe helping his summer romances follow up leads for some dumb story they were working on.

Except, she told herself, tilting her head down as the wind changed direction and began slicing into her cheeks like a razor, it wasn't a dumb story. It had the makings of a great story. The kind of story that really *could* make her a big name in investigative journalism, if she wasn't forced to let the trail go cold now, through lack of funds and support.

She did have other options. She could go to one of the papers with what she had so far. But that would mean handing over control – and credit – to some megalomaniac newsdesk editor, and she'd rather stick pins in her eyes than do that. Besides, she thought, clutching the worryingly thin manila envelope that represented her 'evidence' more tightly, she really didn't have that much on paper – yet.

Anton Tisch, she was rapidly discovering, was a master at subterfuge. No matter which avenue of inquiry she tried to pursue: his love life, business life, even his childhood, she was met with roadblock after roadblock. And all along the way were littered the dead careers of reporters who'd trodden the path before her, whose editors had been either bribed or threatened into squashing their stories.

Whatever his secret – or secrets – Anton Tisch had gone to inordinate lengths to hide them. Which of course only piqued Sian's interest all the more.

Passing John Adam Street, she could see the top two floors of the impressive Adelphi building, where Tisch had his offices, jutting proudly into the skyline. She wondered if he was inside right now. The thought made her shiver even more violently than the cold, with the same mixture of excitement and fear that had propelled her through the last few weeks of late nights and dead ends on nothing but adrenaline and caffeine.

Ben's offices were another mile's walk at least, along the river toward the City, London's ancient financial district. Looking around in vain for a taxi with its light on, Sian stepped up her pace and began to jog. The sooner she got there, the sooner she'd get it over with. And at least the exercise would warm her up.

Up in his third-floor office on King William Street, Ben flipped through the pink pages of the *FT* without much interest. The FTSE and Nasdaq were both up. But the dollar was having its third bad month in a row against the euro, which would certainly mean more redemptions from Stellar investors.

Bollocks to the lot of them.

Outside the sky was a dull silver and the few trees in the City's green spaces looked spartan and spindly, waving their leafless limbs in the biting winter wind, as though sending a distress signal. Everyone's spirits seemed to fall on a day like today and Ben was no exception. Christmas and New Year were over. All that stretched ahead were endless dreary weeks of work, and cold, dark, miserable afternoons. Oh, and wedding planning. Even bloody worse.

'For God's sake, cheer up. You could curdle milk with that face.'

Tammy, who'd returned from a winter break in Barbados with a bright orange tan and her blond hair streaked platinum, brought him his post. 'You've only been engaged five minutes,' she added helpfully. 'Aren't you supposed to still be in your honeymoon phase?'

'I am,' said Ben, moodily. 'Can't you tell?'

Tammy frowned but said nothing.

'I know you women think weddings are the answer to everything. But just 'cause I'm getting married, doesn't mean I have to like the sodding weather. Or the fact the dollar's going down the shitter.'

He'd finally given in to the inevitable and proposed to Bianca on Christmas Day, having run out of reasons not to. For a couple of days, he actually felt quite good about it. She was so happy when the ring fell out of her cracker at lunch, she burst into tears on the spot, and didn't stop crying until dinner. It made him realize how much she really did love him, and he thought what an idiot he'd been to have prevaricated for so long.

But soon his doubts came creeping back, invading his peace of mind like a guilty lover stealing back into the marriage bed after dark. Bianca was already on about having a glitzy engagement bash, and getting *Tatler* to cover the wedding. It *so* wasn't his thing. But when he'd tried to explain that to her it all came out pear-shaped and she got furious with him, accusing him of having second thoughts.

It didn't help that his mum and sisters were totally on Bianca's side about everything. Within days of the engagement, they'd filled the Canvey Island house with wedding magazines and started banging on endlessly about dresses and flowers and Chantilly fucking lace. Bianca was in seventh heaven. But the happier everyone else got, the more Ben felt the pressure piling onto his shoulders. He wished he could feel like they did, all giddy and excited. But he couldn't. He just couldn't.

Tammy left him leafing through his post. Half an hour later he was deep in the legal language of an offering memorandum when she barged into his office again, looking even more orange and furious than before.

'You need to come to reception,' she announced.

'Not now, Tam, all right?' he said. 'I'm busy. Can't you deal with it?'

'If I could deal with it,' said Tammy, in a martyred, God-give-me-strength voice, 'I wouldn't be stood here, would I?'

Wearily, Ben put the memo down. 'What's the matter then?'

'A mad cow has chained herself to the settee in the lobby,' said Tammy.

'I'm sorry. A *what*?'

'A girl. A very rude girl turned up without an appointment demanding to see you,' Tam explained. 'She wouldn't tell me what it was about, so I told her to sling her hook. She then padlocked herself to the settee.'

'Are you serious?' Ben laughed.

'Do I look like I'm joking?' asked Tammy, who didn't. 'I've called security, but every time one of them comes near her she starts screaming the bloody place down, saying she'll only talk to you. She's a complete nutcase. She'll be singing "We Will Overcome" in a minute I 'spect. It can't be good for business.'

'I see,' said Ben, still smiling. And here he'd been thinking today was going to be dull as ditchwater. 'Well, I'd better come and have a look then, hadn't I?'

Coming down the grand, sweeping staircase into reception, he could see a small crowd of staff and visitors, who effectively obscured his view of the girl.

Stellar's back offices were dull and functional, but the public areas were lavish, designed to scream wealth and permanence to potential investors. With this in mind, the lobby boasted a polished marble floor, overhung by a glittering antique chandelier, and the artfully placed furnishings were all of the ornate, eighteenth-century French variety. One of these, a walnut sofa with intricately coiled arms, was the focus of the current drama.

'Excuse me.' Ben cut a swathe through his gawping staff and walked up to the girl. She was bent double, apparently securing the chain, so all he could see was the top of her dark head and a pair of white fluffy snow boots.

'I'm Ben Slater,' he said. 'Can I help you?'

Sian looked up and smiled at him ruefully. 'Yeah,' she said, blushing. 'You can help me undo this padlock. The key just snapped in half.'

Twenty minutes later, once Jimmy the handyman had arrived with a hacksaw and a mutinously grumbling Tammy had been dispatched to make some tea, the two of them were alone in Ben's office.

'I'm sorry for the dramatic entrance,' said Sian, gnawing nervously at her fingernails.

'Yeeeees,' said Ben. 'I did wonder what that was all about.'

'The chain was a last resort. But that bizarrely colored woman wasn't going to let me see you.'

'You carry a *chain* around with you?'

'Only for emergencies,' said Sian, as if that explained everything. 'What is that woman anyway? Half human, half citrus fruit?'

'Tammy's all right,' he said. 'She was trying to protect me. I think she thought you were a nutter.'

Sian blushed. 'I guess I can see why.'

She started to peel off layer after layer of coats and scarves and jumpers, dumping them all unceremoniously on the floor at her feet. Ben watched, feeling like the lucky winner in a game of human pass the parcel. When she finally got down to her pink skinny-rib sweater and jeans, her cheeks were flushed from heat and embarrassment, and her hair made her look as if she'd just been electrocuted. But to him she looked absolutely perfect.

'So, what's this all about?' he asked, genuinely curious. 'I'm assuming it's something pretty important for you to go all Emily Pankhurst on me. Rather than try something more traditional. Like, ooh, I don't know, picking up the phone.'

'It is,' said Sian. 'Important, I mean. And maybe I should have called you first. But it's kind of hard to explain. I wanted to do it in person.'

Handing him her manila folder, she waited for him to leaf through its contents.

'I don't understand,' he said eventually, pulling out one of many similar photographs of semi-naked teenage girls. 'Who are these kids?'

'They're hookers,' said Sian. 'But you're right, they *are* kids. Every one of these girls is under age. And look what else they have in common.'

She pointed out a piece of paper with a bunch of names on it, six of which had been highlighted in bright green pen. The letterhead at the top of the page said *Children of Hope Care Home, Southwark*.

'They were all in care?' said Ben, shrugging. 'Is that really so surprising? Most British prostitutes started out that way, I imagine.'

'Yes, but they're all from the *same* home. And they've all posted their pictures on the same website, *www.hothookups. com*.' She handed him a second piece of paper. 'Guess who's on the board of Children of Hope? And guess who *also* holds a majority stake in Delta Media, the company that owns hot hookups?'

'Who?' Ben looked blank.

'Look!' Reaching over, Sian pointed to one of the names in the small print at the bottom of both documents. 'Anton Tisch, that's who. And that's just the beginning.'

She walked him through more pictures, and testimonials from past lovers who'd accused him of everything from in-decent assault to rape, until they were paid – or threatened – into retracting their claims.

'This is all very well,' said Ben, trying not to sound too discouraging, as he could see the passion and expectation written across Sian's face. 'I can see he doesn't exactly come across as Santa Claus. But then, don't people know that already? That he's, you know, a bit dodgy with women?'

'A *bit dodgy*?' Sian looked at him, incredulous. 'He's pushing vulnerable children into prostitution! Children he has a legal duty to protect. He's probably fucking them himself, for Christ's sake.'

'You don't know that,' said Ben reasonably. 'None of what you've shown me here proves it.'

'Sorry to interrupt.' Tammy appeared at the door and gave Sian a look of purest contempt. 'But your *fiancee*'s on line two.' She gave the word as much emphasis as possible. 'She wants to know if you've remembered you're interviewing the wedding planner at lunch.'

'Oh,' Ben looked awkward. 'Yeah. I forgot, but that's cool. Tell her I'll see her at home at one.'

'You don't want to tell her yourself?' Tammy held the portable phone out to him.

'No,' said Ben, getting irritated. 'I don't. And please don't put any more calls through to me, all right? I'm busy.'

He turned back to Sian, who had a fixed smile glued to her face, not unlike a corpse in the early stages of rigor mortis.

'You're engaged?' she said, still smiling. 'I didn't know. Congratulations.'

'Thanks,' said Ben, wishing he didn't feel so empty when he said it.

'Bianca's incredibly beautiful,' said Sian.

She had no idea why she said it. The words just seemed to fall out of her mouth, like lines in a play.

'Er, yes,' said Ben absently. 'Yes, I suppose she is. Thank you.'

A horrible, awkward silence fell between them. They looked at one another, each willing the other to say something. In the end, Ben spoke first.

'You and Paddy must come to the wedding.'

'Of course!' said Sian. Right after I've finished pulling the shreds of my heart out of the blender. 'We'd love to. We'll probably be next down the aisle ourselves. You can give us some pointers.'

More silence.

Oh God. What had possessed her to say that? If she'd happened to have a cyanide tablet to hand, she'd happily have swallowed it in that moment. She was no more planning to marry Paddy than fly to the moon.

'Good,' said Ben, his tone brusque and businesslike all of a sudden. 'Fine. Now look, about this Anton business.'

'I know what I've got so far is shaky,' said Sian, grateful that he'd changed the subject. 'I do know that. But I really feel like I'm on to something here, Ben. First there are all the stories already in the public domain, about that lap dancer and him not paying child support. Then, according to you, he set up that whole Tina Palmer thing.'

'So Lucas tells me.'

'And that tape, by the way, also first came out on the net via another Delta Media site – what a coincidence.' She was barely pausing to draw breath now, so convinced was she of her own argument. 'And now these girls from *his* care home mysteriously find their way onto *his* website ... Come on. You don't find any of this even the least bit suspicious?'

Ben was silent for a moment. He found it all highly suspicious. But suspicion and proof were very different things. His dislike of Anton might be prejudicing his judgment.

'What are you looking for?' he asked. 'From me, I mean?'

Sian started mumbling incoherently. She hadn't got as far as thinking up a specific figure, and didn't want to be the first to suggest one.

'I assume you need money to fund your research?'

Sian nodded, blushing red as a double decker.

'Is a hundred grand enough?' said Ben.

Her jaw dropped. 'A hundred ... oh, no, goodness, that's way too much. I couldn't possibly ask for that much.'

'You didn't ask for it,' said Ben. 'I'm offering. Look.' Reaching forward, he took her hand in his. 'I have to be very careful. I don't want to be seen to be supporting some kind of witch hunt against my biggest business rival.'

'Of course not,' said Sian, horrified. 'And it isn't a witch hunt. I'm only interested in the truth.'

'Nevertheless, my name has to stay out of it,' said Ben firmly. 'Understood?'

'Absolutely,' she nodded vehemently. 'On pain of death, I swear.'

'The truth is, if Tisch goes out of business, that'll be worth a lot more than a hundred grand to me,' admitted Ben, squeezing her hand. 'But more importantly, if he *is* trafficking kids, he deserves everything you can throw at him. Besides, after all the shit he pulled on Lucas, I'd like to see him get a taste of his own medicine. I'm happy to help.'

Sian, whose heart had practically stopped beating when he took her hand, immediately pulled it away at the mention of Lucas.

'Why do you even still care about that guy?' she said, shaking her head. 'He's such a jerk.'

'He's changed,' said Ben. 'People do, you know. You should give him another chance.'

'Hmm,' said Sian, skeptically. 'Maybe next lifetime.'

Gathering up her ridiculous pile of outerwear, she thanked Ben again profusely, and promised to call with regular updates on her progress.

'Email me your account details and I'll have Coutts wire the money first thing in the morning,' said Ben, as she made for the door. 'Oh, and don't forget this.' He handed her her broken padlock and chain. 'You never know whose sofa you may need to lay claim to next, right?'

'Right,' Sian blushed, kissing him briefly on the cheek. 'Sorry again. About that.'

When Tammy bustled in to his office five minutes later, Ben was still standing in the exact same spot where Sian had left him, staring into space.

'Good,' she said briskly. 'She's gone. Right then. D'you want me to book you a car at twelve forty-five, or are you driving?'

'Hmm?' said Ben.

'The wedding planner,' said Tammy, with a lot more patience than she felt. 'Remember?'

'Oh. Yeah. Book the car,' said Ben. But wedding planners were the last thing on his mind. He now had a legitimate reason to talk to Sian, and even to see her regularly. Bianca was so wrapped up in bridesmaids dresses and *placements*, she wouldn't bat an eyelid. And who knew, maybe he'd even get a bonus out of it and knock Anton Tisch and the unstoppable Excelsior off their market-dominating pedestal?

Today was starting to look up after all.

Anton grabbed Petra's breasts with both hands and squeezed tightly, sucking in his paunch as he thrust inside her.

Not bad for fifty-two, he thought smugly, feeling his glutes contract and his lower back muscles give a satisfying ripple as he moved. Fucking Petra was like driving a Bentley Continental: smooth, easy and immensely satisfying. She was always wet for him, but he made sure to slather her between the legs with a generous dollop of astroglide anyway. It made it easier for him to shift gears from drive into reverse, as he liked to think of it. And although it didn't take her pain away completely, listening to the woman's muffled, high-pitched squeals was all part of the thrill of anal sex – yet another activity that Petra excelled at.

'Ah,' she hollered now, right on cue. 'Not so hard, Anton, please. It hurts.'

But the arching of her back and stiffening of her nipples beneath his palms told a different story.

'Be quiet,' he said, smiling as he felt her tighten the muscles gripping his cock, in an involuntary little spasm of excitement.

Her body, displayed in front of him on all fours and to spectacular effect in the mirrored walls of the hotel bedroom, was a work of art. Her skin was white and smooth, her breasts and buttocks full but firm (he despised scrawny women), and her legs long and infinitely spreadable. Between them was a neatly trimmed landing strip of pubic hair, dyed the same white-blond as the hair on her head, around which everything else had been waxed into oblivion: perfect.

Better in bed than a prostitute, more discreet than a KGB agent, well bred and smart to boot, she was the best lover he'd ever had, as well as one of the finest managers he'd ever employed. Thanks to her daddy Oleg, a Russian press baron, she was also independently wealthy – for Petra, her career was purely about ambition, never money – and she had as little interest in marrying him as he did in marrying her.

In short, he thought, grabbing hold of her hair as he felt his orgasm building, she was his ideal woman. He must be careful not to attach himself emotionally, or he'd be sunk.

'Turn around,' he grunted, pulling his twitching dick out of her body and holding it in his hands. She complied, positioning herself the way she knew he wanted – kneeling, but very low, so that he could kneel over her. Grabbing her skull, he yanked her head backwards, then came, showering her alabaster cheeks with warm spurts of semen, one after another.

When he was finished, he sank back against the fluffy white pillows and gazed contentedly at the ceiling. He liked the Hotel Pennsylvania. There was something so very New York about it that appealed to him. Not the minimalist, modern, self-conscious Schrager New York. This was the old-school version: classy, luxurious, stylish in its own understated, confident way. He adored the fact that Duke Ellington and Glen Miller had once been guests. Miller had even written a song incorporating the Pen's telephone number. Best of all, they let him bring Mitzi here, a concession Anton considered highly civilized.

In normal circumstances he'd have stayed at the Herrick. But East Hampton was so desolate and dreary in winter and he couldn't face the trek out there. Besides, he was only in New York for two days, on fund business, so it didn't make sense to stay out of town.

'Tell me more about Vegas,' he called after Petra, who'd disappeared into the bathroom to clean up.

'Oh, it was hilarious,' she said, re-emerging still damp from the shower and crawling under the sheet beside him. 'I wish you'd been there. You'd have laughed.'

That was another thing he loved about her. No matter how much he degraded or controlled her in bed, as soon as sex was over it was back to conversation as usual. Sitting up naked in bed, she looked as clean and flushed as if she'd just finished an energetic game of tennis. Certainly she wasn't remotely ashamed.

'Would I?' he said, kissing her indulgently.

'Lucas was strutting around like Mick Jagger, talking up his new hotel.'

Anton had tried his damnedest to stop Lucas acquiring any land in the Hamptons, but he'd underestimated the strength of local hostility towards the ever-brasher Herrick. All his bribes to the planning committee were rejected, and his threats – perhaps foolishly – ignored. As a last resort he'd promised the owner of the plot that Lucas had eventually bought three times Lucas's offer not to sell to him. But the seller was rich enough not to need Anton's money, and stubborn enough not to appreciate being bullied. The deal had gone ahead.

'You know he's calling it Luxe America now?' Petra gave a short, derisive snort. 'Talk about megalomania! Why not Luxe Planet Earth? Luxe Cosmos? He's so ridiculous, with his pathetic little postage stamp of land. It's not even on the good side of town.'

'Has he started building works yet?' asked Anton casually. Though irritated Lucas had found a site, Anton didn't feel threatened by him. The tiny scale of what he was proposing in the Hamptons would barely impact the Herrick, like a flea on the back of a camel.

Petra shook her head. 'No. I drove by the site yesterday morning and it was deserted. He's cleared planning though. Fuck knows how he managed that.'

'Indeed,' growled Anton.

'And he's hired a site manager, a Frenchman, who's been running around town telling everyone they'll be open by Christmas.'

'Has he indeed?' said Anton. 'Well, we'll see about that. Who's funding him, do you know? He's only just opened in Paris, so he must be stretched pretty thin.'

'If he is, you'd never know it, the way he was strutting around like cock of the walk,' said Petra sharply. 'Word is, he's had a serious falling out with his partner and is scouting about for someone new.'

Anton raised an eyebrow. That was interesting. He made a mental note to find out the name of Lucas's partner and get in touch.

'The funniest thing of all wasn't Lucas, though,' said Petra, her eyes lighting up with cruelty like a cat before a kill. 'It was Honor Palmer, running around the Wynn with her little bag of architects' plans, trying to find someone to cough up for a complete rebuild. If I didn't hate her so much, I might actually have felt sorry for her. Talk about the mighty fallen.'

Anton smiled. He didn't share Petra's passionate loathing for Honor, but he could still relish the image of East Hampton's one-time princess wandering Las Vegas cap in hand like a pauper.

'No takers?' he asked.

'Of course not!' Petra sneered. 'Well, unless you count Fred Gillespie, who agreed to lend her a couple of hundred out of pity. She needs ten million for that project, at least; the insurers aren't budging and all the Palmer family money's gone up Tina's nose. She'll probably end up laying the bricks herself. I can just picture her in a pair of overalls and a hard hat, can't you? Or perhaps she and her humanitarian sister can shoot a new home movie. That should raise a few bucks.'

'Not to mention a few dicks,' said Anton, and they both laughed.

It was a novel sensation for him to feel so companionable with a woman. But Petra really did feel like a partner. An equal, even. He was also flattered that she found him funny. In England people continually made jokes about Germans being humorless, and though he pretended to laugh along, inside these jibes needled him more than he liked to admit. He'd always considered himself to be really quite witty. It was a pleasure to have finally found a woman who thought so too.

'Let's have a party,' he said, out of the blue.

Petra looked perplexed. 'A party? What for?'

'To celebrate our being voted Relais Chateaux's number one.'

Throwing back the covers with a sigh, Petra got out of bed and started pulling on her clothes. 'You're jumping the gun a bit, aren't you?' she said, doing up the fly on her white Calvin Klein jeans with an audibly brusque *zip*. 'The results aren't out until next month.'

'Actually,' said Anton smugly, 'I got a call from Matthieu Fremeau in Geneva yesterday. Strictly off the record, of course, but he says we've got it.'

Shrieking like a banshee, Petra dropped her bra and sweater on the ground and made a flying leap, topless, back onto the bed and into his arms.

'Really?' She beamed, her face flushed with triumph and excitement. 'He's quite sure?'

'Quite,' said Anton, laughing, and cupping her soft, milky

white breasts in his hands. 'We'll do the party in the summer. Make sure it's so fabulous that the press lose interest in Lucas and his pathetic efforts to compete with us.'

'Oh, don't worry,' said Petra. 'It'll be fabulous all right.'

Flipping onto her knees, she lowered her head and wrapped her lips lovingly around his cock, her tongue caressing him expertly until he hardened like cooling lava.

Closing his eyes, Anton relished the sensation. Did life get any better than this?

He had the number one fund, the number one hotel and now the number one woman in the world.

He deserved a fucking party.

Chapter Twenty-six

Honor leaned heavily on the handle of the strimmer, and peeled off the blue cotton shirt that was glued to her back with sweat. Tying it around her waist, she took a moment to get her breath back.

In front of her was a thing of rare beauty, at least in her eyes: a wooden skeleton of a building, half finished on the west side but still open to the elements everywhere else, its slate-tiled roof just beginning to take shape beneath a blindingly bright April sun.

The great Palmers rebuild had been underway for ten weeks now. Sometimes, waking up in the little cottage she'd rented in town, her muscles aching from the previous day's labor, she still found it hard to believe that it was really happening. That the dream that had seemed so utterly hopeless in Vegas was actually coming to fruition.

After her disastrous one-night stand with Lucas – an error of judgment that still haunted her daily – Honor's luck had finally changed. First Fred Gillespie, bless his triply bypassed heart, had agreed to an interest-free loan of two hundred and fifty thousand to 'get the ball rolling' as he put it.

'Of course I'll help you, kiddo,' he said, taking her hand between his own great bear paws over lunch at the Venetian. 'Your father was like a brother to me. And I know he may not always have shown it too well, but Trey loved you. If he'd still been in his right mind at the end, he'd never have behaved the way he did, leaving your trust so vulnerable.'

Honor was so choked, she burst into tears. The fiasco

of her night with Lucas, on top of the stress of the last few months, had left her seriously tired and emotional. Fred's kindness was just too much.

The quarter of a million he was offering was barely a drop in the ocean of what she needed, but his faith in her marked a turning point in her own thinking. How could she expect an outsider to invest, with no security beyond an insurance payout that now looked ever more unlikely, if she wasn't prepared to lose the shirt from her own back?

As soon as she got back from the conference, she met with a bunch of contractors, hired one, and set them to work at once, blowing almost all of Fred's money on their first retainer and initial materials. Knowing that if she didn't raise more cash immediately she would lose everything, her next step was to meet with the mortgage company and come to an agreement for paying off her debts slowly that stopped just short of declaring herself bankrupt. After that, she put her old Boston bachelorette pad on the market and began systematically selling off every last asset, from stocks and premium bonds to valuable family paintings. With gut-wrenching regret, she even sold the jewellery her mother had left her as a keepsake – two valuable ruby bracelets and a topaz and diamond choker, so precious to her that she'd never even worn them once, for risk of losing them.

'Are you quite certain, Miss Palmer?' the kind man at Christie's in New York had asked her, watching her lovingly finger the stones as she handed them over. 'I'm sure we can fetch a good price for them, but sentimental items like this ... you may live to regret parting with them.'

I'm already regretting parting with them, thought Honor with a pang. All she had left of her mother now were some dog-eared photographs and a few letters she'd gleaned from the chaos of Trey's home office after he died. She tried not to think about Tina, lounging around getting stoned in Santa Fe while that blood-sucking cult bled her bank accounts dry. She must stay focused on Palmers – keep her eyes on the prize, as Trey always used to say. Besides, she reasoned with herself firmly, it was only jewellery, and no more part of her mother than Palmers had once been.

Depressingly, even after turning her entire life into one big yard sale, she was still a long way short of what she needed to finish the building project. Day to day, week to week, she lived on a knife-edge, watching her funds deplete, sucked into the black hole of construction far faster than she could replace them. Desperate, she swallowed her pride and allowed gossip and lifestyle magazines to write features on her. They all wanted to know about her relationship with Tina, who by now had achieved iconic pin-up status similar to Pam Anderson's as America's favorite slut-turned-saint. Honor quickly learned the art of providing them with exclusive 'new' information, without actually revealing anything significant, and soon became a regular on the pages of *US Weekly*, *In Style* and even European magazines like *Hello!* and *OK!* She tried to tell herself that it would all be good publicity for Palmers when they opened next year (please God let them open next year!) and that in any case she needed the money and had no other choice. But she still felt like a prostitute every time she saw air-brushed pictures of herself lounging on a couch looking pampered and privileged. They normally had her in floaty John Galliano dresses, holding a flute of champagne. What a joke! She seemed to spend most of her time these days in overalls or sweatpants, schlepping bricks and tiles around like a carthorse.

Not that she was complaining. Despite the back-breaking work and constant financial worry, coming on site every morning was a joy, and she wouldn't have sacrificed her hands-on involvement for anything, however much Petra Kamalski might scoff. Whether looking at spreadsheets, arguing with suppliers, or getting down onto her hands and knees to inspect the damp proofing, this was Honor's dream made real. She needed to be a part of it, to live it and breathe it like the oxygen that, for her, it was. All the old magic from her childhood – the Palmers magic – was still there. She could feel it in the air. But this time, Honor controlled it. *She* was the sorcerer, conjuring the building and the gardens to her will. Even now, in its half-built state, it was so fucking beautiful it made her want to cry.

The toughest times came at the end of the day, when she was forced to leave the magic behind and go home. It would be many months yet until she could move in to the hotel. Until then, 'home' was a quaint but impractical cottage slap bang in the middle of town – impractical because there was nowhere near enough space for the mountainous piles of paperwork that the building project seemed to generate on an hourly basis; and because there was no privacy. Many a morning Honor had woken to the sound of clattering downstairs, and charged into the kitchen with the nearest blunt instrument only to find it was Mrs. Miggins from next door returning the cup of sugar she'd borrowed, or Joe, the site manager, letting himself in to look for some plans, or just in search of a cup of coffee. While it was nice to feel part of a community, and to feel that local people – Petra aside, of course – were rooting for her and for Palmers, Honor was discovering that you could definitely have too much of a good thing.

Last week, to her passionate relief, she'd received a phone call from her old bank manager and former family friend, Randy Malone.

'You've come a long way with your rebuild, I see,' he told her warmly. 'In the light of what you've achieved, and the investment already made, the bank might be prepared to reconsider that loan you asked for a few months back. Why don't you pop in for a chat?'

On cloud nine, Honor skipped into town to meet him, but her euphoria soon vanished when she heard the rate of interest they were offering.

'That's daylight robbery!' she gasped indignantly, the

figures swimming before her eyes. 'You've known me since I was born, Randy. How can you even think of ripping me off like that?'

'It's a competitive rate, Honor,' the old man insisted sanctimoniously. 'If you'd prefer an equity partner, by all means go and look for one. But I think you may find it harder than you anticipate. Hotels are always a high-risk proposition, especially when you've got one as successful as the Herrick already established up the road. All commercial real estate's looking very soft right now.'

Not as soft as your backbone, thought Honor, mutinously. But she desperately needed the money. With a loan this size she could guarantee finishing the construction on time. She couldn't afford to refuse, and they both knew it.

At least she could enjoy the small comfort of knowing that Luxe America, the grand project Lucas had been so insufferably arrogant about in Vegas, had yet to get off the starting blocks. Bogged down in a complicated, multi-national lawsuit with Connor Armstrong (funded, or so it was rumored, by Anton Tisch) he and his new American partner were forbidden to start work until the case was settled. Crushed under a pile of injunctions fatter than the Koran, they had no choice but to sit on their hands for the foreseeable future.

Lucas's enforced absence from East Hampton was a bonus for Honor, but it didn't mean he wasn't on her mind. Ever since Vegas she'd been plagued by flashbacks of their night together. She tried hard to focus on the negative: his arrogance the morning after, how dismissive he'd been of her plans to rebuild Palmers. But the physical memory of his touch still haunted her. More than once she'd woken in the middle of the night, after a particularly erotic dream, feeling so frustrated that she'd had to throw on her gym shorts and go for a run, just to get it out of her system.

Reaching the end of the strip of turf, she switched off the rickety old strimmer and turned around to admire her handiwork. Not bad, especially considering that the closest she'd come to manual labor growing up was handing her dirty laundry to the maid.

Petra and her cronies could make fun of her all they liked. Honor didn't care. When this place was finished, they'd all be eating their words. Trendy, flash-in-the-pan hotels like the Herrick always burned themselves out in the end. That was the nature of the beast – no one place could remain the 'it' spot forever. However high-end they were, and however hard they tried to differentiate themselves, the Tischens were a chain. So were the Luxes, whatever Lucas might claim. Only Palmers was a one-off. Unique. Only Palmers had the magic.

It was hard to define what made a hotel a classic. Even Honor wasn't sure she could put it into words. All she knew was that whatever alchemy it took, the Palmers of her grandfather's day had had it in bucketloads.

And she vowed that, by this time next year, *her* version was going to have it too.

Walking back to her hotel room in the sweltering, ninety-degree heat, Sian felt the weight of the world on her bony, sunburned shoulders.

She was in Grand Cayman, on the last leg of an exhausting paper trail that might or might not throw more light on Anton Tisch's links with the corrupt Azerbaijani government. Right now, unfortunately, her money was on the latter option. Or rather, Ben's money, seeing as that was what she was spending.

The last three months had been the most exciting, hardworking and frustrating of her life. Tisch was a uniquely compelling subject, and unraveling the murky depths of his past had rapidly morphed from a professional interest into a deeply personal obsession. Regularly putting in eighteen-hour days, which often involved skipped meals, she'd now reached the point where she even dreamed about Anton at night, his pale, waxy, emotionless face competing with Ben's freckled, broken-nosed loveliness for her subconscious's attention.

But as driven as she was, she constantly seemed to be moving one step forward and two steps back. An unexpected source would suddenly pop up from nowhere, providing her with the name and address of one of Anton's underage poppets, then she'd travel halfway across Europe to discover that the girl was too drugged out of her mind to make a statement. Unsolicited letters, hinting darkly at possible involvement with the Russian mafia and ex-KGB underworld, had Sian buying an air ticket to St. Petersburg, only to find that her British Press Association accreditation wasn't recognized and she was denied access to even the most basic documentary evidence. Other letters, threatening letters, had also started hitting her and Lola's doormat with depressing regularity. Sian told Ben about the first one, from some illiterate Eastern-bloc hood with an overactive imagination and a well-developed knife fetish. But Ben had overreacted so massively, threatening to pull the plug on the whole story if she put her personal safety at risk, that she'd kept schtum about the rest of them.

The frustrations of the investigation were as nothing, however, compared to the torture of working with Ben. As the weeks rolled by and the case against Anton built, Sian spent more and more long evenings over at his flat, poring over documents and planning the next prong of attack. At the beginning, Bianca had pushed off and left them to it. But lately, perhaps sensing the longing that poured out of Sian like water through a sieve and wanting to guard her territory, she'd taken to hanging around, even taking a nominal interest in the story herself. Never anything less than physically perfect, she lolled on the couch next to Ben in her skinny-rib vests and spray-on fucking jeans, resting a flawless manicured hand on his thigh in a gesture of casual possessiveness that made Sian want to leap up and bite her, like a snake. Of course, she felt desperately ashamed of her hostility. Bianca was so self-evidently a good and loving person, and much more deserving of Ben than she was. But she couldn't help it.

Like a horror movie she couldn't switch off, she played every glance, touch and gesture over and over in her mind, analyzing Ben's responses to Bianca and to her with the obsessive precision of a microbiologist poring over a single cell. Often she thought she noticed him distancing himself from Bianca, withdrawing eye contact or shifting positions when she came and sat next to him. Occasionally, he even seemed to look lingeringly at Sian herself, or to jump with the same high-voltage shock that she did when their hands accidentally brushed against one another. But perhaps this was just wishful thinking, in both instances? His wedding to Bianca, scheduled for this August, was still very much on. And despite numerous opportunities, he hadn't made the slightest pass at Sian in the twelve long weeks they'd been working together.

She would have loved to confide in Lola about her feelings, and her fears. But ever since the story had hijacked her life, a growing distance had been developing between the two girls. It got worse about a month ago, when Sian had finally bitten the bullet and broken up with Paddy.

'But you can't,' said Lola incredulously, and not a little tactlessly, when Sian told her the news. 'You two are so perfect together.'

'Believe me,' said Sian sadly, 'we're not.'

'But he's such a wonderful guy. And he really loves you.'

'I know,' snapped Sian, guilt and lack of sleep making her more than usually irritable. 'OK? I know. Why d'you think I dated him for so long? We just ran out of steam, that's all. I can't explain it.'

She couldn't admit that Ben coming back into her life had so completely poleaxed her, sexually and emotionally, that she felt physically sick every time Paddy touched her. That seeing his loving, unsuspecting face come home in the evenings, clouded with doubt and rejection that he didn't understand, made her want to sob out loud with guilt. Paddy *was* a lovely guy, the best. He deserved to be with someone who could love him properly, who didn't have to pretend.

Knowing that Lola thought she was simply being selfish, and that it was her obsession with work that had come between her and Paddy, made the whole awful episode even more painful. Unable to deal with the criticism, or to bear watching Lola and Marti so happy and cocooned in love for one another, she started working even longer hours, coming home later and later and sneaking out of the flat at the crack of dawn. Inevitably, the distance between the two girls grew, at the very time when Sian most longed to be able to bridge it.

Boarding the plane for Cayman had been a relief, a welcome escape from Ben and Bianca, and Lola's ever-present resentment. But as soon as she landed in the famously secretive tax haven, and official home of most of Anton's businesses, she'd felt her positive spirits fading.

Less than five hundred miles south of Miami, the so-called 'Caribbean paradise' of the Cayman Islands was Sian's idea of hell: luxuriously soulless hotels, like the Hyatt Regency where she was staying, loomed up out of the surrounding poverty like insensitive giants, their gazes focused firmly on the sunny blue sky and still waters of the ocean beyond, and not the slums at their feet. Like Miami, extreme wealth and extreme poverty walked hand in hand here. But somehow, lacking Miami's vibrancy and the hope and energy of its ethnic melting pot, the division of wealth seemed starker and more brutal in Cayman. To Sian, it felt like a Swiss version of an island paradise: Jamaica, run by civil servants. She could quite imagine Anton feeling at home here, even without the tax breaks, and was unsurprised to learn that, unlike most of the internationally wealthy with accounts and trusts on the islands, he'd actually bought a villa on Grand Cayman and used it regularly for a number of years.

She'd hoped he might have had some neighbors from that time who remembered him and could fill in some of the many blanks in her narrative so far. Perhaps he'd joined the local golf or yacht club? Become buddy-buddy with the Ferrari dealership in the harbor? But no. If he'd made any social contacts on Cayman, he'd taken pains to keep them as discreet as his business dealings. After three exhausting days here, Sian had still not found the lead she'd hoped for. There had been one interesting development today, a bank account number that hadn't cropped up before on any of her searches, which she'd traced to a personal account at Uneximbank in Moscow.

When she finally got back to the Hyatt, she slid her key-card into the door of her room and sighed with relief as she walked into a cooling air-conditioned breeze. Peeling off the linen jacket that had stuck to her skin like a cheesecloth, she kicked off her shoes and flung herself back on the bed, luxuriating in the soft welcome of the mattress.

She only intended to take the weight off her feet for a minute, but the next thing she knew she was woken by the insistent ringing of the phone by her bedside. Groggily lifting the receiver, she noticed it was dark outside. How long had she been asleep?

'Hello?' she mumbled.

'It's me.' Ben's booming cockney voice sounded crackly, diminished by distance. But Sian's innards turned to liquid just the same. 'Just wondering how you got on today?'

'Fine,' said Sian. Still half asleep, she stifled a yawn.

'Shit, I didn't wake you, did I?'

'No, no, not at all. Of course not.' Desperate to prolong the conversation, she forced herself to pep up, and launched into a garrulous monologue about the day's progress, or lack of it. 'I did come up with one new lead though,' she said, and told him about the Russian bank account. 'I'm thinking of leaving here early and flying out to Moscow in the morning to do some digging.'

'I don't think that's such a good idea,' said Ben, who suddenly had visions of her being pursued down a dark alleyway by a bunch of murderous Kremlin hoods. 'If Tisch *is* involved with anything dodgy out there, and you show up sniffing about, things could get very nasty very quickly. Those Ruskies don't just put the frighteners on people. They mean business, and they don't give a shit if you're a woman or what country you're from.'

'Come on,' said Sian teasingly. 'Don't you think you're being just a teeny bit melodramatic? What are they gonna do, slip strychnine into my tea?'

'They might,' said Ben, trying not to sound as desperately anxious as he felt. Sian was so obsessed with getting her scoop, she might easily do something reckless. And the former Soviet underworld was no joke. 'Or they might just shoot you in the head, like poor old Anna Polly-what's-her-face.'

'Politkovskaya,' said Sian. 'And they won't. She was after Putin. I'm after a German financier the Kremlin probably haven't even heard of. Don't worry.'

But Ben did worry.

Sitting alone in his empty office – it was half past nine in London, and apart from the poor drones in M&A, the rest of the City had long since gone home to bed – he launched the Google home page. Typing in 'Russia, Journalist, Murder' he was horrified to read that almost three hundred members of the press, many of them foreign nationals, had been killed since the fall of communism in Russia. Sian was incapable of being discreet. She was bound to go barging in there like Ruby Wax on speed, demanding 'airn-sers,' as she would put it. You could hear her American accent from a hundred paces, he thought lovingly.

Why the fuck had he written her that stupid cheque up front? Now he had no control over where she went, or what she did.

Switching off his PC, angry at himself, he grabbed his jacket from the back of the chair and flicked off the light, wishing that the thought of going home to Bianca didn't make him feel so irrationally depressed. Tammy was right. For a soon-to-be-married multi-millionaire, he really was turning into a miserable old git. He had to get a grip.

Chapter Twenty-seven

Six weeks later, Lucas was sitting in the spectacular vaulted Gothic waiting room of the Palais de Justice in Paris, waiting for the latest round in his case with Connor Armstrong to be called. He'd begun the morning angry. After months of legal wrangling that had seen him flying back and forth from Paris to Madrid to the European courts in Strasbourg like a fricking shuttlecock, they were still no nearer a resolution. But now, after three hours numbing his ass on a hard wooden bench, he was simply bored.

There weren't even any good-looking women to distract him. He shared the waiting room with a shaven-headed, French-Arabic boy in a light polyester suit three sizes too big for him, who had the word 'defendant' written all over him (although it was his tailor who deserved the life sentence), two lawyers and a middle-aged matron with tightly curled red hair, whose bottom seemed to spread across the bench like dough, threatening to engulf Lucas at any moment.

'Would you like to have a look?' Smiling warmly, the matron offered him the copy of *Hello!* magazine she'd just finished reading. 'It's a good one.'

'Thank you,' said Lucas, who wouldn't normally have wiped his arse with *Hello!* but who was so bored he welcomed any distraction. Flicking through the glossy, picture-filled pages, he sneered inwardly at the ludicrous pretensions of the 'celebrity' subjects. Horse-faced minor aristocrats burbled on shamelessly about their relationships with royalty while posing outside their crumbling piles. Trained for nothing and having never done an honest day's work in their lives, this was probably one of the few ways they knew to make money, money they so clearly needed to prop up their over-sized houses. Lucas pictured them once the cameras had stopped rolling, sending the ball gowns and jewellery back to the pawn shop and retiring to the two rooms of the stately home they could still afford to heat, to rustle up some Tesco 'value' baked beans on toast. Everything these magazines pedaled was a sham.

But a few pages later, his internal diatribe came to an abrupt halt when he found himself face to face with a quite stunning photograph of Honor. In a wood-nymph-green silk dress, sprayed onto her tiny body like gold leaf, five-inch Jimmy Choo heels and with a simple but exquisitely cut amethyst pendant resting on her bronzed chest, she looked sexier than he'd ever seen her. Her hair, which had been mermaid-long in Vegas, was now cut into shoulder-length layers that had been streaked alternately in honey and chocolate, a perfect shade for her darker, sunkissed skin. She was lying on a stone bench in the rose garden at Palmers, propped up on one elbow with her haunting, angular face cupped in one, long-fingered hand, and her green cat's eyes burned out of the page like two nuggets of kryptonite. Lucas, for one, felt his super-powers waning when he looked at her, so regally, coolly beautiful and yet at the same time so vulnerable and slight, like a leaf that might blow away on the wind at any moment.

The piece was about Palmers, a three-page spread combining archive shots of the old hotel with bigger, sunlit pictures of the rebuild that Honor had famously commissioned now. Tucked away in the corner was a small shot of the charred remnants of the old building, taken the day after the fire. Looking at it, Lucas felt sick, thinking how close Honor must have come to being killed that day.

'The insurers are still refusing to pay our claim, even though the police have said they're forensically certain the fire was a deliberate act of arson,' she was quoted saying to the reporter.

'Disgusting,' said Lucas out loud, surprising his fellow

wait-ees with this burst of indignation on Honor's behalf. 'Fucking bloodsuckers.'

'*Without an arrest and a conviction, they say, the causes are still open to question.*' He read on. '*It's been a tough slog to raise the money to rebuild her. But I'm really proud of what we've achieved.*'

I bet you are, thought Lucas, looking at the pictures of the new hotel rising up from the earth, as white and pure as a spring snowdrop. He was still angry at Honor for the hot and cold signals she'd given him in Vegas, and for being too stubborn to call him and apologize afterwards. Why was it that women could *never* admit when they were wrong? But he had to admit she'd had more balls than he'd given her credit for when it came to rebuilding Palmers. They weren't finished yet, but Honor had already pulled off what he and most others in the business had considered an impossible feat. She deserved serious kudos for that.

Still, she must be absolutely desperate for money to have agreed to a cheesy *Hello!* feature like this one. Gossip mags were complete anathema to Honor – she considered them very much Tina territory – and Lucas could only imagine the frantic pride-swallowing that must have gone on before she poured herself into that deliciously revealing dress.

It was ironic that, even with her money problems, Honor was storming ahead at Palmers whilst he (who thanks to his new investor, the oil heir Winston Davies, had money coming out of his ears) was stuck not passing Go at Luxe America. Perhaps he'd been naive. But Connor had complained so vociferously about the business before Vegas, it hadn't occurred to Lucas that he would object to being bought out. And indeed, he'd already accepted Winston's more than generous offer for his shares both verbally and by email by the time Anton had got involved in February, stirring the pot as only he could do.

Everybody knew what had happened. But unfortunately none of them could prove it. Tisch had got in touch with

Connor and started throwing money around like a newly signed footballer in a brothel, promising him the earth and all its riches if he refused to sign the contract and stayed on at Luxe as a 'spoiler' partner, preventing further expansion, including Luxe America. Lucas and Winston countered, citing their verbal agreement and the emails, not to mention the fact that Connor had already taken receipt of the first tranch of Winston's funds by the time of his sudden change of heart. In the end, it was highly likely that the courts would rule against Connor, but that wasn't the point. With Anton's legion of international lawyers behind him, Connor was quite capable of dragging out the case for months or even years, flitting from one jurisdiction to the next each time a decision went against him, and lodging appeals every time Lucas's attorney opened his mouth.

So far, Winston had been very patient. He had the sort of wealth that made it easy to shrug off a million-dollar-plus lawsuit. Besides, he believed in Lucas and the Luxe brand, and didn't take kindly to people trying to bully him out of his business decisions. But as grateful as Lucas was for his support, it still left him nowhere in terms of getting his new hotel off the ground. And in the meantime, not only had the Herrick been voted the number one luxury hotel, with Petra planning the mother of all victory parties to celebrate this summer, but now Honor looked set to revive the Palmers franchise for a second time.

Time, in this instance, was not only money. Time was everything, and Lucas was fast running out of it.

'Monsieur Ruiz?' The sour-faced woman clerk, a gallic Barbara Walters who reeked of Jolie Madame and Elnet, emerged through the wooden double doors and nodded curtly in his direction. '*Suivez moi, s'il vous plaît.*'

'At last,' said Lucas, handing the magazine back to his dough-bottomed neighbor, who blushed and smiled as she took it. Getting wearily to his feet, he followed the clerk into the almost empty courtroom with a heavy heart. Despite all the waiting, he knew today's hearing would be just like all the others: a monumental waste of fucking time.

'Yes, yes, I can see a lot of work goes into them,' said Ben, trying to keep his temper.

'It's more than just work, duckie,' Maxwell, the flamingly camp wedding coordinator pouted furiously. 'It's artistic genius. Ice sculptures of this sort of scale and complexity are ... well,' he dabbed his brow with a monogrammed linen handkerchief, 'they're the stuff dreams are made of.'

'Not my dreams,' said Ben bluntly. 'Twenty grand and by the end of the night it's a dirty fucking puddle. Come on, B, don't you think this is just a bit extravagant?'

Bianca bit her lip and fought back tears. It wasn't that she cared about the ice sculpture so much, although she did think that the scale model of Notre Dame, complete with miniature frozen gargoyles, was exquisite. But would it really have killed Ben to show just a smidgen of enthusiasm for *any* of her and Maxwell's proposals?

The three of them were in Wedding World's offices, which took up the entire top floor of a trendy converted warehouse in Clerkenwell. The place was a cross between a New York loft and a giant padded cell. Every surface was soft, even the walls, which were covered in some sort of foam-filled white fabric that looked like stuck-on clouds, and the rounded, rubbery desks scattered around the room like so many colorful children's toys. Ben and Bianca were at one end, ensconced in a white sofa so ridiculously soft it kept threatening to swallow them whole, opposite Maxwell in a pink sixties bubble chair that had an annoying habit of swiveling and creaking whenever he moved. Between them was a white rubber coffee table, on which were spread out various books and magazines, all depicting the gruesomely vulgar weddings of Maxwell's former clients.

Ben was there on sufferance. He'd said from the beginning that he didn't want a big, flash wedding, just a traditional ceremony in a pretty country church some-where with a meal and dancing afterwards. But Bianca had had her heart set on a fairytale from the beginning and, encouraged by his mother and sisters, had pressed ahead regardless, concocting ever more extravagant and, to Ben's mind, ridiculous plans with bloody Benny Hill over there. He'd already been steamrollered into having the wedding at some damn stupid castle in Ireland, and signed off on jugglers and fire eaters and God knows what else. Next they'd be flying in Siegfried and Roy, or processing up the aisle on fucking unicorns.

'The sculpture was only an idea,' said Bianca coldly. 'If you don't like it, perhaps you'd like to suggest another centerpiece? You haven't exactly been awash with contri-butions so far.'

She knew she sounded waspish and nagging and she hated herself for it, but her nerves were frayed to ribbons. Things had been so horribly strained between them lately, ever since Ben got involved with Sian and that stupid story. Not a naturally mean person, Bianca made valiant efforts not to hate Sian, or to blame her for Ben's distancing and patent lack of interest in the wedding. But it was hard. This morning he'd been banging on about her again, even try-ing to wriggle out of their appointment with Maxwell to go and meet her from the airport.

'She's coming back from Azerbaijan this afternoon,' he said plaintively. 'She says she really needs to talk to me.'

'Well, she can join the fucking queue.' Bianca snapped. 'I need to talk to you, Ben. About our *wedding*. It's less than two months away now, you know.'

'How could I not know?' he snapped back. 'You remind me often enough.'

'And why do I have to remind you?' she yelled hysteri-cally. 'Because you're always holed up with bloody Sian in your little club of two, that's why! Obsessing over Anton

Tisch. Anyone would have thought it was her you were planning to spend the rest of your life with, not me.'

'Well, it isn't,' said Ben guiltily. 'It's you.' He knew he'd been neglecting Bianca, but it was hard when all she wanted to talk about was a wedding he was increasingly coming to dread.

'Look, all right,' he said now, flicking through one of Maxwell's magazines with about as much enthusiasm as a mother superior with a copy of *Playboy*. 'What about something like that? That'd make a good centerpiece, wouldn't it?'

Maxwell wrinkled his nose in a 'did I just tread in dog shit?' way, and looked at Ben pityingly. 'A cake?' he said. 'A bog standard, common or garden wedding cake?'

'What's wrong with it?' asked Ben.

'It's hardly very original,' said Bianca, gently.

'So? Do we have to be original about everything? Does it always have to be skydiving angels leaping off chandeliers?'

'Oh, no, of course not,' said Maxwell snidely. 'Tell you what, why don't we just have a nice bunch of flowers on the top table and be done with it? Perhaps you could pick them up from the Shell garage on your way to the service, Ben?'

'I've had enough of this,' said Ben, getting angrily to his feet. He'd given Bianca a blank cheque for this wedding and resented the implication that he was being a cheapskate. Why couldn't people see that the reason he didn't want a big, fuck-off do was that it was, A: naff as shit and B: was turning the whole thing into a performance? Couldn't Bianca tell he was nervous enough already?

'Where are you going?' she asked, getting up after him. She looked anguished and he felt awful leaving her, but the whole thing was doing his head in.

'Back to work,' he said, picking up his briefcase by the

door. 'Look, I'm sorry, B, but I'm no good at this stuff. You and Maxwell pick what you want. I'll pay for it.'

I don't want your money, thought Bianca bitterly. I want your interest. I want your heart.

As if reading her mind, Maxwell plonked his ample backside down in Ben's vacated seat and wrapped a comforting arm around her.

'There, there, duckie,' he said. 'He'll come round. The grooms are all like this in the last few weeks. It's only nerves.'

'Really?' Her eyes welled up with tears and her beautiful, full lower lip began to tremble.

'Definitely,' said Maxwell, who couldn't understand why such a show-stoppingly gorgeous girl was throwing herself away on a philistine like Ben Slater anyway. 'Trust Uncle Maxwell. I've seen it all before.'

Chapter Twenty-eight

'Truly, Mr. Tisch, we can't thank you enough.'

The painfully earnest charity worker pumped Anton's hand with her clammy palm and stared at him with her bulging bug-eyes. She must have some sort of thyroid problem. The woman looked like a blowfish with earrings.

'The difference you've made to these children is incalculable. Incalculable!'

'Not at all,' said Anton magnanimously, retrieving his hand and wiping it with distaste on his starched white handkerchief. Honestly, wasn't it enough to give money to these people, without having them paw at you afterwards with their sweaty hands, like vermin?

He was in Vauxhall, an area of London he would typically go out of his way to avoid. But tonight was the grand opening of an arts center for troubled inner-city teens, a spin-off from the Children of Hope charity of which he was patron.

Personally, he found the whole place deeply depressing. All the garish, primary colors, and walls covered with the dreadful, talentless daubs that the kids had produced. To call it art was an affront to common sense, and probably a blatant breach of the trade descriptions act. But then what could you expect from a bunch of dead-eyed crack heads, brought up on council estates? The only children with any 'hope' were the girls pretty enough to make a living off their nubile young bodies, a few of whom he'd been happy to help out personally. As for the rest, they had no future. The mindless optimism of charity workers like the blowfish woman never ceased to amaze him. Did she honestly believe a few afternoons a week throwing paint around was going to change the lives of these pond scum?

Noticing that a *London Tonight* TV crew were hovering just behind her, Anton gave her a second, ingratiating smile. 'I'm thrilled to be able to help in my own small way,' he said. 'What the children have achieved here is truly magical. You must be very proud.'

'Oh, I am, I am,' she beamed. 'God bless you.'

He was pleasantly surprised by the good press turn-out. Most journalists expected more from a charity 'do' than orange squash and a few plates of curling marmite sandwiches, but all the major papers and news channels were here. He supposed he had Saskia to thank for that.

Saskia Kennilworth, the PR girl he'd hired last year to oversee his charity work and personal branding, was already proving herself to be quite an asset. Her sloaney 'bubbly blonde' persona hid a steely business acumen that was rare in public relations, an industry largely staffed by the inbred daughters of British aristocrats, whose combined IQ would be unlikely to impress a self-respecting earthworm.

But Saskia was a pearl among swine. She was the one who'd steered him toward teen charities, and away from the more elitist opera and polo events he used to be associated with. It had turned out to be an inspired move. He'd read more positive articles about his philanthropy in the last six months than ever before. And his star definitely appeared to be rising in those all-important establishment circles.

Saskia was attractive too, albeit in a completely opposite way from Petra. She had tits the size of barrage balloons, wore far too much makeup and had a raspy, filthy, smoker's laugh that was as infectious as it was sexy. She'd come on to him like a train in their initial meeting, but he hadn't slept with her yet, as much from a lack of opportunity as anything else. He'd been traveling an awful lot lately. But Saskia was definitely on his 'to do' list. He needed to break the unhealthy cycle of monogamy he'd gotten into with Petra, and Ms. Kennilworth should provide the perfect antidote to the Slavic hauteur he'd grown to find so addictive.

'... don't you think, Mr. Tisch?'

Damn it. The blowfish was speaking to him again, and he'd been miles away. Now the cameras were trained on him hopefully, waiting for a response.

'Absolutely,' he said, smiling broadly.

Saskia was big on smiles. They made him more approachable, apparently.

It was a further twenty minutes before he was finally able to extricate himself from the glad-handers and escape to the safety of his waiting Daimler.

'Thank God,' he sighed, as the driver glided across Vauxhall Bridge, back towards civilization. The MI6 building loomed above them, illuminated an ethereal green at night, like a comic book Gotham City. Below them, the Thames oozed as shiny black and sinister as an oil slick. Anton flipped open his laptop in the back seat and went straight to his emails.

The top four were all from Petra. Two were about the arrangements for next month's 'number one' party at the Herrick. As always, she'd done a stellar job at organizing things, and had already put together a guest list and entertainment program to rival the Oscars. Scrolling down the attached list of confirmed attendees, Anton felt a warm rush of contentment: Hollywood Royalty, Rock Royalty, Fashion Royalty. There wasn't a C-lister amongst them. Only real royalty had failed to succumb to Petra's charms – they'd had a 'no' from Lady Helen Taylor. Uptight bitch. But looking at the last page, he brightened considerably, and let out a half-stifled squeal of delight: the Duchess of York was listed as a 'maybe,' along with both her daughters. Put that in your pipe and smoke it, Lady Helen!

He wondered how Petra would react if he brought Saskia

in to help corral the press coverage. Not well, he imagined, chuckling quietly. Petra responded to other attractive women the way that the majority of her sex responded to spiders. You could visibly see her flesh crawl in their presence. A brassy, British ball-breaker like Saskia would be Petra's equivalent of a fat, hairy tarantula. Throwing the two of them together was bound to result in some serious fireworks.

But he'd save that particular bombshell for later. For now, he kept his responses to Petra's messages as neutral and businesslike as usual.

By the time he clicked open her third email, with its multiple JPEG attachments, he was almost home. But the title 'Palmers Pics' piqued his interest, and he instructed his driver to make a detour through Shepherds Market and around Berkeley Square, so he could finish downloading it in the car.

'Thought you might like to see these,' Petra had written. 'From this month's *Hello!*'

Opening the first image, Anton gave a little snort of surprise, bordering on admiration. Honor had made startlingly rapid progress.

The building wasn't finished, but it couldn't be more than a couple of months from completion, and what he saw here was impressive. The facade was strongly reminiscent of the old hotel, but fell short of the sentimental replica he'd been expecting. It was grander, for one thing – the portico was taller by a good three feet, he reckoned, and it was rendered in stone, rather than the cutesy Huck Finn whitewashed wood of its predecessor. The landscaping was also done on an altogether bigger scale, although to his mind it was still drearily conservative: rose gardens, topiary, lavender-lined gravel paths. No vision. No daring. It reminded him of a slightly grander version of Southampton's 1708 House.

'Did you know she was this far down the line?' he instant-messaged Petra, before moving on to the interior shots: simple, classic bedrooms, with heavy mahogany four-posters and lots of white linen and ceiling fans; bathrooms with freestanding copper tubs, and big enough proportions to accommodate the comfy antique armchairs and paintings that gave them the feel of living rooms.

Petra IM'ed him back.

'I've been trying to tell you for months. You didn't want to know.'

Anton scowled. He didn't appreciate being upbraided by his staff, or his lovers. He'd always felt that Petra overestimated Honor's significance as a threat, her judgment clouded by her own, personal hostility. But perhaps he should have heeded her warnings after all?

Clicking open more of the pictures, he saw that Honor had given more than a nod to her family's colonial heritage. There was bound to be a pretentious, walnut-lined library in there somewhere, crammed with first editions of Hemingway. And she'd eschewed all the modern touches normally considered to be *de rigeur* in a top-flight hotel these days. There wasn't a plasma screen in sight, and the doors all had traditional locks and keys. Still, for a woman whom most of the industry had written off as a crackpot, she'd done well. He wondered how on earth she'd raised the money.

'Interesting, but not important,' he wrote back to Petra. 'She can't touch us now.'

Ninety-five percent of him believed this – that with the Herrick so firmly established, and now at world number one, Palmers stood no chance of regaining its old supremacy. But the five percent of doubt irritated him almost as much as the pictures of Honor looking so effortlessly beautiful in that green dress, a perfect match for her defiant eyes, as she lounged on the hard stone bench.

He cheered up when he read the next email, a gloating note from Connor Armstrong about yesterday's hearing in Paris. Lucas, apparently, had first shot himself in the foot by turning up to court without a tie – Madame Justice Dubois, the lesbian battleaxe judge, was not remotely impressed – and then damned himself further by losing his temper when she'd quizzed him about employing illegal immigrants in the Luxe kitchen.

'Show me a hotel chef in Paris with a kitchen full of legal workers, and I'll show you a liar,' he'd apparently roared at her. 'What does any of this have to do with Mr. Armstrong deliberately sabotaging my business?'

Needless to say, she'd ruled against him.

Anton was no admirer of Connor's. He found him pompous, and his pretensions at being a 'big hitter' in property nothing short of pathetic. But he'd really outdone himself with this court case, devoting an energy and effort to destroying Lucas that was almost a match for Anton's own. As well as the endless legal wrangles, Connor had had a hand in most of the other blows that had rained down on the nascent Luxe chain in recent months: drugs raids in Ibiza, strikes in Paris, a lurid kiss and tell with a girl from the Crazy Horse in last month's *Paris Match*. He'd been worth every penny of the blood money Anton had paid him.

So much for Lucas's boasts about opening Luxe America by the end of the year. At this rate he'd be lucky to open at all. As irritating as Honor's progress at Palmers was for Anton, he knew it would be a thousand times more galling for Lucas to see his old rival storming ahead while his shitty little business foundered in the muddy shallows, like the dying fish that it was.

'D'you want me to keep circling, sir?' The driver had already gone past Annabel's four times, and was starting to think about his bed.

'No, Michaels,' said Anton imperiously, switching off his computer. 'I've seen all I need to see. We can go home now.'

★

461

Bianca stared at the pile of dirty mugs and overflowing ashtrays in the kitchen sink and pursed her lips with annoyance.

'There are three fucking adults in this house,' she muttered furiously under her breath, scraping used cigarette butts and congealed takeaway remnants into the bin, before filling up a second sink with hot water and detergent. 'How come I'm the only one capable of cleaning up after themselves?'

It was the day after Ben had stormed out of the meeting with the wedding planner, and she'd hoped he might have shown a little sensitivity to her feelings. But no, he'd been on the phone to Sian first thing this morning, unable even to wait until he got into the office, and promptly invited her over this evening for a progress meeting.

Progress my ass, thought Bianca bitterly, peering through into the drawing room to see the two of them laughing together over yet another dumb piece of paper. They'd been working on Sian's scoop for five months now, but she'd yet to mention a publication date for the piece, and seemed as far away from finishing the damn thing as ever. Bianca tried not to believe that both of them might have an ulterior motive for dragging the thing out indefinitely. But she couldn't be sure of anything anymore.

Mindlessly dropping dirty plates and cutlery into the sink, she thought back to how much she'd liked Sian when they'd first met at that wedding in New York, and how long ago that seemed now. Back then she'd seemed spunky and fun, a real girls' girl. But Bianca had evidently misjudged her spirit of sisterhood. Sian was round at the flat all the time now, whenever she was in England anyway, shamelessly monopolizing Ben without a thought for Bianca's feelings, and pointedly excluding her from their discussions. The pair of them would smoke up a storm (Ben knew Bianca loathed smoking) emerging from their stinking den only to order huge, revolting-smelling Dominos pizzas and leaving the empty boxes and grease stains for Bianca to deal with.

She'd never been one of those up-herself, high-maintenance models that expected minions to clean up after her. Nor was she afraid of a little housework. But she wasn't a doormat and she was tired of being treated like one.

Feeling left out and taken for granted wasn't even the worst of it. It was the horrid, creeping realization, a sort of slow-growing panic, that Ben prefered Sian's company to hers. She'd tried to talk herself out of this a thousand times – to tell herself that his interest in the story was purely business, about exposing Anton as a crook so that he could win Stellar's investors back. But each time she watched him giggling with Sian over a shared joke, or even fighting with her about which angle to pursue, she felt the fear start to crawl back over her body, like lice.

Last night in bed, she'd finally plucked up the courage to voice her anxieties to Ben.

'You're being ridiculous,' he assured her. 'Sian and I were over years ago.'

But Bianca couldn't help but notice that he turned away from her when he spoke, as if his face might give him away.

'Well, if you do love me,' she said, stroking the bare curve of his back, 'why don't you make love to me?' She hated herself for sounding so weak, and jealous, for having to ask. But she needed the reassurance. 'You haven't touched me for weeks.'

Turning around with a sigh, Ben pulled her into his chest and kissed her on the forehead.

'I'm sorry,' he said gently. 'I'm just tired, that's all. It's got nothing to do with Sian. Honestly. Work's hellish, and this story's taking up a crazy amount of my time.'

'So leave it to Sian, then,' said Bianca, pulling back and kissing him on the mouth, desperately hunting for some sort of a response that went beyond brotherly affection.

'You're *paying* for the stupid thing. Let her do the bloody detective work.'

'She is doing most of it,' he said. 'She sometimes needs a sounding board, that's all.'

Bianca raised a skeptical eyebrow.

'I'm the one who stands to gain the most financially if we do nail him, so I want her to succeed,' said Ben. 'If Excelsior goes down, that would be a huge coup for me. For us.'

Reaching for her breasts, he started to stroke them, something he hadn't done in ages. Bianca closed her eyes and tried to feel comforted. They made love afterwards, and though the sex was clumsy and brief, it felt so good to be connected again, she barely noticed. Then, this morning, they'd slept in an extra hour. He'd been so sweet to her, promising they'd spend more time alone and even setting aside a whole evening next week to go through wedding plans properly with Maxwell.

But just as she was starting to relax, he'd picked up the phone to Sian, and the whole downwards spiral began again. Stacking the dripping plates to dry, Bianca was horrified to find herself fantasizing that Sian might be hit by a bus on the way home.

'Hey, chica.'

She jumped out of her skin as two strong, deeply tanned arms coiled themselves around her waist. Spinning around, she squealed with delight to see Lucas, who had let himself in.

'I can't believe he's got you barefoot in the kitchen already,' he joked, standing back to admire her flat, toned belly, exposed between a midriff-bearing tie-dye T-shirt and sexy low-cut jeans. She was Ben's girl, but he could still look. 'You're not even married yet.'

Bianca smiled. Lucas had always had an uncanny ability to make her laugh in even the blackest of circumstances. Standing in front of her, a lit Gitane in one hand and a bottle of beer in the other, he looked mightily pleased with himself. His grin was almost as broad as his shoulders.

'At this rate, I'm starting to wonder if we ever will be,' she said ruefully. 'Married, I mean.'

Lucas frowned. 'What on earth makes you say that?'

'Oh, nothing.' She turned back to the dishes so he wouldn't see the tears welling in her eyes, but it was obvious she was upset. Stubbing out his cigarette on one of the takeout boxes, Lucas gently spun her back around to face him.

'Come on, angel,' he said gently. 'You can tell Uncle Lucas.'

Bianca gave a sob. Desperate to confide suddenly, it all came flooding out: Sian's investigation into Anton and Ben spending more and more time with her, the growing distance between herself and Ben, the fights over the wedding. When she'd finished, Lucas looked stony-faced.

'That bitch,' he said viciously. 'No wonder Ben's been so bloody evasive with me recently. He didn't want to admit he's let that little gold-digger back into his life.'

'I wouldn't say she's a gold-digger, exactly,' said Bianca, shocked by the strength of his reaction. 'It's just that she's incredibly ... intrusive. Getting Ben to focus on the wedding when she's around is like trying to teach astrophysics to a goldfish.'

'Where is he?' Lucas still looked far from pleased.

'He's next door in the living room. With her.'

'With Sian?' his eyes widened. 'She's here now?'

Bianca nodded. 'But listen, darling, please don't say anything. Ben already thinks I'm overreacting and—'

'Don't worry,' Lucas said firmly. 'You leave this to me.'

The row that erupted over the next five minutes was so loud it could be heard on the street below.

'I can't believe you lied to me about this!' Lucas could be heard yelling at Ben. 'All this time Anton's been crucifying me in court, and you never even mention you've been spending the last five fucking months investigating him? I could have used some of that information. I thought we were friends.'

'No one lied to you,' said Sian furiously. 'This is my story, and it's none of your damn business.'

'You keep out of this, you poisonous little shit-stirrer,' Lucas roared at her. 'What the fuck are you doing here anyway? Still trying to get your grubby little hands on Ben's money?'

'That's enough,' said Ben, who was still recovering from the shock of Lucas's presence, never mind his tirade. 'Don't speak to Sian like that.'

'Why the hell not?' Lucas was incandescent with rage. 'And *you* ought to spend less time worrying about this tramp and more time worrying about poor Bianca. I just found her in the kitchen in floods of tears, cleaning up your mess.' He glared in disgust at the half-eaten pizzas and empty beer cans littering the room.

'I would have done it myself later,' mumbled Ben guilt-ily. 'Is she all right now?'

'No,' said Lucas. 'She's not. She's miserable as hell and she thinks you don't love her. You should get in there and sort it out.'

Ben headed for the kitchen, then looked at Sian and hesitated. 'You all right?'

'Hey, don't worry about me,' said Sian, looking daggers at Lucas. 'I can handle this prick. Go do what you've got to do.'

Ben left the room and for a few seconds the pair of them stared silently at one another, basking in mutual loathing. Then the fighting began in earnest.

'I'll give you this, you're a tenacious little cow,' said Lucas. 'Just when did you get your claws back into him exactly?'

'No one got their "claws" into anyone,' she shot back

indignantly. 'Ben's a friend. The only money he's given me has been to fund my research into Anton, a guy who, believe it or not, turns out to be an even nastier piece of work than you are.'

'At last, something we agree on,' said Lucas sarcastically. 'So Ben was the only person in the world you could have gone to for help, was he? It had nothing to do with you still holding a torch for him, or wanting to come between him and the only woman he's ever really loved?'

Sian tried to hide how stung she was. Had Ben said that to Lucas? That Bianca was the only woman he'd ever loved?

'He wasn't the only person, but he was the person with the most to gain from seeing Anton brought down. Apart from you, of course. But frankly I'd rather have taken money off Ted Bundy than let you back into my life, on any level.'

'Something else we agree on,' said Lucas bitterly, though inside he was impressed by her poise, and thinking how much she'd matured since her days as a summer maid at Palmers. He still didn't trust her an inch, especially not where Ben was concerned. But it took a tough cookie to take on the likes of Anton. She must have known that digging into his affairs would be dangerous and difficult, but if the thick slab of a file spilling its contents all over Ben's coffee table was anything to go by, she'd already got a lot to show for the risks she'd taken.

'So,' he said, idly flicking open the file and pulling out a couple of documents, 'what sort of a return have you shown him on his investment? Other than a weeping fiancée.'

'Oh no you don't.' Sian was across the room in a flash. Whipping the papers out of his hand she shoved them back into the file and, not knowing quite what else to do, sat on it. 'You think I'd trust you with my story? You can read it when it's finished like everyone else.'

'Right,' said Lucas, languorously stretching out his long

legs as he sat down on Ben's leather Chesterfield sofa. 'And when will that be? The twelfth of never, evening edition?'

'Actually, I hope to be ready to run with it next month.' Despite his needling, Sian couldn't entirely hide her excitement. 'That's why I came to see Ben tonight, before we were so rudely interrupted. I just got back from Azerbaijan. Let's just say that in the last forty-eight hours things have taken a quantum leap forward.'

Ben came back in looking tired and shut the door behind him. Lucas noticed for the first time how gray and drawn his complexion had become and how much weight he'd lost. Bianca obviously wasn't the only one with pre-wedding nerves.

'How is she?' asked Sian, earning herself a withering look from Lucas.

'She's upset,' said Ben. 'It's my fault. I was being a bit of a dick to her yesterday about this wedding planner she's hired. And then tonight, spending so much time in here with you, I think I might have added insult to injury.'

'But didn't you tell her what's happened? What we've found?' said Sian, who still found it hard at times to remember that not everyone was as obsessed with bringing Anton Tisch to justice as she was.

'No.' A soft voice came from behind Ben as Bianca opened the door. 'He didn't tell me anything. He never does.'

Having washed off her tears in the bathroom and changed into a clean sleeveless T-shirt and hot-pink cut-off Bermuda shorts, she looked like a darker, more mysterious version of Gisele Bundchen on a really, really good day. Sian, who by contrast looked tired and washed out in a sludge-brown shift dress the same color as her ancient, over-washed panties, felt a stab of envy so violent she actually clutched her chest. Pointedly ignoring Ben, Bianca made a beeline for Lucas, her protector, curling herself up next to him on the sofa. The message was clear: it wasn't two against one anymore; Lucas had arrived to even the odds. Sian got it in a heartbeat.

'We didn't think you'd be interested,' said Sian, trying not to sound as hostile as she felt. She knew she had no right to be. 'You're always complaining about how much time we spend working on it.'

'I complain about how much time *Ben* spends on it,' interrupted Bianca. 'Frankly Sian, I couldn't care less what you do with your time.'

This sudden boldness was completely out of character and took Sian by surprise. Meekly, she shut up.

'But seeing as you're here, again, monopolizing my home and my boyfriend, again,' Bianca smiled at her rival thinly, 'I think I *would* quite like to know what all the fuss has been about. And I'd like Lucas to know too.'

Sian gave a splutter that was half laugh, half naked outrage. 'Yeah, well, sorry, but it'll be a cold day in hell before we tell that scheming bastard anything. Lucas's secret-keeping record is right up there with Judas Iscariot's.'

'OK, OK.' Ben held up his hands, like an overwhelmed referee trying to separate rival teams at a football match brawl. 'I don't think any of this is particularly helpful. Bianca does have a right to know what's been going on.'

'But—' Sian tried to argue, but Ben wouldn't have it.

'No, come on, Siany, she does. She's put up with a lot.' He looked sorrowfully across at Bianca, whose eyes immediately started welling up again as she tried to smile back. Sian felt winded with jealousy, but said nothing.

'And I also think we should tell Lucas.' Ben went on, 'on the understanding that whatever gets said tonight remains between these four walls, and none of us breathes a word of it outside this room.'

'No way!' Leaping back to her feet, Sian sounded properly panicked. 'Ben, no, you promised. You promised not to tell *anyone*. That was our deal!'

'I know,' said Ben. 'But that was before we knew what

we know now. Before Azerbaijan.' Walking over, he put a reassuring hand on her shoulder, unconsciously increasing the 'them and us' atmosphere of two opposing teams, himself and Sian versus Lucas and Bianca. 'I honestly think Lucas can help. He wants to see Anton finished as much as any of us.'

'That's the second time someone's mentioned Azerbaijan,' said Lucas, who had calmed down now and whose curiosity was well and truly piqued. 'What's the connection? I mean, I know Tisch made his fortune from Russian oil.'

'It goes a lot deeper than that,' said Ben.

'First you have to swear,' said Sian. 'Swear on ...' She tried to think of anything that was important to Lucas other than himself, but drew a complete blank. 'Swear on your *honour*,' she finished sarcastically, 'that you will keep what we're about to tell you to yourself, until I tell you you can do otherwise.'

'Fuck off,' snarled Lucas. 'I don't take orders from you.'

'You do on this,' said Ben firmly. 'This is Sian's story and she's sweated blood to pull it together. You can either respect her authority or get out.'

It was hard to tell who was more pissed off by this show of support for Sian, Lucas or Bianca. Both of them looked as if he'd just offered them a bite of a dog-shit sandwich. But in the end, Lucas's curiosity got the better of him.

'Fine,' he said grudgingly. 'I swear. Now come on, what's all this about?'

Ten minutes later and, for once in his life, Lucas was lost for words.

'Pretty incredible, isn't it?' said Sian, with more than a touch of pride. 'Up until this point, most of the shit I had on him was sexual. And a lot of that was pretty fucking creepy: underage girls, prostitution, the odd sexual assault allegation here and there, although the girls always changed their tune before things got to court. But this shit?' She shook her head, still astonished by the revelations herself. 'This puts us in a whole new ballgame.'

'I don't understand,' said Bianca eventually. 'He's committed a serious crime. Surely it's your absolute duty to go to the police?'

'And lose my exclusive? Are you out of your mind?' snapped Sian. 'I haven't worked my tits off for half a year to lose my scoop at the last hurdle. We finish the story. We print it. *Then* we get dickhead locked up.'

'Darling?' Bianca turned to Ben, who'd suddenly developed a burning interest in his cuticles. 'Surely you don't agree with that?'

Ben shrugged awkwardly. His instinct was to defend Sian – this was her story, after all – but it was hard to stick up for her when she got so strident and hostile. 'It's not really up to me,' he mumbled, lamely.

'Rubbish,' said Lucas. 'You're implicated up to your eyeballs, and so are Bianca and I, now that we know, too. Suppressing evidence is a crime.'

'Please,' Sian snarled, fear making her even more aggressive. Lucas and Bianca were threatening to flush her entire story down the toilet and Ben wasn't lifting a finger to help her. 'Like you're such a fricking boy scout all of a sudden. Tell it to someone who doesn't know what a scheming little player you are, Ruiz.'

Lucas started hurling abuse back at her, but Sian ignored him.

'In any case, we still don't have all the bank account numbers we need, for the police or the papers,' she said defiantly. 'The worst thing we could do is make a move before this thing is watertight. The slightest weakness and Tisch will pounce on us like *that*.' She clicked her fingers for emphasis. Not even Lucas could argue with her about that. 'I'm going back to Azerbaijan the day after tomorrow for some more meetings.'

'What? You never mentioned another trip.' Ben, all

animation suddenly, looked pained. 'What meetings? With whom?'

Sian, who'd sat back down again, now shifted uncomfortably in her seat, tugging at the hem of her shapeless dress like a schoolgirl hauled before the principal.

'With some rebels, OK?' she said, then seeing Ben's face, added: 'I know what I'm doing. I trust these guys.'

'Then you're a bloody moron,' shouted Ben, so loudly that Bianca and Lucas both turned to stare. 'How can you possibly know who to trust? It's the wild fucking west out there. They're terrorists, for God's sake.'

'Rubbish,' said Sian sulkily. 'They're freedom fighters.'

'I don't care,' said Ben. 'Call them what you like but you are not going back out there. It's too dangerous. I'm not having you risk your life over this. It's insanity.'

Watching him, Bianca felt her heart lurch. His face was a study in anguish. Obviously the idea of Sian coming to any harm was tearing him up inside, so much so that his usual diplomacy seemed to have deserted him and he hadn't even made an effort to hide it.

For her, it was the last straw. Turning on Sian, she sprang across the room in two, long-legged bounds and physically yanked her up out of her seat.

'Get out!' she whispered, shaking with rage. 'Get the fuck out of our house and don't come back.'

Sian, who before tonight had never known Bianca to be anything other than painfully polite and accommodating, was too shocked to react. Ben had no such qualms.

'Jesus, B,' he said, pulling the two of them apart. 'What the hell are you doing?'

But Bianca was not for turning. 'I'm doing what I should have done months ago,' she sobbed, tears of anger and hurt and frustration rolling down her perfectly chiseled cheeks. 'I'm getting this bitch out of our lives before she poisons everything. She's all you fucking care about these days,

Ben. She's all you see!' Wriggling free from his grip, she lashed out at Sian again wildly, landing a painful kick to her shin before covering her face with her hands and fleeing the room in tears.

'I'm so sorry,' stammered a shell-shocked Ben, as Sian bent double, rubbing her bruised leg. 'She's never normally ... I have no idea what's got into her.'

Lucas, who'd sat back and watched in silent horror as this little drama unfolded, now shot Ben a 'who are you kidding?' look.

'It's OK,' said Sian, who was actually deeply shaken. 'I'm fine. I should go.'

'You don't have to.' The mark on her leg was already spreading, he noticed, and would no doubt soon morph into the deep plum shade she so often wore as eyeshadow, which gave her pale face an even more ethereal, other-wordly beauty. Life would be so much simpler if only he didn't want her so dreadfully much.

'I do,' said Sian, forcing a smile for his sake. 'Really. I can see myself out.'

The front door slammed shut behind her, followed by a second slam from the bedroom door at the far end of the corridor. For a few seconds Ben just stood there, forlorn, like a little boy dumped on a station platform.

'I'm going after her,' he said eventually, patting his various pockets frantically, looking for his car keys and only stopping when Lucas laid a hand on his shoulder.

'No you're not,' he said firmly. 'Bianca's the one who needs you. You stay here and sort things out with her.'

Ben looked torn. 'But Sian ... what if she? She mustn't take that flight back to Russia. I'm serious, Lucas. What if she got killed? I'd never forgive myself.'

'Give me her address,' said Lucas.

Ben looked dubious.

'For fuck's sake, give me the girl's address, all right? I

promise to go easy, and I promise to keep her on the ground, at least for the time being.'

Grabbing a piece of paper from the desk, Ben scrawled something down and pressed it into Lucas's hand.

'She lives with Lola Carter, you know,' he said. 'You might want to take a bullet-proof vest.'

'Thanks,' said Lucas grimly, nodding down the corridor in the direction of Bianca's still audible sobs. 'So might you.'

Back at the flat on Tite Street, Sian was relieved to find that Lola was out, no doubt staring doe-eyed across a candle-lit table somewhere at Marti, who'd been staying with them again for the last few weeks. She truly couldn't have faced Mr. and Mrs. Love's Young Dream tonight, nor was she in the mood for 'talking things through,' which was always Lola's answer for everything.

Flinging herself down on her bed, still unmade from this morning, she pummeled her fists into the pillows and howled for a few minutes until she felt marginally better. Then she walked into the bathroom, splashed a sinkful of ice-cold water on her face, half of which splattered down the front of her dress, and tried to marshall her muddled and depressing thoughts into some sort of order.

How the fuck had it all gone wrong tonight? She'd been so happy on the way over to Ben's, armed at last with the breakthrough they'd both been hoping for. OK, so he might not love her, and he might be about to marry officially the most beautiful woman on the planet. But their work together, this story, had built a bond between them that was uniquely theirs. Anton Tisch, of all unlikely people, had brought her and Ben together. It was a closeness that she knew couldn't last, but she'd cherished it all the more for that. And now it was gone. Just like that.

For all she knew Bianca might be at the police station right now, ruining everything. Spurred on, no doubt, by that shit-stirring motherfucker Lucas, her own personal bad penny.

'Open up!'

She was disturbed from her moping by a loud and very insistent knocking at the front door. Christ, it couldn't be the cops already, could it? She hadn't even begun to get her story straight.

'Just a minute.' Frantically scraping her unruly hair back into a bun and slipping her bare feet into slippers, she hobbled to the door. Her shin was still throbbing from where Bianca had clocked her one. Naturally Miss Fucking Accomplished At Everything turned out to be a black belt in bloody karate, too. 'I'm coming.'

Pulling open the door she was equally shocked and enraged to see Lucas, pushing past her and swaggering into the sitting room as though he owned the place.

'Lola here?' he asked, looking around.

'No,' said Sian furiously. 'What the fuck—'

'Good,' Lucas cut her off. 'We need to talk in private.'

'We most certainly do not.' Sian looked murderous. 'You have no business being here, and you know it. Why don't you fuck off and leave me alone?'

'I knocked. You let me in,' said Lucas, with maddening nonchalance, picking up a glass paperweight from one of the side tables and examining it idly before setting it back down.

'I didn't know who it was,' said Sian. 'Obviously.'

'You shouldn't have opened the door then, should you? Those the kind of survival skills you're going to use in Azerbaijan, are they? With a bunch of lawless, crack-head rebels with Uzis stuffed under their trenchcoats? You won't last a day.'

Suddenly too tired to argue, Sian retreated to her bedroom, climbed under the covers and pulled the rumpled sheet up to her chin. Maybe if she simply ignored him, he'd give up and bugger off. But apparently not. Following her, Lucas closed the door behind him, calmly removed a pile of dirty clothes and underwear from the chair by her dressing table and sat down, crossing his legs and looking at her with his head cocked to one side, in the manner of a psychiatrist assessing a new patient.

Irrationally, Sian found herself wishing that she'd bothered to put makeup on earlier, or at least had the foresight to tidy up her tip of a room. Lucas looked ludicrously out of place in his Savile Row suit and silk, sunflower-yellow tie surrounded by her journalist-on-a-deadline squalor (complete with used tissues on the floor and old mug of tea growing mould on the windowsill), like a Hugo Boss model posing on a Baghdad bomb site.

'I have a suggestion for you,' he said coolly.

'Does it involve you dying? Or having your testicles surgically removed and bequeathed to the women of the nation in a pickle jar?' asked Sian, deadpan.

'Sweet, but no,' said Lucas. 'It involves you making a much bigger splash with your story than you would do by simply selling it to one newspaper.'

'Oh, so now you want to *help* me with my story?' Sian gave a hollow laugh. 'What happened to rushing off to the police with your pal Bianca? Over our law-abiding citizen phase now, are we? That was quick, even for you.'

'Look,' said Lucas. 'You can bitch or you can listen. It's your choice.'

Sian was silent for a few seconds. 'Go on,' she said skeptically.

'Petra's throwing a party next month to celebrate the Herrick being voted number one luxury hotel.'

'I know,' said Sian, with an unimpressed shrug. 'So?'

'So she and Anton have invited half the world's media to be there. I'm not just talking print press either, but TV, news crews, all the LA gossip shows like *Entertainment Tonight* and *Extra!* None of them give a shit about the hotel, obviously; they're there for the celebrity guests. But it's turning into one big circus. Now, if you could hijack that event,' he raised an eyebrow temptingly, 'you'd have coverage beyond your wildest dreams. Here, the US, Asia . . .'

Sian allowed herself to imagine this for a moment. It was certainly an appealing fantasy. But it wasn't long before reality and reason reasserted themselves.

'There's no way,' she said. 'Anton'll have major security at that party, and that's aside from all the personal heavies the stars'll bring with them. It'll be like Fort Knox.'

'I agree,' said Lucas. 'I'm not saying it'd be easy. We'd need a lot of inside help, and someone on the ground out there to co-ordinate things. Someone with access.'

Sian looked at him quizzically. 'I don't get it,' she said. 'You don't give a shit about me.'

'Correct,' said Lucas.

'So what do you care what happens with my story? What's in it for you?'

Lucas stood up and walked over to the window. Outside the Victorian streetlamps glowed orange, illuminating kissing couples as they strolled home after dinner on the King's Road. When it wasn't raining, London could really be quite charming, especially on warm summer nights like this one.

'Anton set me up,' he said quietly. 'He's spent the last three years systematically trying to ruin me. He's even backing Connor in this damn court case. I want revenge. I want to see his reputation shredded, the way he shredded mine. And I wouldn't mind seeing Petra Kamalski brought down a peg or too either. We go back a long way.'

Sian could see the muscles of his back and shoulders tighten visibly beneath his suit jacket, and his left hand coiled itself unconsciously into a fist. She'd heard Lucas's version of this sob story from Ben many times, and wasn't sure how much of it she believed. But there could be no doubting his anger. That was palpably genuine.

'So what are you saying?' she asked. 'Do you *have* insiders at the Herrick who could help us?'

Lucas turned around. 'I can probably call in a few favors, yeah. Petra pays her staff well but she treats them like shit. I don't imagine it'll be too tough to find some bitter, disaffected soul to help us.'

'I don't know,' said Sian. 'I don't like the idea of sharing information with some random bell boy we barely know. What's to stop them selling whatever we tell them to the highest bidder?'

'We don't have to tell them anything material,' argued Lucas. 'Come on, you're the investigative journalist here. Surely you're not above a little spin?'

But Sian wasn't budging. 'It won't work,' she said. 'It's too complicated; there are too many wild cards. Besides, I can't be in the Hamptons to pull it all together. I have to go back to Azerbaijan.'

'Forget that,' said Lucas, walking over to the bed and sitting down next to her, to Sian's unspoken alarm. God, the man was pushy. 'Ben's right, it's far too dangerous.'

'No, Ben's wrong,' said Sian, starting to lose patience. Why was she even having this conversation with Lucas? 'I need that information.'

'Then get it,' said Lucas. 'There are other ways. You can stay in London and work on that from here. I'll take care of things in the Hamptons.'

Sian wavered. He was so forceful, so sure of himself, it was hard not to get swept along. And though she'd die rather than admit it to him or Ben, she *was* in fact scared shitless about the thought of going back to meet the rebels on her own.

'What about your court case? Won't that keep you in Europe?'

'Yeeeees,' Lucas admitted, acknowledging a snag in his argument for the first time. But the doubt was gone as soon

478

as it had appeared, and with a Eureka click of his fingers he suddenly said: 'Honor!'

'Excuse me?' said Sian.

'Honor Palmer. We should bring her in on this. She'd be the perfect person to manage things on the ground. She and I can work together when I'm there, and when I need to go to Europe—'

'Whoa, whoa there,' said Sian. 'Have I missed something? Doesn't Honor, like, *loathe* you?'

Lucas shook his head. 'That's just a front, because she wants me so badly. Women always get aggressive when they can't handle their own desire.'

The arrogance was breathtaking. Sian opened and closed her mouth in wordless fury, before finally managing a disbelieving, 'My God, you are *such* an asshole.'

'One thing I would like you to do, if you have time,' said Lucas, ignoring the insult, 'is to do a little digging into the Palmers fire.'

'I don't have time,' said Sian, truthfully.

'Those bastards at the insurance company really did a number on Honor, and they won't pay out until someone's actually charged with arson,' Lucas went on, once again ignoring her objections. 'The Hamptons police are a lazy bunch of donut eaters; they're never going to find anything. But you're obviously ... good at this.'

She could see how much it pained him to bestow this compliment, and smiled. 'Thanks.'

'Maybe you could, I don't know ... come up with something? Once you've got what you need on Anton.'

Again, Sian looked puzzled. 'You want me to help Honor Palmer. Why?'

'Look, it's not a big deal, OK?' snapped Lucas, defensive all of a sudden. 'If you have time, that's all. So what do you think?'

'About?'

479

'About holding off going to the papers? Ambushing this party?'

Sian was silent for a moment. The ridiculousness of her current situation had not escaped her. Here she was, lying in bed, casually chatting to the man she loathed most in the world about a plan so audacious and fraught with difficulties it would almost certainly see her ending up with egg on her face. But the combination of Lucas's boundless confidence, his unexpected faith in her abilities, and the tantalizing possibility of worldwide coverage for her story proved too much to resist.

'I think,' she said, grinning, 'it's a crazy idea. But what the hell. I'm in.'

Watching her face light up with excitement, Lucas realized for the first time what it was Ben saw in her. She'd always be too pale and scrawny for his taste. But there was a charisma about her, a combination of intelligence and courage, that could floodlight a stadium if she put her mind to it.

'Listen,' he said, fishing a Gitane out of his pocket and lighting it without asking her whether she minded. 'There's one other thing we need to talk about.'

'Oh? And what's that?' she said, humoring him.

'Ben,' said Lucas. Inhaling deeply, he blew out a long stream of smoke through his nostrils.

Sian's eyes narrowed. 'There's nothing to talk about.'

'You're in love with him, aren't you?' Lucas cut right to the chase.

She thought about denying it. But after everything that had happened this evening, it seemed a little late for secrets.

'I always was in love with him,' she said, throwing caution to the wind. 'But you could never accept that, could you? You always knew better. I was a chambermaid; he was a millionaire. So *you* decided it must have been all about the money. But it never was. Not for me. Not then, and not now.'

The tears in her eyes were obviously genuine. Lucas felt a pang of guilt. Maybe the real reason he'd taken against her from the start was not that she was a gold-digger, but that she reminded him so much of his younger self, a poor, desperate self he wanted to forget, a self with ambition oozing out of every poor like sweat. Or maybe he'd simply been afraid that she was going to take Ben away from him? How pathetic if that were true.

'I'm sorry if I misjudged you,' he said, lighting a second cigarette from his first and offering it to her. Warily, Sian took it. 'I made a lot of mistakes back then. Perhaps that was one of them.'

'Jeez,' said Sian, relaxing slightly as the nicotine flooded her system. 'Lucas Ruiz, apologizing? Stop the press.'

Lucas looked awkward.

'What happened? First you want to help Honor Palmer, now you're apologizing to me. You're not in therapy, are you?'

'Don't be ridiculous,' said Lucas.

'AA?'

'Hardly.' He forced a smile. 'My doctor says I should think about donating my liver to science, and he's a Frenchman.'

'NA?'

'Stop avoiding the issue,' he said gently. 'I'm not in any kind of A. I admit I was wrong for the things I said about you back then.'

'You said them tonight, too,' Sian reminded him.

'Fine, so I'm a dickhead, OK? Maybe I should never have come between you and Ben in the first place. But the point is, it doesn't matter now.' He looked her squarely in the eye. 'He's getting married. Bianca's made him happy, happier than I've ever seen him. He loves her, and she loves him.'

'I know,' said Sian miserably, twisting a loose strand of hair round and round her fingers.

'Bianca's a good person,' said Lucas. 'I mean *really* good. Not like you and me.'

'I know that, too,' whispered Sian.

'So don't ruin it for them,' said Lucas. Stubbing out his cigarette on a dirty plate on the bedside table, he did the same with hers, then took her hand in his. 'If you really loved him – I mean *really* – you'd let him go.'

'You sound like a Hallmark greeting card,' said Sian. But she was only bitching at him out of force of habit. She knew he was right. What could she possibly offer Ben that Bianca couldn't? She couldn't even say 'her heart,' because Bianca's feelings were obviously every bit as deep as her own.

The next thing she knew, Lucas had pressed her hand to his lips.

'You're a beautiful girl,' he said, softly. 'You'll find someone else.'

'I don't want someone else,' said Sian, the tears in her eyes at last brimming over.

'You and Ben would never work. He needs a calming influence. Someone steady. A home-maker. That's not you.'

'It could be,' she said desperately.

'Not in this lifetime, sweetheart,' Lucas laughed. Leaning forward, he kissed her full on the lips. Shocked for a second, Sian found her mouth tentatively opening in response. Before she knew it, she was kissing him back, with more passion and longing than she could remember feeling since Ben.

'Oh my *GOD*!'

Lola's screech was car-alarm loud. Lucas jumped out of his skin and off Sian's bed, turning around mid-leap to see Lola standing in the bedroom doorway like a red-headed angel of retribution.

'What ... what the hell is he doing here?' she screamed at Sian.

'OK, calm down,' said Sian. 'I can explain. It's not what you think.'

'No?' Lola gave her a look so laden with bitterness and disappointment it made Sian blush scarlet. 'Well, what is it, then? Because it sure looks a lot like Lucas Ruiz is in my fucking apartment, making out in bed with my so-called best friend! How could you let that freak in here?'

'It's business. He's here about the story,' said Sian, realizing at once how ludicrous an excuse it must sound, given that she'd just had her tongue halfway down the man's throat.

'You can talk to me directly, you know,' said Lucas, regaining some of his usual sangfroid. 'I *am* here.'

'Shut up!' yelled Lola and Sian in unison.

'What's going on?' Marti, a little unsteady on his feet after two very good bottles of Chilean cabernet at dinner, washed down with a couple of grappas, appeared behind Lola, resting his chin on the top of her head as much for his own support as for hers. 'Why all the shouting?'

Lola gave a hollow laugh. 'This is Lucas,' she said, pointing at Lucas like she was picking the killer out of a line-up. 'You know Lucas, the guy who ruined my family's life? But it's OK,' she added bitterly. 'He's here on business. As long as it's for the good of the story, right, Sian? What's a little thing like friendship and loyalty, if he helps you get your precious scoop?'

She was more than a little drunk herself. In a micro-short gold dress from French Connection that clashed gloriously with her wild, Titian hair, she looked like a space-age cave woman who'd just been ravished by a group of marauding martians and was pretty bloody furious about it. Lucas, already aroused from his kiss with Sian, felt his budding erection start to strengthen and edged behind a chair in an effort to hide it.

'My mom tried to kill herself because of this guy,' said Lola, getting increasingly hysterical.

'I know, I know,' said Marti gently, trying to calm her down. He hated seeing Lola upset, but he especially hated seeing her upset with Sian. The two of them used to be such good friends. 'He went to the press about your dad's affair.'

'Actually, he didn't,' said Sian, unthinking. 'Anton was behind that story, not Lucas.'

'Again, I am here,' muttered Lucas, to no one in particular.

'Oh, what, so you're *defending* him now?' said Lola. 'Unbelievable. So what else don't I know about him, huh? Please, enlighten me! Has he brokered peace in the Middle East since we were dating? No? Won a Nobel Prize for physics? No, really, I'm serious. I'm dying to hear what a great guy he really is, and how none of the shit he did to me, or my family, was actually his fault at all. Please, go on. I've got time.'

'Well, it's been lovely, but I should go,' said Lucas, emerging from behind the chair now that his ardor had died down, replaced by a splitting headache. 'Nice to almost meet you.' He nodded at Marti, who nodded back. 'Sian, call me in the morning to discuss where we go from here.'

'No.' Darting back into the doorway, Lola barred his way. 'You stay and have your discussion now. I can't stay in this building one more minute. Not until it's been fumigated.' She looked at him with such hatred, Lucas shivered. It was hard to believe that they had once been lovers.

'But Lola, you live here,' said Sian, stating the obvious.

'That's right,' Lola hissed. 'I do. And as of tomorrow, you don't. Marti and I'll spend tonight in a hotel. I want you gone by the time I get back in the morning.'

'Honey, come on,' said Marti, following his furious girlfriend as she exoceted into her own bedroom to grab some underwear and a toothbrush. 'Don't you think you're overreacting just a tad?'

Clearly Lola didn't think so. Cramming her stuff into an overnight bag, she grabbed his hand and physically dragged him to the door. On the way out she turned for one last parting shot at Sian, who'd now made it as far as the sitting room.

'You know what? I'm glad you broke it off with Paddy. I figure he had a lucky escape. You and Lucas deserve each other.' And with a slam that echoed around the building like a lone gunshot, she was gone, the hapless Marti following in her wake.

'She'll come round,' said Lucas, putting a comforting hand on Sian's shoulder. 'Her boyfriend seems like a decent guy. He'll talk some sense into her.'

With no one else to rage at, Sian turned on him like a pet cat gone feral. 'What *is* it with you?' she yelled. 'Every relationship I have, you have to destroy it. Now, because of you, I'm fucking homeless!'

'Because of *me*?' Lucas looked astonished. 'What the hell did I do?'

But Sian was done arguing.

'Get out!' she roared, manhandling him towards the front door with surprising strength for one so slight. 'Get the hell out of my life, Lucas. And don't come back!'

Chapter Twenty-nine

Two weeks later, at the Carters' summer home in East Hampton, Lola helped Marti into his tuxedo.

'You know what?' he said, as she fiddled with his tie. 'This whole dressing for dinner thing is starting to make me real nervous. I feel like I'm in a bad episode of *Falcon Crest*.'

Lola laughed. 'Don't let my mom hear you say that. My parents think soap operas are the root of all America's problems. Them and MTV. And women being allowed membership of the Bridgehampton Polo Club.'

'Yeah, that was a big one,' said Marti, deadpan. 'Didn't that knock the Iraq invasion off the top spot on CNN?'

He always made jokes when he was nervous. It was a defence mechanism he'd learned in childhood, when kids at school in Queens used to tease him for being so skinny and wearing such thick, nerdy glasses. He hadn't grown into his looks until his early twenties, but a childhood marred by acne and bullying had had some positive side effects on his character. Wit was one of them. A ferocious drive and determination to succeed was another. Sadly, he doubted very much whether either of these attributes would mean as much to Lola's family as the right surname. And that was the one thing he didn't have.

When Lola first floated the idea of a few weeks in the Hamptons, the morning after her titanic row with Sian, he'd been all for it. Though she put on a tough front, he could tell that Lola was deeply upset by what had happened, and that she needed to get away. Returning to Tite Street to find Sian and all her things gone, with not so much as a note or a forwarding address, must have been like a bullet to the chest. Though he hadn't dared ask her whether she regretted being so harsh to her friend last night, Marti was pretty sure that she did, and that the trip to the Hamptons was her way of running away from that guilt and sadness. Not that she'd presented it like that of course.

'I just need a break from the business. We both do,' she said, forcing the cheerfulness into her voice. It might have been an excuse, but it also happened to be true. Marla had been consuming both of them for months, and Marti also had his other online businesses to run. Physically, he was shattered.

'Besides,' Lola added, 'it's high time you met my folks properly.'

This was also true. The last and only time Marti had seen Devon, he'd been hiding inside a broom cupboard with his pants round his ankles, which didn't really count as a meeting. So they'd made plans for the trip, with Marti spending the next week imagining long, lazy days on the beach with Lola, just the two of them exploring her childhood haunts together.

Unfortunately, as so often with vacations, the reality turned out to be rather different.

His first misgivings came on the drive from the airport, when their little Volkswagen hire car was overtaken by an eye-popping series of Porsches, Lamborghinis and Bentleys, all heading for Water Mill, the Hamptons' hippest and most exclusive beach.

'I thought you said it would be low key?' He looked at Lola nervously.

He could easily have afforded to hire a flash set of wheels – since his internet company took off four years ago, money was no longer an issue – but cars had always bored him. Now, though, he wished he *had* gone for something a bit further up the food chain. He wouldn't want Devon to think he was a cheapskate who couldn't take care of his daughter.

'It is low key,' said Lola. 'I mean, you know,' she added breezily, as a gleaming silver Vanquish roared past, burying them in a cloud of dust. 'It's all relative.'

Their arrival at the Carter house had done nothing to calm his nerves.

Karis greeted them at the front door in a daze, looking like a younger Miss Haversham, all white-blond hair and jutting bones.

'Holy crap, she's gotten skinny again,' whispered Lola, squeezing his hand for moral support.

'No shit,' he whispered back, a terrified grin of welcome fixed across his features. 'She looks like Mary-Kate Olsen on Valium.'

Lola had conveniently forgotten to mention that this was the first time any of her family had been back to East Hampton since her dad's affair had been made public. Karis, highly strung at the best of times, had insisted she could face it, but since arriving had spent most of her time wandering around the house like a shell-shock victim, permanently on the brink of tears. She point blank refused to venture into town, even for groceries, in case she ran into Honor, which meant that Devon and Nick, strapped for cash and visiting on sufferance from LA, were under virtual house arrest too. By the time Marti and Lola showed up, the strain on everybody was already starting to show.

At least Karis had made a token effort to be welcoming. Devon, on the other hand, made a great show of bear-hugging Lola, before stiffly offering Marti his hand as if he were greeting the guy sent to unblock the drains. After that he'd disappeared off to his study for the rest of the evening, not to be seen again until the following morning.

After four days spent climbing the walls in the house, the last thing Marti felt like was tonight's ludicrously formal at-home dinner.

'Did you happen to see tonight's menu?' he asked, as Lola finished with his tie and smoothed down the lapels of his gleaming new tux. 'It wasn't Grilled Jew, by any chance?'

'Don't be silly,' she said firmly. 'You'll be fine.'

'Can I please not sit next to Nick?' asked Marti, feebly. Lola's brother had turned out to be even more obnoxiously arrogant and dull than she'd described him, which was quite a feat. The way he talked about his business, anyone would have thought he was Warren Buffet, yet it was painfully obvious that the only reason he was here was to screw some more money out of his poor, tapped-out parents.

'Not my call,' said Lola. 'Mom'll seat us.' Flinging her arms around his neck, she gave him a long, lingering kiss.

'What was that for?' he asked, smiling. She looked more beautiful than ever tonight in an empire-line, blue chiffon dress, with her glorious red hair flowing long and loose over her shoulders. Like a pre-Raphaelite goddess.

'For being here,' she said. 'I know they're difficult. But they're my family. And so are you now.'

Incredibly touched, he pulled her closer. 'I love you,' he said. 'But if they sit me next to your brother, I can't promise not to strangle him.'

'Oh, please,' laughed Lola. 'Don't hold back on my account. I'll bring the rope if you like.'

Dinner was predictably ghastly.

'So,' said Devon, swirling the burgundy round his glass and sniffing appreciatively at the deep purple whirlpool he'd created, 'tell us a little more about yourself, Martin.'

'It's Marti, Dad,' said Lola, through clenched teeth. 'No one calls him Martin. And you know all about him. He's an internet entrepreneur, and he's brilliant.' She beamed across the table loyally.

Marti smiled sheepishly back. 'I wouldn't say brilliant, exactly,' he mumbled. 'Well, maybe I would.'

Devon didn't laugh.

Miserable sod. He was a classic closet-antisemite, Marti had decided. Loads of Jewish clients, even Jewish friends, staunchly pro-Israel. But to have his daughter marry a Jew? Forget it. He'd rather die.

'Online business, it's a tough game,' piped up Nick self-importantly from across the table. 'Of course, I was lucky. I got in in ninety-eight. First mover advantage. But guys like you, coming late to the party?' He shook his head knowingly. 'Not easy. *Not* easy.'

'You got in in ninety-eight?' Marti looked baffled. 'Weren't you in, like, ninth grade in ninety-eight?'

Nick's model-perfect features clouded over with irritation. 'I was young,' he admitted. 'But then I've never been a time-server.' He waved his hand airily to indicate his devil-may-care, entrepreneurial credentials. 'Very few of the big guys are. Trump. Branson. Gates. None of them went to college. It's all about starting young.'

'Did you compare yourself to Donald Trump?' Lola sniggered, choking on her wine.

'Yeah,' said Nick aggressively. 'So?'

'I'm pretty sure Bill Gates went to college,' said Marti.

'Did not, too,' said Nick.

Nice comeback. Maybe he was still in ninth grade?

'Well,' said Marti, deciding to be the bigger man and take the high road. It'd be too easy to shoot Nick down, and it was unlikely to win him many points with the parents. If the looks on their faces were anything to go by, Mr. and Mrs. Frosty McFreeze didn't need another reason to hate him right now. 'I've nothing against people not going to university, or starting work young. Your sister's business has been incredibly successful already.' Lola smiled at him gratefully. 'But I guess I *am* what you would call a time-server. I had a wonderful time at college.'

'Where did you attend?' asked Karis.

'Wharton,' said Marti. 'My grandfather came from Pennsylvania. He worked the mills in Pittsburgh. His side of the family always had this big thing about Wharton.'

'Pittsburgh?' said Karis. 'Did your people know the Mellons?'

'Er, no,' laughed Marti. 'I don't believe their paths ever crossed.'

'His grandfather worked in the mills, Mom,' said Lola, crossly. 'Didn't you hear that part?'

'And what do your *own* parents do?' asked Devon. 'Are they educated?'

'*Dad!*' Lola looked suitably horrified. 'You can't ask people questions like that!'

'It's all right,' said Marti, determined to keep his temper. Devon was a petty-minded snob, but he was here for Lola, not anyone else. 'No, they aren't educated, not beyond high school, anyway. My mom's a part-time nurse at the old people's home down the street. And my dad runs a kosher deli. We're not kosher ourselves,' he added, 'but it's a good business. He used to run a hardware store, but then they opened a Home Depot four blocks away and wiped us out.'

'A *Home Depot*?' said Karis, turning the words over as she spoke, as if examining a rare stone. 'How fascinating.'

Clearly, ordinary people with ordinary jobs were completely outside her frame of reference. With two such out-of-touch parents and a megalomaniacal fantasist for a brother, it was a miracle Lola had turned out so normal.

Somehow Marti made it to dessert – a sinfully creamy tiramisu – without losing his cool, and at last the general conversation changed tack.

'This party at the Herrick should be fun,' said Nick, helping himself to a second slab of dessert and greedily cramming a spoonful into his mouth. 'From what I hear, that Ruski chick's really pulled out all the stops. Alex Loeb said the Clintons are gonna be there.'

The Herrick party, less than three weeks away now, was the talk of the town.

'Good for them,' said Devon, without looking up. 'However, we won't be going.'

'Speak for yourself,' said Nick. 'I'm going. Gisele Bundchen's on the guest list, along with half the Brazilian Elite girls. I'm not missing that for anyone.'

'Yeah, right. Like you have a chance with *them*,' muttered Lola.

'Enough!' roared Devon, losing his temper and banging his fist down on the table so hard the crystalware shuddered. 'None of us is going and that's final. We're here to enjoy a quiet, family summer together, not go running around town chasing after tarts.'

'You'd know all about that,' muttered Nick under his breath.

Unfortunately he wasn't quite quiet enough.

'What did you just say?' Devon's voice had dropped to its normal level again, but his lips had gone white with rage.

'Darling, leave it,' whispered Karis. 'Please.'

Marti shifted uncomfortably in his seat. This was going to get ugly.

Nick pushed back his chair and got defiantly to his feet. 'I'm sick of being stuck in this house, creeping around like a criminal because you two are running scared of Honor stupid Palmer.'

'Nicky!' hissed Karis, on the verge of hysterics. 'Do not say that name in this house. Ever.'

Lola reached across the table and squeezed her mother's hand, but Karis seemed not to notice. Meanwhile Devon's face had gone from white through every shade to purple and was now, Marti noticed, roughly the color of a baboon's backside.

'Get out!' he yelled at Nick. 'I mean it, Nicholas. Get out of this house, before I throw you out.'

'Fine,' said Nick, kicking his chair to the floor as he stormed off, slamming the dining room door behind him.

For a few precious moments silence fell. Then Devon looked up and smiled round the table as if nothing had happened.

'Would you like some coffee, my dear?' he asked Karis.

'Yes,' she said, a little nervously. 'I think so. Why not? As long as it's decaf. Lola darling? Will you and Martin be having any?'

Half an hour later, up in their bedroom, Marti undid his tie with relief.

'Was it just me or was that like something out of the *Stepford Wives*? Your mom was smiling so hard she looked like her jaw might go into spasm.'

'I know,' said Lola, unzipping her dress and kicking off her gold stiletto shoes.

'How can they live like that, in such a constant state of denial? I've never seen two people more repressed.'

'I did warn you we weren't exactly the Waltons,' said Lola ruefully. 'Look on the bright side. At least Nick's buggered off.'

'Not for long, I bet,' said Marti. 'Your dad hasn't written him a check yet, and isn't likely to if he doesn't stick around to eat some humble pie. Something tells me he won't be going to that party at the Herrick either.'

'Poor Giselle'll be sooo disappointed,' giggled Lola.

Crawling under the covers together, they soon fell asleep, content as always just to lie in one another's arms.

At eleven the next morning, Honor sat at a table in the newly finished Palmers dining room, sampling some mouthwateringly delicious roast monkfish.

'What do you think?'

'Fantastic,' said Don Bradford, her saintly accountant whose own mouth was still full of the succulent, juicy fish. 'Fucking amazing, if you want the truth.'

Don had been brilliant this year, guiding her gently through the minefield of IRS demands and escalating interest payments that had become her life since the rebuild, never complaining when his bills were settled months after they were due. It was so rare to find someone kind and decent in the financial world, Honor had been hugely touched by his generosity, and was always looking for ways to repay it. Knowing he was a paid-up foodie, she'd invited him along this morning to help her choose one of three Michelin-starred chefs to run the new Palmers restaurant. He was clearly having a whale of a time.

'You know, the food is great,' he said, dispatching the last of the monkfish parcels. 'Truly outstanding. But don't you think it might be a little rich for some people, with all the cream and garlic and drizzled balsamic *jus*?'

Honor laughed. The menus were a little pretentious.

'Have you considered trying something simpler? I know an awesome Mexican chef in the city who might consider a move.'

Honor laughed. He was joking, wasn't he?

'No offense, Don. But when people pay a thousand bucks a night for a room they expect a little bit more than enchilladas, guacamole and a bucket of re-fried beans for dinner.'

'They wouldn't if they'd tried Tito's food,' said Don, affably.

Looking around the dining room, with its dramatic floor-to-celing windows and limed oak floor, Honor felt her chest swell with pride. Her financial worries were far from over, but after so many months of hard work and sleepless nights, she was finally getting to the fun part: finalizing the soft furnishings, arranging contracts with florists, hunting around local antique markets for the perfect grand piano for the cocktail bar.

She remembered, the Christmas before her mom died, Santa had brought her a beautiful hand-crafted dolls' house in the style of a French chateau. For years afterwards, she'd spent every cent of her pocket money buying furniture for it. Her favorite piece was a tiny working replica of a chandelier, which attached with red wires to a switch on the back of the house. At night she would turn off all the lights in her bedroom in Boston and switch it on, watching with delight as the dolls' house and its residents were bathed in a magical red glow that seemed to imbue them with a life of their own.

Decorating Palmers gave her the same thrill. She'd even found a similar light fitting for the dining room. By any rational standards it was far too ornate and completely at odds with the rest of the decor. But she couldn't resist. Hanging above their table now, she thought it looked absolutely magnificent. And Don adored it.

He also approved of her hiring decisions – which was a good thing, as she didn't know what she'd have done if he'd told her the money couldn't stretch to more than a skeleton staff. The chef they were choosing today would be one of only a handful of new appointments, since almost all the old Palmers staff were coming back, a testament to the excellent working relationship Honor had built with them over the years. After the ruthless cull she'd initiated when she first took over, it took a while for the remaining workers to feel secure again. But they soon came to realize that their new boss was as quick with her praise as her censure, and scrupulously fair.

When Petra took over at the Herrick, she'd given all the workers there a blanket pay-rise, and made sure that everyone at Palmers knew they could make more if they jumped ship. But Honor hadn't lost so much as a single waiter. There was a camaraderie at Palmers that simply didn't exist anywhere else. Certainly not at the Herrick, where staff turned over almost as frequently as the bedlinen.

Of course, after the fire, Honor's workforce had been forced to move elsewhere, and some had gone to the Herrick then, out of necessity. But almost all were taking pay cuts to return to the new hotel in the fall. There was a palpable sense of excitement about getting the old gang back together, and for the first time in years Honor felt that perhaps, this time, the gods were with her.

She'd promoted Enrique, her old head barman, to overall head of hospitality. He and a handful of core staff were already living on-site, as was Honor herself. They shared the unfinished space with a legion of workmen, painters, plumbers and gardeners who still showed up daily, and whom Honor was still scrambling to pay on a week-by-week basis.

Even with the constant hammering and disruptions, it was bliss to be out of her pokey little cottage at last. Her new rooms were considerably smaller than the old ones: a modest, wood-paneled bedroom that opened out onto a secluded terrace, just big enough for a wrought-iron table and two chairs. She also had a simple sitting room, with a pair of matching, white denim couches, an antique thirties standard lamp and her grandfather's old writing desk tucked into the corner; and a bathroom, as yet unfinished, although the shower worked and the toilet flushed which was all she needed right now.

Her old suite had had a kitchen, but she'd never used it – more wasted square footage that could have been used for another paying guest. The new Palmers was all about economy. If Tina turned up next summer demanding a free room, she could forget it.

'Excuse me, Miss Palmer?' Agnes, the faithful receptionist Honor had so terrified when she first arrived at Palmers, but who adored her boss now, appeared at the table looking uncharacteristically anxious. 'There's a visitor ... someone ... here to see you.'

'Oh?' said Honor, springing automatically to her feet and dabbing the corners of her mouth with her napkin. 'Is it that guy from the tiling company? Because I told him already, a quote is a quote. I'm not about to renegotiate now just because he lost a ship somewhere. I need those bathrooms finished this week or he doesn't see a red cent from us – right, Don?'

'No. No, it's not him,' Agnes stammered. 'It's ... I did tell him you were in a lunch meeting, Miss Palmer. But he wouldn't go away.'

'*Who* wouldn't?' said Honor.

For one awful moment, it crossed her mind that it might be Devon, come to try to wheedle his way around her yet again. That would explain Agnes's embarrassment. The last she'd heard from him was after the fire, when he'd had the brass balls to send a Get Well card to the hospital, in which he'd scrawled the sort of self-pitying, half apology she'd come to expect from him. She'd heard he was in town – bad news traveled like wildfire in East Hampton – and had resigned herself to the fact that she would almost certainly run into him at some point. But she could have done without it right now, in front of Don.

But it wasn't Devon.

'I see they set three places. Were you expecting me?'

Lucas strolled casually over to the table, extending his hand to Don, who'd stood up.

'I don't believe we've met,' he smiled. 'Lucas Ruiz. I'm a friend of Miss Palmer's.'

'Don Bradford, her accountant,' said Don, shaking his hand with the same warmth with which he greeted everyone. 'You're just in time. I'd have woofed that last bit of fish myself in a minute.'

Lucas had already helped himself to the last plate of monkfish and was halfway through it by the time Honor had time to blink, never mind tell him to take a running jump. Grinning at her all the while, wearing a loud pair of Bermuda shorts, an open Hawaiian shirt and flip flops, he looked disgustingly relaxed for someone in the midst of a major court battle and whose business was supposedly in crisis.

'Great job you've done here, sweetheart,' he said, nodding

appreciatively at the decor whilst cheerfully shoveling food into his mouth. 'Don't you agree, Mr. Bradford?'

'Absolutely,' said Don, who seemed not a bit put out to be joined by an unexpected guest.

'Food's good, too,' said Lucas between mouthfuls. 'Could do with a *leetle* more coriander. But not at all bad.'

'OK, that's enough,' said Honor, looking daggers at Lucas.

Belatedly, Don realized that perhaps something was amiss. 'Is everything all right, my dear?' he asked.

'Everything's fine,' said Honor. 'Mr. Ruiz was just leaving. Weren't you?'

'Was I?' said Lucas, holding her eye contact. 'I don't think I was, actually.'

An awkward silence fell.

'Perhaps *I* should go,' said Don, getting to his feet. 'Let you two talk.'

'No, no, no,' said Honor. 'Please, you really don't—'

'Thanks,' said Lucas, shaking his hand again with friendly finality. 'Under the circumstances I think that might be best. Honor and I have some very important business to discuss, you see. It's a little ... delicate.'

'He's kidding,' said Honor, laying a restraining hand on Don's arm. 'Lucas and I have absolutely nothing to say to one another.'

In a short, fitted red dress, with her hair slicked back into a pony tail and her emerald eyes flashing fury, she looked like a fire hydrant about to explode.

'I think I know you well enough, my dear, to see that that is quite patently untrue,' said Don with a chuckle. He lived a life so free of dramatic passions that he had always found other people's amusing. 'Thank you for a wonderful meal, but don't get up. I can see myself out.'

'Nice guy,' said Lucas once he'd gone. A second course of rack of lamb had arrived while Don was saying his goodbyes, and Lucas was liberally grinding pepper onto his helping now, looking for all the world like a paying guest. He'd be ordering a cold beer and a doggie bag in a minute.

'You know what?' said Honor, pulling her hair out of its elastic band and letting it fall loose, a gesture that made Lucas automatically look up. 'I'm actually too tired to do this.'

'To do what?' he said, taking a bite of lamb. It was so soft, it melted on his tongue like a truffle.

'To fight with you,' said Honor calmly. 'To play whatever dumbass game it is you're playing this time. So why don't you tell me what it is that you want. And then go away and leave me in peace.'

Dropping his knife and fork with a clatter, he gave her a look so intense and serious it made her momentarily nervous.

'Do you remember that night in Vegas?'

'Barely,' she lied, taking a leisurely bite of her own food. 'I was very drunk. And the sex really wasn't that memorable.'

'I'm not talking about the sex,' said Lucas. 'Although I'm flattered that was the first thing *you* thought about.'

Honor blushed beetroot. Bastard. How did he always manage to *do* this to her? To twist things around? He was the one who brought up Vegas, not her.

'You'll be flatt*ened* in a minute,' she shot back furiously. 'So what are you talking about?'

'Anton,' said Lucas. 'You remember I told you how he set us both up that summer?'

'Of course I remember,' snapped Honor. 'You think I'd forget a thing like that?'

'And you told me we ought to fight back? Get revenge?'

'I said *you* should get revenge,' said Honor, looking proudly around her. 'I've already gotten mine. I've built this place back up from nothing.'

'Yeah, yeah, yeah,' said Lucas, waving his arm impatiently.

He hugely admired what she'd done with Palmers, but he wasn't here to massage her ego. 'I'm talking about *real* revenge.'

'It's a damn sight more than you've done!' said Honor indignantly.

'Something that would destroy him,' said Lucas, ignoring her. 'The way he tried to destroy us.'

Honor was silent. She didn't like him using the word *us*. It scared her.

'I've come to see you because I have a plan,' he said. 'And it's a pretty damn good one. It involves some other people, people you know. But we won't be able to pull it off without your help.'

Honor sighed a deep, heartfelt sigh and closed her eyes. 'I know I'm gonna regret this,' she said. 'But go ahead. I'm listening.'

Chapter Thirty

'What the hell do you call that?'

The gardener froze halfway across the polished marble floor. He was carrying a cripplingly heavy potted bamboo through the Herrick's lobby, and had rivers of sweat streaming down between his shoulder blades, not to mention a steady stream of lactic acid coursing through his aching biceps. But when Petra Kamalski yelled at you, you stopped.

'These are the plants you ordered,' he panted, staggering from foot to foot under the weight. 'For the party?'

'I know what they're for,' said Petra scathingly. 'But they most certainly are not what was ordered. I said black bamboo, and I said a minimum of eight feet. That's practically a pot plant.'

'A pot plant?' he muttered under his breath. 'You try lifting it, lady.'

'Don't talk back to me,' hissed Petra. Her bat-like hearing was legendary amongst the Herrick staff. 'And don't even think of putting that filthy tub down on my floor. Get it out of here. Out, out, out!'

'But ma'am,' wheezed the gardener, 'we have a truckload of plants outside. I have the order sheet right here. You can check it yourself.'

'I don't have time to waste on your mistakes,' said Petra, 'and nor do my staff. Fix it. Today.'

Even by her own, autocratic standards, she was unusually short-tempered this morning. The 'number one' party was in forty-eight hours and there was still so much to do. The downside of having A-list guests was that they came with A-list requirements, some of them frankly ludicrous. One particular pop diva, for example, had refused to book a room for the night unless she could bring her own bed – not bedding, *bed* – and have twenty Figuera Dyptique candles lit the the bathroom exactly two hours prior to her arrival. Another guest, an actress, demanded that *her* arrival be carefully choreographed to upstage that of a younger Hollywood rival, who'd also been invited. There were people who had to run into one another, and others who must *under no circumstances* run into one another. And overshadowing it all was Anton, who was treating the whole thing like his private birthday party, and who was delighted by the celebrity attendance just so long as it didn't eclipse his own shining star.

Retreating to her office, she barely had time to sit down before she was rudely interrupted.

'Ah, Petra, there you are. Jolly good.' Anton's pet-PR-girl Saskia, the one person whose presence in the hotel, in fact whose very existence, caused Petra more stress than all the other bullshit put together, had barged in without so much as a by-your-leave. 'We've got an awful lot to do today, duckie,' she trilled efficiently, 'so it's all hands to the mill. I've just had the producer from E! on the line asking about the outdoor lighting. Now where are we with that?'

Petra's top lip began to curl upwards, like a sliver of dried orange peel.

There were so many things she hated about Saskia, it was hard to focus on any particular one. She was vulgar, overweight and overbearing. She wore enough cheap perfume to qualify as a biological weapon. Her laugh, forced, loud and braying, was a cross between a witch's cackle and a particularly insidious car alarm. At this moment, she was wearing a tight, luminous orange T-shirt in a material so shinily synthetic it would melt, rather than burn, if you put a match to it (which somebody really ought to); and a pair of white shorts that left nothing to the imagination, beneath which she was plainly pantie-less. The woman had all the class and style of a mongrel puppy, and yet she projected an innately British air of superiority that gave Petra fantasies about tying her to the back of a pick-up truck and driving off at speed. Not since Honor Palmer had she met a woman so sickeningly full of herself, with so little reason to be so.

But worse than any of this was the way that Saskia had muscled her way in on tomorrow night's party. Ever since Anton had brought her on board, she'd been acting like the proverbial queen bee, throwing her considerable weight around with Petra's staff and generally making a royal nuisance of herself.

Anton denied it, but it was perfectly obvious to Petra that he and Saskia were sleeping together. This in itself didn't bother her. She'd never been the jealous type. If Anton had so little taste as to find a blowsy little tart like Saskia attractive, more fool him. But the vile creature clearly felt that as the boss's lover, she had carte blanche to behave as she pleased and flout Petra's authority as manager. And that *was* a problem. A big one.

She'd already grabbed a chair and parked herself on the other side of the desk, and was reaching over to grab the phone when Petra snapped.

'Get out of my office!' she commanded, snatching back her telephone. 'I've told you before, if you need to make calls you may do so from the business center like everybody else. This is *my* private office, not some sort of common room. And I am *not* your *duckie*.'

'Anton's made it very clear he wants us to work together,' pouted Saskia. 'We can't very well do that from separate offices. There's only thirty-six hours to go now, you know.'

Petra's antipathy was heartily reciprocated by Saskia, who considered her rival to be about as sexy as a deep-frozen stick insect, and considerably less pleasant company.

She couldn't fathom what Anton saw in her. It must be like sticking your dick into one of those automatic pencil sharpeners.

'I'm well aware of the time pressure, thank you, Saskia,' said Petra tartly. 'I've spent the last three months putting this party together. You've been here three minutes.'

She glanced out of the window at the hive of activity going on in the grounds. The marquee company had arrived and were busy unloading scaffolding and canvas. The entire Japanese garden was going to be covered by a series of Moroccan tents, turning it into a sort of impromptu souk, although Saskia had put a cat amongst the pigeons at the last moment by insisting everything be opened up on one side to allow easier access for the TV crews. She'd also demanded glaring spotlights be hung from every conceivable tree, but so far Petra had vetoed this idea on the grounds that it would ruin her carefully planned candlelit effect. It was this battle over lighting that the E! channel had been complaining about again this morning.

'You're ridiculous!' snapped Saskia. 'If it weren't for me you'd have had one man and his dog covering your precious party. As it is our TV coverage is under threat because of your ludicrous candle-obsession. Anton gets here tomorrow, and he wants this resolved. Petra! Are you listening to me?'

But Petra wasn't. She'd just noticed a familiar figure milling around amongst the workmen outside.

'I don't believe it,' she muttered under her breath. 'What the hell is he doing here?'

'Who?' asked Saskia.

Ignoring her, Petra prized open the window and stuck her head outside. 'You're trespassing!' she yelled.

Lucas cupped his hand to his ear and shook his head, pretending not to be able to hear her, before turning back to his conversation with the marquee guys.

'Call security,' Petra barked at Saskia, slamming the

window shut and sweeping out of the door in a whirlwind of righteous indignation. 'I may need help getting rid of him.'

'Oh, may you,' said Saskia, once she'd gone. 'Well, that's tough titties, isn't it, duckie? Rude bitch. You can whistle for your help.'

Whoever it was that had got the Ice Queen's knickers in a twist, Saskia felt more inclined to give him a medal than have him thrown off the property. Sinking her ample backside down into Petra's vacated chair – it was so much more comfortable than her own – she returned to her phone call. Someone had to sweet-talk the E! producers, or they'd pull out altogether.

Outside, Lucas saw Petra goose-stepping furiously across the lawn toward him. Knowing it would infuriate her, he flashed her his most winning smile. In a black wool pencil skirt and matching jacket, she must have been roasting, but she didn't have so much as a bead of sweat on her forehead to show for it.

Maybe she didn't sweat. She probably just leaked antifreeze every now and then.

'You're spying.' She looked at him accusingly. Then, turning to the workmen he'd been talking to, demanded: 'What did he ask you? If any of you has breathed so much as one word about tomorrow night's arrangements—'

'Relax, pet,' said Lucas, remembering the nickname she'd so despised in college. Judging by the angrily throbbing vein at her temple, she was none too keen on it now, either. 'We were only making chit chat. I was about to offer these poor guys something to drink. They tell me they haven't had a sip of water all day.'

'That's because they're working,' said Petra. 'Do any of you have any complaints you'd like to make to me?'

She glared at them each in turn, daring them to challenge her further. But no one was brave enough, and one by one they all slunk off back to work, leaving Petra and Lucas alone.

'The next time I catch you spying on this property,' she told him curtly, 'I'll have you arrested. Today I'll make do with having security throw you out.'

She looked over her shoulder for the expected reinforcements, but no one appeared to be coming. Bloody Saskia obviously hadn't bothered to call.

'Don't panic,' said Lucas amiably, sussing out her predicament. 'I'll go quietly. You don't need your heavies.'

'So tell me, what brings you to town, Lucas?' asked Petra, trying to regain the upper hand. 'Nostalgia? A longing to relive your glory days? How touching.'

'Hardly,' said Lucas. 'I'm here for some meetings about my new Luxe.'

'Ah, yes, the late great Luxe America. How's it going over there? You were going to open by Christmas, weren't you?' She laughed – a horrible, empty, tinkling sound with nothing but spite behind it. 'Can't see that happening now.'

Lucas bit his tongue. He'd already got what he came for and wasn't about to indulge her by losing his temper.

'I won't keep you.' He smiled. 'Shall we say au revoir, then? Until tomorrow night?'

'What do you mean?' Unusually for her, Petra let her guard down. 'You're not invited tomorrow night.'

'Oh, but I am,' said Lucas brightly. 'Got my invitation three weeks ago. A charming lady by the name of Saskia was kind enough to call me in person.' He clapped his hand over his mouth in mock surprise and gasped. 'Didn't Anton tell you?'

Petra's lips pursed into a puckered anus of fury. 'It must have slipped his mind.'

'Dear oh dear.' Lucas was starting to enjoy himself. 'And to think, you two used to be so close.'

As soon as he'd gone – for all his bravado, Lucas didn't

relish being manhandled off the grounds by Petra's security heavies, who were bound to show up eventually – Petra stormed back into her office. Saskia was on the phone, but she reached down and ripped the socket out of the wall, cutting her off mid-sentence.

'What the hell are you playing at?' she roared. 'Inviting Lucas Ruiz to the party behind my back? And what happened to the fucking security I asked for?'

'You didn't say please,' said Saskia, who wasn't easily intimidated. 'And you aren't my boss, duckie. As for Lucas, it was Anton's decision to invite him, not mine. He's invited the Palmer sisters, too.'

'*Whaaaaaaaaaat*?' Petra was apoplectic.

'I assumed he'd told you,' said Saskia. 'But if you and he don't talk anymore …' She gave a winsome little shrug. 'It's hardly my fault if you've grown apart, is it?'

'Wipe that smug look off your face,' said Petra. 'Let's get one thing straight. I know you're fucking him, and I really don't give a shit.'

Wrongfooted, Saskia blushed, her cheeks clashing horribly with her revolting T-shirt.

'Men like a cheap thrill every once in a while.' Petra looked at her witheringly. 'And let's face it, thrills don't come any cheaper than you.'

'You bitch!' gasped Saskia.

'Go on,' Petra called after her as she gathered up her things and ran out of the office. 'Call him. See how much sympathy you get.'

She wasn't worried about Anton. Whining women bored him. It wouldn't be long before he tired of a sniveling lump of lard like Saskia.

But Lucas was another matter entirely. What was he doing here this morning? He was up to no good, she was sure of it.

She was also sure that inviting him and Honor tomorrow was a mistake, and not just because Anton had done

507

it behind her back. He wanted to gloat, to rub their noses in his success. Petra, of all people, could understand the impulse. But her gut told her that this time, it was a wrong move.

Keeping one's enemies close was all very well. But Lucas was getting too close for comfort. Why wasn't he in Europe, holed up with his lawyers? Something didn't add up.

Meanwhile, in London, Sian tried hard to be patient with the moron at the Virgin check-in desk.

'Look,' she said, willing herself to keep calm as the girl took out a nail file and started ostentatiously fiddling with her cuticles. 'Perhaps I haven't explained the situation properly. I'm a journalist. I have a crucial interview in New York, and I have to make that flight. I'll pay first class. I'll pay cash.' Reaching into her bag she pulled out a wadge of notes and laid them on the counter to emphasize the point. 'Can't you ask anyone if they'd be willing to give up their seat for cash?'

'Sorr-ay,' said the girl, who clearly wasn't. 'We can't do that I'm afride.' She had striped-blonde hair extensions, a fake tan that made Donatella Versace's look real, and the sort of whiny, nasal voice that could double as a garage door opener.

'Why not?' asked Sian. If she didn't stop filing in the next ten seconds, Sian would be forced to reach over the desk and snap off her hideous french-polished talons one by one.

The girl gave her a look of infinite boredom. 'Policy, innit.'

'I'd like to speak to a manager,' said Sian, ignoring the loud groans and mutterings of "bloody Americans" from the lengthening queue of passengers behind her.

'Fine,' said the moron. 'You'll 'ave to wite. Over there.' She pointed to a firmly closed check-in desk with a couple of plastic seats in front of it. Hopelessly, Sian shuffled over and took one of them.

What a day.

She'd been up at five this morning, putting the final touches to her case against Anton, knowing that the slightest flaw in her evidence could bring the whole story crashing down around her ears. And it wasn't just her ears anymore. Ben, Lucas and now Honor Palmer as well were all deeply implicated in what they were about to do. The stakes couldn't be higher.

Having caved in to pressure from Ben and Lucas to ditch her trip to Azerbaijan, she'd spent the last three weeks in London trying to pull together information by phone and through face-to-face meetings with the large, disaffected community of Russian émigrés scattered all across the city. In all that time, she'd barely slept, rushing from interview to interview, tracking down ex-girlfriends, classmates, business associates – anyone who might be able to shed more light on the murky depths of Anton's pre-London life. At night, bone tired, she'd returned to the dingy hotel in Marylebone where she'd been camping out since her row with Lola, and began the arduous process of editing the new information she'd gleaned. But it had been worth it, worth every grueling, frustrating minute. At least, it *would* be worth it, if she made this flight. If she didn't … no, she couldn't bear to think about it. They had to let her on.

Pulling out her cell phone, she scrolled down her address book, stopping at Ben's name and allowing her finger to hover over the 'call' button for a few seconds. She'd never have a better reason to ring him – he was a personal friend of Richard Branson's, and would undoubtedly be able to pull the necessary strings – but she didn't make the call.

Ever since that night at his apartment, the night Lucas had kissed her and Lola had thrown her out of the flat, she'd tried to keep her distance. At the time she'd lashed out at Lucas, blaming him for her fallout with Lola as well as for coming between her and Ben. But beneath her veneer of anger, his words kept coming back to her, haunting her far more than his unexpected (and unexpectedly pleasurable) kiss had done. If she really loved Ben, he told her, she wouldn't ruin things for him and Bianca. She and Ben had never really been right for each other.

All this time she'd been keeping alive a tiny flame of hope that, even if he *did* marry Bianca, he would wake up one day and realize that she, Sian, was the one. But Lucas was right. She'd been kidding herself all along. Ben didn't need her. He needed someone calm and maternal and ... all those other things Lucas said.

She hated him for it, but Lucas had done her a favor and finally woken her up to reality. Ben had been with Bianca for years. He was going to marry her, and soon. Working with him on the story had been wonderful, magical. But it wasn't reality. She'd been allowing herself to exist in a dream, and now she was going to have to pay the price.

She was still staring at her mobile when it rang, and jumped when she saw the word 'Lucas' flash across the screen.

'That's serious ESPL,' she said. 'I was just about to call you.'

'Is everything OK?' He sounded jumpy. Evidently she wasn't the only one shitting herself about tomorrow.

'I have everything we need,' she said. 'It's looking good. But I'm having a *teeny* little problem getting on the plane.'

'What sort of problem?' said Lucas. 'Can't you speak to the manager or something?'

'Doh!' said Sian sarcastically. 'Why didn't I think of that? I'm at the airport, waiting for her right now, but there's no sign. And the bimbo airhead at check-in won't let me on the fucking flight for love nor money.'

Sian could hear Lucas's brain ticking into life on the other end of the line. As infuriating as she found him personally, she had to admit he'd been great to work with these last few weeks, pulling the various strands of their plan together with all the authority and cool-headedness of a field marshall.

'Which airline?' he asked.

'Virgin.'

'Have you spoken to Ben?'

'No,' she said softly.

'Well, why not?' shouted Lucas.

'Jeez, because I haven't, OK?' Sian shouted back. She didn't need shit on that subject, especially not from him.

'OK, OK,' said Lucas more gently. 'Put me on the line with the check-in girl.'

'She won't talk to you,' said Sian. 'She's a bitch and a half.'

Just at that moment a dour-faced woman in a red Virgin jacket that did her florid complexion no favors at all, and whom Sian took to be the manager, waddled over.

'Is there a problem, madam?'

'Yes,' said Sian, thrusting the phone at her. 'This gentleman will explain.'

Lucas couldn't have any worse luck than she'd been having.

Thirty minutes later, she was kicking off her shoes in an Upper Class seat, sipping at a much-needed glass of champagne. Lucas's magic touch with women was apparently just as effective over the phone as it was in person: he'd managed to sweet-talk the battleaxe Virgin supervisor in about ten seconds flat. Not that Sian was complaining. It was nice to have his legendary charm working in her favor for once.

'Do I have time to make a quick call?' she asked the passing stewardess.

'Of course.' The girl smiled helpfully. Evidently they reserved their moronic nail filers for the cattle-class check-in desk. 'We won't take off for fifteen minutes,'

*

Simon Davis was passing a dull afternoon at his desk at the *News of the World*, alternately playing solitaire on his computer, picking his nose, and thinking up imaginary offenses for which he could bawl out his reporters, when his direct line rang.

'What?' he barked, Rottweiler-friendly as ever. Belatedly recognizing Sian's voice, he added, 'Oh, it's you. Haven't you been deported yet?'

But within a minute, his dismissiveness had gone, replaced with rapt attention. Sitting bolt upright, he leaned forward over his paper-strewn desk, with the receiver superglued to his ear, waving at everyone around him to be quiet. One thing you could say for Simon: he might be a miserable bastard, but he knew a good scoop when he heard one.

'Absolutely,' he said, once Sian had finished. 'We can run it this Sunday. How much did you say you wanted again?'

Sian repeated the figure.

'Fine.'

He didn't hesitate and she instantly regretted not having asked for more.

'But if you shop it around to the *Mail on Sunday* behind my back, I'll tear you limb from limb.'

'I won't,' said Sian, hanging up.

Taking another sip of her champagne, she closed her eyes and finally allowed herself to relax. There was no need to tell Lucas or the others about her little back-up deal. But now, whatever happened tomorrow night – whether Lucas and Honor pulled off their ambush of the Herrick party or not – Sian would have her story. While most of America was still asleep and the party was drawing to a close, the first copies of the *News of the World* would be hitting newsagents and corner shops all across England.

She might not ever be Mrs. Ben Slater. But she was damn well going to be the next Lois Lane.

Chapter Thirty-one

Anton sat contentedly in the back of his limousine the next morning with Mitzi drooling loyally by his side, watching the flat Long Island scenery roll by. Tonight was going to be one of the greatest nights of his life, public affirmation of the success he'd worked so long and hard to achieve.

All he needed for his happiness to be complete was for his knighthood to finally come through. But his man in the ministry had assured him he needn't worry on that score. He was a shoo-in for the next honors list, after the obscenely large loan check he'd written to the government last month. The first time he heard himself addressed as Sir Anton would truly be a day to remember. But tonight's party at the Herrick would be a good start – a taste of the recognition to come.

He was also excited about seeing Petra again. Saskia had served a useful purpose. She'd kept Petra on her toes and done an A1 job whipping up press coverage for the party. But sexually he was already tiring of her, like a little boy gorged on too-rich birthday cake. He longed for Petra's skinny, unforgiving body and the icy, imperious way she looked at him when they made love. Knowing that she was furious about the way he'd foisted Saskia on her made the prospect of their reunion all the sweeter. Few things in life gave him more pleasure than fucking an angry, resentful Petra into submission, bending her to his will. Making love to Saskia was like diving into a sea of marshmallow. With Petra, it was more like taming a wildcat.

He was also relishing the prospect of the *This Is Your Life* style presentation that Saskia had planned for this evening.

It was being billed as a surprise, so he'd have to look suitably humble in front of the press and VIPs, and feign embarrassment.

But in reality he'd overseen every detail of the footage, and even gone so far as to run the twelve-minute film past his civil servant friend, to make sure it was 'on message' from a knighthood point of view. He'd been assured he came across as powerful but compassionate – 'a magnanimous magnate,' as the ministry man had put it, a turn of phrase Anton liked so much that he'd suggested it to Saskia as a title for the film.

He wondered what Lucas would make of it.

He'd extended an invitation to both Lucas and Honor, largely so that none of the press could accuse him of grudge-bearing, but he was amazed when Saskia told him that Lucas had accepted. Surely the boy must have twigged by now that he and Connor were in cahoots, and that he was both the brains and the bank behind the court case? Of course, it was possible his intention was to cause a scene, to try to upstage the event by airing his grievances amongst Anton's famous guests. But if he did, it would be his funeral. No one would be interested in the drunken ramblings of a washed-up conspiracy theorist like Ruiz. Not when they had the party of the century waiting to be enjoyed.

Honor, more predictably, had declined to attend, citing pressure of work. The new Palmers was opening later this year, and she was busy putting the final touches to it – much good may it do her. Anyone with even the most rudimentary business sense would have seen it was ludicrous to try to open a niche boutique next door to the most successful hotel in the world. Anton had built up his Tischen empire by building close to big-name hotels, but they were always fading giants, never rising stars like the Herrick. Plus, he had unlimited funds with which to force his rivals out of the market. By all accounts these days Honor Palmer could barely afford to buy a sandwich, and according to Petra had last week been spotted varnishing Palmers' fences herself, by hand. Talk about David and Goliath!

Ruffling the fur on Mitzi's head, Anton closed his eyes contentedly and turned his thoughts back to Petra. Why waste precious thinking time on Honor, or Lucas? As far as he was concerned, they were both yesterday's news.

While Anton savored his impending hour of glory, Lucas was in Honor's old cottage, frantically delving under cushions and piles of paper for his car keys.

He was supposed to be picking Sian up from the airport this morning, but after a late night with Honor working on the master plan for tonight, he'd overslept ad was now hopelessly late.

'Shit.' He sent another two groaning foolscap files flying across the room. 'Honor!' Sticking his head into the narrow stairwell that led up to the cottage's lone bedroom, he shouted into the void. 'Have you seen my keys? I can't find them anywhere and I have to go. Now!'

A few moments later, a sleep-addled Honor appeared at the top of the stairs, rubbing her eyes. In a pair of over-sized men's pyjamas – *whose are those?* Lucas wondered jealously – and with her cheeks still creased from the bed sheets, she looked adorable. All she needed was a teddy clasped to her chest and a Linus blanket trailing on the floor to complete the picture.

'What time is it?' she murmured.

'Ten,' said Lucas tetchily. He was tense as hell about this evening and his brief night spent on the cottage's hard sofa had done little to improve his mood. 'I'm seriously fucking late, and this place is a pigsty. No wonder I can't find anything.'

'Hey,' said Honor, getting annoyed herself, 'if you lost your keys, that's *your* fault, not mine. As for the pigsty, I didn't see you in a rush to clean up after yourself last night.'

It had been a long night and they were both strung out.

With another two months to run on her lease, Honor had held on to the cottage as a sort of overspill office, a place to store the mountains of as yet unfiled paperwork relating to the new Palmers building works.

Since Lucas's unscheduled arrival, it had morphed into the nerve center for 'Operation Anton' and served as his temporary base while he was in town. Normally *he* would have slept in the bed, and Honor would have gone home to her suite at Palmers. But it was so late when they'd finished last night, there was no point in her going home. In an uncharacteristic display of chivalry, Lucas had offered to take the tiny couch.

He regretted it now. He hadn't slept a wink. Quite apart from the logistics of trying to get comfortable on a piece of furniture designed by a sadist for a midget, just knowing that Honor was upstairs, probably naked, in his bed, kept him tossing and turning through the small hours like a prisoner on the rack. The combination of sleep deprivation, sexual frustration, and stress about what lay ahead of them – what if they blew it and got thrown out, or worse, arrested? – conspired to make him moodier than a teenage girl in the throes of PMT.

'Your keys are on the counter,' said Honor, coming wearily down the stairs. 'I can see them from here.'

Snatching them up with an irritated frown, Lucas thrust them into the back pocket of his jeans.

Grabbing a bagel from the bread bin on his way out, he left, slamming the cottage door behind him so hard that the sea of papers fluttered up into the air like wind-blown leaves.

Honor surveyed the mess he'd left behind.

'A simple *thanks* would have been nice,' she mumbled, crossly. But she still hoped he'd drive safely on his way to Kennedy. He could be awfully reckless when he was stressed out, and on two hours sleep those single-track roads out of town could be lethal.

When Lucas saw Sian struggling through customs with two battered suitcases and a groaning briefcase, she looked distinctly travel worn. Notwithstanding their kiss in London, he'd never been the biggest fan of her looks, but he didn't think he'd ever seen her looking quite so preternaturally pale as she did now. Her dark hair was greasy and hung long and lank to her shoulders. As for the clothes she was wearing – combat shorts, tatty sneakers and a faded orange T-shirt covered in coffee stains – they were only a small step above bag lady.

'You look tired,' was all he said, relieving her of both suitcases.

Uncharacteristically, she let him take them without a fuss. Her shoulders were killing her, and she was too shattered to take a feminist stand about it today.

'You've been pushing yourself too hard.'

'Yeah, well, I had to, didn't I?' said Sian grudgingly. 'You made it pretty clear you wouldn't wait around for me to get the rest of the evidence together. It had to be this weekend or never. I haven't slept in two weeks.'

'Me neither,' said Lucas. 'Jesus.' He frowned at the heavy bags in each hand. 'What the hell did you pack in here? Lead?'

They'd reached the elevator, and he put down both cases while he pressed the call button.

'No.' Sian grinned triumphantly. 'Tapes.'

'Tapes? What tapes?' The lift arrived and they stepped inside.

Sian looked at him witheringly. 'Anton's high-school reunion. Jeez, what do you mean *what* tapes? It's the sexual stuff, you idiot. Your hors d'oeuvres for the party tonight, before we pull out our big guns.'

'You do have the big guns, though?' said Lucas nervously.

'Relax,' said Sian. 'I got it all. This stuff is just interviews with some of the girls from his homes who went on the game. All on the record, mind you. Sixteen hours of audio, five and half of visuals. You would not *believe* some of the stories. It goes way beyond what we thought.'

'We're gonna have ten minutes up on that podium tonight, total,' grumbled Lucas. 'Maybe less. Honor and I have it timed to the last second. What are we supposed to do with five hours of footage?'

'Hey, you wanted pictures, remember?' said Sian. 'Don't fucking whine when I bring them to you.'

Why was he being so negative? He ought to be ripping her arm off. This stuff was white hot. It would certainly focus people's attention, so by the time they got to tonight's real shock they'd have a captive audience.

The elevator doors swooshed open at the fourth floor. Lucas walked over to the car and began loading the bags silently into the trunk.

He knew he was being churlish. If Sian had brought another nail to hammer into Anton's coffin, that was great news, and the American press were bound to salivate more over a sex scandal than any other sort of wrongdoing. This was a nation who'd impeached their own president over a blow job, for God's sake. But part of him resented the fact that it was Sian's work, her research, that was ultimately going to bring Anton down. In his mind, tonight was the culmination of *his* revenge, his private, personal battle against the man who'd set out to ruin him.

'We've got the whole afternoon,' said Sian, climbing into the passenger seat beside him. 'We can edit it.'

'I suppose,' he grunted. 'We're cutting it a bit fine, though, don't you think?'

Sian struggled to keep a lid on her anger. She'd flown halfway across the world to get these tapes and the rest of her evidence here on time. A little pat on the back might have been nice.

'You don't have to worry,' she said bitterly. 'I'll do all

the editing. I already know where the money shots are.'

'As it were,' said Lucas, raising an eyebrow.

Despite himself, a smile had started to creep across his features. Despite herself, Sian returned it.

'I spoke to Ben earlier, by the way,' said Lucas, changing the subject. 'He wished us all luck.'

'I wish he was here,' said Sian, her tiredness making her drop her guard of indifference.

To her amazement, Lucas stretched out an arm and wrapped it around her shoulder in sympathy.

'I know you do, sweetheart,' he said. 'So do I.'

It wasn't until they'd pulled out of the airport and onto the Expressway that Sian remembered the other thing she had meant to tell him.

'Oh!' she said suddenly. 'There's something else. I can't believe I didn't tell you before.'

'What's that?' asked Lucas, keeping his eyes fixed on the road ahead.

'The Palmers fire,' said Sian. 'You know you asked me to check it out?'

Lucas looked up. She had his attention now.

'Well, I did,' she said. 'And I'm pretty sure I know who started it.'

Chapter Thirty-two

Petra adjusted the vintage Dior brooch at her décolletage, and admired her reflection for one final time in the mirror. The gown she had chosen for tonight, a black, Narciso Rodriguez column dress, was elegant rather than sexy, a deliberate statement designed to contrast with Saskia's vulgar, neon-pink Dolce & Gabbana mini-dress. Honestly, if that woman got any tackier you could use her as human fly-paper.

Anyway, it worked. Petra's white-blond bob and flawless milky skin looked even more striking against the severe black taffeta. The overall effect was positively regal, appropriate given that tonight she intended to show Saskia up in front of Anton and their many illustrious guests as the cheap pretender to her throne she really was.

Outside, the party was beginning to warm up. Twisting her office blind a fraction she could see the swelling crowd, and in the midst of them, Anton, glad-handing the media and more important corporate guests. Only two hours ago, he'd been in her office, arguing furiously with her about Saskia. She was still livid that he'd had that fat slug issue invitations to Lucas and Honor behind her back, and had let him know her views on the subject in no uncertain terms.

Anton always got turned on by confrontation. But after this afternoon's row he'd been positively foaming at the mouth, so desperate was he to fuck her. For once, Petra had resisted and decided to make him wait. Submission in the bedroom was all very well, but after all the shit he'd pulled with Saskia, he needed to be taught a lesson. By the time he'd stormed out of her office, with a hard-on the size of Canada bulging visibly in his suit pants, he was angrier than she'd ever seen him. But she wasn't worried. Later tonight, once the party was over, he could have what he wanted. And by then he'd want it so badly, he'd be prepared to make ample recompense. Saskia's remaining hours in his employ were now officially numbered.

She opened the blind a little further. Only a few big-ticket names had turned up so far: Teri Hatcher was here with her new toy-boy, and Oprah and Stedman were deep in conversation with the head of Random House at the entrance to the moroccan marquee, sipping the Dom Perignon that Petra had insisted on. (Saskia had wanted the irredeemably naff Cristal, of course.)

Petra was quite relaxed about the paucity of celebrities. Stars always liked to make an entrance, and that meant turning up late. But she could tell Anton was fretting. In yet another of her craven bids for his affection, Saskia had put together a cringe-making mini-biopic, *A Magnanimous Magnate*, which was scheduled to run at ten thirty. In his typical German way, Anton was obsessed about the thing starting on time, but he also wanted as many VIPs as possible to be there to see it.

Gliding back outside to join him – if she left his side for too long, Saskia would swoop in to try to play hostess, and she wasn't having any of that – Petra drew him to one side for a pep talk.

'You must try to relax,' she whispered in his ear. 'The film is for the media, not the guests. If you run around looking antsy and like you're not having a good time, believe me, so will everyone else.'

'I'd be a lot more relaxed if you'd opened your fucking legs two hours ago,' he hissed back.

Surreptitiously she allowed the back of her hand to brush against his crotch. 'Temper, temper,' she said. 'Good things come to those who wait. Didn't your mother ever tell you that?'

Meanwhile, back in the kitchens, Sian was battling with her own nerves. Honor had done a meticulous job stage-managing the plan for tonight. With the help of some of the disaffected Herrick staff, she'd managed to wangle a job for Sian as a temporary waitress, and get access to the detailed timing of the night's festivities. All Sian had to do was follow instructions. But as everything was based around the timings Honor had been given, they could only pray that Petra hadn't had a last-minute change of mind and reshuffled something. This was the part that worried Sian.

'We'll be OK,' Lucas had tried to reassure her this afternoon, whilst simultaneously taking the piss out of her French maid's outfit. 'Petra's a compulsive organizer, and Anton's even worse. Trust me, they don't do spontaneous. They'll stick to the schedule.'

Sian prayed he was right. Yanking down her much-too-short skirt – she was sure Lucas had had a hand in ordering her uniform, which had clearly been intended for a child, or one of those miniature Filipino women, not a strapping Irish Jersey girl like her – she picked up a tray of canapés and ventured out into the grounds.

But as soon as she turned into the Japanese garden, she caught her breath and dived for cover behind the nearest shrub. There, right in front of her, was Lola's brother Nick. He had his arm around the waist of a vacuous brunette, a twig-like giantess who could only have been a model, and his whiney, insistent, arrogant voice cut through the general buzz of conversation around him like a chainsaw.

'So you see, I'm all on my lonesome,' he was saying. 'My folks have officially become East Hampton's first agoraphobics. And my sister's too caught up with Super-yid to care about anything else. They're probably at home making matzo balls together.'

The twig laughed dutifully. Crouched behind the

bush, Sian's heart was pounding. Nick being here was bad enough. If he saw her he'd blow her cover in an instant. But since when was Lola in town? Lucas hadn't mentioned anything, and the last Sian heard, the whole Carter family were avoiding East Hampton like the plague.

'Come on.' Nick led the girl by the belt of her dress toward the marquee, much as one might a recalcitrant puppy. 'Let's check out the Ruski's attempt at La Mamounia. I bet it's lame.'

Once she was sure he'd gone, Sian re-emerged, brushing the dirt and leaves off her apron and legs. Please God, don't let Lola and Marti show up tonight. Any more stress and she was going to go completely bat-shit.

On the other side of the gardens, at one of the myriad outdoor bars, Petra shimmered beside Anton like a towering black shadow. Saskia, she noticed happily, was still stuck behind the newly built podium, sorting out technical difficulties with the sound system. Petra watched her scurrying around amongst the technicians like a fuschia-pink mother hen – the tiny dress she was wearing made the absolute worst of her chunky, shot-putters thighs, and even from here you could see her breasts spilling over the top of it like cookie dough. Better still, she appeared to be having a perfectly miserable time.

Much as she would have liked to spend the entire evening watching Saskia squirm, Petra was distracted moments later by another voluptuous blonde. Along with her sister, she was making quite an entrance, preening and pouting in front of a vast bank of cameras, whose flashes were going off one after another like sheet-lightning.

'I don't believe it,' she muttered furiously to Anton, under her breath. 'Tina Palmer's here. With Honor. I thought you said they weren't coming?'

Excusing himself from the Viacom CEO, Anton pulled her to one side. 'They weren't,' he said. 'Honor declined, and as far as I know Tina was never even on the list. But I don't see that it matters much. Do you?'

'Hmm. I suppose not,' said Petra, grudgingly. But inside she couldn't shake the feeling that it probably did matter. That the Palmer sisters' unexpected presence was a danger signal they ought not to ignore. 'Don't you find it odd, though? I'd have thought this was the last place Tina would want to show her face, wouldn't you? And look how pally she is with her sister. I thought they hated each other.'

Anton shrugged. 'So they kissed and made up. Who cares?'

'Apparently they're not the only ones,' said Petra, her concern mounting. 'Take a look at that.'

Lucas had just arrived, looking dapper in a Paul Smith suit and Hermès tie. Marching straight up to Honor, he kissed her warmly on both cheeks, then proceeded to offer the same friendly greeting to her sister. Once again, Anton didn't seem bothered.

'You knew we'd invited Lucas,' he purred, running one finger languorously up the length of Petra's spine and massaging the nape of her neck. 'Now who's getting too tense?'

'I knew he was *coming*,' she said tetchily. 'But look at the three of them, thick as thieves. Not so long ago those girls had a death warrant out for Lucas. What's changed?'

'I don't know,' said Anton. 'Luxe is going down the toilet faster than a lead turd, and Tina Palmer seems to have money to spare again these days. He's probably trying to butter her up for a loan.'

'And Honor?'

Anton shrugged. 'Maybe she's doing the same.'

Petra looked skeptical. 'I don't like it.'

'You're being paranoid,' said Anton. 'Besides, what do you want me to do about it? Have security throw them out?'

'Don't be facile,' snapped Petra. Grabbing a flute of

champagne from a passing waiter, she drained it in one long gulp and put the empty glass back on the tray. 'You invited them. I just think we should keep an eye on them, that's all. A close eye.'

Finding himself enveloped in a bear hug by Tina, Lucas tried to breathe through his mouth, and wondered how long it would be before he passed out from the fumes of her cloyingly sweet scent.

'Shalom,' she whispered breathily in his ear. 'It's been too long, my friend.'

With typically appalling timing, Tina had turned up at Palmers six hours ago, although Lucas hadn't actually seen her in person until now.

As usual, her arrival had been unscheduled. Wafting into the hotel lobby barefoot, wearing some sort of Hari Krishna kaftan (but incongruously followed by two minions weighed down with six massive Louis Vuitton trunks) she noisily demanded to see her sister.

'I'm afraid Miss Palmer isn't here,' the receptionist told her meekly. 'She's over at the cottage on Main Street.'

'Fine,' said Tina serenely. 'Give me the adress. And find rooms for my staff, would you, please? They all need feeding and watering.' She waved airily at her entourage like Marie Antoinette to the peasantry.

'But ... we aren't open for business yet,' stammered Agnes. 'We don't have rooms. Or a kitchen staff. Miss Palmer?'

But Tina wasn't listening. She'd already set off into the village in search of Honor.

When she eventually found her, she was sitting cross-legged on the living room floor with a dark-haird girl Tina didn't recognize, surrounded by a jungle of editing equipment, CD burners and wires, and staring intently at the TV screen.

'Peace!'

Standing in the doorway, Tina threw her arms out wide. But Honor and her friend were so engrossed, neither of them looked up.

'I said, *peace*!' said Tina again, more sharply. When no one looked up, she resorted to shouting: 'Is anyone going to tell me what's going on?'

In the end, Honor had decided it would be easier to let her in on the plan than to try to come up with a cover story at this late stage.

'She's got as much of a reason to hate Anton as any of us,' she reasoned with a deeply skeptical Lucas over the phone. 'And as nothing I say or do will keep her away from that party tonight, we may as well have her help us. She's actually not as stupid as she looks, you know.'

'No one's as stupid as your sister looks,' said Lucas moodily. 'Can't you send her back to LA?'

'Oh, sure, like she does what I tell her!' Honor laughed. 'Look, she's here now, like it or not.'

Lucas definitely didn't like it. But as he couldn't come up with a viable alternative, other than have Tina motor-mouthing her way through the party, asking awkward questions and drawing unwanted attention to all of them, he'd reluctantly agreed to clue her in.

Looking at her now, though, dressed about as discreetly as a transvestite at Mardi Gras, his misgivings returned with a vengeance. Feeling increasingly like a rodent in the grip of a Chanel 19-soaked boa constrictor, he gently prized himself free from her embrace.

'It's good to see you too,' he lied, wondering not for the first time what had ever possessed him to sleep with her. She was an attractive girl underneath, if you liked that sort of thing, but with all the makeup, and the diamonds and the hairspray she looked much older. She actually reminded him of Zsa Zsa Gabor, and not in her young starlet days, either.

By contrast, Honor's simple white empire-line dress and

face almost completely bare of makeup was so much more alluring. She'd changed beyond recognition from the spiky tomboy of old. When he'd kissed her earlier, she'd smelt of some faint lemony cologne, like the stuff they used to put on babies back home in Ibiza – fresh and natural. He loved it.

'You know, we shouldn't spend too much time together,' he warned Tina. 'Not here. Petra's already looking over. I think she can smell a rat.'

'Takes one to smell one,' said Honor. 'Honestly, just look at her, glued to Anton like the Grim Reaper.' But she took Lucas's advice and, dragging Tina by the hand, disappeared across the lawn and into the crowd to mingle.

Seconds later, Lucas felt a tap on his shoulder.

'Well, well, well.' The familiar, put-on British accent with just the faintest undercurrent of German menace, made Lucas's blood run cold. 'Look who it isn't.'

It was the first time he'd seen Anton in the flesh in almost five years. If you could call it flesh – the man had so much botulism and fillers running through his veins these days, he looked more like a Madame Tussauds waxwork than a human being. Despite himself, Lucas felt his pulse start to race with nerves.

'Anton,' He held out his hand. After a brief moment's hesitation, Anton shook it. 'Congratulations. Great party.'

'I'm thrilled you're enjoying it.' Anton smiled. 'Although I must say, Petra and I were surprised you could spare the time away from your own ... empire.' He injected the last word with enough sarcasm to sink a ship. 'Some might say you were fiddling while Rome burns. Or in your case, while Paris burns. How's the court case going?'

'Oh, you know what the EU contract laws are like,' said Lucas breezily, determined not to betray any hint of weakness. 'These things take an age, but there's no doubt we'll win in the end. Luckily Winston, my partner, is a patient man. We'll get through it.'

'That remains to be seen,' said Anton frostily. Not even the powerful freezing agents in his face could completely suppress the spite suffusing his features as he spoke. Lucas felt his own hatred bubble inside him like lava, but he kept his cool, and smiled affably.

'True,' he said. 'None of us can predict the future, can we? Even a great hotel like this one can fall from grace.'

Sure that he was being provoked, but unsure how to respond, Anton let out an impotent mewl of annoyance.

'If I were you,' he said curtly, once he'd rediscovered his voice, 'I'd focus on what was left of my own pitiful business, before throwing stones at others.'

'Again,' said Lucas, draining his glass. 'Good advice. I'll do that. Now, if you'll excuse me ...'

And handing his empty flute to a speechless Anton, he walked off.

By ten thirty-five, Saskia decided she could wait no longer. Anton was positively twitching with impatience, chatting distractedly with a radiant Christie Brinkley twenty feet away, and shooting her looks that got more and more agitated by the second. With any other client she'd have held off. Madonna and Guy Ritchie were still not here, nor were Donald and Melania, or the Hilton sisters. But if she didn't start soon, she ran the risk that some of the A-listers who had shown up might start leaving. And wouldn't that bitch Petra just love that? She'd already contrived somehow to turn Anton against her, quite *how* Saskia had no idea, but she wasn't about to hand her any further ammunition.

'Ladies and gentlemen.'

Up on the podium, microphone in hand, she made a brave bid for the now massive crowd's attention.

'People!' She shouted louder, signaling to the sound guys to up the output on her mic. 'If I could ask you all to look this way for just a moment.'

Slowly but surely, the noise levels began to dim, as an

enormous, multiplex-sized screen loomed up behind her on the stage, apparently out of nowhere.

'As you know,' she went on, her braying British accent strangely at odds with her mutton dressed as lamb, crotch-skimmer dress, 'we're here today to celebrate the Herrick being voted world number one.' A polite ripple of applause, punctuated by a few drunken whoops and cheers, echoed around the grounds, bouncing off the hotel's glass walls. 'But some of us also wanted to take this opportunity to pay tribute to a remarkable man,' Saskia simpered.

On cue, a lone spotlight made a great show of sweeping searchingly across the crowd before alighting on an apparently unsuspecting Anton.

'A man whose vision, hard work, and above all generosity of spirit, have made not just the Herrick, but the entire Tischen family, such an outstanding global success story,' said Saskia.

Lucas laughed out loud at Anton's blatantly fake surprise, complete with hand on chest, possum-wide eyes, and 'surely you don't mean li'l old me?' expression. He'd have liked to catch Honor's eye, but couldn't find her in the crowd. Instead he saw Sian, slipping unnoticed through the guests and looking whiter than her starched apron with nerves. He prayed she wasn't going to bottle it.

'The following short film, *A Magnanimous Magnate*, from award-winning director Bowen Langford,' Saskia went on, 'is a tribute to your host, and my friend,' she beamed at Anton adoringly, 'Mr. Anton Tisch.'

'Who is that creature?' a woman close to Petra could be heard asking her friend as the footage began to roll, earning herself untold brownie points by adding in a sotto voice whisper, 'She looks like a billiard ball with legs.'

Clearly, no expense had been spared on production values. *A Magnanimous Magnate* opened with some rousing, John Williams-esque music, accompanying a number of stills from Anton's childhood: Anton as a baby in an old-fashioned Silver Cross pram, wearing a frilly sun-hat; Anton aged about eight, standing at the foot of a ski slope clutching a medal with an oddly endearing, gap-toothed grin; Anton looking groomed and preppy at sixteen in an official high school photograph. But it wasn't long before the stills gave way to a series of high-profile talking heads, each giving suitably glowing testimonials about the great man himself.

'Tisch is a fighter,' a smiling, casually dressed Richard Branson spoke straight to camera, his legs dangling from a swing seat on the verandah of his Necker mansion. 'I've known the guy fifteen years, and I still wouldn't want to meet him in a dark alley.'

More polite laughter from the crowd.

Testimonials followed from a slew of British politicians and business leaders. From where she was standing Petra could see the eyes of a number of the Hollywood contingent glazing over.

'What's ICI?' one starlet could be heard asking her friend.

'I think it's a studio,' the friend replied earnestly.

But just when it seemed she was about to lose her audience's interest altogether, Saskia suddenly began pulling out the big guns. Arnold Schwarzenegger told a genuinely funny joke about Anton's golfing prowess, or rather lack of it, then praised him for his charity work on both sides of the Atlantic. He was followed by a glowing Brangelina, neither of whom said anything particularly interesting but whose impossibly beautiful features were enough to ensure the rapt attention of every sexually active person there, male or female. Finally, warm words from Kofi Annan and the chairman of the international Red Cross were interspersed with shots of smiling children, mostly cancer or liver transplant patients, thanking Anton for his generous contributions to their various hospitals/research foundations.

'Mr. Tisch doesn't have children of his own,' an adorable,

wispily blonde girl of six lisped in finale. 'But he's been like a father to me. Thank you, Mr. Tisch. I hope you enjoy your party.'

The screen went blank, to wild applause. Anton, still hamming up his surprised and embarrassed schtick, was beckoned up to the podium by Saskia. At yet another pre-rehearsed cue, the press were ushered further forwards and space was miraculously created for the TV crews with their bulky boom mics and camera equipment. Only once the media were all in place did Anton start to speak.

'I won't bore you with a long speech,' he said, taking the microphone, 'not least because I had *no idea* they were going to spring this on me.' He wagged an admonishing finger at Saskia. From their various posts, Lucas, Honor and Sian all cringed. 'So I have nothing prepared. But I would like to say a few words of thanks, off the cuff as it were. To all of you,' he held his hands out magnanimously, 'for being here tonight to help celebrate the Herrick's remarkable achievement.' More cheers. 'To my loyal staff, especially Ms. Petra Kamalski, my outstanding manager here, whose hard work is in large part responsible for this happy occasion.'

Despite herself, Petra flushed with happiness. He'd singled her out publicly, without giving Saskia even a passing mention. Knowing how crushed her rival would be filled her with a warm inner glow.

'But most of all, I'd like to thank the children, like little Leila whom you saw there, with whom it has been my honor and privilege to work over the last twenty years. I can truly say that they have given me more, far more, than I have ever given them.'

'Ain't that the truth,' muttered Sian.

Reaching for the perfectly pressed white handkerchief in his breast pocket, he dabbed at his eyes with one swift gesture: manly but compassionate. It was a bravura performance. Even Lucas, at the back of the audience, was impressed.

The applause for his speech, respectable at first, swelled to an almost deafening crescendo. Standing on the podium, basking in the adulation, it took some seconds before Anton realized that it wasn't, in fact, he who was the focus of this rapturous reception, but Tina Palmer, who had somehow appeared behind him on stage. Wearing a (for her) conservative creation in blue-gray bias cut silk, she nevertheless looked every inch the star, with Elizabeth Taylor-sized diamonds at her throat, ears and wrists and her blonde hair piled on top of her head in a solid hairsprayed mountain. The drag queen look that Lucas found so off-putting up close seemed to evaporate with distance, as well as on camera. To the partygoers below, and all the viewers at E! and beyond, Tina looked Screen Siren perfect.

She was holding up an enormous bouquet of lilies, freesias and roses, a vulgar but impressive riot of color finished off with a red silk bow the size of a small child's head. Leaning forward, she presented it to a bewildered Anton. More than a little annoyed to have his limelight so shamelessly usurped, but with the spotlights trained firmly on him, he had little option but to smile and take the flowers, which obsucred him from view almost completely. As he reached for the bouquet, Tina deftly relieved him of his mic.

'What the hell is going on?' hissed Saskia, stepping forward looking officious. 'You shouldn't be up here.'

But Tina held her ground, shooing her away with all the languid unconcern of a cow flicking its tail at a fly. Saskia reviewed her options silently for a moment, then withdrew into the shadows. Tina Palmer was bona fide A-list these days. She could hardly have her manhandled from the stage.

Watching proceedings from the audience with a rigid-jawed stare, Petra shared Saskia's sense of impotence. Tina was clearly up to no good, but there wasn't a lot they could do about it, not unless she really overstepped the mark.

'I apologize for this unscheduled diversion,' breathed

Tina huskily, channeling her best Marilyn Monroe. 'But given my own work with Unicef, I felt it was appropriate. I believe many of you here tonight are familiar with my work.'

Suddenly a still from her infamous porn movie flashed up on the screen behind her. The crowd gasped as one, then erupted with laughter.

'Thank you; you're too kind,' giggled Tina, camping it up.

Honor, who'd worked her way to the front of the crowd, blushed scarlet. The naked image had been her idea – a surefire attention-grabber – and she was relieved Sian had managed to commandeer the projector as planned. But looking at her sister like that, all creamy, udder-sized breasts and candy-pink nipples, still floored her with embarrassment.

'Anyway, given my own charity work – and Mr. Tisch's involvement with it, of which more later,' Tina smiled mysteriously, 'I felt I couldn't let this evening pass without a small, personal tribute. So if you'll bear with me ... Sian?'

Inside the summer house, coverted by Saskia into a makeshift projection room for her tribute film, Sian's hands were shaking like someone in the final stages of Parkinson's. Thanks to Honor's careful planning, everything had gone seamlessly. As soon as the credits rolled on Anton's biopic, she'd been able to slip unnoticed into the building and lock it from the inside. But now that she was actually here, with her finger on the button both metaphorically and literally, she felt sick as a dog. Media from across the globe were lined up outside, their cameras trained on the screen behind Tina: *her* film, *her* story. Back in London, Simon would have already gone to print. The first copies of the *News of the World* would be on the newsstands within hours, with her exclusive exposé plastered all over the front three pages. It wasn't just Anton Tisch's life that was about to be changed forever. It was hers, too.

Christ, she hoped she hadn't fucked up the editing. Weaving her extra footage into the film they already had had been painstaking work, and everything had been so rushed this afternoon at Honor's cottage. What if she'd somehow cut out something crucial? Or what if they had technical problems? Basic editing she could just about do, but Sian was no technician.

Seconds later, she had the surreal experience of seeing her own face pop up on-screen in front of her.

'Good evening, ladies and gentlemen.' Sitting in a black leather chair in a nondescript white room, she spoke directly to camera. 'My name is Sian Doyle. I'm a journalist. And I'd like to show you all another side to Anton Tisch.'

The camera panned outwards to show a very young girl sitting opposite her in a second, identical black leather chair. Bug eyed and visibly shaking with nerves, she was hauntingly beautiful but didn't look a day over fourteen.

Up on stage, Anton's hands tightened involuntarily around his bouquet. He didn't even notice when the thorns from the roses skewered his palms and blood began to trickle over the flowers' plastic wrapping.

'Find Petra,' he mouthed urgently over his shoulder to Saskia. 'I want this stopped. Now!'

'At first, I thought Mr. Tisch was just being friendly. I was very grateful to 'im for trying to help me,' said the girl, in a childish whisper littered with cockney cadences. 'The first pictures I done was all right. Tasteful and that. But then there was this other man, Bill or Billy I think 'is name was, who worked for Mr. Tisch on his website. He wanted me to do ... other things.' She looked away. 'He showed me pictures what some of the other girls from the home had done.'

Three stills filled the screen in quick succession, all of nude underage girls in sickeningly graphic sexual poses. A collective gasp of disgust erupted from the crowd.

'These images were posted on a website that's a wholly

owned subsidiary of the Tischen Group.' Sian was talking directly to camera again. 'All three of these girls spent time in care homes paid for by Anton Tisch. All three were known personally to him.'

'This is preposterous!' spluttered Anton. Dropping the flowers on the ground, he made a lunge for Tina's microphone, but she stepped back, whipping it away like a matador taunting a bull. She had no idea what any of this was really about – Honor's explanations earlier about some sort of movie exposé sounded boringly convulted to Tina. But she was definitely starting to enjoy being a part of it now.

Those of the guests who weren't still reeling with shock began giggling as they watched Tina Palmer evading Anton's grasp. Aware that he was starting to look like a laughing stock, as well as a pedophile, Anton cut his losses and stormed off stage.

'Where's Petra?' he roared at the hovering staff behind the podium steps. 'Can none of you switch off this fucking thing?'

'Whoever's in the summer house has locked it from the inside, sir,' piped up one brave soul. 'They're trying to break in there now. Saskia's got a bunch of guys down there.'

Back in the summer house, Sian could no longer hear her own projected voice over the frenzied rattling of the door behind her. As well as locking it, she'd managed to wedge it shut with various bulky items of furniture, but the guys outside weren't giving up in a hurry. Aware that she was running out of time, she made an executive decision to skip the next section of footage altogether and cut straight to the finale. Activating her wire for the first time that evening, she sent a warning message to Lucas.

At the back of the garden, he clutched his ear trying to make out what she was saying through the heavy crackle. 'Need a minute. I'm g ... second tape. Can you get Tina ... cover?'

Getting the gist, he stood up on an empty champagne

crate and waved a pre-arranged signal to Tina. Please God let her have remembered ...

In fact, he needn't have worried. With Sian reloading the tape decks, the screen faded to black, but Tina stepped forward quite unfazed and kept everyone occupied with a little show of her own.

'The story doesn't end there, folks,' she said huskily, her diamond choker dazzling in the spotlight. 'In a moment, our lovely hostess Sian will be back with some even more shocking revelations.' The crowd ooed and aahed. Their earlier disgust apparently forgotten, Tina had suddenly transformed them into gullible participants in a cheap reality show. 'But in the meantime, I'd like to share my own personal experience of Mr. Tisch,' she went on. 'Unfortunately for me, his interest in the sex-tape industry wasn't entirely restricted to teenagers. I now know that Anton Tisch himself was personally responsible for my own debut in the adult movie world. That's right.' She gave a wounded pout, preening for the TV cameras all the while and making sure she kept her chin firmly down. '*He* was the one who entrapped me, not poor Lucas Ruiz,' she wagged her finger playfully at the press, 'whom you awful swine were so quick to blame at the time.'

A shocked murmur rose up from the hotel industry people scattered amongst the crowd. No one in the US would forget in a hurry how Lucas had been pilloried over that tape, and the self-righteous fever of condemnation that had swept the business at the time.

'But the good news,' said Tina archly, 'is that we've raised over two million dollars to date, ladies and gentlemen. Well, I guess it's primarily the gentlemen I have to thank.' Another loud burst of laughter. 'So please, keep watching!'

She might be best known as a porn star, but there was no doubt Tina Palmer was East Hampton's sweetheart tonight.

'And on behalf of Unicef and the poor children of Africa, I'd like to propose a toast of my own: to Anton Tisch. A *true* humanitarian!'

Just as the roars of applause were dying down again, the screen behind Tina lit up once more.

'Atta girl,' whispered Lucas under his breath. He'd lost radio contact with Sian again, but she'd obviously come through.

'We now come to the final, and most disturbing aspect of tonight's short film.' Still in her black chair, talking straight to camera, Sian's clear, steely voice filled the night air. 'Most of you probably don't know much about Azerbaijan, so let me fill you in on the headlines. It used to be part of the Soviet Union. It's got a lot of oil – expected oil revenues over the next twenty years of around a hundred and twenty *billion* dollars. And it's run by one of the most corrupt regimes on the planet. Oh,' she added, breaking into a rare smile, 'and it's where Anton Tisch first made his fortune.'

A couple of stills followed of rugged mountainous scenery, some enchanting coastline, and vast pipelines built to ship the country's oil to the West. But just as people were starting to wonder quite where Sian was going with this geography lesson, another, horrifying image filled the screen. It was the body of a young boy, no more than eleven or twelve, his torso riddled with bullets, still clutching an ancient Kalashnikof rifle to his chest.

'We don't know his name,' Sian's voice, somber again now, drifted over the speakers, as they cut to more shots of dead children, some burned and tortured beyond recognition. 'Or his. Or his.' Relentlessly the pictures kept coming. A number of people in the audience looked away.

'I think I'm gonna be sick,' said the starlet to her friend.

'What we do know, and what I can prove, is that Anton Tisch supplied arms to boys like these, children forced to become armed warriors against President Aliev's ruthless regime. And this is what he bought with the profits.'

A shot of Anton's stunning Geneva mansion loomed into view, followed by another of a child soldier, this one still alive but malnourished, his eyes wide with terror and confusion. More of the same followed: Anton's yacht, and a pile of rebel bodies; Anton smiling as he shook hands with President Bush, and an Aliev labor camp, complete with emaciated faces pressed up against the barbed wire. Then the screen abruptly went black.

'They must have got into the projection room,' mumbled Lucas to himself, trying in vain to raise either Sian or Honor on their wires. So much for state-of-the-art communications technology. But it didn't seem to matter. They'd been on air long enough to get the point across. Within seconds, pandemonium broke loose. Everybody wanted a piece of Anton, but he seemed to have melted into the melee. Happily, Tina was still up on stage and more than willing to step into the breach in his absence, sacrificing herself to the media feeding frenzy.

'Tina, can you prove any of this?' yelled reporters, thrusting microphones and cameras at her from all angles. 'Who is this Sian Doyle? How do you know her?'

'Please.' Holding up her hand, Tina did her best to look harassed, and perhaps just a touch little-girl-lost. 'One at a time, OK? Don't crowd me.'

'Why didn't you go straight to the police?' A pretty Asian TV reporter from one of the local news shows forced her way to the front. 'If you had proof of criminal activity, why'd you wait?'

'To be honest with you, I'm just the front woman here,' said Tina. 'You'll have to ask my sister about that sort of stuff.'

'Honor's behind this?' The Asian girl swooped on this new information like a hawk diving for a shrew.

'Well, no, I wouldn't say behind it exactly.' Tina sounded wrongfooted.

'Where is she right now? Is she here tonight?'

At that moment Saskia came careering through the lines of press like a furious pink canon ball and hurled herself at Tina, knocking her to the ground.

'You bitch!' Climbing on top of her, she clawed at her face and neck like a savage, much to the delight of the TV crews. Her heavy mascara was running in thick black rivulets down her face, and her fuschia lipstick was smudged everywhere, making her look like a psychotic clown. For a moment Tina was genuinely frightened.

'Do you know how much effort went into this party?' Saskia shrieked. 'Do you know how *hard* I worked?'

As she raised her arm for another blow, Tina closed her eyes and flinched. But instead of the expected sting of talons ripping into her cheek, she felt a weight being lifted off her.

'Take her inside.' Petra's voice sounded as ice cool and imperious as ever. 'She's hysterical.' The only hint that the crisis was affecting her at all was that her Russian accent had become slightly more pronounced. 'And help Miss Palmer to a chair, please.'

Opening her eyes to see two burly and by no means unattractive security guards looming over her, Tina decided not to put up a struggle. Though it pained her to yield the limelight, she *was* feeling a little shaken. Honor never mentioned anything this afternoon about the risk of being assaulted by fat British lunatics.

With Tina temporarily out of action, the reporters lost no time in cornering Petra instead.

'Ms. Kamalski, I take it tonight's allegations against your employer have come as a complete surprise to you?'

'I'll be making a full statement later, once I've had a chance to speak with Mr. Tisch.' said Petra calmly. 'Right now, you'll understand, I have over a thousand guests I need to deal with. I really don't have the time for questions.'

'But you must have been shocked by these revelations,

the abuse of young girls, the terrible lives and deaths of those poor children ...'

Petra gave a magnificently dismissive wave of the hand. 'None of which has anything to do with Mr. Tisch. To be honest with you, I'm not surprised to hear that Honor Palmer orchestrated this entire debacle. Clearly she and Lucas Ruiz dreamed this up together as some twisted form of industrial sabotage.'

'A little extreme, don't you think?' A paunchy print journalist from the *LA Times* looked at Petra skeptically. 'To make up a pack of lies that elaborate? Why would they do that?'

'Because the Herrick is number one, of course,' said Petra scathingly. 'We're the best in the world, while their respective hotels are foundering.'

'But according to Ms. Doyle ...' the reporter pressed on bravely.

'Miss *Doyle?*' said Petra sharply, her paper-thin facade of politeness beginning to crack. 'Sian Doyle is a money-grabbing former waitress, nothing more. The police are on their way here as we speak and when they arrive, they will arrest her. She is not to be taken seriously.'

'What about the girl's evidence?' The Asian girl piped up again. 'Or Tina Palmer's accusations? You can't dismiss all of them out of hand, surely?'

'A few teenage hookers and a porn star with an axe to grind?' Petra snorted in derision. 'I most certainly can dismiss them. This is nonsense. What Mr. Tisch decides to do about these libelous and quite frankly ridiculous accusations, is a matter for him. My priority right now is to ensure that the people responsible for destroying tonight's celebrations are brought to book. Aha!' she looked up glee-fully, 'here come the police now.'

A troop of uniformed officers, eight or nine of them, pulled up in front of the hotel and began spreading out in various directions. Two made straight for Petra, who greeted them with a brusque professional smile.

'Thank goodness you're here,' she began. 'The girl, Doyle, is in our summer house in the care of my security. If you follow me, I'll take you there. But it's clear she wasn't acting alone. Lucas Ruiz and Honor Palmer were both here earlier, although I suspect they may have taken off by now. I—'

'Actually, Ms. Kamalski, it's you we need to talk to.' The older, more senior officer laid a hand on her shoulder. 'I need to bring you downtown for questioning. If it's not too much trouble.'

'Don't be ridiculous. I can't possibly leave the hotel,' said Petra, with a look that left the word 'moron' hanging in the air. 'Whatever you need to ask me, you can do it while we walk. But I want these people off hotel property.'

The senior cop gave a nod to his colleague. Before she even had time to register what was happening, Petra found herself being handcuffed and escorted toward the podium steps.

'We could have done this the easy way, you know,' said the officer, shielding his eyes from a sudden barrage of camera flashes. 'This is your choice, lady. Petra Kamalski, I'm arresting you on suspicion of instigating an arson attack on Palmers hotel. You have the right to remain silent. Anything you say—'

'This is ridiculous.' Petra's voice was shaking. 'I had nothing to do with that fire. You can't possibly link me to it.'

'On the contrary, ma'am, we have some very strong links, courtesy of your friend Miss Doyle, and two solid witnesses who say they saw you entering the hotel kitchens that morning.'

'Anton!' Catching sight of him across the garden as she was dragged down the steps, Petra called out in panic. It was so long since the fire, and the police had drawn such a

541

total and consistent blank, she'd long ago started thinking she was home free. How on earth had Sian found witnesses? But she'd done it for Anton, for both of them. He'd see that, surely? He'd help her.

Having gone awol for the last twenty minutes, Anton had suddenly popped up arm in arm with a scowling, obese man in a suit, whom Petra recognized instantly as his lawyer, Bob Singer. Swarms of people were pressed around them on all sides, but they, too, were flanked by cops and being ushered politely but firmly in the direction of the waiting squad cars.

'Anton!' As they got closer, she shouted again. 'Darling!'

Glancing up, he caught her eye. He had never seen fear on her face before – never seen any kind of weakness, in fact. It unnerved him so much, he dropped his gaze. Moments later he was bundled into the back of a squad car with Bob.

On his attorney's advice, Anton hadn't uttered a single syllable to either reporters or the police. To be honest, he hadn't needed the advice. He had no idea what to say and was still in a state of stupefied shock, wondering if this was some sort of nightmare from which he would imminently wake. He also knew that in the long run, the US police were likely to be the least of his worries. Even if, by some miracle, Bob could talk him out of these charges, Aliev was not a man known for his mercy towards his enemies. Anton had taken what he could from his government in the early years, and for a while had been happy to take his money and run. But seeing so many of his former Russian buddies surge past him in the wealth stakes these past few years, greed had got the better of him and he'd decided to get back in, switching allegiance to the rebels, who for a while had looked set to seize control of the pipelines in Azerbaijan's east. Supplying arms was the easiest and cheapest way to buy himself a slice of that pie. What did he care if a few young boys took a bullet along the way? They were born into lives of such unutterable misery anyway, it hardly seemed to matter.

Through the windscreen, he saw Sian being ushered into the car in front of them. She wasn't handcuffed, as Petra had been – and what was that about? Petra had nothing to do with any of this – but she did appear to be under arrest. Nevertheless, she looked not just relaxed but happy. When her sixth sense kicked in and she caught him staring, she flashed him a grin that he could only interpret as one of triumph.

Whatever happened to him now, that girl would have made her name in the tawdry world of investigative journalism and, he imagined, her fortune too. He didn't think he'd ever hated another human being quite so much. Why hadn't she come to him with what she knew? He'd have paid her fifty times whatever she'd been offered for her story. They could both have been rich, safe and free.

'Do you know her?' asked Bob, catching the exchange of looks.

Anton shook his head. 'No. I never laid eyes on her before tonight. Although she sure as hell seems to know me.'

'Quiet,' ordered Bob, nodding at the cops in the front seat. 'No she doesn't. She's a fantasist, got it? Let me do the talking.'

Hidden in the shadows of one of the Herrick's perfectly clipped yew hedges, Honor watched as the cars containing Anton and Sian sped away, followed by a clamoring press pack. With Tina there to work the crowds and the media, she had been able to hang back and focus on making sure the plan ran smoothly behind the scenes. Which it had done, until Sian had been arrested. That was most definitely not supposed to happen.

'Hey.'

Honor jumped like she'd just been jabbed with a cattle prod. Lucas had crept up behind her and, wrapping both arms around her waist, begun dragging her further back into the shadow.

'Let go of me!' she said crossly, wriggling free.

'Shhhh,' he whispered in her ear, clapping a hand across her mouth. 'Someone will hear you. You don't want the press on your case, do you?'

Honor shivered. It was late and getting cold, and all this standing still was making it worse. Plus Lucas's warm breath on her neck tickled.

'You've got goose bumps,' he said, staring at the upright hairs on her forearms. 'Am I making you nervous?'

Honor looked at him witheringly. 'No,' she said. 'I'm cold. And I'm worried about Sian. Did you see the cops take her away just now?'

He nodded.

'I think they arrested her,' said Honor. 'Why would they do that? We have to get down to the station, right now. We have to straighten this out.'

She made a move to go, but Lucas grabbed her arm.

'No,' he said firmly. 'Trust me. Whatever it is, Sian can take care of herself. She knew what she was getting into.'

'What's that supposed to mean?' said Honor indignantly. What a classically selfish, Lucas response. 'We can't just abandon the poor girl!'

Just then, the gaggle of media parted like the Red Sea and an ashen, handcuffed Petra was shoved unceremoniously into a third waiting police car.

'Oh my God.' Honor turned back to Lucas. 'Petra too? This is ridiculous. What's going on?'

Lucas shrugged and gave her an innocent 'beats me' look. But Honor wasn't buying it.

'What don't I know?' she asked, her eyes narrowing suspiciously. 'What haven't you told me?'

Lucas took a deep breath. Now was probably as good a time as any. 'Come with me,' he whispered. 'We need to talk.'

Chapter Thirty-three

'You can't do this to me!' yelled Sian at the top of her lungs. 'I'm a reporter! Whatever happened to freedom of the press? And where the hell is *he* going?'

Anton, still glued to his attorney like a barnacle to a rock, was being escorted across the lobby and out of the back door of the East Hampton station. His brows were corrugated in concentration, and he seemed not to notice the racket coming from the holding cell behind him, or Sian's furious little face glaring at him through the wooden porthole.

'He's going to New York,' said the duty sergeant patiently. 'Thanks to you he has a date with the FBI. That's what you wanted, right?'

'What I *want*,' said Sian, 'is the key to this door. Or failing that an attorney, a phone and something to eat. A Big Mac'd be nice.' It was hard to be taken seriously whilst wearing a semi-porn French maid's outfit, but she did her best to sound like she meant business. 'And I'd like a copy of the early edition of the *News of the World*.'

'News of the *what*?' The sergeant looked blank. 'Listen, kiddo, you'll be outta here just as soon as one of your rich buddies shows up with your bail money.'

The East Hampton police station had a retro, *Leave It to Beaver* ambience that, under other circumstances, Sian might have found endearingly quaint. The lobby looked like it hadn't been touched since the fifties, all heavy wooden fixtures and fittings, with a polished brass hand bell on the desk for attracting the duty officer's attention. But appearances could be deceptive. It might look like the kind of place where the worst that ever happened was some old lady's cat getting stuck up a tree, or a bunch of kids getting a little over-enthusiastic with the trick or treating at Halloween. In fact, in the last two years alone, three local murders had made the national news, not to mention a mafia money-laundering operation that had seen two brothers from Bridgehampton arrested and sent down for consecutive life sentences. Anton Tisch was hardly the first big fish to pass through these musty old halls nor, she imagined, would he be the last.

The sergeant returned to his sudoku puzzle, and Sian skulked over to the chair at the back of her cell. This was so annoying!

The cop who'd dragged her out of the projection room muttered something about trespassing and impersonation, false pretenses, or some other bullshit. Didn't these guys realize what undercover reporting *was*? What was she supposed to do, wander up to Petra Kamalski bold as brass and say: 'Excuse me, my name's Sian. Do you mind awfully if I ruin your party, expose your boyfriend as a gun-running pedophile, then have you arrested for getting kerosene-happy at Palmers last year? You don't? Great! Thanks!'

If the police had done their job properly, and smelled Anton and Petra for the rats they were, she wouldn't have had to trespass and take matters into her own hands. But for some reason, the arresting officer hadn't been swayed by the obvious logic of this argument and had gone ahead and booked her anyway. Worse, the bastard had only allowed her two phone calls before shutting her in the lock-up. She'd tried Honor's cell, then Lucas's, but both were switched off. How the hell was she supposed to make bail if she couldn't call anyone to come get her?

Half an hour passed, and soon her stomach was rumbling so loudly you could have measured it on the richter scale. Too nervous to eat all day, she found she was suddenly famished. Given the option of burger or phone, at this point she'd have gone for the Mac and fries hands down.

Outside, she could hear the low hum of the chattering TV crews, no doubt pitching camp in the hope of getting a decent shot of Anton being led away.

'I should be out there,' she moaned to no one in particular. 'This is *my* story that's breaking. It's not fair.'

A few minutes later, she was distracted from her pity party by the arrival of Petra. Looking like a death's head in her funereal black dress and staring straight ahead, she was whisked away immediately to an interview room at the rear of the building, followed moments later by another black-suited woman, presumably a lawyer.

'Spoilsports,' said Sian, as the detectives closed the door behind them. 'You might at least let me watch. Haven't you got one of those see-through glass thingies you could put me in? Oh, come *on*. I won't tell.'

The duty sergeant laughed and shook his head. 'You know, the time'll pass a lot quicker if you just go to sleep. There are blankets in there and a pillow. It is almost midnight.'

'Yeah, right,' grumbled Sian. 'As if I could sleep. I'm too fucking hungry to sleep.'

The next thing she knew, she was being jolted roughly awake by somebody shaking her shoulder.

'Hey, sleeping beauty.'

It was a different cop, a weasel-faced little man with a nose so long and thin and protruding it could have been designed to search out termites. His friend must have finished his shift and gone home. How long had she been out?

'Wake up. Looks like your prince has come.'

For one fleeting, mad, sleep-confused moment, Sian thought he meant Ben. But she was almost as pleased when she opened her eyes and saw who it actually was.

'Don't say anything, OK?' said Lola. 'I know I look like shit.'

547

In a pair of green sweat pants-cum-pyjamas, with one of Marti's thick fisherman's sweaters over the top and with her feet thrust into a pair of frankly filthy Ugg boots, she had clearly just been dragged out of bed. But even without makeup and with her long red hair matted and tangled, she somehow managed to project an aura of sexiness that had weasel-face and his buddies staring at her like dogs slavering over a steak.

'Yeah, well, check out my outfit,' quipped Sian, throwing off the blanket to reveal her ridiculous frilly apron. 'Talk about fashion forward, right?'

But Lola was way too over-emotional for banter. Stepping forward with tears in her eyes, she opened her arms, and Sian ran headlong into them, hugging her back like a long-lost sister.

'I'm sorry,' they both said simultaneously, then giggled.

'How did you know I was here?' asked Sian.

'Nick told me,' said Lola. 'Marti and I were sound asleep when he got back to the house and … oh, hi!' She smiled at the weasel-faced cop, whipping out her black Centurion card along with a killer Carter smile. 'I need to pay her bond. Do you guys take Amex?'

'That'll do nicely, thank you,' said the cop with a leery smile, then turning to Sian added, 'Looks like you got yourself some friends in high places.'

The girls spent the first ten minutes of the car ride shaking off reporters. Thankfully, Lola knew the local back roads like the back of her hand, and only the most dogged of the press pack dared follow her once she started weaving in and out of the maze of lanes and bumpy beach tracks at rally-driver speed.

'You know, I could just get out and talk to them? Give them a quote or whatever,' said Sian queasily, as the jeep made another lurching left-right-left combination of turns and almost veered into a ditch. 'Holy crap, Lola, please slow down. I know I told Simon that I wouldn't talk to any other papers, but it's not worth dying for, you know?'

'We aren't gonna die,' said Lola, in the same breath switching off her headlights and plunging them, the road and everything into total, abject darkness. 'Try and catch me now, asshole.' She grinned in her rear-view mirror.

Sure enough, within minutes they'd shaken off the last of the stragglers and Lola pulled over into the deserted parking lot of a diner, so that they could finally have a chance to talk.

'Thanks,' said Sian, a little nervously, once Lola had killed the engine. 'For coming to get me. And for paying that bail money.'

'No problem,' Lola smiled. 'Now that you're a world-famous investigative reporter, you can pay me back, right? So you sold Satan the exclusive, huh? How much d'you manage to screw out of him for that?'

'More than he wanted to pay,' said Sian. 'But less than it's worth, I reckon. I knew it was gonna be a big story as soon as I got the girls from Children of Hope to talk. But the arms dealing was more than even I expected. Those poor little boys.' She shook her head sadly.

'Well, those assholes chasing us certainly seemed to think it was big news,' said Lola.

An awkward silence fell, which Sian was the first to break.

'About Lucas,' she said, staring straight ahead, tracing patterns in the stars through the windscreen. 'What you saw. Believe me, I didn't want him in the flat that night anymore than you did. And that kiss ... it totally took me by surprise. There's nothing going on between us, truly.'

Lola raised a hand for her to stop. 'Forget about it,' she said.

'No, really,' said Sian. 'It's important to me that you know. I don't have any feelings for Lucas. But I do have to admit he's been phenomenal in getting everything together

549

for tonight. And, please don't yell, but he actually *does* have a nicer side to him. I wouldn't have believed it myself until now.'

'It's OK,' said Lola. 'I'm sure he does. I needed someone to blame for Dad's affair, that's all. For what it did to my mom.'

'Oh, don't, please don't cry,' said Sian, watching the tears welling up in her eyes.

'It's OK,' Lola sniffed, wiping at her face with the back of her hand. 'The point is that Lucas was a handy scapegoat. But it was never his fault. My dad was the only person to blame.'

'Well,' said Sian reasonably, 'I don't know if I'd go that far. Honor was there too, remember? It takes two to tango. And Anton was the one who leaked it to the press.'

'Yes, but it's not just the affair.' Lola shook her head angrily. 'All my life, my father's set himself up as this big moral example. He used to criticize Mom for being shallow – and maybe she is – but at least she's honest, you know? Dad's such a fake. In his eyes Mom was shallow, I was spoiled and my brother was a lazy jerk.'

'Your brother *is* a lazy jerk,' said Sian, reasonably.

'I know.' Lola smiled. 'Dad always acted so *baffled* by that. Like "How could such a great guy like me wind up with such a selfish kid?" And yet underneath all the bullshit, he and Nick aren't so different. Marti was the one who made me see it.'

'Really?'

'Yeah. I always knew my parents were conservative. I even knew they were snobs. But bringing Marti home really opened my eyes. My dad is so racist, so self-righteous, so full of . . .'

'Shit?' offered Sian.

'I was gonna say hate,' said Lola, shivering despite the warmth of the car, with the heaters turned up full blast. For a moment the word hung in the air between them,

550

like a stale smell. 'He actually looks down on Marti,' Lola went on. '*He* looks down on *Marti*. Where does he get off? Anyway.' She smiled, abruptly shifting gears. 'The point is, it was never really about Lucas, or you. I'm glad he helped you get your story.'

'Honestly?' Sian's face lit up.

'Absolutely,' said Lola. 'Are you kidding me? Anton Tisch is clearly, like, the world's biggest asshole. You totally nailed him.'

They hugged again, all traces of awkwardness gone.

'So what now?' Sian asked warily, as Lola turned on the ignition again. 'I can't go back to Palmers, or the cottage. The press'll be everywhere.'

'You can sleep in our guest house,' said Lola. 'It's private, alarmed, and we have dogs.'

'Sounds perfect,' said Sian. Suddenly she longed for a bed, any bed. There'd be time enough to savor her triumph, and catch up with Lucas and Honor, in the morning. After five minutes with her head lolling exhausted against the window, she suddenly sat up. 'Hold on. Isn't your house in the other direction?'

Lola smiled. 'Er, yeah. We're making a quick detour.'

'A detour, really? Now?' said Sian. 'I don't wanna sound ungrateful, Lo, but couldn't it wait till tomorrow? I'm wiped out.'

'Not really,' said Lola. 'You'll see.'

They'd reached the bottom of an unlit dirt road. Winding down her window, Sian could hear the lapping of waves. Somewhere in the near distance, she could also make out a dying buzz of chattering voices and revving engines – the remnants of the Herrick party heading home.

'Lola! You moron,' she said good-naturedly, climbing out of the car onto the deserted beach. 'You took us in a circle, we're right outside Palmers, aren't we? I thought you wanted to avoid the press. This place'll be crawling with them soon, if it isn't already.'

'Actually,' the voice came from behind her, close to the shore, 'most of them sloped off once they realized Honor and Tina weren't here.'

Sian froze, unable to bring herself to look around. She looked for Lola, but she seemed to have mysteriously vanished.

'And you, of course,' the deep cockney rumble went on. 'They all wanted to talk to you. But some bright spark convinced them you'd been whisked off to New York for interviews. Don't know his name, but I heard he was English, charismatic, and looked a bit like Brad Pitt. Only fitter.'

Sian felt her stomach crunch itself into a fist, then flip over like one of those jumping frog bath toys she used to have as a kid.

'Shouldn't you be in London?' Turning around at last, she put on her best platonic smile.

'Oh, well that's nice,' said Ben, walking slowly across the sand toward her. 'Would you rather I was in London? That's just charming, that is, after I've flown halfway across the world to see you.'

He was wearing the same tattered pair of shorts he'd had on the day she first met him, and a Rolling Stones T-shirt that had seen better days. He looked tired and pale, and his hair, as usual, was all over the place, sticking up at all angles in the night breeze. But his smile was like a sunburst, so big and broad and joyful that it dominated not only his face, but all of him, from his scruffy bed-head to his threadbare tennis shoes. If she'd wanted him anymore, she would have burst into flames.

'I didn't see you at the party,' she stammered. 'Were you there?'

It seemed easier to focus on facts and logistics than feelings, and she hadn't the courage to ask him why he'd come.

'No.'

As he moved closer, Sian could hear the rumble of Lola's engine fade into the distance. So much for sisterhood!

'It all went great,' she babbled. 'Better than I could have expected, actually. Although they did book me for trespassing.'

'So I heard.' Slowly extending one arm, Ben laid his hand on her hip and drew her toward him.

'They took Anton straight into the city.' She couldn't seem to stop talking. It was as if she hoped her words could form a physical barrier between them. 'The FBI want to interview him – I expect you know about that already – and I'm sure Interpol won't be far behind. They're gonna want to talk to me, too, I'm sure, but the local cops are so hopeless they let me leave with Lola, so at least I'll get one full night's sleep before I face the music. Anyway, I saw Anton leave with his lawyer, the fat guy, but I don't think he saw me. Maybe he did, though. And then they brought Petra in—'

'Sian.' Ben put his index finger to her lips. 'I don't care.'

Ba boom. Ba boom. Someone seemed to have turned up the volume on her heartbeat to full. She finally stopped talking.

'I don't care what happens to Anton, or Petra. I don't care about Interpol. I don't even care about the fund anymore. Not if I can't have you with me.'

'But ...' Somehow Sian forced the sound from her lips. 'What about Bianca?'

'Bianca's lovely,' said Ben, tenderly stroking a stray tendril of hair back from her face. 'And I've tried to love her. Really tried. But I don't.'

'Oh,' said Sian, who knew it was wrong to grin but couldn't seem to help herself. 'I see. Probably not the greatest idea to marry her, then. Is it?'

Ben burst out laughing, sweeping her up into his arms and spinning around on the sand. 'No, you cheeky cow,' he said. 'It probably isn't. Then again, I'm not so sure I should risk it with a gold-digging slapper like you, either.'

'*Slapper*?' she laughed, hitting him on the head. 'How dare you! Anyway, I'll have you know I don't need your money. I'm a woman of independent means now, thanks to the dear old *News of the World*. I have a big career ahead of me, traveling the world, exposing injustice.'

Ben's face fell. He set her down on the ground again. 'You can't, he said. 'You can't travel the world.'

Sian looked up at him quizzically. She couldn't tell if he was serious or not. 'Why not?'

'Because,' he said, frowning. 'Because it's dangerous. There's ... terrorism. And stuff.'

'Oh, for heaven's sake!'

'I'm serious,' said Ben. 'And anyway you'll be too busy in London to go gallivanting around the globe.'

'Busy with what?' said Sian.

Ben grinned. 'Having my babies.'

Sian's eyebrows shot up. 'Oh, will I now?'

'Yes,' said Ben firmly. 'You bloody well will.' And leaning down he kissed her so hard and for so long that she started to feel dizzy. 'By the way,' he said, finally coming up for air. 'Whose idea was the maid's outfit?'

'Anton's,' said Sian, blushing. 'All the party staff had to be in full uniform. Fucking pervert.'

'You know, maybe we've been a bit too harsh an old Anton,' Ben whispered, his fingers creeping slowly up beneath her ludicrously short skirt. I'm starting to think he wasn't *all* bad.'

Closing her eyes, ensconced in Ben's arms at last, Sian was almost inclined to agree.

About ten miles away, in the passenger seat of Lucas's hire car, Honor was starting to get concerned.

'Are you sure you know where we're going?' she asked,

again. 'Because I've been coming here my whole life, and *I* have no idea where the hell we are.'

When they'd left the party, Lucas had sped off in the direction of the city, then forked right into remote farmland where a dizzying latticework of lanes seemed to be leading them further and further into the boonies, before jack-knifing back in the direction of the coast.

The drive had been eventful. As soon as they were out of sight of the Herrick, Lucas dropped the bombshell that Petra was the one responsible for the Palmers fire. Honor's first inevitable question: 'How do you know?' was more shell-shocked than accusatory.

'Sian told me this morning, on the way back from Kennedy,' said Lucas, 'and we tipped off the police just as Tina got up on stage. I asked her to look into it back in London, but to be frank with you, I never thought she'd come up with anything, and certainly not with this.'

'But Petra ... she could have killed me,' Honor murmured to herself, after a long initial silence. 'She could have killed a lot of people. And she was already so far ahead of us at the Herrick. Why would she take that risk, when there was no need?'

Lucas shrugged, keeping his eyes on the road. 'Why did Nixon bug Watergate when he was about to win a landslide? For some people, getting to the top is the easy part. It's staying there that panics them. Petra's always been obsessively ambitious. And she hates your guts. Maybe she wanted to impress Anton. Maybe she just wanted you gone.'

Honor shuddered. Did he mean 'gone' as in not a commercial threat, or 'gone' as in dead and gone? It was a scary thought.

'Sian thinks Tisch didn't know what she was up to,' said Lucas. 'If she's right that's just about the only dirty pie he didn't have his finger in.'

But Honor was barely listening. 'Did you say *you* asked

Sian to look into the fire?' she asked, suspiciously. 'Why would you do that?'

'We're here,' said Lucas, not answering the question as he brought the car to a screeching, dust-spraying halt. 'Come on. Out you get.'

'We're here?' Honor stepped gingerly out of the car, lifting up her long dress with her hands to stop it from trailing in the sand. 'Oh my goodness, we're *here*. How did we get back to town so fast?' They were at the entrance to one of the many winding paths leading to Water Mill, the beach where the two of them had first met so inauspiciously all those years ago.

It was pitch dark. The stars were out in force, but the moon was only the merest sliver of a crescent, and with the car's headlamps off it was hard at first to make out anything in the blackness. But once her eyes adjusted, Honor could see the familiar slope of the ground, and the tufts of spiky, wind-blown grass bursting through the sand at intervals, like an old woman's beauty spot sprouting unwanted hair.

'Follow me,' said Lucas, taking her hand to help her over the uneven ground.

'Would you slow down?' she pleaded, stooping to remove her stilettos as she felt the white chiffon on her dress catch and tear on some brambles. 'I almost broke my ankle on that last slope.'

'You shouldn't wear such ridiculous shoes then, should you?' said Lucas, scooping her up into his arms without breaking stride.

'They're party shoes.' Honor looked at him indignantly. 'I didn't know I'd be going moonlit hiking, did I?'

But she allowed him to carry her the final few yards down to the beach, closing her eyes and taking instinctive comfort in the warmth of his body. Her own body rocked in sync with his big, loping strides, like a child swinging in a hammock, a motion that stirred dim memories of being picked up and carried across the lawn at Palmers by her father. She must have been very young then. It would have been before her mom died. Afterwards Trey could barely bring himself to touch her, never mind hold her close, as Lucas was doing now.

'Here we are.'

Setting her down on the sand, he stood back and watched for her reaction. Laid out in front of them was a midnight-blue cashmere blanket, weighted down by heavy onyx candle holders that glowed orange from the tea-lights within. It was simple – nothing over the top or cheesy – but it was an undeniably romantic gesture.

'What else did you bring down here, Casanova?' she teased him, trying to hide her own nervousness by going on the offensive. 'Barry White CDs and a cocktail shaker?'

'Of course not,' said Lucas defensively.

'What is this, your lover's lair? Bring all the girls here, do you?'

'Don't be ridiculous,' he snapped, sitting down grumpily on one side of the blanket and leaving her no option but to do the same. 'It's just somewhere off the beaten track where I figured we could talk in peace.'

'OK.' Honor sounded less than convinced. 'So, now that you've *lured* me here, what do you want to talk about?'

Lucas stared awkwardly at his hands, as if the answer to her question might be revealed by the calluses on his palms. He had so much to say to her, but in that moment, watching her provoking, elfin, defiant little face flickering in the candlelight, his carefully prepared speech tumbled out of his head like so many rice grains through a colander. He felt his mouth go dry and swallowed hard.

'You asked me a question earlier,' he began awkwardly, 'about why I had Sian do some digging into the arson attack at Palmers.'

'Oh yes,' said Honor, feigning unconcern. She was regretting having shown him her vulnerable side yet again by letting him carry her down here, and thought some aloofness might help her regain the upper hand. 'I just wondered, that's all. It's not important.'

'I did it because I knew you were struggling financially,' said Lucas.

'What do you mean?' said Honor, immediately defensive. 'I'm doing great, thanks. I'd worry more about your own business if I were you.'

Lucas laughed. 'After tonight, our worries are over,' he said confidently. 'Connor won't want anything more to do with Anton after this, just you watch. The court case'll go away, he'll pay my costs without a murmur, and we'll be back to business as usual.'

'Whatever you say,' said Honor, who was feeling more and more rattled.

'Look,' said Lucas, exasperated that once again things were not going according to plan. Why was it that whenever he tried to do something to impress Honor, she ended up throwing it back in his face? 'If you'd stop ranting for a moment and listen—'

'I am not ranting!' Honor ranted.

'I'm trying to tell you that I did this because I wanted to help you. I wanted to help you get your money. The insurers will have to pay out now, right?'

'Oh, come on,' said Honor robustly. 'You don't do anything unless there's an upside. There must have been something in it for you. So what was it? Getting your own back on Petra for taking the Herrick job? Or do you get a cut of Sian's money?'

'Neither,' said Lucas.

'Well, what then?' said Honor.

'Why is it so hard for you to believe I'd do something good and decent and right without an ulterior motive?'

'Erm … because I know you?' said Honor, only half jokingly.

'OK,' said Lucas defiantly. 'OK, fine. It was you. *You* were what was in it for me.'

'Me?'

'Yes, you stupid bitch. You!' he shouted, so loudly that Honor jumped. Standing up, he began prowling around the blanket like a lion guarding his territory, or perhaps sizing up a possible kill. 'Does that really surprise you so much? That I might want to help you, because I care? Because I care about *you?*'

The last sentence came out with all the reluctance of a pulled tooth.

'You care? About me?' Honor repeated, aware she must sound like a parrot, or a lunatic, or both, but not sure what else to say. 'But you're Lucas. You don't *care*. You don't care about anyone.'

'Thanks,' he laughed bitterly.

'Oh, you know what I mean,' said Honor. 'You're so ambitious.'

He looked at her, incredulous. '*I'm* ambitious? And you're not?'

'Well, yes,' she admitted. 'Maybe a little bit. But that's different. I have a responsibility for Palmers. My family ... anyway, this is beside the point!' she added crossly, back on the offensive. 'If you care about me so much, why were you such an asshole in Vegas?'

'An asshole?' Lucas looked genuinely hurt. 'How was I an asshole?'

'You took advantage of me,' said Honor.

She did at least have the decency to look shamefaced when she said it.

'Oh, please,' said Lucas. 'Bull-*sheet*!' His Spanish accent was always strongest when he was angry. Grabbing her by the wrists, he pulled her to her feet and, without thinking, kissed her. 'You wanted me so badly in Vegas, you were practically begging.'

Honor opened her mouth to protest, but he kissed her again, with such force that she staggered backwards, tripping over one of the onyx candle holders and landing

559

ass-first on the sand. The next thing she knew Lucas was lying above her, propped up on his elbows, while she tried ineffectually to writhe out from beneath him.

'Admit it,' he said, smiling for the first time since they'd got there. 'You wanted me from the beginning. From the first day I met you, right here on this beach, when you were still doing your best to convince the world you had a dick between your legs.'

Honor shook her head violently. 'You are so fucking delusional. If anyone wanted anyone, it was *you* who wanted *me.*'

'All right, yes,' he admitted, rather throwing her off stride. 'I did want you, despite how awful you looked.'

'I did *not* look awful!'

'But you were too busy making a fool of yourself with that middle-aged jerk-off Devon Carter to notice.'

Honor blushed scarlet. 'Well, *you* were too busy screwing my sister, along with every other female that moved.'

'Fine,' said Lucas, sensing the mood deteriorating. 'Let's say we were both fools, shall we? Can't we make up for it now?'

For a split second, Honor thought about keeping up the fight. About telling him to fuck off and berating him for meddling in Palmers and her life. But then he bent his head, brushing his lips along her collar bone and down, tantalizingly slowly, towards her breasts. And she changed her mind.

'I'm too tired to argue with you,' she murmured, closing her eyes and sighing as he slipped a hand between her thighs. 'I don't have the energy.'

Lucas grinned. 'Really? I'm not so sure. Let's see how much energy you have, shall we?'

Three hours later, lying naked in his arms with the blanket curled around them as the waves lapped softly against the deserted dawn shoreline, Honor extended her limbs in a long, luxuriant stretch.

'It's gonna be tough, you know,' she whispered, her lips brushing the top of Lucas's ear. 'Making this work. The whole long-distance thing.'

'What long-distance thing?' Flipping over onto his side he turned to face her, pressing his broad nose against her cheek.

'Well, you'll be in Paris, won't you? Or Ibiza.'

'What makes you think that?' asked Lucas.

'Well ...' she stammered. 'Luxe America is kind of ... dead, right? There's no reason for you to stay here.'

'On the contrary,' Lucas smiled. 'Now that Anton and Petra have rather bigger problems on their plate, I'm anticipating a miraculous easing in our legal and planning problems. As long as I'm on site to push it, I can't see why we wouldn't be up and running by this time next year.'

'I do admire your tenacity, darling,' said Honor, kissing him chastely on the lips. 'But you must realize you're wasting your time.'

'Oh, am I indeed?' Cupping his hand around her right breast he squeezed it tightly. 'And why's that?'

'Because,' she said, without a hint of irony, 'Palmers is the greatest hotel in the world, and *we'll* be up and running by Christmas. I'm sure your Luxes are lovely in their own way. But you can't seriously hope to compete with me.'

Lucas laughed. 'Actually, my darling,' he said, 'I'm looking forward to spending the rest of my life doing exactly that.'